AUTHOR		CLASS	
	ARDEN, T.		A F F

TITLE	
	Sultan of the moon and stars

Sultan of the Moon and Stars

Sultan of the Moon and Stars

THIRD BOOK OF THE OROKON

TOM ARDEN

VICTOR GOLLANCZ
LONDON

Copyright © Tom Arden 1999
All rights reserved

The right of Tom Arden to be identified as the author of
this work has been asserted by him in accordance with the
Copyright, Designs and Patents Act 1988.

First published in Great Britain in 1999 by
Victor Gollancz
An imprint of Orion Books Ltd
Orion House, 5 Upper St Martin's Lane, London WC2H 9EA

To receive information on the Millennium list, e-mail us at:
smy@orionbooks.co.uk

A CIP catalogue record for this book is available
from the British Library

ISBN 0 575 06372 6

Typeset by Deltatype Ltd, Birkenhead, Merseyside

Printed in Great Britain by
Clays Ltd, St Ives plc

The Sultan Song

Purple stranger
  Sadly roams,
He shall be Sultan of the Catacombs:
Standing fast by the last of the skeleton jars,
  Not like the Sultan of the Moon and Stars.

Alien creature,
  Seldom seen,
Shrouded in mystery in the jungle green:
Turn and twist in the mist with a crazy picaroon,
  Never with the Sultan of the Stars and Moon.

  – Sultan of the Stars! Sultan of the Moon!
Can we hope to catch you if you're coming by soon?
  – Simpletons, down from your spars!
You might soar through the heavens in triumphal cars,
  But never catch the Sultan of the Moon and Stars!

Scarlet angels,
  Azure too,
Come to the caverns of the what-to-do:
Where the wild and a child and the strangest avatars
  Pray to the Sultan of the Moon and Stars.

  – Sultan of the Stars! Sultan of the Moon!
Tell us what you see beyond the mountain and dune!
  – Simpletons, look to your scars!
You might batter at your walls, beat at your bars,
  But never know the secrets of the Moon and Stars!

Players

JEM, *the hero, seeker after the Orokon*
CATA, *the heroine, beloved of Jem*
RAJAL, *loyal friend to Jem*
POLTY (POLTISS VEELDROP), *their implacable enemy*
BEAN (ARON THROSH), *loyal friend to Polty*
LORD EMPSTER, *mysterious guardian to Jem*
'JAC' BURGROVE, *a ruined man of fashion*
CAPTAIN PORLO, *a crusty old sea-dog*
BUBY, *his pet monkey, tending to the mangy*
SCABS, *his cabin boy, tending to the pustular*
KALED, *Sultan of the Moon and Stars*
SIMONIDES, *his old tutor, most senior of his Imams*
PRINCE DEA, *the Sultan's son and heir*
THAL, *Novice of the Flame, friend to Dea*
MOTHER MADANA (1), *a slave-woman, nurse to Dea*
MOTHER MADANA (2), *mistress of a fine caravanserai*
MOTHER MADANA (3), *Keeper of Palace Women in Qatani*
SEFITA *and* SATIMA, *the names of her many charges*
EVITAMUS, *formerly a Teller, now in retirement*
AMED (AMEDA), *his tomboy daughter*
FAHA EJO, *a goatherd, friend to Amed*
ELI OLI ALI, *his cousin, a great man in Qatani*
CASCA DALLA, *hated business rival to Eli Oli Ali*
LITTLER, *a small boy, son to Eli Oli Ali*
THE BLACK RIDER, *destined to die*
CALIPH OMAN ELMANI, *brother to the Sultan, ruler of Qatani*
VIZIER HASEM, *puller of his puppet-strings*
BELA DONA, *the 'Shimmering Princess'*
DONA BELA, *a beautiful mute girl who looks just like her*
RASHID AMR RUKR, *fearsome leader of the Tribes of Ouabin*
ALMORAN, *master of the House of Truth*
THE GIRLISH YOUTH, *his servant*
MYSTERIOUS GUESTS *in the House of Truth*
RAINBOW, *a most remarkable dog*
FISH *and* BLUBBER, *thieves, members of the 'Unners' gang*

3

CHEESE and STORK, *also of the Unners*
LADYBOYS *in the Place of Cobras*
OLD LACANI, *madman across the water*
PATCHES, *a member of Captain Porlo's crew*
THE DOOM-DANCERS, *tricksters, but also holy men*
EBAHN GUARDS *at the Sanctum of the Flame*
ELDERS *of the College of Imams*
WHISPERERS *in the walls*
TARGON RETAINERS
COURTIERS, GUARDS *and* PILGRIMS
SAILORS, SLAVES *and* EUNUCHS
TRADERS, MIXERS, RABBLE
&c.

IN ZENZAU:
'BOB SCARLET', *highwayman and rebel leader*
HUL, *his deputy, once a great scholar*
BANDO, *friend to Hul, veteran rebel*
LANDA, *a beautiful young Zenzan Priestess*
RAGGLE *and* TAGGLE, *sons to Bando*
THE FRIAR, *object of their frequent torments*
THE OLD LADY *on the Agondon stagecoach*
BAINES, *her one-eyed companion*
GOODMAN OLCH, *a respectable married man*
GOODY OLCH, *a respectable married woman*
MISS TILSY FASH, *the Zaxon Nightingale*
FREDDIE CHAYN, *scion of a worthless principality*
COACHMEN, BLUEJACKETS, INNKEEPERS
&c.

IN THE REALMS OF THE DEAD:
SULTAN EL-THAKIR, *father to Kaled, the present Sultan*
CALIPH ABDUL SAMAD, *brother to Sultan El-Thakir*
THE AMBASSADOR OF LANIA CHOR
LADY YSADONA, *his beauteous daughter*
LADY YSABELA, *his other beauteous daughter*
MALA (LORD MALAGON), *childhood friend to Kaled*
PANDARUS, *father to Simonides, Evitamus and Almoran*
MOTHER *of Simonides, Evitamus and Almoran*
MESHA BULAQ, *Sultan of the Red Dust*
PRINCE ASHAR, *his sickly son*
THE 'GEDEN BRIDE', *betrothed of Prince Ashar*
THE SHAH OF GEDEN, *father of the bride*

NOVA-RIEL, *who defeated the serpent Sassoroch*
TOR, *mysterious uncle to Jem*
The warrior-woman ILOISA, *wife to Bando*
The philosopher VYTONI, *author of* Discourse on Freedom
Other GREAT AUTHORS *and* SCHOLARS
KINGS, QUEENS *and* HISTORICAL FIGURES
Various DEAD RELATIVES, FRIENDS, ENEMIES
&c.

WAITING IN THE WINGS:
EJARD BLUEJACKET, *unrightful King of Ejland*
QUEEN JELICA, *his wife, the former Miss Jelica Vance*
TRANIMEL, *his evil First Minister: see also* TOTH-VEXRAH
LADY UMBECCA VEELDROP, *evil great-aunt to Jem and Cata*
EAY FEVAL, *her spiritual advisor, or co-conspirator*
CONSTANSIA CHAM-CHARING, *once a great society hostess*
TISHY CHAM-CHARING, *her Greenstocking daughter*
SILAS WOLVERON, *father to Cata*
BARNABAS, *a magical dwarf: still missing*
MYLA, *missing sister of Rajal*
MORVEN *and* CRUM
Many other OLD FRIENDS, ENEMIES
&c.

GODS AND STRANGE BEINGS:
OROK, *Ur-God, father of the gods*
KOROS, *god of darkness, worshipped by the Vagas*
VIANA, *goddess of earth, worshipped in Zenzau*
THERON, *god of fire, once worshipped in Unang Lia*
JAVANDER, *goddess of water, worshipped in Wenaya*
AGONIS, *god of air, worshipped in Ejland*
TOTH-VEXRAH, *evil anti-god: see also* TRANIMEL
LADY IMAGENTA, *his daughter, beloved of Agonis*
JAFIR THE GENIE
The HARLEQUIN
'BOB SCARLET', *the bird of that name*
PENGE, *a particular part of Polty*
BURNING BIRDS
&c.

The Story So Far

It is written that the five gods once lived upon the earth, and the crystals that embodied their powers were united in a circle called THE OROKON. War divided the gods and the crystals were scattered. Now, as the world faces terrible evil, it is the task of Prince Jemany, son of the deposed King of Ejland, to reunite the crystals.

Already the anti-god, Toth-Vexrah, has burst free from the Realm of Unbeing. If Toth grasps the crystals, he will destroy the world. Only Jem stands in his way.

An unlikely hero, Jem was born a cripple, but gained the power to walk after falling in love with the wild girl Catayane and finding the first crystal. As Jem set out on his quest, Cata was captured by the sadistic army officer Poltiss Veeldrop. Delivered over to the evil Aunt Umbecca, the wild girl was forced to become a lady. She has now escaped. Disguised as a man, Cata is part of Bob Scarlet's rebel band in Zenzau, but remains desperate to find Jem.

Polty longs to find her too, for only if he marries Cata shall he inherit his father's title.

Meanwhile Jem has acquired a mysterious guardian, Lord Empster. From the first, Jem has wondered if his guardian is really good or evil. Jem's fears seemed allayed by the end of his second adventure, when, amidst the chaos and battles of Zenzau, he found the second crystal. Now, as Jem, with his companion Rajal, sails for the desert realms of Unang Lia, he shall soon find whether he was right to trust his guardian.

But first, in a place called the Sacred City, strange evil is stirring. Events there may seem distant from Jem, Rajal, and especially Cata.

But they are not. Not at all.

PART ONE

The Vanishing Song

Chapter 1

SANCTUM OF THE FLAME

Deep within the desert realms of Unang Lia lie the rocky red peaks of the Theron Ranges. Rising sheer and sudden to unclouded skies, the great mountains loom impassively over a sea of shifting sands. When the sun is high, the jagged peaks glow with vermilion fire; when day declines, the bright blaze gives way to darker flames, of purple, green and blue. But always, amongst the glimmerings, there is one that is brighter, sharp and golden, flashing like a beacon from a high plateau.

To the traveller who has crossed these arid wastes, the first sight of this beacon must come as something alien, alarming. An outlander, perhaps, might screw up his eyes, staring into the splendour with a heart-hammering awe; a Unang would prostrate himself in the sands at once, blurting out the name of the Sacred City.

Kal-Theron!

This is the gold on the high plateau. In far Sosenica, in Yamarind and Emascus, on the isles of Zoebid and the Qatani coast, the very name must be accompanied by a blessing. To Kal-Theron, year on year, the pilgrims come, leaving their pale hillsides, their pungent groves, their market-places and palaces and their shadowy alleys. Many are sick, many are old, but on they travel, undaunted. Many shall die, but what does it matter? To a Unang, it is a promise of eternal bliss to end one's life on the way to Kal-Theron.

Tonight, as the sun sinks behind the mountains, the Sacred City is aflame with life. Torches blaze; tabors beat; incense and chanting rise to the skies. It is the Festival of the Prophet: in the Great Calendar of Unang, with its elaborate reckonings of orbits and rotations, starshifts and moonturns, there are many sacred times, but none more so than this. For five days, the faithful have fasted and prayed. Now, on the evening of the fifth day, crowds jostle before a vast edifice that towers at the head of a sweeping boulevard. Encrusted redly with rubies, garnets and amethysts, this is the place called the Sanctum of the Flame, the greatest temple of Theron's faith. Few shall ever see what lies within. Gathering in their masses, the awed people know only that it is here, in this immense bejewelled casket, that there burns the Sacred Flame.

Excitement pulses on the hot night air. The festival's climax is looming near. Soon Kaled, Sultan of All Unang, will ascend to the Sanctum, disappearing through the immense doors; inside, it is said, he will gaze into the Flame, communing, like his ancestors before him, with Theron's spirit. Then will come the moment that all have awaited. Emerging, standing at the top of the ruby steps, the Sultan will look down to the masses below. Eagerly every eye, every ear will strain towards him, longing for the balm of the words he will – *must* – let fall:

The Flame still burns.

It is enough – it is always enough. Then come the screams, then the prostrations, then the wild wailings of joy.

✳

But this is yet to come. Now the frenzy lies coiled in wait, shivering in a fever of anticipation. *Sultan of the Moon! Sultan of the Stars!* come the murmurous chants. Sweat oozes from the tight bands of turbans. Veils flutter across the faces of the women, rising and falling with the heavings of emotion.

Then come the gasps, then the cries. The time has come! Now, from the far end of the boulevard, horns sound at the gates of the great edifice known as the Whispering Palace. Spasms thrill through the crowd as the Sultan, richly bedecked, emerges in glory to his adoring people.

Strutting before him come troops of guards, dressed like their master in the imperial hues of fire – guards with spears, guards with scimitars, guards with lions on straining leashes. Milling round are gorgeous eunuchs, beating at drums, trilling on pipes, whirling, dancing in swathes of silk and damask. Sturdier slaves bear the ornate litter, a riot of tassels, pillows, swaying lamps. Sailing along the boulevard, high above the crowd, the monarch sits in the posture of benediction, cross-legged, head bowed, arms raised high. *Sultan! Sultan!* comes the cry from every throat; there are moanings, ululations, upstretched hands; some, clapping and swaying, burst spontaneously into the anthem, known to all, that proclaims their leader's greatness:

> – *Sultan of the Stars! Sultan of the Moon!*
> *Can we hope to catch you if you're coming by soon?*
> – *Simpletons, down from your spars!*
> *You might soar through the heavens in triumphal cars,*
> *But never catch the Sultan of the Moon and Stars!*

At first, all eyes are only for the Sultan; then, swaying in his wake, come two further litters. If each is less magnificent than the first, still they are objects of frenzied excitement, for here too are those who shall enter the Sanctum.

The Sultan's companions are beautiful youths, their hands clasped together, raised in prayer. One, tall and willowy, twined in wreaths of lotus and jasmine, is Prince Dea, the Sultan's only son, making his first visit to the Flame. Boys gaze in envy; girls swoon. The Prince is barely at the brink of manhood, but soon the time shall come when he will take his first bride, binding his destiny to the Line of the Prophet.

Behind him, garbed in the simplest of robes, is the young member of the College of Imams known only as the Novice of the Flame. A day ago, the Novice had another name, but already that name is lost to him, seared away in the fires of forgetting. Each sunround, a youth from the college is chosen for the Flame. Symbolising the bond between Sultan and Order, it is the Novice, tonight, whose eyes shall first alight upon the Flame; but when the time of communing has passed, the Novice will never leave the Sanctum. The Sacred Flame is the last thing he will see.

No greater honour could befall any Unang. Reverence greets the Novice, prayers and submissive bows, for in the instant of his appearance this unknown youth has taken upon himself the mantle of a saint.

What thoughts must pass through the Novice's mind? Rocking upon his litter with tight-shut eyes, his face is blank, his pose serene. Perhaps by now, as his spiritual master has counselled, he has swept himself clear of all thought; perhaps already his awareness floats free, oblivious as much to the crowd below as to the face that twists towards him from the litter ahead. It is Prince Dea, ashen with fear, who cries out the name the Novice shall never bear again.

'Thal!'

The lapse is brief. The willowy boy commands himself, clasping reverent hands again, squeezing his eyes shut tight like the Novice's. Indeed, he hopes the boy behind him has shut his mind, too – to memory, and most of all to desire. They must do their duty; there can be no question. But how hard is fate – how bitter that Thal, of all the Novices, should be chosen for the Flame!

Thal had been the Prince's dearest childhood friend. But that was yesterday, and today he is Thal no more.

※

The ceremony begins. The Sultan stands upon the ruby steps, his tall son and the Novice beside him. Behind them, ranged in reverent lines, are Imams, guards, eunuchs. The music, the chanting rise to a frenzy; then the monarch stretches forth his hands and silence descends across the scene like a pall. All down the boulevard the faithful abase themselves, scraping their foreheads on the paving stones. Great doors swing open above them. Now it is the Novice who must go forward first. Someone places a censer in his hand; guards, Imams part like a sea; eunuchs look on, crooning high and wordlessly.

Thal – for of course, he is the same boy – stares ahead. He swallows hard. Trembling, he enters a cavernous blackness, and is confused, for he had imagined these doors opening to a furnace-like blast. Where is the Flame?

But only for a moment is the darkness complete. The doors clang shut and a glow appears, flickering orange, red and gold, beckoning the Novice on his final walk. Slowly, reverently, he makes his way forward, as his master has told him to do.

How coldly the fear grips his heart! How his resolution flickers, flutters! In his hand, unbidden, the censer sways; the curling smoke makes his eyes water – or perhaps it is tears that are streaming down his face. Before him is only a vast blank wall of rock, but in the corner of the wall is an archway, leading to a flight of descending stairs. His steps falter. For a moment he wishes he could run back to the Prince; instead, turning his head just a little, the condemned Novice finds himself staring into the glittering visor of an Ebahn guard.

Bedecked in gold, clutching a scythe, the guard looms forward from the shadows like a phantom. Thal snaps his eyes away, but at once he is aware of another guard, and another, moving spectrally out from the darkness. He trembles, gasps. So it is true about the Ebahns! All his life he has heard of this corps, but never before was he sure they were real.

He knows their legend well enough. Selected from the finest Ebahn slave-boys, trained in cellars beneath the Sanctum, it is the destiny of these guards never to leave this holy place. All their lives must pass in the presence of the Flame, but it is a flame no Ebahn ever sees. At their time of induction the slave-boys are blinded, but all their other senses are then trained to the highest pitch.

Sweating, shaking, the terrified Novice bends his reluctant steps towards the stairs, flanked by the phalanx of fearsome guards. By now, he has forgotten everything about his sacred destiny, his privilege, his honour among the faithful. If he could escape, he would – but there is nowhere to turn, nowhere to run. The heavy steps of the blinded guards echo harshly against the cold stone walls. Round and round go the spiral stairs, descending far beneath the level of the boulevard. In the epicycles since the Prophet first found the Flame, many have forgotten that the great bejewelled Sanctum had been built, like a tomb, over a craggy mountain cave. Around them the light is at first a chill pallor, but rapidly it gets brighter, more lurid. A dull roar grows louder in Thal's ears.

Then comes the last turning of the stairs.

Now he cries out. Violent spasms course through his frame. His legs give way and he sinks to the floor, gazing into the dazzling column of fire. Rising from deep beneath the floor, shooting up from within a great ring of rock, the Flame surges far above, terrifying in its ferocity.

The Prince screams, runs towards his friend. It is no good: the Ebahns separate them, holding them fast. In moments, they will fling the Novice into the Flame – but not yet, not yet. The ritual must proceed as it has always done. First the boys are pushed to their knees, forced into the posture of prostration. The Sultan sweeps between them, abasing himself, moaning to the Flame like a lover, like a slave. Abjectly he implores the fiery god to receive him, to bless him, to pardon his vileness; ardently he begs the fire god to receive his paltry offering.

The Ebahns drag the Novice forward.

'No!' comes a cry again, wild and pealing. But this time it is the Novice who screams, struggles, kicks, while the Prince can only look on, numb with shock. There is nothing he can do for his friend now.

In a moment there is nothing anyone can do.

The Sultan looks wryly at his stricken son. Deafeningly the roar of burning fills the chamber, booming and bursting immensely, like a storm.

Chapter 2

GHOST IN THE GARDEN

'Have a little nectar. Your Royal Majesty, please.'

With a sad smile the slave-woman held out the medicine, but still the young Prince would not turn towards her. From the moment he had burst back into his chambers, it had seemed that nothing could allay his grief. On and on he sobbed into his silken pillows, his thin shoulders heaving beneath his rich, embroidered robes.

'Lammy, go away. Just leave me alone.'

The old slave sighed. It was long after midnight. From the alcoves in the walls, the konar-lights cast a diffuse glow, shimmering in the tears that filled her own eyes. She wiped them quickly with a gnarled hand. How she cursed the rules that bound her! A moonlife ago, she would have flung herself upon her young charge at once, mingling her tears freely with his, holding him tightly in her withered arms. No more: now that he was Heir Unquestioned, an intimate of the Flame, Prince Dea's person was inviolable, subject to the touch of no vulgar hand.

It was cruel, but Mother Madana dared not question the cruelty. For fifty sunrounds she had nursed the royal children, and knew well enough the penalties of transgression. Even now, alone with the Prince, she could take no risks. Not for nothing was this imperial seat known as the Whispering Palace. Spyholes riddled the walls, assuring that only the most loyal were certain to live to the end of their days. Mother Madana's life was drawing to its close. She cared little for herself any more, yet still she had a pride in her that would not be broken. The old slave had seen many of her friends, too many, die by the swords of the palace guards. She was determined to die in her bed.

The goblet of nectar was still in her hand as she paced to the far side of the wide chamber. It was a hot night. The long, latticed doors to the terrace stood ajar and a breeze wafted from the scented gardens, stirring the curtains and ornate hangings. For a blissful moment, Mother Madana basked in the fragrance. How often, with her young charges, she had wandered happily along the high, broad terraces, then up into the lush roof gardens above.

In her long life, Mother Madana had known much sorrow, but never quite as much as she had expected. Sold into slavery as a young girl, she had grieved, of course, for her loss of freedom, but had known that

18

perhaps it was a secret blessing. Her father had been a poor man, with an older daughter and a son, too; never could he have given her an adequate dowry. Her older sister had married the master of a fine caravanserai, the finest, said some, on the Dorva Coast. What became of her brother she had never been sure; she had heard, and hoped it was true, that he was a great man, rising in the court of the Caliph of Qatani.

Mother Madana had not resented her luckier siblings; after all, she had been a plain girl, unlikely to attract the eyes of men. This, too, had been a blessing of sorts. Pretty slave-girls were destined for a fate she was only too glad to have been spared. Assigned to the royal nurseries, Mother Madana had been at first relieved, then relief had turned to pleasure as she devoted herself to her work.

No, she had lived a blessed life – for a slave. Not a day passed when she was not grateful, but in the very fact of her blessing, she knew, there lay the seeds of this present sorrow. What a fool she had been, to love her young charge! But how could she have helped it? Dea was the Sultan's only son, and a sickly, sensitive boy. If, in this last sunround, he had grown to the height of a man, still he had yet to attain a man's strength. Often it seemed that he never would. Willing her eyes not to fill again, Mother Madana thought of the times she had kissed the young Prince, had smoothed his brow, had fluffed the dark down of his little head. Never again would she be suffered to touch her lips even to the hem of his garment. After his wedding, he would be taken to new apartments on the far side of the palace, and if she ever saw him again, she knew she would mean nothing to the boy. They would turn him into someone different, someone alien.

Mother Madana shuddered. She had seen it all before, but this time it was worse. Could it be natural, could it be right, that the boy should assume the mantle of Heir Unquestioned so soon? And was it coincidence that Thal, his dear friend, had been sacrificed to the Flame?

She breathed deeply, struggling to calm herself. From long familiarity the old slave picked out the subtle, delicious scents of the garden, of jasmine and Javander-root, of malak and night-narcissus, and the spores of moon-nectar, most delicate of all. Ah, but that came from the goblet in her hand. Stirred into a potion, it was said to cure all heartaches. She arched back her throat, downing the precious medicine. Goldenly, like the glow of the konar-lights, a warm radiance spread through her body.

She turned, fearful of the eyes in the walls. What had she done? Such potions were not for the lips of a slave!

From the terrace came the tread of a slippered foot. A slave? A message? Quickly Mother Madana hid the goblet, just as the imposing figure of a man appeared before her, stepping in through the long latticed door. She gasped, clapping a hand to her mouth. No slave, the man wore a dazzling robe of red and gold. Jewels flashed in a band round his skull, but even his eyes glowed like precious stones and a hundred little points of light, sharp in the lamplight, glittered in the blackness of his smoothly oiled beard.

What could the Sultan be doing here?

Awkwardly, Mother Madana abased herself. 'Sacred One!'

A smile came to the Sultan's lips. 'Can this mantle of greatness deceive even my old nurse? Come, Lammy, we are friends, are we not? Do you not remember when you dandled me on your knee?'

Flushing, the slave-woman could not reply, managing only a strangled sound midway between a sob and a laugh. Whether it was astonishment that tied her tongue, or fear, or the medicine that coursed through her veins, Mother Madana did not know. She knew only that she could not speak to this man, not this alien, evil creature who came to her in the depths of night and called her *Lammy*. It was a taunt, it had to be, a cruel taunt. That once he had been dear to her, as Dea was now, only made the old slave suffer still more. To think, that her young Prince would one day be like this! She could only be glad that she was old, and death must take her before that time would come.

'Off your knees, Lammy.' The Sultan extended a hand to her, raising her up. He gestured towards the boy on the bed. Insensible of his father's presence, the young Prince still sobbed, his face turned away. 'My son's first visit to the Flame has left him shaken. It is to be expected in one so young – expected, even welcomed. Should a boy's heart be light on so great an occasion?'

Blankly, Mother Madana shook her head. She cast down her eyes with a submissive air, but in her mind the fury bubbled like lava. Was the man saying he was glad that Dea was so distressed? Oh, he was a monster, a black-hearted monster!

The Sultan went on, 'Can the sorrow he feels unman my son? I cannot believe it. Likewise, can it unman me to come to him now? Who better to comfort my poor boy than one who bears the burden that one day shall be his? Come, Lammy, you may withdraw to the terrace. Leave me with my boy, but for a moment.'

Mother Madana bobbed with an appearance of duty, but she struggled to command herself. Stepping out through the latticed windows, the old slave could not resist a backwards glance. How bitter was the pang that filled her breast as the Sultan enfolded Dea into his arms!

Reluctantly, Mother Madana slipped into the shadows.

※

'My son,' said the Sultan, 'it is time to dry your tears.'

Stiffly the bejewelled figure lowered himself to his son's narrow couch.

20

Sniffing, blinking back his tears, the boy gazed blankly at the oiled black beard, at the many-ringed hands, at the crinkles in the corners of his father's eyes. The robes his father wore were sleek and cold, like lizardskin. Dea felt sick. All he wanted to say to his father was *Why, why?*

'Why, why?' said the Sultan.

Dea started.

'That's what you're wondering, aren't you?' The Sultan attempted a smile. 'Ah my son, be not afraid of your own father! Do you not know how much I love you? What happened tonight was a test, and you have passed that test.'

Now Dea was astonished.

'These womanish tears?' The Sultan laughed. 'Why, they are nothing! Do you think I am ashamed of you, my son? Since the ceremony you have sobbed without end, but you have sobbed in private. To the common folk who lined the boulevard, to the Imams, to the Ebahns of the Sanctum, what was Prince Dea but a steely young hero?'

Dea's astonishment could only increase. Since the ceremony he had been filled with shame, cursing the cowardice that had paralysed him, leaving him only to watch in shock as the Ebahns hustled Thal towards the column of fire. How he wished he could have burst forward, wrenching his friend from the murdering guards! But Dea was too weak, too frightened. He had not even cried out, not even to beg Thal's forgiveness.

'Father, you are mistaken. I am no hero.'

The Sultan smiled. 'My son, you forget yourself. Can the Sultan of the Moon and Stars ever be mistaken? I say you are a hero, for you appeared as such, and in time, my son, we become what we appear to be.' He paused, his eyes narrowing. 'So we must be careful what we appear to be.'

'Father?'

'You are puzzled, and think me cryptic; but in time, my words will be clear to you.'

Now Dea bridled. He brushed away the last of his tears. 'Father, I think your words are clear enough, and I am not sure I like them. Would you deny the first lesson I learnt from Lammy, that honesty is the virtue above all others?'

At this, the Sultan laughed again, if a little awkwardly, and enfolded the boy in a stiff embrace. 'My son, can you say you have no courage? My finest counsellors would go to the stake for less impertinence than you have shown me in these last few moments. Ah, but how gratified you make me! I had feared you were a milksop. Instead, I find you a true son of mine!'

Dea stared at his father wonderingly, then winced as the beringed hands gripped his shoulders tightly, almost painfully. His father's voice was a hot, eager whisper.

'My son, sorrow has wracked your frame tonight, but what was tonight but a stage through which you must pass? A boy must empty his eyes of tears before he is ready to become a man. Sleep now, and when morning comes this night of weakness will lie behind you, soon to be forgotten. I too, when I was a young Prince, was forced to watch a friend sacrificed to the Flame.'

'A ... friend?' Dea felt the pressure of tears again, but struggled to hold them back. How he wished his father would turn away the eyes that looked so intently, so piercingly into his own.

Instead, his father breathed deeply and said, 'When I was a boy, Dea – a boy like you – I had a friend called ... called Malagon. In the roof gardens that lie above the terrace here, how happily Mala and I would play together, in the days when our voices were high and piping, our chins yet smooth of beards! Rapturously we filled long afternoons with hide-and-seek and wrestling and games of catch. Our imaginations stretched and grew wings. In armour made of tinsel, we were soldiers bold and true. On wooden steeds we crossed the furthest reaches of these realms, searching for treasure, slaying dragons, rescuing maidens from mysterious towers. In the evenings we sprawled on the floor of my father's library, eagerly unravelling the scrolls to read about intrepid heroes of old. Often we ventured forth again, this time on the chessboard, bargaining fiercely with the imaginary lives of little carved swordsmen and holy men and monarchs.'

At this, Dea almost sobbed again, for he had played just such a game on his last night with Thal, before his friend was taken to the College of Imams. The boy looked with sudden trust into his father's eyes. It was difficult to believe that this big, fearsome man had once been young, as he was now, with a friend just like his own. But Dea knew it must be true. How else could his father speak with such feeling?

The Sultan swallowed hard. 'Yes, my son, all that you have known with your friend, I knew with mine. But my friend, like yours, was a mere commoner, and had been chosen for me for that very reason, to bind me in love to the people I was to rule. And like your friend, mine ... mine had to die.'

Dea said, 'Father, but why?'

'Why? That I would feel the loss sorely, as you have done in your turn. What better proof could there be that a Prince is ready to be bound to the Line? Tonight you have proved the honour of your heart. My son, rejoice! It is true, you are younger than I was when Mala was ... lost to me, indeed much younger. But if the test you have faced was a crueller one than mine, so the challenges before you shall be greater, in the long sunrounds that lie ahead.'

Earnestly the Sultan pressed the boy's hands, and the fire flamed brightly in his eyes again. 'My son, I cannot say how much longer I shall live! No, be not startled – but heed me closely. In a settled time, I should have allowed you a longer childhood, and gladly would I have done so. Now I can afford no delay. The affairs of these lands are at a crucial pass, and the Heir Unquestioned must be in place.'

Dea quavered, 'Father, I don't understand.'

'Fear not, my son – or perhaps I should tell you to fear indeed, for soon, too soon, much of which you are now ignorant must be revealed to you. Would a foreigner, observing the frenzies of this night, guess that my empire is deeply riven, my reign in dire peril? Never: but such is the power of public spectacle. Tomorrow we shall meet the wisest of my Imams, the Councillor Simonides, and you shall hear of threats so deep, of villainies so profound that for ever afterwards your heart will be scarred. Tomorrow, you shall hear of one called Rashid Amr Rukr.'

'R-Rashid Amr Rukr?' Dea shuddered. It was a name he had never heard before, but he knew at once that it frightened him. Gulping, he said, 'Sire, I know not this evil thing. Is it a man?'

The Sultan gripped his son's hands painfully. 'A man, or some loathsome Creature of Evil, dressed in the stolen garb of a man! Ah, if only I could preserve your innocent heart, but alas, it must be sacrificed – as your friend was sacrificed.'

Solemnly the Sultan cast down his eyes.

'But my son, spoil not this night with further distress. Sleep now, and ready yourself for the morrow. Dream not of what is past and gone, and if you would dream of the future, dream of the lovely bride who shall soon be yours, to relieve the rigours of your new-found manhood.'

Dea said uncertainly, 'Then it is true, that I am to marry?'

The Sultan smiled. 'Of course! Already my black-garbed messenger goes forth, bearing a command to the fair city of Qatani, Jewel of the Shore. My boy, mark well what I say to you now. Tonight you lament the death of your friend, but soon – I tell you, it must be so! – the Novice of the Flame shall lodge in the dustier chambers of your memory.

'My brother, the Caliph of Qatani, has a daughter who is known as the Shimmering Princess, though the real name she bears is Bela Dona. Reports of her beauty have flown throughout my empire. Why, she is said to be a creature so fair that the sun herself should weep, feeling herself surpassed. There are many who would sue for Bela Dona's love, but only one who shall lie between her thighs. Since the time of her birth, this Shimmering Princess has been your betrothed.'

'M-Mine, Sire?'

23

'You are Heir Unquestioned, are you not? To marry my heir is Bela Dona's destiny.' Dea started as his father's hand reached caressingly for his son's loins. 'My son, you have attained the height of a man; soon, too, you shall feel a man's longings. Do you not know what I mean, Dea? Ah, but you shall! Rejoice, my son, at the pleasures I have procured for you! When you are grown, perhaps, you shall take many wives; but with none shall you know the bliss you are to know with Bela Dona!'

Dea's heart was hammering hard as his father smiled knowingly and withdrew. Left alone, the boy lay back uneasily on his couch. He was exhausted, but there was no question of sleep. For brief moments, he would feel a surging excitement; then a wash of sorrow; then the fear returned in force. In the violence of his emotions he would have leapt up, pacing back and forth as his father had done, but just then he heard Mother Madana's familiar footsteps, returning along the terrace.

Dea shut his eyes tightly, feigning sleep. If the child in him longed for his nurse's caress, something else in him, something new, did not even want to see her face. He thought of his father's fondling hand and a burning flush crept up his neck.

※

Mother Madana looked sadly on the gawky, huddled boy. With a sigh, she covered him with a blanket, careful that her profane hands should not touch the sacred person. The temptation was strong to kiss his cheek, to smooth his hair, but she resisted. Nervously her eyes flickered about the walls, into the shadows between the konar-lights.

Moments earlier, Mother Madana had been less cautious, lingering close to the latticed door, straining to hear all that passed within. Only at the end, as the Sultan took his leave, had the slave slipped further away on tiptoed steps, holding herself still, flattened against a pillar as the fearsome figure swept past. After he had gone she had exhaled deeply, slowly, but the turmoil inside her was just beginning. Returning along the terrace with a measured tread, Mother Madana seethed with secret anger.

How she cursed her own cowardice! There had been a time when she thought herself the Sultan's loyal subject. Now only fear for her life kept her in thrall to this vicious man. When she had heard what he said about Lord Malagon, it was as much as she could do not to burst back into the Prince's chamber there and then, denouncing her lord and master as a liar. Yes, the Sultan's friend – a commoner, indeed! – had died in the Flame, but who had it been who ordered him killed? Oh, at the time Mother Madana had convinced herself that the Sultan must have been right, that indeed Lord Malagon – gentle, sweet Mala – was a traitor

24

deserving only torture and death. She knew now what a fool she had been.

The old slave's heart throbbed painfully as she moved about the walls, slowly extinguishing the konar-lights. At last, when only the glimmerings of the moon cast pale patterns of light across the floor, she padded back swiftly to Dea's couch, kissed him lightly, and repaired to her own narrow bed.

Later she would shudder at the risks she had taken that night. But she could not help herself, she could not!

❄

'Dea,' came a whisper. 'Dea.'

Dea started. 'Thal?'

But of course, there was no one there.

The Prince rose from his couch, staring into the pale squares of moonlight through the lattices. Perhaps he had slumped into a fitful sleep; dimly he was aware of a troubling dream. Then it came back to him, all that had happened; not a dream, but the harsh truth.

Dea moaned, but there was a blankness in his voice. By now he had no more tears to cry; desolation hung upon him like a heavy, trailing cloak as he padded out on to the terrace. Like a ghost, the willowy boy slid towards the white, curving staircase that led up to the roof gardens. Pushing his way through the thick, fragrant foliage, he leaned against the trunk of a lemon tree, peering desolately into the perfumed places where once he had played so happily with Thal. In the thin moonlight there was little he could see, but it hardly mattered. Dea's imagination filled in the parterres and mazes, the groves and grottoes, the winding paths and sinuous, burbling rills.

Oh Thal, Thal.

The night was still. Not even the gentlest breeze rustled the leaves and vines or shook a headier incense from the lush, exotic flowers. Dea felt his eyelids growing heavy again.

That was when he saw it.

It was a human figure, a boy, or rather a figure in the shape of a boy, shimmering with an eerie, silvery light between the parterres.

Dea's heart turned to ice. 'Thal?'

The figure stretched forth an inviting arm, as if inviting Dea to join it. To come and play.

25

Chapter 3

ANOTHER COUNTRY

Scarlet, scarlet, his coat was of scarlet,
With a hey-zown zerry,
Zerry-zown;
In Viana's kingdom he was often seen,
In the years after they had killed the Queen.
With a hey-zown zerry,
Zerry-zerry zown,
With a hey-zown zerry,
Zerry-zown!

It was Bando who was singing. His song drifted softly into the darkened woods. Sadly the Zenzan stared into the dying fire, but did nothing to stir it back to life. It was late, and the fire was only for cooking. In a moment he must stamp it out, making sure no mischievous spark leapt into the tinder-dry undergrowth. But not yet, not just yet. Slumped against his fat belly, sleeping deeply, were his little sons, Raggle and Taggle. The boys were exhausted after their long day's march, and Bando was reluctant to make them stir. Smiling, he smoothed Raggle's tousled hair – or perhaps it was Taggle's, he could never quite tell.

In the Zenzan woods the heat hung heavily, burdening the leaves and branches like insidious, unwanted fruits. The glory days – Viana's days – were long moonlives ago, when the first stirrings of new life had burst back greenly, decking the ancient trees with rapid, riotous garlands. Now Theron's season had risen to its height. In daytime the sky was a fierce blue, insisting its brightness into all but the most shadowy caverns of the woods. Leaves and grasses, flowers and fronds had taken on a dusty, exhausted air. In the dark of night the heat barely retreated, but lingered like a vast mocking presence, hunched and waiting. If only there could be thunder.

If only there could be rain.

Murmurously Bando kept on singing, gently rocking the boys. There was no significance in his choice of song. He had snatched at any melody that came to mind, but there was an irony in this eulogy to their leader. Even in Zenzau, the highwayman's legend was passing rapidly into memory, and beyond. Everything was changing in the conquered kingdom since the rebels had been crushed in the Battle of Wrax.

Evil evil, he fought against evil,
   With a hey-zown zerry,
      Zerry-zown;
Though scarlet may be the colour that's true,
There's too many who say that it's blue!
   With a hey-zown zerry,
      Zerry-zerry zown,
   With a hey-zown zerry,
      Zerry-zown!

The Zenzan yawned. On the other side of the fire, another of his companions had slumped into sleep. The Friar, after grumbling all day about his bunions, his prickly heat and his miserable rations, was snoring at last. In the morning, inevitably, he would bemoan his mosquito bites, and wonder when he could sleep in a proper bed.

Often Bando had wondered why their leader did not dismiss so useless a companion. What was the capon – so Bando called the monk – but a waste of rations? Young Wolveron, for all his follies, was worth a hundred capons. It seemed that Bob Scarlet had religious scruples, and no more would turn away the Ejlander monk than he would banish Priestess Landa.

Grudgingly Bondo had agreed not to torment the Friar, though for a time he enjoyed remarking, when the little man was near, that rations would be worse when Koros-season came, and maybe they would never sleep in beds again.

But Bando no longer laughed at the Friar's horrified looks. The future that lay before them was too real for jesting. Instinctively the Zenzan hugged his sleeping sons. For himself, he had no fear – since Iloisa, the warrior-woman he had loved, had lain down her life in the rebel cause, Bando would gladly have joined her in death. It was when he thought of the fate awaiting his sons that the Zenzan shuddered in horror.

The days with Jem, in the woods by Oltby Castle, had been the last happy days the rebel band had known. How things had changed! Jem had gone his own way, Rajal too, pursuing a quest that Bando did not pretend to understand. Blackjaw was dead; so was Priestess Hara; Dolm and Mother Rea had remained behind, too sick and old to join them on this journey – what Bando had come to think of as their *final* journey.

Sometimes – the feeling was a new one for him – Bando wondered if he could go on with this rebel life. How he longed to find his way back to the little village he had left so long ago – how peacefully, how sweetly he could live there, raising his boys. Of course, this was only a fond dream. It was too late: Bando Riga was a wanted man, a traitor to the usurper king. If the Bluejackets found him, they would torture him, then kill him, and what was left of him would hang in the village square until the picked carcass was no more than bones, and the bones crumbled at last into a dry, clattering heap. What would become of his little sons then? No, Bando could not go back – not to live his life in fear of discovery. Whatever his destiny might hold in store, the Zenzan knew he must face it squarely. His sons would not grow up to believe their father a coward.

꽃

Carefully Bando shifted the boys, arranging a blanket over their sleeping forms. Stamping out the fire, he looked round the camp. On a mattress of leaves, the girl Landa – the Priestess, as they must think of her now – was sleeping like the child she had barely ceased to be. Close by, Recruit Wolveron leaned against a tree, keeping guard.

For a moment Bando gazed at the motionless form. He was an odd one, that Wolveron. They had fallen in with him on the day of the battle, but for all the adventures they had shared since then, the lad had never ceased to be surly and distant. Even Raggle and Taggle could not draw him out; only with beasts and birds did he reveal any tenderness.

To Bando, it seemed strange – but perhaps it was not – that a fellow whose bayonet had run with human blood should recoil in horror from killing a bullfinch or a rabbit. Once, when Bando had a fine hare in his sights, Wolveron grabbed suddenly at the barrel of the gun and the shot had gone awry. How angry Bando had been that day – but not as angry as he had been at other times, when the lad had been reckless in more dangerous ways. Once he had sneaked into a Bluejacket base. Once he had taken pot-shots at a passing patrol. Of course, Bando understood why, but he was damned if he would allow the lad to get them all killed. Several times they had nearly come to blows, until Hul or their leader had intervened.

But Bando could not bring himself to dislike young Wolveron. The lad was raw, but his heart was in the right place, that much was certain. When battle came again, Bando had no doubt that their new companion would be a brave fighter. They could not afford to lose him.

Clutching his rifle, the lad looked out intently into the darkness of the woods. His would be the first watch. Later he would wake Hul, but Hul was not yet sleeping. Beneath the branches of a tall pine, the scholar hunched earnestly over a battered volume, reading by the light of a single candle. Bando looked affectionately at his old comrade. 'You're on watch tonight, Hul. Should you still be straining your eyes?'

'They are well strained, my friend, if their straining brings me wisdom.'

'Why Hul, I thought you had enough of that already.'

Hul laid down his book with a thoughtful air. In a better time, he might have been a professor at the University of Agondon. Instead, the unlikely rebel had fought side by side with Bando in many a perilous campaign. Seldom had two friends so little in common; seldom had two friends been so fiercely loyal. 'You think a man can have too much wisdom, Bando?'

'Hm.' The Zenzan squatted down, stuffing his pipe. 'I sometimes wonder if a certain fellow – I don't mean you, Hul – may have too much.'

'Old friend, who might this fellow be? And tell me, why should you wonder such a thing?'

Bando's eyes darted about the clearing. There was little need for wariness: Bob Scarlet had withdrawn from the company. As always, their leader slept apart from the others, his pistols, Bando was certain, poised at the ready. Loyalty prevented the Zenzan from saying their leader's name, so instead he merely sighed and said, 'I'm a simple man, Hul – not like you. This fellow – well, often I don't understand what he does. Or rather, what he does seems foolish to me.'

'What he does, or what he's going to do?'

Bando ignited a tinderstick. 'Both. Either way I am left confused – but certainly this fellow has more wit than I.'

'You're so certain?'

'What do you mean, Hul?'

Hul's spectacles glinted in the candlelight. 'Perhaps you're not being square with me, Bando. You say he has wit, and you have little. But really, perhaps you think it is the other way round?'

The Zenzan drew back thoughtfully on his pipe. What Hul said was true, though Bando would never have admitted as much. There had been a time, before the Battle of Wrax, when he had regarded their mysterious leader with awe. Now, crushed in defeat, the masked man seemed only a sad, solitary figure. Spiralling down slowly towards inevitable doom, still he clutched tightly to secrets that none of them were trusted to know – none of them, that is, except perhaps for Hul.

Bando had long suspected that his old friend knew more than he would tell about this so-called Bob Scarlet. To be sure, he must do – otherwise, would Hul have been so insistent that they join this little band after the loss of their first leader? Bando had been happy to bow to Hul's wisdom, but the highwayman was a very different character from the harlequin – and hardly a fair trade, in Bando's eyes.

His thoughts flickered back to their first, lost leader. Poor Tor! To think, he had died in the very manner Bando most feared – hanged by the neck in his own childhood village, another victim of Bluejacket 'justice'. An old, familiar hatred surged through Bando's veins. If he did not like their new leader, still he knew the one thing that kept him loyal.

He said suddenly, 'Hul, you think ill of me.'

'What's this, old friend? Never!'

'For all his strange ways, the one of whom we speak is the implacable foe of evil, is he not – of all the evil that wears a blue jacket? You would have me disloyal to a rebel who has been a legend in story, song and rhyme?'

'Perhaps you think the legend is tarnished?'

Bando looked down sadly. Day after day, their party scudded like animals through the thickly wooded hills. How far they had come, he did not pretend to know. All he knew was that they must move, and keep moving, towards a new and more terrible confrontation – undoubtedly, towards a new and more terrible defeat. Their leader was decided: they must make for Ejland, where his agents were raising a new rebel army. It was madness – but perhaps there was nothing left for them but madness.

Bando said, 'It is the times that are tarnished.'

Hul smiled. 'Well said, old friend! I think there is more wit in you than you would allow.' He reached forward, clutching his companion's arm. His voice was a hot, earnest whisper. 'Bando, there are things I am pledged not to reveal. Just believe this: that there is a design in this course we follow. For now, it is a design too deep for you to see, but one day, all shall be clear to you. Our course is a dangerous one – it has always been dangerous – but Bando, it has never been foolish, and is not foolish now. Clutch your rebel faith close to your heart; for in time, I promise you, it will be rewarded amply.'

Bando looked wonderingly at his companion. For a time the two men sat in silence, until at last the old rebel extinguished his pipe, grinding out the embers, and the scholar laid aside his book. He blew out his candle. They reached for the blankets from their saddlebags, and lay down to rest in the warm, straw-like undergrowth.

'It was different when young Jem was with us,' murmured Bando, after a lengthy yawn. 'How I wish those days would come again!'

'Poor Jem!' sighed Hul. 'I wonder where he is now?'

Chapter 4

PIECES OF EIGHT

'Jem . . . Jem?'

Rajal nudged his friend.

Jem started. The trance again! The last he knew, he had banged down his tankard, wiping his mouth on the back of his hand. It had seemed just for a moment, though it must have been for longer, that he stared into the bright flame of the candle, shimmering in the middle of the captain's table. He had not meant to be rude, but now he had missed the end of the old man's latest story. How he wished he could speak to his guardian! How many times had it happened now, this strange, silent awe before a candle, a taper, a lamp?

It had happened a lot since they left Port Tiral.

Through the open casement the sea hissed softly, dark but for the silver gleamings of the moon. It was a hot night – below decks it would be sweltering. Jem rubbed his eyes. Around him, Captain Porlo's cabin was a cave of strange treasures, ranged about the walls or suspended from the low, smoky ceiling. There was a tiger's head and a rhinoceros horn, a Rivan pennant and a Torga-shield, a brass musketoon and a rusty scimitar that once must have flashed in the hand of a fierce Wenayan pirate. Yellowed maps and charts lay all about, and musty volumes of the captain's log. The old man's cabin was like a picture of his mind, shabby but glittering, and stuffed full with memories of a hundred fabulous adventures.

Jem looked down at the heavy plates, greasy with remnants of salt-pig and mustard.

'Don't mind my friend,' Rajal was saying. 'Our guardian once arranged for him to learn to be a gentleman, but – truth to tell – he killed his teacher before the lessons were complete.'

The captain's eyes twinkled. He gestured to the weapons about the walls that clinked with the sluggish shiftings of the tide. 'With what, me lovely? A cutlass? A claymore?'

'Shot him in cold blood.'

'Hah!' The captain slammed the table. 'The hot vigour of youth! Ah, Master Jem, you be a dark horse and no mistake.' The old man took a hearty swig of rum. He winked at Rajal. 'I dare say he's a devil with the lasses, too?'

'A devil? Why, he's Toth-Vexrah himself!'

'Raj!' Jem protested. 'Don't jest with the name of the anti-god!'

Rajal only laughed. Jem's friend was drunk – they were all drunk – and revelling in a certain innocent glee. Even the captain might have been a child, liberated from the stern gaze of his guardian.

For a moonphase now, since they had left Port Tiral, Lord Empster had kept to his cabin. Without him, the little party soon abandoned the pretence that really, they were in a respectable drawing-room, and salt-pig and rum and weevily biscuits were pheasant and Varl-wine and flame-of-orandy pudding.

But the easing of tension was only apparent. Still their for beat beneath the surface, even as laughter hooted from their lips. The time was drawing close when the *Catayane* would reach Unang Lia. Surreptitiously Jem felt for the leather bag he wore like a talisman round his neck. Hidden inside it was the Crystal of Viana; Rajal bore with him the Crystal of Koros, but there were still three crystals left to find, and already Toth-Vexrah was abroad in the world, hiding in the guise of Tranimel, the Ejlander First Minister. Soon, somewhere in the burning southlands, they must seize the Crystal of Theron – before Tranimel, or his agents, found it first. But where the crystal might be, who could say? Could Jem's trances offer any clue?

Rajal was goading the captain. 'I'm sure *you* were a devil, Captain – still are, I'll wager. Is it true you tarry fellows have a lass in every port?'

'Hah! I dare say every sailor *has* a lass in each port, me lovely,' replied the captain, with a mischievous wink. 'There's always lasses who'll lift their skirts for a copper coin or two – and a great comfort to us menfolk they be. But alas,' the old man added with a sigh, 'that sort of thing's beyond me now. Me animal spirits have long been dry as dust.'

'Nonsense, Captain!' Rajal burbled merrily. 'Can decrepitude have overtaken – so soon! – a man who once bounded over the wall of a Caliph's harem?'

'Raj!' This was dangerous territory. This time Jem aimed a kick at his friend, but missed and kicked Buby instead. Buby was the captain's mangy pet monkey, who often lay, as now, beneath the table, comfortingly curled around her master's wooden leg – a finer piece of lathework you never did see, as the captain was wont to remark. From time to time certain gaseous emissions brought Buby to the attention of the company, but the creature seldom stirred except when this or that clumsy guest forgot her presence sufficiently to tread on her tail, squash her ribs or kick her in the head.

A shriek sounded from below, but fortunately was masked by a clattering from the decks as a sailor rang the bell for the next watch.

Besides, Captain Porlo was preoccupied. Tears flooded the old man's eyes. 'What a hot-headed young fool I used to be!' he blurted, and Jem knew they must listen yet again to the tale – at once extraordinary and absurd – of how the captain had lost his leg. 'It were lust that brought me low, wicked lust! If only – ah, if only I'd never climbed that Caliph's wall!'

'If only,' Jem agreed, and sighed.

The captain took a fortifying swig from his tankard. 'Many's the chap that says he'd die for a sight of them lovely harem-lasses; but how many would live on without their trusty Lefty, answer me that? (I means me leg, me lovelies, me poor left leg.) Mind you, I suppose I was lucky – would have lost me jewels, I would, if them guards had had their way!'

'Jewels?' Jem enquired dutifully.

'Jewels them harem-guards don't have none of, if you know what I mean! Ah, they be brutes in that Unang-land, me lovely, make no mistake. Still, I suppose they thought I'd had enough, after they pulled me out of the cobra pit.'

'C-Cobra pit?' Rajal mustered the required alarm.

'Ever seen a cobra, me lovelies?' The Captain pronounced it *cobber-a*. 'Rummest serpent this side of Sassoroch!' There was a grim pause. 'Thought no one could climb like young Faris Porlo, I did. And ah, I was eager for the sight of them lasses – only the sight, mind, I meant no disrespect. Hide something from a man and there's those of us won't rest until we've clapped our eyes on it, aren't there?' The captain shook his head. 'Got over the spike-wall, I did, but didn't reckon with the pit below.'

'You fell?' Jem feigned surprise.

'Fell!' Rum spluttered from the captain's lips. 'Young Faris Porlo? Not a bit of it! Leapt over them cobber-as, I did, and had a good shufty round on the other side. Big palaces? Tell me about 'em. Corridors? Tell me about 'em. Lovely lasses? You tell me about lovely lasses!' For a moment the captain leered, but then his face clouded. 'It was when them big jewelless fellows got me – that's when things went wrong. Hustled me back to the balcony they did – threw me down without so much as a by-your-leave!'

Jem and Rajal looked suitably appalled.

'Let me lust be a warning to you, me lovelies. I've known chaps been shot by angry husbands; I've known chaps lose their every jit. More than a few ends up rotted with pox – high price for a moment's pleasure, eh? Why, there's some, they even ends up married – to a wife, like!' The old sea-dog shuddered. 'But I think there's only one like your poor captain, lying in that there cobber-a pit. If it just been old Lefty broke, I might have got him fixed, but when them evil cobber-as come slither-slithering near – *sss*, they go, *sss*, *sss* – nuzzling their hoody heads into the weeping wound, what chance has a chap got? – answer me that! Drank their fill, them cobber-as did, and left poor Lefty all a-swim with venom! Ah, they be evil things, them cobber-as – *sss, sss,* a-hissing all the time, like they was having a fine old shindig! Ah, me lovelies, you'd better pray you never meets them cobber-as!'

Rajal – his theatrical training had not gone amiss – looked as if he might be moved to pray there and then. Jem attempted to emulate his friend, but even in the absurd story were reminders enough of his deeper fears. He thought he should ask the captain more about Unang Lia, this strange land of harems and eunuchs, but at that moment the captain banged the table again, declared it was no good to get morose, and swivelled his head this way and that, in search of his concertina.

'Time for a song, me lovelies, eh? And more rum?' He tilted up the pitcher over Rajal's tankard, but the pitcher was dry. 'Hah!' The captain flung it to the floor, tilted back in his chair and bellowed, 'Scabs!'

The cabin boy, bearing more rum, appeared as if by magic, or rather, as if he had been waiting just outside. Indeed, one of his ears was bright red: perhaps it had been pressed against the low wooden door. But then, much of Scabs was red, or so one surmised from the pustular sores that splotched his face and neck. Carefully the ugly creature leaned across the table, glugging more rum into the captain's tankard, which he had retrieved from the dusty corner where it had rolled.

'The new lad is a fine one, eh me lovelies?'

Jem smiled, but looked distastefully at the boy's raw knuckles. Even his hands were ringed with sores. Scabs had joined the *Catayane* only at Port Tiral, southernmost base of Ejland's empire, but it seemed unlikely he could be a Tiralon. Under the disfiguring markings, his skin was pale as a ghost's.

The ship shifted and a spurt of rum leapt across the tabletop.

'Steady on, lad! What do you think it is – *u-rine piss?*' With playful violence, the captain aimed a cuff at the new boy's tousled head. 'That's precious balm, that is – but don't you go sticking your scabby snout in it, me lovely, or there'll be trouble, I'm telling you now!'

Sniffing, Scabs filled the remaining tankards. But poor Scabs was a clumsy fellow, and as he withdrew he stepped back too sharply and trod on Buby's tail. This time the monkey's shriek was louder. In a flash she clambered up the table leg; an instant later, she was clinging to the ceiling, hissing and beating her tail back and forth.

Laughter burst from the captain's lips. 'Me poor pretty!' The old man stumped upright, plucking the frightened monkey into his arms. With coarse fingers he smoothed her mangy fur. 'There, there – never mind old Scabs! Poor lad, he's mostly made of pus. I expect he'll burst one day, and then where will we be? Swimming in yellow muck, the lot of us!'

The cabin boy flushed beneath his raw blotches, gathered up a pile of greasy plates and retreated in haste. From through the door, inevitably, they heard the plates clattering. The captain laughed again and raised his tankard. 'To Theron's nectar!'

He took a hearty swig.

'Theron's nectar?' said Rajal.

'Because it burns, me lovely! Ah, but don't expect none of this where we're going! String you up in the marketplace for knocking this back, they would. Very devout – fearfully devout. But let's have us a bit of a shanty, eh?'

With that, the captain gave his squeezebox a violent tug, and roared:

> *Pieces of eight! Pieces of eight!*
> *Gold and diamonds, rubies and silver plate!*
> *Are they lying in a wreck at the bottom of the sea?*
> *Where, tell me where can me treasure be?*
> *Yo-ho-hee! A sea-dog's life for me!*
> *But where, tell me where can me treasure be?*

It was a song the captain had sung before, during the many times when he was deep in his cups. Jem had once asked the old man about the treasure, thinking that perhaps the captain had a quest like his own. The captain laughed and said it was just a silly old sea-dog's song.

> *Bullion bars – stamped with a crest!*
> *Ah, how they'll flash when I opens that chest!*
> *Is it buried in the sand 'neath a far-off desert sky?*
> *Where, tell me where can me treasure lie?*
> *Yo-ho-hee! A sea-dog's life for me!*
> *But where, tell me where can me treasure be?*

Rajal joined in eagerly with the raucous tune, incongruously adding his higher, purer voice to the captain's tuneless caterwauling. Jem struggled to do the same, but instead found himself gazing into the candleflame again, his face blank and stricken. Before the song was over, he juddered back his chair.

'Sorry, Captain – I'd better get some air.'

'Air?' Captain Porlo gestured to the window. 'You can do your *u-rine piss* out there if you likes, me lovely!'

But Jem had gone already. As the wooden door bashed shut behind him, the candle on the captain's table flickered out. Buby shrieked, scurrying about the floor and walls. The captain only burst into a hearty laugh, clanged his tankard hard against Rajal's, and drank another toast to Theron's nectar.

Chapter 5

THE FIRST VANISHING

Dreams hovered thickly above the clearing. Hul slept in silence; whining little snores came from the Friar; from Bando, deeper and more guttural gruntings. The boys had kicked away their blankets, but were still fast asleep, the risings of their breath barely stirring the air. Stillest of all was Landa; she seemed not to be breathing at all. Somewhere an owl hooted; somewhere, little paws scurried through the undergrowth.

Recruit Wolveron shifted his musket and turned, sensing something. It was not danger – it was Landa. Suddenly the Priestess raised her head and looked about her warily, this way and that. Wolveron caught her eye and nodded. Swiftly, silently, Landa scrambled up.

They swished through the undergrowth.

'I thought they'd never sleep,' Landa whispered.

'The old rebels? Their memories make them restless. Did you find a place?'

'I looked when it was still light. Deeper in the woods is a burbling brook, and by the brook is an immense oak, its branches gnarled and twisted, its roots rippling over the bank like . . . like the coils of a vast serpent.'

'Not Sassoroch, I hope!'

Landa did not smile. 'Sister, speak not the name of evil!'

'Priestess, speak not the name of sister!'

'The tree is not Sassoroch. But you are my sister.'

Looking back cautiously, Cata whispered, 'Only when we are certain that others cannot hear. Our comrades would think me no warrior if they knew I were a woman.'

'Sister, that is not true! Have you not heard the story of Bando's wife?'

'The noble Iloisa? Indeed, and I honour her memory; but she was a woman from the steppes of Derkold, trained from birth to wield axes, arrows and knives. What am I in the eyes of the world but a runaway graduate of Mistress Quick's? Better it is, far better, that our comrades think me a man – Recruit Wolveron, never Catayane.'

'Dear Cata!' With a sigh, Landa spoke the forbidden name. She clutched at her companion. 'Sister of my spirit, can you think I doubt you? Be assured, all my powers are ready to assist you. But how sad I shall be if you must leave me!'

36

'Priestess, I know it. But you have found your destiny – I am still in search of mine. On the day of battle, did I not feel the presence of my beloved, closer to me than he has been since the time we were parted? Then the power was broken, and I lost the trail again. I know only that I must seek him, and not for myself alone: with him I shall forge the destiny of our realm.'

The Priestess murmured, 'Alas, that such a destiny is no longer mine!'

'Priestess?'

Landa said no more. The lapse was for a moment, and a moment only. Mere moonlives ago, the new Priestess had been the betrothed of Prince Orvik. By his side she would have been Queen of Zenzau, as Cata hoped one day to be Queen of Ejland. How strange, how winding are the ways of destiny! Landa brushed her eyes and moved swiftly onwards. She must think no more of her dead, foolish lover. Time and again she prayed in her heart that Cata would not suffer as she had suffered.

They parted a curtain of pendulous leaves. Moonlight glimmered on the waters of the brook and flashed on the point of Cata's bayonet. If it worried her to leave their comrades unguarded, still she knew she must take the risk. The ritual was vital. With sudden reverence the Priestess knelt down, gazing up into the branches of the oak. The trunk was immense, a spreading, corrugated monolith of stone-hard bark, garbed thickly with moss and wreathing vines.

'This tree – it's one of the ancient ones?' said Cata.

'Few remain from the time of the Sisterhood. We shall be lucky to find another such one, as we move ever further from the Hills of Wrax. The trees here are newer than those of my childhood, but this oak, I am certain, is the oldest among them. Let us but hope that its aura is strong enough.'

'The goddess may not come?'

'I am sure she will come. But much energy may be needed to summon her, now we have left the places of greatest spiritual power.'

The ceremony began. Landa lay full-length before the tree, her robes vanishing into the reeds and fronds, her long hair twining into the roots and vines. Cata lay beside her, feeling the strange coolness from the dank, fecund earth. The brook babbled close by, rolling and tumbling through the eerie darkness.

'Ul-ul-ul-ul-ul!'

It sounded like birdsong, flashing through the night. But the cry was Landa's. She raised her head, clawing and clutching at the sinuous roots; with serpentine swayings she drew herself upright, moving forward to embrace the tree. Entranced, she traced her fingers over the mossy, pungent bark.

'Daughter of Orok, see your supplicant. Sister of Koros, hear her words. Most sacred Viana, soft as leaves, come to me now in this woodland place, where I bring before you a sister who has stumbled in blindness, lost alike to knowledge of your majesty and your mercy. By what design, goddess, you have raised this child of nature, far from the grace of your own sacred woods, your mere daughter-servant cannot presume to say. Know only, goddess, that this child has been true to you, dwelling in harmony with your element of earth; only through the machinations of the evil ones has this faithful servant ever left your side. Daughter of Orok, see your supplicant. Sister of Koros, hear her words.'

In moments, Cata would rise to join the Priestess, and their voices would twine into complex mantras, *Viana-Vianu, Viana-Vianu* and *In the greenwood let me lie* and – even though it was a hopeless plea – *Let no axe fall in the Hills of Wrax*. Tumbling over each other, pitching and tossing, the words became sounds and sounds alone, and the sounds became a music of incantation. Enraptured, Cata whispered to the primaeval oak,

> *Goddess of the living, consume me like a fire,*
> *Goddess of the dying, grant me my desire.*

If the music was strange to her, it did not matter. Instinct guided her where knowledge failed; instinct, and a sense of deep, abiding rightness. When Landa had declared her to be a daughter of Viana, Cata had never even thought to doubt her. After the chaos of the Battle of Wrax, for a time Cata had despaired of her quest. Dedicating herself to a rebel life, she had thought she could only bury her nature, concealing herself in her manly disguise. But the call of blood was strong in her, and Cata had to worship.

※

It had been early one morning on the journey out from Wrax that Landa had come across the new recruit communing in secret with the beasts and birds and flowers. Recklessly Cata had shed her disguise; Landa had rushed to her. *Sister, I knew it! Sister, I knew you!*

Cata gasped and scrambled up, but Landa showed not even a trace of surprise. Sobbing, the Priestess embraced the naked girl; Cata, marvelling, shook her head. When she said they could not be sisters, Landa only smiled; when Cata said she was a Vaga, Landa laughed aloud. *In your father's veins there may have run the Koros-blood – but in your mother's? Sister, can you not feel it? You have lived in ignorance of your true goddess, yet has she not called to you from the earth, from the trees?*

Cata had known at once that the Priestess spoke the truth.

Now the mantras had twined for long enough; with a gesture, Landa brushed them aside. She flung back her head. 'Sacred Viana, send my sister a sign! Assist her, goddess, in her mystical quest! Help her to find

38

the one she seeks! Show her where the crystal of your powers has travelled, clutched against the heart of the one they call the Key!'

Now the declamations rang loudly, too loudly, battering at the walls of the dark silence. High, wild echoes escaped into the woods, but already a mysterious green glow was burning like phosphorus in the reeds and moss; already the goddess was gathering, growing, enfolding her worshippers in the mantle of her powers.

Cata's heart thundered. Landa reached out, grabbing her hand. They joined in a dance, capering and cavorting like mad things under the web of moon-shadowed branches. Still the phosphorus burned on, growing brighter. Now the green light was rising higher, raging through the branches of the oak like fire; now a column of dazzling brightness came spinning between them as they danced round and round. Violent, impossible teemings of life came fizzing into being beneath their feet – flowers and ferns, grasses and vines, slithering and burgeoning, rippling and writhing. Brighter, brighter grew the column of light, but now it was more than just light. Cata's eyes blurred. Gasping, astonished, she could only look on as the image of a crystal – a green crystal – appeared before them, spinning in the blistering light.

'Jem!' she burst out. 'Jem, where are you?'

'Goddess!' cried Landa. 'Sacred Viana, show my sister the path she must follow! All-merciful one, show her where—'

But before Landa could say any more, her voice was swallowed in a wave of sound. Power exploded up from the earth.

The women cried out.

Torn apart, they were flung to the ground. Violently the beam of light began to flicker. Cutting across the greenness came a flash of gold, then another, then another. All at once the crystal was gone, and in its place, spinning above the ground, was the naked statue-like figure of a man, his head flung back and his arms outstretched. Only in shape did the figure seem human. His skin was gold, and golden light streamed searingly from his eyes.

'No!' cried Landa. 'This cannot be!'

'What is it?' Cata shouted. 'What's happening?'

'Interference! Some other magic!'

'Is it evil?'

'I don't know!'

Around them, all the elements were a churning maelstrom. The light was flashing. First the green crystal, then the golden man; green then gold, green then gold. Then the crystal and the man were gone, and in their place was only a hurricane of light. Reeds were flattened, flowers torn free, sucked into the shrieking, uprushing beam. Even the brook became a churning mass. Branches and vines twisted and contorted, dancing in a terrible, crazed ecstasy.

Landa screamed, 'It's sucking me in!'

Desperately she clawed at the roots and grasses. Wildly her robes fluttered about her. In any moment she would vanish, spirited away into the swirling fury.

'Hang on—'

'Cata, I can't—'

'Just hang on, hang on—'

With one hand, Cata clung to a sturdy root; with the other, she grabbed at Landa's billowing robes, clutched and clawed at her flailing limbs.

No good, no good: she needed both hands. There was nothing for it: Cata flung herself forward. With a surge of energy she tore at Landa's shoulder. Landa cried out. Gasping, she splashed into the surging brook. She was saved!

But in the next instant, it was Cata who was screaming.

'No—!'

Landa scrambled back to the bank, to no avail. With horrified eyes she could only look on as Cata surged upwards into the beam of light.

'*Cata!*'

But it was over – all at once, it was over. Suddenly the terrible magic was gone; gone were the lights and the swirlings of the air; gone were the wind and the ragings of the brook. All these things were gone as if they had never been.

And so was Cata.

Chapter 6

THE SECOND VANISHING

'Jem . . . Jem!'

Jem's eyes snapped open. He had been dreaming, and though his dream vanished at once, for a moment he seemed to smell burning on the air. Before his eyes was a dance of flame.

'Fire?' he breathed, but the fire had been an illusion. There was only the night, pressing all around him – night, and the hand that was shaking his shoulder. 'Raj?'

'Jem, listen – there's something going on.'

Jem listened. The hour must be late, or some of the sailors would still be huddled round a lamp, splitting the darkness with their jokes and violent gaming. Now there were only muffled snores; there were scurryings of rats; there were the softest of sloshings, creakings, knockings. The ship was becalmed and the sails were furled. Through the rigging the moon shone clearly, webbing the deck with grids of gold.

'Listen? There's nothing.'

'I don't mean listen, I mean look. I mean – Jem, just come. Come to the stern and I'll show you – quick!'

Jem groaned, struggling out from the hammock he had strung up in the bows. Rajal's bedroll lay a little distance away. Only on the coldest nights had the two friends slept below, and there had been no cold nights since they left Port Tiral. Just as well: the bowels of the ship were cramped and dirty, there were no windows and the air was foetid with the reek of salt-pig, lingering from the galley, and the foul odours of the men. Sometimes Rajal would pine for a cabin, a proper cabin of their own, but there was only one for passengers, and that was Lord Empster's.

Jem did not mind: he liked to sleep up here, close as he could be to the ship's figurehead that reminded him so strangely of his lost beloved. Often Jem would gaze upon this mysterious wooden lady, falling into reveries of his golden days with Cata. Several times he had asked the captain about the figurehead, and how it could be that the ship had got her name. *Catayane, Catayane?* was all the old man would say. *A fine old name, is it not? A fine name for a lass!*

Jem could only agree.

Rajal staggered, for all the world as if the *Catayane* were pitching, suddenly, on a high sea.

'Raj, you're drunk! What's this all about?'

Jem guessed that his friend had not yet been to bed. Shipboard life had been bad for Rajal. He was drinking too much rum, and at times his behaviour was distinctly odd – but then, they were all behaving oddly. Jem thought of his own hasty exit from dinner, of the waves of fear that had swept over him suddenly. Now, in his pounding temples, he still seemed to feel their subsiding wake. He swallowed hard, his mouth dry and acrid. The night no longer seemed so warm. Jem became aware of a descending chill, bringing with it a layer of briny mist. He rubbed his arms.

Stumbling, they made their way through the darkness.

'So what should I see?'

'Shh! Just follow.'

With a theatrical furtiveness, Rajal glanced up at the crow's nest where Scabs, by now, would be fast asleep, then backwards and forwards to the bow, the stern. Now he led Jem across the quarterdeck, lurching his way round the glinting cannons, the coils of rope, the heavy spokes of the capstan. From the edge of the poopdeck he pointed, as if in triumph, to the waters below. Jem's brow furrowed, but when he looked down, there was only the sea, glimmering about the rudder and the rounded stern.

Rajal burst out, 'But it was there, it was!'

'Shh! Raj, what?'

Exasperated, Rajal turned away. Suspended above their heads was a Wenayan ensign, one of many different flags the captain kept on board. This particular flag was useful, so the captain maintained, to deter privateers – or rather, other privateers. On a fleeting breeze the flag flapped once, weakly, like the wing of a dying bird. Rajal slumped far across the wooden parapet, his head in his hands. 'Oh, I can't be mad, can I?'

'Careful – you'll be overboard! What do you mean, mad?'

Rajal tugged at his hair, as if he wanted to pull it out in tufts. 'I stayed too long with the captain after you were gone – made myself sick on all that rum.'

'That's not hard! But Raj, all this drinking ever since we came on board: it's not like you.'

Jem remembered Rajal as he had been before, back in the days they had spent on the road. Then it had been Jem who was the rackety fool, Rajal the careful, sensible one. Already it seemed so long ago. Since he had lost his sister, Rajal had changed. Jem was worried for him – worried, too, for the crystal that Rajal now wore. He wanted to comfort his friend, but what to say, and how, he did not know.

42

His friend was saying in a flat voice, 'At last the old man's head crashed forward. The monkey danced round me and I pushed her away – then staggered up here and fell asleep, I think, slumped across the side like this.'

'That wasn't smart!'

'But that's when I saw it, you see,' said Rajal.

'In your sleep?' Jem thought of the flames that had sent him into a trance, and his dream came back to him. Fleetingly he saw a human body, screaming inside a flame – a towering, rushing column of fire. He shook himself. 'But Raj, what did you dream?'

'It wasn't a dream – I mean, I woke up. Lean over here and you can see into the windows—'

'Of the captain's cabin?'

'Lord Empster's. There was a light—'

'A lamp?'

'A rod of light. A spinning, unearthly rod of light—'

'Raj, you were dreaming.'

Rajal tugged his hair again. In the moonlight, his face was the colour of ash. 'Why should I be dreaming? We've seen so much magic—'

Jem shrugged. 'Yes, when we're close to the crystals.'

Rajal gestured to his chest, then to Jem's. 'Couldn't be much closer.'

'Not to the next one.'

'We're getting there, aren't we?'

'Actually, we're becalmed. You were dreaming, Raj.'

Rajal breathed deeply. A strange disappointment clouded his face and this time he tugged his hair harder, painfully. Jem winced. In the silence of the night, the murmurous sea had in it a quality of mocking insistence. The mist was growing thicker, churning into a fog.

So quickly? thought Jem.

That was when he felt something touch his leg – he gasped, but turning, saw it was only Buby the monkey, loping around them, hunched silently. He shuddered. Captain Porlo was so affable a fellow, but something about the monkey filled Jem with alarm. Once she had taken up the captain's concertina, squeezing out a high, eerie semblance of a tune. The captain had thought it delightful and laughed, but Jem had been overcome by a rush of strange fear.

Now Rajal touched him and Jem jumped again.

'I wasn't dreaming,' Rajal said softly. 'Jem, don't you think there's something about him—?'

'Lord Empster?'

'Yes! Something not quite right—'

Jem sighed. 'I've always thought that, Raj – since the first time I went to his house, just as the harlequin told me to do. Do you know, I half thought he would *be* the harlequin?'

'Empster?'

'Yes! The harlequin, in another disguise—'

'He's someone else. But who? Jem, what has he told you about the quest?'

'This time? Only that we'll be landing on the Qatani coast. We know he's got papers, diplomatic papers—'

'Faked?'

'But why? He's an important man—'

'Oh come on! Mustn't they be looking for him now?'

Jem scoffed, 'On the Qatani coast?'

'Why not? What do you know?'

'No more than you! Only that we're headed for Qatani, and that somewhere in the Caliph's Court, there's – well, I suppose there's a clue.'

'At the Court?' Rajal considered this. 'This Caliph – I wonder, is he the one with the cobber-as?'

Jem had to smile. He snaked his hand forward, like a hoody head. '*Sss!*'

But all at once Rajal grabbed Jem's wrist. 'Jem! Look – it's happening again!'

Startled, Jem gazed below. Fog was churning thickly round the hull, but through Lord Empster's diamond-paned windows, cutting sharply through the clouded darkness, came a spinning rod of light. It was as Rajal had said, just as he had said.

'But what can it be?'

'Something evil, I know it!'

'Raj, hold my legs.'

'What?'

They spoke in urgent whispers. 'That's no lamp, no flame – no ordinary flame.'

'I told you!'

'Yes – and now I want to see what it is. If I lean over far enough, I can look through the window.'

Rajal was aghast. 'He'll see you!'

'So? He's my guardian!'

'A guardian who locks himself in his cabin and won't come out! Why don't you just go and bash on his door?'

'He'll hide it then, won't he – whatever makes that light?' Why Jem was sure of this, he could not have said, but somehow he knew the light was a secret – a dangerous secret. 'Now hold my legs.'

Rajal grimaced. By now, his drunkenness was the merest throbbing

44

memory. Suddenly their positions were reversed and again he was doleful, sensible Raj, trying to restrain his exuberant friend.

As Jem clambered into place, Buby began to shriek. Back and forth, back and forth her tail beat the deck and her spindly fingers grabbed first at Rajal, then at Jem.

'Oh, fling her overboard!' cried Jem, exasperated.

They both swiped at the mangy creature, but just in time she darted out of the way, scurrying into the rigging. Only later would it occur to Rajal that the monkey had only been trying, as best she could, to prevent the disaster that was shortly to happen. Rajal braced himself, digging his nails hard into Jem's straining calves. Jem protested, but Rajal would not relax his grip. 'Be careful, Jem!'

'You're the one who'd better be careful!'

Jem hung upside down over the side of the ship. Almost at once, he began to regret this escapade. The blood rushing to his head was bad enough; the bile to his throat was worse. He swallowed hard. He gripped the cracking ledge of the window frame, edging his way down towards the spiral of light. How bright it was!

'Over a bit.'

'This way?'

'The other. Now down a bit – just a bit.'

Empurpled, Jem's head bobbed beneath the level of the window. Now the strange light played across his face. He screwed up his eyes, fending off the radiance.

That was when things began to go wrong. First the crystal, in its leather bag, slipped towards his jaw. Only Jem's tunic-button kept the bag from falling, splashing into the sea. He clutched his throat.

Then he saw it.

Jem cried out.

※

At that moment, far away in the desert dunes, another curious scene was about to be enacted. Beneath the clear, many-starred sky, reclining round campfires, was a party of wanderers in long white robes. It was a large party, spreading far across the starlit sands. By now, like the camels they would ride at dawn, many were sleeping, but some were still joking, gaming, smoking. They were all men, and formidable ones, sinewy and steely-eyed.

To an observer, coming upon them there, it would have been clear at once that these were no ordinary travellers. They were not merchants; they were not pilgrims; nor did they wear the uniforms of a Unang army. But if the observer were a Unang, he would know at once who they were, and know that, in truth, they *were* an army of a sort. Fear would fill his heart, and he would hope only that the Ouabin[1] were bound anywhere but the place from which he had come, or the place to which he was going.

Now, from the late revellers, a song breaks forth. Ringing above the dunes, the song has about it something strangely sinister, for all that its melody, on the verse at least, is an innocent lilt. It is a song that is to prove of great significance in events that are to follow.

VERSE

Time may run swiftly or time may run slow,
Marriage brings pleasures that all men should know:
First fix your sights on the girl you desire,
Win her, enrich her and bathe her in fire!

CHORUS

Marry and burn!
The wheel shall turn!
What bold lover needs ever to yearn?
Seize your treasure from the gleaming py-y-y-re—
Marry and burn,
Marry and burn!

But now we turn from the revellers to one who is not of their number, but who is, nonetheless, very much awake, and stealing away into the wild, lonely dunes. Soon he is concealed from all eyes, and no sound comes to him but the distant echo of the song.

Wives may cost dearly while lovers come cheap,
Still, they bring pleasures that all men should reap:
Ah, for the day when you give her your name,
Clutch her, ignite her and douse her in flame!
Marry and burn, &c.

The man smiles. He almost laughs. Yes indeed, there is a maiden that soon he shall douse in flame! He sinks to his knees, flinging his hands to the skies. On and on comes the echo of the song as the golden presence forms in the air before him. Yes, yes, he had known he was right. He had felt the summons, felt it like a physical ache.

'Golden One, it is true? You shall soon be in this land?'

'Ouabin, would you doubt my word?'

'Never! I trust only that all goes well.'

'Ah, trust! But can I trust you to play your part?'

---

[1] Pronounced *Wah*-bin.

'Is my name not Rashid Amr Rukr? I only hope, my lord, that I may trust *you*.'

'Fool! Do you not know my name?'

'I could guess, my lord. I believe, indeed, that I have.'

And Rashid Amr Rukr, with the boldness of his breed, looks into the eyes of the golden apparition. Another man, at that moment, might have been struck down. Instead, the Sheik's unearthly visitor only smiles, extends a hand and raises up the Ouabin leader. Now the golden light bathes the Sheik too, and much understanding, and many promises, pass like magic into his mind. Ecstasy fills him as he thinks of the power that soon, soon shall be within his grasp.

Back in the camp, the song has reached its climax.

> *Deserts are places the gods have accursed,*
> *There men live harsh lives of heat, drought and thirst:*
> *Give them a future unburdened with dread,*
> *Rashid and Qatani's princess must wed!*

> *Marry and burn!*
> *The world must learn*
> *Ouabin power is our sole concern!*
> *Princess Bela Dona holds the ke-e-e-ey—*
> *Marry and burn,*
> *Marry and burn!*

✺

'Jem, what is it?'

But Jem could only gaze, astonished, into his guardian's cabin, where the golden creature revolved slowly, just above the floor. Light streamed from its eyes and its mouth opened and closed as if speaking to an unseen stranger, far away.

If there had been no more, perhaps Rajal would never have let Jem go. It was what happened next that made him stagger back, releasing his precarious grip.

The night cracked open.

Massively, a bolt of lightning – green lightning – fizzed from the skies.

Now it was Rajal's turn to cry out. He was flung to the deck. From the cabin below came an unearthly shriek, and at the same time there was another shriek, all too earthly – and a mighty splash.

'Jem!' Rajal scrambled up, but collapsed again at once, doubled over in pain.

The next moments were all confusion.

They would end in greater confusion still.

First there was Rajal shouting for help, then furiously ringing the ship's bell. Around his feet, Buby capered wildly. Scabs, started awake by the lightning flash, shinned down rapidly from the crow's-nest; then there were the sailors milling up from the hold.

There was even Captain Porlo, bursting on to the quarterdeck, stumbling and roaring, 'Man overboard? Who's overboard?'

'There he is!' cried Scabs excitedly, leaping and pointing until the drunken captain struck him a blow to the side of the head. Then someone – but it was not Rajal – was jumping into the sea. Desperately, his back aching where he had fallen, Rajal could only look on as a lantern swung on the foggy air, as harsh voices bellowed, as ropes span down over the side of the ship.

The captain grabbed his arm, wrenching at it brutally. 'What would you young scamps be playing at, eh?'

'Captain, we didn't mean—!'

'Didn't mean, didn't mean—!'

The captain – enraged, perhaps, at his sudden awakening – only flung Rajal aside again. There were things to be done. All at once a driving rain was scattering the fog and far off, through the murk, dawn was breaking. Buby leapt down on to her master's shoulders, urging the old man into bellowing life.

'Haul up the anchor! Unfurl the sails! You swabs, can't you feel the wind's come back?'

With that, the captain stumped away, and only Rajal was there to exclaim when the man overboard lay before him at last. The figure was blue-skinned, but still breathing hard.

Only something was wrong.

'That's not Jem,' Rajal whispered hoarsely.

Dripping sailors shambled away. Rajal called after them, clawed at them. *'That's not Jem!'*

Someone had taken the lantern away. In the darkness, the sailors could not see – they thought Rajal was raving, that was all. Distraught, he rushed to the ship's side, looking down desperately into the shifting waves.

Where had Jem gone? Where could he be?

He turned back helplessly to the figure on the deck. The figure wore the garb of a Zenzan peasant-boy. Seaweed-like tendrils of raven-dark hair splayed out from around the fine-featured face.

The eyes opened, gazing in astonishment at Rajal.

'Wh-where am I?' Cata said.

Chapter 7

GIRL-BOY AND BOY

On the Dorva Coast the cliffs rose steeply, dividing sea from land like a rocky, jagged wall. A road clung perilously to the clifftops, rising here, plunging there between chasms and curtains and narrow ledges of blazing white boulders. It was morning, still early, but already the heat filled the sky like fire.

Rapidly along the road came a rider. Pale dust clouded the air behind him; his camel whinnied and harsh hands, jerking at the reins, snapped its gaze brutally from the depths below. Beneath the rider's headdress were steely, unblinking eyes – the eyes of a Sosen messenger. One of the finest cameleers from the Sosen Plateau, like all his people he wore flowing robes, but his robes were black instead of white, and secured at wrists and forehead with flashing golden bands. Embossed on the bands was the Crest of Kaled. Common folk trembled at the sight of the rider, for they knew he bore with him the Sultan's Resolve.

He turned a rocky corner. Staying his mount, he surveyed the scene before him. One last village, one last paltry caravanserai, jutted from a spit of land a league or so ahead. From there, his path was clear. Around the curve of a bay the cliffs shelved slowly, sinking at last to meet the glimmering sea. From the head of the bay came flashings of marble, glass and gold. Sails billowed colourfully on the deep blue water.

It was Qatani, Jewel of the Shore. Principal seaport of Lower Unang, the city-state was the seat of the Caliph of Qatani, brother of the Sultan and greatest of the princelings who were suffered to rule under his imperial sway.

The rider touched his heart. It was a sacred gesture, a sign of luck, habitual amongst his tribesmen when their destination loomed near. Soon his spurs would dash at his camel's flanks again, but first he had to perform a second sacred observance. His eyes gauged the angle of the sun. Hardly necessary: as if by instinct, he knew the time.

Green. It was the time called Green.

Dismounting, the rider made the stay-sign before his camel's eyes. The eyes glazed and he stepped a little away, raising his arms high above his head. Now giving forth a strange high wailing, the black-garbed figure turned and turned about, then cast himself down, prostrating himself in the direction of the Sacred City.

49

It was the second of the Five Submissions, enjoined daily upon all the faithful. From an ancient prophecy, which told of five great mortal rulers who would reign over Unang in the days before the gods returned to this world, the Submissions were known as Catacombs, Green, Dust, Wave and Stars. All over Unang, in cities and towns, women and men of every type and class went through the same motions. Desert caravans ground to a halt. Milling crowds were suddenly still. In the fields, lone workers cast down hoes and scythes; in noble courts, as in muddy swineyards, all was silent but for the sound of prayer.

For long moments the rider remained thus, mumbling and bobbing. The sea below the road was a vast field of blue, glistening but unmoving in the bright morning; barren hills stretched inland, spiky with grey-green clumps of ugly, coarse vegetation.

Following the litanies he had learnt as a boy, the rider prayed for the Sultan, for his health, his wealth, his wisdom, his mercy, for his hands and feet, for his eyes and mouth, for his lungs and liver and stomach and bowels and the vigour and fecundity of his virile member. Only at the end, as he had always done, did he add an appeal for his own well-being, wishing that his life should be spared, and that in time he should know the love of a certain young maiden from the far plateau that was his home.

It was a modest prayer, but would not be answered.

The rider was a loyal man, steadfast and true, but he also had in him a foolish streak. Many phases had passed since he had set out on his mission. Now, so close to delivering his message, he should have made for Qatani with all dispatch. But the day was early yet; he could be there by nightfall. In the village ahead, a pleasant caravanserai would tempt him to linger.

It was to be a fatal temptation.

※

Ameda, Daughter of Evitamus – Amed, as she was known – crept on tiptoe across the cool tiles of her father's chamber. On a shabby mat by the window, the old man still prostrated himself, his prayers rolling from his lips in a sweet, high singsong. How Father loved that window! Framed in bright sunlight, he was a tableau of devotion. From here, he liked to think, his words fluttered like starlings over the dunes to the Sacred City.

The far side of the chamber was deep in shadow. Glancing back at her own abandoned prayer mat, Amed felt a twinge of guilt, but not much. It was not slipping away that worried her: that was easy. Oblivious in his sacred rapture, Father never knew when his daughter had left his side. The hard part was getting back in time. Amed winced – already she seemed to feel the sajana-strap lashing across her back. If only she'd made Faha Ejo come to the caravanserai!

But no. Would she have a mixer think her a coward?

Amed was no ordinary Unang girl.

By the door of the chamber was a dark, ornate chest. Amed braced herself. Glancing back one more time, she lifted the heavy lid. She had meant to raid the chest last night, while Father was sleeping. Instead, and as usual, after a day of chopping wood, stacking shelves and winching up water, she had fallen asleep as soon as she lay down, waking only when Father nudged her in the morning.

Now she had to be quick. Rucking up the cloth that lay beneath the lid, Amed jammed the hinge with a wedge of velvet and plunged a hand into the soft depths.

The musk of fabric was intoxicating. For as long as she could remember, Amed had been fascinated by this pungent chest, filled with memories of Father's old life. When she was small, she had urged Father to don his robes again, but Father had only smiled. Once, when the old man was out, Amed had dragged out a cloak spangled with stars, parading down the stairs and all the way round the yard of the caravanserai, trailing the glittering cloth behind her. Travellers and servant-girls had laughed and applauded, but when Father had found out his face had been black with rage. A moonlife passed before the sajana-weals vanished from Amed's back. If Amed would behave with the boldness of a boy, then she must be treated as one, her father had said, as he always did when he whipped her.

After that, the girl – the *girl-boy*, as Faha Ejo called her – had been careful, but still she would often repair to the chest. Everything inside it was as well known to her as a friend: the star-cape, the pointed cap, the cylinder of gold, the thick book that had to be opened with a key.

She loved these treasures, but there was rubbish in the chest as well – empty scent-bottles, a scratched dinner-plate, a chessboard with no pieces, a ring with no stone. There was a little ivory camel, missing one leg. There was a sand-timer with cracked glass and no sand inside. Then there was the konar-light. Lying in the very bottom of the chest, jammed beneath a roll of musty carpet, the lamp was a shabby, battered thing that Mother Madana would never allow to be used in her caravanserai. Hardly the priceless thing Faha Ejo had demanded – still, it would just have to do. Father, at least, would never notice it was gone. Amed felt for the shape and drew it forth. Well . . . it wasn't so bad, was it? Perhaps, to a mixer, even this old brass lamp would be a luxury beyond his dreams!

So Amed hoped.

Father's singsong still fluttered from the window as she quickly closed the chest, padded from the room and down the stairs. Like lightning she flashed past Mother Madana as the crone, impiously ignoring the time, passed in and out of her kitchens. The formidable mistress of the caravanserai would be sure to punish Amed if she knew what the girl was doing. Only at prayer was Amed free from the demands that she haul this, heave that, fetch this, carry that, all day long.

She dashed across the yard. A moment later she was bounding up the hills behind the village, leaping over the sharp rocks and salty grey-green bushes.

'Infidel!' she called. 'Infidel!'

A grin gleamed in a dark face. 'Girl-boy!'

On a curve of white boulder, Faha Ejo the goatherd lolled in the sunshine, smoking a clay pipe.

'Better girl-boy than infidel.'

'Infidel than girl-boy!'

It was their customary greeting. The friends slapped palms together, hard enough to sting. Breathless, Amed cast herself down on the boulder beside the goatherd.

'I've got it,' she said proudly.

'Hm?' Faha Ejo blew out a smooth stream of smoke, his eyes flickering over his scrawny flock. Some slumped forlornly on the slopes below; others, with a thwarted air, nuzzled at the stonecrop.

'I said I've got it!' Amed thrust the lamp under Faha Ejo's nose.

'This is it?'

It was a very ugly lamp. Dubiously the goatherd took the mean offering, running a hand over the bulbous burning-bowl, the ear-shaped handle and the jutting spouts, one for oil, one for konar-powder. Impatient, Amed plucked the pipe from Faha Ejo's mouth, sucking back too deeply on the rough tobarillo.

Faha Ejo drew down his mouth. 'It's battered.'

Amed coughed. 'It's old.'

'So I see. And dirty.' The goatherd snatched back his pipe again.

Amed swallowed hard. 'Old things are valuable.'

'If they're gold or silver, girl-boy. Couldn't you do better than this?'

'It's a fine lamp!'

'For a hovel!'

Affronted, Amed quite forgot the truth of the matter. Grabbing the lamp, she would have run back to the caravanserai, but Faha Ejo leapt up.

He clutched Amed's arm. 'Still, Cousin Eli might take it.'

Amed brightened. 'You think so?'

'We'll have to ask him. Come on, let's find him now.'

Nervously Amed glanced back downhill. The flat roof of the caravanserai flamed accusingly in the sunlight. 'Supplications are nearly over.'

'What, you're frightened?'

'I've got to be back.'

Faha Ejo snorted. 'Tell the old man you were taken short – Mother Madana's sheep-eye stew!'

Amed had to laugh – Faha Ejo always made her laugh. With a grin, the goatherd snatched the lamp again, careering away.

'Infidel, your goats!'

'Where will they go? Come on, race you!'

It would be no contest. Faha Ejo had all the litheness of his mountain-bred tribe. Struggling to keep up, Amed almost slid down the stony hillside. Wheeling out her arms to keep her balance, she took in the scene that lay below – not just the village but the clifftop, the sea, and somewhere in the distance, the dazzle of riches that was Qatani.

How mean was her village!

How large, how splendid, was the great world!

With Faha Ejo, Amed always saw the larger view. Though she had lived for – oh, at least fifteen sunrounds, the girl from the caravanserai had known nothing beyond this village of her childhood. Often she had feared that she never would. It was true that the prospects before her were bleak. Who, as her father said despairingly, would marry a girl-boy? Amed knew only that she dreamed of more than marriage, and of a life that was more than drudgery. By now, her dull days might have damped the fires within her, convincing her that life was a drab affair after all. Instead, last Koros-season, the mixers had come to town. Time and again, Mother Madana had told her to keep away from them; time and again, Amed had disobeyed.

Soon the sparks inside her had flamed back into life.

Faha Ejo had never meant to inspire his new friend. Nonchalantly, without the faintest sense of wonder, the goatherd would speak of the places he had seen, the jewelled cities, the mountains capped with ice, the far realms of pink and purple dunes, shifting like mirages in the shimmering heat. Like a painter, summoning pictures on the air, Faha Ejo showed Amed the Dead Sea of Geden, the Jungles of Janaga. In casual words he called back into being the Great Fire of Faqbar, the Nardac murders, and the time the Sultan's troops had sacked the Chasm of Ryn.

From Faha Ejo, Amed had learnt that the world was an extraordinary place. She had also learnt to smoke, to blaspheme, to lie and to steal. Now, if only the lamp were payment enough, would come a still greater forbidden pleasure.

'Come on, slow-wheel!' Faha Ejo called back.

Chapter 8

A GREAT MAN IN QATANI

They skidded into the mixer-maze, the warren of shanties and tents and wagons that huddled behind the flat-roofed houses. Cookingpots, pisspots, curtains of laundry, strung-up seaweed and strung-up goatmeat obstructed their way through the noxious alleys. Flies buzzed, babies squalled. Smoke and shit-smells lingered on the air. There was laughter and music.

All good Unangs despised the mixers. Some said they were as bad as Vagas, though no one nowadays could say for sure – no Vaga-tribes were left in the southlands. Still, there was Vaga-blood in many a mixer's veins. Others, like Faha Ejo, were Xladins, scattered in the diaspora of the Xlada Wars; most were a crazy-quilt of races, Harand and Yuqi and Geden, Faqbar and Nardac and Ryn. In some, there was even Wenaya-blood, or traces of Zaxon, Varlan, Tiralo. In any case they were all infidels, and all, as Mother Madana often said, dirty and shiftless and not to be allowed in her caravanserai – no, not for the world. They were pedlars, indigents, harlots and rogues, but never servants and seldom slaves.

Everyone knew you could not trust a mixer.

Faha Ejo grabbed a runny-nosed little boy. 'Where's Cousin Eli?'

The boy looked blank and snuffled his snot.

'Papa?' Faha Ejo rounded his hands on the air, suggesting an enormous belly.

Delighted, the boy laughed and pointed.

In the gap between a tumbledown shack and a rickety van, Faha Ejo's cousin – the little boy's father – squatted in the dust, smoking his pipe and gnawing intermittently at what looked like a dog-bone. The dog, whose bone it perhaps was, lay miserably at his feet. Behind him, Faha Ejo's mother stood over a stewpot, ripping feathers from a dead seagull. At the sight of her son, she cawed through brown teeth, 'Eh, Faha-boy! Goats, goats!'

Faha Ejo ignored her. Hiding the lamp behind his back, he punched his cousin's shoulder.

'Eh!'

'Eh-eh!'

Man and boy slapped each other back and forth several times until

Faha Ejo jumped away, grinning and beckoning. At first his cousin would not come, but at last, with a display of weariness, he struggled up on his flabby legs and waddled after the boys. With the dog following, and the snot-boy as well, they wound their way out of the maze.

Amed did not like Faha Ejo's cousin. The fat man had not arrived in the village with the rest of the band, but instead had appeared only a few days ago, driving a shabby old Vaga-van. Breaking the journey that had taken him to another, more distant maze, far along the coast, he was on his way back to Qatani. If he claimed his journey was an urgent one, food and comfort could nonetheless delay him. Eli Oli Ali was lazy, and a troublemaker too, but it seemed it was as well to keep in with him. In Qatani, according to his nephew, he was a considerable man of business.

Amed found it hard to believe. A mixer, a man of business? The fat fellow claimed that he had been to fetch his sister, whom he hoped to sell in the city. He kept the girl locked in his van, and none of the others had seen her; but she was said to be a beautiful girl, more beautiful than any she-mixer had a right to be. If anyone could get a good price for her, Eli Oli Ali could, or so all the mixers admiringly claimed.

Amed could only feel a confused disgust. Yesterday, in a wild moment, Faha Ejo had declared that they must run away to Qatani, hitching a ride with Cousin Eli. Eli would take them, of course he would! But if the fat mixer had laughed at the goatherd, he had laughed even more at Amed. Pawing her arm, leering at her, he had asked if she were a girl or a boy. If a girl, he said, he might just have a use for her!

In the middle of the night, waking on her bedroll in the caravanserai, Amed had heard raucous songs, echoing from the maze. Clasping her arms about her ears, she had felt a strange, desperate helplessness, and her cheeks had burned with shame. But still she had fallen in with Faha Ejo's latest foolish plan.

※

They emerged on the clifftop, gulls scrabbling round them until the fat man, with a cry of 'Pah!', flung his dog-bone down towards the sea. The dog howled and Eli Oli Ali kicked him; a pained look shot across the snot-boy's face.

Grinning, Faha Ejo produced the lamp. 'What do you think?'

With a sigh, the fat man took the offering, turning it round and round in his pudgy hands. He stuck out his lip; he scratched his moustaches and his stubbly chin. His face was greasy and beneath each of his nails was a half-moon of dirt.

He said at last, 'For Kua? Pah!'

'Pah?' Faha Ejo affected a look of amazement. Pacing back and forth along the clifftop, he proclaimed the splendours of the lamp with a conviction that, in the artistry of its sophistry, would not have shamed the Vizier of the grandest royal court. Was this not a lamp of rare beauty? A product of the finest craftsmanship? A lamp not unfit for the most splendid palace, for the most sacred altar? By such a lamp, the wisest Imams might intone the Threnody of Theron; by such a lamp, a Prince of royal blood might consummate his marriage vows.

Lowering his voice, Faha Ejo stepped close to his cousin. 'By such a lamp, might not the beauties of the fair Dona Bela shine forth all the more?'

The fat man bridled. The lamp clattered to the stony ground and he seized Faha Ejo's throat. 'Speak not of my sister with disrespect!'

Faha Ejo gasped, 'No! I speak only of the lamp—'

'Trash!' Eli Oli Ali kicked the lamp and it would have skittered over the cliff-edge if the snot-boy had not bounded forward, grabbing it. Laughing, the little boy danced on the clifftop, holding aloft the battered lamp like a trophy. It flashed in the bright sunlight.

Faha Ejo broke from his cousin's grip. 'Cousin Eli,' he sputtered, 'you promised—'

'For a price!'

'I bring payment—'

'Some luxury of the Court, you said!' Contemptuously the fat man looked at Amed. 'What do you think I am, girl-boy? Eh?' He gestured over the glittering bay. 'Why, in your fine capital, there are those who'd pay purse after purse of gold for a skin – one skin – of Kua-ferment. And you come up with a dirty old konar-light! Don't you understand, I'm a man of business? Don't you understand I must fight and fight against Casca Dalla?'

This was a name Eli had often mentioned, even in the short time he had been in the mixer-maze; the name belonged, it seemed, to a hated rival who threatened to steal his business away. In bringing his beautiful sister to market, Eli hoped to score a masterstroke in his eternal war against Casca. Triumphantly he claimed, once and for all, he would show that if a man wanted quality, it was to Eli that he must go.

'You think it's easy in Qatani?' he wailed, gesticulating. 'Think I loll in luxury, with wealth to give away? For an honest man to make a living, it's a never-ending struggle! A konar-light? Why, if I were such a fool, Casca would have triumphed long ago! Pah! Konar-light, indeed . . .'

With that, shaking his head at the ignorance of the young, the fat man waddled disgustedly away, his scrawny dog shambling after him.

'Theron!' Faha Ejo blasphemed. Swiping back the lamp, he might have flung the thing into the sea, but something stayed him and instead he shoved it under his jacket.

The snot-boy protested at losing his new toy, but Faha Ejo chased him away with a threatening roar.

Stabbing his pipe back between his teeth, Faha Ejo slumped against the side of a van. Amed felt guilty. For a moment she feared her friend might turn on her and was relieved when the goatherd muttered instead, 'The fat pig! What's Casca Dalla got to do with us? I'll bet Eli's drunk all the ferment himself!'

Amed echoed her friend's outrage, but secretly she was relieved. To drink ferment was a fearful transgression. In the city, smoking-dens might swirl to fumes of esh and masha and other potent harvests of the Jarvel Coast; in every bazaar were powders and potions, seeds and leaves to set the brain spinning merrily, or drifting into a haze of vision and dream. But ferment was different. In the Tablets of Theron, handed down by the Imams of Old, it was said that the fall of Agonis, the deluded sky god, came about when he supped from the glass proffered to him by an evil enchanter. So it was that *dreams from a glass* were forbidden in all the lands where Theron was worshipped.

Perhaps that was why they seemed so beguiling. Ferment-drinkers spoke of a vision beyond vision, of a joy beyond joy; ferment-sellers soon became rich. But if they were caught, buyers and sellers alike were punished severely. Some lost their lips, some their tongues; some were bastinadoed until all their bones were broken. Amed could – yes, definitely could – find it in her heart to wish such a fate upon Eli Oli Ali.

'I'd better be getting back,' she muttered miserably.

'Wait!' Faha Ejo grabbed her arm. 'You want to see something?'

'I can't!' Amed shrugged her friend away. In her mind she saw the sajana-strap, whipping back behind her father's head. She blundered into the maze again, pushing past the curtains of seaweed, the cookingpots, the fly-blown meat.

Faha Ejo tagged behind her. 'I was going to wait till you were reeling on Kua—'

'Infidel—'

'In a Kua-haze, I thought, it would be a vision of the gods—'

'I said I've got to go—'

'But girl-boy, I was wrong! Why, it would be a vision to a blind man—'

Amed turned, exasperated. 'Infidel! What are you talking about?'

Faha Ejo thrust his face into Amed's. The goatherd's breath was rich with tobarillo, his voice a hoarse whisper: 'Cousin Dona Bela!'

'What?'

Faha Ejo grinned. 'The fat pig thinks he's got her so safe. But there's a hole in the side of the van! You want to see?'

Amed's heart thumped hard. She knew she should run back to the caravanserai, but curiosity overcame her. Since hearing about this mysterious captive lady, she had been filled with a desperate pity – pity, and anger too.

In an instant she had forgotten the sajana-strap. An instant more, and she was squeezing with Faha Ejo into the rank space behind Cousin Eli's van. The timber was cracked and the bright paint was peeling.

Slithering slowly to a crouching position, Faha Ejo put his eye against the wall. The clatter of the maze rang all around them, but here they were concealed. Shadows dulled the brightness of the day as Faha Ejo let out a long, low whistle.

'A vision of the gods indeed!'

Eagerly Amed pushed her friend aside. She squatted on her haunches. The hole was no more than the size of her little finger, and at first she saw only blackness. She was about to protest, sure that Faha Ejo had played her for a fool.

Then came a bright blur of gold.

Amed shifted and the scene came into focus. A gasp escaped her. She had never seen inside a Vaga-van before. If this was a moth-eaten, mildewed affair, still it had remnants enough of its former glory. A lamp, far finer than her own shabby offering, cast its soft glow over plump upholstery, carved panelling, trailing beads and cloth. Incense wafted on the air and from the ceiling hung chimes of silver and glass, ready to jingle when the van was in motion.

But these things were not what arrested Amed. What made her gasp was the fair form, reclining on cushions on the floor of the van. Clad only in the sheerest of silks, Eli Oli Ali's sister was turned away from the spyhole, but even from the dark hair that cascaded down her back, from the flawless olive skin of her curving shoulder, Amed knew she was beautiful.

With a sigh, the girl lifted a many-bangled arm and strummed the hanging chimes above her head. Music like the running of a crystal stream filled the air as the lovely prisoner, swaying gently from side to side, intoned in a voice of matchless purity the following cryptic words:

> In my mind there are
> Five vanishings,
> Vanishing one by one:
> One is done in a soaring canopy,
> Two is blue down below.
> The third vanishing comes in the sun,
> The fourth through a darkened glass,
> But only after there are
> Five vanishings
> Shall I be real again!

Amed watched in silence. The song saddened her, troubled her, but most of all she was simply transfixed. Tears sprang at once, unknowingly, to her eyes. Never had she felt so strange an enchantment.

The enchantment was broken by a hand, grabbing between her thighs. Angrily Amed pushed Faha Ejo aside, but her friend was persistent.

'You're stiff! I felt it!'

This was not the first time they had played this game, but now Amed was angry. 'I'm a girl! Don't be stupid!'

'You're half a boy, aren't you?'

A moment later, the two friends were fighting, pummelling each other in the dirty alley.

'Eh!' came a rough voice.

'Eli!' With a wild laugh, Faha Ejo took to his heels. Amed scrambled up. Only the narrowness of the passage behind the van prevented the fat man from accosting her at once, dragging her out by the scruff of her neck. Amed would have time, just time enough, to escape. But first, she could not help herself.

Just one glimpse. One glimpse more.

Eli Oli Ali roared again, but Amed did not care.

Inside the van the girl called Dona Bela had turned, alarmed, to the sounds of the fray. Her veil had fallen and her beauty flamed out, dazzling in the golden light.

Amed cried out. Never, never would she forget that face.

Chapter 9

THE GOLDEN APPLES OF THE SUN

'Scabs! Scabs, where are you?'

Billowing through the windows came the tang of salt. A slant of sunlight, shifting with the tide, warmed the mouldering books and charts; little silver glitterings played on the scimitar and the musketoon and the tiger's head, flashing in the shallows of the fixed glass eyes.

'Scabs! What are you doing, squeezing your sores?'

There was a clattering in the gangway, but not a catastrophic one; Scabs must be struggling with his laden tray. On this tide, it would be like walking up a steep hill, a shifting one too, but Captain Porlo was hardly sympathetic to the trials of fellows blessed with the luxury of more than one leg. What did they know about walking?

Impatiently he clashed his knife and fork. It was a morning to make an old sea-dog ravenous. The sudden storm of the night before had given way to a sustained surge of wind, rippling through the sails like the breath of an impatient god; the very timbers of the captain's cabin juddered with the high, heady surge of the sea.

'Scabs, hurry up, you dirty swab! Really, is a man to wait all morning for his breakfast? Begging your pardon, miss,' the captain added, flashing Cata a shy, blackened smile. 'You'll excuse the roughness of old Faris Porlo, but never you mind, his bark's worse than his bite.'

Cata smiled back, jogging the monkey that had settled, like a contented infant, in her arms. If Buby were smelly and hardly clean, Cata did not mind; she sensed the benevolence in the captain's shabby friend, and loved her as she loved all the wild things of the world.

Rajal looked on resentfully; cruel he was not, but if only it had been the mangy old monkey, not Jem, who was caught in the flash of green lightning! Cata, it seemed, could explain the magic that brought her here, but neither Cata nor Rajal understood what had happened to the young man they both loved. Rajal shifted uncomfortably. Jem's fate was a catastrophe, and all they could do was sit with the old sea-dog, waiting for their breakfast!

'Scabs! At last!' bellowed the captain as the door was flung open. It was as well that the distance to the table was small; at that moment the ship lurched alarmingly and Scabs, for all the advantages of his two legs, did not so much stagger into the cabin as fall.

Buby shrieked, scrambling from Cata's grip, but there was no crisis; the tray crashed into the middle of the table, just where it should go. Scabs, it was true, had fallen face-first into the food, but Captain Porlo hardly cared. At once his eyes were big with greed. Pushing the cabin boy aside, the old sea-dog stuffed his mouth with a weevily biscuit, tore with impatient fingers at the salt-pig and mustard, and berated Scabs for not yet bringing him his rum.

The captain remembered himself a moment later; or rather, remembered the presence of the lady. He gestured after the departing Scabs. 'Don't mind that clumsy oaf, miss, none of his pustules have popped over the salt-pig. No, that's mustard ... just mustard, see?'

Cata was dubious, but hunger soon overcame her scruples. In her Wildwood days, she had kept to Papa's vow never to eat the flesh of a fellow creature. How appalled Papa would be if he knew all the things she had eaten since!

The captain urged her on. 'And Master Raj, you'll tuck in, won't you? That's right, show the lass the way. It's as well we're not having eggs, is all I can say. I likes a nice egg, I does, when we're in port. Scrambled. Ever tried them scrambled, miss? Now there's a dish fit for ... why, fit for a Queen, if you'll pardon me saying.'

Cata could only smile, acknowledging the gallantry. Since her strange arrival, she had exchanged her peasant's rags for a rich brocade gown, coloured green and brown like the earth. Retrieved from the plunder in the captain's chests, it gave her the air of a quality-lady, abroad upon some important visit. Cata would have preferred the garb of a man, as she had worn in Zenzau, but Lord Empster had other ideas. In the Courts of Unang, he claimed, no man would dare harm a foreign lady, and she would be more useful to them in that guise than another. Cata was doubtful, but bowed nonetheless to the nobleman's wisdom. From the first she sensed the power in him, and knew she must be wary.

The captain continued his efforts at polite conversation.

'I see Buby's taken to you at once, miss,' he observed, as the monkey came snuffling round the table again. 'Appreciates the delicacy of a fine lady, she does, after an old ruffian like me. Trust you found me cabin comfortable? And the bedroll? I shook out the fleas as best I could, but you know there's only so much a man can do, after them cobber-as have been at his leg. Poor old Lefty! Should have got Scabs to do it, I suppose, but I wouldn't have him sniffing round a fine lady's bedding, now would I, miss? If you'll pardon me again.'

Cata said she would, and assured the captain that really, she was no fine lady, and he need not have given up his bed for her. The captain could only reply that Faris Porlo might be accused of many things, but impoliteness to a lady would never be one of them.

'Not that I be an expert on ladies, miss, never having had the blessing of a wife, I mean. There was a sweetheart I had once, it's true, but I ask you, would Faris Porlo leave so fine, so fair a flower of womanhood pining, pining while her husband was at sea?'

'Couldn't she have come with you?' said Cata.

The captain looked shocked. 'Well really, miss! The sea's no place for a lass, now is it?'

'I'm at sea,' said Cata.

'Yes miss, and if I could put you ashore, somewhere nice and safe, I'd do it this instant! Ah, there be dark magic afoot in this world, when an innocent young maiden is snatched from dry land where she belongs, to find herself suddenly in an old hulk like this, surrounded by coarse, tarry fellows, and far from all the feminine fripperies she needs!'

Cata was about to tell the captain that her life on land had hardly been one of lacy frills and samplers when the door opened again. The sea-dog looked up eagerly, expecting his rum; his face darkened just a little when, instead of Scabs, he saw Lord Empster.

'Me lord,' he blustered, 'you'll take breakfast with us? I declares, you hardly eat, and this high wind's enough to make any man ravenous . . . Scabs! Scabs! Where's me rum? And His Lordship's, too?'

Lord Empster only smiled tightly and, without staggering at all, made his way to the table. Rajal looked intently into the nobleman's face; as always, it seemed mysteriously shrouded, concealed beneath the shadows of the broad-brimmed hat. Rajal thought again of the golden vision he had seen the night before. Had it been real? Could it have been real? Now, in the morning, it seemed a bad dream.

But if it had been a dream, Jem would still be here.

The nobleman lit his pipe. 'Porlo, we must talk. How long now till we make Qatani?'

'Why, another day should do it, at this rate,' said the captain. 'We've only got to round the Cape of Kept Promise, then hug in tight to the Dorva Coast. Ah, me lord, but what's to become of this treasure-hunt of yours, now the young fellow's gone and got himself drowned?'

Cata burst out, 'Drowned? Jem's not drowned!'

'He can't be dead, he can't!' Rajal cried.

'Hush, my young friends,' said Lord Empster kindly, and as if to allay their fears he produced from his pockets two bright golden apples. They took them gratefully. 'Porlo, you speak out of turn.'

'It's only what you told the tars, me lord. The young fellow's drowned, and the girl's the last survivor of a wreck. Just happened to be there, hm, hanging on for dear life? Went to rescue him, we did, and rescued her instead. A likely story, if you ask me . . . well, if you ask me tars! Let's just hope they don't notice the lass looks like me figurehead, that's all I can say. Or find out she calls herself Catayane! Best crew in Ejland you wanted for this voyage, me lord; that's what I got you, and they be no fools. There'll be mutterings of witchcraft below decks, you mark me words!'

Cata, forgetting the salt-pig, was biting into her golden apple; Rajal turned his own apple curiously in his hand, watching the sunlight play on its skin. Now how had Lord Empster, in the middle of the sea, procured such fresh, luscious fruit? Oh, he was a strange man, a strange man indeed!

Rajal's stomach rumbled. He bit into the apple.

'Porlo, what we tell the men and what we say amongst ourselves are two different things,' his guardian was continuing. 'But come, my young friends, I must instruct you in the part we are to play, for soon we are to reach a place stranger than any you have visited before. This would be dull for Porlo, who has already plumbed the secrets of all the lands of this world. Perhaps we shall go up on the deck, hm, and leave Porlo to his salt-pig and mustard? And his rum. And his monkey.'

Buby let out a hissing cry. Moments earlier, she had scrambled to share the food; now she cowered uncertainly in the corner, beneath the rusty scimitar that was fixed to the wall. Lord Empster produced a third apple and handed it to the monkey. Her manner softened and she grabbed the apple excitedly in her small, alarmingly human hands.

※

'Daughter of Orok, see your supplicant. Sister of Koros, hear her words. Most sacred Viana, soft as leaves, come to me now in this woodland place and show your mercy to an erring sister. By what fate, goddess, my magic has gone awry, I cannot say; by what fate my lost sister has been entangled, I shudder to contemplate. Know that I meant to achieve only good, and would not have meddled in the arts of darkness; know, goddess, that I have been true to you, as my sister has too, and if it lies within your grasp to return her to me, I beg you, return her to me now. Evil stalks this world, and the trials before us are sore ones; how much sorer must they be, I fear, if my sister shall never be restored to us! Daughter of Orok, see your supplicant. Sister of Koros, hear her words . . .'

But Landa's words were trailing away, becoming the merest whisper, as she crouched in the shadows of the ancient oak. Reeds and fronds pressed softly all around her. The little brook babbled close by, rolling and glimmering in the gathering sunlight. Landa sighed, resting her forehead against the cool bark. All night she had struggled to bring Cata back, praying and pleading, calling on all the magic she had learnt from

Priestess Ajl. It was to no avail. Never once had Landa felt even the faintest presence of the goddess. Again and again the thought came to her that she must not give up; again and again she felt the stabbing fear that Cata was gone, really gone, and would never come back.

She raised her arms, wearily determined to try again, when she heard a rustling behind her, and a kind voice. 'Priestess, come away. Come away now, child.'

Landa turned, and Hul was beside her. She flung herself into his arms, sobbing bitterly; the scholar, a little awkwardly, stroked her coppery braids.

'Poor Landa, I know how you suffer. All of us suffer at this grievous loss, but there is nothing more we can do here now. Remember, Bluejacket patrols are abroad, and Agondon is still far, far away. The day is upon us, and we must be on the move.'

Landa struggled to contain herself. Hul was right – besides, she thought, it was Recruit Wolveron who was lost, the surly young soldier, not her dear friend Cata. If she were not careful, Hul might think – why, he might think . . . She shook herself, brushed her eyes, smiling bravely when Hul added that Bando was presiding over breakfast and if they were quick there might be something left before the Friar had gobbled up their shares.

They pushed their way through the entangling branches. The heat of the day was descending swiftly, cutting its dazzling shapes through the dry, dusty leaves. In this Season of Theron, it seemed to Landa there could be no refuge for green, growing things, and the earth from which they sprang. Theron's land, she knew, was a desert of searing sands. An image came to Landa's mind, vivid as life, and she was puzzled, for she had never seen such a place before.

Fear filled her heart. She had wanted only to bring Cata a sign, a clue, to give her hope that one day she might find Jem again. Now who knew what terrible dangers Cata might be facing? Who knew, indeed, if Cata were still alive? But Landa would not think that way. She could not. She looked back, one last time, at the immemorial oak.

I won't give up, she said beneath her breath. *Cata, believe me, I won't give up.*

'Oh Hul,' she said aloud, 'I blame myself so terribly.'

The scholar considered this, a little more deeply, no doubt, than Landa would have wished.

'Philosophers have written much on the subject of blame,' he said, 'for what is the conundrum of the "Korosan Creation", foundation of all our mythologies, but an allegory of blame? In these Lands of El-Orok, blame and its cognates and corollaries – I speak, of course, of responsibility, vengeance and spite – might be considered the very elements in which our beings find the most enduring of their lodgings. For my part, I think of Vytoni's *Discourse on Freedom*. What did that greatest of authors say, but that no good could come from blame, endless blame, and that if we were to save ourselves, we must move beyond it?

'For that matter,' Hul could not resist adding, 'he also devotes a chapter[1] to the folly of meddling with gods and magic, arguing that we must win our freedom for ourselves, by our own efforts, in the daylight world. I fear I have seen a little too much, by now, to accept this view quite so wholeheartedly as once I did; certainly I shall provide extensive footnotes to this chapter, should I ever come to revise my edition, and indeed perhaps add a paragraph or so to my introduction; nonetheless, my dear, I do find myself wondering if *you*, perhaps, might not have done well to heed Vytoni's advice.'

Some moments passed while Landa endeavoured to find a meaning, should there be one, in this torrent of words, then suddenly she broke from her companion, wailing, 'Cruel Hul, you blame me!'

The scholar reddened, and caught her arm. 'Landa, no! I was only philosophising, I didn't mean to hurt you! You meant to do good, and there can be no blame. I only wonder if your ways are the best.'

Landa brushed at the tears that had started again, too quickly, in her eyes. A shaft of sunlight speared down through the trees, surrounding her young figure in a haze of gold. Rather to his surprise, Hul found himself thinking that Landa was a lovely girl, a lovely girl indeed; then, as if to chasten him, the girl sniffed and said, 'You are not of my faith, Hul; indeed, I fear you are a man of no faith. But the goddess is real, and so is magic. How otherwise would . . . would Recruit Wolveron be gone?'

Hul said softly, 'I think you mean Catayane, don't you?'

Landa gasped, 'Hul . . . you knew!'

'Just guessed, Landa. Jem's Uncle Tor, The Red Avenger, told me long ago of a man called Wolveron. Caused quite a stir, did Old Wolveron, in Tor's childhood village. Well, I knew the old man had a daughter, and I knew there was something strange about Recruit Wolveron.'

Landa had to laugh. 'Oh Hul, and we thought we were so clever! Do the others know?'

'Let's say there's no point in hiding the truth now. Hm?'

Landa nodded, then suddenly she was sad again, and repeated to herself her private vow:

I won't give up. Cata, believe me, I won't give up.

---

[1] 'On the Iniquity of the Mystic Persuasion': see pp. 223–231 in the edition edited by Hul (Eldric Hulverside) in his youth (Agondon: Free Philosophical Society, AC 994*a*).

'Rum! Scabs, where's me bloody rum?'

Captain Porlo was not displeased when Empster took the young folk away; they had barely touched their breakfast and after all, a tarry fellow could not afford to let good food go to waste. Not that the captain was greedy; he considered throwing Buby a biscuit, but the monkey was intent upon the strange apple.

Apples, indeed! Knowing little of such landlubbers' fare, the captain assumed that Empster must have been keeping the wretched things in his cabin all this time. Was that what he ate, when he didn't have his dinner for days on end? It was another mark of the nobleman's madness. Really, what did a man want with apples, when he could gorge himself on salt-pig?

With mustard, of course.

The captain sat back in his chair, looking round his shabby domain. He would not go on deck in this swell. With Scabs to wait on him, a chamberpot by his chair and the wafting, salt tang of the sea through the window, what need was there to stir?

But if he was comfortable, the old sea-dog was sad too, thinking of the lovely girl who looked so much like his dear wooden lady, the only bride he had ever known. Could it be true that her name was Catayane? The captain had no lust for the girl – he was past the time for that – but how she made him think of all that might have been. Had he never met them cobber-as, Porlo often thought, he might have been a different man, a bolder man. His reverie turned to the dear girl, a Varl-lass she was, who might have been his real bride, long years ago. Married a fellow called Crum, last he'd heard of her. Farmer Crum. Had a boy, soon after. Why, the lad could have been his own son!

The captain wiped a tear from his eye, shook himself and called again for rum. It was no good dwelling on the past, was it? He must take a leaf from Buby's book. Affectionately he looked at his dear little friend as she turned the apple round and round in her paws, her cheeks bloated with munching. To Buby, nothing else seemed to matter; she thought only of her treasure. Now the captain thought of treasure too, and hummed, softly to himself, the song he had bellowed for the boys last night.

> *Yo-ho-hee! A sea-dog's life for me!*
> *But where, tell me where can me treasure be?*

The captain grinned, his mood suddenly brighter. He reached for a familiar, yellowed map that lay amongst the clutter on his table, studying it with glowing eyes. Did Empster, foolish Empster, think he had old Faris Porlo under his thumb? If the nobleman was using the captain, the captain was using the nobleman too. Why, the poor old *Catayane* had been languishing in dry dock, ready to be scuttled, when the captain met again, so unexpectedly, the mysterious nobleman he had first known many years before. In those days, Faris Porlo had been a cabin boy, as Scabs was now, setting out on his first voyage. But Empster? Same as now, hadn't he been? Strange, that it seemed so hard to remember. Strange, that the fellow seemed no older.

What of it? What did Porlo care? Without Empster, he could never have got the old ship rigged out and crewed for this last voyage. Yes, her last voyage, and her captain's too; but of all the voyages he had taken, Porlo knew this would be the most important. To be sure, he must keep in with Empster, for now at least; the time had not yet come to break away. Besides, the fellow had powers; ah, but what powers would be the captain's when he found the treasure he had sought for so long?

The captain's grin grew wider, and he held out his arms for his darling Buby. The monkey leapt, nuzzling against her old protector's chest.

Only one thing tempered the captain's contentment.

'Rum! Scabs, where's me bloody rum?'

Chapter 10

VISION OF THE PROPHET

Bright light slanted over the floor of Dea's chamber when strange servants came for him. Starting awake, the boy looked up to see five brightly garbed Targon Retainers, members of his father's special retinue, standing over his couch with fixed, inscrutable faces. Bowing their heads solemnly, they intoned a brief blessing upon the Heir Unquestioned, then gestured in unison for the boy to rise.

Dea looked round uncertainly. 'Wh-where's Lammy?'

'We will serve you now,' came the five voices, high and twittering and strangely mechanical. Until now, Dea had seen members of the Targon Guild only at a distance, moving through the far vistas of palace corridors. Even then they had frightened him, and at close quarters they frightened him still more.

'Wh-why do you all talk at once?'

But the Targons made no reply, and a rush of dread surged through Dea's frame.

'I want Lammy!'

Springing up, he would have rushed to Lammy's cell, but the Targons surrounded him like a wall. What could this mean? With a pang of guilt, Dea realised he had slept through Catacombs, the first of the five daily calls to prayer. He looked at the sun. Why, perhaps he had slept through Green too – Lammy would never have let him sleep so long! He had committed a grave sin and at first he feared the Targons had come to punish him.

He was mistaken.

'Calm yourself, O Heir,' came the voices again. 'The Sultan of the Moon and Stars has decreed what is to pass, and it is his will that you come to him now. Eagerly he awaits you in the Grand Chamber of Presence. First, we will dress you in the Suit of Flame.'

As if by magic, each of the Targons produced an item of rich, exotic clothing. Helplessly Dea gazed at the slithery silken fabrics of breeches, shirt, cape, cravat and the golden length of turban cloth. Moving about the Prince with a prim, relentless efficiency, somehow without touching him at all, the Targons spirited the garments on to his willowy frame. The boy could only submit to their ministrations.

When he was dressed, they marched him through a labyrinth of corridors, immense and echoing, that sparkled with encrusted gems and intricate patterns of tiles. Spaced evenly against the length of the route, holding their scimitars ready at their sides, were palace guards with oiled muscles and black, sprouting topknots of tightly wound hair.

Dea was filled with dread, but it was a strangely unreal, disembodied dread. Overlaid on the present scene were the mysterious events of last night. Had he truly seen the vision of Thal, beckoning to him from the darkened garden? It could not have been real, but if that was not real, what else had been merely a cruel delusion?

Dea had never been into the Great Chamber of Presence, but he knew that it lay at the top of a sweeping marble staircase. With faltering feet he ascended the steps, alarmed at the strange intensity of a glowing, coloured light that streamed down from above. At the top of the stairs his heart lurched, for he found himself looking through a huge stained-glass window, framing the great boulevard he had travelled last night. In the centre of the window was a vast panel of red, flanked by lesser pillars of purple and green on the one side, blue and gold on the other.

Only for a moment did the Prince stare from the window, gazing in alarm towards the Sanctum of the Flame. Then the Targons surrounded him again. They made him turn; they led him forward and Dea found himself looking along an expanse of red carpet that ran like a river of blood to a golden throne, surmounted by a canopy in the shape of a flame. There sat the Sultan, in his finest robes of state. Courtiers in their hundreds stood in silence with their heads bowed low.

'Come, Prince of the Line! Come, Heir Unquestioned!' The Sultan's voice echoed fearsomely down the corridor-like room.

Dea willed himself to move forward, borrowing the strength of the flanking Targons. From somewhere near the throne a gong crashed, and a party of holy men intoned prayers and blessings. All this seemed the prelude to a grand ceremony, but even so, Dea was going to be surprised by what happened next.

❄

The five Targons vanished into the crowd, leaving the tall, shy boy standing before his father.

Dea was intensely aware of the watching courtiers, but they had no part to play; they were an audience, that was all. The boy looked into his father's eyes, glowering blackly beneath the bright turban. The scrutiny was too much; he looked down, studying the big hands that hung over the arms of the imperial throne. The sharp nails. The glittering rings. The dark, thick whorls of hair.

'Come, Dea,' said the Sultan, 'be not afraid. We meet today in a more formal setting, but formality is appropriate when a young man passes from one stage of life to the next.'

He gestured down the blood-red carpet.

'You see I look directly from my throne to the Sanctum – as one day, my son, shall you. It is as well we keep that sacred place in view, for in the lesson you will learn this morning, and remember for all your life, there is nothing more important than the Flame.'

Murmurs of assent came from the courtiers, and a quiet cough from an old man who hovered beside the throne, holding a crisp sputum-cloth to his mouth. Dea had never seen the old man before. He was dressed in the robes of an Imam, but he had not been one of the party who came last night to the Sanctum. Bent double, the old man leaned unsteadily on a walking stick topped with a ruby-studded orb. Cascading down the front of his robes was a long white beard.

'This is Councillor Simonides, and he is very dear to me,' said the Sultan. 'Once Simonides was my tutor, and taught me all I know of my sacred duties. Since then he has risen in the ranks of my Imams to become my Chief of Elders. Alas, my old instructor is infirm now, his duties curtailed; but in all these realms there is still no man of greater wisdom. For this important day, he has risen from his sickbed. Come, Simonides, instruct my son as once you instructed me.'

His back bowed like a question mark, the old man doddered forward, looking up at the young Prince through watery, red-rimmed eyes. His flame-shaped mitre wobbled on his head and as he quavered out his words he frequently dabbed at his loose, moist mouth.

'Prince of the Line, you have wondered why it is that you are called upon (so soon, so immoderately soon) to assume the mantle of Heir Unquestioned, have you not? Why, Heir Unquestioned, this morning you shall learn the answer to this – ah – question. But ah, to think I must call such a child (but your pardon, I mean no disrespect) by the name of Heir Unquestioned! Heir Unquestioned, if only it were the case that your father could afford, indeed, to leave *unquestioned* the – ah – question of . . .'

The old man seemed to have lost his thread.

'As concise as ever, Simonides,' smiled the Sultan. 'But come, old friend, you have told me yourself that the time before you is short. Sad shall I be to see you pass into The Vast, but sadder still if this last of your pupils misses the wisdom you would share with him.'

The old man stood blinking for a moment, then nodded, as if in reluctant assent, cleared his throat and began again, 'Prince of the Line, you have been kept in ignorance, as (naturally enough) a child must be. But I have heard it said you are an apt pupil (of course, for are you not your father's son?) and I know you shall grasp easily what I am about to impart to you. But first . . . tell me what you know of the history of our faith, and the founding of the Line of which you are the newest . . . ah, *twig?*'

Dea's brow furrowed. Many times had he been called upon to rehearse this history, but it surprised him that he should be asked this on such on obviously important occasion. His father made an encouraging gesture; there were shiftings amongst the courtiers.

The gangly boy looked about him, gulped, and began, 'Why, good my lord, I know there was a wicked time, before the coming of the Prophet Mesha. In those days our people were divided amongst themselves, lost to the faith that had once been theirs.'

'Once?' Phlegm gurgled in the old man's throat.

'My lord, yes. In the Time of Vagabondage, when our peoples came forth from the Vale of Orok, they were united in the Faith of Theron. Then, as epicycles passed, that faith was lost. Like grains of sand, blown by the winds, our peoples scattered across this great subcontinent. Alas, that they divided into many sects and nations, forgetting their allegiance to their common god!'

The Sultan smiled. If his son were merely reciting a lesson, still it was a lesson the boy had learnt well. The great man leaned back against the cushions of his throne, stroking his oiled beard with a single, gentle finger. Closing his eyes, he might almost have believed that he was himself a boy again, piping out the same answers to his tutor's questions.

But the lesson was turning into a lecture. Unsteadily, Simonides paced before the Prince, planting his stick before him with an old man's care. Enthusiasm filled his voice as he warmed to his theme.

'Indeed, young Prince,' Simonides was saying, 'these realms were in a parlous state. Few recalled their duty to the true god, who stands at the centre of Orok's Line as you (*you*, Heir Unquestioned!) stand at the centre of your father's. What vile blasphemies were then but common currency through all these Lands of Unang! There were Cults of the Five Gods, there were Cults of Imagenta. Some worshipped the sun, some the moon. There was much idolatry; there were sacrifices of beasts. Wisely indeed do the Books of the Imams speak of those days as the Time of Profanation . . .'

'Simonides?' Now the Sultan made a throat-clearing noise.

'Hm?' The tutor realised he had become carried away. 'Hm yes . . . so what happened then, Prince of the Line, to redeem these benighted kingdoms?'

Dea gulped again, painfully this time.

'My lord, you speak of the Coming of the Prophet. It was five epicycles ago, in the sunround reckoned on the old calendars to be SC 34/124, or NU-1 on the new, that the simple cameleer who was to become the

71

Prophet Mesha was vouchsafed a vision of the True God[1]. This was in the far Wilderness of the West, where our peoples lived a harsh, joyless life, scraping a subsistence from the arid soil, offering their oblations to worthless idols, and fending off raids from the godless Tribes of Ouabin.'

'Good, good,' urged Simonides.

Dea's mind whirled, struggling to remember all he had learnt. As he spoke he was turning slowly round, following the pacings of the old tutor. Staring along the length of the blood-red carpet, the boy found himself drawn towards the Sanctum, itself a blazing flame through the red stained-glass.

He plunged on, 'One day, at the height of the midday heat, the Prophet-to-be was stumbling in the dunes far from his village, fruitlessly seeking the camels he had lost in the last raid. There it was that the True God appeared to him in a – in a column of flame . . .'

Dea found it difficult not to stare at the Sanctum. Like a vicious mockery, proud in its supremacy, the great edifice chastened even the richest domes and minarets of the fine city around it. Trailing off, the young Prince cast down his eyes, remembering the horror he had seen the night before. He struggled to shake off the terrible vision, thinking of the courtiers, of all the watching eyes.

'Go on, Dea.' A tone of harshness had entered his father's voice.

The boy continued flatly, 'Then the True God showed Mesha the way. He told him to lead the people in the path of righteousness, for a time was coming when the present degenerated age would end. Then the good – those who followed Theron's way, his way alone – would be rewarded in The Vast, while the wicked would be consigned to the Realm of Unbeing.'

'Hm. And what else did the True God say?' said Simonides.

Dea hesitated. 'He – he told Mesha to lead his peoples on a pilgrimage to the mountains where this city now stands. There, said the True God, Mesha would find the – the Sacred Flame . . .'

---

[1] In Unang Lia, time has been reckoned differently from in Ejland, but the basic principle of the epicycle has remained constant in the two empires, and throughout the lands of El-Orok. An epicycle is a unit of 125 years. SC (Sosenic Calendar) 34/124 therefore refers to the 124th or penultimate year of the 34th epicycle since the beginning of the Time of Atonement. (Atonement had at that time begun some 4374 years ago; by the time of the present action, AC 999d on the Ejland calendar, 4999 years have passed.) In honour of the Prophet's vision, SC 34/124 was later redesignated NU (New Unang) Sunround 1, or NU-1 (that is, the beginning of a new cycle of time) by the College of Imams. Because all time takes its meaning only from the Vision of the Prophet, 'sunrounds' are simply numbered consecutively from that point onwards, with no further subdivisions. The present sunround (the Vision being 'five epicycles ago') is thus NU-625. Cf. the Appendix, 'Time in The Orokon', in the First Book in the sequence, *The Harlequin's Dance*.

72

At this, the boy might have faltered again, but now it seemed that his father had heard enough. Springing up from his throne, the formidable man swept the tutor aside with a surprising lack of grace. Clasping his hands behind his back, he spoke in a rapid, excited voice, sweeping between the ranks of intent courtiers, pacing the length of the crimson carpet. Uncertainly, his son followed him. They were headed towards the window.

'The Sacred Flame!' The Sultan gestured expansively. 'Yes, my son, it is the vital thing, for what is it but the Flame that ensures our power – mine, and yours too, in the life that lies before you? When Mesha took possession of the Flame, he founded our Line. He who holds the Flame holds All Unang; but though you know the power the Flame confers, what do you know of its origins?'

'Origins?' Dea did not understand.

The Sultan snapped, 'Boy, did you think the Flame *really* eternal? Did you think there was never a time when the Flame did not burn? That one day the Flame might not gutter and die?'

His father's anger alarmed the Prince, but then the Sultan softened and added, 'Ah, but your delusion was once mine too.'

Dea's lesson was just beginning.

Chapter 11

A CORRUPTED TEXT

'Dea?'

Dea stared from the vast red window.

'Dea?' The Sultan's voice was a little harsher.

The boy turned, shaking himself, and looked into the eyes that were almost, incongruously, level with his own. In the moments that followed he would forget the gaze of hundreds, perhaps a thousand, of the empire's finest courtiers. There was only himself, his father – and the old man, Simonides.

'Dea,' his father went on, 'you have studied well in the Book of Mesha, and know all you must of the Prophet's coming. You are young yet, but soon, now that, like your father, you are bound to the Line, your eyes shall pass over a certain ancient manuscript that lies in the keeping of the College of Imams. I speak of the El-Orokon. Corrupted versions lodge in the libraries of Ejland, perhaps in Zenzau and Wenaya too, but ours is the only true copy ... Is that not so, Simonides? Simonides?'

Irritation filled the Sultan's voice as he repeated his old tutor's name. Simonides stirred himself to nod in assent. The elderly man was evidently exhausted. Lingering at the far end of the long carpet, he appeared to be fighting a strong temptation to slump himself down in the vacated throne. There were no other chairs in the Presence Chamber.

'The El-Orokon!' cried the Sultan. Linking his arm in Dea's, he swept back towards his golden throne. 'In that sacred text,' he boomed, 'is told the story of the Crystals Five that embodied the powers of Theron and his four inferior siblings. My son, you have spoken of the Vagabondage, when our peoples came forth from the Vale of Orok, but do you know why they were compelled to make this journey?'

Dea looked blank. His father cast himself into the throne again; again, Simonides he cruelly brushed aside. The courtiers had no eyes for the old man; all they could see were the Heir Unquestioned, and the one they acknowledged Sultan of the Moon and Stars. In the Line of the Prophet, or so it seemed, was embodied the destiny of their race. How vital it was that Prince Dea should understand this destiny – the hopes, the glories, and the terrors, too.

The Sultan expatiated on the Crystals Five. He told of The Orokon, that once had ensured the harmony of life. He told of the warmaking that had ravaged the Vale of Orok, until at last, when the devastation was complete, the five races of humankind were compelled to leave that first place of their dwelling. 'That is so, is it not, Simonides? And then? And then?'

Simonides swayed on his stick. When he replied, he spoke with difficulty, his breath coming in laboured gasps. Many of the courtiers could not catch his words, but what did it matter, so long as Dea could hear? The Prince, in the tenderness of his heart, wished he could intervene on the old man's behalf, but fear held him in check.

'Then?' puffed the old man. 'Why, what miseries came then, what miseries, when earth's peoples learnt of their separate destinies. Each race was to undergo a trial, that it might prove its worth to the Ur-God ... each race was sent to a place befitting its nature ... icy mountains for the passionless Agonists; forests, islands, paltry womanish hiding-places like these for the races of the inferior female gods ...'

The old man applied his sputum-cloth to his lips.

The Sultan prompted impatiently, 'But one race was favoured above others, was it not?'

This time he did not wait for an answer. Many a courtier drew in his breath, exalted by the passion of the Sultan's address.

'Our race, my son, was the favoured race, for if there is a harshness in these Lands of Unang, what better field of training could there be for a people who are destined to conquer all the world? The world, I say, for how can it be otherwise, when Theron, red of hair and eye, is the favoured Child of Orok?

'Five epicycles have passed since the Vision of the Prophet. In each epicycle, as the Prophet foretold, a great Sultan has blessed these lands with a reign of especial magnificence, extending our dominions, conquering all enemies. Think, my son, what your history scrolls have told you – of Purple King Mesha, Sultan of the Catacombs, who drove the evil spirits from the City of the Dead! Of Zultan, Sultan of the Jungle Green, whose empire, at its height, reached deep into the tangled, mysterious Lands of Orokona! Of Bulaq, Sultan of the Red Dust, who brought all the great southlands under our imperial sway, in a grip of iron that would never be lost! Of Abu Makarish, Sultan of the Blue Wave, who extended our reach to island realms, far beyond our shores! Of Mesha Kaled – yes, child, of your own father, whose glory is such – has not the flame god told me so? – that he can be known only as Sultan of the Moon and Stars! Child, think what glory must lie in wait for the son, the Heir Unquestioned, of so great a monarch! Child, think – truly think – how no race can be greater than your own!'

Restlessly, the Sultan had slipped from his throne again; he was pacing, and his voice had risen to an echoing roar. 'Corrupted texts make different claims – let us not speak of the blasphemies of the Agonists – but is it not clear that the Ur-God most favoured his second son? In the mighty Theron, did he not create a bold and fearless warrior? What was Koros but a misshapen villain; Agonis but a canting milksop? Why, the Agonist god even refused to fight – refused, when the Vale of Orok was in its direst peril!'

The great monarch shook himself, turning back decisively to his shuddering son. All through the crowd, eyes were bowed, as if daring not even to look upon a man of such magnificence, such potency, such power. How could his reach not extend, indeed, to the very moon and stars?

'I digress,' said the Sultan, 'but how can I not? The destiny of these lands is my consuming passion. I have said that we were favoured of the Ur-God, and never more than in that sorrowing time when it fell to us to leave the Vale of Orok.'

'But Sire,' Dea said nervously, 'was not the Ur-God punishing *all* his peoples?'

The Sultan's eyes flashed, but he laughed indulgently, inviting the courtiers to do the same. 'Some more than others, ignorant boy! In truth, Orok showed mercy, for though he damned the Children of Koros – I speak of the verminous Vaga-breed, now mercifully exterminated in these Lands of Unang – to each of the superior races he gave a parting gift. What were these gifts but the crystals of the gods, to protect these peoples in the times that were to come? Of these crystals, none could rival the Crystal of Theron, that glowed magnificently with vermilion fire.'

At that moment there was a guttural cry. Simonides, who had been staggering, had now fallen to the floor. Dea would have gone to him; instead, the Sultan gripped his son's thin shoulder, spinning him away from the prone old man.

But Simonides raised himself up and wailed, 'The crystal was entrusted to the Imams of Old, and was to have remained in their eternal keeping! Had this been so, it is certain our peoples should never have strayed so grievously, as was the case during the Time of Profanation. Alas, that a dire fate befell those ancestral Imams, during the crossing of these Theron Ranges! Whether it was but an accident, whether they merely lost their way, whether they were victims of some evil treachery, we shall never know. There have been shocking stories, even evil ones. Some say the Imams (the holiest of our race!) fell into warring factions, victims of the sins of envy and pride; some say mighty Theron, watching from afar, decreed them unworthy of their precious burden; some that

Vaga-blood had tainted our breed, for how else ... how else could this suffering have befallen us?'

The old tutor would have attempted to say more, but he was breathless again and besides, the Sultan was impatient.

'The truth remains shrouded in the veils of time, as much about the past always must,' said the great monarch. 'Suffice to say that the Imams vanished, and with them, the sacred crystal was lost! That's what you meant to say, isn't it, Simonides?'

The old man had slumped to the floor again. Only a strained wheezing came in reply.

The Sultan went on, 'To the common folk, perhaps, this loss was of little import, for already they were sinking into the vile debaucheries which soon were to overwhelm them during the Time of Profanation. But to those who knew better, it was a disaster, and so it proved to be. Hm, Simonides?'

The old man was struggling to stand again, scrabbling awkwardly at the carpet with his stick. His flame-shaped mitre had fallen from his head and rolled some distance across the floor. Veins strained dangerously at his bald temples as he floundered, 'Great One, you have truth,' and slumped again.

Wonderingly Dea looked from the Sultan to Simonides, from Simonides to the Sultan. For the first time the thought came to the boy that his father was mad, actually mad, not merely vicious and cruel. But if this were so, Dea knew that the madness was gripping him too, gripping him as hard as his father's hand. In his mind, Dea seemed to see a glowing crystal, searing the air with its fiery rays.

Suddenly he didn't care about Simonides.

'But Sire, was the crystal never found again?'

'Hah! You are sharp, my son, sharper even than your tutors have reported. But no, never again have human eyes lighted upon the crystal, except perhaps in the realm of dreams. Legends tell of holy men, even in the darkest days of Profanation, who sought the glowing treasure which, they believed, would restore the true faith. Alas, even the holiest were disappointed, as all such seekers have been disappointed since. But think, my son, of the Vision of the Prophet. Mesha led his people in quest of the Flame that springs from the rocky depths beneath these mountains. And where, my son, did I say the Imams had lost the Crystal of Theron?'

Dea's eyes grew wide. 'Sire, in these mountains. In Theron's Ranges.'

The Sultan smiled. 'Now think, think more! When the Prophet found the Flame, so it was that the worship of Theron spread like purging fire through all these Lands of Unang. So it was that our true faith was restored, our destiny secured. How could this happen without the crystal? All through my reign my wisest Imams have stared into the heat of the Sacred Flame, in all its mystery, in all its majesty; again and again, in the Litanies of the Prophet, I have asked them what it can be that supplies this Flame. The answer they have given has never altered, and how could it alter? For who could doubt that Theron, in his mercy and wisdom, ensured that all should bow to his might – but that never again should human hands seize the sacred token of that might!'

Dea whispered, 'So the Flame is ... the crystal?'

The Sultan smiled mysteriously, sweeping his gaze across the assembled courtiers. The boy was doing well. Very well indeed.

Chapter 12

JEM IN A PREDICAMENT

'Black. White. Yellow. Pink.'

Squatting in the dust by the wall of the caravanserai, Eli Oli Ali's little son sorted pebbles into heaps. From time to time the boy snuffled, or wiped his nose on the back of his wrist. He did not look up at the bright sky, or down towards the sea, or along the clifftop road. He was a serious child, very skinny and very dirty, with big sad eyes and a sensitive mouth. Perhaps Papa had given him a name, but the only name the boy knew was Littler, and that just meant he was small. Small and weak.

Littler had collected the best pebbles he could find, pushing them into his pockets until the seams were bursting. He could not have said why, nor could he have said why he was sorting them now, only that it was something he wanted to do. He dug into his pocket for another handful.

'Purple. Grey. Brown. Green.'

From a distance all the pebbles were a washed-out white. Only when you really looked could you see the colours. It was as if they had a secret, Littler thought, and though they made no effort to conceal it, still it remained secret – except to those who looked.

'Gold. Orange. Red. Blue.'

From the caravanserai came the clatterings of pans, and over the clatterings a sound of shouting. It was Mother Madana, yelling at Amed – Ameda, as she called her. First she said the girl was stupid, lazy, vicious and disloyal, then she told her to sweep the dining-hall, lay the tables, and bring in more wood for the kitchen fire.

Littler ignored the commotion. He was used to angry voices. Just that morning Papa had raged and cursed, cursed and raged, declaring he would tear Cousin Faha limb from limb. As for the girl-boy, why, the little bitch would be roasting on a spit if she dared show her face in the mixer-maze again!

With a grin, Littler tried to imagine Faha Ejo's friend turning round and round over a roaring fire.

Then he heard the Rider.

At first the clamour from the caravanserai had masked the approaching thunder. Only now did Littler look up. He saw the billowing dust, the dark robes, the flashing golden bands. He scrambled to his feet, scattering pebbles.

The Sultan's messenger!

Even a little mixer-boy knew enough to be frightened.

Kaled's messengers always rode alone. Perhaps this was to illustrate the Adage of Imral, that the traveller is swiftest who treads a lonely road; perhaps it was to show that their master was fearless, imagining no impediment to the passage of his will. None would be fool enough to harm a Black Rider. To do so would be a crime against the Sultan himself, punishable by the most rapid and vicious of reprisals. Memories were long in Unang Lia; legend lasted longer. Whole villages had been razed to the ground where one man within them had dared defy the Sultan.

The village square was empty in the midday heat. Littler skittered across the road. He should have run back to the mixer-maze, but if he was alarmed, he was excited too. He wanted to see the Rider pass.

Crouching low, he hid behind a boulder.

Littler was six sunrounds old, no more, but he had seen much of the world – too much. With Eli Oli Ali he had been part of the Kua Exodus, one of the many thousands who fled into the coastlands after the Siege of the Man-Dragons. His earliest memories were of a jolting cart, making its way into Lower Unang through the treacherous reaches of the Vorgon Pass. Then came the mazes and camps and caravans, where Eli Oli Ali would ply his trade. In a hundred hole-in-corner places Littler had heard the hissing of urgent voices, the clink of furtive coins; in the backstreets and squalid docklands of Qatani, where Eli had rapidly prospered, his son had grown accustomed to the roar of drunken laughter, and the roar of tradesmen after he had stolen their bright trinkets, running with the gang of thieves that lived in the cellar beneath Papa's dirty khan. Time and again Littler had escaped from strangers, and often from Eli Oli Ali too; more often, he had taken the slaps and threats and curses Papa intended for his rival, Casca Dalla. Littler was used to it, just as he was used to being dirty and hungry. But all the time a dull rage burned inside the boy, hidden like the colours in the unregarded stones.

Rage cannot be damped down for ever. Sooner or later it bursts forth, sometimes unexpectedly. Fear hammered at Littler's heart as the Rider turned into the village square.

Then all at once, fear became rage.

A sharp stone whizzed through the air.

❋

The suck. The hiss.

Jem moaned. Only slowly did he return to consciousness, ascending through layer after warm layer. Warm, yes; feeling the warmth, like a restoring balm, for a moment he fancied he was drifting on a strange, sustaining sea. But no; Jem felt the raggedness of rock beneath his limbs; then the pain that the warmth could not allay. Slowly he focused on a greyish clump of weeds, clinging to the chalky whiteness of the rock; he turned his head upwards to a dazzling pallor. Birds wheeled high in the incandescence, echoing back their distant cries; from closer, from below, the suck, the hiss.

He was lying on a ledge, halfway down a cliff.

Above him: a sheer, jagged wall of rock.

Below him: the sea.

✳

'Ameda! Yargaberries!'

The Black Rider winced.

'Yargaberries, do you hear? Ameda?'

The Rider winced again at the bawling voice. He was slumped over the kitchen bench and his headdress was beside him, exposing the shaven pate and golden earrings of his tribe.

Mother Madana turned back to him. His head was in his hands and blood soaked through his fingers. 'Eh, my poor sir! My yargaberries, they fix you up, eh? Bottled last god-season, only the best. Why, for my yargas I charge – oh, many zirhams. Forty, fifty a bottle! But for you—'

There was the bang of a door, the slapping of feet over flagstones. Amed held up a dusty jar. Pickled in viscous liquid were long greenish stalks.

The mistress bristled. 'Stupid girl! Did I say hamali-stalks? Yargaberries, Ameda, yargaberries!'

Flushing, Amed scurried away again. Only moments had passed since the cry from the square, the rearing camel, the Rider collapsing, bleeding, into the dust. Mother Madana had assumed control at once, yelling for Amed to help her with the injured man.

Whoever had thrown the stone had run away.

'Some mixer-brat, I'll be bound. Why, sir, it can happen anywhere, anywhere! But what can we do?'

The old face beneath the headscarf smiled. Already Mother Madana had rung the midmeal bell and the guests had assembled in the dining-hall. But for once the mistress had no thought for her regulars, the few lonely camel-traders and small-time slavers, the couple of pedlars and a parvo-troupe, on their way to Qatani. Cauldrons bubbled and steam filled the kitchen; unleavened bread and dishes of spices, peppers, olives stood at the ready. But Mother Madana's eyes were all for the Rider.

'The Reds are not far behind me,' he snarled. 'They shall destroy this wretched village!'

The Red Riders, and the Yellows, were imperial patrols. They rode in bands and administered justice, if justice it could be called. Some would have quailed at the mention of a patrol; Mother Madana only laughed.

'Eh, sir, let them destroy what they like, but they'll need somewhere for refreshments afterwards! Why, I've seen you black fellows often enough – the red ones, too, and the yellows – and what do I say to myself but *Why don't they slow down? Don't they know this is the finest caravanserai on the Qatani Road?* Eh, I know what you think – the rates, the rates. Why, it is nothing. In Qatani, the zirhams, the korzons flow from your pockets like sand through a hole. I say to you, why stay in that wicked town? Go, give your message, come back to Mother Madana, eh? Everything you need, here and waiting. In Qatani, you pay – oh, korzon on korzon, and for what? A pail of slops! A bedroll full of fleas! And the servants? Don't talk to me about the servants!'

Mother Madana did not consider that the Rider and his ilk would repair to barracks. She was in full flight, drumming up business. Only once in her life had she been to the city, but the shocking standards of service she had experienced there had marked her, she would say, marked and marred her. Often she would enlarge upon this theme, and was about to do so now when a breathless Amed came skidding back before her. The old woman grabbed her yarga-jar. With muttered curses, she waved the girl away. Snatching up a cloth, she poured pickled berries into the folds, squashing them into a paste.

Impatiently she pulled away the Rider's hand. Across his cheek, close to his eye, was a savage cut. He drew in his breath sharply as Mother Madana applied her remedy. 'What are you doing, crone, burning me?'

Mother Madana did not flinch. 'There! All better now, eh?'

The Rider glowered, reaching for his headdress. 'Where's my camel?'

The old woman laughed, 'Why, sir, you can't be in such a hurry! Are you not hungry after your dreadful ordeal?' With a smile she watched the dark fellow's nostrils twitch, taking in the heady, familiar reek of jama-rice with goat's cheese and dahl. Gimlet eyes flickered over the dishes of olives, the spices, the chewy flat circles of bread.

A different greed filled Mother Madana. In old tales she had often heard of this or that legendary khan or caravanserai – here, the place where Warrior-Prince Ushani had lain down to die; there, the most splendid of roadside palaces, known through three kingdoms as the Sultan's Blessing. The old woman knew that legends, like runner beans, had their beginnings with the smallest of seeds. Had she not saved the Sultan's man? Perhaps, in time, they might say it had been the Sultan!

She breathed deeply, steeling herself to the necessary sacrifice.

'Why sir, you can hardly be on your way so soon! Come, the finest midmeal this side of Qatani awaits you. Why, you arrived just in time! It must be fate ... Charge? No charge! Am I a woman driven by mere venality? The very thought! I seek only to serve the Sultan's cause.' She dropped her voice, close to the Rider's ear. 'But tell your fellows of the splendours of my establishment – that is all the payment I ask.'

✳

'Blue. Red. Orange. Gold.'

Again, Littler laid his stones out in lines. His hands trembled and he swallowed back his snot in rhythmic, bubbling gasps. It was no good hiding, he knew that. But then, he wasn't hiding, not really. It was cool here, beneath Papa's van. Besides, Eli Oli Ali would find him soon enough, when the time came. Why be frightened? Littler knew what was coming, and how much it would hurt. He dug into his pockets for more stones.

'Green. Brown. Grey. Purple.'

The little boy was lying on his belly, knuckles pushed into a sharp cheekbone. Beside him, panting lightly, lay the nameless dog, flopping his tail lethargically on the ground. Through the spokes of the wheels, they could look out at the world like prisoners from a cage. On one side they saw pale rocks, shelving rapidly towards the cliffs; on the other, an upended pisspot, discarded gull bones, and the bulbous trailings of a seaweed curtain. Everyone had flocked to the village square, curious to know if the Rider would die. In the maze the buzz of flies was louder than before, a steady, thrumming insistence.

'Pink. Yellow. White. Black.'

For a long moment, Littler lay looking at the stones. Hanging beside his head was the end of a rope that coiled round and round one of axles of the van. Idly, he flicked the rope-end back and forth; it swung like a pendulum, and the dog barked.

Waves of misery descended over Littler. He scrambled out on to the cliff, snuffling furiously. Dashing a hand against his nose and eyes, he called out a curse and gouged into his pocket for the remaining stones, flinging them over the cliff in a vicious shower.

Two things happened, almost at once. A voice cried *Hey!* and Littler wheeled round. That was when he saw them, beating up dust in the far distance. The Red Riders! Yes, they were distant, but what did it matter? He saw the flash of their crimson uniforms and knew what they meant, well enough. Terror filled his heart and he lurched, almost collapsing.

But it was not from the Riders that the cry had come.

The dog barked and Littler saw the stranger, spreadeagled halfway down the side of the cliff. The little boy gasped; less, for an instant, at the stranger's predicament than at his pale skin, at his yellow hair. Chalky rocks slithered down the side of the cliff. Inexorably, the ledge was crumbling into the sea.

'Help me!' mouthed the stranger. 'Please, help me!'

Littler floundered back into the mixer-maze, his heart beating hugely and his eyes wide. Flies buzzed around him and he beat them away. How he wished Cousin Faha were here!

There was no time to find him. There was no time to find anyone. What was he to do?

Then he knew.

The rope!

He dived back under the van.

A crunch of footsteps sounded in the maze. 'Littler! Where are you, brat? Come on, we're harnessing the camels and leaving – now!'

For a moment, Littler froze. With sudden horror he imagined Papa on the cliff-edge, laughing contemptuously at the stranger below. Perhaps he would kick down a heavy stone. Quickly the little boy unravelled the rope. He scrambled back to the yellow-haired one.

'Here! Quick!'

He played out the rope. Would it be strong enough? Anxiously Littler switched his glance between the distant Riders, the struggling figure below and the van, from behind which Papa would burst forth in fury at any moment.

'Damn you, Littler, where have you gone? What, would you have Casca cackling to all and sundry that Papa was killed in this dirty place? I'll leave you behind, I will! Don't you know Riders eat little boys ...?'

The ledge crumbled away.

The stranger clambered to safety.

'Little boy, I owe you my life!'

Littler snuffled excitedly. All through his long travels, he had collected stones, hoping that one day he might find a magic talisman. Had another, different magic come to him at last? Questions filled his mind, but there was no time, no time.

The voice was closer. 'Littler! Pah! You don't deserve a Papa like me ... beat you black and blue, I will ...'

Littler looked desperately at his new friend. 'Quick! You must hide!'

In an instant Jem scrambled into the van, the door slammed behind him and Littler turned guiltily, just as Eli Oli Ali burst round the corner, caught him and cuffed him.

'Wretched brat, it was you who threw that stone, wasn't it?'

'Papa, no!'

Littler braced himself for a savage beating, but the Red Riders saved him.

Eli Oli Ali glanced into the distance. 'Pah! They're coming fast! By this evening, this place will be a ruin!'

Quickly, secretly, Littler bundled up the rope again while Papa harnessed the camels.

Chapter 13

MY SECRET BURDEN

'Ameda! Zorga-cream!'

The Black Rider winced.

'Zorga-cream, do you hear?'

The voice rang in the rafters of the long cool room. All around, at low benches, the regulars ate in silence, from time to time glancing furtively up at the dais. For a guest to sit beside the mistress was rare enough; for the guest to be a Black Rider was unprecedented. Had Mother Madana been cowed and trembling, the awed regulars might have understood. Instead, she seemed to be quite in command, treating the fearsome messenger as an honoured guest.

But then, when had Mother Madana ever been cowed?

Between bawlings for Ameda, the old woman boasted of the splendours of her establishment. The guest acknowledged, did he not, that hers was no commonplace caravanserai, no shabby little wayside mud-hut? – noted, did he not, the capacious chambers, the sturdy walls? – divined that the place had once been a sea-fort, guarding the approach to Qatani back in the days of the Wenaya-raids?

Details followed of its illustrious history. Would the guest like to see the cannons on the battlements, the powder-pocks, the punishment cells? Why, the very spirit of this noble empire breathed, veritably breathed from these walls! Where, Mother Madana demanded, could riders in black, riders in red, riders in yellow find lodgings more eminently suitable?

It was a bold campaign, but what effect it had was hard to say. The guest made no replies. Indeed, he seemed barely to be listening. Lurid with the impasto of the yargaberries, the skin beneath his eye was bloated and purple. His brow remained fixed in a scowling furrow and his gaze did not rise from the food before him. Still, he ate heartily enough – empty bowls soon cluttered the table.

This was encouragement enough for Mother Madana.

Amed skidded back with the Zorga-cream. Weaving between benches, the clumsy girl almost slopped the precious cargo. Cursing her, Mother Madana seized the jug. But her scowl quickly faded. Almost at once she became the image of smiling benevolence. Leaning towards her guest, she poured the potion generously over his spicy meal.

Amed gasped. A dash of Zorga-cream, she had heard it said, would make of the plainest meal a dish fit for the Sultan. Mother Madana's was legendary, but mostly because she never shared it. She made it only seldom, then kept it for herself, covered by a damp cloth in the cool-chamber under the kitchens. Amed, of course, would frequently dip a finger into the mixture, but only when she was certain – very certain – she would not be caught. If Mother Madana had freely offered her even a taste, let alone poured the cream on to her plate, Amed would have gasped in astonishment.

The Rider gave only a surly grunt.

Mother Madana was undaunted. 'But sir, what can I be thinking of? I give you all the best from my kitchens, but do I give you what a man most wants? Eh?'

The Rider looked up sharply.

She rushed on, 'Ameda! Bring my late husband's Jarvel-pipe, and the best esh. Eh?'

Amed leapt down from the dais again. Serving at table was never easy, not with Mother Madana giving orders. But today was the worst day she had known. She was exhausted. Still, it could have been worse – much worse. She had expected her back by now to be reduced to bloody weals.

Only because she returned so close to midmeal had Amed avoided the sajana-strap. The camel-traders, lounging on the portico, had laughed when they saw her running across the square. One of them mimed the action of the strap, and Amed had quailed. In the hall, Father was waiting. Crying that his daughter had defiled the Faith, the old man would have beaten her there and then, but Mother Madana burst forward instead, ordering the girl savagely into the kitchens.

Blundering back between the benches now, Amed avoided Father's eyes. Hunched over his bowl, the old man sat apart in a far corner. On an ordinary day, his loneliness would have stood out painfully. Then the benches would have rung with voices, the braggings of traders, the wily talk of pedlars, the eager bets cast upon the flip of a coin. Jarvel-stained teeth, yellow and brown, would have widened into grins at coarse jokes.

Today, even the scraping of spoons in bowls was subdued, and Father's wary eyes matched the eyes of all the others.

'Ameda!' The old man caught his daughter's wrist.

'Father?'

The voice was a hoarse whisper. 'You break my heart, don't you know?'

Amed bit her lip. As she clattered about the kitchens she had resented Father. Spiteful thoughts sprang readily to her mind. What did Father do but pray and eat and mope? Amed worked and worked. She tried to be good, but was she to have no friends, no pleasures? More and more now, the girl burned with restlessness. In her rare moments alone she would roam along the clifftops or climb to the ruined battlements above the caravanserai, where Mother Madana had forbidden her to go. There she would gaze longingly across the bay to where Qatani shone splendidly, mysteriously, like a jewel.

Once, in a past Amed could barely imagine, Father had lived in that great city. How he could put it behind him, Amed did not know. All she knew was that she too would not live out her life in this dismal caravanserai. If Eli Oli Ali provided no escape, Amed would find another. More than once, she had thought she would run away. Then it came to her that it was her labour, hers alone, that paid for Father's lodging. In truth, this old man who beat her, cursed her and despaired of her was helpless without her. He was weak; he was sick. Only at the height of his rage could Father wield the sajana-strap.

With a strange foreboding Amed gazed into the faded eyes. She was about to speak when Mother Madana's voice rang out again, demanding the Jarvel-pipe. Quickly Amed broke from Father's grip. It had lasted only for an instant, but in that instant the girl had plumbed the depths of sorrow.

※

At the dais, the Rider turned to Mother Madana. During the meal he had spoken little. Now a sly look crossed his face. 'Woman, I had not thought you treacherous.'

'Sir?'

'I carry with me a precious burden, secreted in a vessel I guard with my life. Already I have encountered one who would shatter that vessel. Now perhaps there is another who would tilt it over till the ichor is drained?'

Mother Madana's brow furrowed. 'Sir, I am a simple woman – I fear you are too deep for me.'

The Rider leaned closer, hissing out his words through camel-like teeth. 'You are unaware, then, that I am forbidden the vice with which you tempt me? Why, for the men of my corps, Jarvel is proscribed as heavily as ferment! Wicked woman! Not with a stone would you possess my secret, yet still, it seems, you desire it ardently.' He tapped his forehead. 'For where is my burden but here?'

'S-Secret? B-Burden?'

'The Sultan's words! The very words that have passed from his lips! What am I but the voice of His Grand Imperial Highness, echoing from the fastness of the Sacred City to the furthest reaches of his realm? To the palace of your Caliph, in the city they call the Jewel of the Shore, I bear my trust. Until my words are delivered my person partakes – but can you not know it? – of the sanctity of the Sultan.'

Mother Madana had turned pale. What the Rider said was true, of course. But what could it mean? Below, all the eyes of the men at the benches – fifteen pairs, and a single – gazed up at the dais with furtive avidity.

All the ears strained to catch even a word.

The Rider said, 'Throughout the Lands of Unang, I had thought my trust was honoured. Have I discovered the one canker in these kingdoms – a canker to be torn out, root and branch?'

Now the old woman drew in her breath. If she did not quite understand her guest, still she heard the threat in his words. Alarm and indignation fought inside her. Was this the reward of all her hospitality? She had a good mind to present the fellow with a bill.

Then she changed her mind. It might be dangerous.

For a moment the Rider gazed over the benches below. Swiftly, fifteen pairs of eyes – and the single – avoided his scrutiny.

'Yet perhaps,' he muttered, 'there is a way.'

'Sir?'

'A way,' he went on, 'for this wretched little town to redeem itself.' The Rider smiled. 'That old man in the corner – what is his name?'

Mother Madana looked towards her oldest guest. 'Evitamus. His name is Evitamus.'

'And his beard – is it not forked?'

'I dare say.'

'Thrice-forked?'

'I suppose it is.' Mother Madana screwed up her mouth. She wondered where this could be leading.

'Hm. He is far from us, but – is that not a star, graven on his forehead? This Evitamus – he is a Teller, is he not?'

Now the old woman understood. 'Why sir, but long retired. Many years have passed since first he came here, wisely leaving the discomforts of Qatani. (Oh, the service! How one could tolerate it for a day is quite beyond me!) Hardly could the old man be called a Teller, as you, for your part, are the bearer of the Sultan's will, or I the mistress of this caravanserai.'

The Rider smiled. 'A Teller, retired? But Telling is a gift, is it not? Can he eradicate the star at his brow, or the scars on his chin that make his beard grow forky? Likewise, can he forgo his gift of divination?'

'It is your desire, sir, to profit from that gift?'

'Profit?' The Rider sighed. 'What profit can there be, for one whose destiny has been loss?'

'Sir?'

The discussion seemed to be taking a new turn, and one still more mysterious than the last. It occurred to Mother Madana that she had placed a little Jarvel-powder – perhaps a little too much – in her last batch of Zorga-cream. The Rider's eyes looked distinctly clouded as he leaned closer to her now and whispered, 'Woman, there is a part of me that is troubled sore.'

Mother Madana felt a flutter of alarm, and hoped her guest recognised that hers was a respectable establishment. 'Your wives give you no ease?' she replied frostily.

'Ignorant woman! The men of my corps are not permitted to marry until they leave the Sultan's service, after the passing of their fortieth sunround. But for me, that time is fast approaching.'

'Then the ease you seek shall soon be yours.'

'Would that it were so! In the plateau whence I come, there is a beauteous young maiden for whom my heart has burned, burned and raged since first she was nubile. Still she remains unwed, but her father is an impatient man and I fear he will give her to another suitor before I am ready to take her to my bed. Should this fair one be lost to me, my life should indeed be a desolate waste. But I must know my fate: I can bear to wait no longer. Woman, let the Teller approach me now, and stare into my future. Bring this to pass, and I shall forget the incident that has taken place in this little town.'

'That, sir, is all the recompense you seek?'

Mother Madana almost laughed. Already her imagination was vaulting forward, far beyond the confines of the present scene. Great possibilities sprang into her mind. That the old man was a Teller had obviously been known to her from the first, but never until now had she thought it significant. That was part of his old life, the life he had fled many sunrounds ago. In the beginning there had been gold enough to sustain him; then the girl, soon enough, had proved her worth. That had been all that mattered. Telling, divination? Mother Madana was a practical woman, and spat on such mumbo-jumbo. Now she realised that she had – what was the expression? – *missed a trick*. Hadn't she heard that Tellers were well rewarded, plying their trade only to the rich? Her regulars, of course, were the merest riff-raff – why, they could barely afford the food she provided them! But the Riders . . . ?

Mother Madana breathed deeply. At once she determined that Amed's father must demonstrate his powers – here, now, this very afternoon. Why, this could be the beginning of a new era! Who knew what torrents of trade might follow?

She looked up sharply. 'Evitamus!'

Fear filled the eyes of the old man in the corner.

Intent on her strange conversation with the Rider, Mother Madana had forgotten her last command for Amed. It was just as well: the girl was ransacking the pantry cupboards, wondering where the old woman had put the esh, when suddenly a hand stole round her face.

She gasped. She writhed.

'Eh!' came a taunting voice. 'Eh-eh!'

'Infidel!' Amed broke free. 'What are you doing? Why, Mother Madana would scream to the rafters if she knew there was a mixer in here!'

'She's not screaming already?'

'What?'

'I thought she had a bit more to worry her – and I'm curious. Don't you know half the village has gathered out front?'

Faha Ejo ushered his friend into the yard. There, clambering up a rough stone wall, they could peer into the village square. It was as Faha had said: a crowd milled before the caravanserai. In the front stood an old peasant-woman, swaying her covered head, chanting murmurous prayers. Her companions set up an answering hum.

'The fools! What do they think they're doing?' Amed leapt down, scooping up a handful of stones.

Faha Ejo grabbed her wrist. 'Don't throw stones. That's what started all this, I've heard.'

'What?'

'They're worried. They think the village is going to be destroyed.'

Amed grinned. 'Only if the Rider blows up – from too much Zorga-cream!'

But Faha Ejo was solemn. 'Where the Blacks ride, the Reds aren't far behind. Then the Yellows, just to set the seal. There'll be trouble of some sort, mark my words.'

'Trouble?'

Faha Ejo only shuddered. 'Oh, I've seen it before, girl-boy – time and again. Forget those fools! What's to pray for? Me, I'd run and keep on running.'

Amed's eyes flashed. 'So why don't you?'

'Oh, I'll be gone soon enough. I'm fast, don't you know? Let's just hope that little bastard's fast too!'

'Little bastard?' Amed echoed blankly. All she could think of was that her friend would soon be gone, and had not even asked her to run away with him.

'Little bastard? Littler!' the goatherd was saying. 'He always goes round with a pocketful of stones. Just wait till Eli Oli Ali catches him!

Poor Cousin Eli! There he was, looking forward to another nice night in our maze – all the comforts – and now it's back on the road!'

'With his sister?' Amed slumped against the rough wall.

Now it was Faha Ejo's turn to grin. 'Hah! So that's what you're worried about?'

Amed flushed darkly. Since the incident in the mixer-maze, she had barely had time to think about the girl. But all at once, her image came back – sharply, too sharply. She doubled over, moaning.

Laughing, Faha Ejo tried to fondle Amed between the thighs again. 'Why, half-boy, there are girls enough if you look hard – *look hard*, get it? What about the ferment, answer me that?'

Amed bridled. She leapt up, punching Faha Ejo's arm. 'Ferment? Shut up about your stupid ferment!'

'Hah!' The goatherd skipped back. 'You'd be singing a different song now if you'd come up with something better than this rubbish!' Snatching the konar-light from his pocket, he swept it contemptuously through the air, as if about to fling it over the wall. In an instant, the friends would have writhed in the dust, pummelling each other viciously. Instead, they were suddenly still.

A scream rent the air.

Already the bright day was filled with moanings, murmurings, but this was something wilder – closer, too. Then Amed realised it was not a scream, but a strained, deliberate keening.

It was a voice she knew well.

'Father!'

Distraught, rushing back towards the dining-hall, Amed barely noticed that Faha Ejo had followed, and would look on illicitly throughout the strange, terrible scene that was about to be enacted.

Chapter 14

TELLER AND TALE

With a furtiveness she could not quite have explained, Amed crouched behind the hushed traders, peering between their high, bulbous turbans. The dining-hall was in darkness. Someone had closed the shutters and a burning taper stood on the dais, illuminating in a diffuse circle the eager, glittering eyes of the Black Rider, the pursed lips of Mother Madana and the old man who stood before them, dressed in a cape spangled with stars. Arms outstretched, beard jutting high, Amed's father shuffled in a slow circle as the strange, high keening issued from his lips.

Then the old man was still. Staring directly at the taper, now he turned his keening into a song. It was a song as strained and wild as the sounds it replaced; it sent a hot shudder through his daughter's veins. With a horror she could not have explained to herself, Amed seemed to recognise the mysterious, contorted words, though she never recalled having heard them before:

> *Theron, god of the sacred flame*
> *Come to the one who bears the name*
> *Of Evitamus, servant true*
> *Of all your glories.*
> > *All you do*
> *Shall be reflected in his eyes*
> *That widen to a massive size*
> *To see through mists and shrouding fogs*
> *The workings of your secret cogs*
> *In time that far beyond us lies –*
> *The time of one before me now*
> *Who burns with longing to know how*
> *His future life shall be.*
> > *Theron, come!*
> *Grant me vision or strike me dumb!*

When the song was over there was a long silence as Evitamus kept staring into the flame, as the Rider and Mother Madana kept staring at Evitamus. All round the hall the watchers drew in their breath, traders, pedlars, parvo-troupe alike. Small-time slavers forgot their profits and losses, looking on eagerly at the strange scene.

What would Evitamus say? Still he did not move, but for the involuntary shakings of his raised hands, but for the soft swayings of his trailing, starry cape.

Then suddenly the old man collapsed to the floor, clutching his eyes and shrieking.

'Father!' Amed gasped. She would have rushed forward, but a hand gripped her arm.

'Fool! Have you never seen a Teller before?'

It was Faha Ejo, his voice a harsh whisper. The mixer-boy had crept into a shadowy corner, but Amed registered no shock that he was here, and only hissed back, 'What do you mean, a Teller?'

'Girl-boy, don't you even know your own father?'

'That cape . . . he told me never to wear it . . . *he's* never worn it before.'

'Never? Then there's some mystery here, girl-boy!'

They might have said more, but Amed gasped again as the Rider leapt from the dais. With pitiless eyes he stared down at the figure that slumped, moaning now, on the chill flagstones.

'What is it, old man?' he demanded. 'What have you seen?'

Slowly Evitamus raised his head and, drawing back his hands from his eyes, said only, 'No.'

'No?' Exasperated, the Rider swung round, demanding of Mother Madana, 'Woman, what foolery is this? Has the old man the power, or has he not?'

The hostess tried to placate him. 'Sir, but of course! Evitamus the Teller is famed in these parts – why, as famed as my own caravanserai!' Lumberingly she came down to join the Rider. Standing beside him, she wrung her hands, attempting an unctuous smile. 'You must understand, sir' – she was inventing freely – 'that the deepest visions take their toll. What does this collapse show, but the strength of my Teller's gift? Come, Evitamus, you are well again, aren't you? Your strength is returning? Tell our fine guest what you've seen, hm?'

Again the old man only muttered, 'No.'

※

By now the Rider was growing impatient, and so was Mother Madana.

The Rider stamped on the floor. With a sweeping gaze he took in all the watchers, the dark brows beneath his turban furrowing, as if suddenly he suspected they were conspiring against him, laughing at him in secret. A gleam of threat came into his eyes and for the first time Mother Madana was frightened.

'Evitamus! Tell the man what you know!'

'Hah!' cried the Rider. 'This Teller is a fraud!'

With that, the haughty guest would have swept from the scene, but the accusation stirred the old man into life. He scrambled up, drawing his long cape tight around his shoulders.

A proud defiance came into his voice. 'Rider, do you not know it is the code of my guild, and my sworn oath, that I can reveal the truth, the truth alone? There are those who would hear only pleasing lies, but always I have defied them, as I defy them now!'

'What's this?' spat the Rider. 'There is a truth you would *not* reveal?'

'I say only that I must be silent, or say what I have seen!'

The Rider cried out. Seizing the burning taper from the table, he swooped close to Evitamus. In an instant his doubts were forgotten; he was desperate only to know what the old man was concealing.

'Teller, tell me, or I burn out your eyes! What is my future with the Lady Jamia? Shall her cruel father deny her to me? Shall another man take her to his bed? Teller, I must know! Tell me, tell me!'

The Rider grabbed the old man's shoulder. Lurid in the flames, their faces were a study in fear, but which was the more fearful was hard to say. Violently, wildly, the taper-light juddered as the Rider shook Evitamus back and forth, back and forth.

Suddenly something in the old man snapped. 'Rider,' he shrieked, 'you shall never enjoy your lady, or any pleasure – ever again!'

'What?' rasped the Rider. 'What can you mean?'

Now it was Mother Madana who wailed, flinging up her hands, dancing about absurdly like a jerking puppet. Desperately she cried that the old man was mad, that he had made some mistake, that he could not possibly have meant what he said. 'A joke, good sir,' she floundered, 'a Teller's joke – why, all the best Tellers tell them all the time!' She burst into high, strained laughter. 'So droll, so droll . . . but good Evitamus, the truth now, the truth! Oh, how can you banter with our fine guest so?'

There would have been more, but the Rider snapped, 'Woman, be silent! Teller, speak again, and mind well what you say.'

A hushed expectancy fell through the hall, but when Evitamus spoke again, his words brought no comfort to the listeners. Trembling, the old man looked only into the Rider's eyes, and the voice that came then, as if pushed through his lips by some alien force, was pitiless.

'Rider, I say again that you shall never enjoy your lady. I say again that your pleasures are at an end, for before night falls and ends this day . . . Rider, you shall be dead!'

There were gasps, and Mother Madana screamed again, but her scream was as nothing to the Rider's crazed '*No!*'

'Father!'

It was Amed who cried out next, breaking from Faha Ejo's restraining grip. In sudden terror, she knew what came next, knew it with a certainty that was absolute. Viciously the Rider swung back the taper, striking the Teller a savage, searing blow.

Evitamus crumpled.

With a second cry the Rider hurled himself from the hall, but not before he had flung the taper to the floor, igniting the old man's starry robe.

In the next moments, all was chaos. Evitamus shrieked; Mother Madana capered uselessly up and down; Amed and others struggled to smother the flames. In the fray, Amed would have no time to see what became of Faha Ejo; but like all of them she heard the savage words of the Rider, flung back from the doorway:

'Flee for your lives, fools, or die! For there is a Teller of sorts in me too, and before the sun rises again, this much I know: this village shall burn!'

Chapter 15

SUBMISSION OF DUST

From the spires of Kal-Theron the bells rang for Submissions. All over the Sacred City, from the mansions that abutted the Boulevard of the Flame to the lowliest haunts of the functionary classes, women and men abased themselves in the direction of the Sanctum. Whether they were in the streets when the call came, or lolling in luxury, or toiling in the menial labours of a slave, none – well, few – dared contravene the summons. In the marketplaces, hagglings abruptly ceased. In the schoolrooms, tutors held up their hands, signalling their pupils to unroll their prayer-mats. Even in the dens of vice, bubbling Jarvel-pipes were set swiftly aside and other pleasures virtuously postponed. Music fell silent. Mud-black coffee was left to cool.

Only in the Whispering Palace was there confusion. Dea's lesson had lasted longer than expected, and was not over yet. What to do? Simonides had just succeeded in standing again, but prostrated himself at once. Dutifully, Dea fell to his knees beside him; then, to his surprise, his father raised him up. His surprise only increased when he saw that the courtiers were standing too, looking expectantly to the Sultan for direction. Dea's mind reeled. What was power, what could it be, when even the sacred injunctions must rest upon its pleasure?

The Sultan smiled; his smile said that he was beyond the rules that bound others, and could extend to his companions, at will, the privileges of his greatness. All through the Submission of Dust, his son's lesson continued, riding imperiously over the mumblings of Simonides. From time to time the Sultan would fling further questions to the old man, oblivious of his sacred communion. The courtiers smirked dutifully.

The Sultan pointed through the red window.

'My son, we have come to call it the Sanctum of the Flame, that mighty edifice, but equally it might be the Casket of the Crystal. What else could it be that fuels that column of fire? In a chasm deep beneath the holy chamber, there the Crystal of Theron lies, secure in the fastness of its searing heat. On this fact all the Imams are agreed, are they not, Simonides – hm? On this fact depends the truth of Revelation; on this fact, the authority of the Prophet's Line. In a world besieged by doubt, pushing and pressing, clutching and clawing at us every way we turn, this truth must remain, incontrovertible as the stars, unyielding as the rock on which this city stands.'

The Sultan sighed. 'Alas for these realms, that all did not believe it!'

'Sire?' Dea said uncertainly. The boy was troubled, and found himself asking, 'But if this truth is incontrovertible, how can it be that some do not believe it?'

A cloud passed across the Sultan's face, but cleared quickly as he laughed and said, 'Ah, the sweet innocent! Again he asks what I might once have asked, in the days before the beard grew thickly round my lips!'

With a smile the Sultan looked to Simonides, perhaps expecting him to smile in his turn, but the old man was unswayed from his sacred duties.

The Sultan grew earnest again, and gripped his son's hands. 'Dea, you speak from a heart that is honourable and true! How could you even imagine the monstrous, all-consuming evil of our mortal enemy, Rashid Amr Rukr? Ah, if only I could preserve your innocence and tell you nothing of the wicked Ouabin leader.'

'The Ouabin?' said Dea. 'But that was the tribe that raided our ancestors, long ago in the Wilderness of the West. In those days they must indeed have been fearsome, but how can the Ouabin be a threat to us now, fast within the walls of this mountain city? I thought they were primitive nomads, no more.'

'No more, indeed! Remember, my son, epicycles have passed since the Time of the Prophet, and as the Ouabin were a trial to us then, so they remain a trial to us now.'

'Sire, but why?'

'Their intransigence! Their treachery! There are some who say that Vaga-blood must flow through their veins, but my Imams are convinced they are Creatures of Evil – not Vagas but something still worse, beings allowed to flourish through the Vaga-god's folly.' He raised his voice. 'That is so, Simonides, is it not – hm? Ah, if only we could exterminate the Ouabin, as once we exterminated the Koros-children!'

Dea looked into his father's hate-filled eyes.

The Sultan rushed on, 'All through this subcontinent, through faith or through force, the many tribes of humankind bow low to this city. Only the Ouabin have resisted our power, held fast as they are in the grip of dark forces. In the past, the Ouabin have been but an irritation, if a sore one. Now the fanatical Rashid Amr Rukr has forged the murderous tribesmen into a mighty army.'

'But Sire, your forces are supreme in all the world!' Dea burst out.

The Sultan bridled. 'Supreme? Why, the moon and stars, if they descended from the firmament, could not shine brighter than our imperial power! Is that not the meaning of the title I bear, the title

vouchsafed me in my communion with the fire god? In the past, we have
repelled the Ouabin time and again. Only now, under Rashid's sway, do
these evil beings threaten us with real and terrible danger. Like an
infection they have lingered at the edges of our realms, but now that
infection breaks through and spreads!'

'Sire, what can you mean?'

'Never before have the Ouabin made followers among our people.
Why, the very thought would have been absurd! What were the nomads
– what are they still? – but plundering, pillaging murderers? Through all
our realms they were loathed and feared, as such villains must be – until
the coming of Rashid Amr Rukr!'

'This Rashid must be a great enchanter!'

'There is no greatness in wickedness, Dea. Call him a monster in the
semblance of a man, no more. What else could this abomination be, when
not only does he press deeper into our realms, filling our cities with his
spies and assassins, but wrenches our people from the path of true faith?'

Dea gasped, 'Sire, but how?'

'My son, you have attained the height of a man, but in all else you are a
child. Alas, that I must even tell you of the perfidies our enemy has
spread abroad, for it is the charge of Rashid, and the burden of his
rebellion, that those who prostrate themselves each day to Kal-Theron
are the merest dupes of delusion.'

Inevitably Dea glanced at the old tutor casting his breathless prayers
towards the Sanctum.

The Sultan's eyes glittered. 'Of course, the truth is exactly opposite,
and it is Rashid's followers who are mistaken – nay, viciously and
wantonly led astray. Who can account for the power of wickedness? Lies
such as Rashid's are shocking to relate, but to the fools who have placed
their trust in this villain, no crystal burns beneath the Sanctum, no god
flutters in the Sacred Flame.'

'Sire, such persons must be fools indeed!'

'Dea, they are blaspheming mongrel dogs! Many times, many, have
my Imams prayed to Theron, begging that thunderbolts of righteous
wrath should burst suddenly from the desert skies, burning the world
clean of Rashid Amr Rukr! His wickedness knows no limit, for to Rashid
all the history of these realms since the Prophet's coming has been based
on lies. Hah!' The Sultan struck his forehead. 'But ask how it is this
villain should be believed, and I shall tell you of the greatest lie in all the
annals of Unang!'

What happened next startled Dea. Reaching into the folds of his
imperial robes, the Sultan produced a golden box. Solemnly he extended
it towards his son. The boy looked upon the box with an admiration that
was more than merely dutiful. His eyes were accustomed to luxury, but

this was a work of rare craftsmanship. Even in the brightness of the stained-glass window, the little casket shone like a fragment of the sun, carved with painstaking hands. Mysterious hieroglyphs patterned the lid.

'Open it, my son.'

'Sire, may I?'

'At such a privilege, even a Prince demurs? I see then it is a privilege indeed. This box is the work of a Marak guildsman, a relic of the celebrated First Flowering under the reign of Mesha, Son of Mesha.' The Sultan shifted the box in the light. 'Would you think such a treasure a mere outward shell, at once to be forgotten when its contents were produced?'

Dea shook his head.

'But lift the lid, my son, lift the lid.'

Courtiers drew in breath, and the Sultan smiled. For a moment Dea looked wonderingly into his father's dark face. Gingerly he reached out, touching the box as if he expected to feel a shock. But the shock came instead when he lifted the lid, for he saw that the box was indeed an outward shell, no more.

On a bed of crumpled velvet was a massive gemstone, glowing with a deep and dazzling red. With sudden rapture, Dea scooped it into his hand. The priceless casket fell to the floor, unregarded, as the boy stared into the flame-like jewel.

'Do you know what it is, Dea?'

'Sire, I—'

'The Crystal of Theron!'

Dea gasped, 'But you said—'

'Lies, all lies! What, would you believe these legends of a jewel beneath the ground, casting up its fire through a vent in rock? A tale for credulous children!'

Contemptuously he gestured to the prostrated tutor. The Sultan's voice was a hot, urgent whisper.

'Let me tell you the truth about the crystal: could it be that something so precious, so powerful was entrusted into the hands of doddering, quarrelling Imams? The very notion is an insult to the gods! Why, the true bearers of the crystal were men of fearsome strength and honour, men of heroic valour. From the common folk of the Theron tribe – from you and I, Dea, even you and I – such men were a class apart. As time passed, few would think them even of the same stock, but these special men never forgot they were guardians of their people's heritage. How could they, when they carried this precious crystal?

'But the crystal, they knew, must be guarded jealously from the touch of vulgar, blaspheming hands. What a task that was, with Theron's children debauched first by war, then by exile, as they ventured ever further from the Vale of Orok. Taking their measure of the common people, the guardians bore their burden away into the far Wilderness of the West, vowing to keep it safe – and secret – until the Time of Atonement reached its end.'

Staring into the crystal, Dea seemed to have fallen into a trance. He said slowly, 'Sire, then the keepers of the crystal . . . they are the Ouabin?'

❉

Dea's confusion could only increase. The Sultan leapt forward, snatching the crystal. The Prince started, crying out as the precious thing was wrenched suddenly away from him.

'The Ouabin!' his father cried angrily. 'Foolish boy, are you credulous as the dirtiest western sand-peasant, scratching his fleas in some shabby wayside khan? You are my son! You are my heir! Is there in you, even you, the slavering stupidity, like the palsy-sickness that infected all the fisher-folk of Vacos Island, who cast aside their faith in a single day when a lone seasick Ouabin came a-sailing up to their shores, spilling out his lies between his gouts of vomit? Fool, it is what I have told you now that is lies! Could Ouabin-kind be part of our species – a superior part? Could Rashid Amr Rukr have blood purer than mine? Could the hands of that profane dog come even close to the Crystal of Theron?'

As he spoke, the Sultan was twisting back and forth, here, there in agitatation. All the time Dea's heart fluttered with alarm, his head jerking as the crystal swung this way, that way, in his father's hand. Afterwards, the boy would see that all this was a grotesque joke, a joke at his expense, designed for the diversion of the clustering courtiers. How could a Ouabin be the bearer of the crystal when the crystal was here, now, swinging on the air? But then, how could this be the crystal here, now? It was all astonishing, but Dea had no time to be astonished any more, only to cry out as his father suddenly flung the crystal to the floor.

It shattered into fragments.

'Paste!'

'Sire?' Dea was shaking violently.

'Worthless paste, fashioned by the hands of some deceiving Ouabin! Over epicycles the vile tribe has perfected all the arts of cunning and fraud, polluting our realms with their false valuables. Child, can you see now that Ouabin-evil knows no bounds?'

The Sultan kicked the fragments that glittered on the carpet, scattering them wide.

'This is but one of their bogus gems, seized by my agents in the Kardos Hills. Yes, it is magnificent, and the crystal that they now blasphemously call Theron's is, without doubt, more magnificent still. Is it to be

101

wondered that the Ouabin gain followers, that their influence spreads and grows? What they cannot achieve by force they achieve by fraud.'

The Sultan grabbed his son's shoulders.

'Now do you see the danger these realms are in? Now do you see why my heir must be in place? Already Rashid's assassins may be within these walls! Already too many of my people turn from me! Dea, you have been called upon to become a man, and a man you shall be!'

He turned to the courtiers. 'Nobles of Unang, look upon your future! Has this child not proved himself a worthy heir? In mere moonlives, he shall be married, as was ordained, and bound for ever to the Prophet's Line! Already my Black Rider makes for Qatani, there to bring back his betrothed, whose beauty, famed through all my empire, shimmers like the sun in a gleaming glass! Have I not done my duty well, securing the succession which alone can ensure the glorious destiny of these Lands of Unang? Am I not Sultan of the Moon and Stars? Hail my power, my people, all hail, and hail, hail, the Heir Unquestioned!'

'Hail, Sultan of the Moon and Stars!'

'Hail, hail Heir Unquestioned!'

Staggering back, Dea was pale and gasping. But it was not only his father's violent words that shook him, or the thunderous chanting of the assembled courtiers.

'Sire – look!'

The Sultan turned, his gaze travelling over the shards of false crystal towards the slumped, inert figure on the blood-red carpet.

It was Simonides, worshipping no more.

Chapter 16

THE THIRD VANISHING

'Father . . . Father!'

The Teller's eyes kept drifting shut, and when they were open they seemed barely focused, staring blankly at some point among the rafters. Fighting back an impulse to shake the old man, Amed could only gaze helplessly into the wizened, bearded face. Father was shivering, as if he were cold. A blanket covered the ashy remnants of his robes, but Amed dared not draw it tighter.

They were alone now in the darkened dining-hall. The parvo-clown and one of the pedlars had offered to carry the old man upstairs, but Amed had shaken her head. What use would it be to disturb Father now? Carefully she reached for his hand. It was the time of Dust, but for once no one cared. Through the doors came the clamour of hurried departures, and Mother Madana's high voice, riding over the clatterings, thumpings, jabberings. Several times, grabbing guest after guest, the hostess went through the same wheedling cycle. First she would dismiss what had happened with a laugh, declaring it to be nothing, nothing at all; then she would plead with the guest not to go; then, pretence abandoned, she would curse and rail, demanding sums she insisted she was owed.

Amed leaned close to her dying father. The old man's voice was trembling and laboured, forced out on gulping, painful breaths. 'My daughter . . . it is you who must take on my mantle now.'

'Father?'

'You know, don't you? Ah, but you must! In my folly I have left you untrained, your skills no more focused than these eyes are now; yet still the awareness has lodged within you . . . bidden or unbidden, the kernel shall grow.'

Understanding came only slowly to Amed, and her eyes grew wide. With a strange wonderment she studied the star on Father's forehead, the seared, colourless stripes between the forks of his beard. 'Father, but is it my destiny to bear scars like these? Tell me, Father, shall I see *all*?'

'Is that desire I hear in your voice?' A smile played over the old man's lips. 'Daughter, wish not for the powers of the gods! One who saw *all* would see only sorrow, and without such skill I have seen sorrow enough. No, only when I intone . . . when I *intoned* the Rhyme of

Divining did clear sight come to me, that which I was commanded to see. But often, always, there were flashes, glimpses . . . such as when you saw the Rider would strike me. You knew this would happen, did you not, my daughter?'

'Father, apprehension gripped me like a hand! But now I am possessed of a further apprehension, and it is one I can support even less – oh, much less!'

Tears flowed freely from the girl's eyes, but again her father smiled and said, 'Ah my daughter, you need no powers to predict what shall become of your father now. But what a fool, what a wicked fool I have been! Alas, that your memories of me shall be so bad!'

'Father, no!'

The old man took a stertorous breath. Beneath the blanket, his flesh was cruelly blistered. Sweat rolled from his forehead, but still he shivered in the cold clasp of death.

'Ameda,' he said now, 'seek not to beguile me. Grant me no mercy that is not my due. Consumed as I have been with guilt and pride, like a fool I have turned my back on my talents . . . but worse, far worse, I have turned my back on *yours*. Daughter, you shall never be scarred as I am, nor wear the robes I wear, for I was trained in a guild in a city far away, where all was done according to ancient precept, and the harsh disciplines were for boys, boys alone. Yet one day, I know, the power shall burn in you, if . . . ah, if . . . you can right the wrong I have done. Otherwise, I fear, doom shall befall you, too! There is no time now to tell you of my history, but assuredly you shall learn it in the task that lies before you.'

'Task? Father, I don't understand.'

'What happened today was my just punishment, but oh, that it should come before I repaired my great wrong! Daughter, that task must now fall to you. Lean closer . . . closer now, for this Realm of Being is fading around me with each breath that passes these lips. Listen, and carefully, for nothing I have said to you in all the years you have lived was so important as the injunction I must lay upon you now.

'Daughter, a time of great trial has come to these lands. This Rider's approach was but a harbinger of evils that soon shall descend like swiftly flowing rain. My strength is gone, but even if my powers were at their height I could not tell you all that lay ahead. Only . . .'

'Father?'

The old man's eyes flickered shut, and for a moment Amed was frightened that death had come too soon. But her fear did not abate, only gripped her harder still, when her father heaved in another painful breath and said, 'Daughter, you know the chest in my chamber upstairs?'

Amed nodded blankly.

'In the bottom of that chest is a battered object, bearing the appearance of a konar-light. Contained in that object are great and secret powers, powers that I have used once and once only, but to enact a great wrong. Such is the konar-light that those who profit from its magic, common folk who stumble on its secret, forget at once what marvels it has wrought; when its magic is done, they think the battered thing but a konar-light indeed. Alas that I, too, might not forget! But I say, my powers have been a curse, as much as the wrong ... the wrong that I have done. My child, that wrong must now be righted, or ... or this land is doomed!'

Amed breathed in sharply at the fearful words, but cried aloud as her father suddenly struggled upright, clutching, clawing at his daughter's arm. For an instant, life blazed again in the dying eyes and the quavering voice became an urgent cry.

'Daughter, take the konar-light to Qatani ... take it to the Caliph and kneel to him ... beg him ... beg him to forgive your foolish, wicked ...'

'Father!'

If the old man would have said more, there was no time to say it. All at once the fire was gone from his eyes and the force from his hands. He slumped back. At another time Amed might have flung herself forward, collapsing in tears over the lifeless form; now she could only gaze on her dead father, ashen-faced, her temples pounding like ominous drums.

The konar-light! But where was Faha Ejo?

※

Mother Madana burst back into the hall. By now all her guests had left, fleeing into the hills; maddened beyond reason, she burst out, 'Ameda! What are you doing, skulking in the shadows? What's that old man doing, lazing on the floor?'

'He's dead,' Amed breathed, but the mistress of the caravanserai did not heed her.

Instead, she aimed a kick at the inert old man. 'Evitamus, you ungrateful wretch! To think, all these years I've sheltered you, fed you, and now you've ruined my business! For what? The truth, indeed! Truth? I'll give you truth! Off my clean floor, I say! By Theron, where's my broom?'

Amed shrieked, 'He's dead, you stupid old bitch! He's dead!'

'What, girl? What did you call me?'

'I said my father's dead, and it's all your fault!'

'Dead?' Now the hostess wailed in despair. 'What, and left me to bury him?'

'Shut up! Just shut up, you wicked woman!'

Amed lunged at her, pummelling with her fists, but Mother Madana was too strong. Grabbing the girl, the old woman tore at her hair, clawed her eyes.

'Wretched girl, I'll beat you myself! Why, I'll beat you till you can't stand or sit!'

Only with a mighty effort did Amed break free. Long years of resentment gave her strength. She kicked Mother Madana and the old woman staggered back, howling. Amed reeled round, frenzied.

'I'll kill you, I'll kill you!'

'Help!' Mother Madana cried. 'Help, murder!'

But it never went that far. Amed kicked Mother Madana again and the old woman lost her balance, collapsing over the corpse on the floor. In the next moment, piteous shrieks rang behind Amed, beating like lashes across her back as she ran from the doomed caravanserai.

※

Sunlight beat harshly on the white walls and glimmered in the sandy dust of the ground. Amed slumped against a wall, breathing hard. She must find Faha Ejo, find him and get back the konar-light. She sniffed and looked round the square, angrily dashing the tears from her eyes.

Emptiness. Emptiness everywhere.

'Infidel!' Amed shouted.

Only an echo came in reply.

Her gaze swivelled to the left, to the right. She ran back into the mixer-maze, but the alleys were as empty as the square. There was much evidence of hurried escapes. Here a cauldron still bubbled over a fire; there a line of laundry lay in the dirt, squashed down hard by the press of many feet. Flies buzzed thickly and the stench seemed worse than before.

'Infidel?' In the silence, Amed found herself whispering. She breathed lightly, a hand held to her face. Her friend could not be gone yet, could he? Cautiously she ventured deeper into the shadows, fearful as she had not been when Faha Ejo was with her. Once she kicked a pisspot and it clanged loudly; once she stepped into something soft, squelching. She shuddered – a dead bird. On and on the flies droned, but something was droning in Amed's brain too. She thought of the Riders, the black one, then the red ones, then the yellow who followed. Would they really burn the village? If everyone believed it, perhaps it was true. But Amed was aware of something else too, something more, first droning inside her like the flies, then thudding painfully.

Cousin Dona Bela!

This way, then that, Amed looked down the alleys. Indeed this place was a maze, but she would know the shabby Vaga-van at once. She traced the way she had come that morning, passing a tumbledown driftwood shack with a curtain of sacking where the door should be. Yes, this was the way. Nailed to a post beside the door was a distinctive arrangement of dried seaweed, hung out to ward off the Evil One. In the Caliphate of Qatani, a law said that mixers were not allowed to take the produce of the sea, but in a defiant gesture they would gather seaweed and hang it up like this, as if to say they feared nothing, no one.

'Except the Riders!' Amed said aloud. She almost laughed, but her laughter vanished as she turned the corner. In the line of the maze was a jagged gap.

Already Eli Oli Ali's van was gone.

Amed beat a hand against her forehead, cursing herself for a fool. Of course the van had gone! Faha Ejo's cousin was no ignorant peasant, ready to abandon all he had and run up into the hills. By now he would be far off, bearing his precious burden to the markets of Qatani.

Amed moaned. Again the vision of the lovely prisoner rose before her, but there was no time to think of Dona Bela now.

She stepped out through the gap in the maze. Now she was on the clifftop again, where Eli Oli Ali had refused the konar-light, dismissing it as trash. For a moment Amed almost laughed again. A warm wind whipped at her tunic and she screwed up her eyes against the glittering sea. Had Faha Ejo gone with his cousin? But no, the goat-boy had been with Amed in the dining-hall, disappearing only at the end.

Amed imagined him running down the road, chasing after his cousin's van.

She looked along the line of the coast. The road branched up to pass through the village, but clung for much of its length to a ribbon of rock, halfway up the cliff. On the other side of the village was a high promontory. That would be the best lookout point. Amed skirted round the cliff-edge towards it. There, many times, she had sat with Faha Ejo and followed the coast road with her eyes, towards the distant gleam of Qatani, Jewel of the Shore. Many times Faha Ejo had laughed and called her a fool, daring her to set off for the city at once. *If you want to go, go now*, he had taunted. Sometimes Amed had thought she would, if only Faha Ejo would agree to come too.

Foolish thought! The goatherd was hardly to be relied upon, and in any case he was daring Amed to act alone, to prove her courage. Often Amed wondered if she had any courage at all. Perhaps it was merely that it had never been tested.

But her chance was coming soon.

※

The sun burned over the promontory like fire, tumbling down the steep rise of rocks and sand. First Amed saw the scrabbling footprints, then she looked up into the glare and cried out, 'Infidel!'

At the highest point, where they had sat and watched the world, Amed's friend was standing now. For a moment he turned, only for a moment, and Amed saw the flash of the konar-light's handle, hanging from the pocket of the boy's shabby coat. But it was not this that made Amed's heart lurch. In his hands, Faha Ejo held a huge, heavy rock, swinging it back behind his head.

Hoofbeats sounded from the road below.

'Infidel!' Amed cried again. She struggled up the hill, but she could not be in time. Later she would wonder what Faha Ejo had thought he was doing. Perhaps he was showing his contempt for the Unangs, putting their superstitious cowardice to shame; perhaps he was offering testimony of a friendship that had been stronger, after all, than Amed could have guessed, extracting a revenge that Amed would never have dared to take. Perhaps Faha Ejo was just a fool.

With a cry, he flung down the rock.

He staggered back. He had overbalanced, and as he fell to the ground the konar-light rolled out of his pocket. Amed lurched forward. In one moment more, she would have grabbed the precious thing, but again she was too late. Faha Ejo's hand darted forward, clutching the lamp. He muttered something.

Then it happened.

First came the thunderclap. Then the blinding flash.

'Infidel!'

Staggering, Amed blinked and shook her head, willing away the glare that filled her eyes. Only slowly did her vision come back; only slowly did she realise what had happened.

'Infidel?'

But where Faha Ejo had been were only rocks, pebbles, sand.

Then Amed heard the sound of hoofbeats again, and looked down over the rim of the hill. Beating up dust, a riderless camel was pounding away towards Qatani. In the road below lay the Black Rider, sprawled and unmoving.

Amed scrambled down the side of the cliff. Gasping, she collapsed to her knees before the Rider, but though her hand darted to the pulse in his neck it was only to feel the last departing throbs of life. The dark turban had been knocked askew and rich red blood was soaking into the dust, pouring out freely like squandered ferment.

Amed breathed, 'No! Infidel, no!'

That was when the bright day suddenly darkened, and Amed realised she had heard the sound of more than one camel on the road.

She leapt up. She would have run, but there was nowhere to run. Round the curve of the cliff came the Red Riders, and Amed could only look up in terror.

'Murderer!' came the cry. 'Murderer – and traitor!'

Chapter 17

A NEW ADVENTURE FOR JEM

The Vaga-van had stopped at last.

At first the jogging had been so violent that Jem could only huddle against the upholstery, bracing his limbs against the jarring blows. Later, the speed slackened, and for a time he had even drifted into sleep, lulled by softer rhythms close at hand: the clink of chimes and trailing beads, the shifting bangles on the girl's arms. His eyes flickered open and he gazed at her again. The van had no windows, but from the ceiling swayed a lamp that filled the interior with a low, golden light. In such a light, it seemed to Jem, the girl was almost a goddess: beautiful, but with a beauty to inspire not desire, but awe. The shimmering veil! The dazzling jewels! More than once he had whispered his name and attempted apologies for his sudden intrusion. It was to no avail: the girl would not speak. Now she sat with a sad serenity, eyes cast down, and Jem wondered if she *could* speak.

The voices of the little boy and his father sounded, loud in the silence, through the wooden walls.

'Well, that should do it. We'll camp here.'

'Papa, we're not going on to . . . to the city?'

'Tonight? Stupid boy, we left the coast long ago, didn't we? Did you think I'd travel on the road tonight, when the Riders are out? We've a precious cargo here, Littler, and I'm not risking it for those Unang lackeys!' There was a thump, as of some heavy item falling into sand. 'Now come on, get that saddlebag unloaded and light the fire. I want my dinner. Oh, and Littler?'

'Yes, Papa?'

'Bring her out. After all, it's our last night.'

Jem gazed, wide-eyed, at the beautiful girl. Only now did she gaze back at him, and he knew there was something imploring in her eyes. Of course: why should so beautiful a maiden, a lady of quality, travel in the company of such shabby companions? The girl, it was clear, was the precious cargo. But what did it mean, her last night? There was a rattling, a clunk of a lock. Jem braced himself, ready to fly at Littler's father.

Instead, it was Littler himself who clambered up into the van. With tearful eyes, the girl embraced him, smoothing his dark hair. But he squirmed from her grasp. 'Dona Bela, quickly . . . you must come.'

110

The girl's eyes were a dumb show of sorrow.

Jem hissed, 'What's going on? She's his prisoner, isn't she?'

'Shh!' said the boy. 'Yellow-haired one, you must hide! Papa Eli's calm now, but if he finds you, he'll kill you, I swear.'

'I'm not afraid of him!'

'Please!'

The girl, with much clinking of bangles and jewels, was clambering dutifully down the steps of the van. Jem reached for her, as if to restrain her, but the gauze of her gown slithered through his fingers.

'We'll be in the city tomorrow,' whispered the boy. 'Hide yourself in here . . . just hide yourself in here.'

'I can't!'

Now the boy was clambering down the steps too. Jem launched himself towards the door, but the boy slammed it hard against the yellow-haired head.

Jem slumped down.

'Littler, what are you doing back there?' called Eli Oli Ali.

'Nothing, Papa! Nothing at all!'

The bolt of the door clunked back in place.

✳

What was that song?

Jem held his head in his hands, struggling not to moan. A high, unearthly melody was playing on the air – wafting, it seemed, from an impossible distance. Jem could not hear the words, but the voice was of incomparable purity and sweetness. Then he realised that it was not distant at all, but coming from just beyond the walls of the van. The girl? He had thought her mute! He struggled to hear what she was singing, but her accent was strange to him, and the melody seemed to carry away all sense and meaning.

It was then that something extraordinary happened. First it was a feeling, a familiar heat, spreading round the region of Jem's heart. Could it be? Slowly he edged himself up on to his haunches, careful not to make any creakings, any knockings. He clutched the leather bag he wore beneath his tunic. Yes, it was happening! The lamp had guttered out and the van was in darkness, but now Jem saw the green glow, pulsing through his fingers from the hidden crystal.

But how? Why? The purple crystal, when Jem had worn it, had come alive only in the presence of this second, green crystal that he bore with him now. Not even a day had passed since his sudden, strange arrival on the coast of this land. Could he be so close, already, to the next object of his quest? Jem held his breath and trembled in bewilderment, hunching almost guiltily over the eerie light. Then, suddenly, came a stab of fear. It

111

was not only in the presence of its fellow crystal that the first crystal had glowed. No. There had been another time too.

In the presence of the anti-god.

All this time, the strange melody had been twining like a stalk round Jem's troubled awareness; now the twining stopped and the green glow faded.

Darkness again. Jem's heart beat hard. In an instant, even the heat had vanished from the crystal, and he wondered if the light had been illusion, no more. The blow on the head? There was still a dull throbbing in his crown; gingerly he smoothed his haystack hair. Then he pressed his ear against the door, listening hard. The voice he heard now was Eli Oli Ali's, and the fellow's words were clear enough.

'Dear sister, you have entertained us much upon our journey . . . to think, I shall never hear your sweet song again, ringing round the campfire in the desert night! Well, perhaps you shall sing it for me one more time, hm? Before you sleep? What's that? Ah yes, I see the worry in your face . . . you may not speak, but a man can read your looks. Make sure they're sweet, that's all I ask, when . . . Ah, but how could a man not be enchanted by such beauty? Do you know, my dear, I have a good mind to parade you by Casca's windows, as soon as we get to Qatani. Why, he shall foam at the mouth, he shall beat the ground!'

There was an ugly guffaw, then a slosh of liquid. In the van, Jem felt a growing unease. He didn't like the sound of this, not one bit.

'Ah, fine ferment this . . . worry not, my dear!' Eli went on. 'Haven't I seen a thousand girls like you? Well, not quite like you, perhaps, but girls in . . . your position. It's the fear that gets them, mark my words! Fear? Pah! It won't last long . . . I tell you, the fellow who's paid for your maidenhead will break you in good and proper, make no mistake!'

There was a gasp, a sob. The fire crackled. Jem's fingers pressed against the door, and he began to wonder if he could break it down.

Meanwhile, the little boy was playing with the dog.

'Here, boy!'

There was panting, gasping.

'Boy, go fetch!'

There was a flurry of barking, then the imperious voice of Eli Oli Ali, calling out angrily. Jem heard a sharp slap, followed by a whimper.

'Now leave that mongrel alone and go to sleep, hm? My sister and I are having a lovely conversation . . . and we don't want a little brat like you spoiling our pleasures.'

The dog was silent; the boy, too.

'But come, sister, draw a little closer to your brother, hm? Did I say he's a foreign fellow, the one who's booked you first? Yes, a girl should be excited! Good customer, very good . . . one I want to keep out of

Casca's clutches, that's for certain ... Now, what did I tell my foreigner friend? Hm ... all the beauty of the Shimmering Princess, I said – the resemblance is remarkable, after all – with the wanton ways of a harlot! Well, not yet, perhaps, but you'll learn!'

The guffaw came again. Recklessly, Eli Oli Ali glugged his ferment. By now, Jem was furious. Gladly he would have killed the dirty whore-monger, there and then. He tested his weight against the wooden door.

'Where's that brat gone?' called Eli Oli Ali. 'Littler, where are you?'

'A piss, Papa!' came the nervous reply.

'Pah! Well, sleep in the van ... my sister and I have intimate matters to discuss, hm?' The whoremonger dropped his voice to a teasing lilt. Sickened, Jem imagined greasy fingers stroking the girl, fondling her. 'Not still frightened? Well, funny tastes, these foreigners sometimes have ... be prepared for anything, that's my advice. You know, my dear, I wonder if we might not try a little experiment before ... the big event. Just a bit of ... practice, hm? Casca's girls usually have a bit of experience ... well quite a lot, if they're Casca's. Just bend your neck, hm? Yes ... ah yes ... after all, there are ways a girl might please a man, yet still retain her virgin purity ... come, my dear, don't pull away!'

Suddenly the voice was violent. 'Bitch, come here!'

Jem lurched back through the darkness. He braced himself. In the next moment, he would smash through the door like a battering ram. He flung himself forward. In the same moment, Littler clambered up to the door.

The boy pulled back the bolt.

The girl pulled herself away. She ran.

Drunkenly Eli flailed up after her, just as Jem hurtled from the van, cannoning into the whoremonger and bringing him to the ground.

'Ugh! What the—'

'Dirty beast! Leave that girl alone!'

There was a struggle, but Jem had the advantage. He punched the whoremonger savagely between the eyes and the fat fellow was still. Triumphant, Jem sat astride his greasy opponent, breathing heavily and peering into the night. For the first time it occurred to him that he was in the desert, surrounded by a wilderness of dark, mysterious dunes. Awe-struck, he looked up into the starry sky.

'Did you kill him?' came a piping voice.

'Hm?' said Jem. 'Oh, he's breathing. Stunned, that's all.'

'So am I!' Littler struggled up from the sand. 'Will he come round soon?'

'He's a sturdy fellow. I should think so.'

'Shall we ... you know?'

'What?' said Jem.

Littler sniffed back a rivulet of snot. 'Kill him.'

'Not quite what I had in mind!' Jem squinted ironically at the boy. 'This is your father, isn't it?'

'I wish he weren't!'

'Well, that's all right then. We'll kill him – but not just yet. Where's that rope? How about we tie him up first?'

Littler grinned enthusiastically, and dived under the van. In moments, Eli Oli Ali might have been bound and helpless, and Jem would have had command of his own van. It nearly happened. But one thing was wrong. Jem looked round uncertainly in the orange glow of the fire.

Dona Bela! Where had she gone?

A barking sounded from across the dunes. Jem sprang up, sprinting after the excited dog.

❋

'Dona Bela! Dona Bela, where are you?'

It was intensely dark. The unfamiliar stars made a hard, clear pattern, but conferred no light on the dunes below. There was no moon. Jem peered through the night, but still he could see neither the girl nor the dog.

By now, he had run some distance from the van. If he was worried about the girl, he was worried about the boy too, left alone with his vicious father. How long would it be till the whoremonger came round? Jem turned back uncertainly. Already he was not sure which way he had come.

He turned again. Blackness. Only blackness. The fire could not have burned down so soon!

But then, the dunes were high. Very high.

Jem was breathing hard.

The dog barked again, and Jem began to think the desert played tricks on the ears as well as the eyes. He called to the girl. He called to the dog.

That was when he saw something strange.

Jem gasped. It was the dog, but the dog transfigured. In place of the drab, dun-coloured mongrel was a creature glowing with unearthly light. A purple light.

The dog barked again and bounded away.

'Wait!' Exhausted, Jem struggled over another dune. What could it mean, this mysterious glow? One thing was certain: he would not find his way back to the van again.

A new adventure had claimed him.

He felt giddy and staggered, clutching his forehead. He saw the dog again, but the colour had changed.

Green! Again the dog barked; again he bounded away.

'Wait, please!'

Next time, the dog was red.

A cackle of laughter filled the air. Jem reeled round. That was when someone grabbed him from behind. He struggled, but at once his face was covered with a thick, reeking cloth.

Chapter 18

THE BURNING BIRD

'Amazing!'
  'Magnificent!'
  'So blue!'
  'So white!'
  'Those cliffs!'
  'Those ships!'
  'The colours!'
  'The sails!'
  'Feluccas!' interrupted a gruff voice.

'Captain?' Rajal turned to the portly old sea-dog. Captain Porlo stood apart from his two young companions. Like them, he leaned intently over the prow, gazing at the harbour; but his face was grim while theirs, for the moment, were lost in wonderment.

'Feluccas,' the captain said again. He had drawn forth his telescope, sweeping the long glass across the cluttered docks. 'Not to mention xebecs, caiques and dhows. Foreigners, the lot of 'em! It's like going into a cobber-a's lair, and we know about them cobber-as, don't we, Lefty? Why, even a Laniard trader or two, I do declare.'

'Laniard?' said Rajal.

'From Lania Chor,' said Cata. 'Haven't you studied geography, Raj? At Mistress Quick's I was always poring over the atlas.'

'Really? I'd have thought you'd be balancing it on your head!'

Cata laughed. 'Well, that's all most of the girls ever did! I used to steal into the library when the rest of them were in bed, and learn the things they didn't teach us in class – all the important things, the things they think girls don't need to know. I suppose I had a feeling I'd be travelling one day.'

'I'll bet you didn't expect it to be like this!'

'Hardly!'

For a moment the brightness faded out of Cata, and once more she was filled with sorrow. If only Jem were here! In the last day, Cata and Rajal had told each other their stories time and again, as if in this repetition they would find a clue. But all they could do was torment themselves with questions. What had happened? Why had Jem gone? When Cata, steeling herself, had asked Lord Empster to help them understand, the

116

nobleman only looked at her kindly and offered her another golden apple.

His voice came now. 'So, Porlo, you've made a good running!'

Cata started. She had thought Jem's guardian was in his cabin below, but he had stolen up on the bridge beside them. Strange, the way this nobleman would suddenly appear! His cloak billowed behind him and he drew back deeply on his ivory pipe.

'Aye, me lord,' the captain was saying, 'we've had a good passage round the Cape of Kept Promise, make no mistake. A following wind the whole way, ever since me wooden lady turned up in the flesh. Begging your pardon, miss,' he added, in deference to Cata.

If Cata were hardly so delicate, nonetheless a troubled look passed across her face. Not for the first time, she pinched herself, as if she still could not believe she were here. Marvelling, she glanced at her companions on the bridge, then at the cluttered decks below, where tarry fellows with backs like bronze heaved and hauled, sweated and strained, cursed and guffawed and spat black streams of chew-tobarillo. Then she had to smile, thinking how worried the captain had been that the tars would notice her resemblance to the figurehead. In truth, if any of the coarse fellows caught Cata's eye, he would turn away, abashed, not daring to gaze upon the fine lady. Sometimes, Cata had to admit, there were advantages to being a member of what gentlemen liked to call the fair sex.

'Porlo, you'll oblige me with your glass?' said Lord Empster. Admiringly, he gazed through the telescope. 'Qatani, Jewel of the Shore! Many years have passed since last I was here, and still there is no more splendid sight.'

'You've been here before?' said Rajal suspiciously.

'Oh, indeed. The old Caliph, the present Caliph's uncle, was a friend of my youth. Many an evening I whiled away amongst the marble of his magnificent halls, before I moved on to see more of the world. Why, Vaga-boy, I dare say in my green years I travelled as much as your restless tribesmen. It is as well, for the Caliph has been apprised of my arrival, and shall welcome my party as valued friends.'

'Hmph! I dare say *I'm* an enemy,' the captain said glumly.

'Nonsense, Porlo! I hardly think *you'll* be remembered.'

The captain gave a second *Hmph!*, muttering that if they remembered young Mathanias Empster, might they not remember young Faris Porlo too?

Lord Empster laughed. 'Come Porlo, had you been the fine commander you are now, then of course. But after all, you were only a cabin boy – like Scabs.'

The captain bridled. 'Scabs! Why, me lord, you torment a man so! I were a good-looking lad, I were, not like that blister full of yellow pus! Ask Miss Catty here – begging your pardon, miss – if she can't see I were once a good-looking lad. Well, until I met them cobber-as, I were. It was the ferment they sell in these parts, that's what done me in, and no denying.'

'Ferment?' said Rajal. This was an addition to the oft-told tale. 'I thought they weren't supposed to drink.'

'Supposed and do are different things, Master Raj, I'm afraid. Unang rotgut? Lethal stuff! Why, I thought I could walk on air, and now look at me!' The captain thumped his wooden leg loudly against the decking. 'If you wants a warning from experience, lad, them's two: keep away from that ferment, and keep away from them cobber-as!'

Rajal said he would take the advice, and Cata had to laugh, but Lord Empster was grave. 'Alas, I fear our young friends shall meet greater dangers before we leave the shores of this land. But Porlo, look to your flags. Are the colours correct?'

Like other sea-dogs of his type, Captain Porlo kept flags of all nations on board the *Catayane*; indeed, their manufacture and repair constituted a minor industry among the tars. It was a wise policy, but often confusing. Several times already during the voyage they had rapidly had to change this or that flag when a dubious-looking vessel was spotted on the horizon.

The captain cursed. In all the excitement of the following wind, they had never taken down the Wenayan standard they had flown to deter a suspicious sloop, lingering near the mouth of the River Orokona. Angrily he called for Scabs, but just as he was about to bellow out his commands, the air was rent by a different cry.

It was Cata's. The girl had suddenly felt a stab of agony, twisting inside her brain like a knife. She screamed, collapsing.

'Cata! What is it?' Rajal cried.

Then he knew. In the crow's nest, Scabs was leaping, pointing, and all the men were gazing where he pointed. It came from the headland, searing through the brightness of the sky like a comet.

It was a hawk, and its wings were burning.

Now the bird's cries split the air above them, shriek after shriek of hideous pain. Alarmed, a lonely petrel veered from its path. Then came the cormorants, sea-shrikes, gulls, wheeling away and calling out their own wild alarm.

In the rigging, Buby screeched and scrambled.

On and on soared the blazing bird, vanishing into the brightness above Qatani.

Then it was over. Cata rubbed her forehead, staring up into the faces of her three concerned companions.

'Cata, what happened?' asked Rajal.

'The bird's pain was mine. And mine the bird's.'

'What? Was it a portent?'

Awkwardly, Captain Porlo leaned forward, patting Cata's hand. 'The poor lass thought it was a cobber-a, I dare say. Now don't worry your pretty little head, miss, them cobber-as don't come out of the sky.'

But Lord Empster said, in a voice quite unlike his normal voice, 'The girl has the empathetic power. Perhaps, before this quest is over, that power will prove vital. Or perhaps . . . perhaps not.'

Rajal would have asked the nobleman to explain, but in that moment came a new shock. An explosion rang from the shore. In the next instant, a cannon-ball whizzed through the air, splashing into the sea on the starboard side. A geyser of water sprayed over the decks.

The ship lurched. Struggling for his balance, Captain Porlo tottered heroically on his wooden leg for a moment, then, as he crashed like a toppled idol, cried out urgently, 'A warning shot! Across our bows! Scabs, Scabs! Run up them Bluejacket flags, or I'll put your ugly head between me thumbs and squeeze!'

Through the fray, Cata gazed intently, fearlessly at the shores of the strange land. What the future held she neither knew nor guessed, but one thing was certain.

Danger lay ahead.

END OF PART ONE

119

PART TWO

Lady in a Looking-Glass

Chapter 19

THE CURSE OF KALED

'Simonides?'

The old man had drifted into reverie again, gazing sadly into the dappled sunlight. Prince Dea reached out, touching the withered hand. It was afternoon, and they were sitting in the most pleasant of the fragrant groves that opened amongst the lush, bright roof gardens. Simonides was in a wicker chair; his pupil, cross-legged, in the grass at his feet. From time to time there were twitterings through the foliage; not birds, but the Targon Retainers. At all times, it seemed, they must accompany Prince Dea, but at least they had agreed to withdraw from view.

Since his collapse in the Presence Chamber, Simonides had rallied, and today his strength was returning in force. That morning he had risen from his sickbed, determined to do what the Sultan wished and prepare the boy for his impending marriage. That afternoon, as the sun burned high, Simonides had spoken of modes, of manners, of morals. His voice lulled Dea into a pleasant torpor, but strange gaps, as now, would come in the old man's discourse. His voice had trailed into silence, and Dea was aware again of the sadness he felt, there amongst the ferns and flowers and trees where once he had played so happily with Thal.

'Simonides?'

In the first of the silences, Dea had recalled his fears of the day before, when it had appeared that Simonides was dead. Alarmed, the young Prince had almost called for the Targons; now he knew that the old man's mind, like his own, was burdened heavily with sorrows. It could hardly be otherwise. How ashamed, how appalled Dea had been, when it seemed that his father's brutality had ended the old man's life! How sad the old man must be, when he saw the evil that twined, like an entangling vine, round the heart of one he had once instructed!

Tenderly, Dea stroked his tutor's hand. All through his lesson he had barely listened, caring nothing for the forms and conventions that from now on were to rule his life. Looking up into the aged face, Dea sensed that behind that high, domed forehead were many tales the old man could tell, tales that would mean more than the dry, formal phrases he must have recited so many times before.

'Simonides?'

With kindly eyes, the old man looked down at the boy, returning the pressure of the concerned hand. Tears pressed behind the Prince's eyes, for he thought of his father's hand, caressing his loins, then of another hand he would never hold again.

'Simonides,' he found himself saying, 'my father told me of a friend he once had, a friend called Mala. Did you ever know of this friend and his fate?'

A flicker of alarm crossed the old man's face; then his alarm was replaced by sorrow. Deeply he gazed into the eyes that looked up so innocently, but intently, into his own. Indeed, indeed, he knew of Lord Malagon, and the bitter history that had led to his death! Whatever the Sultan had told the young Prince, Simonides was certain it could not have been the truth.

He breathed deeply. Aeons had passed since he had been accepted into the College of Imams. His career in Kal-Theron had been a glorious one, fulfilling abundantly all the promise of his youth. But ah, at such cost! Had it been worthwhile, all the suppressions, the lies? For too long he had done what he thought was his duty, even when doubt had nagged at his heart; now Simonides found a new doubt within himself and knew that, this time, it would not be allayed. His duty, or rather the task before him now, was to speak to Dea of immemorial things, the lessons laid down in the Books of the Prophet. But the child was barely listening, as his father, long ago, had barely listened. The old man's brow furrowed. If he were to do good before he died, must he not ensure that the Heir Unquestioned became, in time, a better man than his father? Perhaps there were lessons this boy should learn, lessons not prescribed in the sacred books.

Through the foliage, the twittering of the Targons came again. Simonides looked round furtively. His voice trembled as he leaned close to Dea. 'Should you like, Dea, to hear the story of your father . . . the story of your father when he was young?'

The Prince nodded, wide-eyed. In what followed, Simonides would keep his voice low. The Targons, hearing merely a dull murmur, would assume that the sacred lesson had resumed.

※　※

'Dea, your father is a strong and powerful man, in the full vigour of his prime. Can you imagine him as a young boy – of your age, or younger still? Yes, it is hard to think of your father then, is it not? But time brings transformations stranger than any in the old tales. As once your tutor – this decrepit fellow before you now – was a smooth-limbed youth with a beardless face, looking forward eagerly to the life that lay before him, so the formidable ruler of these lands was a thin child in a tunic of white, running hither and yon through these fragrant gardens.

124

'How fondly I remember him: his neck a spindly stalk, his voice high and piping. He was bright-eyed, excitable, endlessly curious. I think now he was too curious, and there were times when I should have stretched forth a curbing hand, drawing him back from this or that brink over which a young boy should never have peered.

'Alas, for a recklessness in me that would fan at flames I should hastily have dampened! But I had lived for too long without intellectual food. Your great-father had been the merest dunce, immune to the ministrations of my scholarly arts. In your father, by contrast, I found the pupil for whom every teacher longs. Greed overtook me. Delighting in the quickness of my young charge – ambitious, too, for my own advancement, when the time came for him to assume the throne – I assisted him all I could, encouraged and applauded him in his dangerous ardours.

'He was passionate for knowledge; I soon learnt how passionate. When your father was very young, there was a nightingale that would sit upon a branch by the window of his chamber. Always it was there when I repaired to him in the mornings, pouring out a song that filled my heart with joy. One morning the nightingale was gone, and so was your father. From the gardens I heard the raised voice of Lammy, calling earnestly for the missing Prince. In the event, it was I who found him, secreted in this very grove, hunched over the body of the dead bird. By his side sat his friend, the young Lord Malagon, playmate and companion of his boyhood years.

'What fell work these two had undertaken! Carefully they had plucked away the bird's feathers, and with a sharpened stick had opened the flesh of the neck. Fascinated, they were staring into the interior of the throat. I was shocked, and would have called them wicked; Lord Malagon, at the least, I might have berated, thinking he had led the young Prince astray. Had he not learnt it was a blasphemy of the first order, wantonly to destroy the Ur-God's blessings? But as your father looked up at me, there was not the faintest hint of shame in his eyes, only wonderment at the mysteries of nature. How I remember the words he spoke next, lisped in the innocent cadences of youth!

'"Good Master Simonides, if you please . . . *I wanted to see what made the song.*"

'From that time forth, your father devoted himself to the natural sciences. Fascinated, he sought the secrets of life, the messages hidden in the pulsings of the heart; then, too, in the shudderings of the earth; then in the motions of the moon and stars. He peered through far-glasses, he pored over maps, he prodded the glittering guts of animals after he had peeled away the fur and skin. To your father, the world was a series of questions; to know the answers was a matter of urgency. In all this he was accompanied by the faithful Mala, and both were abetted in their labours by me.

'I think of those years as an idyll. What a happy trio we made then, in the days before the heavy mantle of royalty had yet to descend upon my young Prince's shoulders! Could it have gone on, I have no doubt your father would have become – by dint of no boot-licking, no base flattery – renowned as perhaps the greatest man of learning in all these Lands of Unang. Alas, that duty was first to intervene, then – more terrible still – the passions that divorced his heart first from the love of Lord Malagon, then from the love of humankind itself!

'At the beginning of his sixteenth sunround, your father was declared Heir Unquestioned. Like you, Dea, he was thus to be married, and your great-father chose for his First Blood an exotic young Princess named Ysadona. The Princess – your mother, Dea – was a native of Lania Chor, one of the far kingdoms of Amalia, but for many sunrounds she had lived in Kal-Theron, where her father – a brother of the Lanian King – had been Ambassador to the Courts of Unang. As is the custom with unwed girls, your mother had been kept in seclusion, but rumours of her beauty had spread abroad. When news of the marriage was cried through the city, there was great rejoicing, for who could make a finer bride for the Sultan-in-Waiting than this noble daughter of Lania?

'Now it happened that your father was very little perturbed by thoughts of his wedding. Indeed, his royal destiny seemed hardly real to him. Many sunrounds were sure to pass before he was called upon to assume the throne, and I suppose he imagined he could go on living much as he had done in his boyhood years, spending his days in his cluttered laboratory. One day I even heard him assuring Mala that this marriage was a duty of state, no more, that nothing need change when that duty was fulfilled, that nothing need diminish their scholarly passions. Alas, your father did not yet know the truth. This marriage was a curse, waiting to claim him!

'To be sure, I was moved to wonder at his dedication, for if even my cold scholar's heart – alas, a stranger to the love of the fair sex – was stirred by thoughts of the fair Ysadona, what must be the nature of a taut-limbed youth who could regard with indifference, or so it seemed, the fact that he was soon to possess those beauties?

'Ah, but I did scant justice to your father if I concluded that his heart was cold. After all, he was young yet, and raised within the strict decorum of the Court. So vital was he, so quick of parts, that one could forget that your father – like you, Dea – had seen little of the world beyond these palace walls. What could he know of feminine charms, when Lammy's were the only caresses he had enjoyed?

'As is the custom in these Lands of Unang, your father was not to meet

126

his bride until the wedding. Later, when he had become a man, he could assume the ways of his own father, picking new wives as an epicure selects the finest dishes from a laden table. What a richly stocked harem might one day have been his, in which he could rove as through a garden of pleasure! In a harem, there are no secrets, no veils. But First Blood is different. Only on the bridal night would your father see, at last, the treasure he now possessed, as the Eunuchs of the Bedchamber, with accomplished hands, guided his initiation into the mysteries of love.

'Naturally I assumed that, after this initiation, your father would be conscious of the prize he now possessed. I was happy for him, but sad for myself, and sad for young Lord Malagon too. To be sure, the changes your father had thought would never happen must now inevitably, swiftly come to pass. I feared that he would be lost for learning, deserting library and laboratory alike; I feared too that poor, faithful Mala would lose his place in your father's heart. I was right on both counts, for indeed these things happened; but very differently from the way I had expected.

'After his marriage, your father moved freely through the Sultan's Court, liberated from the strictures of his childhood years. Mala moved beside him, and soon the young nobleman was admired by all. Many were those who said that Lord Malagon was certain to be Grand Vizier when your father ascended the throne. Even now, my fond heart tells me that somewhere, in another, better world, these lands have been blessed by that happy outcome.

'Some moonlives after your father's First Blood, news reached Court that the Tribes of Ouabin had once again breached the Sultan's domains. Secure in his newfound manhood, your father petitioned your great-father that he might ride forth with the Imperial Army. The Sultan dismissed the application with a smile. Heir Unquestioned, yet still so green? Was a Prince of the Line to imperil his life? More than that, was he to lower himself to the level of the herd, consorting with warriors and common folk? The mere thought was monstrous. Unang royalty had never behaved thus, and never would. Your father's protests were to no avail.

'There was an irony in the situation, to be sure. For sixteen sunrounds your father had seen nothing beyond this palace of his childhood, contenting himself with pictures and library-scrolls and objects brought from afar, borne to the palace in the hands of others. Now, when he had ventured forth a little into the world, the thought that he was to go no further was a bitter blow to him. He was a young man, hungry for all that life could give. The knowledge that he was to taste every sensual pleasure, safe within his imperial stronghold, was scant consolation. Soon the delights of marriage began to pall, and I fear your father resented the bride who had been chosen for him by another.

'It was then, I am afraid, that Lord Malagon made his great mistake, the mistake that was to cost him his life – though not directly. Fired by his old friend's talk of battle, of the glories that awaited in the imperial fray, Mala came to your father one day in the mantle of a warrior. Mala had taken a commission, and was to ride forth against the Ouabin. Fond, foolish Mala! He told me he only wanted to help your father, doing for his friend what his friend could not do for himself. I restrained the tongue that would have execrated his folly. For all his learning, Mala showed that he was yet a novice in the ways of the heart.

'Your father's reaction was curious. Later, I would see in it the first sign of the cunning that was soon to become paramount in his behaviour. He embraced Mala, and they prayed together, but inside, I knew, your father seethed with rage. From the whispers in the palace, I soon learnt that he went to your great-father, demanding that Mala's commission be revoked; again, your great-father denied him, this time angrily. What was Kaled's friend, said the Sultan, a servant to be harried hither and yon? Lord Malagon was a young man of noble birth. If one day he was to be an ornament to the Court, must he not disport himself upon the fields of praise, as became a nobleman? Your father protested that it became him too. Again he begged his father to let him ride forth with the troops; again the Sultan said it was impossible. The royal ways of Unang were not to be questioned; nay, not even by those who held the royal titles.

'Your father could only assent, bowing respectfully, but secretly, I am sure, he cursed your great-father for a blackguard and a fool. From that time forth a deep discontent lodged in his royal heart, never to leave, and it pains me to record that your mother paid a heavy price for your father's secret miseries. Stories that reached me from the bedchamber left me sorrowing and angry. When informed that his bride was to bear him an heir, it seems your father displayed neither joy nor concern, and was merely heard to remark, with an accompanying curse, that soon he would need a new receptacle for his lust.

'But Dea ... Dea, my child, I am so sorry!'

❋   ❋

No further would the story proceed that afternoon. Hearing of the idyll of his father's childhood, Dea had been entranced; then, as he learnt of the envy that had riven his father from the love of Mala, tears began to bank behind the boy's eyes. It was the cruelty to his mother that forced them forth.

Suddenly Dea was sobbing loudly.

There was a swish of foliage. In the next moment the Targons were fluttering about, their expressionless voices muttering in unison, 'Heir! O Heir, what ails you? The Sultan of the Moon and Stars would not have you upset, no, not for the world! Are your long legs cramped? Is the sun too hot? These flowers, are they too bright for your eyes?'

'He's tired. Tired, that's all,' said Simonides sadly. 'It's been a long lesson. A long lesson for a young boy.'

The old man could only hope that the lesson would resume.

Chapter 20

A DOG CALLED RAINBOW

When Jem awoke, his first awareness was of the taste in his mouth. He winced and swallowed, but the taste was still there, sharp and acrid. For a bleary moment he wondered what it could be, then he remembered the hand over his mouth, the rank fumes of the night before. With a gasp, he struggled up on his elbows. He seemed to have slept for a long, long time.

Where was he? He lay on a huge, low, slab-like bed, enclosed within a screen of billowing gauze. Through open shutters, the reddish glow of morning disclosed a chamber of extraordinary luxury. Walls, floor and ceiling alike were covered in elaborately patterned tiles; there were rich rugs and hangings, sofas and divans, braziers of incense and bowls of fruit and flowers. Beyond the shutters lay a vista of hanging gardens. Jem heard the burble of running water and the carefree twitter of birds.

He rose, parting the curtain of gauze. Still he was conscious of the acrid taste and swallowed again, grimacing at the dryness in his throat. It was at that moment that he became aware of a figure standing beside him, a tall girlish youth in gorgeous robes. Jem started, but the youth remained impassive. 'Drink this, young master,' was all he said, proffering a small golden beaker.

Jem looked into it and saw a thick, nectar-like substance. At once it seemed the most desirable thing in the world, and he poured it gratefully into his ravaged throat. Even as the liquid slipped past his lips, Jem could feel the pain vanishing and a cool sweetness filling his mouth. The thought flashed through his mind that they had drugged him again.

But then, who were *they*?

Jem turned to the youth, but the fellow was gone, every bit as suddenly as he had appeared.

Jem turned again. In the corner of the chamber was an archway. He moved towards it and saw a chamber beyond his own, then another, then another, all of equal magnificence, vanishing into a long perspective. Why, this place was a palace, a palace more splendid than any in Ejland! How long had he been unconscious? Had he been taken to the Sacred City? Surely only the Sultan could live in such splendour!

'Hello?' Jem called uncertainly. 'Hello?'

The place seemed deserted. But that was absurd!

Jem cupped his hands round his mouth. '*Hel-lo!*' he cried, but only an echo came in reply. He slumped against the archway, the questions thudding insistently in his mind.

Then he heard a noise: the click-click of claws. Looking round sharply, Jem was astonished, less by the sudden presence of the dog than by the new alteration in the creature's appearance. Gone was the phosphorescence of the desert night; now his fur was brightly striped in purple, green, red, blue, gold: the five colours of the Orokon. Eagerly the creature bounded towards Jem, as if to a long-lost master.

'Hm!' Squatting down, Jem fluffed the furry head, looking quizzically into the dog's bright eyes. 'I'm not sure if you're friend or foe, Rainbow. You're going to have to earn my trust. Now tell me, who else have *you* seen in this place?'

The dog barked excitedly, and bounded towards the windows. Jem looked out on to the broad terrace, then down the long vista of the gardens. Reddish-purple in the dawn light, they looked quite as empty as the mysterious palace. Did the dog know something that Jem did not?

Jem felt a rumble of hunger and wondered when it was that he had he last eaten. No wonder he felt so light-headed! Pausing at a brimming bowl of fruit, he filled his pockets with figs, mandarins and pomegranates, then followed Rainbow out into the glimmering morning.

❉   ❉

'Rainbow?'

Jem, turning back on a petal-strewn path, realised that his new friend had gone again. He smiled; the dog had a habit of vanishing. If Jem had thought Rainbow was leading him somewhere, he soon decided that this was not the case. The dog was exploring, that was all, revelling in the size and splendour, the fecundity and fragrance of the palace gardens.

Jem popped a fig into his mouth and peeled another mandarin. He would not worry about Rainbow: soon enough, the dog would come bounding back through a curtain of branches, or from behind another fragrant, flowered hedge.

Idly, Jem tried to imagine the life Rainbow must have lived in his dun-coloured days. It must have been a harsh life; to be sure, such a creature could only be grateful for the strange translation that had brought him here.

But what, Jem wondered, of himself? The panic he felt had subsided swiftly, lulled by the sweet fruit, the warmth, the thousand perfumes that drifted on the air; still, he was aware of his troubling questions, as of little sudden shivers, coursing over his flesh, even in the gathering heat of the day.

By now, the sky had foregone its reddish tinges, assuming a hard cerulean sheen. Jem looked up through a canopy of leaves. Strange; the day seemed more advanced than it should have been. Where was the sun? Jem fancied it was directly overhead. How long had he been making his way through these walks? He had eaten all his fruit, but was feeling hungry again, very hungry.

He turned, troubled. 'Rainbow?'

※   ※

Jem found himself in a grove of willows. Flowers carpeted the ground at his feet and the silence was intense; here, not even birdsong disturbed the perfumed air. He sank down, wondering what to do. Where was the dog? And what was wrong with the day? Already the purple of sunset darkened the sky; soon it would be evening, yet it seemed to Jem that a mere fifteenth, at the most, had passed since he had left the mysterious palace.

He toyed with the petals, rubbing them in his hands. That was when he first considered their colours. Of course: just like the dog. What could this mean, what could it all mean? If he were a prisoner, where were the guards? Had that potion been drugged, after all? Was this garden an illusion – was it all an illusion?

Once, twice, Jem screwed up his eyes, then opened them again.

No good.

Three times, four . . . five.

The same.

He pressed his face into his hands and moaned, wishing he could wake up back on the *Catayane* . . . no, back in the Castle of Irion . . . no! Jem gazed upon the Orokon rainbow, lying in aromatic shards all around him. Suddenly the grove reminded him of the place where he had lain, so long ago, with a wild girl. Reverently he clutched the crystal at his chest. A vision of his beloved rose before his eyes and, as if it were a prayer, he whispered, 'Cata. Cata. I shall not fail your love.'

Jem rose, strengthened. He heard a friendly barking; stepping out from the trees, he saw Rainbow, his colours muted in the evening light, standing on the rim of an artificial pool.

Jem gasped. That day he had seen other pools, but this was by far the most spectacular; an immensely long rectangle of water, glimmering greenly, dotted with lily-pads, stretching before him as if to infinity . . .

But no, not quite. At the far end, shining in an intense moonlight, Jem saw the massy edifice of the palace. No doubt so vast a building presented many façades; still, Jem thought it strange that he had not seen the pool that morning . . . nor encountered it, indeed, in his wanderings before now. The geography of this place was very confusing, but then, everything was large, and laid out on principles Jem could not understand.

He looked in the water and saw his reflection – his, then a girl's, standing beside him.

Jem swivelled round. 'Cata?'

Illusion, of course. Only illusion. Longingly Jem looked into the water again. Ah, but if only! An impulse seized him and he cast aside his clothes, plunging rapturously into the cool purity. His limbs and hair golden in the moonlight, Jem swam with smooth, steady strokes, thinking only of the splendour of the gardens, the palace, the pool.

When he reached the other end, not tired at all, Rainbow was waiting for him. So was the gorgeous youth from that morning, holding out a set of magnificent robes.

A smirk played across the girlish face. 'Young master, you have refreshed yourself? That is good, but now you must hurry. It is time for dinner, and my noble lord awaits.'

Chapter 21

PALACE OF PERFUMED STAIRS

'Aiee-ee! Aiee-ee! Ai-ee-aiee!'

'What are they doing?' said Rajal.

In an alley just beyond the high walls, three old men in dirty white turbans turned round and round in the sunset light. Revolving in a tight circle, beating at the dust with their hard brown feet, they waved their hands high above their heads; their long beards billowed, writhing together like their eerie voices. More than once since arriving in Qatani, Rajal had heard the call to prayer, but this was something different, something stranger still.

'A quaint custom,' Lord Empster said urbanely.

'Quaint? They be men of portent, me lord,' shuddered Captain Porlo. 'I remember just before I met them cobber-as, there was fellows like that, a-wailing and a-carrying on like savages, they were. It be a nasty sign, make no mistake. See, Buby knows, don't 'e, me pretty?'

With a brown grin, the old sea-dog struggled to keep his monkey on his shoulder. In the cool of the evening, the three men had gathered on a long, low terrace shielded from the street by an ornate grille. Cunningly constructed, it would present from below only a geometric pattern, but afforded to those within a splendid view over the city, sweeping down towards the harbour. Palm trees rustled in the evening breezes. Domes and minarets gleamed in the sunset, but the strange song of the three old men cast a sinister pall over the scene.

'I see you have been entertained by our doom-dancers,' came a voice.

'Doom-dancers?' Alarmed, Rajal turned to the tall, elegant form of Vizier Hasem, who had graciously welcomed them to the palace that afternoon.

The Vizier replied with a little laugh, 'Just a name, I assure you, Empster-ward. Of what do they sing but the doom that awaits us all – all, that is, who are tethered to the joys of this world? The sound they make is sometimes unpleasant to our foreign guests, it is true. But the doom-dancers are holy men, and go unmolested in these Lands of Unang. I am sure the ward of so noble an Ambassador is much accustomed to the ways of alien tribes?'

Rajal flushed, but before he could say more the Vizier asked him if everything else had been to his satisfaction. The young man nodded eagerly, with an enthusiasm that was unfeigned. None could gainsay the luxuries of the Palace of Perfumed Stairs. After bathing and resting in magnificent chambers, Lord Empster's party had been dressed in rich robes, complete with jewelled turbans in the Unang fashion. Even Buby wore a golden collar and a sleek silken cummerbund.

Wonderment, like a heady drug, coursed through Rajal's veins. Outside the palace there was much squalor, concealed beneath the bright façades of the city; but inside were splendours far in excess of any he had ever seen before. He knew he could easily be seduced by such luxury, and found himself almost grateful for the ominous wailings winding up from the alley below.

One other thing troubled him. 'Where's Cata?'

On their arrival, Cata had been taken to a different part of the palace. Rajal had been expecting her to join them again, but still she had not appeared.

'The female Empster-ward shall dine with the ladies,' said the Vizier. 'We have not the Ejlander custom of mingling the sexes. Except, of course, when ladies are required,' he added archly.

Captain Porlo dug Rajal in the ribs. 'That be a good one, eh, Master Raj? When ladies is required! Cobber-as or no cobber-as, they know a thing or two in these Unang-lands!'

The Vizier turned to him. 'Then I trust we are forgiven, noble commander, for the shot a hasty watchman fired across your bows? It seems he thought you were a Wenayan privateer, when plainly you display the Ejlander standard. The hasty fool has been blinded, of course.'

Rajal gasped. 'No!'

'Such is our way,' said the Vizier, smiling. 'Our city, after all, is the nexus of the southlands, and we pride ourselves upon our hospitality. For those who shame us, there can be no mercy. But come, the time of banqueting is upon us, and my master is eager to receive his guests.'

❋   ❋

'C-Cat?'

'C-Cata?'

'C-Catayane?'

Stumbling over the name, the girls grinned foolishly, then broke off, giggling. Really, was it so hard? But if Cata thought them stupid, she forgave them as Sefita – or was it Satima? – swept a golden bowl through the water again. Warm cascades flowed over Cata's limbs. She lay back, luxuriating, inhaling the steam, the foam, the oils.

'Mm, I think I'm going to like your Qatani hospitality.'

Giggles.

'Hospi—?'

'—tality?'

'Never mind,' smiled Cata.

Already the girls had scraped her skin, peeling away layer after layer of dirt. Now, with firm but delicate hands, they laved her long hair. Cata closed her eyes. Had she ever felt so clean? Not since her days at Aunt Umbecca's had she bathed in hot water, and never like this. Sunk deep in a marble floor, the bath was filled by concealed pipes that brought forth the water already heated.

Magic?

A fine magic, if so!

Cata's mind drifted. She thought of her aunt's maid, poor Nirry, toiling up the stairs with one scalding jug, then another, then another, boiled laboriously over the kitchen range. *Slosh, slosh,* went the water on the carpet. She thought of her walks with the maid, round and round the Lectory gardens, up and down the orchard path. She thought of herself as a feral child, swishing barefoot through the Irion Wildwood. Exulting, she felt again the ferns against her thighs; then she was lying by the burbling river, soft and safe on the warm bank. But no, not on the bank. In the water. The water . . .

Cata came back.

'Her skin . . . so soft!'

'Her hair . . . so long!'

'So pale . . . so dark!'

'Her eyes . . . her lips!'

'Ah, Sefita!'

'Ah, Satima!'

Giggles. Sighs.

'*Sefita! Satima!*'

The girls jumped. Accompanying the bark had come a sharp clapping. A large woman waddled forward. She was very fat, much bejewelled, and dressed in a saffron sari. Pinned to her chest was a large flat golden object, which might have been a medal.

'Useless girls, isn't my Ejlander ready yet? How is she to be the ornament of my dinner table if she lies here broiling her lovely skin? Why, the poor thing shall be red as a lobster!'

Flustered, the girls sprang into action. One helped Cata from the deep bath; one enfolded her in a drying-wrap, immense, soft and highly perfumed.

Cata faltered, 'Good lady, I'm grateful . . .'

Uncertainly she looked at the formidable woman.

The woman looked at Cata, quite certain.

Of what, Cata could not be sure.

136

'Yes, Ejlander, I think you'll do. I think you'll do very well indeed.'

❈ ❈

Rajal marvelled at the new splendours that surrounded him. They had passed through a succession of anterooms, each one more wantonly luxurious than the last. At every doorway were guards in ornate armour, glittering and impassive; the rich doors and curtains slid back unbidden, as if at the promptings of hidden mechanisms. To Rajal, this Palace of Perfumed Stairs had about it the quality of an immense labyrinth, and how the Vizier found his way around it was a mystery. In the few moments since they had left the terrace, Rajal felt lost already.

Captain Porlo merely felt exhausted. Energetically he swung his single crutch, struggling to keep up; his wooden leg clumped loudly over the marble floors.

They came at last to a large golden screen. The screen was embedded with rubies, forming the shape of the royal coat of arms. The Vizier snapped his fingers and four solemn slave-boys appeared at once. Kneeling submissively, each was holding up a tasselled cushion. Upon each cushion there rested a curious spiky object, shaped like the wings of a bird. Three of the objects were fashioned from a red, horn-like substance; the fourth was made of bronze. The Vizier picked up the latter, fixing it to his face. Only his mouth was left exposed.

'This is the Mask of Manjani, the burning bird. Before he appears before the common folk, my master dons such a mask, though his is made of gold. When he dines in cabinet, as tonight, his face is bare, but it is the protocol that his guests should then be masked, to indicate their inequality.'

Rajal longed to ask about the burning bird, but something restrained him. Moments earlier, the Vizier had seemed so affable; in his bronze mask, he seemed threatening instead, and Rajal was abashed. Compliantly, like his companions, he donned his own mask. Now they all looked mysteriously evil, and Buby capered and shrieked. Enraged, the monkey would have torn the masks away unless Captain Porlo had restrained her, cradling her beneath his arm and holding fast to her tail.

'Hush, me lovely . . . hush now, hush.'

'Ready?' smiled the Vizier, after a moment.

The screen slid back and they entered a dim, pungent chamber, lit by perfumed tapers. To Rajal's surprise, the chamber contained neither table nor chairs, but in the centre was a long, low slab laid abundantly with golden dishes and goblets. Cross-legged at the head of the slab, raised high on a big puffy cushion, sat a roly-poly little man with a moon-shaped face, simpering beneath the biggest turban Rajal had ever seen. Rajal was surprised, for he had imagined the guests would gather and wait, perhaps for long moments, before the monarch made his appearance.

'Ah, Hasem!' The Caliph flapped his hands. 'Our guests are all here? Why, if I weren't such a model of diplomacy, I declare I'd have devoured everything already, so hungry have I been. Ooh, the pangs, my dears!' he added with a sigh. 'Burdens of state, you know, burdens of state.'

Three further figures, all wearing bird masks, squatted already down one side of the slab. Introductions were concluded quickly, and Empster-lord, Empster-ward and Porlo-commander, noblest admiral of the Ejlander navy, took their places on the empty side of the slab. Vizier Hasem sat at the foot, facing his master at the other end.

Slaves appeared like ghosts from the gloom, lifting the covers from the golden dishes. For all his own greed, the Caliph was generous, and urged his guests to make a hearty meal. Rajal complied with alacrity, realising only now how hungry he had been. The banquet was magnificent, and if he palled at some of the offerings – jellied eyes, fried tongues, spiced scrotum-of-bull – there was an abundance, too, of the vegetable foods favoured among the Vaga-kind, and Rajal made his best meal for many moonlives. When each dish was empty, it was whisked away and another appeared as if by magic.

In the Unang custom, there were no intoxicating liquors, but the bubbling hookah that did the rounds between courses more than supplied the lack. Rajal drew deeply on the sweet smoke, feeling his head spinning pleasantly, but it was as he leaned back in these moments of repose that he was also aware of a welling unease. Perhaps it was because in these moments he was obliged to look into the row of masks that faced them on the opposite side of the slab.

In their fine silken robes, the fellow guests looked just the same as the Empster party, except that their masks were blue instead of red. The Vizier had explained that the three men were a trade delegation from Outer Wenaya, who spoke only in an alien tongue. By day they negotiated with the royal interpreters, but tonight their mission was only to eat, as the Caliph conveyed not through mere words, but through the bounties of his kitchens, the depths of his friendship for their island race.

The Wenayans seemed to enjoy the hospitality, but to Rajal, there was something unnerving in their silence. From time to time, behind this or that mask, he would catch the glimmer of an observing eye, and he wondered if their fellow guests really understood nothing of what was being said. More than once during the meal, for all the laughter, all the good cheer, Rajal felt that he had become involved in some kind of game. But what could it mean?

He shook his head, a little too abruptly, when the Caliph offered him a scrotum-of-bull.

Chapter 22

THE CUSTOM OF THE COUNTRY

There was no end in sight to the royal banquet. Still the exotic dishes appeared, some grotesque, some sublime: still the droll banter flowed up and down the long, laden slab. By now, the Caliph had taken Lord Empster to sit by his right hand and was flattering him grossly; the nobleman, skilled in the arts of diplomacy, knew this was merely a prompt for his own reciprocal flattery.

'Why, Empster-lord, I declare you don't look any older than when I was a boy.'

'You see through my mask? Your Magnificence, I am in awe of your powers.'

'Ooh, you! It's your hands, my dear. Not a liver-spot in sight, and so smooth! Asses' milk? Blood of the innocents? Do you know, when you visited all those sunrounds ago – of course, I was the merest child then – I often used to look at your hands and admire them. I said to myself – Oman, I said – what you would do for a hand like that, and do you know, my dear, I don't mind admitting it? As I say to Hasem, you can take pride so far, but there comes a time when you have to face it, a hand is not is a hand is *not* a hand. Hm? But what, no rings, no paint? Such continence, if that's the word. I dare say you'll think *I've* gone a bit far.'

The Caliph held out his own hands, the plump little fingers barely visible beneath the jewellery.

'On the contrary, Great One,' said Lord Empster, 'I can but admire the acumen with which you have adorned yourself, avoiding the twin vices of false modesty and ostentation.'

The little man giggled and smacked his lips. 'Now, Hasem, did you hear that? I said there was no finer fellow than Empster-lord, didn't I? A few nice compliments, that's all I ask, and he supplies in abundance. Fairly pumps it in. I declare, you can be my regular right-hand man, how about it? No offence, Hasem, no offence!'

The bronze mask bowed respectfully, then turned to Lord Empster. 'Indeed, Empster-lord, His Magnificence looks forward to many more learned conversations with you. His uncle, the Caliph-that-was – blessed be his memory – often spoke of your wisdom, and wished that our Caliphate might one day profit again from the beneficence of your presence.'

'Good Vizier, my thanks.'

'The thanks, Empster-lord, are all upon our side.'

The compliments would have continued but for a loud burst of wind, erupting from Captain Porlo's direction. The Caliph simpered, and slaves were milling round the banqueters at once, spraying the air with a lemony scent. The captain sniffed it sullenly, tightening his grip on Buby's tail.

Though evidently much under the influence of Jarvel, the old sea-dog did not appear to be enjoying the evening quite so much as his fellow travellers. He was not used to rich food, Buby was a trial, and besides, it was difficult for him to sit cross-legged. Furtively, beneath his Unang robes, the captain had unfastened the straps that kept his wooden leg secured to Lefty's stump. Unfortunately, he felt vulnerable when his leg was not attached, and resentful memories of the *cobber-as* preyed upon his mind. He would have asked if the Caliph still kept them, but now the conversation took a new direction.

'Come, Empster-lord, you must tell us all the news from Agondon,' said the Caliph, skewering a sheep's eye with a metal prong. 'I hear they're wearing nothing but blue – blue, blue, wherever you look! Now surely there's a little more variety than that?'

The Vizier took a more elevated line. 'These late wars in your empire, Empster-lord, have caused us much concern. I take it all the traitors have been well and truly routed?'

'I'm sure your ward is a young man of fashion,' the Caliph went on obliviously. 'The red mask he wears tonight looks most becoming – doesn't it, Hasem? Would he be a wearer of *red* when he's at home, then?'

'Great One,' Lord Empster attempted, 'red is a pretty colour, and a sacred one, I know, within these Realms of Unang. Alas, that in Ejland it should be a colour of treachery!'

'You don't say?' Eye-jelly dribbled down the Caliph's chin.

The Vizier cleared his throat. 'Is it true,' he went on, 'that all the docks in Agondon have gone underwater? Such a tragedy for the commerce of a great city! To be sure, I'd heard they were built on infirm foundations.'

'Infirm!' Captain Porlo was moved to protest. Though he kept flags of all nations in his trunk, the sea-dog nonetheless remained a loyal Ejlander. 'Agondon-docks be the finest in the world,' he bellowed, 'not like your rickety foreign rubbish!'

'I say,' said the Caliph, 'that's a bit rich!'

He was talking about the lung-and-udder curry.

Lord Empster laughed. 'In his patriotism, my friend forgets that our imperial city was largely built upon reclaimed land. It is true there has been flooding in parts of Agondon, in the extremity of recent weather. But I think both the city and my friend's docks are safe.'

Captain Porlo muttered to himself and took another draw on the bubbling hookah.

Buby was becoming increasingly restless. The little monkey was fascinated, it seemed, by their silent companions behind the blue masks. Several times she had leapt across the slab, and perhaps would have ripped the masks away if agile slaves had not caught her in time.

Now the captain had tied her tail to the tasselled waist-cord of his Unang gown. Fretting, Buby chafed at her confinement, then dug her little hands beneath her cummerbund, scratching hard at her patches of mange. She had not much enjoyed the nuts and sugared fruits the slaves had been offering her throughout the evening, but calmed down a little when she sucked on the hookah.

❋   ❋

'One may assume, then, Empster-lord, that you give no credence to these time-will-end types?' the Vizier was saying now. 'Those of us in the southlands cannot but observe that they grant a particular consequence to your Ejlander calendar.'

Lord Empster smiled. 'There are those who say that calendars are made by men, and should not be thought the handiwork of the gods. Yet your own calendar dates from the time, does it not, when your fire god appeared to the Prophet in the wilderness? A calendar is always half the work of the gods, for even if it is men who begin to count the years, it is gods who have decided how long the years shall be. But when Ejlanders say their thousandth cycle marks the end of time, one can only hope they are wrong, for there is little time remaining, should that be so.'

'Ooh, indeed!' said the Caliph. 'Why, imagine if time should end before I'd finished my dinner! Or before I get the new elephants we've ordered – ceremonial, you know. Frightfully swish – Big Boy will be green. At least, I hope so!'

Rajal said suddenly, 'What about portents?'

'What does he say?' said the Caliph, licking out a sorbet-glass.

Rajal was thinking about the burning bird. 'Some say there are signs.'

Lord Empster gave the young man a warning nudge, but he was too late. Rajal had indulged too freely in Jarvel and his tongue had grown loose. Folk might go about their business obliviously, but there were signs, he said, that the Time of Atonement was coming to an end. A new age was dawning for the women and men of earth, but whether it would be an age of terror or of bliss was knowledge yet hidden in the womb of fate.

Lord Empster cleared his throat and would have asked the Caliph about his ceremonial elephants, but the Vizier suddenly raised his hands above his head like claws and cried, 'Creatures of Evil!'

Buby shrieked.

Rajal gasped.

The Caliph dropped his sorbet-glass.

Then, after a moment, the little man laughed, 'Ooh Hasem, you had me going there – didn't he have you going, boys? Why, for a moment I thought he'd been possessed – and not in a pleasurable way, I hasten to add. But really, there is so much of this evil about nowadays, isn't there? Hasem, did you tell our friends about the Black Rider?'

'Not yet, Great One. But I shall of course be inviting them to tomorrow's execution.'

'Execution?' Rajal felt the Jarvel-warmth subsiding within him, to be replaced by a chill of fear.

'Ooh yes,' said the Caliph, stuffing his mouth with candied fruits. 'Would you believe, Big Boy – I speak of my brother, you understand – was sending me a message, and very polite of him too, when his Rider – that's his messenger – was struck down and killed! On my lands! Fortunately they caught the little beast who did it, didn't they Hasem?'

'I have yet to inspect the villain personally, Your Magnificence, but I understand the child languishes at this moment in the dungeons below.'

'Hm. Well, *he'll* get his just deserts tomorrow, won't he?'

'Indeed,' smiled the Vizier. '*He* will indeed.'

❈   ❈

Rajal felt a guttural stirring in his throat, but whether he wanted to protest or to throw up he was not quite sure. The Caliph turned to him pleasantly, and in the event Rajal could only think to stammer, 'D-Did you r-receive the message?'

The Caliph flung up his hands. 'My dear, of course not! The Rider keeps his message in his head. I dare say it was nothing much – orders for more Wenayan slaves, greetings for Shimmy's name-day, who knows? – but there it is, splattered with the Rider's brains by some paltry caravanserai on the Qatani Road. What a place to spill your last, if you'll pardon the expression. Now we'll have to wait till Big Boy gives it again – his message, I mean. Still, if it was anything exciting I dare say he'll be double-quick on the re-run.'

'Your ways are not ours, Great One,' observed Lord Empster. 'In Ejland, such a system would be thought cumbersome, and all would not depend upon the life of one Rider.'

'Now *that's* cumbersome,' said the Caliph. 'After all, who would harm a Rider? Well, except for this little creature from the caravanserai – to think, that my lands should harbour such depravity! The shame of it, Hasem: shall we ever live it down? Well, I dare say we shall.'

The Caliph popped a large fig into his mouth, realising only too late that it was rather too large. His cheeks ballooned with chewing, then his brow furrowed and he went on thoughtfully between mouthfuls, 'Now remember, Hasem, I want this to be *exclusive* to the royal engravers, not like last time – pirate pictures to every corner of the empire, and not so much as a by-your-leave. Would you say gelding, flaying, disembowelling – in that order? Should we have the limbs off, one by one? Always a bit boring after the first few, don't you think?'

'Indeed, Great One,' said the Vizier, 'but may I counsel against gelding, too? I think perhaps it would be . . . inappropriate in this case.'

'Inappropriate? For killing a Rider?'

The Vizier might merely have smiled again, but instead mused, 'Studies show that applications for the Eunuch Service fall markedly after a public gelding. Makes it seem like a punishment. Your Magnificence, let us recall that your daughter is to appear on the balcony. To be sure, the mob will abide less mutilation – just a little less – if they know that so great an ecstasy of the spirit is shortly to be vouchsafed to them.'

'Ecstasy? Really, Hasem, you make it sound as if we're offering up my daughter for the pleasures of the crowd!'

'But Great One, in a sense we are.'

'Well, really!'

'You'll pardon me,' Rajal attempted, curiously, 'but I was unaware that . . . that Your Magnificence had the blessing of a daughter.'

Lord Empster's eyes flashed behind his mask, perhaps a little wryly; the Caliph arched a well-plucked eyebrow, as if to hint that, for all impressions to the contrary, he was, after all, a house of many mansions. It was left to Vizier Hasem to observe that rather less news of Unang Lia must reach Ejland than travelled the other way. Could Empster-ward really know nothing of Qatani's most priceless jewel?

'Jewel?' said Rajal, swallowing hard. Furtively he touched a hand to his chest, feeling for the Crystal of Koros. Perhaps it was just the Jarvel, but the sense came to him that some clue might be forthcoming, some hint, however distant, that might help in their quest. If only Jem were here!

It seemed the Vizier had no clues after all.

He began, 'Empster-ward, there is a custom in our country called the Royal Revealing, in which the Caliph, whenever he appears before his people, displays to them his finest womanly treasure. There before the eager mob she stands, unveiled and dressed only in the flimsiest of gowns, that women might see in her all there is to envy, and men, all there is to fuel their desire. In times gone by, Caliphs would bring forth this or that exotic new concubine, or luscious slave-girl fresh from the market-place. In any case, the girl was a different one each time, but the crowd's response was always the same, a rippling chorus of cheers, jeers and exclamations of mingled loathing and lust.'

'Barbaric,' said the Caliph, with surprising feeling.

'Indeed,' returned the Vizier, 'but a potent symbol, Great One, of your manly prowess.'

'*My* prowess? Really, Hasem!'

'I mean, of the Caliph's. I mean, it would be, if you . . .' The bronze mask turned back towards his guests, and though the voice was flustered, Rajal felt that he was now about to receive the clue. How he would recognise it, he did not know, but he felt himself possessed of a strange excitement. He cleared his throat and smiled, for again he was aware of observing eyes behind the blue masks.

The Vizier continued, 'This was in the past, you understand, this distasteful lust and envy. Now all is altered, for it was the wise decree of our present ruler that no treasure of the fairer sex could be greater to him than his daughter. It seems all the peoples of our province are agreed, for when the Princess appears upon the balcony, the crowds grow hushed and reverent. Now there are cries neither of lechery nor of spite, but only waves of spiritual power, flowing between the people and the one they have come to call – such is her beauty – the Shimmering Princess. Through all these Lands of Unang, her fame has spread, and few do not bow down their heads to bless such beauty, or pray that the gods may cherish Princess Bela Dona.'

'Bela Dona?' It was the first time the Vizier had said the name, and Rajal, like his companions, found himself repeating it under his breath. Could this be the clue? In the very name there seemed to be some curious magic, some breath of the spirit rustling though the worldly, sensual scene.

Terrible as the morrow's execution would be, Rajal found himself longing for it, that he might see this mysterious Bela Dona.

Chapter 23

ANOTHER MOTHER MADANA

Jem's astonishment had not abated. For immeasurable moments he had trailed behind the girlish youth, eyes darting here and there through chambers that were now lit brilliantly, glowing with all the splendours they contained. Behind Jem came the click-click of Rainbow's claws; from ahead, drifting into his awareness like unravelling coils of smoke, were the sounds of music, excited voices, pealings of laughter.

The banqueting-hall still came as a shock. To think, that Jem had thought this palace deserted! The guests numbered perhaps a thousand, and all were carousing merrily.

'Ah, my young friend!' The girlish youth melted away and a tall, exotic figure swept towards the newcomer, enfolding him in a rapturous embrace. 'Let me look at you . . . ho, but you are not fully recovered, I see.'

'Recovered?' murmured Jem, amazed.

His host was an elderly man with glinting eyes and a long, flowing beard. The fellow wore a black turban, crusted in jewels, and a glittering cape; on his long hands were many rings, and chains of gold and silver circled his withered neck. With a fond smile, he patted Jem's arm. 'It takes time . . . time. You are pale, and I see the trouble in your eyes. But come, you are to take your place beside me. You see your . . . your companion has joined us already.'

The old man gestured with a flashing hand. On a dais raised above the hubbub of the hall, Jem saw a vision that made his heart lurch. He started forward. 'Cata!'

But no. The girl from the van.

Jem staggered, clutching his forehead. Waves of lassitude swept over him and he stared blearily into the brightness, at the sheen of exotic foods, at the sparkle of jewels, at the lush fabrics. He screwed up his eyes. To be sure, Agondon's most exalted offerings could not begin to compete with so resplendent a display of finery, or tables laden so lavishly. All around him, faces had turned to him with friendly smiles and merry, dancing eyes.

'As I say, you are not fully recovered.' A many-ringed hand alighted on his arm. 'The Ouabin are treacherous, and these parts have seen many abductions in these last, fraught moonlives. How I thank the mighty

145

Theron we were able to save you ... but not, alas, before the oblivion-cloth had overwhelmed your senses. You shall find yourself prey to the most curious illusions ... for some days to come, I am afraid, for some days to come.'

The old man sighed, then brightened again. 'But how rude I am! Permit me to introduce myself. I bear the name of Almoran, and you are most welcome to my humble villa ... most welcome indeed, Prince Jemany.'

'You know who I am?'

Jem's host laughed. 'Prince, I am an old man, it is true, and my faculties are fading, but do you think I would not know the heir of the world's mightiest empire?'

Wonderingly, Jem gazed into the glinting eyes.

✳   ✳

'Pale. So pale.'

'In my country, dark.'

'They call you dark?'

'Yes.'

'Your hair?'

'Skin.'

'No!'

'Yes.'

'No! Creamy, creamy.'

A hand fondled and Cata, not for the first time, fought the urge to slap it away.

A bark: 'Sefita!'

The hand retreated.

Turning back to her hostess, Cata smiled – again. But her smile was growing strained. How she longed for this meal to end – how she longed to see her friends again!

'Ah, Satima,' her hostess smiled back.

'Cata,' said Cata.

How many times?

'To me, Satima. All my girls, all of them: Satima. Or Sefita.'

Cata clenched her teeth. 'How do you decide? Which is which, I mean?'

'Ah, Sefita, most would ask why!'

At once, Cata decided she would not. She was tired of these games, tired and uncomfortable. Her legs were cramped. The sari they had made her wear was chafing her skin. She shifted on her cushion. She plucked at the sari. Curtly she waved away a second sorbet.

'Come, Satima, we must make you plump!'

'I'm not a chicken,' Cata said quietly.

'Ah, Sefita, such quick wit. But hold it back, mind, when you meet the men.'

'What men?'

A merry twinkle played in the old woman's eyes. Cata struggled to control her anger.

Mother Madana – for such, it seemed, was the name of her hostess – presided over a long, low table surrounded by a clutter of cushions, carpets, screens. Fifteen, perhaps twenty girls flanked the formidable woman. Like her, all were dressed in saffron, refulgent in the light of many candles. Large, dark men – strangely feminine men – passed back and forth, serving a meal that seemed never-ending.

Not since she left Aunt Umbecca's had Cata been presented with such extravagant fare. She supposed she was meant to feel honoured. Flattered. But how could she? Her requests to dine with her friends had been met only with laughter. Mother Madana, the Sefitas and Satimas seemed bent on trying her patience. But there was worse, much worse. Whispers, whimperings, muffled sobs sounded from behind the divans and screens. From time to time came the clankings of chains, but even then it appeared that only Cata noticed. Could the chamber be haunted?

Gigglings, whinings came from closer at hand.

'Shift.'

'No!'

'Fair's fair!'

'You pinched me!'

'Shift!'

'Ooh!'

The girls vied to sit beside her. Cata braced herself, and the pawings resumed, fresh hands this time, stroking, pinching, prodding. It was more than she could bear. Why should these girls think her such a marvel? Why should these girls be such simpering fools?

In the corner, between the screens, she saw a glint of chains.

'Ah, Satima, I see your future!'

Sharply Cata looked at Mother Madana.

'My girls, how they love you! Then how shall the men?'

Cata's brow furrowed. 'How shall they what?'

'Why, love you, of course! Whitebait, Satima!'

'What?'

'Silly girl, can't you see? You're in Qatani now. See – why, feel! – how an Ejlander is valued!' And laughingly, as if in demonstration, Mother Madana stroked the golden medal-like disc that was pinned to her chest.

'I'm not an Ejlander,' Cata said coldly.

Again, not for the first time.

147

And again: 'Nonsense! Come, Sefita, you're a bit rough round the edges, but I saw you unfold your napkin! Don't you think I recognise a Quick-girl when I see one?'

'You know about Quick's?'

'Satima, who does not? Who, that is, among the world's connoisseurs? Why, does not my own little school – for so I think of it, so I think of it – follow in the footsteps of that great academy?' Mother Madana looked down, swirling sherbet in a balloon-like glass. 'You don't have your certificate, by the by?'

This was too much. All through the evening Cata had restrained herself, reining in her anger, damping down her fears. Now this apparently casual aside made her passion burst forth. Roughly she broke from the pawing girls. She staggered back from the dining-board.

'Who are you? What do you want from me?'

'A feisty new piece!' came a voice from behind.

Cata span round. While the scene was in progress, a visitor had stolen into their midst. It was a man, but a man quite unlike the smooth, elegant slaves who had served their meal. This was a fat, shabby fellow in an ill-wrapped turban, unshaven, greasy, low-bred. He staggered a little. He stank of ferment.

But Mother Madana burst out excitedly, 'Eli! Eli Oli Ali!'

She floundered up from her cushion.

Kisses. *Mwah. Mwah.*

They slapped palms. 'Eh!'

'Eh-eh!'

Cata seized her chance; or rather, she would have done. The doors were open. She darted. But there was no time. At once, ten, fifteen, twenty Sefitas and Satimas surrounded her, smiling, cooing, pawing.

'Pretty, pretty!'

'Mm, her skin!'

'Her lovely hair!'

'Let me go, let me go!'

Eli Oli Ali looked delighted. 'What's this, Mother? Catfight lessons?'

'Pah! The new whitebait's excitable, that's all. Hold her, girls. She'll calm down.'

'Whitebait, now? And feisty?' An eager grin.

'Not for you, Eli.'

'Mother, you're cruel!'

'Cruel? She's a Quick-girl. A bit more training here, and think what she'll fetch! You know our deal, Eli. Common ones for you. Quality, that's my department. I make the choice, and this one's quality.'

'Pah! Looks like trouble, if you ask me.'

'Too much trouble, and she's yours – I promise. But Eli, it's her first night. Make allowances, hm? Why, don't you remember the Empress of Zalaga? Spitting and fingernails and blasphemy all the way, till I managed to break her in. And look at her now! The old woman thrust forward a glittering bosom. 'You've seen my Royal Export Medal, haven't you?'

'Many times, Mother,' said the fat fellow glumly.

Mother Madana rubbed her hands. 'But come, Eli, did you bring your sister? Speaking of quality, I mean – hm?'

There was a pause. Eli Oli Ali sniffed deeply.

'Eli?'

'Alas!'

'Eli, no!'

'The Ouabin!'

Mother Madana screamed. She stamped her feet. She flung herself down on a cushion-strewn sofa. 'The beauty of the Shimmering Princess, you said, and all the fleshly charms of a harlot! Another medal, I was sure of it! And lost, lost! Violated in the desert, in a Ouabin tent!'

The whoremonger sniffed again. 'But there's worse.'

Mother Madana looked up. 'What can be worse?'

'I'd promised her to the Ejlanders. Tonight.'

'What?' cried Mother Madana.

'What?' cried Cata.

But her hostess did not hear her. 'You fool, Eli! Fool and turncoat! Would Casca Dalla have served me so? Oh, I knew you were losing your touch, I knew it! That girl was mine to train – you promised me, *me*, not those rutting pigs! You would squander such a find on common whoredom, when I could make her a royal bride?'

Had anyone else spoken to Eli Oli Ali like this, he should certainly have remonstrated, perhaps violently, but the Keeper of Palace Women was, after all, a vital link in his business empire. Without her, he could never keep his place as Whoremonger Royal, a place that Casca Dalla coveted openly. To be stripped of his royal seal was Eli's worst fear. He blinked innocently at Mother Madana. Caution was of the essence. Besides, what was he, if he couldn't placate the passions of this raddled old hag? She liked him – why, loved him!

Just let her calm down, that was the way.

'Royal bride?' he said after a moment, as if the harsh words had never been spoken. 'Your plan for the new girl?'

'Precisely,' flung back Mother Madana.

'Then content yourself with her. But Mother, I must go to the Ejlanders, and what am I to offer? Call it common whoredom, but they pay well.' The fellow leered at Cata. 'They will need distraction, when they find my prize is lost. Might one of their own kind provide it, do you think?'

149

Mother Madana rolled her eyes. 'Why should they want whitebait, when they can get it at home? The flame-haired one's had more Quick-girls than you've had skins of ferment, mark my words!'

'Flame-haired one?' Cata gasped.

Eli Oli Ali persisted, 'Mother, please! If I can't have the whitebait, give me *something*.'

'Something?'

The greasy fellow nodded.

'None of my quality, mind!'

Now he shook his head.

From behind the screens came a clanking of chains.

Mother Madana pursed her lips. 'A distraction, Eli? What would your flame-haired fellow say, do you think, to a Baba-girl?'

'You've got one?'

'Three. Just came in, while you were away.'

'Three! Fresh?'

'As the dawn. I was going to put them up for auction tomorrow. Quite unsuitable for quality brides. Sullen, none too clean, run to fat. And of course those stalky necks, easily snapped. But for an evening's pleasure?'

'Dear Mother!'

'Dear Eli!'

Mwah. Mwah.

Mother Madana clapped her hands; slaves pulled away a screen; Eli Oli Ali exclaimed, delighted. Candlelight glinted on golden chains and Cata saw three frightened, dark-hued girls, nearly naked, with coily hair and long necks circled with rings.

Eli Oli Ali grabbed a chain.

'Monster! Dirty monster, leave them alone!'

All this time Cata had struggled. Now she lashed out, kicking and screaming. For a moment, just a moment, she broke from her restraints.

To no avail.

Mother Madana turned on her, suddenly, fiercely.

'Shut your noise, whitebait!'

Cata staggered, slumped. She had known Mother Madana was a formidable woman; just how formidable, she had not foreseen.

The woman's fist was like a rock.

'Feisty indeed!' cackled Eli Oli Ali. 'You think you'll really break her in?'

'Pah! I'll break her, or my name's not Madana!'

The whoremonger grinned. 'I've heard that before. Remember, Mother, auction tomorrow! High prices, after a Royal Revealing, hm?'

'Oh, take your Babas and be off with you. Off, off!' Mother Madana signalled to her girls. Cowed, they gathered around the prostrate Cata.

'Now, what happens to Mother's naughty girls, hm? Sefita? Satima?'

'Darky-dark!' giggled one.

'Smelly!' Another.

'Old clothes!'

'Beetles!'

'Spiders!'

'Rats!'

Then, an ecstatic squeal: 'Snakes!'

'There are no snakes in Mother's storeroom, Sefita.' But the formidable woman smiled, satisfied. How well she had moulded her young charges! These were no Baba-girls, fit only for casual venery! All through Unang and the neighbouring realms, gentlemen of quality would pay high prices for these kittenish playthings.

But the new girl looked quite a challenge.

She prodded Cata with her foot. 'Our friend's not quite one of us yet, is she?'

Giggles. 'Mother, no!'

'Let's see how she is in the morning, after a night in the darky-dark.'

Chapter 24

DANCE OF THE FIVE VEILS

'The heir is hungry, hm?'

'I'll say!'

Smiling, stroking his long beard, Almoran looked on as his young guest fell eagerly upon the lavish offerings. Moments earlier, questions had filled Jem's mind; for now, he thought only of the brightly coloured rice, the lamb stuffed with walnuts, almonds and pistachios, the creamy yoghurt and the coconut dahl. There were yams and artichokes and cucumbers and lentils, spiced to perfection and superbly garnished; chutney made from mangoes, quinces and limes; sherbets and sorbets and delicious nectars. Never, it seemed to Jem, had he eaten so magnificently. The flavours, the aromas, even the colours: all were astonishing, all were strange.

Under the table, Rainbow tucked excitedly into his own lavish meal, his stripy tail flapping back and forth, his muzzle jammed into a golden bowl. From the tables below the dais came the sparkle of finery, the merry clamour of voices, laughter, clinking goblets. Almoran clapped for music; Jem sat back, luxuriating in a warm, dreamy contentment.

Only Dona Bela seemed uneasy. Sitting on the other side of Almoran, she looked uncertainly in Jem's direction, her eyes heavy-lidded and her brow furrowed. Almoran reached out, taking her hand. The girl's mouth twisted; after a moment, she pulled her hand away.

'My Lord Almoran,' Jem murmured heedlessly, 'it is a fine palace you have here, a fine palace indeed. To be sure, you must be one of the greatest of men.'

'Young Prince, you are mistaken,' smiled Almoran. 'What am I but a man of business, a mere man of business, retired from his trades to this provincial fastness? No, I am a simple fellow, blessed only in the many friends I have gathered around me, to sweeten the sorrows of my declining years.'

Jem found himself rubbing his eyes. Waves of tiredness rolled over him like clouds and he struggled to reply to his generous host. Dimly, but too dimly, he was aware of the strangeness that pressed, insistent and troubling, beneath the bright scene. 'Then indeed, good sir ... indeed, you are one of the greatest of men, for your capacities for friendship must be remarkable ... why, as remarkable as this house which, for all your modesty, I shall not forbear to call a palace.'

This time Almoran did not demur, but said simply, 'I call it the House of Truth.'

'Why such ... a name?' By now, Jem's voice was a distant moan and he found himself cradling his head in his arms. He peered up hazily. Was it his imagination, or had all the guests turned their eyes towards the dais? Had the music ceased, and the merriment, too?

'Young Prince,' said Almoran, 'this is a place of love, and what truth is there but love? All else is illusion.' Fondly, the old man reached out, smoothing Jem's hair. 'May I not hope that my newest friends shall become as dear to me as those you see below?'

This time, Jem did not reply. When he opened his eyes, he found himself lying on the vast bed where he had woken that morning. This time, the chamber was dark, but through the open windows he saw the sharp gold of the moon, shimmering on the waters of the long pool. On the end of the bed lay Rainbow, sleeping contentedly. Careful not to disturb him, Jem parted the curtain of gauze and padded towards the terrace.

The gardens were still and the silence was deep, deep as if this strange estate were empty after all. Jem looked up at the moon. It was full, hovering over the gardens like a vast, impassive face. Only now did the thought come to him that last night, in the desert, there had been no moon. How long had he been here? Crouching on the edge of the pool, he trailed a hand in the water, recalling his swim. Heat pressed around him in the alien night and he thought he might plunge into the pool again.

His knuckles scraped against something hard.

Curiously, Jem peered into the water. His brow furrowed. He stepped into the pool, sloshing forward cautiously, then more rapidly. He turned, gazing at the house, the moon, the gardens. How could it be? The pool was shallow, impossibly shallow, barely deep enough to cover his ankles.

❈   ❈

The royal banquet was almost over. Rajal was tired and could have slept there and then, but the Caliph clapped his hands and called for entertainment. While coffee and a fresh Jarvel-pipe did the rounds, three masked musicians took their places in a corner. One played a tabla, one a curly horn, one a mysterious stringed instrument, midway between a lute and a harp.

It was as they launched into a slow, rhythmic divertimento that a figure all in black came gliding into the space between the dining-slab and the corner. Evidently the figure was a woman's, but in the fashion of strictest Unang piety she was concealed from head to foot in flowing robes and veils. Even her hands were covered by gloves and her eyes could be seen only through the merest slits in her headdress.

Slowly, billowingly, the woman began to dance.

'This should please our Wenayan friends,' said the Vizier. 'Alas, I fear we have spoken too much, and left them confused and wondering. It is poor policy; but this is a dance to which any man may respond, be his language what it may.'

'Hm,' said the Caliph. 'All about concealing, of course.'

'But revealing, too,' said the Vizier.

'Revealing, yes!'

'You're enjoying yourself, Great One?'

'Greatly.'

'But you'll enjoy yourself more in a moment.'

'Ooh, I know!' The Caliph slurped greedily at his thick, mud-like coffee.

Rajal was confused. In a short space of time the Caliph's character seemed to have changed, and then changed again. This enthusiasm for the black-garbed dancer seemed out of keeping with his earlier manner, but undeniably there was fervour in his eyes as the sashaying woman began to remove the first of a series of garments. For a wild moment Rajal wondered if the flowing materials might conceal the Caliph's daughter. But no, that was absurd. The Princess Bela Dona was a sacred icon; this woman before them now was not sacred, but profane.

As she danced, she sang a Unang song.

> *Whither do I roam? Whither do I wander?*
> *Taken from the only home I've known,*
> *Knowing nothing of my destination,*
> *Only that it must be yonder, yonder!*
> *Shall I be a slave or a concubine?*
> *Pray, shall I find a love that's mine*
> *In the unseen realms that lie before me now?*
>
> *Whither do I roam? Whither do I wander?*
> *Taken with my seeds left still unsown,*
> *Knowing only that there's dark before me,*
> *In whatever land lies yonder, yonder!*
> *Shall I be a whore or a rich man's wife?*
> *Pray, shall I find my love, my life,*
> *In the clouded realms that lie before me now?*

The woman's voice was high and fluting and contained in it a sadness, perhaps even an irony, that seemed, like the words of her song, to be strangely at odds with the lewd writhings of her gloved hands, the rhythmic grindings of her hips. Slowly she cast away the first of her garments. As a silken skein fluttered over the banqueting-slab, Rajal saw that only that the dim light had made the fabric appear black. In truth it was purple, the same rich, deep purple as the secret crystal he wore around his neck. Now he understood the profane dance. What the woman wore was a cunning arrangement of wrappings, each almost transparent, that had contrived at first to give the semblance of a single dark costume. Really it consisted of many colours – or rather, five. Beneath the purple, Rajal saw veils of green; beneath the green, he knew, would come red, blue, gold, the colours of the Orokon.

He watched, entranced, but only moments were to pass before his entrancement turned to terror. The blue-masked figures across the slab had turned intently towards the sensual performance. Rajal glanced at them. Through much of the meal he had avoided their eyes; only now could he try to take the measure of this silent delegation. One was tall and thin, perhaps a little nervous; one, the one in the middle, a solid, imposing presence; the third had a hunched, dingy air, evident even in the cast of his mouth.

The middle one – he must have been their leader – was tapping his fingers on the table-top, in time to the slow rhythm of the dance. Not for the first time, Rajal noted the pallor of the man's skin. He had assumed that Wenayans would be dark-hued; it seemed he was mistaken. Then he considered the ring the man wore on his middle finger. Rajal knew a little of jewellery; all through his childhood he had seen it traded on the brightly laden stalls of the Vaga-fair. This ring did not appear to be of foreign design; indeed, Rajal wondered dimly if he had seen the ring before. Or one just like it.

He raised his eyes slowly to the blue mask. Over the mouth that was visible beneath the mask had crept an expectant, sensual leer. Rajal shuddered, as if at intimation of evil. Then the mask turned back towards him. For a moment Rajal would wonder if Jarvel had disordered his wits. First the hand – the hand that wore the ring – gestured towards the dancing woman. Then, almost in a whisper, the lips let fall the question, *'Doesn't remind you of Catayane, does she?'*

The mask turned towards the dance again. By now the red skeins had fluttered away, leaving the woman garbed in Wenayan blue. The colour of the delegates, thought Rajal. But then, the colour of the Bluejackets, too. He was trembling violently. Had he heard correctly? He could not have done! The man had been murmuring; they were foreign words, and one of them just happened to sound like Cata's name.

Nervously Rajal glanced at his own companions. Between Buby and his own eagerness for the dance, Captain Porlo had noticed nothing, and Rajal could not catch Lord Empster's eye.

'Ah, concealment!' the Vizier was saying.

'Concealment!' sighed the Caliph.

'A fine thing, is it not?'

'But not as fine as revealing!'

'Great One, indeed!

By now the woman had removed most of her coverings, but still nothing could be seen of her naked flesh. Rajal wondered why. Perhaps it was the light, dim and flickering, with all its masking shadows; perhaps it was the exceptional cunning of the costume; perhaps, he would think later, it was an evil, beguiling magic that allowed no hint of revelation until the final moment had come. In any case, Rajal found himself focused intently upon the dancing woman, eager for the first glimpse of flesh beneath the veils.

It was not desire that thudded in his veins, nor any cooler pleasure in the performance. To watch it at all filled him with a certain hot shame, and Rajal was only glad that Cata was not here to see his discomfiture. But there was more to it, wasn't there? Rajal had seen performances like this before, in the more degraded of the Vaga-camps. Always they had ended in whistles and catcalls and coins flung contemptuously at the naked creature who had seemed, in her veils, to be a goddess of desire. But this time would be different. With a certainty that frightened him Rajal knew that the performance would end in more than the display of a woman's naked form.

Now the blue veils were gone and only gold remained; now the music was faster and the gold skeins were waving, flying on the taper-lit air, but still no part of the woman could be seen; still even her face was concealed from all eyes. Rajal knew these last veils would vanish suddenly when the music stopped, but that first the musicians would tease and tease, always seeming to be ending, then starting up another measure.

Dimly he was aware of the Caliph and his Vizier, and the bantering words they flung back and forth. The Caliph said there was much deception in the world, and deception, to be sure, should be rooted out and punished; the Vizier assured his master that indeed it would be punished, punished severely. Rajal felt shivers running down his spine.

The music stopped.

There were gasps, for suddenly all veils were gone and standing before them was no goddess of beauty but a hideous, withered crone!

The Caliph cackled with laughter.

Coolly the Vizier turned to Lord Empster. 'An old Qatani trick, said to be a moral lesson of sorts. My father had it played upon me when the lusts of manhood first fired my loins; I believe, too, it is played upon girls when womanly vanity comes knocking at their hearts, eager to enter. Now, perhaps, this Dance of the Five Veils may teach us a further lesson.'

Lord Empster shifted, his mask glinting in the taper-light.

Rajal restrained an impulse to cry out.

Captain Porlo restrained Buby.

'We have thrilled to the dance, but the dancer was an impostor,' Hasem said softly. 'Like you, Empster-lord, and your Ejland delegation.'

Rajal burst out, 'No!'

The Caliph collapsed into fresh peals of laughter, rocking back and forth. But Hasem was angry, on his feet and shouting.

'Did you think we were fools – primitive fools, to fall for your smooth-tongued lies? Lord? Admiral? Ward? Pah! You are Ejlander war-criminals, seeking sanctuary for your foul crimes! Guards! Take them to the dungeons!'

The doors burst open. There were running feet, scimitars flashing; golden goblets and dishes crashed; there were the Vizier's cries, the Caliph's laughter, and Buby the monkey leaping free at last, tearing a blue mask from a face before cruel hands caught her, beating her mercilessly.

In the moment before he was bundled from the chamber, Rajal twisted back to see, just for an instant, the face the monkey's rage had revealed.

Then he knew everything.

Chapter 25

MADE FOR PLEASURE

'Success!'

'Victory!'

'Free at last!'

Polty leapt up, punching the air. Bean flapped his skinny arms and danced a little. Mr Burgrove tripped on an edge of carpet, overbalanced and sprawled to the floor.

Of the three of them, only Polty was truly overjoyed. Bean's joy was dutiful, to please Polty, while Mr Burgrove was pleased only to be liberated from the constraints of a long evening with nothing to drink but hava-nectar.

Besides, he didn't like foreigners.

Polty was beginning to like them very much indeed. Resplendent in his exotic robes, he cast himself down on a huge, soft divan. Idly he surveyed the luxurious apartment that the Qatanis had provided for their distinguished guests, all cushions and curtains and ornate hangings. It was a place made for fleshly joys, and Polty had soon discovered how to procure such joys, even within the strictly ordered society of the palace. He was expecting some this evening. With a smile he drew forth a tobarillo, tamping it against the top of his little silver case. Since leaving civilisation – or rather, Ejland – he had rationed this particular pleasure, but this was a special occasion.

The tinder-strip flared.

'Polty?'

'Bean?'

'What will happen now? I mean, the traitors. What will happen to them?'

'Hah! To the old sea-dog and the noble lord, nothing.'

'Nothing?'

Polty smiled knowingly. 'We just thought we'd frighten them, that's all. The young ward's the only one we want. Or rather, the only one we'll take now. Let's see how Empster reacts when he hears he's been harbouring – unknowingly, of course – a traitor who's been sought since my father's days in Irion! We'll let the nobleman roam free for a while. I've a feeling he may prove a very interesting acquaintance, one way or another.'

Bean considered this, but was puzzled. 'And the ward?'

'Our young friend? Death, I think, don't you? Why, perhaps in the little theatrical they're planning for tomorrow – disembowelling in the public square! After all, a play needs more than one act, doesn't it? But first we're going to question him. Or rather, I am.'

'Tonight?'

'In the morning – let him stew. Let them all stew. Tonight was made for pleasure.'

'Really, Polty?' Bean said uncertainly.

'Well – pain, if your name is Jem Vexing.'

Bean screwed up his forehead. 'Jem Vexing? But that's—'

'But we're expecting visitors,' Polty said abruptly.

'Again?' Bean was alarmed.

'Of course,' Polty smiled. 'Besides, our mixer-friend's back from the desert, and I'm sure we're eager to hear about his journey. We must gain all the knowledge we can about these Unang-lands, Bean. Carnal, in particular!'

'Oh, Polty!'

But Bean was happy. With sudden eagerness, he began a circuit of the apartment, picking up snot-filled handkerchiefs, discarded stockings, tobarillo-butts. That his duties were unnecessary made them all the more pleasant to him. As – so it was supposed – an important trade delegation, Polty and his friends had been accorded every distinction. Had Polty wished, a team of slave-boys would have been on call, ready to attend to his every whim. Polty had refused their services. The Vizier was astonished, but Bean was not. Had the slaves been girls, Polty might have changed his mind, but he didn't want prying foreigners hovering about, even here in their place of retreat.

Bean would look after him. Just like the old days!

❈　❈

Polty leaned back, crooking an arm behind his head. Sensually he sucked upon his tobarillo. 'I wouldn't mind some knowledge of that Princess,' he continued. 'Carnal, that is. Though I shouldn't like another fool trick like the one they played tonight. Dance of the Five Veils, indeed! Poor Penge tumbled like a house of cards!'

'Oh, Polty!' Bean said again, with an affectionate laugh. Several times he stepped over Mr Burgrove; once he kicked a misplaced pisspot, sloshing its contents across the floor. He sopped it up with a shaving towel. As often, Bean hummed a little tune – one of Polty's favourites – but then something seemed to trouble him, and after a moment he looked up, his brow furrowed.

It was something Polty had said, just a little earlier.

'Polty, that wasn't Jem Vexing.'

'What?'

'That boy in the middle. The crippler-boy from the castle was fair, wasn't he? Very fair. Polty, that boy was dark – his hands, his chin. And he was taller, too – the Vexing, I mean.'

Polty sighed. 'Bean, really! The Vexing, as you well know, is a master of disguise. And he has powers.'

'Powers?'

'Remember that dirty old Vaga that lived in the woods?'

With a grin – it would please Polty – Bean cupped a hand to his mouth and called faintly, 'Eyeless Silas! Eyeless Silas!'

'Precisely. Vaga-magic – and that wicked Vaga taught the Vexing all he knows. Why, I hardly think a crippler-boy who can *walk* is going to have much trouble looking different, do you? To put us off the scent? Or try! Don't you remember he got struck by lightning once, and lived to tell the tale?'

'Then how are they going to put him to death?' said Bean.

Polty did not quite take the point. 'I think the Caliph told us tonight, didn't he? I hope they don't spare the castration, is all I can say.'

Polty's tobarillo had burned down and he flipped it to the floor. Rolling on to his side, he glimpsed his reflection in a cheval-glass, tall and murky, that stood a little away from him in a spindly frame. His eyes flickered to the bulge beneath his robes. Idly he caressed his manly treasures.

'He had a friend,' Bean said after a moment.

'Hm?'

'The Vexing had a friend. A Vaga-boy. *He* was dark. And shorter – the Vaga, I mean.'

'Like the boy at the banquet?'

Bean nodded.

'Bean, don't be absurd. What would Lord Empster want with a Vaga? He called that boy his ward, and we know full well that his ward was the Vexing.'

On the floor, Mr Burgrove moaned. He had hauled himself up on his elbows, but instead of rising, succeeded merely in flopping over on his back. His gown had fallen open and underneath he still wore his Ejlander costume. Polty surveyed it wryly. Some seasons ago, the garments had been the most fashionable that Quisto's could provide. Now the handiwork of Agondon's finest gentlemen's tailor was in sad disrepair.

'Some special agent!' Polty laughed. 'Some gentleman! To think, this man was a legend among the ladies, famed as the handsomest bachelor in Varby!'

'He's never been the same since that business with Miss Pelligrew.'

Rolling on to his side, Mr Burgrove threw up.

'Foreign muck!' he spluttered.

'I don't think the meal agreed with him,' Bean observed.

Polty lit a fresh tobarillo. 'Up you get, Jac!' he called, not quite kindly. 'You could at least lie on your divan. What, am I going to trip over your ugly carcass every time I get up for a piss?'

'I think he's passed out again, Polty,' said Bean.

'Oh, Jac! Give him a good kick in the ribs, Bean.'

Bean hesitated.

'Kick him!'

Bean kicked him – hard.

Had he the energy, Mr Burgrove might have retaliated, turning on his attacker. As it was, he only gasped, coughed, and dragged himself to his divan at last. It was not a steady progress; during its course, he blundered into the cheval-glass, managing to send the tall frame toppling. There was a sound of cracking.

Bean sighed; Polty jerked a thumb at Burgrove. 'Funny, isn't it, how he acts drunk even when he's not? Well, he can't be, can he?'

'He's had a lot of Jarvel.'

'Jarvel? Jac's sodden. Juiced!'

'I think it's running through his veins all the time, Polty. Like my old dad,' Bean added sadly.

'Old Ebenezer?' Thoughtful for a moment, Polty recalled the drunkard from the Lazy Tiger. He sighed. 'Ah Bean, our Irion days seem so long ago!'

'Not that long,' Bean said, brightening.

'But look how far we've come.'

'How far you've come, Polty. Major Veeldrop! In such a short time!'

Bean was well-practised in the arts of flattery.

'It's true,' Polty said, preening. He patted a space on his divan and Bean scurried happily to sit beside his friend. Polty draped an arm round Bean's shoulders. 'You know, friend, I think you can be proud of yourself too.'

'Really, Polty?'

'Why, here you are in Unang Lia, playing your part in a vital mission! For an ignorant potboy from a squalid, provincial ale-house, that's not bad going, is it?'

'I suppose not, Polty,' Bean grinned.

'Suppose not! Why, for the son of a shambling, mad drunkard and a pox-ridden old harlot, I think that's damn good, damn good indeed!'

Polty was on form tonight, it was clear. For much of the evening, Bean had felt sorry for the Redjacket traitors, dreading the moment when the trap would be sprung; now he felt basely glad for the miseries they would be suffering. Had anything gone wrong, Polty would now be in a black rage, laying about him with any objects to hand.

Bean ventured, 'I'm only your servant, Polty.'

'Really, friend, a side-officer is not a servant.'

'No?'

'But your fidelity is touching. Were you my servant, I could not imagine one more loyal, more true.'

Bean's eyes misted. 'May I take your boots off, Polty?'

Blue smoke twined round Polty's curls as he leaned back, permitting Bean to tend to him. Sometimes, thought Polty, life was satisfactory, very satisfactory indeed. To be a military hero was a fine thing; to be a special agent, finer still. Imagine the glory that would soon be his, now that Jem Vexing was in his grasp!

It was Polty's fond belief that a grateful nation would one day reward him as he deserved to be rewarded. Seldom did he consider the miseries of his late father, which proved – if nothing else – that military fame can be a fickle thing. Nor had he considered – at least, not yet – that the work he was undertaking now, being secret, would bring him no additional glory, none at all. What was he, in the eyes of the world, but a government official, sent to procure slaves for the Ejland colonies, in return for shipments of arms to Qatani? It was squalid work, and dull too, hardly befitting a gentleman – trade, indeed! – but the she-slaves provided a diversion or two, for which a man had to be grateful.

If only he could find his wretched heart-sister! Polty had been back in Agondon only for a short time before embarking upon this new mission. There had been no time to look for Cata; nor had there been time to sit for portraits, busts, or statues, receive splendid gifts or attend commemorative dinners. That these things would be forthcoming, Polty had no doubt. They had to be: but oh, how much sooner they would come to a man with wealth and a title!

In an instant, Polty's contentment was gone, and a dull, familiar rage churned in his belly.

He leapt up, pushing Bean aside.

'Damn the bitch, damn her!'

'What bitch? Polty, what's wrong?'

But Bean knew, and Polty did not reply. He paced to the window, looking moodily through the lattices. To think, that riches and a peerage would be his, if only he married his missing heart-sister!

A gong sounded in an antechamber.

Polty breathed deeply. If he were overwrought, still he was hardly impervious to the prospect of pleasure. Turning, he smiled broadly at the fat fellow in long, curly slippers who waddled towards him, arms outstretched.

'Major-sir!'

'Oily!'

Warmly Polty embraced the newcomer, inviting him to sit, to lie, to put up his feet. Did he want Jarvel? Ferment? Food?

'Major-sir, you overwhelm me! Why, is it for you to provide my pleasures, when it is my mission to tend to yours? Pah!' But the fat fellow lowered his voice. 'Perhaps one of your Ejlander-rolls, hm?'

Polty snapped open his tobarillo-case. 'Bean, the tinder-stick! And the best ferment! Why, we'll have a toast to Oily, and sing a rousing song!'

The fat man beamed.

Polty beamed back. 'New turban, Oily?'

'You like? Pah! It's a rag.'

'No! Cost a few korzons, I'll be bound.' Polty had been pacing; now he sat suddenly beside his guest. 'You're late, Oily.'

'Eli.'

'Hm?'

'Eli – my name.'

'I'll call you Oily.'

'Pah, your Ejland voice! Strange to my ears, strange!'

'As yours is to mine, Oily. But you've got the girl?'

There was a clanking of chains in the anteroom.

'But of course you've got her! Bean, ferment! The golden goblets, I think, not the pewter.'

'It's gone, Polty.'

'What?'

Bean held up an empty wine-bladder.

'Jac, you pig!' Striding across the apartment, Polty seized the bladder. Eli Oli Ali jumped as the Major-sir, wielding the floppy skin, beat the drunken Ejlander about the chops.

Mr Burgrove spluttered and coughed.

Polty turned and smiled.

'Ah, Major-sir, your anger knows no bounds!'

'Nor should it, Oily, when I am forced to be rude to so valued a guest! Doesn't the fool know that ferment's hard to come by in these Unang-lands? Ah, but he cares only for his own pleasures!'

The mixer's eyes glittered. 'Major-sir, I've brought you a barrel.'

'You have? Why, and I was only expecting a girl! Roll it in, Oily, roll it in.'

The mixer clapped his hands and two ragged urchins, barefoot street-boys, propelled an exotic, ornately patterned keg into a corner of the apartment. Bean watched them nervously. That the Palace of Perfumed Stairs was a corrupt place, he had no doubt. That the guards could be bribed was a safe bet. But if only Polty would be more careful! What if they were to incur the royal displeasure? Polty insisted that he had Vizier Hasem wrapped around his finger. Perhaps it was so: the Vizier, it was clear, was keen to keep in with the Government of Ejland, and not merely to receive weapons in exchange for slaves. Might he not need to call on the Ejlanders one day, if his position in Qatani ever become parlous? So Polty would argue, yet still Bean was alarmed that the Ejland delegation had betrayed all trust, broken all rules, violated all the sanctities of the Unang faith.

He shot a resentful glance at Eli Oli Ali, then began an attempt to refill the wine-bladder.

Now how was one to open a keg like this?

Polty was saying, 'Oily?'

'Major-sir?'

'How long have we known each other?'

'Why, a moonlife or more.'

'Old friends, aren't we?'

'Indeed, Major-sir.' The mixer looked admiringly at his burning tobarillo. 'Clever, you Ejlanders. Why, you could have these with Jarvel, too.'

'We've thought of that. Oily?'

'Major-sir?'

'Why do I feel you're holding out on me?'

'Pah! I said you were clever!' A doleful look crossed the mixer's face. Reaching up, he pulled at his loosely wrapped turban. Underneath, his head was bound in bandages.

'Oily! What's happened?'

'Ah, Major-sir, I have been attacked!'

In the corner, Bean had turned the barrel on its side. With the scabbard of Polty's regimental sword, he prodded uncertainly at the layered timbers. Really, this was quite different from the good old Ejland kegs they had kept in the Lazy Tiger . . .

'Ah, Major-sir, they came in their hundreds. There was nothing I could do!'

Eli Oli Ali brushed a tear from his eye. His lower lip jutted outwards, trembling. There he was, on his way home, he explained, eagerly bearing back his precious cargo, when down from the hills swept a band of Ouabin raiders. How they knew he was coming, and what he had with him, he could not say, not for sure . . . but bank upon it, he had been betrayed by a Qatani. Yes, a Qatani . . . a villain of the blackest dye . . . Ouabin agent if ever there was one . . . name of Casca Dalla . . .

By now, Polty was barely listening. He said softly, 'Then the fairest of the fair—'

'The dream within a dream—'

'The jewel beyond comparing—'

'My sister? Gone.'

※　※

Meanwhile, Mr Burgrove's nose was bleeding. Stanching the blood with his golden cravat, he looked about him miserably. The sight of the keg raised his spirits at once.

'Have I died and gone to The Vast? A whole keg!'

He staggered upright.

Polty looked levelly at Eli Oli Ali. He reached out, carefully taking his guest's tobarillo. The whoremonger looked on sadly as the burning column hovered for a moment above his plump forearm.

Then Polty flung it to the floor and sighed.

Bean was attacking the barrel, first with the hilt, then the blade of Polty's sword. Mr Burgrove hovered over him, staggering, urging him on.

'O brave knight! O valiant knight!'

A new gleam came into the mixer's eyes and he leaned close to Polty. 'Major-sir, have you heard of Baba-girls?'

The mixer's breath was foul. Polty wrinkled his nose, but had to ask, 'What's a Baba-girl?'

'From the Baba Coast. Black as beetles. Stalky necks.'

'What are you saying, Oily?'

The mixer clapped his hands. A clanking sounded from the anteroom again, and this time the boys led in three exotic beauties clad only in chains. Iron muzzles secured their mouths, making it certain they could not cry out.

Polty's mouth fell open. 'Oily, I like you again!'

The mixer salaamed. 'Ah, Major-sir, you are good, so good!'

'I know, Oily,' Polty smiled, rummaging inside his robes for a purse of gold. He weighed the purse in his hand, considering. 'They're clean, of course?'

'Untouched! Why, Major-sir, I inspect them personally.'

'I'm sure you do,' said Polty, palping the full breast of the nearest girl. Revolted, the girl flinched from his touch.

Polty grinned. Resistance could be such a pungent sauce.

But something troubled him. 'Oily?'

'Major-sir?'

'Your sister. Tell me again: what did she look like?'

The mixer sighed deeply. 'Major-sir, there was only one who could compare to her. Major-sir, I mean the most beautiful woman in the world ... Major-sir, I mean the Princess Bela Dona. Why, we had even given her the name Dona Bela, for all the world as if she were the Princess in reverse, shimmering in the magic of a looking-glass. A Shimmering Princess indeed!'

The mixer sighed again. Polty eyed him wryly.

Two things happened to end the touching scene.

First Polty turned, his hand dropping from the Baba-girl's breast. 'Take them away.'

'Major-sir?'

'Take them away!'

Then from the corner came a sudden sound of cracking.

'No!' cried Bean. 'Oh no!'

Face first, Mr Burgrove collapsed into a flowing red tide.

Chapter 26

A LIGHT IN THE DARKNESS

Marry and burn!
The wheel shall turn!
What bold lover needs ever to yearn?
Seize your treasure from the gleaming py-y-y-re –
Marry and burn,
Marry and burn!

Campfires. Camels. Long white robes. A song, ringing above the dunes. We have been here before, or so it seems. But now the Ouabin are closer to Qatani. Much closer.

Tonight, stealing away to his secret meeting, Rashid Amr Rukr feels an impatience that is almost anger. The ache, the longing has been in him all night, but only now, later than usual, has he been certain that the one he seeks will be here. Is this not a time for urgency, for impassioned zeal? How, with events moving to their climax, can the Golden One have kept him waiting? How, the Sheik almost thinks, can the Golden One have *dared*?

Remembering all he stands to gain, the proud man struggles to suppress these thoughts as the figure forms before him at last. With ill grace, he abases himself in the sand.

'Fool,' comes the voice, and it is almost bantering, 'what is this rage I sense in you? I vex you, do I?'

'Golden One, no!' The Sheik looks up, alarmed. 'What could I feel but ardour, with our object so near?'

Golden eyes glow brighter, and the Sheik feels a sudden, sharp pain spreading through his being. He gasps, doubles over, but the pain is brief.

A hint, no more – a promise, perhaps.

'Do not even *think* to lie to me, Ouabin! Omnipotent you may be amongst your filthy desert nomads, but what is your earthly power against the godly power that is mine?'

The golden figure turns, glowing in the moonlight, revolving slowly just above the sand. The Sheik trembles, then curses himself, for never before has he acknowledged fear, nor known himself the inferior of any man . . . No, not of any *man* . . . For an instant he wonders if indeed he is

167

a fool, to trust to the promises of this mysterious tempter, to stake his fortunes on this bargain, this alliance. Then he thinks again of the power he has been promised, and his doubts are no more to him than the grains of sand that lie all about him in the desert night.

And then he thinks that the Golden One needs him, needs him as much as he needs the Golden One. His eyes grow bold and when his strange visitor turns back to him, the Sheik looks at him squarely, directly. Such defiance might invite further punishment, but when the Golden One speaks again it is in a tone very different from before.

'It is true, Ouabin, that we need each other, if we are to attain the power we seek. The world for you – for me, the moon and stars! It is what we have agreed, is it not? Our destiny is at hand – but Ouabin, we must not fail each other now. Even in the time since I spoke to you last, your part in these affairs has grown yet more urgent. You wonder at my delay in appearing to you tonight? In truth, my earthly manifestation has been held in captivity.'

'Captivity, Golden One?' The Sheik flares into a new, different anger. 'What, have the Qatanis already revealed their vile, cowardly treachery? The wrath about to descend upon them shall be double what I had planned!'

'In any case, let it be so; but no, they have yet to reveal their true colours – as have I.' The figure pauses – considering perhaps, contemplating. 'It is as well I chose to endure this captivity, for it was brief, and I should not – not yet – wish to appear before others as I really am. The proceedings of this night were a game, or so they would have it, an entertainment for the Caliph. Yet am I a fool? Already, Toth's agents have got to the little potentate – or rather, to the Vizier who pulls his puppet-strings. This has been no game, but a warning. One of my companions remains imprisoned – then, too, another is missing and, to be certain, there is foul play at work, for my consciousness, roam as it may across this arid land, can locate him nowhere! Already things are at a desperate pass. Your speed is all the more vital, Ouabin. Your speed – and your strength.'

If much of this speech remains mysterious to the Sheik, the last words are clear enough. 'Golden One, it shall be as we planned! On the morrow I liberate the city—'

'Liberate?' And his visitor, for the first time, almost laughs.

'Golden One, I liberate it for us! As for others, let them use what words they may! What care I, so long as they tremble beneath the power of the Ouabin? Has not my tribe, under my leadership, shaken this very empire itself? Do not the very walls crack already – shall they not soon fall? Think of the hundred fearless campaigns I have led in the course of my long career—'

'Forget your career! What are the petty triumphs of the past to the glories of the morrow? What is the power you have known until now, compared to the true power we seek? The girl, Ouabin, think only of the girl! Come, let us steel ourselves for the coming triumph!'

With that, the strange allies link hands and a searing light passes between them. When he sinks into the sand again and finds himself alone, for long moments Rashid Amr Rukr shall feel as if the power for which he longs possesses him already, consumes him like a fire. Tonight this will fade – but soon, mere moonlives from now, shall he not have this power for ever?

> *Marry and burn!*
> *The world must learn*
> *Ouabin power is our sole concern!*
> *Princess Bela Dona holds the ke-e-e-ey –*
> *Marry and burn,*
> *Marry and burn!*

❋   ❋

That night, as he retired to his apartments, the Caliph Oman Elmani felt rather less satisfaction than he might otherwise have done, after the conclusion of so successful an evening. The capture of the Ejlanders had provided a droll spectacle, it was true, but the Caliph's troubles were deep, and richer diversions were needed if he were ever to forget them. He thought of the trials of the morrow, when his daughter would once again appear before the mob. What a terrible secret her fame concealed! The Caliph sighed, and felt the pressure of tears behind his eyes. He blinked angrily. What would tears avail him?

He had just stretched out on his couch when there was a rapping at the door and Vizier Hasem entered. For long moments the two men embraced, as it was their custom to do before retiring. Rumour had it that their relations were more extensive still; in truth, though the duties of the Vizier included the procuring of certain pleasures for his monarch, he had never been called upon to provide these in, as it were, his own person. Indeed, he could not have done so; the Caliph, after all, had specialised requirements, which in time, I dare say, we shall have cause to reveal. Suffice to say that the Vizier was wholly unsuitable for these, and glad, indeed, to be so; nonetheless he was solicitous of his master's needs, and asked if a little . . . a little *solace* might be appropriate now.

The Caliph sighed again. 'Alas, Hasem, my dear Shimmy fills my heart! What could drive her away?'

'I have not yet introduced you to the new Amalian. Or what about the sweetest flower of Lania Chor?'

'They would, I doubt not, be greatly beguiling, but Hasem, tonight I must sleep. Oblivion is the best solace of all.'

'As you wish, Oman, as you wish.'

'But watch me a little, Hasem, as I sink away. You know I like it when you watch over me.'

'Of course, Oman. Of course.'

Sadness filled the Vizier's heart as he sat beside his fat little master. There had been a time, long ago, when he saw the Caliph only as a duty, and a tiresome one at that; long since, he had come to love his difficult charge, and dedicated himself to serving him well. How he wished that the Caliph loved him too, and did not think of him always as a substitute for another! Sometimes Hasem feared that one day, that other would return – but no, it could not be.

The genie had gone, gone long ago.

Now it was the Vizier's turn to sigh, and he let his thoughts drift back to the past.

THE TALE OF JAFIR THE GENIE

From his appearance, and his manner too, none would have guessed that Caliph Oman Elmani was brother to the formidable Sultan Kaled, and son of Sultan El-Thakir. Growing up in the shadow of so fine a brother, Oman's boyhood had been miserable. As it happened, he had seen little of his brother after the sunrounds of infancy, but always he had been aware of his brother's superior talents, his brother's superior looks, his brother's superior prospects. From the first, Kaled was certain to be Heir Unquestioned; Oman's lot was to be a mere courtier, sweltering dutifully in the flames of his brother's glory. To many in Kal-Theron, and to Oman himself, it thus came as a surprise to learn that Sultan El-Thakir had marked this inferior son for a greater destiny.

It happened that El-Thakir stood in the relation of cousin-by-cousin to the Caliph of Qatani, at that time one Abdul Samad. For long sunrounds, courtiers in landlocked Kal-Theron had looked jealously on that Jewel of the Shore that was Abdul's royal seat. Without doubt, Qatani was vital to the Sultan's imperial power; vital, in particular, if he was to hold his grip on his dominions over the seas. True, like all lesser rulers on this great subcontinent, Abdul had sworn fealty to his cousin in Kal-Theron; but Sultan El-Thakir was not alone in thinking that this was not enough. For some time he had suspected Abdul of imperial urges of his own; rumours had reached him of certain plans which, had they even been meditated upon, would have constituted the utmost treason.

El-Thakir decided against open accusations; instead he determined that his son Oman, and none of Abdul's many sons, should succeed to the throne of Qatani. Had Abdul been informed of this scheme, he should certainly have protested; as it happened, protests were never necessary, for some moonlives later, a party of masked men – Ouabin agents, there could be no doubt – broke into the Caliph's palace, putting every one of Abdul's sons to the sword. The distraught Abdul could only bow to his cousin's wishes, and Oman Elmani was declared Caliph-in-Waiting.

It need hardly be said that El-Thakir had no intention of conferring great power on his inferior son. On the contrary, Oman was to be the merest puppet-king, dancing on the wires that were pulled from Kal-Theron. To this end, one of the most trusted of El-Thakir's courtiers was appointed to the post of Oman's companion, his protector, his prop and stay: this was Vizier Hasem. The arrangement, we have seen, was most satisfactory; over the course of many sunrounds, only two things had marred it. Unfortunately, they were two very major things indeed. The first was a genie by the name of Jafir; the second, another man of magic, who resented, amongst much else, the genie's power.

Now, Hasem had not been present when the genie first appeared, but he could imagine the scene vividly enough. One wet afternoon, shortly after succeeding to his illustrious title, the new Caliph was rifling through his late uncle's chambers when, at the bottom of a chest stuffed with fine fabrics, he came upon a battered lamp of the type known as a konar-light. Idly, Oman rubbed the lamp; all at once a mighty cloud billowed forth and the genie stood before him.

This was astonishing enough; more astonishing still, the genie resembled the fat little Caliph in every feature.

The Caliph staggered back, fearing a terrible enchantment.

'Fear not,' simpered the genie, his face overspreading with joy, 'for you are the liberator I have always sought. I am Jafir Al-Jazan, and I am your friend. Epicycles ago, I was apprenticed to a great but cruel enchanter, and as punishment for – why,' he smacked his lips, 'the most *trivial* of misdemeanours, he bound me to the servitude of this wretched lamp – without so much as a by-your-leave, and a long servitude it's been, let me tell you! But I see the enchanter was good as his word, for he said my trials would end when at last I met my twin. I can tell at once that twin is you.'

'Twin?' Joy filled the Caliph's eyes, for all his life he had felt inferior to his brother, and hated him; now here was a brother he could love.

Jafir went on to say that he would serve the Caliph freely. To others, he said, he had given but three wishes, but the Caliph could have all the wishes he wanted. 'Do you know, those others forgot me at once – once they'd had their WISHES, I mean. I suppose it was part of my curse. Why, they even thought this enchanted lamp was *really* just a shabby konar-light, fit only to be thrown away. My dear, you have *no idea* how long I used to wait, sometimes, for someone to come and let me out again. Really, I don't know which is worse, to be shut in that lamp or have to grant the WISHES of – oh, the commonest people! I don't know, but you have to be polite, don't you, even when you want to scream?' The genie grimaced, rolled his eyes, then reached out, taking the delighted Caliph's arm. 'But that's all behind me now. Come on, Oman, let's have some fun!'

So it was that a period of great wonderment began in the life of the Caliph. That afternoon, with Jafir at his side, he commanded the drizzly sky to resume its accustomed cerulean shade; he whizzed invisibly above the rooftops of Qatani; he doubled the size of his late uncle's palace; he made himself as tall and handsome as Kaled; he turned all the men in the bazaar into women and all the women into men; he ate the biggest banquet he had ever seen, without feeling sick.

It was clear that the Caliph's powers would now be immense, but when the Vizier discovered what had happened, he was aghast. Stern warnings left the foolish Caliph feeling chastened and reluctantly he commanded his new brother to change everything back to the way it had been before. Patiently, as if to a child, the Vizier was obliged to explain that any hint of such powers would be sorely resented in Kal-Theron. Oman might play with his new friend, but they must limit themselves to modest feats of magic, lest the Sultan call down upon them all the wrath of the fire god.

As it happened, in the end neither Caliph nor genie found hardship in these restrictions. They would soon have tired of their ecstatic games, and the Caliph hardly had wit enough to turn the genie's powers to political ends. Soon they had settled into a quiet round of companion-ship, in which ever more magnificent banquets and filmy illusions projected on the walls were their only real indulgences. Seeing the two fat fellows together, Vizier Hasem was not displeased; it was as well that Oman should be distracted, and nothing could distract him so effectively as Jafir. If the Vizier felt a deeper, welling sadness, he suppressed it; he must think only of affairs of state, and what was best for the empire. In those days, when he bade goodnight to Oman, Hasem would even run a protective hand over the lamp, sitting safely by the Caliph's bed, in which the genie lodged for the night. For all that he complained about his battered home, Jafir would not have been without it.

Such were the glory days of Oman and Jafir. The idyll was not to last. It was at about this time that the Caliph's brother, in far Kal-Theron, married the beauteous Lady Ysadona; word came from Sultan El-Thakir that the Caliph, too, must marry. Of course, it fell to Hasem's lot to search for an appropriate bride, and the Vizier gave much thought to the question. He was proud of his choice; many thought it brilliant; but from the first, the marriage was hardly a success.

For long moonlives, the Vizier had struggled to keep Jafir a secret from the courtiers; now the Caliph's strange companion must be kept from his bride too. Soon rumours were flying abroad that the Caliph was cruel to his lovely wife. It was a foul calumny; the terrified Caliph had spent barely a moment in her presence, and indeed had gone so far as to call upon Jafir's powers, and not his own, to ensure the production of a son. Why the genie disobeyed him, and brought forth a mere daughter instead, Oman was never to be certain, but if this was disobedience, he was glad of it. Often, when he would hark back to his days with Jafir, he would say that, for all his other sorrows, at least he had Shimmy, a child touched by magic.

It was the Caliph's misfortune that other magic lurked in wait for his daughter. There were those in the palace from whom it had been impossible to conceal the secret of the genie. Chief amongst these was the Teller Evitamus, magical assistant of the late Caliph Abdul Samad.

Late in life, the Teller had married and produced a daughter. Marriage and fatherhood had softened the old man, but the early death of his wife filled him with a bitterness from which he could not recover. In youth, by all accounts, he had been an ambitious man, but had not fulfilled his ambitions as he wished; old troubles still rankled his heart and he had made many enemies. Only political cunning prevented the Vizier from banishing him forthwith. The Teller had powers, though how great they might be was difficult to determine. Banished, reasoned the Vizier, the Teller might be more trouble, much more, than while he was suffered to remain. So, in the event, it proved.

Envy filled the Teller's heart when he saw the favour that the genie now enjoyed; often, while the Caliph was enclosed with his special friend, Hasem would come upon the Teller lurking, with a scowling face, in the corridors outside, as if seeking knowledge of what passed within. Surprised, the Teller would fling up his hands in strange, mystic gestures, and scurry contemptuously away.

After events had reached their climax, Hasem would tell himself that indeed he should have banished the old man in the beginning, banished him and been done with it. The Teller's revenge, at such a point, could hardly have been worse than what he did in the end.

It was on the day of Shimmy's betrothal that tragedy fell. The Sultan commanded that his brother's lovely child be promised in marriage to his

Heir Unquestioned, thus binding the Caliphate of Qatani yet more strongly to the imperial thrall. Now it happened that the betrothal ceremony, in its traditional form, involved the services of a Teller, and the Sultan would have all done according to ancient precept. In vain did that great man's closest companion, an old man named Simonides – as if himself, perhaps, possessed of the Telling power – urge his master to suspend this part of the ritual. So it was that Teller Evitamus predicted not glory for this marriage, but doom. The betrothal ceremony was ruined and broke up in confusion. Evitamus was banished, escaping death only at the urging of Simonides, who mercifully insisted that the old man was crazed, his powers long ago corroded and warped.

What no one foresaw was the terrible curse the Teller would lay upon the Caliph's daughter, nor the simple, but immensely effective means he took to ensure that Jafir could not reverse his spell.

The spell *was* Jafir's; the Teller's powers permitted him only to see the future, but his cunning was like a dark magic in itself. What happened was this: the wicked old man stole the konar-light while the genie was trapped inside; then, using the unwilling genie's magic, he cast a terrible spell on Princess Bela Dona, spirited himself and his daughter away, then laid around them a web of blindness, ensuring that none from Qatani should ever be able to find them.

Three wishes. The genie could not have disobeyed.

✸   ✸

Vizier Hasem reached out, extinguishing the new, shiny konar-light that stood, for purposes of illumination only, by the Caliph's bedside. The fat little fellow was sleeping now, his breath rising and falling like a child's. Sighing, Hasem smoothed his companion's hair, rose from the couch and paced restlessly towards the window. Ships bobbed in the harbour, far below; high in the sky hung a bright, golden moon.

The Vizier laid his head against the window-lattices. Long sunrounds had passed since the day of the curse. He thought back to the horror that had gripped Oman then, when he realised all he had lost. Since that day, he knew, Oman had dreamed only that Jafir would return, and all would be well again in the troubled Court of Qatani. Suddenly, for all he had thought to the contrary, the Vizier knew that it was his wish too. If he had come to love the fat, foolish Caliph, still he knew that he was no more, in the end, than Oman's gaoler. He was weary of his life, and his long servitude to the Sultan's empire. Let the genie return, giving Oman the powers that would make him not only happy, but free!

Tears glistened in Hasem's eyes as he stood back, at last, from the moonlit window.

'Dea,' came the whisper. 'Dea.'

At that moment, in far Kal-Theron, Prince Dea was waking from a troubling dream, which had begun with Simonides, whispering his story amongst the hot, fragrant gardens; then Dea had seen again the gardens in darkness, and his frightening, ghostly vision of Thal. Trembling, the boy lay gazing into the night, thinking with a mingled horror and sadness first of his father, then of Thal, then of his own royal destiny. Moonlight, silver and sinister, crept across the floor. There was a light breeze, carrying with it faint sounds of rustling from the gardens above.

Then came the whisper again. 'Dea, Dea.'

The boy had thought it part of his dream; now he knew it was more. He rose from his couch, padding towards the terrace, expecting the Targons to appear at any moment. Instead, as if indeed he were still dreaming, he found himself gliding up the pale stairs again, then through the curtaining foliage. Now he stood again amongst the parterres and mazes, the groves and grottoes; he heard again the burbling of a sinuous rill; incense enfolded him like a special, different air, as again he saw the vision of his dead friend.

'You're real, Thal?' breathed Dea, his lips barely moving.

'Friend,' came the reply, 'of course I'm real.'

'But I see through you.'

'Friend, I am no less real.'

Dea trembled, sinking to his knees in a border of grass. His hands covered his face, and if he still dreamed, he would have awakened now, longing only that this torment would end.

But if this were a dream, it had barely begun.

Quite why it was that Dea uncovered his face, he did not know. All he knew was that somehow, with a vision that came not to his eyes but his mind, he was aware of the ghostly hand that first reached towards him, then curved back, beckoning him to come.

To come and play.

Chapter 27

MADMAN ACROSS THE WATER

'I've got him—'
  'Quick, stab!'
  'Dirty big brute—'
  'Stab, you fool!'
  'He's too quick—'
  'Skewer him!'
  'Cowards! That's not the way—'
  'Shut up, scum!'
  'Cowards! Grab his tail—'
  'What, scum?'
  'Chuck him up in the air, and slice!'
  The cornered rat squealed and squealed. Rajal blocked his ears, but if he managed to muffle the oaths, the boots, the blade striking at stone, still he heard the cries of the rat, suddenly louder as it swung up through the air.
  Swoosh! went the scimitar, and Rajal scrambled back as a shower of guts came splattering through the bar of his cell.
  'Ha-ha!'
  'Enjoy!'
  'Mm, fresh!'
  'Special treat!'
  Drunk on ferment, the guards were doubled over, while the prisoner across the way, who had teased and taunted them, rattled at his bars, cursing, crying.
  He must have hoped the guts would fly in his direction.
  'Back, scum!'
  A torch fizzed forward. Laughter came again, then the guards were gone, sloshing away merrily through the stinking water that lay all along the corridor. For a moment there was silence, and the darkness was deep; then Rajal heard again the muffled sobbings, the moanings, the furtive scurryings that echoed through the dungeon, perpetual as the slime that dripped from the walls. Moonlight, seeping through a tiny grille, glimmered down evilly on the splattered guts. The rat must have been huge.
  Rajal shuddered, kicking a clump of straw over the steaming mess. He

176

hugged himself tightly. How long he had been here? His head swirled with Jarvel, and the Qatani food, too rich for him, had left his stomach bloated, churning and bubbling noisily. But already the banquet seemed far in the past, as if nothing now existed but this terrible confinement, in all its stench and darkness.

The madman opposite let out a scream, yelling for the guards to come back, calling them cowards again, daring them to take on another rat, a real one this time. Perhaps he meant himself. The young man across the way could only be glad not to share a cell with so desperate, so pitiable a creature. But when the madman cried out, Rajal knew why. His own confinement had lasted less than a night, and already he could have beaten at his bars in useless, despairing rage.

Instead, Rajal huddled deep into himself, drawing his knees up close to his chest, knitting his fingers across his face. He stuck his thumbs in his ears; he shut his eyes tightly; when he breathed, he breathed through his mouth, and shallowly, as if he could resist the foul stench that pressed all around him like a tangible thing.

He dozed at last; for a time he even dreamed.

Rajal's Dream

I am standing on a ship, on the prow of a ship, looking ahead as the vessel cleaves a deep, blue-green sea. It is the Catayane, *this ship, though her sails are whiter, her decks scrubbed cleaner than they have ever been before. Strange; for the crew and Captain Porlo are nowhere to be seen. In the dream, I know these things, though still my gaze remains fixed ahead, focused only on the rippling waves. Am I alone on the ship? It seems I am; though the thought leaves me strangely unalarmed.*

Then I am aware of the figurehead beneath me, stretched precariously above the heaving ocean. With a pang, I remember how lovingly, how longingly, Jem had gazed upon this wooden lady; then how sad she had made him too, with her painted face, her rigid neck, her hard bodice, chipping, fading, cracked. But in the dream, it seems to me, this Cata-lady is new; more than this, her cheeks, her eyes glow with life, while the stiff corrugations of her gown are gone, to be replaced with billowing fabric.

The half-body is alive, and over the wash of the waves, over the wind, I know she is speaking, though I cannot make out the words. But ruefully, it comes to me that I am not Jem; that I shall not lean dangerously as my friend would have done, eager for what falls from the wooden lady's lips. I only sigh; I stare ahead. On and on sails the Catayane, *through a blue blankness of sea and sky, sky and sea, no land in sight.*

The sky is darkening, and I hear the rasp of a storm, approaching fast. Then I know more: first I hear the words of the wooden lady. He's not yours, he's mine. He's not yours, he's mine. *It is a chant, a mocking chant. Later, I know, I shall think on this dream, flushing at the memory as if with shame; in the dream – here, now – I understand nothing, neither the chant nor to whom it could refer.*

Then I turn, for as the chant fills my ears, now I am aware of a presence behind me. In gathering darkness, I slide across the decks – slide, it seems, like a heavy stone, dragged laboriously over a stubborn surface. The helm is before me, and standing at the helm, turned from me, is a figure I know.

Of course it is Jem. I touch his shoulder. The figure turns; but I see, to my surprise, that the face is not Jem's. It is Cata's, and her expression is blank, stiff like a doll's, as she says only, mechanically, He's not yours, he's mine.

Confused, frightened, I blunder away.

Then I am standing in the prow again, but something has happened to the figurehead below. The chant has ceased. Again the figure is fixed, unyielding, but suddenly I am aware of something else, too. I am reckless now, like Jem, and shin out on to the bowsprit, swinging down to look. All around me, the sky is dark, the air filled with a terrible stench. Loud in my ears comes the sound of rasping, as if the ship itself, by now, is being dragged slowly forward, a stone over stone. I reach out, clutching at the wooden face.

It is as I had feared, all as I had feared.

'Jem!' I cry out. 'Jem, Jem!'

❊   ❊

'Shh! Quiet!'

'Jem?'

'Shh!'

Through the grille, high above, came a glimmering of dawn, and in the bleak glow Rajal made out the figure that hunched beside him, dusty, dirty, dressed in rags.

'But you're not Jem!'

'Quiet, I said!'

Rajal was quiet. Astonished, he looked into a face dark as his own, the face of a boy perhaps his own age, perhaps younger. Cobwebs draped the boy's curly black hair, and from his chin, like a wisp of beard, hung a whorl of pallid dust.

For a moment Rajal was confused, still half in his dream, and whispered, 'But where's Jem?'

'Oh no, not you too!'

'Wh-what?'

Quietly but firmly, the stranger slapped Rajal's face.

'Hey!'

'Shh, I say! You're not mad, are you?'

'I – I must be,' said Rajal. 'Where did you c-come from?'

But he knew the answer soon enough. His gaze flickered round his mean cell. The door was shut fast, as it had been all night; the bars were unbent, firm as ever, but on the floor beside them, Rajal saw a heavy, sandy block of stone. It was a stone from the wall. Pushed from its place, it made just room enough for a slender boy to crawl through from the neighbouring cell.

For a moment, Rajal had forgotten his dream. Now he remembered the sound of scraping: rock against rock, stone against stone.

'Old Lacani showed me,' said Rajal's visitor. 'We looked for others like it. He said – well, it must be true – that if this one was loose, who knew what others might shift if we pushed them? I haven't found more, but at least there's this one. I mean, one escape route's better than none, isn't it?'

Rajal was sceptical. 'What's the good of an escape route if it only takes you into the next cell?'

'It's a start! Do you know, I think Old Lacani might know where there're more, but just won't tell me?'

A corner of the stone block had broken away and the stranger picked it up, weighing it in his hand. Then he put the chunk in the straw beside him, as if perhaps he had a use for it, but not just yet. He began to say more about Old Lacani, who had been in the dungeons for sunround on sunround, and forgotten the very existence of the world outside.

Already Rajal was irritated by this strange boy and his hushed, excited babbling. 'Who is this Old Lacani?'

As if in answer, there was a piteous howl from the madman across the corridor.

'He's crazy!' said Rajal.

'Damn right he is, and he was in my cell! I mean, I was in his. He was all right for a while, then he tried to strangle me!'

'Why?'

'How do I know? Thought I was someone else, I suppose. I was lucky – they dragged him off me and flung him in by himself, over there. Ever since, there's been nothing from him but mad stuff, howling and all that.'

'So I've heard!'

'Say, I'm starving, aren't you?' Searching his pockets, the stranger found a hunk of bread. Breaking off a bit, he offered it to Rajal, then crammed the rest – most of it – into his own mouth. 'You're not a Unang, are you?' he asked, chewing.

'I'm – I'm an Ejlander,' Rajal lied.

'I thought they were fair.'

'Most. Not all.'

Dubiously Rajal peered at the bread, fingering what appeared to be a prodigious growth of mould.

'Oh give it here!' His visitor swiped it back. 'If you don't want it, there's one who does!'

'Old Lacani?'

'Bother Old Lacani, I mean me. You won't be getting banquets in here, you know.'

Rajal said, 'You know about the banquet?'

'Oh, I heard the guards having a good laugh, before they went up to fetch you. It's an old trick – dress you up, feed you, then you're denounced. Well, that's what happened to Old Lacani – so he said. But don't worry, you won't be here as long as him.'

Rajal looked at his visitor questioningly.

'They'll cool you off down here for a night. But only a night. I don't think they'd want to – well, spoil you.'

'What do you mean?'

The stranger picked up the chunk of rock, tossing it idly up and down. He was standing now, pacing about the cell. 'A boy like you. You've got value, haven't you?'

'Value?'

'Of course! Not like Old Lacani.'

Rajal shuddered. If he did not quite know what his visitor meant, still a shaft of apprehension pierced him.

'What about you? You're just a boy.'

The stranger smiled. 'Am I?'

'What do you mean?'

'What does it matter? I'm going to die.'

'We're all going to die,' Rajal said uncertainly. He was also standing; for a time, the two of them were circling each other, though why this should be, Rajal could not have said.

Still the stranger held the chunk of stone. He explained, 'I mean I'm condemned. I mean, they're going to kill me.'

He was not moving now. Standing wanly in the seeping light, he answered the question in Rajal's eyes.

'Today. In the marketplace.'

Now Rajal remembered. 'You killed the Rider!'

Amed – for of course, it was Ameda, daughter of Evitamus – burst out her denial and raised her fist, the fist that was filled with broken stone. Rajal stumbled back.

'I – I'm sorry,' said Amed. 'But I didn't do it, you see. I mean, did *you* really do what they think you've done?

Rajal thought it best to shake his head.

'Of course not. You're innocent, I'm innocent – why, I dare say Old

Lacani's innocent. We're all the same, aren't we? Some of us are just more desperate, that's all.'

'How do you know?'

But Amed never bothered to answer that question.

Rajal looked down, studying his hands. In the long night, his turban had become unravelled, and a stray trail of cloth hung across his forehead. He did not bother to put it back in place. What would be the use? Trembling, he thought of his visitor, and the fate that soon awaited him.

Rajal's voice came sadly. 'You haven't told me your name.'

'Oh,' said Amed, 'I don't think I shall.'

'No?' Rajal had slumped to his knees again. Still he looked at his hands.

Amed stood above him. 'You know what they want to do to me, that's enough. So perhaps you'll understand what I must do to you.'

At that, Rajal would have looked up at last, but there was no time. The stone-filled fist struck suddenly, and he collapsed into the straw.

❋　❋

Quickly, Amed unwrapped Rajal's turban before the fabric was stained with blood. With equal rapidity she switched clothes with her victim. When she found the bag that hung round his neck, the bag that contained the Crystal of Koros, she peered into it curiously, saw that perhaps the crystal was valuable, and took that too. Then she pushed Rajal's body through the hole in the wall and strained to shift the heavy stone back into place.

Amed lay in the straw, breathing heavily. Her plan had been daring, and perhaps would still fail. But it was all she could do.

Rajal was Amed. And Amed was Rajal.

Chapter 28

GUARDS! GUARDS!

Which was the way to the Sacred City? Amed, in her cell, could not be sure, but as she heard the echoes of the summoning-bells, ringing over the world outside, she prostrated herself in the dirty straw. Intently she murmured the prayers she had spurned so short a time ago. Even Amed could not have said whether she prayed, like others, to the god of flame, or to the spirit of her own dead father.

Often the Teller seemed to be with her now, hovering like a benevolent presence at her side. More than once as she languished in the dungeons, Amed thought she heard her father's voice, whispering to her as if from the walls; but what the voice was saying, she could not make out. Sometimes, in Old Lacani's lucid moments, Amed had wondered if her father, in truth, were speaking wisdom through the madman's lips. How strange, thought Amed, how sad a paradox, that the father who had been so distant in life should seem so close to her, so real to her, in death!

Amed had half-believed she would soon join him – even without the executioner's aid. Already, in the time she had spent in these dungeons, she had learnt that many prisoners died in their cells. Some succumbed at once to the contagions that hovered, ready to pounce, in the filth and foul air; many more died from broken limbs and heads, so vilely were they abused by the ferment-crazed guards. On her first night, Amed had watched in terror as the guards, blundering and cursing, dragged a corpse along the sloshing corridor. Later, she heard the splash as they flung it into the sewers. It was as much as Amed could do to hold back her tears, but she was not sorry, not really, that the man was dead. How she wished she too could die like that, cheating the executioner and all who would come to jeer and bay in the marketplace!

That had been Amed's worst moment. Never since then had she given in to despair. In the luck that had kept her alive so far, she could fancy she detected her father's guiding hand. Perhaps it was so: for Amed had prayed to escape, and now her chance had come.

If only it would succeed!

Amed completed her devotions and sat quietly in the straw, her head bowed. In a matter of days she had changed greatly. By now, it was almost with astonishment that she looked back on what she had been so short a time ago, a callow servant in a caravanserai, scheming for ferment with Faha Ejo. On the day of her father's death, Amed had become – as she fondly thought of it – a man. But oh, how she regretted her last act as a boy! With shame she would think of the konar-light, and pray that Father would forgive her folly.

A groan sounded from the cell next door.

Amed winced. So the Ejlander, at least, was not dead.

The groan came again and she tried to ignore it. She must think only of her mission, her quest, not the Ejlander – if Ejlander he were.

Amed thought about him nonetheless. They were not dissimilar: in height and colouring they were, perhaps, the same. But would they really think the Ejlander was Amed, and drag him out to kill him in the marketplace? Of course Amed had to hope this would happen; but if she were desperate, she was not wicked, and a pang of guilt assailed her. Basely, she told herself that the Ejlander was a coward – a coward or a fool. Might he not have guessed the danger he was in, and made some effort to defend himself? Amed ran her hands over the silken robes that until so recently the Ejlander had worn. Contempt stirred in her. What could be the fate of such a fancy-boy? With a shudder, Amed recalled certain rumours, certain stories she had heard from travellers at the caravanserai. Could the great city really be home to such depravity? Perhaps it was as well the Ejlander should end his life today.

Amed thought: *But I am the fancy-boy now.*

Then she had no time to think any more. Suddenly there was the clunk of a key in the door and Amed looked up, startled, from her reverie.

The guards were upon her at once.

'Come on, fancy-boy!'

'No! Leave me alone!'

'Bah, he's a struggler, this one!'

'Keep still, you little beggar!'

'Ouch! Stop that!'

'Damn you, damn you!'

'Got him!'

'Heh-heh! Shall I give him a good slap in the chops?'

'No, they want him in one piece – the mouth, especially. What for, I can't guess!'

'No?' Ribald laughter. 'What about a good kick in the jewels?'

'He's a foreigner – respect, they said.' Tightly the guards wrapped the chains round Amed's wrists. 'Come on, boy, you're one of the lucky ones. I dare say there'll be pleasures enough where you're going – though a bit of pain first, I shouldn't be surprised!'

The guards laughed again as they bundled their captive away. Why she had struggled so uselessly, Amed could not have said. It was as if some instinct had taken her over, and for a moment she had forgotten

183

that her plan had worked – it had worked! With a kind of rapture she gulped in the air as she emerged, blinking, from the foetid dungeons. Terror filled her at what might be in store, but Amed knew she would rather face the challenges ahead than endure another moment in the dark world below.

❄ ❄

The Palace of Perfumed Stairs, like many a noble house, was divided into distinct zones, and the menials who served in one zone were forbidden to enter the others. Kitchen-slaves would never venture into the fine apartments of state; eunuchs, who tended the royal women, lived in a different world from the royal grooms; the warders of the dungeons were of quite another order from the splendid guards, garbed in gold, who served in the palace above.

At the foot of a further set of stairs was the junction-point, as it was called, where the warders would hand over their prisoner to their golden counterparts. Moments earlier, the guards had been waiting, but a skirmish at the palace gates had called them away.

The warders were not prepared for what happened next.

FIRST WARDER (*stamping his feet*): Bah, where are they?

SECOND (*grinning*): Heh-heh! Don't they know the Caliph's
    aflame with lust? Bit early in the morning, you'd think, eh?

FIRST: It's not the Caliph.

SECOND: What?

FIRST: It's not the Caliph that wants him, it's the red-haired one.

SECOND (*snuffling snot*): Red-haired what?

FIRST: Bah, they told us, remember? The Ejlander with red hair.

SECOND: What is he, a child of the fire god?

FIRST: Shut your blaspheming!

SECOND (*snuffling harder*): Look who's talking! Heh-heh, you can
    hardly stand straight for all the ferment in your belly! Dirty
    old sot.

FIRST: Who you calling a dirty sot?

SECOND: You! Just a dirty sot, you are. Sharif Fez said I'd be
    promoted to the Gold Guards by now – the Gold Guards,
    mind – if I hadn't had you to drag me down.

FIRST: Bah! Without me, you'd be shovelling shit.

SECOND (*wiping nose on sleeve*): At least I'd be shovelling it
    without you!

AMED *stands between them. Chains tether her to the wrist of each
warder. Restlessly her gaze shifts in all directions, or all that are*

possible in her present condition. Wryly she compares the passage in which they stand, a drab affair of raw, sandy bricks, and the glimmerings of marble and mosaic that lie ahead, in the palace proper. Escape seems impossible. Then it happens, the miracle for which she has prayed. AMED *winces. A purple-black light is shining, burning, through the fabric of her robes. For a moment, her captors remain unconscious of this unexpected development.*

SECOND WARDER (*after a pause*): A man's hair can't be red!
FIRST: He's an Ejlander, I said.
SECOND: And an Ejlander's can? What, and blue, too? Heh-heh!
FIRST (*ignoring him*): Bah! I could do with another slug of
ferment.
SECOND (*suddenly frightened*): Stones of Theron!
FIRST: Shut your blaspheming, I said!
SECOND: No, look—!
FIRST: What is it? Ah—!

They double over, covering their eyes against the light. Only for a moment does the mysterious power last, but the moment is enough. AMED's *chains bend and break. She bounds up the stairs, just escaping the golden-garbed guards who return at that moment to see the hapless warders reeling, half-blinded, in the corridor below.*

❈   ❈

'After him!'
'He won't get away!'
'Quick! This way!'
'That way!'
'No, this way!'
'Come back, you fool!'
'He's gone!'
'Gone? He can't be gone!'
'There he is!'
The power must have remained, shimmering round Amed for long moments after the flash that broke her bonds. She would remember this time only as a madness of flight and pursuit, corridor after corridor, chamber after chamber. Gold and jewels, velvet and silk streaked past her eyes; loud in her ears came the cries, the clattering armour, the heavy boots of her pursuers, guards, guards and more guards, rushing after the escapee.
She skidded round a corner.
She looked ahead. Stairs.
Left. Windows.

Right. A door.

Ajar.

Amed slipped inside. The chamber was empty. Breathing hard, she leaned against the door. A key was in the lock. There was just time to turn it before the boots, the clatterings, the cries sounded from the corridor.

'Damn and double damn!'

'Which way?'

'Windows!'

'Stairs!'

'I'll take the door!'

'That door's locked!'

'Locked? Why?'

'The women's wing!' The handle juddered. 'Rock solid, see? Now come on, we'll lose him!'

The footsteps slapped away and on the other side of the door Amed found herself slithering to her knees. Suddenly she was exhausted, more exhausted than it seemed she had ever been before. Magic, she knew, had held her in its grip. Now, it seemed, the magic had gone.

But Amed was wrong.

The magic was only beginning.

Chapter 29

A LADY MADE OF MIST

'Cata . . . Cata.'

The voice was soft, the water warm. Someone lifted a golden bowl. Cata lay back, luxuriating. Dimly she was aware of green caverns of leaves, of sunlight flashing through hanging branches. Was she home again? Lightly she felt the touch of hands, then the hands stronger, firm but delicate, stroking her skin, laving her hair.

Cata looked up through dreamy eyes.

'Jem . . . Jem.'

But only a giggle came in reply.

Cata lashed out. There were scramblings. Squeals. At first she was dazzled, and did not understand. She blinked. She looked about her. From a slit-window, high above, a beam of hot light had been shining on her face. All last night she had lain on a pile of old clothes, deep and soft, in a corner of Mother Madana's storeroom. Hazily she recalled the hands that had lowered her, carefully, caressingly; then the clunk of a key in the door. Now she saw the door standing ajar, and two girls whimpering, close beside her. What had happened was clear enough: unable to resist her, the girls had stolen the key and crept in, bent on resuming their fondlings.

Cata glanced at the open door. She smiled at the girls. She crooked beckoning fingers, one on each hand.

'Satima? Sefita?'

They scrambled back, grinning.

'Dear Sefita. Dear, dear Satima.'

Cata reached out, as if to embrace them. Carefully she cupped their heads in her hands. Imbecile pleasure shone in their faces; pleasure of a different sort shone in Cata's, after she had cracked their skulls together.

The girls slumped, unconscious, on the pile of clothes.

Cata leapt up. She darted to the door. From outside came sounds of breathing, deep and low: all the other Sefitas and Satimas, slumbering. Then there was a murmur of voices, deeper still, more worldly-wise than the girls could possess. One voice, Cata knew, belonged to Mother Madana; the other was familiar, too: a man's voice. Cata heard a burst of coarse laughter. Then came the bubbling of a Jarvel-pipe.

Quietly, Cata shut the door behind her. She made her way forward, edging along the wall. Only the sharp angle of a corner concealed her from Mother Madana. In the chamber where they had eaten last night's meal, the formidable woman entertained her guest; all around them lay the sleeping girls.

Cata peered round the corner.

'Mother,' the man was saying, 'I could barely believe it!'

'But Eli, you said Flame-hair would take anything. Offal from the streets, you said.'

'Yes, but he's fastidious, too.'

'Offal, and he's fastidious?'

'Last night, all he wanted was my sister.'

'Sisters! Hmph! Did I tell you about my sister, Eli?'

'I didn't know you had one.'

'I've got two. One's a slave in Kal-Theron – looks after the Sultan's brats, would you believe? Dear Lammy! She was the one I always loved.'

Bubble, bubble, went the Jarvel-pipe.

'You don't love the other?'

'A bitch, that's what she is! Keeps a caravanserai on the Dorva Coast. Did till a few days ago, that is. To hear her talk, you'd think she was the one who'd lived in a palace – and not just as a slave!'

'The Coast, you say?'

'That's right. Would you believe, she came here and pleaded with me – pleaded with *me* to take her in, now that her miserable hovel's been bashed about by the Riders. Hmph! As if I didn't know it was her – her, the bitch – who took Lammy to the slavers! I looked her in the eye and told her what I thought of her. What do I want with the mistress of a dirty old ferment-den, I said? Yes, I called her that! Well, I won't tell you what she called me ... I told her *you* kept some lodgings down in the docks, Eli, if she needs somewhere to stay. That's true, isn't it? Serve her right to be beholden to a mixer ... no offence, Eli, no offence.'

'Mistress of a dirty old ferment-den, you say?' Eli's voice was thoughtful. There was a pause, as if he were pondering; then Mother Madana burst out:

'Eli, you're not going to employ her? Eli, I forbid it!'

'Mother,' the mixer said innocently, 'would I upset you? Let her go to Casca Dalla – see what she gets from him!'

Bubble, bubble, went the Jarvel-pipe.

'Yes, let her go to Casca,' resumed Mother Madana, a moment later. 'As if I had a korzon to squander on that bitch ... we're out of pocket, Eli. Your sister lost, now these Babas a dead weight on our hands. You

188

know there are rumblings in the Exchequer, don't you?'

'Rumblings?'

'I've had advice. Better to go with Casca, some say.'

'Mother! You can't mean—'

'Eli, Eli, would I betray you? What's Casca, to a man with a royal seal? Business has cycles, does it not? Another moonlife, we'll be solid as rock ... But the Babas. I think we'll put them in the auction, hm? Babas are bad luck, anyway.'

'Now she tells me!'

Bubble, bubble.

'What about the whitebait?'

'What about her, Eli?'

'She'd fetch a few zirhams, eh?'

'I told you: she's for training.'

'She's trouble! Why train her, when we can sell her now?'

'Eli, she's an investment!'

Bubble, bubble.

'Eli?'

'Mother?'

'Your sister. Was she really like the Shimmering Princess?'

'Like her? Her image!'

'Oh Eli, if we could only get her back!'

'Pah! Think how Casca would foam at the mouth ... think how Flame-hair would pay through the nose!'

'Flame-hair? Hmph! The Emperor of Zalaga!'

There would have been more, but just at that moment there was a loud crash.

Screams.

Cata screamed too. Agony stabbed, twisting in her brain. It was an agony she had known before. She staggered out of hiding, but knew already what had happened round the corner. A burning bird, like the one she had seen on the ship, had crashed through the blinds.

Flames filled the air.

❋　❋

First she heard the voice. 'You've come. I knew you'd come.'

It was a quiet voice, pitched low, but unmistakably feminine. What the voice meant, Amed was not sure, for how could it be that she was expected? She turned, slowly taking in the details of the chamber: the long slatted blinds that obscured the windows, filtering the light into a pattern of lines; the frail painted screens; the many looking-glasses, framed in gold and draped in billowing, gauzy fabric. The air was heady

189

with a rich, sweet perfume, but it seemed to Amed that no one was there.

'Lady?' she ventured.

'Girl-boy,' came the voice again.

Amed drew in a long breath. If it troubled her that her disguise should prove so ineffectual, still more was she alarmed that the mysterious voice had in it something familiar. But how could that be? Once before – the day that Father died – it had seemed to Amed that destiny, like a tangible thing, had reached for her, touched her, taken her hand. Now, in the aftermath of her strange escape, she knew that destiny was with her again.

She whispered, 'Lady, I cannot see you.'

The voice returned laughingly, 'But you must! I am gossamer, but not invisible. Girl-boy, you must look harder! Why, look across the chamber from where you stand.'

'I see a glass.'

'Go to it.'

'It is covered in gauze.'

'Gauze is sheer.'

Amed's brow furrowed and she stared into the light that shimmered dimly from behind the fabric.

The voice said, 'What do you see?'

Amed was silent.

'There is a shape, is there not?'

It was true, but Amed was puzzled, for what could this shape be but her own? Then it came to her that the voice, too, might be no more than something of herself; for when the lady spoke again it seemed to Amed – and the thought made her sad – that the words sounded not on the outer air, but inside the cavern of her own skull.

The lady said, 'A shape only?'

'The room is in shadow.' Amed's voice was by now the merest whisper, and she trembled so violently that she could barely stand.

Quickly, clumsily, she pulled away the gauze.

She started, stumbling back, for the figure in the glass was not her own, decked out in its stolen frippery. Instead, Amed beheld an elegant lady in a fine but simple gown. The lady was veiled, but only thinly, and from her eyes alone, Amed knew she was beautiful.

'I shock you?' said the lady. 'But how can that be?'

'Lady,' breathed Amed, 'how can that *not* be?'

But the shocks had barely begun. A gentle laugh came from behind the veil, and the lady stepped out of the looking-glass, as if through an open door. 'Girl-boy, you knew you would meet me, did you not?'

'Lady,' Amed said, 'I know not who you are.'

'Not my name? Not my place?' If there was mockery in the voice, it was a gentle mockery.

'Lady, again I can say only *no.*'

Gracefully the lady reached up to her face, and when her hand dropped again, so did the veil. As it fluttered away, it vanished into the air, but Amed had eyes only for the face. Like the worshipper of a god she sank to her knees, for indeed this lady was a vision of beauty.

But she was more than this.

'Lady, I know you now.'

'But of course,' smiled the lady. 'You have seen me, perhaps, on my father's balcony?'

'Lady, I know not what you mean. I can only wonder how it is that you are here, and how, like me, you have escaped your captivity.'

'Girl-boy' – the voice was wry – 'do you think I am another?'

'Never until now have I been to this palace. But – but I think you are a lady I have seen before.'

The lady looked at her – it seemed with longing – and Amed could only moan, remembering Faha Ejo's lovely cousin. Had that lady a sister, a sister exactly the same? But how could the world contain two such women? Amed would have turned her eyes away, struggling to escape this new and strange rapture that possessed her being.

Instead she added, suddenly bold, 'Lady, I saw you but for a moment, but in that moment, I knew that I loved you.'

The lady gave a cry and turned away, holding a hand up to her face. Amed went to her. She would have pulled the hand away, bold in her desire to comfort, to protect.

Instead, she cried out. Was the lady made of mist?

'Yes!' The lady swung back. In her eyes there was almost triumph, but a sad, bitter triumph. 'You would touch me? Your hand sweeps through me. You would embrace me? I vanish from your arms. Kiss me, and you kiss the air! Girl-boy, look at me closely. You think me real, for I stand before you and speak, but I am not real as you are real. Amongst the luxuries of this palace, I am the merest emanation, and can touch its treasures no more than I can feel the embrace of love. Each day, fine foods are set before me, for my father would have me treated like any other daughter; alas, that I can only sit and watch as the dishes grow cold! Tributes of jewels fall through my hands; frankincense burns on the air and I sense it not.'

Amed faltered, 'I – I don't understand. In Eli Oli Ali's van you were flesh, I am sure of it!'

The lady fluttered to the window, as if afraid. 'Speak not to me of my other life! To me it is the merest blur of pain, a source of troubled dreams, no more. It is enough that you have seen me in my reality, not my illusion! Can you not see me shimmer, shimmer, like an image in the water?'

Now the lady trembled, and as she trembled it seemed as if indeed she were an image in water, after the casting of a stone. She said bitterly, 'They call me the Shimmering Princess, for they think me a precious jewel. Ah, but they know not the irony of the name!'

Amed gasped. Confused, she abased herself. Only now did she realise the identity of this extraordinary lady.

But how was one to speak to a Princess?

'L-Lady – P-Princess – then indeed I have heard your name! Your grace, your b-beauty is famed through all this land! But – oh, say it is so! – can you pardon a mere p-provincial, who m-means no disrespect, who speaks only from ignorance, and – and . . .'

Trailing off, Amed looked up, more boldly than she had intended, into the lovely eyes. With a smile the Princess extended her hand, and for a moment it seemed she could really raise Amed from the floor. The rich, sweet perfume of the apartment seemed suddenly stronger, almost intoxicating.

Still Amed did not dare touch the hand.

'Girl-boy,' came the voice again, 'tell me your name.'

The whisper came back. 'Ameda.' Then, 'Amed.'

A flush of happiness filled the lovely face and the Princess sighed. 'What brought you to me today, Amed, I cannot guess, but my incorporeal form gives me powers of a sort, and I see beyond the mere surfaces of things. For long sunrounds I have implored our fiery god to send me a friend, that this loneliness in which I languish might be eased at last. I look into your eyes and see that you are that friend. Abase yourself not before one who loves you. Girl-boy, you shall be mine – and the Princess Bela Dona is yours.'

And again the Princess reached down, but this time Amed reached up. Carefully she cupped her fingers round the insubstantial hand, then bent her lips towards it for a phantom kiss.

✻   ✻

'Eli, stamp it out!'

'I'm trying, you fat eunuch!'

'You pig, don't call me that!' Mother Madana drew her sari protectively about her, and laid a hand on her Royal Export Medal.

'You know what you are!'

'Pig! Greasy pig!'

'Help me, you stupid bitch! The stock, the stock—'

Mother Madana clapped her hands. 'Sefitas! Satimas! Out on the balcony!'

'The Babas! Get the Babas—'

The fire spread rapidly. Cata writhed, shrieking, but the pain was brief. The bird was dead.

Cata staggered through a curtain of smoke. She heard a cry – *The whitebait!* – but whether they knew she was loose, she could not tell. She blundered behind a sofa. She slipped behind a screen. In her juddering vision she saw a low door, between two hangings on the far wall.

She floundered towards it.

Slammed it behind her.

Cata breathed deeply. The door was heavy, and on the other side, she found herself in a long, almost dark passage, low-ceilinged and with rough stone walls. Echoes of voices sounded from afar. Lights glimmered distantly. This, Cata guessed, was a service corridor, connecting the fine apartments. But could it lead her out of the palace? Peering ahead, she saw forking paths. She scudded through the gloom, cursing the sari they had made her wear.

She had gone only a little way when suddenly she heard louder voices, and a taper flared in her eyes. Slaves, coming close! Cata pressed herself hard against the wall.

Useless. They would see her.

Instead, the wall gave way, and Cata found herself in another fine apartment.

The first thing that struck her was the extraordinary scent. Marigold, lavender, honeysuckle, rose? It was all. It was none. Cata peered round an elegant screen. Filling the chamber were looking-glasses, and all were draped in gauze.

Then Cata saw them, the boy bending, kneeling, cupping his fingers round the girl's hand.

But the boy was not a boy.

And the girl was a phantom.

Fascinated, Cata watched from her place of concealment, through the scene that followed.

Chapter 30

A WOMAN OF SUBSTANCE

Lush fabrics surrounded Amed and Princess Bela Dona as they sat side by side on a claw-footed sofa. Sunlight fell sharply through the slatted blinds, making a gold-black pattern on the floor; before them, a looking-glass was a lustrous haze. Gazing into its depths, Amed studied first the Princess, then herself. Both seemed equally real – or unreal.

She leaned back, savouring the heady, perfumed air.

'Bitter,' said the Princess, 'is the bondage in which I languish, for it is my fate to be a divided creature, riven between two incomplete selves. Splendid would be my life if I were real; cruel is the mockery that I am not. Somewhere in the wilder regions of these realms, my corporeal being lives a life of fear, exposed to what dangers I can barely imagine; all I know is that should she die, I shall die too; should she be ruined, I shall be ruined; should her beauty flee from her, so shall mine.'

'How cruel!' cried Amed. 'But is nothing to be done?'

'Many times, in the sunrounds of my bondage, my father has called upon the art of his physicians, the wisdom of his philosophers, the magic of his enchanters, that they might render me complete again. Each time, my hopes have leapt high, certain that at last a deliverer has come; each time, I have done no more than add to my sorrows.'

Amed burst out, 'Oh, if I could be that deliverer!'

'Girl-boy, your eagerness sets my spirit fluttering, as if indeed you might be the one. But I say, too many times have my hopes withered. Hold back your ardour, and your ready tongue, until you know how this spell was laid upon me, and why.'

Amed listened intently as the Princess told the story of her betrothal, long sunrounds ago, to the Sultan's heir. When she spoke of the Teller, Amed's heart thumped hard. Deep in her story, the Princess seemed barely present; indeed she seemed insensible as Amed, hunched and trembling, whispered what had been – she was sure of it – the Teller's invocation:

Theron, god of the sacred flame
Come to the one who bears the name
Of Evitamus, servant true
Of all your glories . . .

The Princess plunged on, 'How they longed to hear of my happiness when the Prince had grown to manhood, I to womanhood, and he had taken me to his bed! Little did they reckon with the Teller, who rose from his trance with a terrifying roar, thundering not of joy but sorrow, not of triumph but doom! For the Teller said that never would the Prince and I be wed, and that no fate but ruin awaited the Sultan's line!'

Amed could only tremble, possessed by shame and horror. Now she heard of the intervention of Simonides, that had saved her father from certain death; of her father's banishment, and the terrible vengeance he had then enacted. Astonished, she heard about the konar-light, and Jafir the genie, hapless, unwilling agent of her father's curse.

'So it was,' concluded the Princess, 'that this spell was laid upon me, and I became as you see me now.'

'No,' murmured Amed, 'no, no . . .'

For a moment she thought she was going mad. She closed her eyes and saw a terrible darkness, swirling up to claim her. She knew that her father had done something terrible; never had she imagined just how terrible. She held back her tears and clenched her fists.

'Dear friend,' said the Princess, 'how sorely you feel for me.'

Amed brushed her eyes. 'How can I not feel for one of such renown? Before now, I had heard many times of the Shimmering Princess; never did I understand the meaning of her name. But Princess, how many know of your fate?'

'None but those who must. The curse has been a secret to this day, and must remain so. But for the slaves who tend me here, who have no tongues, and the men of wisdom who have endeavoured to cure me – sworn, upon pain of death, to secrecy – only my father and Vizier Hasem know the truth of my condition. My appearances on the balcony are the merest imposition, easy beguilings of the ignorant mob. Never must the mob come close to their Princess, for never must the mob suspect the truth.'

'But why?'

'Girl-boy, are you as ignorant as the commoners?'

'Until now, lady, I should have been amongst them.'

'Then you know how tightly they cling to a hope, however frail that hope may be. What, after all, is the Shimmering Princess, but the future of Qatani? In truth, my father's reign has been inglorious, and often I have suspected he married my mother only that he might rise in the favour of the mob.'

'I thought him a good man!'

'He is a man both good and bad; that is to say, he is a man. For Jafir the genie he showed great love; alas, I fear he had little for my mother. From certain hints I have surmised that he treated her cruelly, barely sorrowing when she sickened and died. His concern was for the security of his reign, no more; and soon that security depended upon me.'

The Princess almost laughed, but it was a sad laugh.

'Yes, not merely upon a mere girl, but a girl who is just an illusion! How could it be otherwise? For when the mob loved their Princess, would they challenge her father? And what of the Sultan? Could he look unkindly upon his brother? He could not; but girl-boy, I have heard my father speaking softly to his Vizier, and learnt more, I fear, than a daughter should know. In truth, my father has no love for the Sultan; more than this, the Sultan has no love for him.

'Girl-boy, what is to become of me? What is to become of Qatani? Swiftly the time of my marriage draws near, yet still I languish in the thrall of this spell. Alas, what fury shall burst from the Sultan when he learns the truth at last!'

Until now, the Princess had kept her equanimity; now she slumped back and tears streamed from her eyes. In that moment, Amed longed to hold her, kiss her. Nothing seemed more terrible than to be a mere witness, helpless in the face of such distress.

But Amed was more than a witness, much more.

The Princess sobbed, 'How weary I have grown of this imposture! Today I must appear again on the balcony, as my father displays me to the hungry mob. Always, at such times, I have held my image fixed; today I long to flicker like a guttering flame, that all may know I am nothing, nothing!'

'Princess! Oh, say not such! How can you be nothing, when to me you are everything? Little more than moments have passed since we met, but on the merest moment a destiny can turn!' Imploringly Amed reached out, as if through the power of her will, her will alone, the Shimmering Princess might suddenly be real. 'Princess, I shall supply the substance you lack!'

'Then you are a fool – or you mock me cruelly!'

'Mock you? Princess, no!'

'Girl-boy, yes! What, you would unite me with my self again? You, achieve what great and learned men have failed, again and again, to bring to pass? It cannot be! You are barely more than a child, and though you affect the manner of a boy, still you have only the weak body of a girl!'

Amed bridled. 'A girl? A woman – and a woman of substance!'

The Princess flinched, as if slapped. 'Indeed, you mock me! I thought you my friend – now I see I rouse you only to hatred!'

This was too much. Amed slumped to her knees, clutching uselessly at the flickering form. 'Hatred? Princess, I love you!'

'Love me? Can I believe it?'

'Believe it? You must!'

The look that came into the lovely eyes then was one that Amed would never forget, a radiance that broke through the tears like the sun through a rainy sky. Then the Princess brushed the tears away and, leaning forward, like a lady in a legend, motioned as if to kiss her new-found champion.

Amed shuddered, almost moaned, with pleasure.

Then a new eagerness flashed across her face. 'Princess, listen. You said the men of wisdom had tried, time and again, to break the genie's spell—'

The Princess sighed. 'They have sought the answer endlessly, but all they do is heap up fuel for their useless disputations. One attempts the sacrifice of a bird. One speaks of chalk marks and magic circles. One says the curse may be removed only by some talisman, some object. A medallion, a ring? Perhaps one of the gifts that marked my birth? No, no and no again!'

Impatiently, Amed brushed all this aside. 'Princess, there's one way, only one. The konar-light. What if I could find it, and bring it back to you?

The Princess moaned, 'But it is impossible! The Teller had the genie cast a web of blindness, ensuring that none from Qatani should find him. If the efforts of all the wisest men avail nothing, how can a lone girl-boy bring back the genie?'

'But I can!' Had Amed been able to clutch the Princess then, she would have done, clutched her and shaken her. 'What can it be but fate that brought me here today? If the wisest of men can do you no service, perhaps it was destiny that a humble girl-child should achieve what they cannot. I swear to you, I – I have seen the konar-light, the very one . . . and I shall bring it to you!'

'Girl-boy, can it be true?'

'Princess, I swear it!'

Fresh tears might have flowed from the lovely eyes, but at that moment a gong sounded, deep and low, in the corridor outside.

Amed started.

'My father!' said the Princess. 'You must go!'

Already the Caliph could be heard by the door, barking instructions to his retinue. Amed looked to the windows, but the Princess shook her head.

'The pit!'

'Pit?'

There was no time to explain. The Princess waved towards a far corner. 'Behind that screen – there is a service corridor. You can escape that way, I am sure of it.'

There was a moment more. Amed's arms circled the shimmering form. Her lips pursed, kissing the air.

Still the Caliph barked.

'Wait,' breathed the Princess, 'you must have a token! Quick – the key you turned, when you entered my chamber. Take it. Wear it.'

Amed darted for it.

She turned back a last time, reaching into her robe. Impulsively, she seized the crystal. The Princess reached for it; it should have fallen to the floor. Instead, there came a burst of dark flame. The Princess gasped. The crystal juddered in her phantom hands. Black lightning rippled up her arms.

Then it fizzed out, and the crystal was gone.

'Shimmy, Shimmy!' A voice through the door.

Amed ignored it. 'Princess, what happened? What have I done?'

'What was that stone?'

'I don't know! I—'

'It was the magic that brought you to me, it must have been. Oh, you should not have given it to me, I fear you should not!'

'Shimmy, Shimmy!' The voice again.

The Princess spun round. It was a game her father played. In the next moment, he would open the door.

'Go now, go!'

'I go, but I shall return.' A last airy kiss. 'And when I return, I shall liberate you, Princess!'

But Princess Bela Dona was troubled, deeply troubled, as she turned, forcing a smile, to face her father.

❄ ❄

'Shh!'

The hand clapped across Amed's mouth. Locked together, girl and girl-boy swivelled back through the door behind the screen.

'Who are you?'

'I know everything. I'll help you. Quick. Come.'

Behind them, the Caliph was fawning over his daughter, urging her in baby-talk to be a good girl, a goody-good girl ... would Shimmy not shimmer this afternoon?

Light filled the chamber. Darkness, the corridor.

Cata raced ahead, Amed behind.

'Which way?'

'This. No – this,' Cata gasped.

Her temples pounded. How she longed to swing back, grabbing the girl-boy, holding her down, demanding answers. *Who are you? What are you? What was that stone?* All Cata knew – but she knew it for certain – was that here was a mystery she had to follow.

Voices.

'Quick!'

Cata drew Amed hard against the wall. A crossways was close. Taper-light flared.

'. . . and all the best cushions!'

'Not the chenille!'

'And an Amali screen.'

'Ooh!'

'My dear, yes. Priceless . . .'

Two eunuchs passed by, far too close. Cata was struggling not to breathe, but sensed, intensely, the tang of smoke.

The fire! She had forgotten.

Not only the furniture had been damaged, it seemed. The eunuchs said it was a heavy blow. At this rate, Mother Madana would soon be bankrupt. If only she weren't so sentimental about that greasy mixer! Losing her touch, some said she was. But the Exchequer would never let the export trade go under. Too valuable. It was only a matter of time, everyone said so, before Eli Oli Ali was out, and Casca Dalla was in, let Mother rant and rail as she would . . .

'. . . First Eli's sister.'

'Now this. Lost the whitebait, who'd believe it?'

'They'll find her. Up for sale then, mark my words.'

'Auction – a cert. Serve her right . . .'

They were gone.

Again: 'Which way?'

'This. No – this.'

'Do you really know?'

'I didn't before. But—'

Cata felt a sharp, instinctual prodding. Animals. Sunlight. Yes, she knew the way.

Then came voices, different ones this time.

Shouts. Echoes.

'She's got to be, she has to be!'

'Whitebait! Whitebait! Give yourself up now, don't be silly!'

'Quick!' said Cata.

They rounded a corner. At the end of the corridor was an open door. The door blazed with sunlight.

They ran towards it.

They were on a balcony. Beyond the balustrade was a spiky wall; beyond the wall were roofs, domes, minarets.

'We'll have to jump!'

'But the gap—'

'The spikes—'

'The wall—'

'How far down is it?'

They looked below. They gasped. Now Cata understood the sharp, sudden sensation she had felt back in the darkness.

'The cobber-as!'

'What?'

'The cobra pit. It's all around the women's wing.'

'Whitebait! Whitebait!' came the echoes, closer now.

Amed leapt up on to the balustrade.

'Wait! Give me a shoe!'

'What?'

'Don't argue!'

Cata tore off her sari. Quickly she twisted the fabric into a rope, tying the shoe into the end as a weight.

'Can you throw?'

'Of course!' said Amed.

'Get the shoe between the spikes – that'll hold it. Jump, clamber up the wall, then over the spikes and down. Get it? You go first – quick!'

'What about you?'

'I'll take my chances.'

'You're naked!'

'Quick – go!'

But one moment more.

Fervently, Amed clutched Cata's hand. 'Stranger-girl, I don't even know your name.'

'Cata. And yours?'

'Amed. You're a friend. Oh Cata, how can I make this up to you?'

'Give me your robe – and your other shoe!'

'Whitebait! Whitebait!'

Eli Oli Ali. Close, too close.

'Quick!'

There might have been time, but something happened. Something small, something golden, clattered from Amed's robes just as she was about to cast them off. It was the key to Bela Dona's apartments. The girl-boy would have blundered back, retrieving it, but Cata snatched the object instead and cried again, 'Quick!'

Amed leapt, but she swung too low. Desperately she hung just above the cobras, floundering, flailing as they hissed and snapped.

Cata cried out. In one hand she held the key; in the other, Amed's shoe.

She threw the shoe at the cobras.

Rrrip! went the sari.

Amed swung lower.

Instinct took over. Suddenly Cata called on all her powers. She moaned, hissed. Her body rippled. She clutched her arms above her like a cobra's hood. She closed her eyes, felt her skin go scaly.

Down, down. She willed the snakes away.

The sari ripped again.

But not too much.

In the next moment, Amed was over the wall, and Eli Oli Ali, bursting from the balcony, had clutched the naked snake-girl in his arms.

Chapter 31

TALE AND TELLER

'Wisdom of the ages? My young friend, you flatter me. No, I could hardly claim to be possessed of such wisdom, though' – Almoran gestured – 'the means to attain it are here all around us.'

It was true. The walls were honeycombed with deep holes, from each of which protruded a roll of parchment; between the banks of parchment were dark oaken shelves, and books bound in the Ejlander manner. In the centre of the chamber was a circular table, covered with a clutter of further books, scrolls, maps. The late morning light burned brightly through the windows; the library was warm.

Almoran looked at Jem, an eyebrow raised. 'Upon my retirement from the great city, I determined to devote my declining years to the scholarship I slighted in my impetuous youth. If the pleasures of friendship have diverted me from my aim, am I to regret a diversion so sweet? Still, there are smatterings of wisdom – smatterings – which I like to imagine I have nonetheless attained.'

Rainbow click-clicked over the parquet floor, shambling round and round the vast circular chamber. Jem found himself watching the dog, intent on the bright, almost flashing fur. Shaking himself, he turned back to Almoran. 'Good sir, your modesty is a credit to your character. To be sure, you must be a man of great wisdom, to have risen to that ... that eminence in the world, to which this tour is a testimony.'

'You think so, young Prince?'

Jem was uncertain how to reply. By now, the tour of the house seemed interminable, and politeness was becoming a strain. He was standing by the circular table, holding a volume idly in his hand. Almoran arched an eyebrow again; Jem feigned a scholarly interest. Peering at the lettering on the faded spine, he was startled to see that it was not the ponderous tome of philosophy he had expected. On the contrary: it was a copy of *Becca's First Ball*. Jem almost dropped the book. He looked up sharply at Almoran, but the old man was oblivious.

'Come, my young friend,' he was saying, 'we have ventured far enough on this hot morning. Let us relax in this pleasant chamber, and I shall tell you the story of my life. Well, some of it.'

Set before the window was a pair of curving, carved chairs. Almoran gestured for Jem to join him, then clapped his hands curtly. The girlish youth, or another just like him, appeared through an archway in the library wall and the old man commanded him to bring them green tea. The youth bowed and withdrew, but returned almost instantly with a laden tray.

Troubled, Jem looked at his mysterious host. In their long journey through the House of Truth, Almoran had expatiated on architectural splendours, on rich furnishings, on intricacies of adornment, but had shown barely a flicker of response to the questions Jem had asked. Who were they, these Ouabin, who had almost succeeded in kidnapping him, and Dona Bela too? – Almoran pointed to a vaulted ceiling. How had it been that Almoran had saved them? By what means had he saved them? – The old man exclaimed over a pattern of tiles. How did he know that Jem was a Prince? – A wrinkled hand smoothed a velvet cushion. In all the many chambers they had visited, they had encountered no other human presences, not a single one. Where had they gone, the thousand revellers who caroused so merrily only last night?

Jem fought against the strange tiredness he had felt before in Almoran's house. Beside his chair, Rainbow lay sleeping already, his head resting on his folded paws. Jem reached down, stroking the dog's ears. Through the window, the empty garden was a bright blaze of foliage, sharp against the dusty haze of the library. Not for the first time, the thought came to Jem that he had a mission, a quest to fulfil. When, he wondered, could he be on his way? And how?

In a dreamy, droning voice, Almoran began his story.

Almoran's Story

1

There are those whose lives begin in the manner in which they are to proceed, and those in whose origins we find no hint of the people they shall become one day.

Three gens ago, in the great city of Qatani, famed through all these lands as the Jewel of the Shore, there lived a poor cobbler. This lowly man had three sons, of whom I was one, and the youngest. My eldest brother was Simonides; the name of my middle brother was Evitamus. No one, looking at us then, three ragged urchins, playing in the dust beside my father's hovel, could have guessed the strange destiny that one day would be ours. Our mother despaired, for it was said that she had once been of a higher station, and wished only that her sons should not be condemned to the poverty that was her lot.

For our own part, my brothers and I were too young to despair. To be sure, our prospects were bleak and we had little chance of fulfilling the ambitions that each of us had, it seemed, from the first.

My brother Simonides was an earnest, pious boy, and longed only to venture to far Kal-Theron, there to be accepted into the College of Imams. Evitamus had in him the lust of courtly power, hoping that one day he might rise to eminence in the service of our monarch, the Caliph of Qatani. My desires were at once more modest, and more grand. Depending on neither colleges nor Caliphs, I aspired to make my own place in the world, becoming a merchant of such eminence that, upon my retirement, I should live in independent splendour, unbeholden to the favour of any man.

No doubt our ambitions should have filled us with frustration, but in truth there was a secret we three brothers shared, which gave us much consolation. At night, lying side by side beneath our single blanket, we would take it upon ourselves to think of a better place, to focus our minds on a grand house with luxurious gardens, which would become the scene for our innocent play. So powerful was the illusion, it seemed to us that indeed we were transported to this paradise, leaving our father's hovel behind. I much preferred these playful dreams of night to the ambitious dreams of day, and would have indulged in them endlessly, but for one curious condition.

It was this. When I was young, I could not dream alone; the grand house seemed real to me only when my brothers joined me in the dream, in a threefold act of sustaining. It was a sorrow to me, therefore, when my brothers grew older and declared they would indulge in the dream no more. Simonides would think only of his piety, and Evitamus only of the Court. When I begged them to dream, they would curse me for a fool, and ask if I would dream my life away. To me, my brothers were the fools, to fret over blessings that could not be theirs, when bliss lay so easily within their grasp.

These then were my brothers; I must speak now of my father, whose name was Pandarus. It is a commonplace that children take their parents for granted, seeing in them little of the peculiarity which, to the greater world, is evident from the first. My father's particular eccentricity was to wear a thick mask, fashioned from the materials of his cobbler's trade, which entirely concealed his face. Through our early sunrounds, my brothers and I never saw the visage that lay beneath, and when once we asked my mother why this should be so, she said that our father had been disfigured in his youth, and would not revolt us with his scars. For me, and for my brothers too, this explanation sufficed. Not until Simonides was in his twelfth sunround, Evitamus in his eleventh, and I in my tenth, did we learn what really lay beneath the mysterious leather mask.

2

It so happened that three great trials came, one succeeding another, to the Caliphate of Qatani.

The first was pestilence, an outbreak of the jubba fever so severe that it seemed that soon no one in the city would be left alive. Women and men fled in their thousands, many embarking upon a desperate pilgrimage to the Sacred City, hoping that in this, they might yet redeem their lives. The courtiers urged the Caliph to make the journey – I speak, you understand, not of the present Caliph Oman Elmani, but of Caliph Abdul Samad, his uncle, and uncle of the present Sultan too.

Now Abdul Samad was young then, and in his youth was a man much given to portents, signs, and all things mystic. In the jubba fever, which burned away the wits of men, he feared he saw the fire god's displeasure, and to allay that displeasure he would have abandoned his very realm. Abdul Samad needed no persuading, and ordered his retainers to ready him for the pilgrimage.

On the way out of the city, Abdul Samad's train happened to pass by my father's hovel. Our little family had no thought of fleeing, for what provisions could we take with us on so long a journey? Poverty would kill us if the jubba fever did not.

As the royal train passed by, my brothers and I clustered by the roadside with other poor folk, eager, like the fools we were, to applaud and cheer as our leader passed, barely thinking that he had rewarded our devotion only by abandoning us in this time of peril. Our role was a virtuous passivity, no more; imagine then our horror when our father leapt out suddenly before Abdul Samad's litter, crying that the Caliph must not go. My brothers and I quailed; my mother moaned; the guards would have slain my father at once, but Abdul Samad looked down from his litter and demanded, in an imperious voice, that the masked man explain himself.

'Caliph,' said our father, 'I should die rather than offend you, for in your city, this Jewel of the Shore, I have known a contentment that never before has been mine, through all the course of a long and fraught life. I beg you, believe me that it is only my devotion that prompts me now to tell you that you must not go. You would avoid the pestilence, as all would have you do; know then that the fever burns already in the pilgrims on the road. Go with them, and assuredly you too shall die, plunging this realm into a misery that shall never be abated; return to your Palace of Perfumed Stairs, and I tell you, the fever shall swiftly pass, leaving you unharmed.'

Indignant cries rose from the crowd, and again the guards would have put my father to death, but Abdul Samad looked thoughtful and commanded his train to turn back. There was much astonishment at this, and many in the crowd would have attacked my father had not Abdul Samad commanded that none, on pain of death, must touch the masked man.

Days passed. Word came from the Kal-Theron road that pestilence had claimed the pilgrim party; another day passed, then another, and soon the fever had gone from Qatani. The city was saved! There was much rejoicing, and that night a royal retainer came to our hovel, there to reward the masked man with the riches he deserved. My brothers and I had been terrified by what our father had done; now our terror turned to joy as it seemed to us that all our troubles were over. Think, then, of our shock when our father turned the retainer away!

'I deserve no reward,' he said, 'and I deserve no thanks. The prediction I made was the merest of accidents. Randomly, the gods selected me for their instrument; I am glad only that the Caliph is spared. Leave me now to resume my poor and anonymous life. It is my lot, and I desire no more.'

My brothers and I could only sorrow at what our father had done; we went to our mother and begged her to make him change his mind. Alas, our mother would not be moved, and said only that there were things we did not understand, and begged us, in turn, that we never question the judgement of our father.

We could barely believe that she could take such a view; from this time on, our discontent grew greater. My brother Simonides, in his pious way, claimed to accede to the ways of fate, but I knew that even he thought of the wealth and finery that might have taken him to the College of Imams. My brother Evitamus condemned our father openly, cursing that his courtly dreams should have been within his grasp, only to be snatched so cruelly away; for my own part, I wished my brothers would but accompany me again, in our threefold dream, to the great house and gardens where once we had known such happiness.

But I said that three trials came that sunround to the Caliphate of Qatani. The second, then the third, followed hard upon the first. A moonlife or so after the fever was dispersed, a great fire broke out in the docks. Spreading fast, it threatened to engulf the city, and there were fears for the Palace of Perfumed Stairs. The nobles urged the Caliph to flee, and he was making his way rapidly from the burning city when once again he passed by my father's hovel.

'Caliph, hold!' cried my father, leaping into his monarch's path. 'Know that I should die rather than offend you, but believe me, it is only my devotion that prompts me now to tell you that you must not go. You would avoid the fire, as all would have you do; I tell you, its destruction shall not touch your palace, but there are Ouabin traitors who have sparked this fire, and would sack all your treasures if you leave! Return to the Palace of Perfumed Stairs, and the fire shall swiftly pass; leave, and a time of terror shall descend upon this land.'

So it happened that once again the Caliph turned back; and once again, all came to pass as my father had predicted. The fire spared the palace; the Caliph's men rooted out and destroyed the treacherous Ouabin agents.

Now great glory would have come to my father, but again he refused all honour and all reward, and again my brothers and I were left in the utmost anger and dismay. Was our father merely a random instrument of the gods? We could not believe it; cruelly we pressed our mother to explain his strange actions, wondering if he could really be a simple cobbler, and whether his mask concealed a scarred face, or the more terrible visage of a powerful demon.

To be sure, our thoughts were the Caliph's too, but I have said that Abdul Samad was a superstitious man; twice saved by my father, he was unwilling to disobey his strange protector. He would leave the masked man be; until, that is, my father's powers astonished him for a third time.

War came to Qatani. Enraged by the reprisals against their agents, the Ouabin hordes descended, surrounding the city and demanding the Caliph's surrender. If he surrendered, they said, he could go free, riding in safety out of his city; if he continued to resist, his city and all its peoples faced certain destruction. The Caliph had no choice. At last, with a sorrowing heart, he rode to meet the Ouabin, and would have laid down his seal of office, giving up his power, when once again my father appeared suddenly before him.

'Caliph, again I tell you to hold! I think only of the sanctity of your person and your realm, and believe me, you must place no trust in the promises of Ouabin. Ride on now, and you shall be killed, whether you lay down your seal or no; while the Ouabin, fearing resistance no more, shall begin their work of destruction forthwith. Return to your palace, sending word that you shall meet the Ouabin on the morrow; in truth, the Sultan's armies shall be here by then, sweeping this city clean of the invading hordes.'

So it was that for a third time the Caliph turned back; so it was that, for a third time, all came to pass as my father had predicted.

This time, Abdul Samad would hear no more of my father's disavowals; this time, he demanded that my father be brought to the palace, and there before the joyous nobles of the land he first presented him with a chest of gold, then embraced him fulsomely and then, suddenly, inevitably, jerked the leather mask from my father's face.

The Caliph leapt back, as if expecting a fearsome visage. Instead, he saw a forehead stamped with a star, and a grizzled beard, which grew by dint of two scars on the chin into a thrice-forked shape.

Pleasure, not fear, filled Abdul Samad's face.

'A Teller! My, my, Pandarus, you have been mysterious! But indeed you have been a blessing to me, for you are a Teller more powerful than any I have encountered before. No more of your mysteries, Pandarus, and no more of the ignominy in which you have lived. You have proved yourself, as I trust it was your intention to do; from now on, you shall be the ornament of my Court, and a more trusted aide to me than any man.'

3

Now it was that my brothers and I knew exaltation, for it seemed to us that at last, and in truth, our trials were over. In what seemed the work of an instant, we were established in luxurious apartments, and dressed in finery we had known before only in our threefold dreams. The meagre meals of poverty were replaced by luxurious banquets, served by slaves. From now on, our father would wear robes spangled with stars, and disappear for long, secret interviews with his royal master. Fondly, my brother Simonides thought of the day, which must now be soon, when he would embark for Kal-Theron, there to become an ornament of the College of Imams; in a species of ecstasy, my brother Evitamus thought of the prospects of his courtly career; for my part, I rubbed my hands, thinking that now I could easily become the great merchant I had wanted to be, and build my private kingdom.

It came as a shock to us to realise that our parents did not share our joy. The face of our mother remained troubled, for all the finery that was now hers to wear; one day we came upon her weeping, abandoned helplessly to grief.

'Mother, what ails you?' said my brother Simonides. 'How can it be that our fortunes are made, yet you feel not the joy you should feel?'

'Alas, my sons,' said our sorrowing parent, 'you know not the cost of all this splendour! Your father and I have lived like this before, but always, always it has ended in suffering. A Teller is a man of great power, it is true, and a power much valued by the world; but his power is a curse as much as a blessing. Swiftly do potentates turn against Tellers when they are told what they do not wish to hear; Viziers, ministers, inferior courtiers plot revenge, such is their envy and consuming spite; the fine life of the Court gives way swiftly to the dirty alley, the dungeon, or the terrible banishment of the desert wastes! In his long career, your father has been denounced, beaten and tortured; he has been expelled in ignominy from Geden, Vashi and Ormuz; he has been captured by the Ouabin, who demanded to know the secrets of his powers. At last, we retired to this fair coastal city, here to live in virtuous and anonymous poverty; alas, that your father's powers, trained to the highest pitch in the Great Guild of Tellers, would give him no rest, and thrice he was called upon to save this city! You ask me to rejoice in the bounty that now is

208

ours; how can I, when I love my husband and know that this time, he faces doom!'

To be sure, we were much troubled by my mother's words, yet such is the folly of youth that we soon dismissed them, revelling instead in our new lives of wealth, and all the privileges it brought us. Now we entered upon the great age of our prosperity, for such was the Caliph's trust in my father's powers that soon he would take no decision, none at all, unless my father would first predict its outcome. Were the prediction unfavourable, the Caliph would devise another strategy, then another, until he hit upon one that would succeed. It was a splendid system, and the Caliph's power grew great; trade flourished, diplomacy too.

Only slowly did we see the dark side, for it emerged that the Caliph, in his vaulting ambition, would now prove his supremacy in the arts of war. For too long he had chafed under the imperial yoke; now he would go into battle against his cousin, the Sultan, and liberate Qatani.

4

My mother trembled, fearing the end had come, but there remained a twist in this last, tragic episode of my father's career. It was at this time that my mother, with a heavy heart, had decided that my brothers and I must be sent away; we were young yet, but now was the time when we must be set up in the world if all our fair prospects were not to be lost.

Alas, that when she told our father of her plans, the old man only looked at her with tear-brimming eyes and said that the Caliph had sent for us – Simonides, Evitamus, and Almoran too. At this, my mother wailed and collapsed, while my brothers and I milled around my father, demanding to know what this summons could mean.

We were to find out soon enough. Trembling, we stood in the presence of the Caliph, as he informed us that his new, imperial ambitions would require more than the services of a single Teller. Our father had been a splendid servant, but was old; yet, to be sure, the power of Telling would persist in his sons. It was the Caliph's plan that my brothers and I be sent in secret to the Deserts of Los, there to train with the Great Guild of Tellers, where our father, long ago, had received the star at his forehead and the scars at his chin. Upon our return, we should be the Three Tellers of Qatani, and none but the Caliph should be more glorious. A Teller of Culture. Of Commerce. Of Conquest. With our united powers, we would build the greatest empire the world had ever seen. Qatani would be unassailable!

His eyes blazing, the Caliph turned to my father, demanding, as always, to know if the words that had fallen from his royal lips were true.

It was then that my father took the bravest decision of his life, breaking all the vows he had made in the Great Guild of Tellers. 'Caliph,' he cried, 'if there are truths that it is a joy to tell you, so too there are some that must pain my heart sorely. But as I am a Teller, I can do no more than say what I see. This I see: that your plan must come to naught, for my sons possess none of the power you suggest, and their destiny it is to live the lives of ordinary men!'

At this, the Caliph's visage darkened, but astonishment overspread him at the next development. Suddenly, Simonides collapsed to the floor, screaming and clutching his eyes. In agony the words were ripped from him, 'Caliph, my father has lied! Know ye that indeed your plan is doomed, for never shall we be the Three Tellers of Qatani; but know too, that the power is in all of us, and shall sear our hearts like flame! My father seeks to protect us, but as the power surges through me, claiming me, I cannot resist its terrible truth! I have the power! But it shall never be yours!'

Suddenly the Caliph was angry, terribly angry, and turned on my father. 'Wicked old man, you would lie to your protector, who has raised you to riches from the squalor of the streets? Guards! Kill the traitor! Kill him this instant!'

With that, the guards descended, running their blades through my father's hapless body. Down he fell, dead; then it was that despair gripped the Caliph, for he saw the ruin of all his plans. Never had it occurred to him that a Teller could lie, but now, if this were so, what trust could he place in his Tellers Three, even if we were to be trained as he wished?

5

The sequel may be swiftly told. The Caliph was not an evil man, for all that he had succumbed to the vice of hubris; great had been his gratitude to my father at first, and much regret did he feel for the death of one he saw, too late, to have been his loyal friend.

Again my brothers and I were called before the great man. He said that he would atone for the wrong he had done us, and asked us what we wished. Thus it was that our long-held ambitions came true after all, if not quite in the manner we had expected.

My brother Simonides forswore the powers that had brought his own father to so terrible an end; he asked only that he be sent to Kal-Theron, to the College of Imams, where he might devote himself to a life of humble piety. In truth, the life that was to come would never, for Simonides, be so simple as he wished. The Caliph, let us recall, was the Sultan's cousin; arriving at the college, as he did, with a recommendation from so great a man, Simonides was marked out from the first as a boy of spectacular promise. True, the Caliph had said nothing of the boy's special powers; nonetheless a long, laborious career of worldly affairs lay ahead for this eldest brother of mine, high in the ranks of the imperial service. Never again, I believe, has he called upon his powers, but many times I have wondered how often he has wished he could, and how often the intimations of the future have stolen upon him, unbidden. Before his life is out, I am certain, he shall have cause to break that vow of blindness he took, long ago, in the Court of Qatani.

My brother Evitamus had no such scruples. He was, as I have said, ambitious of the Court; now, thinking only of the greatness our father had enjoyed, telling himself that he could avoid our father's foolish mistakes, this brother asked that he might yet be sent to the Great Guild of Tellers. Simonides and I were shocked at such a request; I am certain, too, that it shortened our poor mother's life. One might have expected the Caliph to reject the plea, but the lure of the Telling art is strong, and he decided that, yes, the Court needed a Teller; there could be no need to repeat the errors of the past.

Thus it happened that Evitamus was trained after all in our father's dark arts, returning from the Guild with a star at his forehead and deep scars between the forks of his beard. Alas, his powers failed him if he imagined that his life henceforth would be a smooth progress of courtly prestige; in truth, he made powerful enemies, and brought much suffering upon himself and others. I fear that this poor, foolish brother is dead now; yet the feeling is strong in me that he may yet appear again from beyond the grave, to right one of the many wrongs he has done.

As for Almoran, the youngest of the brothers? For my part, I wanted nothing of the Telling arts. In time, certain other powers developed within me – I mean, of course, those powers of commerce that were to lead me to eminence in the world of trade, and bring me in time to this honourable retirement, here in this place I call the House of Truth. My sorrow is only that my beloved brothers are not here to share this place with me, for I have constructed it such that it resembles, wholly and utterly, that house and those gardens where once we retreated in our blissful, threefold dream. How much more splendid it would be, I like to think, had I but my brothers to dream in it with me now!

※　※

Jem started awake. But no, he had not been sleeping, had he? Only listening to the dreamy, droning voice. Yet it seemed to him that Almoran's story, though long, had not been quite complete; perhaps there were parts of it that had yet to be told. For a moment, Jem attempted to formulate a question, as if he would know more; but he could not quite think what he wanted to know, and the question, and the desire, slipped silently away.

He looked out into the garden and saw Dona Bela, wandering idly beneath an avenue of willows. How remote she seemed, how ethereal! To Jem, it was almost as if she belonged to this strange place, as if she had never been the girl he had saved, so short a time before ... or what seemed so short a time.

Almoran smiled. 'But I am an old man, and talk and talk. Poor Prince, you must be hungry – hungry, and you are not yet well! I'm sure the Princess feels the same.'

'Princess?' said Jem, glancing again at the girl in the garden.

Almoran only smiled again. 'Come, shall we join our many friends?'

Chapter 32

DEATH IN THE AFTERNOON

'Peppers!'
 'Spices!'
 'Olives!'
 'Oil!'
The cries filled the crowded bazaar, resounding high above the laden stalls, echoing through cool archways and narrow, cluttered alleys.
 'Alkanet!'
 'Amber!'
 'Saffron!'
 'Sugar!'
All through the southlands, where the sun flamed high, no bazaar was more famed than Qatani's. From across the sprawling metropolis and beyond, from docks where fishing boats knocked and sloshed, from workshops in alleys and gardens in the hills, they came: women in black, men in dusty white, traders in their turbans, robes and veils, converging each day upon the great square.

Round the edges of the square, raised high on stout pillars, was a viewing-gallery, connected by walkways to the Palace of Perfumed Stairs. Here, beneath cool, ornate arches, noble folk could look upon the scene, safe from all vulgar jostlings.

Vizier Hasem strolled with his guests. 'A striking display, is it not?'

'Vizier, thirty sunrounds ago it was striking. If anything, it is more remarkable now.'

The Vizier smiled, 'Empster-lord, but I am forgetting you have visited this Jewel of the Shore before. Accept my humble apologies.'

'Good Vizier, none are needed. When a man has lived so long in the world, may he not find it pleasant to forget the length of his stay? But let us halt here; my salty companion is falling behind.'

Already the gallery was filling rapidly, and Captain Porlo, stumping though the thickets of courtiers, was somewhat without his customary aplomb. His cheeks were flushed, his eyes bloodshot. Buby the monkey quivered on his shoulder, a thick white bandage tied around her head.

Warmly, the Vizier clutched the Captain's hand. 'I trust, noble admiral, you have forgiven us last night's imposture? The Great One enjoys nothing so much as a little theatre, and the denunciation of a trio – I'm sure you'll agree – seemed a spectacle more droll than that of one alone. Of course, we meant no harm by it.'

'Only to Master Raj,' muttered the captain.

'Indeed,' said Lord Empster, 'who could have believed we harboured so vile a traitor? Vizier, we are indebted to you for exposing our folly.'

Smiling, the Vizier would have petted Buby, but thought better of it when the monkey hissed fiercely.

'You're sure the lad be a traitor, then?' said the captain.

'No doubt of it. No doubt at all.'

It was Lord Empster who made this last remark. Incredulity filled the captain's bloodshot eyes, but his employer only smiled and leaned over the balustrade. Packing his pipe, the nobleman gazed urbanely into the carnival of abundance, glittering and glistening in the afternoon sun. Idly his eyes flickered over earrings and artichokes; over mangoes, memory-beads, mermaid tails; over eels hanging from hooks and heaps of honeyed locusts.

In the middle of it all was the Circle of Sacrifice. The grim edifice looked remarkably simple: a plain disc of scrubbed timber boards with a trapdoor in the floor and a rack, raised vertically, shaped like a wheel. Here the victim would be strapped, limbs stretched wide.

'It revolves,' said the Vizier. 'A recent innovation.'

'The wheel?' said Lord Empster, lighting his pipe.

'The stage, too. Of course, the principal knife-strokes occur directly before the royal box.'

'Of course.'

'But afterwards, a little turning is desirable, we have found. Common folk have been crushed as they strain to see. Not to mention when they scramble for the sex.'

'The sex?'

'You have forgotten, Empster-lord? Why, to retrieve the sex is a particular blessing. Of course,' the Vizier added with a laugh, 'often little remains after a hundred hands have clutched and clawed.'

'It is never flung to the gallery? Quality-folk, I trust, might behave more decorously.'

'Our pleasure comes from the scramble below. But today, I venture to add, there shall be an additional pleasure. Shall we say, a novelty – a surprise?'

Lord Empster arched an eyebrow.

Vizier Hasem might have said more, but a new voice greeted him and he turned, perhaps with relief. 'Ah, but here are your Ejlander friends.'

'My greetings, Lord Empster,' said Polty benignly. 'You slept well, I trust?'

The nobleman returned the greeting, just as benignly. 'But your friend Mr – ah – Burgrove is not with you?'

'Alas, Jac is indisposed.'

'He's been throwing up all night,' said Bean.

Suspiciously, Captain Porlo eyed the new arrivals. Last night, in their blue masks, the supposed Wenayans had been a sight both sinister and bizarre. In daylight, their natural faces – Polty's creamily handsome, Bean's freckled and gauche – seemed still more sinister, still more bizarre, combined with the luxuriance of their borrowed robes.

Vizier Hasem inclined his head. 'You will excuse me, my friends? Submissions are almost upon us and I must make my way back to my master.'

But as the Vizier was leaving, Polty clutched his arm, drawing him to the back of the gallery.

'Hasem, is it true?'

'Flame-haired one?'

Polty's voice was a snake-like hiss. 'The Vexing – the Ejland prisoner – has he escaped?'

'There is – shall we say – a small problem.'

'You fool, Hasem!'

The Vizier stiffened. 'Arrogant Ejlander! Must I remind you that you are a visitor in my country?'

'A visitor, Hasem, but a trader, too. Would you have the weapons I promised you, or not? You know what I want: the Ejland-boy.'

'I do not pretend to understand you, flame-haired one. There are boys enough, if you seek but a boy—'

'Don't make me sick!'

'Hardly what I was attempting,' the Vizier returned. Sharply he glanced at the hand that still gripped him. 'Ejlander, if our arrangement no longer pleases you, I dare say we can terminate it at once.'

It was mere bravado, and Polty knew it. Would Hasem give up his valuable Ejland trades – let alone the favour of the Bluejacket régime? Hardly, but he was a prickly fellow and it was as well to soothe him. 'Hasem, I'm sorry, I was overwrought. I know you are doing your best for me.' Polty shot a furtive glance at Lord Empster. 'And the others?'

'Why, we shall observe them constantly, as you wish.'

'Dear Hasem! You have taken your measure of the booty?'

'The ship? The hold groans with pirate treasures. But we shall string the so-called admiral along, just a little longer. The girl, of course, I have disposed of already.'

A strange look came into Polty's eyes and he tightened his grip on the Vizier's arm.

'Girl? What girl?'

'This execution, me lord. I suppose that's what's in store for Master Raj?'

Lord Empster shrugged, studying the bazaar again. His gaze lingered on ornate Jarvel-pipes; on bolts of golden cloth; on pentagon-chessboards with pieces carved from ivory. On the opposite side of the square, across the fray, were the grilled galleries for the ladies, flanking the great central cube of the royal box. Here the Caliph's daughter would make her appearance, standing beside her father. The box was heavily curtained, and the curtains still drawn.

The captain attempted again, 'I may be speaking out of turn, me lord, but what do you think you be playing at?'

'You're right, Porlo, you're speaking out of turn.' The nobleman blew out a long stream of smoke. Deftly he reached into the captain's jacket, plucking forth the little brass far-glass, remarking only, 'Now shall we be able to see the Caliph's daughter from here, do you think? Really see her?'

It was an impertinence for which any other fellow would have walked the plank, or so the captain put it to himself. But he pursued doggedly, his voice a raw whisper, 'I know you're a rum fellow, me lord – sometimes a bit too rum for a simple old sea-dog. But you trust old Porlo, don't you, after all these years? Please, me lord: do you know something I don't?'

With a preoccupied air, Lord Empster adjusted the focus of the far-glass. 'Secret, Porlo? Now it would hardly be a secret if I told you, would it now? Let's just say that destiny works mysteriously.'

The captain cursed. Savagely he gestured to the Circle of Sacrifice. 'What's the destiny of the poor fellow on that? And what does that Hasem fellow mean, a surprise? I tell you, me lord, they're not civilised like us, these Unang dogs!' He stamped with his wooden leg, as if in illustration, and added, rather too loudly, 'Remember them cobber-as!'

While Polty was engaged with Vizier Hasem, Bean had been hovering uselessly. He looked about him, this way and that. By now the galleries were crowded as much as the square below, a heady mix of greetings, laughter, Jarvel-smoke. The young lieutenant looked miserably over the balustrade. With pretended intentness he studied the common folk, milling round the market stalls.

His gaze fell, for no particular reason, upon a fat old woman in the middle of the crowd. Clutching a basket of hard cakes, she cried her wares in a curious open-mouthed cawing, with her tongue in a roll and flapping from side to side. No Ejlander would cry thus; no Ejlander could. Bean found the action both fascinating and repellent; then all at once the woman broke off. A ragged street-boy had slipped through the crowd, snaffled a cake and darted away. Bean watched the woman shake her fist, then marked the boy weaving lithely through a shifting, bewildering forest of legs, arms, robes. Still running, the boy stuffed the cake into his mouth. Bean grinned, but his grin fell as the boy careened suddenly into a protruding, dome-like belly. A cuff about the head, and the cake went flying.

'Hey!' Bean cried uselessly, as if it were the boy, not the old woman, who was the victim of injustice.

Then he gasped.

The belly belonged to Eli Oli Ali. The greasy fellow was endeavouring, with some difficulty, to goad a party of slaves across the square. Bean recognised the Baba-girls. But last night, there had been three. Now there was a fourth, but a fourth rather different from her naked, dark companions. The Baba-girls, broken long ago, seemed resigned to their fate, enduring alike the slavemaster's shoutings, the strokes of his whip, the pawings and fondlings of the leering crowd. The new girl twisted and writhed in her chains, calling out her defiance.

But there was more.

The girl was white, and wore a green gown.

※　※

'Wait!' Oblivious, Polty clutched the Vizier's shoulder. 'Hasem, what did you mean about a girl?'

The Vizier rolled his eyes. 'A girl on the ship. The crew's concubine, I suppose. You said all the portable property was ours, didn't you?'

With that, the Vizier would have gone again, but Polty would not let him. 'What sort of girl?'

'What do you think? Hardly one of your Ejland roses! Let me see – long, dark hair . . .'

Polty struck his forehead. 'Of course! The bitch, she's run off with the Vexing! Hasem, I want her!'

'First a boy, then a girl! Versatile, or just indecisive?'

'Hasem, where is she?'

'I handed her to the Keeper of Palace Women, of course. Oman hardly wants a white trollop round the palace – she'll go up for Blood Market this afternoon, I dare say.'

Polty froze. 'Blood Market?'

'Questions, questions! You're no student of our customs, I see. After the blood, the market. Slaves purchased after a public sacrifice are felt to be specially blessed, didn't you know? Doubly so, when the Princess puts in an appearance. Why, I should expect your bit of whitebait to fetch a high price indeed. Feisty thing, but there's some who like that – so I'm told. Now you'll excuse me?'

'Hasem, I want that girl!'

The Vizier had endured enough. Roughly he broke from Polty's grip, reiterated that the girl would be sold, and swished away decisively.

Meanwhile, Bean fought through the crowd. 'Polty, I think there's something you should know—'

But at that moment there was a clamour of bells, and the scene around them altered with an eerie suddenness. First there was a rumbling like thunder. In the galleries, in the square, the Unangs abased themselves.

All was silent but for the mumbling of prayer.

❋   ❋

'Ah, Hasem, what kept you? Praying, were we?'

'Droll, Oman. You have the girl?'

'Of course! In the glass.'

'Fixed?'

'Not a flicker. Now quick, Hasem, get in place.'

The Vizier took up his position beside the throne. Even through the curtains the sun flamed hotly, colouring the interior of the royal box a dim but intense red. Like conversation through a thin floor, familiar but maddening, the dronings of worship rose up from below.

'I hate that mumbling.'

'Straighten your mask.'

'What?'

'Your mask's not straight.'

Submissions were almost over. Slowly, the curtains parted. When the faithful rose, they would gaze up at their ruler, decked in impossible finery, his face concealed behind a pair of immense golden wings. Sweaty behind the mask, squinting in the sunlight, the fat little man raised his hands in benediction.

Polite applause rippled from the galleries.

A roar went up from the square.

'I never know if it's *for* me, or against me. If you see what I mean.' The voice from behind the mask was sour.

'Of course it's against you, Oman. They're baying, not cheering.'

'Do they hate us so much?'

'Don't you know what they call you? Sensualist. Sybarite. Powerless puppet—'

'Puppet!'

'We *are* in thrall to your brother, aren't we? And frankly, Oman, I don't see how we could have it any other way. Would you like to run this Caliphate without imperial protection? Jewel of the Shore, indeed! I

218

should imagine many envious eyes would be cast upon us, should it be suspected for a moment that we were weak. Wenayan eyes. Ejlander eyes, if we don't keep in with them. And let's not forget the Ouabin.'

The Caliph sighed. 'Pull away the cloth.'

With stiff dignity, Vizier Hasem moved to the side of the stage, where there stood what might have been a door, perhaps a screen, panelled in beaten silver. From the square, even from the galleries, it was only a dazzle of reflected light.

It was a looking-glass, draped in a length of spangled cloth. The Vizier twitched the cloth away and the Princess stepped forth.

This time there was no roar, but a sudden, enveloping silence, leavened only with sighs. Perhaps, in a land where fine ladies were seldom seen in public, and then only when heavily robed and veiled, the sight of a woman in a sheer, diaphanous gown was startling enough; but there was more, much more. For another lady, the moans, the sighs might have been filled with desire; for this lady, they had in them nothing base, nothing earthly. Had the prayers of moments earlier been fulfilled all at once? Enraptured, thousands upon thousands gazed up, as if at a sacred vision.

Then came the whisperings.

'Can she be a goddess?'

'A goddess on earth!'

'Can it be true, she is to marry soon?'

'The Sultan's son—'

'Line of the Prophet—'

'Empress of the Line—'

'Then we shall be blessed!'

Throughout the assembled masses, words like these were spoken. Words of a different sort were exchanged in the royal box. The Caliph looked sadly at his dazzling daughter, then more sadly at the common folk below.

He sighed. 'Can we have the sacrifice now?'

'A moment longer, Oman. Let them drink their fill.'

'I should think they were bursting!'

The Caliph looked glassily into the centre of the square. During Submissions, heathen slaves had made swift preparations on the Circle of Sacrifice. Concealed beneath a black sheet, the prisoner was bound to the wheel. Beside the wheel, the Justice Killer stood stiff at attention, scimitar poised, dressed in his elaborate blood-red uniform.

'Hasem, did you bring the far-glass?'

'Of course! There's a surprise today, didn't I say?'

'I hate surprises! What is it?'

'The sacrifice. The sex.'

'Hasem, what can you mean?'

'The killer. It's a girl-boy.'

'A girl-boy!'

The Caliph spoke more loudly than he had intended; too loudly, since his words sounded in his phantom daughter's ears. Princess Bela Dona had been standing stock-still. All at once, she swivelled towards her father.

'Girl-boy?' she blurted.

✵ ✵

But it was not.

Beneath the shroud, Rajal ached with loss, but joy filled him too. Aeons ago, it seemed, he had abandoned hope, certain that death was about to come. When they dragged him from his cell, he had railed and cried; but when they had bound him on the wheel, he was yielding, sighing as if a thorn had been drawn from his flesh. Like a stone, he sank into sorrow, then memory, then into a darkness without desire. All around him, like a sustaining medium, he felt the deep purple warmth of his faith.

If only he could have seen Jem again – and Myla!

✵ ✵

'Shimmy, you're shimmering!'

'Child, they'll see!'

'Into the shadows!'

'Child, come away!'

The Vizier gives the signal, a vertical dart of the hand. Round and round the galleries, guards do the same. Curly pipe-horns break into flourishes, and all through the square the crowd turns to the circle in the centre.

Now the Justice Killer comes into his own. First he bows, deep and low, paying his respects to the Princess and her father; then, with an admirable elegance, he raises his glittering blade. He passes it over his head; he scythes the air; he dances a swooping, slow dance of death.

The crowd applauds. Cheers.

'Father, make him stop!'

'Shimmy, don't be absurd!'

The wheel turns; the stage, too. Round and round goes the spread-eagled victim; round and round goes the Justice Killer. Red-garbed, lissom, he might be a bizarre, immense bird, intent upon deadly courtship. On the fifth turning of the stage, he shall tear away the coverings from the victim's body, exposing the nakedness beneath; then, as they pass before the royal box, shall come the first of many graceful,

220

almost delicate strokes that turn the tender flesh, with exquisite slowness, into a mutilated, bloody mass.

The crowd stamps. Bays.

'Make him stop, I say!'

'Shimmy, what's wrong with you?'

'The girl-boy! He'll kill her!'

'Really, child! You've seen it before!'

'Not the girl-boy!'

'Shimmy, stop shimmering!'

Exasperated, the Caliph is gesturing to his daughter, leaning forward awkwardly, golden mask askew. Vizier Hasem clutches the girl's arm, or would do, but his forgetful hand sweeps through her phantom being.

To the slaves: 'The curtains! Pull the curtains!'

But at that moment, another curtain is torn away. Already Princess Bela Dona is confused; now, suddenly, her confusion is redoubled as the Justice Killer wrenches the fabric from the wheel.

She gasps.

So does her father. He claps the far-glass to an eyehole of his mask. 'Give me that glass!'

'Hasem!'

'But it's impossible!'

'A girl, you said! Can't you tell the difference?'

'Treachery!' The Vizier shakes his fist at the sky.

❈ ❈

POLTY (*gasps*): I don't believe it!

BEAN: Polty, who is it?

POLTY: Bean, are you blind?

BEAN (*he sees now*): The Vaga-boy! No!

CAPTAIN PORLO: Me lord! Me lord!

Dazed, LORD EMPSTER *stares into the distance.*

BEAN: Polty! We've got to do something—

CAPTAIN PORLO: It's Master Raj! Me lord, make them stop—

BUBY *the monkey shrieks and cries. Still* LORD EMPSTER *stares ahead, but he barely sees the Circle of Sacrifice. Entranced, like a worshipper, he gazes only upon the Shimmering Princess.*

POLTY: Bean, you're brilliant! First you find my heart-sister! Now this! Of course we must do something! Why, the Vaga could lead us straight to the Vexing! We've got to question him before he's killed—

BEAN (*bursting out*): No, no, no—

221

POLTY: Steady on, Bean! Hey, what's wrong with you—?

✳ ✳

Five colours flashed in Rajal's eyes. First came a dazzling glare of gold as his dark shroud was ripped away. For an instant, he plunged into a new, different blindness; then the gold gathered to a point and flashed.

The scimitar, arcing through the turning air.

Blue. The flash subsided. Only the sky.

Red. His killer's arm rose again.

Green. The shimmer of an aqueous glass.

Then came purple. The girl from the glass.

Rajal cried out, but not in pain. The wheel had turned him upright, facing the Princess. Now, in a vision, he saw his lost crystal, glowing like a luminescent heart inside her breast. Could the vision be real?

Suddenly Princess Bela Dona screamed. She flung out her hands. Imploringly, she leaned towards the stranger-boy, as if this boy were in truth no stranger, but really her beloved girl-boy after all.

The wheel turned.

The stage, too.

In an instant, the blade would sweep down, slicing flesh.

'Shimmy! What are you doing?'

'The child's gone mad!'

Then the girl's father cried out, too, as suddenly her form seemed to flicker like lightning. Purple light fizzed from her hands, striking the naked boy on the wheel.

The girl screamed again.

She staggered back, collapsing into the looking-glass.

She was gone.

Then came the explosion. Startled by his daughter's strange magic, the Caliph thought at first that this was more magic still, a magic yet stranger, yet more dangerous.

Screams.

Running feet.

The gallery sagged.

Corpses in the dirt.

'Hasem! What's happening?'

✳ ✳

The Justice Killer fell down, dead.

In the next moment Rajal felt hands tugging at his bonds. A shadow passed across his dazzled eyes. Wildly he imagined Princess Bela Dona, swooping down to save him, magically, from on high.

But it was not the Princess.

222

'Shit, shit!' came a familiar, common voice.

The wooden stage rocked. Powder filled the air. This was no magic, but a Ouabin bomb, then another, and another, exploding in the midst of the crowded square.

'Flee for your lives!' came the cries from all around.

The voice again: 'Quick! Quick!'

Rajal was free.

※　※

'The Ouabin!'

In an instant, it was over. White-clad riders burst into the square, wielding swords and burning brands. A violent battering shook the royal box. Then the door flew open and a Ouabin warrior stepped forward boldly, thrusting a scroll into the Caliph's hands. The fat little monarch pushed the mask from his sweaty face. It clattered to the floor. Shaking, he attempted to unroll the scroll, then thrust it at his Vizier with a frustrated squeal.

'Hasem, what does it say?'

'Not much,' said the Vizier grimly.

'Hasem! I said, what does it—?'

'Read it, Oman. It's for you, after all.'

The little man faltered, '*Greetings, Great One* . . . Now that's nice, isn't it, Hasem?'

Angrily the Vizier snatched back the scroll, spitting out the words into the Caliph's startled face.

Your city is surrounded. Resistance is useless, but needless too. In peace we come, to liberate your realm from the thrall of Sultan Kaled, and your daughter, too, from the bondage of her betrothal. As all these Realms of Unang shall now be mine, so Princess Bela Dona shall be my bride.

I wait upon you in your palace forthwith.

Your friend in faith
RASHID AMR RUKR

END OF PART TWO

PART THREE

Lovers and Strangers

Chapter 33

THE CURSE OF KALED
(continued)

'Young Prince, are you sure?'

'Not sure I can bear it. But sure I must try.'

'I only fear I might do you harm.'

'Good Simonides, but how?'

'How? Indeed, I am a fond, foolish old man. I would have you grow to acquire great wisdom; yet, too, I would not spoil your innocence.'

'Where is my innocence,' Dea said sadly, 'after the night when my friend was burned?'

Simonides nodded and the boy gripped his hand, urging the old man to continue. They were in their fragrant grove again, drinking green tea. Above them, through the whispering leaves, the sky was hard and clear with its cerulean sheen. Laggardly a butterfly fluttered about their heads, and through the foliage came the familiar, strange twitterings of the Targon Retainers. Simonides knew it was dangerous to go on with this story. But he was an old man, and would soon be dead. Dea was Heir Unquestioned, and beyond harm. The truth must be told. Simonides sipped his green tea and drew in a deep, wheezing breath.

'Dea, I have told of the youthful idyll of your father's life with Mala, and the scientific researches which once so entranced them. I have told how your father was declared Heir Unquestioned, and married to the beauteous Lady Ysadona. Then, too, you have learnt of the Ouabin wars, in which young Lord Malagon would fight, while protocol prevented your father from joining him on the fields of praise. What a sad, embittered young man your father became! But alas, his troubles were only beginning.

'The campaign against the Ouabin was a long and vicious one. Eagerly your father awaited the dispatches that arrived with maddening slowness from the Wilderness of the West, poring over the scrolls for any mention of Mala. Imagine his shock when he learnt that Lord Malagon had been captured by the Ouabin! Seething in a turmoil of contrary emotions, your father first felt crushed by a burden of sorrow, thinking of his childhood days with Mala; then, like returning bile, the late bitterness rose in him again and basely he exulted at the thought that Mala had now been certainly and condignly punished. Sometimes your father would curse the Sultan, your great-father, who had not let him ride forth at Mala's side; sometimes he cursed himself for concealing from Mala the rage and indignation that had now, perhaps for ever, been denied their natural vent.

'Now your father was an object of great sympathy in the Court, for all knew – or thought they knew – how he had loved his lost friend. Only your great-father was insensitive. One night, at a royal banquet, he chided your father that he should smile so little when, after all, he was to repair to the arms of the lovely Ysadona. Your father leapt up and would have attacked your great-father, if restraining hands had not intervened. Sadly the courtiers shook their heads, ascribing your father's outburst to the strength of his grief. The Sultan only gazed upon his son with a sour irony and enquired whether even Ysadona was enough to quench such fiery passions. Had the hotness of your father's lust turned his wits? Very well, let him find a second bride, if one was not enough!

'Ah, but your father was to take that taunt to heart.

'For three, perhaps four moonlives this sad situation persisted. Then came the next dispatch, and suddenly all was changed. Mala was free! Far from dying at the hands of the brutal Ouabin, the young officer had led a rebellion behind Ouabin lines, breaking open the way for a glorious Unang victory. The war was over, and young Lord Malagon was coming home a hero! Imagine the rejoicing that filled Kal-Theron! *Mala, Mala* rang the hero's name, shouted from the housetops, shouted in the streets. How warmly the courtiers congratulated your father, that he should be served by so great a man!

'I was with your father often in those days, and knowing him as I did, needed only to look into his eyes to see that all affection for his old friend had now been extinguished. From that time on I was fearful for Mala, though I knew that your father would smile and smile, pretending to share in the general joy. When Mala rode back through the gates of Kal-Theron, your father was there to welcome him, standing at the head of the official party. Passionately he embraced his friend before the crowd. What cheering filled the streets! What prayers rang on the air! That day, or so it seemed, a new era was dawning, symbolised in the embrace of Unang's newest hero and this wise and learned young Sultan-in-Waiting. Who, among that enraptured crowd, could even have dreamed of the evil that festered in your father's heart? Who could have guessed that already he was plotting a terrible, final revenge upon the friend who had loved him and, in loving him, sought only to serve him well?

'The Mala who returned from the Ouabin Wars was, of course, rather different from the Mala who had left. The young nobleman had acquired a gravity, a manhood that put your father's into the shade. I think, too, there was a new wistfulness in Mala, a spiritual quality I would glimpse sometimes when he told of his adventures – not of charging cavalry, of flashing scimitars, of flight and pursuit across the arid wastes, but of shifting sands in a blood-red sunset, of a caravan becalmed in a palm-filled oasis, of the strange high songs of a desert singer.

'I remember the first time he spoke of such things. It was late in the evening and I was alone with him. His voice, like the konar-lights, was gentle and low, and for a moment it seemed I heard a faint, mysterious music, floating on the air like incense smoke. Only slowly did I realise that Mala was speaking of his time not with the imperial army, but with the Ouabin. I felt a shudder of excitement and alarm. In the event I was right to be alarmed, for if the Ouabin had unlocked something in Mala, perhaps it was something that should never have been opened. Thus the sequel would prove; but at first it seemed that evil could have no purchase where Mala was concerned. The new wistfulness in him seemed to bode only good, for certainly it was this that now made the young hero fall hopelessly, desperately in love.

'Dea, you are perhaps still unaware that your mother, the beauteous Ysadona, was one of a pair of sisters. The Ambassador's other daughter was called Ysabela, and familiarly they were known as Dona and Bela. Your Aunt Bela was the younger of the pair. At Court she had always been veiled, but by all accounts was the equal of your mother; some were even certain that she must surpass her. The surmise, I am afraid, was convincing; for through Bela's silken robes were visible the lineaments of a form so fair as to shame even the lady in the moon, in the days before her face was pocked with sickness. What man would not long to clutch her to his heart?

'So it was that young Lord Malagon sued for her hand. To many it seemed a perfect outcome, binding your father and his Vizier-to-be in carnal possession of the two Princesses. Eagerly the Court looked forward to Mala's First Blood. Joyously the eunuchs planned an elaborate ceremony. All this was to reckon without your father, whose own eyes had set upon his young bride's sister.

'Would things have been different, I sometimes wonder, had Mala chosen another as the object of his love? Perhaps any choice Mala had made would have inflamed the envy of his friend. Yes; but I wonder if what began as envy could so soon have grown into passionate love? For this was the tragedy that lay coiled in wait, not merely that Mala loved the beauteous Bela, and that your father, through spite alone, would keep her from his arms . . . but that your father loved her too!

'What happened next has become a legend at Court, one of our saddest, one of our bitterest. In the Adages of Imral it is said that what is brightest, perhaps especially what is brightest, must come to be tarnished in the end; but who could have imagined that Mala's fall from grace should come so soon, so suddenly? Shock gripped the capital. To think that Lord Malagon, hero of the day, was really a treacherous Ouabin agent! Where it came from, the evidence of his treachery, was to remain a mystery; it sufficed that the Sultan, your great-father, was convinced beyond question.

'To this day there are those who shake their heads when Mala's name is mentioned, lost in reveries of astonished sorrow; though if treasonous thoughts mingle with their sorrow, of course they will not say. Then there are those who blaze in righteous anger, not at Mala, not at your great-father, but at the Ouabin-kind who first abducted that brave and loyal nobleman, then twisted his being to their own depraved ends. In any case, all agree that in these Lands of Unang there was no night blacker than the night Lord Malagon was paraded in fetters to the Sanctum of the Flame; no silence deeper than that after your great-father, his head hanging low, emerged again on the ruby steps to declare that the traitor had paid the ultimate price.

'That night your father stood on those steps too, his face held taut. It must have seemed that grief had stunned him like a blow. In truth, how riven his heart must have been, burning at once with secret love and secret hatred! Few indeed were those, like me, who guessed the truth; fewer still, those who even imagined the possibility of protest. Many times, with a heart thudding hard, I steeled myself to remonstrate with my erstwhile pupil; once I would have gone to your great-father's chamber, but cowardice overcame me. I cursed myself for it then, and I curse myself for it now. But Mala had been denounced by sacred decree, and even to question that decree was a crime punishable by death.

'The irony of it all was that your father would not even receive the reward of his perfidy. On the day after Mala went to the Flame, your father summoned his father-by-marriage and declared that, satisfied with the Ambassador's first daughter, he now wished to marry the second. Many were the proofs of passion your father would have cited; noble was the desire he began to state, that he might redeem the stricken woman whose lover had been so base a rascal.

'The Ambassador would not listen, for though he neither knew nor cared how your father had treated his first wife, his sense of royal protocol was keen as a blade. With a cry, he stemmed the fine words, demanding to know if your father would insult him.

'"Insult you? Heart-father, what can you mean?"

'"Prince of the Line, have you forgotten who I am?"

'"You are the Lanian Ambassador—"

'"Yes, and brother of the Lanian King! What do you think my daughter is, that you would use as her as your concubine?"

'Confusion overspread your father's face, and he could only stare as

230

his father-by-marriage informed him that his daughter could never have married a mere Vizier-to-be. The thought was monstrous, but worse still was the proposal that your Aunt Bela should be any man's *second* wife!

'Scarlet with rage, the Ambassador swept from the meeting, declaring that he would have an official apology, or Unangs henceforth would be bitter enemies of all true sons of Lania Chor. To be sure, such words were rash when his eldest daughter was married to the Sultan-in-Waiting, but the Ambassador, a cold and vain man, thought only of the affront to protocol. In the days that followed, much abasement on the part of many courtiers was required to dampen the Ambassador's fury, as slowly he was brought to understand that your father had meant no insult. His mind was disordered by grief, that was all.

'At last the Lanian forgave his son-by-marriage, and when your father asked if there were any further atonement he could make, the Ambassador invited him to send a fine gift to Princess Bela's wedding.

'"H-Her wedding?" said the Prince blankly, for in his heart he still hoped that Bela would be his.

'"Indeed," smiled the Ambassador. "You do not think so fine a lady could long go unwed? Just yesterday I received back the contract, signed and sealed, from Vizier Hasem. The girl is to belong to your brother, the Caliph of Qatani, and a fine First Blood I am sure she will make him."

'Now, had your father been Sultan already, his response would perhaps have been to have the Ambassador killed, then to take possession of the daughter, be the consequences what they may. Instead he was obliged to embrace his father-by-marriage, beg forgiveness for his late follies, and profess himself delighted at Princess Bela's impending joy.

'The strain was great. How I recall the ceremony when your aunt departed for the Caliphate of Qatani! Earnestly I studied my young master, praying that he could hold in the passions that must have threatened to burst from him like lava. On and on went the maddening formalities, but in the event my fears proved needless. Your father only bowed with a stately demeanour, imperturbable as stone as the woman he loved left to be joined in wedlock with his brother.

'Ah, but what must have gone through his mind as her caravan wended its way to Qatani? Perhaps at last he had resolved, in all sincerity, to accede to the dictates of fate. Perhaps he saw the folly of his passion, regretting the evils he had done in your aunt's name. Would that it were so! But perhaps, even then, my young master's mind was evolving some new, more desperate scheme. In the event, I would learn soon enough that he was far from reconciled to the loss of his beloved.

'One thing overshadowed the ceremony of leave-taking. If, officially, it was an occasion of joy, still it could not be concealed from Bela that her sister was gravely ill. Alas for your mother! Undoubtedly your father's brutality had hastened her decline, but this sad young woman was loyal to the last, speaking no word of the cruel truth. Perhaps she was a fool, but after all, what could she say? In these Lands of Unang, a wife can speak freely no more than her husband's slaves; why, she is enjoined to silence as to a sacred duty. But oh, to think that any man, let alone one of royal blood, could harbour so little kindness for a woman great with child! Now, separated from her beloved sister, your mother faced her greatest challenge, and it was a challenge she would fail. Her confinement was to be an agony to her, and she died, poor Dea, on the night when you were born.

'Your father was inconsolable. Sadly – but admiringly, too – the courtiers remarked how much he had loved her, how sorely he would miss her, how tragic it was that a man so young should have suffered so grievously. Some said his emotions had driven him mad, and it is true that for a time he was crazed; but if this were so, it was neither with sorrow nor regret, but with anger, raging anger that he had married your mother, when her sister was all he wanted in the world. Your father vowed that somehow, someday, Bela would be his, and cursed his confinement in the imperial city.

'In the moonlives that followed he became morose, and there were those who despaired of him; but a sunround or so later, his demeanour changed. One day, your great-father was out hunting mountain lions when suddenly he was thrown from his steed and killed. When the news reached the city, your father knew that his hour had come. From now on he was Sultan, with all a Sultan's powers!

'"Tutor," he would say to me sometimes, "my every command is law."

'At this, I smiled at him, and laughed when he laughed, but I was pretending to a gladness I could not feel. What new wickedness would my old pupil unleash, now there were no constraints upon him?

'But of course, there was the Flame.'

'The Flame?' Dea said, with a strained eagerness.

By now, the afternoon was far advanced, and the sorrow in the boy's heart was almost too much to bear. But he knew he must hear the story to its end. His heart thudded hard, and he prayed only that Simonides had strength enough to continue.

'Simonides?'

Suddenly Dea was alarmed. The old man had slumped back in his wicker chair. His breathing was a harsh, painful rasping. Fearfully Dea clutched the old man's hand again. How cold it was! In a piping voice, then a cracking shriek, the young prince called for the Targon Retainers.

'Heir?' came the five voices. 'O Heir, what ails you?'

'It's Simonides, you fools! Councillor Simonides!'

Chapter 34

THE REALM OF UN

'Rainbow? Rainbow, where are you?'

Deep amongst the fragrance of violets and yarrow, henna, bluebells, daisies and a hundred other unexpected flowers, Jem pushed his way through sun-speckled shadows. Through the foliage sounded birdsong and the burbling of a fountain. Somewhere far away, on a path strewn with pebbles of mauve and green, Rainbow had suddenly bounded away, barking excitedly. Jem had started after him, but the brilliant creature had vanished swiftly amongst the twists and turns of the dense, mysterious garden.

'Rainbow? Didn't I hear you bark again?'

Turning another corner, Jem came across the fountain, a curious undulating tower of ochre-coloured rock, bulbous at the bottom, tapering at the top. He cocked his head on one side and surveyed it, wondering what its shape was meant to suggest. Only after some moments did he realise it was a flame – a giant flame. Water slithered down the stiff curves of the sides and gathered beneath the flame in a mossy bowl.

Gratefully Jem splashed his face, then slumped down sleepily against the cool, carved pedestal. The scent from the flowers was like Jarvel-smoke, and heat hovered round him like a tangible thing. He had shrugged off his elaborate robes long before; now he wore only a bright red loincloth. He ran a hand over his chest, clutching at the bag that contained the crystal. The fabric was sleek with sweat and the crystal was warm.

Jem looked up through the canopy of leaves. The sun was at its height; but he had set out, long ago, in the cool of the evening! What had gone wrong with time? Would it ever be right again? By now Jem could barely imagine how long it had been since he had found himself in Almoran's domain. Mornings flashed by; afternoons lurched like a drunken dancer; nights seemed suspended in a timeless void as he lay, sweltering, on his big bed. He was living in luxury, but all the time he was tired and hot, and much of the time he was hungry too. Sometimes the banquets seemed far apart; sometimes there was barely a gap between the end of one and the beginning of another. It did not matter: Jem ate and ate, but as soon as the guests were gone and the dishes cleared away, he felt as if he had not eaten at all. Almoran spoke of the oblivion-cloth, and the after-effects of its dark magic. Jem was beginning to wonder if the magic was Almoran's.

More than once, as he passed in and out of the banqueting hall, Jem had attempted to speak to the other guests. It was useless: they only grinned and laughed and clapped him on the back, or replied in languages he could not understand. The girlish youth went blank if asked the simplest question. How Jem wished Dona Bela could speak! But she had come to be as distant to him as the guests. He knew only one thing: that he must leave this place. At last night's banquet, or that afternoon's, he had suggested politely to Almoran that soon the time would come when he must be on his way.

'You would join your friends in Qatani?'

'Yes, how did you know?'

But Almoran said only, 'Prince, you are hardly fit to travel.'

'It can't be far! We were nearly there when . . .'

'Prince, it lies across vast desert wastes.'

'But that's impossible!'

'Prince, you are unwell. You must rest . . .'

Rest, rest . . . that was always the way, but in Almoran's estate, the comforts of sleep were as delusive, it seemed to Jem, as those of the banquets.

No, he would not sleep, he would not. He would think, think clearly, about this strange place . . . how to get away . . . how to join his friends . . .

❈   ❈   ❈

The voice called back: 'This way!'

Rajal ran, fleeing with the others. In the crush, he could not glimpse his rescuer's face, only the dirty beret and the dun-coloured, flapping rags. He pushed his way forward, shouldering past stragglers, skidding though squashed melons, cabbages and coffee beans, sticky honey and toffee-sticks; winding his way round upended tables, boxes, broken urns, dead bodies bleeding into the cobblestones. For a time he held the black shroud, gripping it round his shoulders; then it was caught, or ripped away. Rajal was naked, but no one cared. Horses reared. There were screams, shouts. Sabres flashed blindingly in the bright air.

The voice again: 'This way!'

They plunged into an alley. Crushed against a wall, while the tide tumbled past of turbans, robes, jingling purses, clutched loot, camels, horses, cats, dogs, rabbits, rats, Rajal saw his rescuer clearly at last. The face beneath the beret turned to him eagerly, but already Rajal had seen the sores that blotched the neck.

'Scabs! How did you get here?'

'Jumped ship, didn't I? Keeping the *Cata* under armed guard, they are, them dirty foreigners. Don't think I'd stand for that, do you, Master Raj? Slipped over the side and held me breath, I did. That there salt water didn't half sting me sores, I'll tell you . . .'

Rajal held out his hand. 'I owe you my life, Scabs.'

'Spit.'

'Scabs?'

Scabs spat in his palm. Rajal did the same and they gripped hands firmly. There was no time to say more. Flames were tearing through the galleries above the square, and the white-garbed horsemen were riding hither and yon, slashing with their sabres at passers-by.

They ran again. Rajal's ribs ached; his sides were scratched; his feet burned in the dust of the alley. Painfully he blundered into a pile of boxes, then into a post.

They turned a corner. The next alley was empty, and deep in shadow. Rajal doubled over, almost slumping to his knees, but Scabs darted back and grabbed him by the arm. The next thing Rajal knew, he was being bundled, like a sack, into a trapdoor that opened in the ground.

Gulls wheeled above. There was a stench of fish.

Rajal fell heavily.

❉　❉　❉

Jem dozed, lulled by the burbling of the fountain. He must have slumped on his side, stretching full-length, for when he awoke, pebbles were pressing into his side and a rough tongue was licking his face.

His eyes flickered open. 'Rainbow! I've found you.'

'Hardly,' came a soft voice. '*We*'ve found *you*.'

Jem looked up. Through the canopy of leaves speared a bright ray of sunshine, enveloping the figure before him in an ethereal haze. For a moment, Jem thought he must be dreaming, but the girl was real enough. He scrambled up, suddenly self-conscious in his near-naked state.

'Lady, I . . . I thought you couldn't speak!'

'Here I can. This is not the real world, and the spell that binds me there need not constrain me here.'

'Spell? Real world? I . . . I don't understand!'

The girl would have replied, but at that moment Rainbow barked and she turned quickly, aware before Jem of a presence behind them. It was the girlish youth, bidding them join their host for the evening's entertainments.

'Evening?' murmured Jem.

There was no need to wonder any longer. Before they reached the house again, the sun had plunged rapidly beneath the horizon. Wild thoughts filled Jem's mind, but a strange abashment too. Confused, he gazed after the strange girl. How he longed to seize her, clutch her and shake her, demanding to know everything she could tell him, at once! With a pang he saw that Rainbow trotted beside her, for all the world as if he were *her* dog. But then, thought Jem, perhaps he was.

On the steps of the house, the girl turned sharply, whispering in Jem's ear, 'Meet me at midnight. At the flame-fountain.'

Jem's heart lurched.

✳   ✳   ✳

'Scabs?'

Rajal came round slowly. In a dingy, subterranean chamber, he found himself lying on a pile of dirty clothes. From beams above his head hung crude curtains of sacking, partitioning the shabby space. The air was foetid. Rajal could see neither windows nor doors, but through the curtain closest to him seeped a sickly light, and the sinister hiss of a burning lamp. Dampness oozed through the walls and he fancied he could smell the sea.

'Scabs?'

A shadow came into the light and the curtain slid back. Rajal looked up into an unfamiliar face, clear of pustules, lean and boyish, with a wisp of beard. Its owner bore some resemblance to a goat and, like a goat's, his expression seemed at once foolish, stubborn and cunning.

'Awake?' the goat-boy grinned. 'You took a bit of a tumble when you came down the hatch.' He jerked his thumb towards a treacherous flight of stairs that seemed to lead up only to the ceiling. Then he indicated the dirty clothes. 'You'd better root round for some habs, eh?'

'Pardon?'

'Habiliments!'

Rajal blushed, realising he was still naked. Quickly he sorted through the pile, retrieving a ragged tunic and a pair of ill-fitting breeches. Among much else, he found a beret like the one Scabs had worn, almost jamming it on his head until he saw a familiar streak of pus, smeared across the band. With a shudder, he cast the beret aside.

His new companion grinned. 'We change each time we go out, usually. Well, we're supposed to.'

'Why?'

'Don't want to be recognised, do we? Traced?'

Rajal's brow furrowed. 'What is this place?'

'There's some who call it the Realm of Un. Me, I wouldn't go quite that far.'

The grin again. Cross-legged, Rajal's companion sat up on a barrel, producing a clay pipe that he proceeded to clean with an intentness rather – inevitably, thought Rajal – like that of a goat, nuzzling at some irritant.

Rajal looked about him. Already he had guessed he must be in the docklands, perhaps in the cellar beneath a sailors' tavern. Here and there hung a hammock, and crude bundles and bedrolls were stashed between the many crates and barrels. A door in the wall was bolted and barred, as if what it contained was an important secret. Through the floorboards above came creakings, murmurs, and from time to time a shout, or burst of coarse laughter.

'You're lucky, you know,' the goat-boy said.

Rajal raised an eyebrow. 'Lucky? Why?'

'Oh, I like that! Bound on the wheel, and wonders *why*. To be here, I mean. Besides, I know what you are.'

'What do you mean?'

'Saw the mark on your leg, didn't I? I mean, we don't see your type much round here. Stamped out in these parts, you lot were. Why, if I were you I'd be glad to have fallen among thieves.'

'Thieves?' Rajal was alarmed. 'Where?'

Laughter. 'Here! Me!' With a taper ignited from the hissing lamp, the goat-boy lit his pipe. 'Oh, you mean the others? Well – out thieving, aren't they? Stands to reason. Good day for it, too. One of us should always hold the fort, Eli says. My turn today.'

'Who's Eli?' Rajal said innocently.

A snort came in reply, 'Who's Eli? Why, he's a great man in Qatani, is Cousin Eli. He's in charge of us, sort of – though of course, Eli's got too many interests to look after the day-to-day operations down here. Needs a deputy,' the boy added, preening. 'And to think, only a moonlife ago I was a common-as-muck mixer, stuck in the outlands, till the magic that brought me here!'

Pipe-smoke filled the cellar, mingling foully with the oil that burned in the lamp.

'Magic?' said Rajal.

The goat-boy screwed up his face. 'Well, must have been, is what I say. Eli just says I had a knock on the head. All funny I was, when I turned up here, see. I remember wishing I were anywhere but where I was when – well, when I made the wish. Fell off a cliff, I think I did. Perhaps that was the knock on the head ... I remember being in the middle of the sea. Then I wished I was dry. Then I wished I was in Qatani, and here I was.'

Rajal could not quite follow, and only smiled politely.

'Funny,' sighed the goat-boy, 'I've wished a lot of things since then, but none have come true like that. No, it wasn't magic. Knock on the head, like Eli says. Silly dream. Still, what would you do if you could really have your wishes? That's what I wonder.'

For his part, Rajal wondered about more practical matters. There were many questions he would have asked, but before he could speak there was a commotion above, the trapdoor burst open, and thundering down the stairs came a band of ragged urchins. Breathless, laughing, they tossed strings of beads, golden goblets, purses of coins, and myriad other valuables into a jumble on the floor.

The goat-boy grinned and with the stem of his pipe pointed out the members of his intrepid little band.

'Vaga-boy, meet Littler . . . Stork . . . Fish . . . Blubber . . . Cheese . . . and I think you know Scabs. If this is the Realm of Un, then these are the Unners. What about you, then, Vaga-boy? Got a name?'

The boys ranged in age, it seemed, from First to Fourth cycle, and their sizes and shapes were just as diverse. They were an extraordinary sight and for a moment Rajal could only study them, astonished.

Again, the goat-boy asked him if he had a name.

Rajal flushed. 'Rajal of Xal-blood.'

The grin again. 'Hand?'

'Pardon?'

A roll of the eyes; grabbing Rajal's palm, the goat-boy slapped it, hard. 'Ouch!'

'Faha Ejo,' came the grin. 'Of blood too mixed to know what, or where, or who. Welcome to the Unners, Raj. Shape up, and it's all the ferment you can drink, a safe place to sleep and a band of brothers. You're with us?'

Chapter 35

TAINTED LOVE

'Up the stairs, bitch!'

'Let me go!'

'Not a chance!'

Taking the stairs two at a time, Polty surged ahead, tugging savagely on the golden chain. Behind him Cata jerked and writhed, heedless of the pain in her manacled wrists. On the broad landing she lunged forward, crashing into Polty as if to send him tumbling back down the stairs. He staggered, but she could not bring him down; she punched him, scratched him, but could not break his grip. Round and round his forearm coiled Cata's chain, just where he had wrapped it when he found her in the rubble. He would not let go, he would never let her go.

He caught her in his arms. She smelled a rankness in his breath, like the odour of evil, gusting from behind the handsome façade. 'Stupid little fool, do you think you'll escape me now?'

'Polty! You're hurting her!'

Breathless, Bean came floundering up the stairs.

'Keep out of this, Bean!'

Polty fumbled for the key to their apartment. With a crash of chains he pushed Cata inside, staggering again as she sprawled to the floor. He turned back in the doorway. Grabbing Bean's collar, he spat savagely, 'Where's Burgrove?'

'I d-don't know, Polty. He r-ran away.'

'Then keep him away. My heart-sister and I have business to attend to, and desire no interruptions. Go and . . . go and find that Vaga, hm? Understand?'

With that, Polty swung the door shut in Bean's face.

'Understand?'

Bean heard the clunk of the turning key. Miserably, like a dog, he slumped outside the door. Afternoon light spilled around him like milk, sour and sickly. He looked about the landing, then down, then up the staircase. Where were the guards? They were nowhere to be seen. Through the windows came sounds of running and cries, some of despair, some of glee. Fires roared through the city square and looters were raiding the market stalls. There were hoofbeats. Shots.

What did it matter, what happened outside? Closer, by his ear, Bean heard Polty pull the key from the lock. Bean swallowed hard and tried to still his pounding heart.

He pressed his eye against the keyhole.

✻　✻　✻

Polty turned, secreting the key inside his robes. He turned his wrists, unwrapping Cata's chain.

'What is this place?' she muttered.

'Heart-sister, where but love's bower?'

'Don't make me sick!'

The blinds were closed, but the sun pressed through the fabric, filling the chamber with a jaundiced light. Cata's eyes flickered over chamber-pots and dirty linen, snot-filled handkerchiefs and dandruff-filled combs. In the middle of the chamber was a long, cracked cheval-glass. In a corner was a huge, blood-like pool of wine, congealed and stuck thickly with flies and ants and moths. The stench was appalling.

'You can't keep me here!'

'On the contrary, heart-sister, I can do as I will. And where do you belong, but with me?'

The chain clattered to the floor.

Still the manacles circled Cata's wrists, but she moved away, as if she were free. Polty had to laugh. Like an eel, the dragging chain swished back and forth.

He stepped on it.

Cata jerked.

He lifted his foot.

She reeled away, crashing into the furniture.

Polty laughed again. He grabbed at the chain.

Cata blundered back to him. 'I'll scratch out your eyes if you touch me!'

He was too quick.

Polty caught her wrists. Grinning, he taunted, 'So, my little puss-cat's claws are sharp? What a pity if we should have to draw them! But heart-sister, I hardly think you shall be so silly. Hurt me, and I hurt you twice over! What will your crippler-boy say, I wonder, should your limbs be mangled as his own once were?'

'Leave Jem out of this! Don't even speak of him!'

'Actually, heart-sister, I had no desire to do so. How pleasant to see we are of one mind.' Deftly Polty pirouetted across the floor. Lifting one leg of a heavy divan, he slipped a link of the chain around it, then flopped himself down in a languorous pose. 'More permanent arrangements can of course be made. But come, heart-sister, join me, join me.'

With a grimace, Cata only tugged at her chain.

Polty leaned back, lighting a tobarillo. Looking at Cata, he could not help but smile. Was there ever a girl he had loved so much? Her lips. Her eyes. Her skin. Her hair. Exaltation swept through his being as he thought of the pleasures that would soon be his.

Needless to say, force would be required.

But only at the beginning, of that much he was sure.

Idly, Polty stroked the bulge beneath his robes. His eyes became hooded, sensual, and his gaze strayed to Cata's reflection, cracked in the mosaic of the broken mirror. Did she know she was reflected there? Polty smiled. For so long, for too long, he had known but phantoms of his lost beloved. Now, soon, he would clutch the living flesh!

Greedily, he eyed the heaving breasts. 'A pretty gown, my dear, if a little soiled. But were you not given Unang clothes?'

'I tore them up.'

Polty tut-tutted. 'A sensual madness?'

'To help someone, if you must know.'

'Help them?'

'Escape!'

Polty arched an eyebrow. 'So that's what you call it? Heart-sister, if I hear some other fellow has seen the treasures that are mine, and mine alone, you understand that my – my *honour* shall compel me to kill him.'

Cata spat, 'Your honour!'

'Indeed, my dear, for what is a husband who fails to avenge the virtue of his wife?'

'You're mad! What are you talking about?'

Polty drew back on his tobarillo. 'I thought we weren't going to speak of your crippler-boy.'

'We haven't.'

'No? Then this . . . escape?'

'It wasn't Jem. I don't know where he is.'

'No?'

Cata clashed her manacles back and forth. 'I'm telling you nothing!'

'So I gather. Never mind, my dear: when I have brought you to a proper submission, I hardly imagine we shall have any secrets.'

Polty flicked his eyes to the engorged Penge, still shrouded, of course, but eager to emerge. Could the girl have forgotten the bliss they had shared? High colour played in her cheeks. Her eyes glistened. No, she knew! She was ready! She was a proud one, that was all, but soon her pride would be humbled in the dirt.

Time to begin.

But softly, softly . . . Cata, dear Cata, was no common conquest, undeserving of tenderness and respect.

'Come, heart-sister, sit by your brother.'

241

'You're not my brother.'

'No? Then perhaps it is as well. After all, I am about to make you a proposal ... of marriage.'

Cata gasped. 'Marriage!'

'But heart-sister, of course. Have you forgotten I was once your intended? What a pity your Aunt Umbecca got ideas above her station – or rather, yours. What a lot of bother we could have saved ourselves! But soon, as it happens, you shall be raised to a pinnacle of which your Aunt Umbecca could hardly have dreamed. Well, not for you.'

Polty's eyes glittered, moist with tears. He cast aside his tobarillo, sinking to the floor, his hands clasped together as if in prayer. Imploringly he looked up at the astonished Cata.

'Darling girl, I intend no lewdness. Don't you understand the destiny before you? Don't you understand it is ordained by fate that you are to be one of the great ladies of Ejland – that you are to be ... Lady Veeldrop?'

Cata could only laugh, but mirthlessly.

She turned away, and still saw Polty's face, cleft in twain in the cheval-glass.

She turned back. 'Your father is dead?'

Polty rose. He clutched Cata's manacles, drawing her towards him.

'Dead? But indeed. Didn't you know, he died on the very day you fled my family home? Now why should that be, do you think? Hm? Heart-sister, you have brought much sorrow to the family of Veeldrop. You would pretend to virtue, but does not guilt, just a little, stir in your heart? Here, now, is your chance to allay it. Become my bride, and your sins against my family shall be expunged – oh, a thousand times.'

Again Cata struggled in Polty's grip, but he was tenacious, and growing ardent now. He crushed her against him, hard. His voice came hotly.

'My darling, think of it! We find ourselves in a far-flung, heathen land, but by the laws of the sea, your own Captain Porlo may perform the nuptial rites. We have wasted much time – why waste more, when the days of youth are fleeting? We can honeymoon here in these exotic climes ... why, your dear Porlo shall take us on a cruise, docking at the islands that line this coast, the many sweet realms of coconut and spice. When the sun flames high, beneath the broad leaves of the banyan we shall quench our hot desires; in the balmy evenings we shall bathe, cavorting and laughing, in the foaming surf!'

'Never!' Cata cried, but Polty barely heard.

'For ever? Ah, but no! Shall we tarry too long, when all Agondon society awaits our return, eager to celebrate this finest, this loveliest, this most incomparable addition to its line of noble ladies? What triumph shall be ours, when I carry you home!'

Now Polty's voice dropped to a whisper, and his hand ran caressingly down the front of Cata's gown. 'And shall we tarry, as my bride grows delicate – as her belly, gorged on noble seed, swells to a fecund dome? Darling, darling, what a world of bliss awaits us, as the smiling mother looks up from her travails, to see her dear husband cradling his progeny – his son, his heir, his Little Polty! With what loving fingers shall I smooth his flaming down! Sister, dear sister, but say you will be mine!'

Enraptured, Polty kissed her hands, her neck, whispering endearments. He sought her lips.

Twisting, Cata swung back her manacles and struck him, hard.

He staggered, but only for an instant.

He swooped towards her.

She darted from him, tugging at her chain, the divan juddering, squealing across the floor.

Polty leapt up on it.

Cata jerked back, collapsing into the pool of sticky wine. In the next moment, Polty was astride her, pinning her down. Her eyes blazed with hatred. Back and forth, back and forth, she swirled the spit in her mouth.

If he struck her, she would not care.

Polty did not even wipe away the spit. Suddenly tears burst from his eyes and he sank, heaving with sorrow, on her breast.

All around them rose the sourness of curdled wine.

'Darling,' gasped Polty, 'don't you understand? Since leaving Irion I have known many women – many, too many have moaned beneath me, gorging like gluttons on the milk of my love. What is the pleasure their flesh has afforded me? A bagatelle ... a trinket ... a tinkling chime! Squandering my substance, defiling my name, with what assiduity have I pursued the sex, from the noblest ladies to the harlots of the stews. Yet what have I sought in every pretty face, in every allurement, but a phantom that went by the name of Catayane? Darling girl, think not that I have been faithless, for never in my heart have I loved another. These others were all but counterfeits, pale reflections of you! Would you condemn me to a life of counterfeits? Forgive me, as I forgive the temporary madness that drove you into the arms of the crippler-boy. Sister, we were lovers! Let me love you again!'

By now Cata was sobbing too, overwhelmed first by disgust, then grief for all the horror that seemed to lie before her, and all the horror she had known before. Could it be true that once she had known the bliss of true love, in a petal-strewn bower deep in the Wildwood? How swiftly her happiness, and Jem's, had been blighted – by this monster who reared over her now. He had never been her lover! With shuddering revulsion she recalled his advances, in the dirty back room of the Lazy Tiger.

'Lovers?' she burst out. 'I was a whore!'

'Sister, never!'

'You threw me copper coins! You made me crawl! You laughed at me! You called me a slut!'

'You let me make love to you!'

'Love? Huh!'

'I had you, didn't I?'

'I had no choice!'

Polty leapt up, dragging Cata with him, her hair ripping painfully from the sticky pool. He kicked over the divan. He grabbed the end of her chain. Savagely he swung her round the floor.

'No choice?' he shrieked, raw-voiced. 'Bitch! Dirty bitch! I told you, I've had a thousand women! Don't you think I know a woman's tricks? Don't you think I know when a woman wants it? You'd lick up the spatters from the sheets, you slut!'

'You're sick! I never wanted you!'

'Cata, I love you! You love me too, you know it!'

'Stop it! Stop it!'

Round and round, gasping, cursing, Cata staggered on the golden chain.

She would not fall, she could not!

Polty screamed, 'Marry me or I'll kill you, bitch!'

'Marry you? Never!' Cata cried.

She crashed into the cheval-glass, sending in it spinning rapidly in its frame. Shards of glass showered the floor.

A thumping came at the door.

'Polty! Polty! Stop it, you're hurting her!'

'Keep out of this, Bean! Open that door, and I chop your spine!'

'Polty, please!'

The lock rattled.

Still the cheval-glass spun round and round.

Crazed, Polty flung Cata to the floor. He ripped open his robes and the part he called Penge sprang forth, massive, like an avenging god. Polty clutched it, brandished it like a sword.

'Slut! Whore! What's your crippler got that I can't give you? Has he got this? Has he got this? Bitch! Dirty bitch! I'll prove that I love you!'

'Keep away from me!'

Cata lashed out, kicking.

Polty kicked back. Lunged.

Spin, spin, went the cheval-glass. Wouldn't it stop? But now something else, something stranger, was happening, as the fragments of glass that had rained about the room gathered themselves into a gleaming orb, and that orb began to roll round and round the floor.

The door smashed open. 'Polty! Stop!'

It was the bravest thing Bean had ever done.

Polty rounded on him. Bean foundered, clutching his shoulder. He sank to his knees, ready for the blow.

It did not come.

All this time the cheval-glass had spun, faster and faster in its spindly frame; now, suddenly, the spinning ceased and from the remnants of the mirror flowed a searing light. Thunder shook the floor. The orb rolled, describing a circle round Polty's feet. Then it was that he dropped to his knees, astonished, agonised, crying out, 'Master!'

Cata gasped.

Bean screamed.

Suddenly Polty's skin was an iridescent blue, and his carrot-coloured hair had burst into flames. He rolled on the floor, shrieking, clutching his face.

What could be happening?

Cata didn't know, but she saw her chance.

'Polty, Polty!' Bean cried, hysterical.

Still the light seared from the glass. Still the orb rolled.

Cata grabbed up her trailing chain. She blundered to the door.

Chapter 36

ELI OLI ALI SEES A CHANCE

'Bean!'

Bean was running. Like a jerking puppet he had floundered through the occupied city, his tearful eyes blinded as much to the mounted Ouabin as to broken barricades, flaming houses and terror-struck, jostling crowds. Pummelling his way through the devastated square, he had skidded into the warren of alleys by the docks. Now, clutching at a stitch in his side, Bean collapsed against a filthy wall.

'Bean!'

Seeping from above came the bruised purple of the evening; from close by, he heard the sloshings of the docks. Bean shut his eyes and saw again, rearing up before him, the terrible spectacle of Polty's hair, bursting into flames.

Moonlives ago, when Polty had returned from the Zenzan campaign, Bean had surged on a tide of happiness. That his friend was safe was reason enough, but how much more splendid to learn that Polty – *Major* Veeldrop, if you please! – had not only vindicated his name, but seen it become a byword for heroism. When Bean had learnt they were to be reunited, setting out on a secret mission, his happiness turned to elation. Ah, but how swiftly it faded away!

From the beginnings of the voyage to Qatani, Bean sensed there was something wrong. When he would ask Polty about his exploits in battle, his friend became surly, pushing him away; when he asked about the orders they were following now, Polty accused him violently of insubordination. It was odd; Polty's moods had always been erratic, but now it seemed that something strange, something alien, was gnawing away inside him. Had the Polty who returned from Zenzau not been quite the same as the one who went away?

In Qatani, Bean's unease could only grow. Their mission, as he understood it, was to trade weapons for slaves; this was repulsive enough, but Bean knew there was something else, something darker still. Now, though there was much he did not understand, it seemed to him that all his worst suspicions had been horribly confirmed.

He opened his eyes and saw a rat scurrying up his long, bony leg. He shrieked and kicked the thing away.

'Bean!'

Only now did Bean hear the breathless voice that had been calling him, ringing above the shoutings and clangings from the docks and the high unearthly shrieks of wheeling seabirds. Brushing his eyes, he looked up blankly. Swaying towards him in the gathering evening came a dishevelled, pale figure with straggling whiskers and a golden cravat.

'Burgrove,' Bean muttered. 'But you were . . . lost.'

'Lost?' came the reply. 'What are you talking about, man? It pays for a fellow to keep his head down when the powder-bombs are exploding, what?'

With a guffaw, Burgrove moved closer, assailing Bean with gusts of reeking breath. Bean squirmed and would have broken away, but Burgrove took no notice as he grabbed the young lieutenant in a drunken embrace. Jerking his thumb towards the end of the alley, Burgrove pointed to a sign emblazoned with stars and a crescent moon.

'Buck up, Bean, I've discovered the most marvellous little place – they call it a Jarvel-house, but there's ferment aplenty! Let's drown our sorrows and forget we ever came to this stinking, rotten land!'

❋   ❋   ❋

'Princess?'

The door thudded shut. Quickly Cata turned the key in the lock and slumped, relieved, against the ornate panels. Her chain clattered round her feet, then there was silence. She breathed deeply, conscious of the mysterious, sweet odour that had so entranced her before. Her eyes flickered about the chamber. Bands of heat fell obliquely through the blinds, painting pale stripes across the richly patterned carpets, the painted screens, the looking-glasses draped in filmy gauze.

When she had blundered out of Polty's apartments, Cata would have run anywhere, desperate only to escape the madman's evil magic. But where could she go? Even on an ordinary day, the streets of Qatani were hardly the place for an unveiled woman in a torn gown – a foreigner, too, and an escaped slave! She thought of Lord Empster, Captain Porlo, Rajal. She thought of Jem. But what could she do? Desperately, hopelessly, Cata had been turning, clutching and unclutching her manacled hands, when she felt, nestling in the bodice of her gown, the key that had fallen during Amed's escape. The women's wing! She needed a disguise and she needed a plan. If she could hide with the Princess, perhaps there was a way.

'Princess?' Cata said again, murmuring this time.

The journey back to the women's wing had been difficult and dangerous. In the chaos of the afternoon, guards had left their usual posts, courtyards were empty, corridors unpatrolled; then, too, there were confused slaves, palace officials darting hither and yon, and sudden white-robed parties of Ouabin. More than once Cata had run wildly, chain jangling, flailing away from a presence, a cry; for long moments, she had squeezed behind pillars or screens, barely breathing, but with a heart that hammered hard.

Now she felt a different, stranger tension. Slowly she moved between the looking-glasses and screens, aware of the silence like a ringing in her ears. Something brushed against Cata's arm. She started; turning, she saw it was only the gauze from one of the glasses, fluttering to the floor. Almost with surprise, Cata gazed on the image of her own dishevelled beauty. She supposed she was alone.

'Princess?' whispered Cata. 'Princess, where are you?'

※　※　※

'Burgrove—'

'What's that, Bean?'

'Burgrove, it's Polty! He's—'

'A pig of a fellow! Ha, ha, ha!'

'Burgrove, I'm serious—'

'Do you know, I heard tell that Polty was once fat as a pig – big as a prize porker! Would you believe it, Bean? Ha, ha, ha!'

'He *was* fat, but that's not what I—'

'What's that? He *was* fat? Ha, ha, ha!'

'Burgrove, please—'

'Drink up, man, you're far behind!' Reaching into his jacket, Burgrove produced a dog-eared set of cards, slapping them down on the table. 'Orokon Destiny?'

Bean caught the drunkard's arm, desperate to make him listen, but Burgrove, with another laugh, only shook himself free. Oh, he was useless! All he could do was drink, drink and drink, destroying all vestiges of his glory days. This mission had been a chance for him to redeem himself, but it seemed that 'Jac' Burgrove was irredeemable by now. Juddering back his chair, he rose up, swaying in the smoky gloom, waving the cards back and forth as he called for willing gamblers. Pigtailed Amalians, burly Wenayans, stripy-shirted Tiralons and tur-baned Unangs turned for a moment, uncomprehending, then guffawed in turn as the cards shot from Burgrove's unsteady hand, raining down around them.

The would-be gambler only fumbled at the front of his breeches, considered whether he could make it out into the alley, shrugged, and relieved himself upon the floor instead. Other men had done the same all evening; the boards were awash, like the deck of a ship, and seemed to lurch like a deck, too. Relieved, Burgrove slumped down again, almost missing his chair, swigged back the last of his ferment and bellowed, 'Mother, more!'

'More, more?' Leering contemptuously, a crone in a black headscarf pushed her way roughly towards the Ejlanders, sloshing ferment carelessly into their goblets. Scratching a fresh line on a much-scored slate, she looked round distastefully at her rank domain. All the shutters were open, breezes blew from the sea, but here there was only heat, smoke, ferment, sweat, vomit and piss. Elsewhere in the city, all thoughts were of the Ouabin; in the Khan of the Crescent Moon, the invaders were of no account, unless to make the carousing still more reckless than before.

'To think,' moaned the old woman, 'that once the finest caravanserai on the Dorva Coast was mine! Oh, to be reduced to this!'

'Poor, poor Mother,' Burgrove slurred in an imbecile voice, and fondled the old woman, for all the world as if she were a buxom young beauty. Long sunrounds must have passed since Mother Madana had felt such a touch, but it filled her only with disgust. Denouncing her customer as a dirty infidel, the crone cuffed him and he fell forward, cracking his head against the table.

Bean shook his companion. 'Burgrove—'

'Wh-what?' It seemed that the slap had released something in Burgrove. He raised his reeling head. For a moment, Bean feared his companion would vomit, but instead the drunkard burst out savagely, 'Bean, have I told you how much I hate your friend Polty? Do you know, before I met him, I was the handsomest bachelor in Varby?'

Bean knew it.

'Why, everyone said I had great things ahead of me . . . a fine house . . . a splendid marriage . . . a place at Court . . . oh, my father's was a trade-fortune, it was true, but if any fellow from my rank would end his life as a peer, who could it be but "Jac" Burgrove? Look at me now, Bean, and blame your friend! That viper's destroyed me, and why? I'll tell you why: he envies me, that soldier's bastard, because he knows, try as he might, he'll never be true quality like old "Jac"!'

With that, the ruined man of fashion raised his goblet high, flinging half its contents into the air, and screeched out before he slumped into senselessness, 'Here's to Major Poltiss Veeldrop . . . may he rot in the Realm of Unbeing!'

'Burgrove . . . oh, never mind!' Bean sat trembling, terrified, as if at the foulest blasphemy that had ever assailed his ears. Recklessly he scoffed back his own rotgut, called for more and downed that too. Fire filled his throat.

Meanwhile, fresh guffaws split the air, and much stamping and whistling, as the tars turned to see a party of harlots come staggering into the khan. They were alley-tarts of the lowest sort, but visions of beauty in the squalor that surrounded them. At once, the drunken fellows launched into a raucous, bawdy song.

> *Tides may run swiftly or tides may run slow,*
> *Wenching's a pleasure that all tars should know:*
> *First fix your sights on the slut you desire,*
> *Toss down some coppers, she's yours for the hire!*

Bean shuddered. In the lamplight, he saw blackened stumps of teeth as mouths opened and closed, opened and closed. Even in the melody, there seemed to him something rancid and depraved. By now he too was feeling an intense desire to piss, and wondered shyly if he could manage it without standing up.

> *Wives can't compete with the girls you have bought,*
> *Still, there's a long wait between every port:*
> *Some may hold out for the right juicy plum,*
> *Some choose their fist or the cabin-boy's—*

The chorus broke up, giving way to a flurry of leerings, pawings and jingling coins. Only then did Bean glimpse the greasy fellow who had entered with the harlots, goading them forward contemptuously. *Oh no.* Bean hated the whoremonger; feared him, too. Could he have slipped away easily, he would have done so, but instead he called again for ferment, glugged it nervously, and slumped down in his chair. Fire filled his throat. He thought again about piss, flowing piss.

The khan, by now, was beginning to swirl.

❊   ❊   ❊

What was that light?

Slumping down at last on a lush divan, Cata had fallen into a trance-like sleep. Now her eyes flickered open again to see that an alteration had come over Princess Bela Dona's apartment. It was not merely that the bands of heat, coursing through the blinds, had been replaced by the pallor of moonlight, or that the Princess, nowhere to be seen before, now hunched, rocking, between the looking-glasses. No, it was the looking-glasses that had changed. Now all the gauze had fallen in filmy drifts to the floor, and from each glass streamed a shifting, unearthly glow. The Princess moaned and rocked, her hands against her temples.

'Princess?'

Cata's brow furrowed. Carefully she gathered up her chain in her hands. The strange light filled her with foreboding as she moved forward, stepping into the circle of looking-glasses. That was when she saw that it was no mere glow that shone from the glasses, but shifting, strange images. Cata let her chain fall again. For long moments, her gaze roved from glass to glass. Transfixed, wondering, she saw a lush garden, heavy-hanging with a hundred bright flowers; she saw an ornate, palace-like house; she saw a long, deep pool, reflecting a sky that shifted rapidly, strangely, from midday to moonlight and back again. Then she saw the Princess swishing through the gardens; the Princess at a formal banquet; the Princess petting a dog whose fur was coloured in stripes of purple, green, red, blue and gold.

Slowly understanding came to Cata. The Princess was in touch with the other side of her being, the corporeal self to which she longed to be reunited. Cata would not intrude upon this magical communion, merely let it play its course. She was about to step back, but felt compelled to take one last look into the field of images. That was when she saw the fountain, fashioned in the shape of a flame. And there, sitting beneath the fountain, a young, blond man.

Cata cried out, 'Jem!'

In her astonishment she started forward. She tripped on her chain and her hand swept through filmy substance. The Princess looked up, blazing-eyed. There was a dazzling flash, as if the eyes had exploded. Suddenly the looking-glass images were gone, replaced by a searing maelstrom. Gasping, blinded by the dazzle, Cata lurched back, desperate only to escape the light, the looking-glasses, the shimmering girl.

She backed into a flimsy painted screen.

She staggered behind it.

She collapsed.

※　※　※

'A fine trade tonight, Mother!'

'Dirty ruffians! Why, in my caravanserai—'

'Crone, forget your old hovel!'

'What? For forty sunrounds, it was my life—'

'Pah! I said I'd pay you well, didn't I?'

'Yes, mixer! Pay me to forget my honour, my faith—'

'Faith? What faith did you ever have but money, money, money? Crone, think: would you moulder in that provincial fastness, or prosper beyond your most extravagant dreams, here in the great city? Or perhaps you'd like to go back to that so-called sister of yours, and see what you get from her? Or should I say, *it*? Hasn't old Eli done you proud, when you could have been starving in the streets?'

'You're a wicked fellow, mixer!'

The whoremonger chuckled, and had to agree.

Business, for the time being, was taking care of itself. In the darkness all round the walls of the khan, tars of all nations slammed at the harlots, while others impatiently waited their turns. Bean was in despair. To push his way out into the alley seemed impossible; even to stand might make him sick. Twice he had shaken Burgrove again, but his companion only mumbled and slumped back leadenly. Besides, a more urgent problem gripped Bean, hard. His foggy mind struggled to think. Trying to hide from Eli Oli Ali, he had already slumped down far in his chair; perhaps if he worked his way to the very edge of his seat . . .

'But come, Mother, how go the 'temper-boys?'

'You mean those poor wretches you've left to die?'

'Mother, don't you know a khan needs its 'temper-cell? Here by the docks – why, the 'temper would burn like fire, were there not the 'temper-boys to draw it away!'

'I've heard it may burn in any case!'

'Pah! Would you accuse me of superstition?'

'I'd accuse you of anything, you dirty mixer,' sniffed Mother Madana, adding scornfully, 'Your poor wretches have gone to The Vast, Eli. First thing I did this afternoon was put them out for the dead-boat.'

'What? Dead, and the cell empty!' The whoremonger slapped his newest employee on the head. 'Stupid crone! Casca boasts he has the finest 'temper-cell in the city – now you tell me I have none at all? Stupid, stupid crone!'

Meanwhile, Bean's lanky frame had almost slithered to the floor. The chair creaked beneath him. He was in position now, wasn't he? Ah, but there was the problem of how to direct the flow. The stream – Bean squirmed – would certainly be a powerful one, a sudden unleashing of intolerable pressure. On no account must it gush upwards, splattering off the underside of the table; perhaps if Bean could turn on his side, just a little . . .

Another slap. 'Don't you hit me, mixer swine!'

'Pah! Feisty, eh? Crone, you're not your own mistress any more! Just remember who pays your wages, eh? Damn good wages, too . . . go to Casca Dalla, see what you get! Now get below and bring up some of those brats, they'll have to do!'

'What, your own nephew? Or would you prefer your son?'

'Don't be stupid, I mean the others! Pah! What do you think I am?'

Bean was in position, or almost; spasms shook his frame and he rocked uncontrollably on the rickety chair. With fingers that seemed bound in heavy cloth, he fumbled ineffectually at the front of his breeches. If only he were equipped as Polty was! Suppressed for so long, the conduit of his relief had shrivelled almost to nothingness; perhaps, if he turned just a little more, just a little . . .

Bean fell to the floor with a mighty crash.

'Dirty infidels!' spat Mother Madana. 'Into the alley with them!'

'Wait, I know those two!' said Eli Oli Ali. Stroking his moustaches, he looked down at the Ejlanders, one sprawled across the table, one a tangle of long limbs beneath it. Rapidly, the hot discharge from Bean's fountaining groin was spreading on the floor round the mixer's shoes. A smile flickered over the greasy face. Of all the races he despised – and he despised them all – he had decided, long ago, that Ejlanders were the worst; and of all the Ejlanders he had met, the one he despised most was Major Poltiss Veeldrop. Here, perhaps, was a chance for a small revenge.

'Quick, crone, give me a hand. My services are required back at the palace, but I've just time to make these fellows comfortable in their new home, hm?'

'You're a wicked fellow, mixer, you really are!'

Chapter 37

ELI OLI ALI SEES ANOTHER CHANCE

Eli Oli Ali was still laughing to himself as he made his way back to the Palace of Perfumed Stairs. Ejlanders, indeed! Thought themselves so superior, did they? The fat whoremonger had a spring in his step as he flashed his royal seal at the guards and made his way towards the royal apartments.

It was hardly possible that Eli Oli Ali could regard Ejlanders as his superiors; so far as he was concerned, he had *no* superiors. In Eli's mind, even the Caliph and his Vizier existed only to augment his own glory. If a man is to be Whoremonger Royal, after all, there must be royalty to provide his title – but who would be the hapless ruler of Qatani, despised by his people, unstable on his throne, staggering under the yoke of foreign dominion? Whoremonger Royal, that was the thing! Could Eli doubt he was the envy of all Qatani – the envy, in particular, of Casca Dalla? For luxurious moments, Eli even forgot the threat posed by his hated rival. Oh, he liked his life tonight, he liked it very much!

If he had a regret, just one little regret, it was that a certain Major-sir wasn't in the 'temper-cell where he belonged. Still, what of it? Not only was the flame-haired one far gone in debauchery, but undoubtedly he was running risks – far too many risks – for a fellow in his position! He'd get his come-uppance in the end, no doubt about it. Perhaps Eli might drop a few hints – inklings of blasphemy, that sort of thing – this very night, as he ministered to certain needs of the Caliph and his Vizier.

It was at this point that Eli realised he had taken a wrong turning somewhere along the labyrinthine corridors. Where was he? Shouldn't he have reached the royal apartments by now? Fear – well, just a little – prickled at his neck. Might he not be late already? Getting those Ejlanders into the 'temper-cell, pleasant as the task had been, had wasted valuable time. True, the ferment had been delivered earlier – Eli had made certain of that – but he needed to check that all was in order before the Caliph and his Vizier came back from their banquet. Damn it, which was the way?

Ahead, the corridor was increasingly dark, with konar-lights turned low, spaced at long intervals, and no guards in sight. Eli retraced his steps a little – hm, but would it really be quickest to go back? The way these corridors twisted and turned, one could hardly be sure which was the shortest route.

Shuttered windows ran down the corridor on one side. Opening a pair of these shutters, trying to get his bearings, the whoremonger found himself looking out into a small quadrangle. Filled with flowering bushes and trees, the aromatic square was only one of many in the vast complex of the palace, and nondescript enough, glimmering greyly under the pallid moon. This was no good. Eli was about to turn away when something – a glimmer that was golden, not grey – arrested his attention amongst the trees below. What could it be?

Then he heard voices, drifting up on the still, hot air.

'Golden One, you are sure we are unobserved?'

'You would doubt my powers, Ouabin?'

'Golden One, never. How could I?'

Carefully Eli swung back the shutters, but left open a crack, just the tiniest crack, so he could still listen. The owner of the first voice he recognised easily enough – the Ouabin leader, Rashid Amr Rukr! But who – what – was this mysterious figure with him, and why was the Ouabin meeting him in secret, hidden amongst these dark trees?

'Ouabin, I have helped you to an easy conquest. But now, have you steeled yourself for the greater conquest that must follow?'

'Golden One, it is as you have commanded! Are not all the preparations in train? All shall be done according to precept, following the immemorial customs – this I have decreed. Yet why, when such profits are at stake, must we tarry? May I not seize the lady at once, forgetting these hated enemy ways?'

'Fool! Will your lust outrun your reason? You know not the kind of lady she is.'

'I know she is a woman.'

'Ouabin, you know nothing! Only, I am certain, if the correct procedures are followed, will she be certain to fall into our grasp.'

'*Only*, Golden One? You speak as if these foolish customs, these ancient traditions, are a form of magic. How can that be?'

'How can it not? Fool, I say!'

There was more in this vein, and much that the whoremonger did not understand. Of course, talk of nefarious campaigns, of women, of conquests, of lust and profit, was familiar enough to him, but there was more here, there had to be. Could they be speaking of the Caliph's daughter? And they spoke of magic: was it magic, some clever conjuring-trick, that made this fellow glow like gold? And why? And was there not something familiar about the fellow – something, at least, about the voice? Eli knew only that there was a mystery here, and wondered at once how he might turn it to his profit. Eli was always on the lookout for

255

chances. A man had to be: after all, if one chance came to nothing, another was certain to come his way soon, so long as he was looking, always looking.

Emboldened by his curiosity, Eli might have opened the shutters wider again, but just at that moment there was a clattering of steel, a tramping of feet and a shout as a patrol of guards rounded a corner. Eli started. Who was he? What was he doing? Such disrespect! The whoremonger bridled, flashed his seal and bade the guards kindly direct him to the royal apartments.

Soon after, he had almost forgotten the golden man – at least for now. Another, more immediate chance was to come his way that night.

✳   ✳   ✳

'It's the end!'

'Oman, no!'

'My beautiful daughter, a sacrifice!'

'Oman, never!'

'My glorious reign, chaff on the wind!'

'Nonsense, Oman!'

Dashing away his tears, the Caliph Oman Elmani looked sourly at his Vizier. 'Really Hasem, I believe you will be saying *no*, *never* and *nonsense* when we are bound upon the wheel! Don't you care that the Ouabin are within our very walls?'

The Vizier rolled his eyes. 'I could hardly *not* care, Oman, when we have spent the evening entertaining the estimable Sheik Rashid. Really, if I had had to watch another of our harem-girls grinding her hips into that leering face, I should have been sick! To think, and he says he must be pure for the wedding – pure!'

They sat morosely for a moment.

'But come, Eli, more ferment!' called the Vizier. 'Oman, sup deeply on this ichor of forgetfulness, remembering the adage of the wise Imral: that of all the mistresses a man shall take, none shall comfort him so much as Oblivion.'

'Mistresses? What are you talking about, Oman?'

Eli Oli Ali filled their goblets again. For the Caliph and his Vizier, such joys were unaccustomed, but not entirely unknown. If, from time to time, they ordered ferment-sellers to be bastinadoed, even mutilated, this was more a show for the mob than any expression of piety on their part. Sometimes, so the Caliph put it, there was nothing for it but impiety, and tonight of all nights was a case in point. Perhaps it was the sanctimonious hypocrisy of the Sheik that drove them to this excess; perhaps the desire for an oblivion deeper than even their habitual pleasures could provide.

Carousing secretly, the two distraught men were becoming unguarded. Eli Oli Ali watched them intently, his face fixed in an obsequious smile.

'Let me choose another adage,' said the Vizier. 'When night is deepest, there is no cause for despair, for darkness is always but a prelude to light.'

'Hasem,' shrieked the Caliph, 'the Sheik wants my Shimmy!'

'Indeed, Oman, but I believe that when he has her, he will leave. The Ouabin are nomads, not colonisers; powerful they are, and much devastation shall they wreak, but not for long. As a badge of conquest, the Sheik would bear away the bride intended for your brother; but when he has her, he will leave us in peace, I am sure of it.'

'Hasem?'

'Oman?'

'You would give away my dear little daughter?'

'Oman, we *always* had to give her away!'

The Caliph swirled the lees of his goblet. 'Hasem?'

'Oman?'

'You would give her away to . . . a Ouabin?'

'There's no choice, Oman!'

The lees, flying across the dining-slab, missed the Vizier by a considerable margin. Grinning, Eli Oli Ali was on hand at once, splashing more ferment into the emptied goblet. Vizier Hasem grinned too, eyeing his master with a wry amusement.

The Caliph took a fresh gulp and resumed his discourse as if the incident had never happened. 'Hasem?'

'Oman?'

'Aren't you forgetting something?'

'Hah!' The Vizier's eyes flashed. 'But what if that something were . . . the very thing?'

'Really, Hasem, sometimes I wonder what you're talking about!'

Eli Oli Ali wondered too. His two distinguished clients were speaking softly; furtively the whoremonger shifted closer. For so great a man to find himself serving at table was, he might have thought, an ignominious thing, but did he mind? Not at all. He was sure it would pay off handsomely, one way or another. Besides, when had Casca Dalla ever been so close to royalty?

'Oman,' said the Vizier now, his eyes shining with enthusiasm, 'for long years we have feared the day when your daughter must marry at last. But think! When she is seized by Sheik Rashid, what thought will the Sultan have for this paltry province? The retribution, which we had thought marked for us, shall be vented instead upon the Ouabin hordes!'

'Hasem, you're still forgetting something, I'm sure!'

Eli Oli Ali's moustaches twitched, and he hoped the Caliph did not refer to that discretion that was enjoined in the company of menials. But no, never. Eli Oli Ali, a menial? Nonsense! The whoremonger sighed to himself, blessing the magical properties of ferment. If only Casca could see him now!

The Vizier was saying, 'Should the Sultan capture the fair prize again, what of it? When he learns the secret of her misty substance, shall he not think this some magic of Rashid's, and merely redouble his fury against the Ouabin?'

'Hasem, indeed you are forgetting something!'

'Never, Oman! You reckon without the Ouabin customs. Rashid will bear his prize away, far into the desert, before he permits himself even to touch her. Did you not hear what he said tonight, about the balm he must apply to his virile member?'

'I thought he had the pox,' said the Caliph, shuddering.

'Hah! It is an ointment to cool the fires of lust, and he must wear it until he returns once more to the lands his tribe believes to be sacred. Only in the far Wilderness of the West will he attempt consummation – moonlives away! Long before then, will not the imperial armies be hard on his tail? Ah, this paltry province shall have little cause to fear Rashid's return!'

'Hasem, I do wish you'd stop referring to my realm as a *paltry province*. But I say you're still forgetting something, and that's this: I know Shimmy has to be married, but if married she must be, I'd rather it was to my brother's little son than that dirty desert creature. Oh, is there no way we can restore her?' Distracted, the little man tugged at his turban; unravelling a long, brightly coloured strand, he cried, 'Cursed, cursed be that wicked Teller! Hasem, there must be a way!'

'Nonsense, Oman! Have we not searched and prayed, prayed and searched? Jafir the genie is gone; we have tried every other means to restore your daughter, to no avail. There is nothing to be done, and what if there were? How can we save her from Sheik Rashid? If the imperial forces get here in time, perhaps . . . but oh, the chances are slim, Oman, slim indeed!'

The Caliph was not listening. He looked thoughtful; then all at once, excitement shone in his flushed little face. 'Wait! Hasem, the Sheik plans a Ritual of Rebonding, does he not – a public ceremony, to establish his claim?'

'Why bother? He'll take her anyway!'

'No, but . . . if a betrothal, a sacred betrothal is to be broken, there must be three suitors, must there not? Three challengers? That's the rule, isn't it? And the one with the most magnificent gift must win poor Shimmy's hand?'

'Oman, you know this ceremony will be the merest sham. The other suitors will be the Sheik's henchmen, and has not he hinted that his gift shall be so splendid as to stun all who see it into shocked submission? Besides, he would kill any real challenger, I'm sure of it.'

'Nonsense, Hasem! He's pious, is he not? Would a man who smears himself with lust-allaying balm defy the most sacred customs? I tell you, if another came forward, Shimmy might at least be saved from this Ouabin!'

'Oman, you're not thinking clearly. Come, leave aside that ichor of oblivion and tell me who, in all the world, would challenge – really challenge – Rashid Amr Rukr?'

By now, so intrigued, so astonished was Eli Oli Ali that he might have burst forward at that moment, declaring absurdly that *he* would be the challenger. Instead, the whoremonger only bit his lip as the Caliph announced in triumph, '*You*, Hasem!'

'Oman, never!'

'Think of it: Hasem, what would a dirty Ouabin know about magnificent gifts? With all my treasures to choose from, how could the contest not be yours? Then if it were yours, then Shimmy should still be ours, then we should have time, more time before the Sultan . . .'

'Oman, no! We've had time enough, and where has it got us? I tell you, mine is the only way.'

'Nonsense!'

'Never!'

But the Caliph could not resist his Vizier's logic, and slumped into moroseness. Calling for more ferment, once again he bemoaned the evil of the Teller, more fulsomely this time, declaring that he would give the world, the very world, to know what had become of that wicked fellow. What joy, what riches would await the man who brought him but a hint of the Teller's fate, but a hair of his beard, but a thread of his coat!

'Oh cursed, cursed be the Teller Evitamus!'

'Evitamus?' Suddenly the whoremonger flung himself forward. 'Your Magnificence, I know of this man!'

The Vizier bridled. 'Scoundrel! You would fall upon your master like a cur?' Stumbling to his feet, Hasem would have called for the guards, but the Caliph stayed him. Swaying on his cushion, he peered blearily at the figure that had now abased itself, cringing, at his feet.

'Whoremonger,' he slurred, 'can this be true?'

The whoremonger looked up with a beaming smile. He rubbed his hands. Yes, this was it. This was it. Casca Dalla would never triumph now!

Chapter 38

A HOUSE IN RUINS

Was it midnight? Who could tell? Jem was aware only of the dark perfumes that surrounded him, and the golden rays of the moon, shimmering in the cool waters of the fountain.

After the banquet he had lain on his bed, certain that the time could not be yet. The thought that he might sleep had seemed absurd; all through the evening his heart had hammered hugely. His excitement, he thought, owed itself to more than the story the girl might soon impart. It troubled him; lying on his bed, he pictured the exotic, beautiful face; then he drifted into a strange reverie. First came the girl's face, then Cata's, then the girl's; then the two together, mingling mysteriously. Why did this mingling fill him with such longing? The reverie became a dream, a beautiful, strange dream . . .

When Jem shook himself awake, the dread came over him that he had missed the meeting. Had he slept too long? Had time swept forward, bearing midnight away? Now he turned, crunching on pebbles. He looked up at the moon. He peered at the fountain. Hieroglyphs were carved on the bowl beneath; Jem wondered what they could mean. He traced his fingers over the strange, mossy characters and another curious delusion filled his mind: the watery flame was truly glowing, shining just a little with a light from within; it seemed then that an answering heat was stirring in the crystal he wore beneath his robes . . .

A crash came through the foliage.

Jem swivelled round. Delighted, he saw Rainbow bounding towards him. Petting the enthusiastic, panting dog, Jem realised how much he had missed him. The dog, it seemed, had left him for the girl. A wave of resentment flooded Jem's heart, for the girl and her strange magic. 'Good boy, Rainbow! Back to your master, hm? Why do you need her, when you've got me?'

'To help me find you,' came the wry, sudden reply.

Jem stood quickly, his face flushed. 'F-Find me?'

Each time he had seen her, Jem had been startled by the girl's beauty; now, in the moonlight, she was a spiritual vision, shimmering like the gold of the moon in the water. 'I didn't think I'd find this place again.'

'I thought you knew it well. You knew about this fountain.'

'Unlike you, I am of this land. Should I not find familiarity in my own

260

sacred symbols?' There was something defiant in the girl's voice, but Jem could see that she was nervous too. She rushed on. 'The flame-fountain seems familiar to me, or does now that I am in contact with the emanation that for so long has been severed from me. But alas, this consciousness is yet new to me, and my powers are weak. Each day since we found ourselves in this dreaming dimension, I have searched for you when Almoran is withdrawn from our sight. But the gardens are immense, his house has many mansions, and—'

'Wait!' Jem had to laugh. 'Too fast!'

Alarm flashed in the girl's eyes. 'You don't understand me?'

'The words, yes. But I think you'd better start at the beginning.'

They slouched together at the base of the fountain. Sitting beside the Princess, Jem found her not quite so ethereal as he had at first thought. Her hair was dishevelled, her face moist, and dark patches discoloured her fine gown. Cross-legged, she toyed with the pebbles on the ground. On the ledge behind their heads, Rainbow lapped happily at the chill water, then slumped down, his head on his folded paws. Heat pressed thickly against the foliage all around them. Jem smiled, and looked encouragingly at his companion.

'How is it that you speak, when until now you were mute? How is it that you were a prisoner of the whoremonger? Can it be true that you are a royal Princess?'

The girl laughed. 'Now it is you who are too fast! Young man, can it be true that you are a royal Prince?'

'It is true. I arrived in your lands on a sacred quest. The fate of the world depends upon my success, but a strange magic has separated me from my companions. Now I am held here, and must find a way to escape.'

'Prince, perhaps this place is a clue to your quest.'

'Princess, have you the gift of sight?'

'No gifts, but the knowledge my fate has given me. In this form I go by the name of Dona Bela, but in my truth, in my Essence, I am Bela Dona, daughter of the Caliph of Qatani. Long sunrounds ago, when I was but an infant . . .'

Jem listened intently as the Princess told him of the strange spell that had divided her, spirit from flesh; of how her physical self, a child devoid alike of speech, memory and desire, had been found in the far provinces and taken in by a kindly mixer-woman. That woman had been the mother of Eli Oli Ali, and had raised the mute stranger as her own daughter. For ten sunrounds, the girl had lived happily with the travelling people. Thus her life might have passed, but Dona Bela was troubled by dreams, dreams so vivid they seemed to be real, of a different life in a palace far away. Often she would wonder how she could even imagine such things; from the first, it seemed to the child that her mind was being invaded by a force from afar.

As Dona Bela grew older, the dreams grew more frequent, and a burden of sorrow descended upon the mute girl's heart. Tearful and withdrawn, she would curse herself that she could explain her mysterious affliction to no one. Her lot was doubly harsh, for as the glimmerings came to her of her divided self, the mixers who had welcomed her as one of their own seemed slowly to sense that indeed she was alien, and to treat her with coldness. Her fate was decided one night in the mixer-maze of Geden, as a party of players strummed gitterns and beat upon tabors and the beautiful young mute, quite unexpectedly, began to sing. She could not help herself. The astonishment she caused among the mixers was considerable.

'Your song! But I heard it! Princess, I am certain it is a song of great power!'

'Prince, I do not doubt it. If I do not understand it, still I know it is vital to my fate.'

'But to mine too!' Jem clutched the crystal at his chest. 'Can you sing it now?'

The Princess shook her head. 'Alas, that cannot be. In this dreaming dimension, I can speak as I could not before; but the song that was once my only comfort has now been taken from me.'

'Your only comfort?'

'After that night in the Geden maze, my life became unbearable. Even my mixer-mother thought me bewitched, and declared me to be her daughter no more. Soon Dona Bela was shunned by all; there was talk that I should be driven from their ranks, cast alone into the desert wilds. For a time I wished that indeed that could be so, but such is the cunning of the mixer-kind that it was decided I had another use. I was no longer a child, and my beauty was burgeoning.'

'Princess, I fear what you are about to say!'

'It is what you think. Mixers are traders, but of the lowest sort. If I was loathed by all around me, still my value to the maze was recognised. Thus I was locked in the van in which you found me, and but for my resistance would have been reduced by now to the condition of the vilest harlot.'

Jem cast down his eyes. With a pang of shame, he thought of the depravities of his Agondon days; with a deeper sorrow, and anger too, he thought of what Polty had done to Cata. 'The gods be thanked you were spared such a fate! But Princess, how could you resist the lusts of these brutes? How came you to be with your pretended brother, on the road and bound for the city?'

'Each time my virtue was imperilled, I would sing my mysterious song. Soon enough, I saw it as my secret gift, a charm to save me from a false destiny.'

'Then I was a fool, to try and save you?'

The Princess caught Jem's hand. 'No fool, no; you were noble and kind, and if we find ourselves imprisoned here, still I know that now I am on the path of destiny – the true destiny, that can be mine only when I am joined again with my bodiless emanation.'

Jem looked in wonderment at the beautiful, strange girl. What remained of her tale was swiftly told. Bitterly the Princess spoke of her days in the mixer-maze, and the many attempts to overcome her virtue. Goaded by her supposed mother, brutal men endeavoured to stop her mouth, to drug her, to deprive her of consciousness, but with the aura that the song had brought her, Dona Bela was able to withstand them all. Despairing, the wicked mother sent for her son, confident that he, of all people, could overcome the girl's tricks.

'This is the man called Eli Oli Ali?'

The Princess nodded. 'When I was but a child, he left for Qatani. There he has become what the world calls a great man; in truth, he has grown rich selling forbidden liquors and the favours of harlots. Scoffing at the incapacities of his brother-mixers, he declared that a glorious career awaited me in the city; you know the rest.'

Jem looked down, troubled. Again he imagined Dona Bela's face and Cata's, mingling as if they were melting together. He shook himself. When would his mind come clear? 'Princess, you speak of this place as a dreaming dimension. What can you mean?'

'Have you not divined it yet? When I crossed the boundary into Almoran's world, many things became known to me, known for certain, that until then I had apprehended only dimly. I knew that my old life had been all unreal; if, though still divided, I seem whole to you here, it is because this is a place where illusion reigns.'

'Almoran spoke of the oblivion-cloth . . . yet I knew he could not be trusted.'

'I do not pretend to divine all his motives, but I know he intends to keep us here. Why he should need us I do not know, when his dream alone creates wealth, beauty, troops of friends. But need us he does. I suspect he wants to marry me. What he wants with you, I can be less sure, but certain only that it is sinister.'

'We must escape his thrall! But how?'

'Praised be the gods that we have met at last, outside the hall of those illusory banquets! Many times, wandering in these gardens, I have sought the limits of Almoran's domain. Alas, too often I have wandered in circles; many times, I have found myself returning to the house, when I thought I was leaving it ever further behind. Prince, together – here, now – we have known more truth than in all the time we have been trapped in Almoran's dream. Perhaps, if we set out together, we might resist the strange intoxicants of this estate and find where its walls begin to grow thin.'

Jem sprang up. 'At once!'

'No, wait. Tomorrow – when it is light, and Almoran expects us to be in the gardens. I have sometimes sensed that he watches me as I sleep. I had to risk this meeting, but now I feel that I must return to my chamber – swiftly, swiftly. Rainbow, come!'

Jem's legs were cramped from sitting on the ground and he had difficulty keeping up with his companions. Once, rounding the corner of a winding path, he thought the Princess had vanished, though she had been in his view but a moment before. Indeed, these gardens were a place of confusion!

Jem heard Rainbow bark, and he turned. Through a vista of trees he saw the long pool, and the Princess beside it, looking up pensively at the mysterious house. He started towards her. Standing there in the moonlight, her resemblance to Cata – for yes, there was a resemblance – was suddenly more striking than it had ever been. She shimmered, and gazed upon him with moist, appealing eyes . . .

Cata? Yes, she *was* Cata!

Jem staggered forward. He caught her in his arms.

An instant later, he was floundering in the pool, startled to realise that the girl – Cata? Of course not! – had pushed him violently away. Jem sank deep beneath the mossy green waters before he heaved himself, dripping, on to the terrace.

That night his sleep was fitful and plagued by lurid dreams, at once both erotic and frightening. In the depths of the darkness he woke up shivering and went to the windows to close them. Looking out, he saw that the pool had become a shallow, dry trough, cobwebbed with cracks, and that all the gardens around it were dead and decayed. He stepped out on the terrace, troubled and entranced, as if to verify that what he saw was real.

When he turned back to the house, he saw it for a moment as a desolate ruin.

'Polty . . . Polty.'

Where did it come from, this moaning voice? Confused, shivering, Bean lay for long moments before he realised that the voice was his own. His eyes flickered open, then closed again. Not morning yet. Vivid as life,

Polty's image floated back, filling Bean's troubled mind. When, he wondered, had he been without his friend? If there had been times when they were apart, still Polty had been the centre of Bean's existence for so long that it might as well have been for ever.

By now Bean could recall only dimly how it had begun, the day when he had found the fat boy with carroty hair, hiding in the stables behind the Lazy Tiger. How long ago it had been – why, it was even before the harlequin came, to dance so strangely upon the village green! Later, Bean had learnt that Polty had been hiding that day from Goodman Waxwell, the fearsome guardian who beat him savagely, but Polty, from the first, had seemed a fearless commander, responding to the skinny boy's nervous challenge with an instant, brutal trial of strength. Of course, Polty had won.

'Polty . . . Polty.'

Bean shifted on to his back. How his limbs were aching! Dimly he became aware that he was sleeping on the floor. Where was his couch? He must find it . . . but not yet. He sank back into his reverie, thinking of Polty in the days – those glorious days – when they had slept side by side in the Nova-Riel Room; of Polty in the waistcoat that Bean's mother had made; of Polty lying naked on Killing Rock, the day Vel had died . . . no, the day that Polty had killed him. Bean had known, he had always known, that Polty was a monster, but what was he to do? Stronger than this awareness was the bond between them; stronger, too, the awe, even wonder his friend had always inspired in him.

'Polty . . . Polty.'

Like a drumbeat, the name echoed through Bean's mind. Oh, but his limbs seemed made of lead! His tongue and lips were parched, and a terrible stench assailed his nostrils. Bean moaned and clutched his face in his hands. But it wasn't morning yet, was it? It couldn't be. He spiralled back down through layers of consciousness, aware again only of his flame-haired friend. He thought of Polty's new-found beauty, after the Bluejackets had taken him away. Had it not seemed a confirmation, a reward for all that Polty had been and done? He thought of the mighty god that was Penge, rising like the glistening sceptre of a King . . . Bean ground his fingers into his eyes. What did he want, what could he ever want, but to serve so great a master? From somewhere he caught a glimmering of light, a murky, seeping greyness. Could it be morning, morning after all? Oh, but he could not lie here! He must see to Polty's linen, his chamber-pot, his hair of the dog . . .

Bean sat up sharply, then cried out as a terrible pain split his forehead. He doubled over, moaning. For a moment he thought he had been lying in some low, tomb-like space, and had cracked his head on the slab above; then he realised that the pain came from behind his own eyes.

The pain subsided to a throb, but as it did so, the terrors of yesterday swiftly rushed in; then, slowly, shuddering, Bean took in the terrors of today. What was this place? Perhaps, after all, it was a species of tomb.

Burgrove lay sprawled on the other side of the cell. At once Bean was certain that his companion was dead.

Chapter 39

BRIGHT DAY

To-whit! To-whoo!

'Oh look, it's a Bob Scarlet!'

On a branch by the roadside, the bird sang merrily. Landa's face brightened and she reached out to him, but the little creature was alarmed and flitted away. Landa sighed. How she wished she had Cata's powers! But then she told herself not to be silly. She was a Priestess, and had powers of her own; she only wished they were sufficient to bring Cata back.

'He's not quite so bold as his namesake,' smiled Hul.

'Hm? Oh, the Bob Scarlet!'

'Poor Priestess, you're not really with us, are you? Must you fret yourself so? I can see you are making yourself ill; your face is wan and there are dark rings under your eyes. Come, no one blames you for what has happened. Great trials lie before us, and we must look to the future.'

Landa nodded; there was truth in Hul's words, but the scholar did not understand how she felt. She knew she was not to blame. Evil forces had been abroad on the night of Cata's disappearance; a dark magic had crossed with theirs, spiriting Landa's friend into its mysterious vortex. Each night since then, the young Priestess had devoted herself to her magic arts, secluding herself in the woods by the oldest tree she could find; each morning she had staggered forth, spent, sadly acknowledging that still her efforts had availed her nothing. Landa only knew she could not give up. Cata was the best friend she had ever known; never, never would she believe her friend was dead.

'I'm not sure we should be on this road,' Bando was saying.

'What's that, old friend?' Hul called ahead.

'I don't like it. Bright mornings are just the time for Bluejackets to be abroad.'

'Bother Bluejackets!' gasped the Friar, bringing up the rear, mopping his forehead with a none-too-clean handkerchief. 'Hot this road may be, but I'm sick of trudging through those wretched woods. My cassock's full of burs and I'm scratched all over.'

'What, Capon, you'd rather be scratched by a Bluejacket bullet?' Bando scoffed.

The Friar rolled his eyes. 'Really, the road's deserted for as far as we can see!'

'That's not that far, Capon. The road bends, or haven't you noticed?'

'Oh, don't talk to me about Zenzan roads. Jog, jog, judder, judder, and that's only if you've got a horse. It's worse on foot. And stop calling me Capon!'

The Friar should have resisted this last remark, for at once, as if on cue, Raggle and Taggle broke the grip of their father's hands and danced irreverently around their clerical companion, improvising a new verse for a rhyme that had undergone many metamorphoses in their long moonlives together on the road:

> Jog, jog, judder-judder,
> Capon, show us your pizzle!
> Jog, jog, judder-judder,
> Capon, show us your pizzle!
> When Capon pees, he squats like a girl
> And instead of a squirt there's a drizzle,
> Jog, jog, judder-judder,
> Capon, show us your pizzle!

The poor Friar could only spin about, spluttering indignantly, 'It's a lie!' and 'I'm not a eunuch!' and 'I tell you, I am equipped as a man!' and 'I'll have you know, there are wenches who favour a Friar!'

It was a cruel game, but if Hul was ashamed that his old friend Bando should permit such behaviour in the boys, at the same time he felt it hardly his place to comment. Besides, he could not help laughing.

Only when he saw Landa's face did Hul snap suddenly into sternness, crying out, 'Boys! Bando, make them stop!'

Bando grinned, clapped his hands, and the boys fell in dutifully with their father again. The dance, at least, had been a diversion. Like pilgrims, the little band trudged on, sweltering in the heat of the day. For some moments there was no noise but the clink of Bando's rifle, the swish of Landa's skirt and the scrape-crunch, scrape-crunch of their weary feet in the dust. Only Bob Scarlet was mounted, and as always the masked man rode well ahead, pistols at the ready, scanning suspiciously for dangers in their way. At present he was somewhere round the bend in the road. For some time, his companions had neither heard nor seen him. This was common for long stretches of the day.

There was an irony in the highwayman's scouting expeditions, for Bob Scarlet was himself perhaps the greatest danger faced by the rebel band. Many times, in the course of their journey, Hul had urged their leader to forgo his mask and his red rebel's garb. It was useless; the man who was, in truth, the deposed King of Ejland, refused to bow to the indignity of any safer disguise. Sometimes it seemed to Hul that their leader was deliberately reckless, caring neither for his own life nor the lives of his companions. It had not always been thus; but alas, the great days of Bob Scarlet's career appeared already over.

The Friar was hoping they would soon find a tavern.

'Really, I've never got used to these Zenzan ways. Why the Bluejackets should want to conquer this kingdom is beyond me, when it doesn't even have the beginnings of civilisation. In Ejland, there's always a fine alehouse round the next corner, where a man may rest his weary limbs and take in a little necessary sustenance.'

'In your case, Capon, hardly *a little*,' Bando could not resist remarking. He might have addressed the calumny upon his native land, but contented himself instead with, 'What, would you put your feet up on a stout bench, fingers laced across your cassocked paunch, only to look across to see Bluejackets leering at you, bayonets gleaming?'

Hul laughed. 'What of it, Bando? We're a troupe of poor players, are we not, bound for the city where we hope to make our fortunes?'

'A likely story! They'll probably ask us to perform.'

'Should that trouble us, old friend? I can see it now: Raggle and Taggle can do their tumbling act; Landa shall be a Woman of Wisdom; I shall recite great classical verse, and you, Bando, why, you can always sing one of your fine songs. How about *Scarlet, Scarlet, his coat was of scarlet*? As for the Friar, so eager is he to fill his throat, I'm sure he'd make a fine show of sword-swallowing.'

'S-Sword swallowing?' gulped the Friar. 'Good Master Bando, I think perhaps you are right, and we should have no truck with these Zenzan taverns! I have always thought you wise; do you think, perhaps, we might repair again to the woods?'

The Friar had scuttled forward and pawed at Bando's arm; delighted, Raggle and Taggle would have improvised another raucous verse, had Bando not demanded quickly, 'And Bob Scarlet? What of our leader, Hul?'

The answer might have been droll, but there was no time to deliver it. From round the bend in the road they heard a commotion, sudden and loud. First came the sound of raised voices, then the rearing of a horse.

Then came the shots.

Bando cried, 'Landa! Hold the boys!'

Tugging at his rifle, banter forgotten, the Zenzan was suddenly racing towards the battle, the crisis, whatever it might be. Raggle and Taggle squirmed in Landa's arms, desperate to join their brave father. Hul looked back and forth between Landa and Bando, torn between helping the girl or racing after his old comrade-in-arms.

The Friar had dived into the undergrowth and was peering out fearfully.

The battle, as it happened, was over already.

But the crisis had only just begun.

❉   ❉   ❉

The hot leaves seemed unnaturally still, not rustling, not even trembling in the thick, blanketing heat. Each way they looked the road shimmered, and the blood was drying already, curling and cracking in the powdery dust. There was something immemorial in the quality of the scene: were the living actors suddenly spirited away, it would seem as if the dead had been lying there for long, long moments.

But the living were left to look upon the dead.

'Sire, what were you thinking of?' whispered Hul, wringing his hands.

Sheathing his pistol, the highwayman turned slowly, muttering through clenched teeth, 'Call me not your Sire! How many times, Hul, how many times?'

Hul surprised himself by the bitterness of his reply. 'What shall I call you, then? Hot-head? Fool?'

Anxiously he glanced at Landa, who was struggling to keep the boys from the corpses in the road. The struggle was too much. Excitedly Raggle and Taggle broke free, whooping and cavorting round the dead Bluejackets. The Friar was struggling to extract himself from a patch of stinging nettles; Bando was down the road, calming the horses.

The highwayman jerked his thumb at the frightened mares. 'We needed more, didn't we? If we kill two Bluejackets into the bargain, isn't that a fair trade?'

Landa overheard this and stepped forward.

'We didn't kill them, you did. Bob, they were just a patrol! Two silly boys, ambling down the road! Remember those two back at Oltby Castle – Morven and Crum? These two could have been Morven and Crum. Bob, you could have killed Morven and Crum!'

The highwayman's mouth only twisted into a cynical smile. The Friar squealed from the patch of nettles; Hul swallowed hard. Watching Landa, he had found himself admiring the girl's feisty spirit. In his scholarly life, then in his rebel life, he had seldom had much to do with the fair sex, assuming vaguely that its members were fey, decorative creatures, hardly suited to the society of a man such as himself. Of course there had been Bando's brief marriage, but the warrior woman Iloisa, for all her merits, had hardly convinced Hul of a need for feminine society. Landa was a different matter, a different matter indeed.

The scholar swallowed again and said, 'Landa's right, Bob. You've been hasty as well as cruel, and who knows what trouble you've landed us in? Where there are two Bluejackets, there are more, many more, not far behind. Or had you forgotten?'

Hul's voice faltered at the end of this speech, and he trembled, suddenly fearful. It was all very well for Landa; she did not know their leader's real identity. Only Hul knew, and the knowledge was becoming a strain. He braced himself. Had the highwayman stepped forward, striking his face, Hul would not have been surprised; he would have felt he deserved it, too.

But Bob Scarlet did not strike his old friend; not, that is, with his hand.

'Hul, I always thought you an intellectual man.'

'What?' Hul did not quite follow.

The answer was simple. 'I see you are becoming a sentimental fool.'

Hul flushed.

From the nettles, the Friar squealed again.

'As it happens,' the highwayman was smiling, 'I am well aware of the dangers I run. Is not Bob Scarlet a byword for derring-do? Thus it has always been; thus it shall always be. I have hardly lived this rebel life for so long to be ignorant of the ways of Bluejackets; you may also consider, Hul, that if there is one area in which I may rival even your formidable scholarship, it is in my knowledge of the Agondon stage lines. I refer, in particular, to their movements and times.'

Hul said, 'Sire? I mean, sir? I mean, Bob?'

The highwayman gestured at the corpses in the road. 'These two won't be missed till this evening, at least. I wanted them out of the way when the stage comes through. I also wanted horses for you and Bando. It's been a while, hasn't it, old friend?' He clapped an arm round Hul's shoulder. 'I think we've had enough of this skulking in the trees. Today, Bob Scarlet's back in business. Now come on, let's help our fat friend out of those nettles, or we'll never hear the last of it.'

Chapter 40

DREAMS FROM A GLASS

'Littler! Fish! This way! Quick!'

Rajal was learning fast. First he looked stealthily from left to right, then waved the smaller boys after him. They darted out of the alley, just at the moment when a party of doom-dancers distracted the Ouabin guards. In moments, Rajal and his new friends mingled with the crowd that filled the square. Blood still stained the dusty ground and the overhead gallery was tumbling down in places, burned black in others, but already the bazaar thrived again, as if the conquest had never taken place.

To the traders, it made no difference; nor did it make a difference to the thieves. Elsewhere in the crowd, with Cheese and Blubber, Faha Ejo worked the stalls laden with calico and muslin, cambric and silk; somewhere nearby were Scabs and Stork, snaffling bright trinkets like jackdaws. Only the Ouabin guards restrained their ardour, but the menacing figures in white, mounted high on dark horses, were hardly concerned with petty thieves. Suspiciously, Ouabin eyes strained for the doom-dancers; weirdly, like a charm, a high, wordless music rose above the hubbub of the bazaar.

Through a crush of bodies, Rajal saw the mysterious figures wheeling, whirling, their bare feet beating the dust as they twirled round and round.

Fish quailed. 'The end is near!'

'So's our chance,' said Rajal. 'To work!'

He had seen enough of the world to forget his fears, but for many in the crowded square, this was not so. Soon a crush of robed bodies had gathered about the strange holy men. Alarmed and fascinated, the eager observers would barely feel the hands that darted into a pocket or tugged at a coin-purse on a golden chain. Faster and faster went the dancers, tambourines beating, long beards flying; faster and faster went the brown, thieving hands.

As they wheeled, as they whirled, the holy men resolved their wailings into a sinister, undulating song:

> *All that we dream,*
> *All that we seem*
> *Is vanishing on the air:*

All things must pass:
Dreams from a glass
Are vanishing on the air:

Crystal at a breast,
Light that shone:
Light into darkness,
Crystal gone!

All that we see,
All we shall be,
Is vanishing on the air—

Had Rajal been listening, he might have been startled by the words they sang. Instead, he was attempting, with some delicacy, to draw a bolt of purple rep from beneath the arm of a black-garbed woman. He screwed up his forehead. He bit his lower lip. But even in this intent moment, a voice inside him clamoured its protest. What was he doing, stealing like this? What was he doing, running with thieves? He could only have replied that it all seemed unreal. Since losing the crystal, Rajal felt he had slipped into a world of illusion. He was outside reality, and his life could only resume when, once again, he clutched his missing prize.

But how?

Far across the sands,
Conqueror comes:
Fires his cannons,
Beats his drums:

All he shall do,
Like me and you—

There would have been more, but the Ouabin were becoming alarmed by the song. Treason? Treachery? Qatanis might tolerate doom-dancers, but Ouabin were not Qatanis.

A shot rang out, a stallion reared; in the next moment, the crowd and the dancers were scattering. For Rajal, it was well-timed, giving him possession of the purple rep in one final tug. But possession was brief. He skittered away, then swivelled back, dropping his prize, as he heard a child's anguished cry.

It was Littler. Desperate, he kicked and flailed, caught in the grip of a fat trader. Whipping a knife from his turban, the trader held it at the boy's throat.

'Let him go!' Rajal would have pushed his way back, risking the slashing blade. Luckily, close by, one of the Ouabin horses reared again.

The trader sprawled. Littler darted free. Rajal grabbed his hand.

'This way!' It was Fish.

Blocking one side of the square was a section of decking, collapsed and hanging obliquely from the galleries above. They leapt on to it, scrambling upwards. Soon they were hidden in the deserted gallery.

✳ ✳ ✳

Little eyes peered from behind a pillar.

The long, cool corridors appeared empty, empty and silent in the afternoon light. Little eyes blinked; little hands scratched beneath a bejewelled collar, and Buby the monkey went loping forth. She was not frightened, but cautious, expecting at any moment to hear the *tramp! tramp!* of guards. Funny, the guards of these last days were different from the ones of that first night, the ones who had tried to drag the poor captain away, before he even had time to fix back his leg. Since then, something had been happening, though quite what it was, Buby did not understand. What could it mean, these explosions, these flashing blades? She only knew that she liked these new guards even less than the ones before. How she wished they could go back to the ship! Buby longed to be sailing again, but what was the captain doing? Right now, he was sleeping in his chamber, snoring away after another big meal. Buby was bored.

Much aimless loping later, and with a little leaping, the monkey found herself padding along a ledge, enjoying the bright sunlight that caressed her mangy back. Being a monkey, she was hardly bothered by the considerable drop to the ground below. It was only when a certain soporific hissing came drifting into her ears that Buby glanced down and saw the pit of long, hoody-headed, writhing things.

The cobber-as!

Buby let out a shriek, and clawed at the catch of the nearest window. In an instant, she had bundled herself into a mysterious, perfumed apartment.

✳ ✳ ✳

'Whew!' Rajal wiped his forehead. 'A narrow escape!'

'I lost my purse!' moaned Littler.

'I lost my rep!' Rajal flung back.

'Some thieves you are!' From the dirty loincloth that was all he wore Fish produced the dried pizzle of a horn-horse, flourishing it triumphantly.

'Good luck charm?' said Littler, aggrieved. 'That's not fair!'

The boy in the loincloth rolled his eyes. 'I didn't have a charm before I filched this one, did I?' He leapt up, stamping on the decking. 'So this is where the fine folk come, hm? Must have had a good view of your bits and pieces, eh, Vaga-boy?'

'Get down!' said Rajal.

'Why?' Fish leaned dangerously over the balustrade. 'Nothing to worry about! Look – all back to normal.'

It was true. With the doom-dancers dispersed, the scene below had returned to what it had always been: the same clamour of commerce, where shouts came only from traders calling their wares, from customers haggling, from angry, inevitable scenes of pushing and shoving in the crowd. Rajal cast his eyes over the bright array, squinting as the sunlight flashed too sharply, first on a marrow, then on a ring, then on the blade of a Ouabin sabre.

No, all was not as it had been before. Still the Circle of Sacrifice towered above the square, but the sacrifices of these last days had been unadorned and swift, with none of the ceremony favoured by the Caliph.

Steadily, like a heartbeat, fear pounded beneath the buzz of the bazaar.

Fish pointed: 'There's Faha!'

To cry the name of a thief in a crowd is hardly fit behaviour in a fellow thief, especially when he jumps up and down and points from a place where no street-boy should be discovered. Again Rajal would have protested; instead, he found himself startled into silence. Just for a moment, he had stared across the galleries, into the shadows of the other side. Just for a moment, he had seen a face.

He punched Fish in the shoulder. 'Look after Littler!'

'What? Where you off to, then?'

Rajal did not reply. Lightly, rapidly, he skittered away, ducking and weaving through the archways that sagged above the square. Whether he had really seen that face, he could not be certain. Twice already he had darted off like this; both times, his quarry had eluded him. Still, Rajal was sure that someone was watching them; sure, too, that he knew who it was. His assailant from the cells! Rajal was not given to violence, but if he caught that murdering boy, he would thrash him to a pulp. To be nearly executed in the boy's place was bad enough. But what had the boy done with the Crystal of Koros?

Again and again in this last day, Rajal had recalled his vision as he was bound upon the wheel. Could he really have seen the crystal, burning at the breast of the Caliph's daughter? Had mystic rays really burst from her hands? More than once, Rajal had asked Scabs if he had seen anything strange. The cabin boy could think only of exploding bombs, heralding the arrival of the Ouabin.

There was much that Rajal did not understand. But if he caught the boy from the cells, perhaps the mystery would begin to unravel. He was certain it would.

Little eyes peered from behind a screen.

The wide, cool chamber seemed empty, empty and silent in the afternoon light. Little nostrils twitched. In her long shipboard life, Buby the monkey had become used to strong smells, but usually they were of rather a different character. To her startled senses, the incense in this strange place was almost as potent as the smoke that the men of this land would suck from those curly tubes, attached to vessels of bubbling liquid. Reeling a little, Buby shambled forward, gazing about her curiously at the ornate furnishings, the frail painted screens, the shimmery, gauze-shrouded ramparts of the looking-glasses.

With a sigh, as if at the prompting of a breeze, one of the shrouds fell to the floor. Buby started, seeing her own image reflected back clearly. She cowered, and the monkey in the glass cowered too. She grinned, and the other monkey grinned. She scratched under her collar; again, the other monkey did the same. Really, it was not a real monkey, it was only a picture! Buby hissed, disgusted at this trick, and wondered who it was that had meant to frighten her. There was some magic here, strange magic, she was sure of it.

Buby turned, thinking she had heard a noise. A moaning. What could it be? The monkey in the glass had made no sound. Then Buby thought the moaning had come from behind one of the screens, a screen painted with a picture of something she did not quite recognise as a fountain. The monkey's little heart began to pound hard, and she wished she had not found her way into this strange place. She padded cautiously towards the painted fountain.

Now it was Buby's turn to moan, for lying behind the screen, slumped and inert, was the girl from the ship, the girl who had appeared so mysteriously on their last night at sea! Sorrowing, Buby looked down at the stricken form, remembered how she had lain in the girl's arms, and how the girl had seemed to speak to her like a friend. What was wrong with the girl?

Then Buby saw the manacles and the chain.

She turned, troubled, wondering what to do. That was when a strange light suddenly filled the chamber, insisting its way even into the shadows behind the screen. What could it be? Buby might have shrieked, but her fear was so intense that she could only be silent. She peered out cautiously, astonished to see a tall golden form taking shape in the space between the looking-glasses. Oh, but this too was a figure she had seen before, in her many lopings round a certain ship! The monkey knew enough to cower back – knew enough, too, to reach a hand towards the prone girl beside her, as if so small a hand could offer any protection.

The man of gold raised an arm and layer after layer of gauze cascaded down, all round the circle of glasses. He revolved slowly, his feet suspended just above the floor, and slowly, with many a colourful swirling, it seemed that images were forming in the glasses. 'Do you see, Ouabin? Here is your dream! But here, too, is the explanation you seek. Here is why all must be done as I say.'

The words meant nothing to Buby; she merely wondered to whom they were addressed. There was no one else here, was there? But no, now there was a grey phantom, hovering beside the golden man. 'Enough,' came the voice, 'of these conjuring-tricks! Golden One, will you try my patience to the death? The girl is not here!'

'Ouabin, she is all around you.'

'What? I don't understand!'

'Look, Ouabin, look.'

It was then that the swirlings of colour resolved themselves, presenting the image of a dark-eyed, beautiful girl, multiplied in shimmering glass after glass. With a cry, forgetful of his insubstantial state, the phantom made as if to lunge forward; the girl's eyes blazed defiantly and something at once dark and bright, purple yet dazzling, shone like a glowing heart inside her breast.

The golden man said, mockingly, caressingly, 'Ouabin, indeed she is beautiful, is she not? But hold back your impatience, just a little longer, recalling the sacred rituals we must follow.' By now, the colours that had swirled inside the glasses were churning instead on the outer air; skein after skein of gauzy fabric rippled and tossed as if in a wind. The girl's eyes grew brighter, glowing like the vision of the crystal inside her, but the golden man only laughed. 'Yes, girl, flash your defiance, but soon you shall be ours! What are you but a vessel for the power that lies within you, the power that soon we shall liberate and possess! This is your destiny, and you shall not escape it!'

'Golden One, make her come forth from the glass! Can you not bring her close to me, just for a moment?'

But the golden man, it seemed, was no longer listening to his grey companion, who flickered, and flickered again, in the billows of gauze and brightness. The golden man's tone grew bantering. 'Ah girl, and I see it is as I suspected – a purple crystal, too? So, the Vaga-boy has lost the burden he was entrusted to bear! Should I not have foreseen as much? Very well, he has played his part in this adventure – he is finished, done with! Indeed, I am certain' – there was laughter again – 'he shall soon meet the punishment which is now all he deserves . . .'

'Golden One,' the phantom pursued, his voice becoming strident, 'make her come closer, just a little closer, please! Let me – oh, let me but brush my hand through her airy form . . .'

But now the images in the glass are flickering, changing, as the Golden One grows brighter. Astonished, Buby sees Master Rajal bound upon the wheel, lying in a cellar, running through the marketplace; then she sees him in a lush, strange apartment; she sees him opening his mouth to scream, and the monkey, alarmed, almost does the same. But Master Rajal is gone, as suddenly as he appeared. Now there is a vision of luxuriant gardens; the girl, the beautiful girl from the looking-glass is there, but strangely altered, and . . . can it be? But it is Master Jem! Now it is as much as Buby can do not to caper wildly up the side of the screen, in excitement as much as fear; then comes a vision of Miss Cata in billowing robes, strangely altered too, and Buby looks confusedly between the girl who lies beside her, still unstirring, and the multiplied images that flicker and flash.

'Enough!' cries the phantom – struggling, it seems, to hold together his insubstantial form. 'What are these dreams that come from a glass?'

There is no reply; the Golden One only glows brighter and brighter; there are more images, and more, and another lady, a lady like the first, yet still more beautiful, now fills every glass. Who can she be? What can be happening?

'Golden One,' the phantom cries, 'I cannot see . . . Golden One, this chamber fades around me . . .'

Then he is gone and there is only the golden man, alone and spinning in the centre of the radiant storm. Now the face of the lady seems to fill the chamber, rushing forward from the looking-glasses to be suddenly, impossibly, everywhere at once, surrounding everything, filling everything, *being* everything. The golden man flings back his head, but whether the sound that bursts forth is laughter or a scream it is impossible to say; Buby only knows that it is wild and crazed.

'Oh my lady,' comes the cry, 'my lady in a looking-glass! One day you shall be real to me, and we shall be together! Soon, these dreams in a glass shall end! The Ouabin is a useful fool, that is all . . . Prince Jemany, the Vaga-boy, the girl Catayane . . . all of them fools, mere useful fools! Cursed be my weakness that I need such servants . . . but soon there shall be no other I need, for I shall have you, you shall have me, and all else that exists shall be to us as nothing! Soon, my darling – soon, soon!'

Then the golden man is gone too; the swirling colours have faded, and the gauze settles into inert disorder. Whimpering, reluctant to emerge from behind the screen, Buby can only cower over the chained, silent Cata.

Chapter 41

A HAZARD OF NEW FORTUNES

Rajal halted, breathing heavily. Sunlight flashed through the shadows and the decking groaned beneath his feet. Twice he had almost crunched through powdery, blackened boards. He shifted, leaning carefully over the balustrade. Littler and Fish were far behind him now. But where was the boy from the cells? He screwed up his eyes, scanning anxiously.

There were voices from behind.

'In broad daylight, I ask you!'

'Yes, yes. Now they came up here, you say?'

'Dear me, it doesn't look safe!'

'Old man, are you wasting my time?'

'Sir, no!'

Rajal turned sharply. He had thought the Palace of Perfumed Stairs provided the only access to the gallery; apparently this was not so. At intervals round the square, there were staircases for functionaries – and guards. Now, up one such staircase, there appeared a supercilious Ouabin, sabre in hand. His companion, puffing behind him, was the fat trader.

Rajal darted behind a pillar.

'Now which direction?' barked the Ouabin.

'D-Dear me,' came the exhausted reply.

'Old man, you are a fool!'

Rajal held his breath. If they came this way, he could only run.

Koros of the Rock, hear your child. Please. Please.

A sound of music wound up from below. Peering into the square, Rajal saw the doom-dancers. Defiantly the strange trio had assembled again, and already a crowd surrounded them. This time the performance was of a different sort. One old man clashed a pair of cymbals; one beat on a tabor; the third played a bulbous pipe, and as he played, a coiled thing at his feet began to unwind, rising slowly.

Rajal started. Were his eyes playing tricks? At first he thought the coils were the body of a snake; then he saw that a long, sturdy rope was weaving its way up above the crowd. He stepped closer to the balustrade and his foot crunched hard, almost crashing through a charred board.

'What was that?'

The Ouabin had been going the other way. Now he swivelled round, sabre flashing.

The trader squealed.

The rope swayed.

Rajal leapt. Clinging precariously, he swayed above the bazaar.

The Ouabin was enraged. 'A trickster, hm?' He lurched forward. In the next moment, the sabre would have slashed the rope; instead, the balustrade gave way and the Ouabin, with a scream, plunged below.

The crowd cheered.

'Dear me!' The trader twisted his beard.

Still the doom-dancers played, but already the guards were rushing forward. The crowd parted. The music stopped. Rajal was falling, but not crashing suddenly like the Ouabin. As the last notes of the pipe died on the air, the magic rope, coiling again, bore him rapidly but gracefully to the ground, just out of reach of the oncoming guards.

Rajal seized the rope and ran.

※　※　※

Those who sequester in the apartments of royalty are used to being treated with the utmost deference. Never should the great of this world be subjected to inelegant or indecorous behaviour, let alone to the irruption of unexpected visitors. Troops of menials exist, after all, to ensure against such vulgar possibilities. When it happens that the defences of these menials are overcome, the great ones must be permitted to feel alarm; doubly so, perhaps, if they are the Caliph Oman Elmani and his faithful Vizier Hasem, writhing in the thrall of invading hordes, and in the middle of a secret, if dispiriting discussion of strategy.

'Is there nothing we can hope for?' the Caliph was saying. 'Surely Big Boy must save us!'

'We can hope so. But can he save us in time?'

'In time? Hasem, you don't mean—'

'Before your daughter is gone? I'm afraid that's just what I do mean, Oman.'

'If only Evitamus could be found!' the Caliph wailed.

'Ah,' said the Vizier sadly, 'I see you think again of the whoremonger. Oman, what hope can there be from that quarter? He is a loyal fellow, and zealous in our cause, but is he to accomplish in mere days what all our resources have failed to do, in sunround after sunround?'

'But he promised! Hasem, how can you doubt him?'

'Easily enough, Oman. Come, think no more of the Teller Evitamus: in magic, I fear, there is nothing for us now. If anything, it is working actively against us – should certain hints I have heard be true.'

The Caliph's eyes widened. 'Hasem, what are you talking about?'

'Suffice to say that a certain nobleman of Ejland may have more to him than meets the eye.'

'Empster-lord?' said the Caliph. 'What has he to do with anything? Why, I'd almost forgotten that shifty character! I never liked him, you know, when he visited us all those years ago – would you believe, he used to look at me as if I were stupid? I hardly think we needed the flame-haired one to warn us about him.'

'You saw through him at once, Oman?'

'Of course. Those hands are far too smooth.'

'You won't be surprised, then, if I tell you he is in league with the Ouabin?'

'What!' cried the Caliph. 'I thought he was a traitor in Ejland! Is he a traitor everywhere he goes?'

'So it would seem, Oman. Thus far I have only the words of certain palace spies, but I gather this dubious nobleman has been seen coming from the Ouabin wing – I mean, Oman, the wing the Ouabin have occupied. Then there are other reports – stranger reports – which I'm not sure we can credit. Suffice to say that this Empster-lord has amply proven himself to be our enemy.'

'Hasem, we must have him executed – bound upon the wheel!'

'No doubt,' said the Vizier dryly. 'If he's still here when the Ouabin are gone.'

'The Ouabin!' With a shriek, the Caliph reared up on his soft couch. 'Hasem, I could strangle them all with my bare hands! And as for that Rashid Amr Rukr . . .' The little man had just launched into a wild and implausible fantasy of retribution, involving a dog-collar, a whip, and a heated poker, when a thumping like thunder came at the door.

'The Ouabin!' squealed the little man, in quite a different tone this time, clutching a cushion and hugging it like a shield against his breast.

'Really, this is intolerable!' The Vizier sprang to his feet, expecting an imperious messenger. Instead, a slave scuttled forward with the news that the Whoremonger Royal had been waiting outside, and was growing impatient. The slave would have said more, but the Vizier cuffed him about the head. Suddenly all thoughts of offence were gone. This was different, entirely different! Why, the Vizier had not even dared to hope . . . ! 'Fool! Haven't I told you, Eli Oli Ali should be shown in at once?'

'Hasem! Can it be?'

'Blessed be Theron, if it can!'

The Caliph flung the cushion from his breast and swivelled round, desperate for what the next moments might bring. His voice cracked into a shriek. 'Whoremonger! Have you found the Teller, have you brought him here?'

Cringing and salaaming, Eli Oli Ali slithered forth, his greasy face glimmering in the afternoon light. 'Pah, Your Magnificence, there is found and there is found. If you mean, does he await outside the door, then no, your loyal servant has not found him; indeed, there is none but mighty Theron who could.'

'Hasem, what's he talking about?'

The whoremonger rubbed his hands, grinning. Such was the fervour of their expectation that neither Oman nor Hasem had remarked that their visitor had failed to don a ceremonial mask. After the familiarities of a few nights ago, did he think he could abandon all respect? The Vizier would have launched into fervent admonishment, but all such thoughts vanished from his mind as the greasy fellow said again, 'I say, I have not found; but if you mean found out, if you mean the truth, then soon you shall be happy. And so shall I.'

'Hasem, make him say what he means!'

'Whoremonger, what do you mean?'

'You ask for but a hint of the wicked Teller. What do I bring you but a story with an ending, and a story that must cause you much rejoicing? A story which Casca could never provide, not if he lived for a thousand epicycles. Your Excellencies, I have discovered the Teller's fate!'

Eli Oli Ali turned, gesturing, and the Caliph gave a second, involuntary shriek. In their excitement, the great ones had failed to register the second, unexpected guest who hovered in their midst, dark and hunched, stealing forward now at the whoremonger's beckoning. Moments passed before the Caliph, to his shock, realised it was a woman, a black-garbed commoner. To bring any female unexpectedly into the royal presence was a violation of the first order.

In this moment, if not before, guards should have rushed forward, dragging Eli Oli Ali to the dungeons. But after all, the crone was hardly a woman, and besides, the Caliph cared only for the meaning, not of the whoremonger's actions, but of what he had said. Proudly the greasy fellow informed his superiors that the crone was a woman known as Mother Madana. He kicked her surreptitiously and she prostrated herself, mumbling a confused but fervent prayer.

'Madana?' interrupted the Caliph. 'Is there not a slave of that name, high in the ranks of the royal service? But this crone is garbed like a common peasant! Who is she?'

Eli Oli Ali was ready with his reply. 'Your Magnificence, this is the sister of that Mother Madana who is Keeper of your estimable women's wing. This too is a woman of great talents, but one whose light has shone, until now, in the far reaches of your Caliphate. Alas, that the ways of wickedness should have driven her from the vocation she has filled with such distinction!'

'Vocation? Wickedness?'

'Keeper of the caravanserai at Dorva,' said Eli.

'Hasem, wasn't that where . . . ?'

'Indeed, Your Magnificence! But what has this crone to do with the Teller? Quickly, crone, is he known to you?'

At first it seemed that Mother Madana had lost the power of speech, but after a second, less surreptitious kick from Eli Oli Ali, she erupted suddenly, as if at the starting of a mechanism, into a babble of reminiscence, regret and rage – none of it, it seemed, pertaining to the Teller. She sobbed, almost keened for the ruined caravanserai, once the finest in all the Caliph's realm; suddenly oblivious of the whoremonger, she denounced the dirty mixers, who had been at the root of the trouble, she was sure of it.

For some moments this continued, with Caliph, Vizier and whoremonger alike unable to resist the surging tide. The Vizier struggled to the surface first, demanding once again what all this could mean. Only several more kicks sufficed to unlock the crone's more pertinent memories.

If he had been anxious for a moment, now Eli Oli Ali permitted himself to smile. Greedily imagining the reward that awaited him, the whoremonger could not forbear from rubbing his hands as Mother Madana first explained how the Teller had come to her, long years ago; how he had taken her finest chamber; how he had paid his bills first with purses of gold, then silver, then bronze, then with the labour of his girl-boy daughter . . . At this point, the old woman's tone darkened; a digression threatened, with her rage directed now towards that useless, disloyal, wicked girl Ameda.

The Vizier interrupted. 'A girl-boy, you say?' He stared between crone and whoremonger. What game was this? Why, from what was visible of the crone's face she looked so much like that fat eunuch in the women's wing that for a moment the Vizier was sure she *was* the eunuch – the real Mother Madana, as it were, dressed up in peasant clothes at the whoremonger's behest. Did Eli Oli Ali think they were fools? Anger flamed in the Vizier's face, but it was the Caliph who cracked first, shrieking, '*Where is he?*'

Mother Madana looked up, blinking. 'Your Magnificence?'

'Crone, were it not for your sex and age, I swear I should have you bound upon the wheel! For long years, since his expulsion from my Court, you have harboured the most implacable of all my enemies – and, it would seem, a second vicious criminal, who escaped from my justice but days ago!' He turned, with mounting anger, on Eli Oli Ali. 'Whoremonger, this is not well done! You come to me, promising what my heart burns to know, yet what do I receive from this crone but torments? Give me what I crave, or leave me this instant for my deepest dungeons!'

It was an uncharacteristic outburst from the Caliph, but such was the passion to which he was stirred by the very thought of the Teller Evitamus.

Eli Oli Ali swiftly took charge. Flushed and shaking, he bowed deeply, and in a swift sentence dispatched the Teller to the death that provided the end of his story.

There was a silence.

Eli Oli Ali peered through his hands.

The Vizier's face was frozen, waxen; the Caliph's reddened, swelling as if it would burst. His enemy . . . dead? The caravanserai . . . razed to the ground?

He screamed.

It was a scream fuelled not only by the rage that had filled him every day since the Ouabin invasion, but by all the frustration of the years since Jafir's loss, as he deferred to the imperial thrall, as he despaired for his daughter, as he dreaded the day when he would receive his brother's orders, demanding her hand for the Heir Unquestioned.

Mother Madana leapt in fear; the whoremonger writhed; Vizier Hasem struggled to silence the enraged little potentate. At this point, a man of reason would have demanded to know if anything, anything had been left amongst the rubble – words, parchments, konar-lights; most men, indeed, would have clutched at any straw that might have lifted the Teller's curse. The Caliph saw nothing but the fact of that death, and with it, it seemed, the loss of any hope that his daughter could ever again be whole. As the blackness of his rage collapsed into despair, he could only shriek at the incredulous whoremonger that he was a villain, a liar and a traitor too.

The Vizier snapped his fingers. 'To the dungeons with him!'

His commands in such matters were usually final, but this time the Caliph cried no, the dirty mixer was not fit to clutter even the meanest apartment of the palace. 'Have him bastinadoed, then throw him back in the street where he belongs – him and his dirty crone, too! But first, strip him of his seal!'

'Your Magnificence, no!' Struggling in the grip of burly guards, kicking his fat legs absurdly in the air, the whoremonger could barely believe what was happening. How had he deserved this? Where was his reward? 'I bring you news! A trace, you say, a trace! Is this not more than a hair, a thread?'

'Strip him of his royal seal, I say! From now on, the post is Casca Dalla's!'

Chapter 42

DARKNESS FALLS FROM THE AIR

To-whit! To-whoo!

'Ooh look, it's a Bob Scarlet!'

'Bob Scarlet!' cried the old lady, jolted suddenly from her reverie. Since they had left the Vendac tavern she had been listening, contentedly it seemed, as her companion, a dour creature with a single eye, read to her murmurously from a tattered novel. Now she clutched her heart; her companion's eye widened; both stared, anguished, at the young lady on the opposite side of the carriage who had made this unfortunate, this most inapposite announcement. Some moments passed before they realised she referred only to a bird on a branch.

'Miss,' said the old lady, in tones of infinite condescension, 'are you unaware that nothing could be more ill-mannered than to allude, even to allude to that vicious creature?'

'What? That little bird?' said the large-eared young gentleman, if gentleman he were, who sat beside the young lady. Like a simpleton, and to the old lady's increasing displeasure, he proceeded to grin foolishly, and could not forbear from mouthing *To-whit! To-whoo!* until the young lady, grinning too, dug him in the ribs.

The old lady grimaced.

'I refer,' she explained with a strained patience, 'to the most notorious highwayman ever to plague the roads of this empire. Since encountering him I have never recovered my composure, never! Why, nothing could more distress any person of quality than even to hear his hated name! I am sure our clerical friend here must agree with me,' she added, with a smile for the fat Friar who had joined the stage only at the Vendac tavern.

'Oh indeed, good lady,' blinked the Friar, wiggling the sausage fingers that rested, laced, across his considerable paunch. 'Yes indeed, miss,' he added, essaying a stern look for the thoughtless young things.

'Miss?' said the young lady, holding up her hand. A golden band flashed on her finger. 'I'll have you know I'm a married woman.'

There was no annoyance in her voice, only pride as she nuzzled against the young fellow, who flushed, grinned again, and adjusted the very white wig that he seemed to have difficulty in keeping on his head.

The old lady only gave a *hmph!* as if, far from standing corrected, she assumed this claim of respectable marriage to be transparently untrue.

Settling her chin into her deep jowls, with a wave of her hand she commanded her companion to resume reading. Really, conditions in this Kingdom of Zenzau were intolerable; she would never have visited Cousin Mazy if she had known. First to be held up by that brutal, vicious highwayman, then to be caught in the middle of a war! A war, of all things! The poor lady had been thrown into a dangerous fever, but once she had rallied, no power on earth, not even Mazy's, could induce her to stay a moment longer in this benighted land.

Now it seemed that she must suffer to the last. In Ejland, would a quality-lady ever be obliged to endure the company of this common little trollop with the butter-yellow curls, and her so-called husband with his silly grin and big, sticky-out ears? Such people! Did they think they could fool anyone, in those cheap imitations of quality-clothes? Clearly they were of the servant class, or worse. Why such persons were suffered to ride inside the coach, and not out on the box, was beyond the old lady, quite beyond her. She could only be glad for the meliorating presence of the Friar; one always felt safer with a man of God on board.

Then she remembered that a Zenzau-canon had been among her fellow passengers when that brutal cry of *Stand and deliver!* had burst upon her ears[1]. She shuddered and signalled for her smelling-salts. From the carpet-bag at her feet her companion produced a little golden, stoppered urn; the Friar's eyes glittered as the bag was opened and he smiled benevolently, as if in a silent blessing.

The coach rattled on in the heat of the day.

Disappointed, the young lady looked at the two old sticks and the fat Friar. She'd tried to be pleasant, hadn't she? Terrible, the way some people thought they were better than some people, when sure as hamhocks they were no better at all. As if she hadn't had enough of that, quite enough indeed!

But she'd make them smile.

The young lady gave a sniff and announced, in a loud and affected voice, 'Prithee, Goodman Olch, is it your view that this dreadful weather displays any signs of alleviation? I declare, I am *fatty-gued*, positively *fatty-gued*, and know not how I shall support myself!'

'Eh, love?' said the young man, grinning uncertainly. 'Nah, you're not fat, not fat at all! Well, I mean you're not skinny, but I wouldn't want you with no meat on your—'

With a little gasp he broke off, feeling the sharp jab of an elbow in his ribs.

'Prithee, Goodman Olch,' the young lady attempted again, 'what thinked thou of the standard of the hostelry at Vendac? It was my view

[1] *The King and Queen of Swords*, Ch. 52.

that it was very common, very common indeed, as I am sure these fine ladies would be the first to agree.'

If the old lady was expected to respond to this, she had no intention of doing so, only settling deeper into her chins; her companion faltered, only a little, in her reading from what was, though her droning made it difficult to believe, a volume of that romantic classic, *The Prickly Path to Wedlock*.

'Prithee, Goodman Olch,' came the young lady again, 'didst thou not think the salt-pig decidedly rank, the taters underdone, and the gravy watery? I am afraid the accommodation also left much to be desired. I declare, had the splinters from that bench worked their way through my skirts, I should not wish to *contemper-late* the effect upon my—'

The old lady looked up sharply; her companion tittered.

'Served a good tankard of ale,' the young man grinned, with a shrug.

'Ale!' cried his wife. 'I declare, ale is but the commonest of the provisions of a tavern! What of that delicacy, that refinement which alone can attract the custom of quality-folk, and not the mere rabble? Thankful I am that' – her voice sharpened – 'as a *woman of means*, I shall shortly be mistress of my own fine establishment, where all may be done to the highest standards!'

Woman of means! This was too much for the old lady. Had she not endured enough? She rapped at the ceiling. 'Coachman! Coachman! I am the cousin of Mazy Michan, wife of the Zenzan Governor! I demand you put out this trollop at once!'

'*Trollop?*' The young lady flushed scarlet.

The coach lurched, turning a corner. In the next moment, the young lady might have returned insult for insult, forgetting all caution; instead, she found herself flung back against her husband as the horses reared, as the coach juddered to a halt, and the cry split the air:

'Stand and deliver!'

The old lady screamed and fainted away.

※　※　※

'You unconscionable blackguard!'

The old lady had rallied soon enough.

'Dear lady,' said the highwayman with a smile, 'I do believe you have addressed me in that manner before. To be sure, such is the number of my engagements that I would be unlikely to remember a nondescript old lady, but your lovely companion lodges in my memory as one of Ejland's fairest flowers of womanhood. Greetings again, my one-eyed beauty.'

The old lady's companion flushed as the gallant highwayman kissed her hand.

'Baines! Stop simpering!' hissed the old lady. 'What, have you lost all shame?'

The highwayman laughed. 'Fear not, my one-eyed beauty; as you know me to be a gentleman, so you must know that with no rough violence would I possess that most inestimable of the treasures beneath your skirts; I speak, of course, of your virtue. As to other treasures, I may be less discerning.'

Baines simpered again, perhaps a little disappointed.

Meanwhile, the young lady whispered to her husband, 'Wiggler, wh-what's he going to do to us?'

'Just do as he says, love, and give him what he wants.'

'What? My hard-earned savings?'

'Shh!'

The highwayman had dismounted from his black stallion. Twirling his pistol, he paced up and down before the coachman, the line-boy and the five occupants of the carriage. Still mounted, keeping watch, were two henchmen, masked like their master. Dusty foliage pressed against the road, barely stirring in the heat, but some of the travellers felt an awareness of other eyes, watching them from the trees. Once, it seemed, there was the giggle of a child, or perhaps it was only the *To-whit! To-whoo!* of the highwayman's namesake.

'Wiggler, I can't!' whispered the young lady. 'Where should we be without my savings?'

'We might be alive, love, instead of dead.'

'What? He couldn't be such a brute, could he?'

'Shh!'

'What are you whispering about?' The old lady turned, eyes flashing, to the younger. 'Oh yes, I see it now! I should have known! The blackguard had an agent on the coach last time, peering and prying into all our valuables. A poor scholar, he said he was! A likely story; about as likely as yours!'

'Hush, my good folk,' smiled the highwayman. 'Down to business, hm? Friar, perhaps you would be so good as to tell me what you have gleaned during your journey from Vendac? Tell me not that you have dozed all the way, or I shall be most displeased, most displeased indeed, and never stand you to a tavern-luncheon again.'

The Friar stepped forward, whispering in his master's ear; the old lady blanched, then quailed as the highwayman turned back to her, expressing what might have been a connoisseur's interest in her delightful little golden vial of smelling-salts, and the other treasures of her carpet-bag.

That was when the droll scene suddenly altered its character. Baines was holding the carpet-bag, and would have thrust it eagerly, with a winning smile, towards their dashing tormentor; instead, her mistress seized it, cried that the blackguard would never take her, and broke from the line, running.

Urbanely, the highwayman had been twirling his pistol.

Just as urbanely, he clutched it tightly.

He fired.

'Bob, no!'

Shrieks filled the air, but the loudest was Landa's. The girl broke from the bushes, grabbing, too late, at the arm that held the pistol. Then Raggle and Taggle were there too, rushing, fascinated, to the fresh corpse, collapsed over the carpet bag. Hul's horse reared; Bando's too. They cantered forward. Baines had sunk to her knees, praying, tears flooding her single eye.

Brutally, the highwayman flung Landa aside.

'I'm tired of this game,' he cried. 'Let it be over!'

It was not over yet. The highwayman was ready to fire and fire again. But just then the coachman, with unexpected courage, launched himself forward; the line-boy, after hesitating, piled in, kicking. Raggle and Taggle shrieked and capered. Bando hesitated. Baines shrieked. Hul looked on, horror-struck, wringing his hands.

A moment more and the line-boy had scurried into the trees, pursued by Bando's whooping sons; a moment more, and the foolhardy coachman lay in the road, the highwayman above him. Now the masked man would kill again.

Instead, a fresh cry split the air.

The highwayman reeled. 'Hul!'

The two men struggled.

The coachman, seeing his chance, blundered away.

'Bob . . . don't,' the scholar pleaded, 'don't do this—'

Easily enough the highwayman overpowered him. Breathless in the dirt, Hul pleaded to Bando, but the old rebel, in his astonishment, had waited for too long. Bob had the advantage.

Three victims, ripe for the taking.

Baines cowered; the young lady and her husband clutched each other, terrified.

Bob aimed.

'Wiggler!' cried the young lady.

'Nirry!' cried the young man.

'No!'

It was Landa who snapped into action, wrenching at the highwayman's arm just as he squeezed the trigger.

The shot discharged into the trees.

The young couple collapsed, but only to their knees.

'Bob,' gasped Landa, 'it's Nirry ... Wiggler. They're on our side, they must be!'

The highwayman reeled. 'What are you talking about?'

Nirry gasped. 'Wiggler, how does she know us?'

'Bob,' Landa was saying, 'Cata told me all about a friend, the most loyal friend she ever had. Cata's friend was called Nirry, and she had a sweetheart called Wiggler ... Wiggler, with big flaps of ears like this fellow here. Spare them, Bob, I beg you, or you're no better than the dirtiest Bluejacket butcher!'

The highwayman's mouth set tightly beneath his mask. Landa gazed at him, ready to plead again; instead, she turned, startled, as Nirry clutched her.

'Miss Cata ... did you say Miss Cata?'

The two women collapsed into each other's arms.

'Eh, what's going on here?' said Wiggler, then let out a *yeow!* as Raggle and Taggle descended upon him, pulling his ears.

'But Nirry, why are you here?' gasped Landa, after a moment. 'Don't you know it's dangerous on the roads?'

'I know!' said Nirry, with a rum look at the highwayman, who was still evidently considering her fate. 'How else are poor Wiggler – I mean, Goodman Olch and I to get back to Ejland? We're married now, and have to look to our prospects. Taken the lease of a little tavern, we have, right in the heart of Agondon – well, very close ...'

'A tavern in Agondon, you say?' said the highwayman; then, as if the horrors of the last moments had not happened at all, he glanced, smiling, at his henchmen. 'Hul? Bando? I think we could use a tavern in Agondon, hm?'

'What's he on about?' said Nirry, her brow wrinkling. With a shudder she glanced at the corpse in the road and almost felt guilty – though she had taunted the old lady, she could hardly have wished upon her so grim a punishment!

'What's going to happen to me?' wailed Baines. The one-eyed beauty had been forgotten; a poor recompense, it seemed, for all the pleasure she had first shown in the highwayman's attentions, and all the noise she had subsequently made.

The answers to both questions would have to wait. Imperiously, the highwayman mounted his horse again, commanding Hul and Bando to dump the old lady's corpse in the trees. With a satisfied air he gazed upon the coach, which was painted a bright shade of 'Ejard' blue.

'Bando, you can be coachman. Raggle and Taggle, you're the line-boys.' He spurred his horse, but called back, 'Me, I'll travel fastest if I travel alone. The rest of you are passengers – respectable passengers, on the Agondon stage!'

Chapter 43

A CHALLENGE FOR RAJAL

Captain Porlo's slumbers that afternoon had gone on for longer, much longer, than planned. With a breeze wafting in from an open window, the sea-dog had drifted into a pleasant stupor, dreaming of the *Cata* on the ocean wave, rolling with the tide and bound for the place where the **X** was marked on his treasure map. Ah, sweet delusion! When his eyes fluttered open, the captain felt a familiar disappointment.

Dry land! Could a sea-dog ever reconcile himself to it? Feeling the maddeningly unmoving couch beneath him, looking up at the unshifting ceiling, Captain Porlo was certain that the answer must be no. Really, what was he thinking of, pretending this latest voyage would be his last? When old Faris Porlo found his treasure, there would be no fine house for him, no liveried coachmen, no landscaped gardens. No, he would have the *Cata* decked out fit for a King, and sail round and round the far isles of the south until the time came when his loyal tars must consign him, at last, to a watery grave. Was a man to lie under clods of earth, with worms tunnelling through his innards and eyes? Never! Down with the sharks and fishes, that was the way for Faris Porlo!

These thoughts brought a tear to the old sea-dog's eye, and he wiped it away with some annoyance. All this dry land was making him soft! He struggled up on to his elbows and looked about sourly at the sickening luxury of his chamber. How much time had passed? Darkness was gathering behind the blinds, and the sea-dog's stomach, which had been bloated from his rich luncheon, rumbled again with the anticipation of food. At this, the captain felt disgusted with himself, but after all a man had to eat, and if foreign muck were all that was on offer, then foreign muck it must be. Why couldn't they rustle up a bit of salt-pig and mustard, that's what Faris Porlo wanted to know. Hmph!

By now, he thought, one or other of those rum-looking slaves might have been expected to come and wake him and help him fix back his wooden leg. Still, everything in this place was in disarray since those wretched Ouabin had come. When would it end? He had told Empster they should just sail away, but Empster had only laughed. Besides, the Ouabin were guarding the docks. Oh it was a rum do, rum indeed!

Wearily the captain was reaching for his leg when he heard a familiar scratching.

In the open window sat Buby the monkey.

'Buby, me girl! Where've you been, then? Roaming hither and yon round this heathen place? I've told you to watch out for them cobber-as, haven't I? Why, it's just at well you can jump high, is all I can say, and swing from your curly tail!'

His bad mood dispelled, the captain opened his arms, expecting Buby to leap into his embrace. He was surprised when she skittered over the floor instead, turning back in the doorway, beckoning him to follow.

'Buby? Buby, what is it, girl? Now just you wait a moment, while I straps on me leg!'

The monkey sat blinking gravely at her master.

※　※　※

'Trust a Vaga-boy!'

'Ran off, you say?'

'Like a coward!'

'What, and left poor Littler?'

'He's lost, isn't he?'

'Weren't you there too, Fish?'

'Am I a dirty Vaga?'

'Dirty enough!'

'But not a Vaga!'

Faha Ejo had to laugh, but mirthlessly. Drawing back on his pipe, the goat-boy looked levelly at Fish, standing defiantly, then at Rajal, slumped on sacking, toying morosely with a coil of rope. The evening was still early, but already uncomfortable in the Realm of Un. Sounds of revelry boomed through the floorboards, but the air below was fervid with different passions. On a barrel in the corner hissed a konar-light, its sepia glow reaching just far enough to disclose the belligerent chorus of Stork, Blubber and Cheese.

'I'm w-with F-Fish,' said Stork.

'They're bad luck, Vagas,' said Blubber.

'They stink,' said Cheese.

Faha Ejo sighed. Perhaps they were right; still, having invited the Vaga into the gang, the goat-boy was in no mood to admit he had been wrong. Besides, who was Cheese to say who stank?

The goat-boy said as much.

'Vagas stink more,' said Cheese, and farted defiantly.

'Much more,' slurred Blubber. Squatting before a sack of seafood, the fat boy was sucking energetically on a large, whiskery creature that still looked half-alive. Sticky juice ran between the boy's fat chins as he added, not quite coherently, 'They should've all been killed, shouldn't they?'

'What? Them f-fish?' grinned Stork.

'Vagas!' spat the fat boy. 'But some weren't. And them that weren't are bad luck. What made you let a Vaga join us, Faha?'

To the goat-boy, it was obvious. 'They're thieves, aren't they? Thieves and liars and cheats?'

Rajal's knuckles whitened as he twisted the rope. He would have protested, but what was the point? If he was proud to be a Child of Koros, his pride availed him little in a place like this. Misery descended over him like a pall and he wished he were back with Jem again, questing for the crystals. He gritted his teeth. Cheese pointed an accusing finger, and the boy's cruel words only echoed the thought that tormented Rajal now.

'He lost Littler!'

'M-Murdered by the Ouabin, I'll bet!' said Stork.

Rajal lashed the floor with the rope, like a whip. 'Why aren't you all out looking, if you're so worried?' He had told Fish to take care of Littler. Was it his fault if Fish were a fool?

'Why, you dirty Vaga!' Fish clenched his fists.

'Dirty? Stinking!' insisted Cheese.

'He's bad luck!' Blubber bawled again, seafood spraying from his moist mouth.

Faha Ejo clapped his hands. 'Listen to you lot! You don't even know if Littler's lost. Scabs is still looking, isn't he?' Admiringly, the leader reflected upon the talents of the cabin boy, another of his fine recruits. Ugly, yes, but agile. All that running up and down rigging, it was, or whatever they did at sea. Good at rooting round in corners, too. Why, if anyone could find Littler, it would be Scabs. 'To think, and we nearly lamed him, didn't we, Blubber? But poor Scabs is a bit too revolting to be a good beggar, hm?'

These pleasantries drew only a scowl from the piggy-eyed boy. From his reeking sack he extracted an eel, ripped off its head and stuffed the slimy column into his mouth. Greedily he sucked out the uncooked meat.

'Littler's the one we should have lamed,' he slurred. 'I told you that, didn't I, Faha? Why, if that brat comes back, I'll chop his feet off, I will. Teach him a lesson, running off like that.'

'Leave Littler alone!' growled Fish, snatching at the sack. He grabbed a raw squid, forcing it down his throat. 'Why don't you chop off the Vaga's feet?'

Rajal burst out, 'Stop calling me a Vaga!'

'It's what you are, isn't it?' said Fish, reaching now for a lobster. Experimentally he licked at a scaly claw, then cursed as he cut his tongue.

Blubber laughed, then almost choked.

Stork, who had lost most of his teeth in a fight, contented himself with a squashy sea-slug or two. Or three. Slime rolled down his receding chin as he stammered that Vagas were s-s-slithery and s-s-s-slippery.

But so were sea-slugs, and eels too. As Stork gripped hard on his oozy snack, brackish liquid jetted between his hands, spurting into Blubber's eye. Yelling, the fat boy dropped his eel and it was snaffled by Cheese, who for some moments had been eyeing the slimey treat. He stuffed it into his mouth, winced, and was about to spit the thing out disgustedly when the fat boy, with a savage cry, launched his bulk upon his smelly cohort. In an instant, the Realm of Un was a chaos of flailing fists. Seafood flew in all directions.

Then came a crash, and the cellar was dark.

'The konar-light!'

'Blubber, you fat fool!'

'It's not my fault!'

'The Vaga started it!'

'Stop calling me a Vaga!'

※　※　※

There was a pause, filled only with heaving breath. A tinder-strip flared, and Faha Ejo loomed above his gang like a goat-faced idol. Retrieving the konar-light, he made an attempt to light it again, gave it up, threw the battered thing contemptuously into a corner and lit a primitive taper instead. He held it in his hand as he paced back and forth, weaving his way between the litter, the sacks, the barrels and the sprawled limbs of his young companions.

He stroked his beard. 'What if the Vaga-boy could prove himself?'

'What?' said Blubber.

'What?' said Rajal.

'Remember when Scabs came into the gang? Kicked up quite a fuss, didn't you, Blubber? And the rest of you.'

'That's different!'

'Scabs isn't a Vaga!'

'Besides, Scabs can climb!'

'That's right! Climb!'

Faha Ejo said, 'But he had to prove it, didn't he? After he scaled the Mosque of the Five Winds, you all thought he might just do, scabby skin and all. How about it, Vaga-boy? Like to prove yourself?'

Before Rajal could reply, there were snorts. Guffaws.

'What could a Vaga do?'

'Vagas c-can't c-climb!'

'Bad luck, too!'

'And they stink!'

But Faha Ejo had an idea. 'We've done the Mosque of the Five Winds, how about the Palace of Perfumed Stairs? I think you've been a guest there once already, haven't you, Vaga-boy? In the lower regions, at least? Well, I'd suggest you go a little higher.'

Blubber said to Cheese, 'What does he mean?'

Cheese shrugged; the goat-boy waved his taper in the air. Making the sharp light dance and blur, he whispered mysteriously, 'Shimmer, shimmer.'

'What's he d-doing?' stammered Stork.

'Who cares?' said Fish. Bored, he extracted the dried pizzle of horn-horse from the folds of his loincloth. Toying with it idly, the boy wished it were really a magic charm. They said it was. But who believed in magic? Shifting on his haunches, Fish felt something hot against his thigh.

The konar-light. He pushed it away.

'Shimmering Princess?' the goat-boy was saying. 'There's been a lot of talk about that girl, hm? Especially since Rashid Amr Rukr came. Now, you don't think he came for our sakes, do you? Because he liked us all? No, no. You see, he particularly likes that Princess.'

'B-But she's betrothed to the S-Sultan's son,' said Stork.

'Pah!' said the goat-boy, 'What's that to a Ouabin? So there was a ceremony? Yes, but many sunrounds ago. Why, Uncle Eli says there's going to be another. A new betrothal. The Ouabin way.'

Stork's toothless mouth hung open.

Rajal twisted the rope in his hands. 'What's this got to do with me, Faha?'

'Yes, what's this got to do with the Vaga?' said Cheese.

'Where's the rest of my eel?' said Blubber.

'Shut up, pig-face,' said Faha Ejo. 'Now listen to me, friends, and listen good. That Princess is the jewel of this city. Within the palace walls or without, is there a finer prize?' He paused, swishing the taper back and forth. 'No? Now, what if a fellow could steal her away?'

'What?' Rajal gasped.

'You d-don't mean the Vaga should t-tup her?' said Stork.

'Tupped by a Vaga!' Cheese burst out, incredulous. Fish was stroking the pizzle of horn-horse; Cheese grabbed it, jabbing it crudely up and down in the air.

'Give that back!' Fish aimed a punch.

'Mind my eel!' Blubber had spied his own prize, languishing in the dirt.

'Friends, friends!' The goat-boy held up a restraining hand. He twirled; the flame followed him like a fiery ribbon. 'You think there's no way a

chap could get to her? Pah! There's a way, for any fellow brave enough.'
He swooped close to Rajal, hissing like a snake.

'The cobber-as!' Rajal breathed.

'What's he say?' said Fish.

'The cobra pit!' said Rajal, his voice cracking.

'Well, well,' Faha Ejo grinned. 'You've learnt a lot about our fair city,
Vaga-boy. In such a short time, too. Well?'

Rajal's face hung in the taper-light like a mask. The apple in his
upturned neck was huge and the magic rope was tight around his wrists,
trapping the blood in his swollen hands. The others stared at him with
intent, frightened faces; only Blubber was preoccupied, brushing the
cockroaches from his dirty eel. There was silence, or almost. Still the
floorboards creaked overhead; still the flame crackled in the goat-boy's
hand; again, the fat boy slurped and sucked, forcing his slimy meal
between the circle of his lips.

The taper was hot against Rajal's face. Beads of sweat slid down his
forehead.

'Well?' Faha Ejo said again. 'Do you accept our challenge?'

❉   ❉   ❉

Later, Rajal would think he should have leapt up suddenly, battering his
way through the trapdoor above, running away into the night. Had he
done so, certain things, decisive things, would never have happened, and
whether that would have been good or bad was a mystery he would
ponder long into the future. But the ways of fate are strange. Undulating.
Painful. Rajal bit hard on his lower lip. Whatever happened, he must find
his crystal. He thought again of the Princess on the balcony. If there was
even a chance that he could search her apartments, it was a chance he
had to take. But how he could he go over that high wall, with the cobber-
as waiting on the other side?

That was when Blubber stuffed down the last of his eel and rummaged
once again in the reeking sack. This time he drew forth a hard, cylindrical
object. Holes dotted the side and at one end of the cylinder was a
rounded swelling; a reed sprouted from the opposite end.

'What's this?' the fat boy cried, disgusted, and would have thrown the
object away; instead, Rajal grabbed it. Cheese was saying it was
something he had found, just something he had found in the market
square, but no one was listening. Rajal rose to his feet. In one hand he
held the long loop of rope; in the other, like a trophy, was the doom-
dancer's pipe.

'Very well, Faha. I'll take your challenge.'

The goat-boy would have erupted into congratulations, turning
triumphantly on his faithless band, but at that moment a ragged curtain

of sacking caught alight from the taper's flames. There were scufflings. Cries. In an instant, the Realm of Un might have been an inferno; fortunately, a drunkard in the tavern above chose that moment to relieve himself of a considerable liquid burden. Through the cracks in the floorboards came the acrid cascade, falling like rain upon the burning curtain.

The Unners let out a hearty cheer.

Chapter 44

A CHALLENGE FOR SCABS

'Buby? Where you be going then, me girl?' whispered Captain Porlo, not for the first time.

The little monkey only looked back at him with the same troubled, grave expression, and skittered on further, ever further. By now she had led him deep into a maze of strange corridors. Darkness had fallen, and lamps in these regions were far apart, casting long shadows from the pillars and grotesque, ornate sculptures that lined the way. It had been a fraught journey, with the captain struggling not only to keep up, but to keep quiet too, muffling the clumpings of his crutch and wooden leg. From time to time they heard the *tramp! tramp!* of patrolling guards, and hid themselves in shadows or squeezed behind pillars.

No guards were in evidence now. It was as well: the captain was exhausted. How he cursed this dry land, that made it necessary to walk such distances! The *Cata* might surge and swell with the tide, but when was a man ever more than a few good clumpings away from where he needed to be? Good healthy clumpings too, none of this hush-hush nonsense!

They turned a corner. A pungent perfume drifted on the air. The captain sniffed, thinking it a rum smell, a rum smell indeed. But it seemed to stir something in Buby, and she grew excited, leaping and scratching at a set of gilt-edged doors.

'Buby?' The captain's voice was uncertain. He clumped forward, trying the doors. Locked. 'What is it then, me girl? Something in here? Something old Faris Porlo should see?' His eyes twinkled. 'Ah, it don't be some fine treasure you mean, Buby? No? What's that?' His brows beetled. 'Someone in trouble?'

It was then that Buby loped just a little further. In the darkness at the end of the corridor was a second set of doors, screens of intricate mesh, leading on to a terrace. She rattled the handles.

'What's that, Buby? Out there, you say? We can try through the windows? I don't think old Faris Porlo's up to clambering through no windows, but let's have a look, eh me lovely?'

The captain was beginning to enjoy himself. To be sure, there was some mystery here, some rum goings-on or other that Buby had discovered. Fondly the captain thought back to his youth, and all his derring-do in the Varl Bombardment, on the far isles of Ananda and in the jungles of Orokona. Leg or no leg, if old Faris Porlo wasn't up to an adventure, what man was? Why, he'd show them foreigners – them wretched Qatanis, and them with the dishcloths on their heads too!

The captain's bravado was short-lived. For one thing, he was becoming aware of a pressing physical urge, the relieving of which was becoming more of a priority than this little adventure, delightful though it might be. For another, there was the memory that lay in wait for him. They stepped out on to the terrace. That was easy; the doors were not locked. Buby skittered forward, clawing at a window. She leapt up and down, hissing for the captain to come quickly, come!

But another hissing arrested the captain's attention.

He turned, very slowly, and looked down from the terrace.

That was when the old sea-dog felt his crutch slipping inexorably, inevitably from under his arm. He slumped down heavily, painfully, his wooden leg skewing back behind him and the contents of his bladder cascading suddenly forth. Trembling, he clutched the balustrade, sobbing and moaning, 'The cobber-as! The cobber-as!'

Frightened, Buby could only creep back, nuzzling uncertainly against her stricken master's side.

So they were when the guards found them, much later, and hauled them back to their apartment. They supposed the old man must have been at the forbidden ferment, and lost his way.

'Senile old fool! Pissed himself, too!'

How they laughed!

❋   ❋   ❋

It was not silent. It was not empty. It was not even dark. Still the creakings and boomings from the tavern echoed round the Realm of Un like ugly music, dissonant against the *drip! drip!* of the sodden curtain, raucous above the scurryings and scuttlings from the floor. Crevices of light disclosed a twitching whisker, a swish of tail, and in a corner, almost concealed amongst the clutter and filth, the cold gleam of the konar-light, lying on its side.

'Home again!'

A trapdoor swung up with a groan of hinges and two ragged figures leapt down. Rats fled.

'Where are they?' Scabs stood peering into the gloom. 'See what you've done, Squirt? They're all out looking.'

'Don't call me Squirt.'

'Littler, then.'

'That's not my name, either.'

'Some gratitude!'

Sniffing, the little boy scuffed at the floor. 'I wasn't lost, just hiding.'

'Huh! Where's the konar-light?'

'There's a taper somewhere.'

'Ugh! This curtain's wet.'

Littler said something under his breath.

'What's that, Squirt?'

'Piss!' said the little boy, in his own triumphant tone.

'Come on, I'd rather call you Squirt.'

After some cursing, Scabs lit the taper. He flopped down on a mattress; then, feeling the damp in the quilted fabric, hauled himself up with a sigh and rummaged for a moment among the sacks and barrels and boxes. He pulled out a tight roll of carpet, furling it over the mattress like a flag. Exhausted, Scabs would have cast himself down again, but for a moment the carpet arrested his attention. The design was one of peculiar complexity, the colours unusually rich. Whorls and spirals, patterned serpents and peacock eyes flared out in the taper-light.

'I haven't seen one like this before,' said Scabs.

'They stole it yesterday. It's a Sultan carpet.'

'A what?'

'Haven't you heard the Sultan Song?' Littler yawned and pointed. 'You know, the Five Sacred Sultans, each with his own domain?'

Scabs did not, but screwed up his forehead and looked hard. He saw shapes like rivers, like hills and trees, like planets and shooting stars; and somewhere in the midst of it all, almost concealed amongst the elaborate pattern, the figures of men. Each man wore a costume of a different colour, and each held a glowing gemstone, like an offering. Lines of radiance shone from the stones, tapering and crossing, travelling in ever smaller stitches to the edges of the carpet.

For a moment Scabs was transfixed, as if by a spell. Then Littler dived impatiently on to the carpet, the taper fizzed out, and the sailors in the tavern above struck up a song, beating out time with stamping feet. The spell vanished and Scabs stretched out beside Littler's huddled form. How soft was the carpet, how sweet its smell! Rolling on to his stomach, Scabs nuzzled deeply into the woven wool, savouring the odours of incense and dye that overpowered the Realm of Un's usual foetid stench.

※　※　※

Scabs was miserable. He was always miserable; but when he had discovered Littler, cowering behind a gable on the broken gallery, he had felt a surge of triumphant joy. It was obvious what had happened. In his terror when the Ouabin came, the little boy had scrambled up the timber slopes, then been too frightened to come down alone. Perched precariously, high above the bazaar, he might have stayed there until he slipped and fell, or until a Ouabin spotted him after all. How frightened he must have been! Littler would not have admitted it, but it did not matter. Leaping like a cat across the chasm between the rooftops, Scabs had gathered up the child in his arms and brought him home. Running back through the alleys to the Realm of Un, Scabs had been filled with love and pride. Fondly he imagined the joy of his new-found friends; more than this, he saw himself celebrated as a hero. They would slap him on the back; they would kiss him; rapturously they would cry out his name.

What a fool he was! In this different homecoming, Scabs saw the vanity of all his hopes. Perhaps the others would be back soon, but he knew they would offer him neither praise nor thanks. It was not their way, and besides, he revolted them. On the rubber plantation where he had begun his life, Scabs had dreamed of escape. How he had longed to run away to sea! But then, on Captain Porlo's ship, he had dreamed again, this time of a new life in a new land; now here he was in a new land, and still dreaming. He reached up a raw-skinned, spindly arm, scratching at the pustular sores on his neck. In the tavern above, the song was reaching its cacophonous conclusion. It was a coarse sailor's song, one that Scabs had heard before.

> *Marry and burn!*
> *Man, you must learn*
> *After the wedding's when you really yearn!*
> *Look for your pleasures with a roving e-e-e-eye—*
> *Marry and burn,*
> *Marry and burn!*

What did it mean? Scabs didn't understand.

The coarse bellowing of the tavern-woman brought the song to an end. In the quietness that followed, Scabs heard the stirring of a rat, the tiny crumblings of a patch of damp, the slow insistent slapping of the sea against the docks. He sighed. Should he go back to the *Catayane*? Should he seek some new place, somewhere in these strange realms of Unang Lia? He did not know; now he knew only that he was tired, desperately tired. He would try to sleep before the sailors grew raucous again, starting a new round of clumping and cursing.

Drawing close to the exhausted Littler, Scabs laid a hand on the boy's side. The breathing was deep and regular, but he did not think his little friend was sleeping, not yet. Dear Squirt! Scabs stroked the downy hair. None of the other boys would have let him lie so near. Blubber was the worst, Cheese almost as bad ... why, Scabs suspected that even Master Raj was revolted by him, secretly if not openly. You could tell, you could just tell. Thinking how he had saved Littler that night, bounding from the gallery gable with the boy in his arms, Scabs wondered what would have

301

happened had any of the others needed saving like this. Would they have shrunk back, revolted by his raw, reaching hands? But then, it wouldn't happen. He wouldn't save *them*, any of them. Not now.

'Are you sleeping, Squirt?' he whispered.

A whisper came back. 'Don't call me Squirt.'

Both boys liked to whisper. They had heard too much of shouting, of screaming, of harsh taunts and laughter. Whispering was a special joy, precious and rare. Anxiously Scabs peered towards the trapdoor. He strained his ears for the slap of feet, running down the alley. At any moment the spell could be broken. He pushed his lips closer to the child's ear. 'What is your name, then?'

'I don't know. I mean, I think Mama must have given me a name, but Papa just calls me Littler.'

'You've got a mother?' said Scabs, as if the idea was extraordinary. 'A father too?'

'Mama's gone. Papa sold her – oh, long ago.'

'And your father?'

Littler sighed. 'But you know him. Everyone knows him, and calls him by his proper name, too. His three names.'

Scabs tightened his grip on the boy. 'Littler, you don't mean Eli Oli Ali?' This seemed more extraordinary still, but Scabs felt the little head nodding three times; once, perhaps, for each of his father's names. 'He's your father, and he put you down here?'

'He had to put me somewhere. Well, that's what he said.' Littler shifted, nuzzling closer to his friend. 'What about you, Scabs? Do you have a name?'

'Once when I was little, they said I did. I think a man wrote it down in a book, when they set me to work on the rubber trees. Before that, I don't remember much.'

'But what was the name?'

'I've tried to remember. I may have got it wrong, but I think it was Jorvel. I asked one of the men on the ship, and he said it was an Ejlander name. Perhaps it was my father's name, I don't know. Why, I don't know anything, except climbing rigging. And rubber trees.'

They fell silent and Scabs, running a hand down Littler's arm, felt the cold in the small body. Here in the Realm of Un, the heat of the day was seldom a visitor and if it did come, seldom stayed for long; often in the night the boys would wake up shivering. Scabs thought he might rummage in the pile of old clothes, seeking more layers to cover his friend; but not yet. He would keep this moment. Just a little longer. He drew the child closer, rubbing at the chill in the tiny arms. If they were hungry, smelly and cold too, they were happy. At least for now.

Littler said, 'Scabs? Shall I call you Jorvel?'

At first, a moan was the only reply. Then, a moment later, 'One day, when my sores have gone away. Until then, I'm Scabs. But I like to think that one day I'll be Jorvel . . . one day.'

There was silence again while they listened to a rat, scratching and scuffling on the other side of the cellar. It seemed so far away; absurdly, they felt safe on their carpet island.

Now Littler mumbled, 'Scabs? Perhaps the Sultan will make you better. Fix you, I mean.'

'The Sultan?'

'In the song. The one in the song.'

Silence resumed; Littler's breathing was deeper still, but Scabs urged softly, 'Squirt? I mean, Littler? Will you sing me the song?'

'I don't know . . . I mean, I can't remember.'

A squeeze. 'Try, Littler.'

But the child had fallen asleep at last. Scabs caressed him again, filled with love and longing. How he wished he could gather Littler in his arms, rising up with him in this moment and bearing him away to a different, better place! Dreams, confused and strange, clustered like clouds in the darkness around him. Soon Scabs would sink into their embrace, but not yet, not yet. Now he was aware of a different, sharper longing, one that had been gathering for long moments as he lay curled against the child's warm body . . .

No!

Scabs rolled away. Miserably he squatted on the edge of the carpet, looking blankly into the darkness around him. Memories of things that had been done to him beat like moths inside his brain. Oh, it was long ago, in the days before he was a hideous thing; it all might have happened to a different boy, but never, never would he forget that pain.

No. Not Littler, too.

From somewhere above, there still came a tiny seeping of lamplight; a glimmering caught the outline of a curved, metallic thing. It was the konar-light, lying on its side. Scabs reached for it, holding the cool brass against his forehead, then his heart.

'Scabs? What's wrong? Scabs, are you crying?'

No, he would not cry; the tears would be painful against his ruined skin. 'I can't sleep, that's all.'

'Shall I sing you the song?'

Scabs murmured assent. Slowly, as if it were a tender thing, he rubbed the konar-light in a circle round his heart, as Littler sang breathily, almost inaudibly:

Purple stranger
Sadly roams,
He shall be Sultan of the Catacombs:
Standing fast by the last of the skeleton jars,
Not like the Sultan of the Moon and Stars . . .

Alien creature,
Seldom seen,
Shrouded in mystery in the jungle green:
Turn and twist in the mist with a crazy picaroon,
Never with the Sultan of the Stars and . . .

There would have been more, and when Littler had finished, Scabs would have urged the child to explain. Perhaps they might have lit the konar-light, hunching together over the figures in the carpet. But all the time Scabs was rubbing the lamp, and then it happened.

Littler broke off.

Scabs cried out.

In an instant, the coloured cloud had swirled up to fill the Realm of Un, churning in bright billows, flashing impossibly with stabs of lightning. Then, just as suddenly, the clouds had cleared and sitting beside them on the carpet, glowing with a strange light, smiling whimsically, was a little man with crossed legs and arms and a bulging pot-belly.

The boys staggered upright, but before they could frame their questions, the little man had answered them – at least, in a manner of speaking. His eyes twinkled and he unleashed a torrent of words.

'Wondering who I am, I suppose? Don't see the resemblance? Ooh, but I suppose you're common boys,' he sighed. 'In any case, my dear brother will insist on that silly mask. Yes, brother I say! Though it's been so long, I wonder if he even remembers me. Poor Oman! Poor me! What an ordeal I've been through! Sunround after sunround in that old man's chest, only to get rubbed – rubbed, I ask you – by that goat-faced creature, and end up here. Why, when goat-face forgot me, I feared I'd languish in this squalid dive for just as long. My dears, the despair!'

The little man rolled his eyes. 'But let me introduce myself. Jafir's my name, and I know who *you* are. Anyway, my scabby friend, I assume you're a little more adventurous than goat-face, hm? I thought you were an adventurous boy . . . yes, you hear quite a lot in that konar-light, you know. See a bit too, even in the dark. Thought I was in for quite a show, just a moment ago.' The genie flashed Scabs a pointed look. 'Now, you're not going to be like that last one, I hope? Such dull WISHES I've never . . .'

Scabs burst out, 'Shut up!'

The little man sniffed. 'Well, I like that!'

304

'Scabs, careful!' hissed Littler. 'He's magic!'

Scabs could hardly doubt it. In his hand he held the konar-light; wisps of cloud still wafted from the spout. The little man was dazzling, but looking down, Scabs was dazzled also by the carpet, glowing richly in the strange illumination.

He looked up again. 'Who are you? What do you want?'

All this time, the little man had smirked; now he laughed aloud. 'Ooh, the babe in arms! Well, that's your friend, but you know what I mean . . . my dear, suffice to say that I am' – a weary sigh – 'the GENIE of that common little lamp you hold in your hands (*such* a common thing – really, it's *that* insult I regard as the worst), which means, I am bound to say, that it is for *me* to ask what *you* want.' And grimacing, the genie added, 'Master.'

'M-Master?' Scabs echoed doubtfully.

The genie rolled his eyes. 'Your WISHES, pus-face! What do you WISH?'

'Scabs,' said Littler, 'do you know what this means?'

'I wonder if *you* do,' simpered the genie, with a meaningful glance at the little boy. Impatiently he turned back to Scabs, sighing. 'Don't tell me you have to *think* about it?'

But Scabs was too astonished to register the insult. He stepped forward boldly.

'I wish you'd . . . take us away from here!'

'Ooh, not another one!' moaned the genie. He snapped his fingers and vanished. In the next moment, the carpet was rising in the air. The boys cried out, then flattened themselves against the fabric. They would strike the ceiling!

Instead, the carpet kept sailing upwards as if the tavern, like the genie's cloud, were made only of smoke. Astonished, they whizzed up through floor after floor of sailors, harlots, servants and slaves, squatting on chamber-pots, puffing at Jarvel, snoring drunkenly, rutting like beasts.

They burst through the roof.

Not until later would they notice that the konar-light had rolled off the side of the carpet when they rose and remained behind in the Realm of Un.

Chapter 45

OVER THE WALL

The moon as my livery,
The stars as my decoy,
I travel through darkness
On a faraway trail;
With no time for marriage,
Still, I'd sell my carriage
For a night with that maiden
In the shimmering veil!

Reeling through the alleys round the Palace of Perfumed Stairs, the prosperous merchant was not to know how close he had come to an unfortunate encounter. Perhaps his lips had last enjoyed the spices and sauces, sherbet and sorbet of a fine dinner, or the kisses of a pretty concubine, or applied themselves to the pipe of a hookah, in the perfumed darkness of a Jarvel-den. In any case, his happiness now bubbled forth in song and his coin-purse hanging unregarded from his plump hip, beat out the rhythm.

Blubber's eyes goggled, for all the world as if he had spied the coils of another eel. Fish, for his part, would have darted forward, but Faha Ejo reached out a restraining hand, tugging him back into the dark doorway.

The merchant staggered away.

'Faha, it's not fair!'

'Fair? Do you want that fool squealing like a stuck pig? Now come on, we're almost there.'

The coin-purse had been one of the few evidences of wealth the street-boys had seen as they flickered through the night. Fine homes clustered round the Caliph's palace, but seldom was wealth outwardly displayed, even by the greatest citizens of Qatani. Sheltering behind high walls, houses hugged their treasures close and secret. Display was to invite thieves; besides, who could compete with the royal residence? Even to be suspected of such presumption was to risk not only derision, but vicious reprisals.

Wraith-like, darting and dancing, Faha Ejo's ragged band stole through a labyrinth of rats, rubbish and spilling sewers, where the moon was a treacherous link-boy indeed, seeping too thinly past the heavy-hanging eaves.

They flashed across the empty market square.

'This way!'

'You know it well, Faha?'

'Shh! Watch out for Ouabin!'

Ducking beneath a section of ruined gallery, the Unners twisted their way, single file, into a chasm between two walls. One, plastered smooth, was the back of a house, blank but for a single dark window, high above the level of the ground; the other, made of large, rough stones, was higher still and surmounted by spikes. Beyond this wall, so Faha Ejo was certain, were the private apartments of the Shimmering Princess. Rajal asked how he could know; the goat-boy only tapped a finger to his nose, mouthing the name of his whoremonger cousin.

Stork and Cheese, grinning excitedly, jammed their ears against the rough wall.

'I can h-hear the h-hissing!'

'Sss! Sss!'

The boys leapt back, writhing their arms in the air like snakes. Faha Ejo rolled his eyes. 'Cut it out, that wall's as thick as Blubber!'

Cheese looked up. 'He'll do his jewels in, going over there.'

'Be one of them ladyboys, he'll be,' sniggered Fish. In his hand he still held the pizzle of horn-horse; grinning, holding it at the level of his loincloth, he mimed the action of a severing knife. 'Don't think you'll be tupping the Princess tonight, eh Vaga-boy?'

'What do you mean?' Rajal said sharply.

But before Fish could reply, Blubber burst out, 'A Vaga couldn't tup the Princess!'

'Neither could you, lard-lump!' Faha Ejo laid a hand on Rajal's arm. 'Listen, you idiots, the Vaga's not tupping her. He'll bring back her veil, that's enough – oh, and as many jewels as he can find.'

Cheese sniggered.

'That sort, too.' The moonlight in the alley was the merest sliver, but revealed the anger in the goat-boy's eyes. 'Over the wall and back, that's all. In and out.'

Cheese sniggered again.

'Look, shut up. After that he's our brother, just like Scabs, and never has to prove himself again. Got it?'

'I'll still say you can't trust a Vaga,' scowled Blubber.

'I'll still say they stink,' muttered Cheese.

'No, you won't,' said Faha Ejo, and pointed curtly to the ends of the alley. 'Cheese. That way. Watch out for Ouabin. Blubber, roll your guts to the other end.'

'Me?' moaned the fat boy. 'I want to watch the Vaga fall!'

'You can watch from there. But watch for Ouabin, too. Ready, Vaga-boy? Now who's going to blow on the pipe?'

'Me!' said Cheese, darting back.

'Me!' said Fish.

Faha Ejo slapped away their hands. 'Stork, you do it.'

'M-me? I can't p-p-play a pipe.'

'You don't have to play, just blow.'

Experimentally, Stork inserted the reed of the pipe into his toothless mouth, producing a high-pitched squawk. Faha Ejo snatched the pipe away.

'Not so loud!'

'How l-l-loud should it b-be?'

'Not very,' said Rajal. 'This rope twitches at the merest toot.'

'Shall we start?' said Faha Ejo.

But there was one more delay. Blubber rolled back from the end of the alley. 'I don't like it,' he hissed. 'The Vaga's cheating.'

'Cheating, how?' said Faha Ejo.

'Scabs climbed the Mosque of the Five Winds all by himself. He didn't use any doom-dancer's magic. Trust a Vaga to be a dirty cheat.'

Cheese slithered back from his own end of the alley. 'Blubber's right. What does it prove, getting over a wall with a magic rope? Besides, Vagas stink.'

The goat-boy pointed to the top of the wall. 'You'd like to do it instead, Cheese? Or how about you, Blubber? That's assuming the rope would rise.'

Blubber was sensitive to remarks upon his weight; which was unfortunate, since few could forbear from remarking upon it, if not at once, then in due course.

'Why, you dirty mixer!' The fat boy took a step forward, but Faha Ejo was faster. With a savage push he sent Blubber sprawling, then kicked him hard. 'Fish! Take Blubber's lookout. Cheese, back to your post or I'll shove one of your dirty feet down your mouth and the other one up your stinking arse.'

Fish sniggered at this, but Faha Ejo hushed the boy viciously, kicked Blubber in the guts again, and commanded Stork: 'Play!'

Stork played; dubiously, Rajal gripped the rope; none of the Unners saw the mysterious, almost ethereal figure that watched them in secret, its hat over its eyes and its cloak drawn tight to conceal its golden form.

❊   ❊   ❊

Turning slowly, like a raft in a stream, the carpet hung in the sky, refulgent under the moon that looked very yellow and very close to the two boys who cowered on the billowing fabric.

There was a puff of smoke and Jafir the genie appeared beside them. 'Well, you're out of there,' he continued, bored. 'I suppose you WISH to *go* somewhere now?'

Leaning forward eagerly, Scabs would have spoken at once, but Littler tugged at his arm, urging him to wait.

Wait? Whatever for? Scabs smiled kindly at his young companion, and spoke all the same. 'Genie, take us to ... to a faraway place!'

Wryly, Jafir twisted his mouth. 'That's it? That's what you WISH?'

Littler scrambled forward, as if to stop his friend's mouth, but Scabs only pushed him playfully away and nodded eagerly. 'I wish!'

'Oh, very well.'

With that, Jafir snapped his fingers again and all at once the carpet was tearing violently through the air, faster than any bird, scudding dangerously over the domes and minarets. Desperately the boys clutched the edges; Scabs flattened Littler, to prevent the little boy from falling over the side. Only the genie seemed to find the speed no trouble at all. His smirk was fixed in place and he kept his arms crossed.

In a matter of moments, the city and its docks were far behind. They flew across the desert.

'Genie, where are we going?' cried Scabs.

'To a faraway place, of course!' Jafir flung back. Then he added, with a gleam in his eye, 'By the way, you *do* know you've only got one WISH left?'

'*What?*' cried Scabs. 'That's not fair!'

'Really, the last one was just like you, too! Three WISHES, that's the rule!'

'You didn't tell me!'

'I'm telling you now!'

And the genie, snapping his fingers, was gone. Scabs howled, but there was no time to think about the wishes now. Faster and faster they flew through the air, until the arid land below, the bright moon and stars, even the pattern on the carpet registered only as streaks in their dazzled eyes.

Faster. Faster.

❈   ❈   ❈

Rajal's heart pounded hard.

The rope began to rise and he looked up, intensely aware of the height of the wall, the spikes and the cobber-as on the other side. It was not too late: even now he could drop to the ground, take to his heels. The temptation was strong, but with a stubborn pride he thought of the Unners, sniggering, sneering that Vagas were useless after all. Rajal would not let them laugh at him, he would not! But was he letting them make him into a bigger fool? He thought of Captain Porlo. He thought of the Princess. Then he thought of his missing crystal, and knew he must take a chance.

This was the plan: when the rope had stretched taut, and Rajal hovered high above, Stork would slowly leave off his playing, the rope would bend gently – as it had bent in the bazaar – and Rajal would be deposited easily, effortlessly on the forbidden balcony of the women's wing. When his work was done, he would signal with a whistle; then the rope would rise again to retrieve him.

Even as he swayed in the gap between the walls, Rajal began to have his doubts. In the bazaar, the rope had moved smoothly, sinuously, like the doom-dancer's melody; Stork's graceless shrillings had an opposite effect. Several times Rajal hit his head against the walls of the alley; more than once he knocked a knee or elbow, but dared not call out his curses. What if the foolish boy should leave off playing? Only when his hip crashed against the bricks, in response to an ill-advised trill, had Rajal almost bellowed; as it was, he bit hard on his tongue. He tasted blood in his mouth, felt water in his eyes. Then he started. A light now burned in the high window, spilling its rays into the alley. Rajal saw figures, moving in a blur. He brushed away his tears and saw them clearly.

Guards.

The guards guzzled ferment and played at cards.

Rajal swayed close to the dangerous spikes. Mouthing silently, he waved to his partners. Had they no idea of the danger? Cheese, at his end of the alley, was only staring up, intent on Rajal's ordeal; Fish, at the other end, toyed idly with the dried pizzle of horn-horse, flipping it up and down in front of his loincloth.

Stork was growing breathless, wheezing – how he longed to break off. The boy struggled to command himself. Desperately he continued his tuneless warblings.

'Not long now,' breathed Faha Ejo. 'Just a little higher, then slowly down.'

'I can hear the snakes, I'm sure of it!' Cheese squealed.

'I hope they bite his jewels off,' muttered Blubber, then moaned as Faha Ejo kicked him again.

'Come on, Stork!' urged the goat-boy. 'One more trill!'

It was not to be. Suddenly Stork gasped. The pipe clattered to the ground.

Rajal cried out, plummeting.

'Idiot!' Faha Ejo seized the pipe, splitting the air with a violent *toot!*

Rajal shot up. A spike ripped his breeches.

A face came to the window. Then came a shout, but the boys below did not hear. Trilling on the pipe, Faha Ejo was kicking Stork up and down the alley. It would have been a comic sight, but for Rajal; each kick made him lurch violently in the air. Between lurchings, he saw the guards in the lighted room, clustering curiously about the window.

'It wasn't my fault, Faha!' Stork was protesting. 'Somebody hit me! Somebody threw a stone!'

The goat-boy blew an arpeggio of annoyance.

'Faha, it's true!' Cheese leapt up and down. 'I saw it, I did!'

A tremolo of temper.

'Someone's there, Faha, in the shadows!'

A cadenza of contempt.

Then something crunched beneath the goat-boy's foot. The pizzle of horn-horse! His playing faltered.

'Fish!'

The boy in the loincloth was lying senseless.

Rajal plunged.

Faha Ejo thrust the pipe back at Stork. 'Play!'

A sharper whistling split the air; Rajal swooped up again, but not before he had sunk low enough to see the glimmer of something shifting, moving in the deep pit between balcony and wall. Terror filled him; bile rushed to his throat. Like a swimmer in trouble, he flailed towards the balcony, but his own efforts were powerless to direct the swaying rope.

In the lighted room, the guards seized their sabres, thundering towards the stairs. In the same moment there was a scuffling at one end of the alley.

'Hey!'

It was Cheese, struggling with an assailant. There were kicks, blows. Cheese collapsed; Faha Ejo ran forward. A stone whizzed, striking his face. He cried out, staggering, and the assailant would have skittered away; but Cheese rallied, blocking his end of the alley. Now the assailant would have blundered back the other way, pushing past Faha Ejo, Stork, and the floundering Fish.

Instead, Blubber reared up suddenly. The assailant darted from the first ungainly lunge, but the second was too much. Three things happened quickly: Blubber's bulk bore down; they cannoned into Stork; the doom-dancer's pipe was knocked from Stork's hand, then crushed, like the assailant, beneath Blubber's weight.

Rajal screamed.

But there was another scream, not from the air. 'Get him off me! Get him off me!'

Faha Ejo staggered forward. Could it be? 'Girl-boy!'

'Infidel, I've been looking for you! You thief . . . murderer! I nearly died because of you!'

'What . . . what?'

There was no time for questions. A rapid *thump! thump!* of boots filled the air and the startled Fish leapt up, desperate, goggle-eyed.

'Guards!'

A moment later, when the guards burst into the alley, they found it empty but for three items, revealed in the glare of their lantern. One was a dry, cylindrical object that might have been an old and very mouldy carrot; one was a curious pipe, its bulbous end crushed; one was a commonplace coil of rope.

There was no sign of Rajal, but nearby, unseen by the guards, a cloaked figure looked on, laughing silently.

✳ ✳ ✳

'Wh-where are we?' Scabs moaned.

They had come back to earth with a bump. Some moments passed before their dizziness subsided. The night was ending and filling their eyes were the rays of a desert dawn. Scabs brought a hand to his forehead like a visor, but at first he could barely make out their surroundings.

Snap.

'Yes, do have a look around,' smirked Jafir. 'I think I'll do the same. So kind of you to let me choose our destination. I think I've chosen well, but caution is of the essence. After all, I must be sure this is a place I'd like to stay. Or should I say, a dream I'd like to dream?'

Scabs furrowed his brow. 'I . . . I don't understand.'

'You realise you left that konar-light behind, by the way? Clattered down to the floor, it did, in that wretched cellar. Oh, how I've longed for someone to lose it, all these sunrounds! Do you know what this means? One more WISH, and I'm free!' The plump face broke into a broad grin. 'I'd thank you, my dears, but gratitude's not quite my line. I'll be back when you need me. One more WISH, remember – just one more!'

'Wait!' cried Scabs. Why should he delay? Already he knew his last wish, or thought he did; indeed, it should have been his first, had he known there were only three. He would wish to be beautiful.

Yes, that was it.

But Jafir had snapped his fingers and gone again, and Scabs did not know how to call him back. The wish would have to wait. Unsteadily, Scabs rose to his feet, extending a hand to Littler. Stepping cautiously off the magic carpet, each wondered if it would vanish or fly off suddenly. It did not, but as Littler looked back it seemed to him that the five Sultans were shifting, just a little, in the dawn light.

Then suddenly it seemed later, much later than dawn. Before them lay a lush vista of gardens, a long, deep pool, and in the distance, dazzling in the bright sun, the massy edifice of the House of Truth.

Chapter 46

A BOY'S INITIATION

Hush, my pretties.

That voice again. Rajal had heard it somewhere before, the same words, the same tone, low, insistent, a sibilant hiss. His eyes flickered open. Moments passed before the scene around him was more than a blur of shifting shapes, but from the first he had an impression of red and gold, shimmering darkly in a sensual lamplight. He rolled back his head and was aware of silk. Somewhere in the background figures moved, sashaying in long, rustling robes or gowns. The air was thick with a potent incense. There was whispering. Giggling.

Hush, my pretties.

The voice came again, and Rajal remembered where he had heard it before. Already the moment when he had swayed on the rope seemed lost in the past, an eternity ago – but this was false. It was the last thing he had known. Now he played the events out in his mind with a dreamy slowness: the heady rush as he plunged down, like a monstrous bird shot from the air; the cobber-as, arching up their hooded necks; then the figure standing in their midst, formidable, unafraid, reaching out. The tall man must have braced himself with expert judgement, for he barely staggered as Rajal crashed into his arms. Who was this man? Dimly, before his shocked mind had sunk into blankness, Rajal had been aware of rich robes, billowing unmolested through shrinking snakes; then the voice again, always the voice.

Hush, my pretties.

But who were these pretties who surrounded him now? Rajal's vision swam back into focus and he saw that he was lying on a slab-like bed, raised unusually high, in the middle of a large, luxurious chamber. There were lush red cushions with golden tassels; there were swaying screens of brightly coloured beads; here and there sprawled an exotic, sharp-eared cat, and around his bed, jangling and glittering, was a constellation of gorgeous, veiled creatures.

At the sight of them, Rajal felt a surge of alarm. But why should this be? Confused, he recalled that he had, after all, been attempting to break into the women's wing. Should it startle him to be confronted with so many women? Perhaps it was their novelty, for since arriving in this country he had seen few of their sex – few, that is, except the common

313

folk, who concealed themselves in shapeless black. By contrast, these women were images of beauty – dazzling, almost brazen in their charms.

Dutifully, in subservience to the tall man, the gorgeous creatures had hushed their chatter. Idly one fed a bird that perched on her wrist; one petted the throat of a purring cat; one dragged a brush, again and again, through the long strands of her hair; one held a hand poised, toyingly, above a lyre.

But there was something else. Something more. In the silence, Rajal sensed a foreboding. Dark eyes gazed over the gauzy veils, and he saw that all the eyes were intent upon him, lingering over the contours of his sprawled body. With a surge of panic he wondered if he were naked again, but no: his rags were gone; someone had dressed him in an ornate robe.

He swallowed and said, 'Wh-Why am I here?'

The question was a foolish one, perhaps, but not completely. His head had been turned towards the gorgeous creatures; there were no replies from them. Here and there, dark eyes looked down.

Then came the echo, in the voice Rajal knew.

'Why? Why? Or do you mean what? In any case, these are questions that might with more pertinence be put to *you*, Empster-ward. To *you*, hm?'

'I d-don't understand.'

'Empster-ward! Is there anything for *you* to understand?'

The voice, Rajal surmised, was mocking him, but not unkindly. In a corner, face averted, its owner stood before a steaming bowl. There were sluicings, sloshings; it seemed that the tall man was washing his hands.

He turned, tightening the cord of his robe.

'Vizier Hasem,' Rajal said blankly.

'Of course. Among my many duties, do I not take care of the Caliph's ... *recreational* interests?'

'The women's quarters?'

'Is that doubt in your voice? Empster-ward, remember you plummeted to the ground. This is not – hm – not *quite* the women's quarters. One might say we are beneath them – though, for my part, I should not care for the implications. Nor, I suppose, should you.' The Vizier smiled. 'But let me introduce you to your new sisters.'

'Sisters?'

There followed a series of names, but Rajal's mind was blurring; the names, it seemed, floated towards him like boats on a slow current, changing mysteriously in the time they took to reach him. This plump girl? Blubina. This tall one? Storkela ... Empster-ward, meet Fishia ... the fragrant Cheesia ... step forward, Littlina, don't be shy ... For a crazed moment it seemed to Rajal that he was back in the Realm of Un,

314

but the Realm of Un transformed by a strange, taunting magic. Bundles and barrels were cushions and couches; curtains of sacking, curtains of beads; rats, cats; cockroaches, birds; and the boys ... the boys ...

Rajal shook himself. What was wrong with him, what could be wrong? His brow furrowed and he looked at the girls, looked at them squarely. Oh, but there *was* something strange about them, there *was*! He sat up sharply and would have flung himself from the bed, but a hand pushed him effortlessly back, and Rajal realised he could not escape. Of course not: there would be guards, snakes, high walls; besides, a strange weariness had possessed him, a leadenness in his limbs. That was when he remembered the Vizier's voice, crooning to him in the aftermath of his fall, *Drink this, Empster-ward. Here, drink this* ... Now Rajal swooned and the Vizier stepped forward, sliding a soft finger over the boy's lips, his chin, the apple in his throat ...

'Empster-ward,' came the crooning again, 'there is much in this world to puzzle us, and there will always be; but there are certain truths, too, that we may come at last to realise, after which many things seem clearer to us. Truths about the stars, truths about the moon; truths about the powers of gods and men. Then, too, there are truths about ourselves. To be sure, you have come here on a quest, a mission, but was not your real quest to find yourself?'

Confusedly, Rajal struggled to think. He thought of the Crystal of Koros, and his longing to retrieve it. He thought of the Crystal of Theron, that they must find, and find soon. Jem and the crystals, that was all that mattered, all that would ever matter. What was the Vizier talking about? What could he mean?

But on and on went the beguiling voice; on and on ran the smooth, thrilling fingers. As he spoke, the tall man leaned over the bed; he almost hovered over Rajal's supine form. His breath came hotly, rich with pungent spices.

'Dear child, can you imagine that you fooled me for a moment? The red-haired one spoke of a bold young man, enemy of your homeland's people and crown; why, it is as if he spoke of another! From the first, I saw what you were – or longed to be. By what strange destiny it was that you, and not the girl-boy, were bound upon the wheel, I neither ask nor care. What is this but a bagatelle, mere chaff in the wind against the greater, more profound fate that brought you back to me?'

The Vizier parted Rajal's robes.

'No, child, doubt not my ardour, for I am aware even of this stab-mark of the gods that aches so mysteriously, so redly upon your thigh; why already, as you lay swooning, it has felt the moistness of my tongue and lips! Feel no shame at what you are! In this Place of the Cobras, what care we for the world and its foolish superstitions? Outside, you are

315

condemned to die, but what of it? Within these walls, you shall fulfil your destiny!'

Rajal would have twisted, writhed, cried out, but he could neither move nor speak. A thousand, a million torments churned in his mind, but nothing could be more real than this moment, unfolding now. Fervently the girls eyed his naked flesh; still only the Vizier dared to touch him. First the hand caressed the thin, boyish chest, then travelled lower, lower. Lust flickered in the tall man's eyes, but the flames ignited a passion in Rajal too. With a sickening lurch, the young man became aware of his own gathering excitement.

The Vizier stepped back, stretching out his arms. Girls went to him, stripping him of his raiment with slow, reverent gestures. There was the sound of fingers sweeping across a lyre, and all at once a heady, sweet rush of odour, stronger than all the perfumes that already filled the air. Rajal's head lolled and his vision was blurred, but he guessed that when the man returned he would be smeared with pungent oils. Desperately Rajal's chest thudded with desire. Tears filled his eyes. *Here, drink this.* It was something they had done to him, it must have been! Slowly he became aware that the girls were pulling him about the bed, positioning him. Cushions raised his hips.

The man returned. This time his caresses were harder, fiercer, and his whisper burned like fire.

'No shame, no shame I say! Did I not say I knew what you were? From the first, I saw the womanish weakness in your eyes.'

Womanish? thought Rajal. *What are you talking about?*

'But why call it weakness? The passivity of a woman is her glory and pride, for what power is greater than the sway she holds over the pleasures of men?'

But I'm not a woman!

'You have heard that your kind is despised, but how can that be, how could that ever be, when you are to be the conduit of a monarch's pleasures?'

Can't you see I'm not a woman? Rajal screamed inwardly.

'How I should like to have you cleansed at once, cleansed and ready for the glory that awaits you! But no, the time is not yet ripe. As ever, we must follow the age-old customs. First, for ten nights – ten nights, my pretty! – you shall know the pleasures I am about to afford you. As in affairs of state, so in love: if the monarch is to enjoy an easy yielding, first his minister must prepare the way. By day, your new sisters shall instruct you in other arts; then, when you are ready, and only then, shall you be made clean, clean and pure as they are, and ready for the Caliph.'

The man moved into position.

'Sisters, hold her limbs, hold them tight. True, we have administered our potions with a merciful liberality; true, we have stirred a receptive longing; still, it may be that there is thrashing, it may be that there is writhing, in the first moments before the pleasure takes hold.' Tenderly, a hand stroked Rajal's hair. 'Ah, child, indeed there shall be pain, but what is pain when it pushes open a portal to a lush new land of unexplored delight?'

Rajal's head rolled back. First came a desperate, hopeless withholding, then suddenly, inevitably, the searing fire. For a moment it seemed that his spine would break, snapping link by link from the base upwards; he screamed, but no sound left his lips. Still a hand swooped across the lyre; somewhere, far away, a girl was singing. Silent screams became silent sobs. It was no good, no good, there was only this pain. On and on went the terrible stabbings; then, from the depths of Rajal's being, came a different stabbing, more urgent still, a rippling, a bucking. The bursting came like lava, and Rajal's shame was complete.

In that moment, it seemed to him that everything was over. How could it go on? How could life go on? But the Vizier's ardour was heightened, not diminished, and sweatily, smiling, he leaned close to Rajal's ear, insisting again that there could be no shame.

'Child, in time you shall learn control, but how are you to know the dangers you face, unless experience is to be your teacher? It is a commonplace accident, no more; to the palate of an epicure, a pungent sauce. In your new life, you are to know pleasures beyond those of ordinary men – ordinary women, too. You feel pain, but is it not ebbing now? Ah, but it shall, for in the depths inside you lies a buried jewel. In that jewel is the secret of joy. Look through the mud to the buried jewel. Child, think of the jewel, the jewel.'

※　※　※

Later, Rajal would wonder if the words had been a spell. Incense swirled; there was the lyre, the song; there were croonings of comfort, caressing hands, and in what followed, it was not the pain but the words, the spell that thudded like a mantra in his mind. Now, glimmering before his eyes, he saw the jewel, purple and shining. What need had he to search? Yes, what he sought was inside him, inside him! Sobs racked his frame as he pictured his hands, scooping eagerly in the viscous mud; then he saw the jewel rising in his hands and his body rising too, upwards, ever upwards.

The next eruption was a blazing whiteness.

Long after it was over, the drugged young man lay moaning and gasping on the soiled sheets, thinking only of the jewel, the jewel.

Chapter 47

THE FOURTH VANISHING

Cata felt herself stirring at last. How long had she slept? It seemed like days. Images from strange dreams swirled through her mind, of lush gardens, of a palace-like house, of a long, deep pool, of sky that shifted rapidly from midday to midnight, then back again. She put a hand to her head, peering out from behind the screen where she had lain. Pale bands of moonlight shone through the blinds, shimmering in the threads of the lush carpets and the gauzy corrugations of the looking-glasses. There was nothing else to be seen. Where was Princess Bela Dona? Where had she gone?

Then Cata heard a voice, whispering from the gloom. Some moments passed before she understood the words, or realised that they formed a strange and malignant rhyme:

> Lamp that has glowed beside a father's sleep,
> Lit his foolish smile, listened to him weep,
> Come, be the bearer of my vengeance-spell:
> Hating a viper, shall I love its spawn?
> Soon he shall wish she had never been born!

It was a man's voice, powerful but distant – carried eerily on the wind, perhaps, across wide desert spaces. Then came a glimmering in the centre of the chamber, and as the voice whirled from the vortex of darkness, so too came an accompanying vision. The gauze billowed, the moonlight seemed brighter, and Cata stared, astonished, at the ghostly figure of a man.

> Tiny flame, glow like the bright rays of dawn,
> Watch as the spirit from the flesh is torn:
> Now, let this spell be a secret you keep,
> Curled deep within you, as inside a shell,
> Until the tolling of a different knell!

The man was very old, but moved, almost writhed, with a peculiar suppleness. Round and round he went. He had trailing white hair and a long beard, fashioned into three forks. He was dressed in star-spangled robes. In one hand he held a glinting object that might have been gold or merely brass. At first Cata could not make it out; then she saw that it was one of those curious, exotic lamps she had seen so often in the Caliph's palace. A konar-light, no more.

But no. Much more.

As the strange incantation writhed on and on, Cata found herself trembling violently.

> *Yea, ere the ringing of the next time-bell,*
> *Down sinks Elmani, as into a well:*
> *Lost to a daughter's touch, condemned to mourn!*
> *Come, genius of the lamp, come, let us reap*
> *Vengeance! You hold the blade! Drive it in deep!*
> *– Spirit and flesh, DIVIDE!*

At this last command, Cata almost burst from her hiding-place, as if indeed the ghostly, murderous figure had a child at his mercy.

Instead, she woke with a stifled cry. A dream, another dream? But it had seemed so real! She brought a hand to her forehead, conscious suddenly of her manacles, her chain. They at least were real. So was the moonlight. So was the screen.

Now, from behind it, came a different voice.

In the middle of the gauzy looking-glasses, the Caliph Oman Elmani sat slumped like a supplicant, rocking a little from side to side; and there, shimmering before him, elevated above the carpet, was the mysterious girl Cata had last seen communing with visions. Fascinated, horrified, Cata watched as the little man poured out, as if to an icon, all the miseries of his heart. He was sobbing, almost incoherent, but often enough he mouthed the words *wedding* and *Ouabin* for Cata to understand what was soon to happen. Like a vision of compassion, the Princess gazed upon her stricken, swaying father as if she longed to take him in her arms. Helplessly, uselessly he cursed the Ouabin Sheik, then the Teller Evitamus, too.

'My child, how I had hoped you might yet be cured! What pains have we taken, what trials undergone, in the hope that somehow a way could be found! Had we but found the Teller, I believed . . . but alas, he is dead, and the konar-light lost!'

There was more in this vein, much more, but soon Cata was no longer listening. Dimly she began to understand her dream, and saw that perhaps it was no dream at all; in a vision, she saw herself staggering forward, crying that the Caliph must not despair, for the Teller, through he be dead, was not yet gone. Instead, as the little man collapsed into a heap, Cata stared with growing entrancement into the brilliant, auroral form of Princess Bela Dona.

At first the beauteous figure was a luminescence of whiteness, a billow of gauze like the covers over the looking-glasses; then Cata saw the coloured glow, pulsing inside the strange girl like a heart, seen miraculously through walls of flesh. The glow at first was purple, then green, then red ... the colours of the crystals! It seemed to Cata then that a sudden, vital knowledge had filled her mind, but what that knowledge could be, she could barely tell. Princess Bela Dona stretched out her arms, turning like a dancer; Cata slumped to her knees, chain clanking, astonished, then frightened as the rays stabbed into the air in great revolving arcs, spinning faster and faster like a whirling wind of light.

Purple. Green. Red. Blue. Gold.

The wind, as if it were real, spirited away the gauze from the looking-glasses. Still the Caliph slumped, moaning. Cata staggered out into the roaring eddy, struggling towards the radiant, turning girl. Somehow Cata knew she must touch the girl's hand; somehow, she knew something vital was at stake.

'Princess!' she cried out, but her words were swept away. Cata sank to the floor. She clawed at the carpet. Her hair whipped wildly in all directions.

Then came a different, stranger screaming, higher, fiercer, than the ragings of the storm, and Cata gasped to see a terror-struck face, magnified hugely in a looking-glass. Then in another. Another. Then in them all. It was the Princess; for a moment it seemed there was nothing in the world but the girl's stricken face, screaming, screaming and screaming again.

Then the screaming stopped and a voice – but not the girl's – boomed hugely from the multiplied faces.

The Caliph scrambled back, shrieking in terror.

> Long years have passed since my terrible bane
> Bound this Caliphate in its iron chain,
> Scourging a father with the cruellest lash:
> Lost from this world now, shall I feel remorse?
> Ah, but I cannot change the spell's harsh course!

Crazily Cata's vision veered back and forth, darting from looking-glass to looking-glass. Again she struggled to stand, tripping over her chain, cursing her manacles, crying out defiance to the wildness all around her. That was when she saw the figure from her dream, rolling and tumbling through the dizzying air.

'Monster! Vicious, taunting monster!' shrieked the Caliph.

> Yet still I know we may mend this divorce
> Temporarily. Child of secret force,
> Traveller, stranger, touch this daughter's pain:
> Link your hand with hers, beat not an eyelash,
> Wait, be still. There shall come a searing flash!

Cata reached out, and though her hand swept through the girl's hand, still the touch was enough. In an instant, the manacles fell from her wrists. The magic was beginning! Was it good? Was it evil? Cata knew only that she must submit. Suddenly she was spinning beside the girl.

But no, not beside. Inside. *Inside.*

'Shimmy! Shimmy!' sobbed the terrified Caliph, but all that came in reply was the Teller's rhyme, booming on and on through the looking-glass faces, but now the faces were first Bela Dona's, then Cata's, Bela Dona's, Cata's, Bela Dona's, Cata's.

> *Caliph, perhaps my solution seems rash?*
> *Compared to your deserts, it is a cache*
> *Of gold. My mercy is for my child, source*
> > *Of true salvation, should she but regain*
> > *The light, that alone shall redeem these twain!*
> > *– Spirit and flesh, UNITE!*

It was over. The Caliph looked up and, seeing only a blaze of light, thought he had been blinded. He whimpered. Sobbed. Then the brightness faded and again there was the moonlight, the carpet, the screens, all as they had been; only the scattered curtains of gauze bore testimony to the magic of moments before.

Only the curtains, and the figure before him now.

It was not Cata's, for Cata had vanished.

The Caliph said uncertainly, 'Shimmy?'

A smile played across his face. Then a frown. Could it be true? Could his daughter be real?

Cata – for no, she had not vanished, not really – turned slowly, staring first into the haze of one moonlit looking-glass, then another.

'My face,' she whispered. 'My face.'

 END OF PART THREE

321

PART FOUR

The Flight from the Enchanter

Chapter 48

THE CURSE OF KALED
(concluded)

Purple stranger
Sadly roams,
He shall be Sultan of the Catacombs ...

Alien creature,
Seldom seen,
Shrouded in mystery in the Jungle Green ...

Dea, staring into his green tea, broke off his murmurous singing. Dappled sunlight played around him, warming the fragrant flowers and leaves. Through the foliage came the twittering of the Targons. Simonides was silent, but for his heavy, laboured breathing. Dea looked up. 'Simonides,' he said, 'what does this song mean? This Sultan Song?'

'Dea, you know it is a celebration of your father's greatness, and the greatness of his ancestors.'

'Yes, but what does it mean? The purple one, the green one were Sultans, I know, but still this song seems mysterious to me. Am I a fool?'

'On the contrary, Dea, you are one who sees deeply. Indeed, the song tells of the five God-Sultans, prophesied to reign over us before the end of this Time of Atonement we live through now. Then too, each represents a spiritual state. Purple Catacombs. Jungle Green. Red Dust. Blue Wave. Each of these is a stop along the way, as we journey to that oneness with the gods which is our destiny. Do we not follow this pattern each day, as we observe the Submissions?'

'Our destiny, then, is the Moon and Stars?' Dea bit his lip, but resumed after a moment, 'Good Simonides, from what you have told me of my father, I wonder how it is that he rose to such a pinnacle.'

The old man sighed. Of course, he had known this would come. To be sure, Dea was a sweet boy, struggling carefully to avoid the painful subjects they had discussed before. Ah, but he could not help himself. Slowly, slowly he had been working back to the one thing he must know.

Simonides reached out, gripping the boy's hand. If the old man were still weak from his last attack, what did it matter? What reprieve could there be? Affairs in the empire were at a desperate pass. The Ouabin, if whispers were true, had converged upon Qatani; imperial forces now

325

converged in their turn. Simonides was troubled by dark intimations, stirrings of the powers he had renounced so long ago. Nothing could distress him more than these, and whatever happened, he would die soon. He had started this act of treason; he must see it through to the end.

'Fear not, young Prince, I shall finish the story.'

The long-limbed boy only nodded, barely breathing. Huddling close to the wicker chair, he stared intently into the old man's faded eyes.

Yes, it had to be.

This time, this time, the story must end.

❈   ❈   ❈   ❈

'My child, I have told you of the envy that eradicated from your father's heart all love for his dear friend Mala. I have told how Mala was found to be a traitor and paid the ultimate price; how your father sued for the beauteous Ysabela, whom once he thought would be Mala's bride. I have told how this maiden, your mother's sister, was married instead to the Caliph of Qatani; then how your great-father died suddenly and your father became Sultan. But what was the pomp of position to this young man, who believed himself to have lost the one thing he wanted? I speak, of course, of the love of Ysabela.

'It was now, in the desolation that possessed him, that your father turned once more to his scientific studies. Again I would repair with him to library and laboratory, this time not as tutor – for who could teach a Sultan? – but as assistant. At first your father sought only distraction, and our investigations were desultory. We studied the movements of the constellations; we dissected snakes and earthworms once more; we tested various poisons upon the lesser royal slaves. Only after some moonlives did our work acquire direction. It was then, walking one day in the palace gardens, that your father confided to me a startling, nay, a shocking fact.

'Since becoming Sultan, it was his duty to commune with the Flame, in the ceremonies held each moonlife in the Sanctum. Time and again he had seen your great-father, writhing in the grip of the sacred rapture; likewise, my young master would now abase himself, waiting for the wisdom that the Flame would impart.

'"But Simonides," he said gravely, "there is none."

'"Sire?"

'"Simonides, I tell you I have heard no voice, seen no visions." The Sultan's voice was the merest whisper. "Am I to fear some lack in myself? Am I really of the Sultan's breed at all? Ah, old tutor, there are times when I have been hot with shame, hugging my secret tight against my breast."

'My mind reeled at your father's words. I was a loyal son of Unang,

326

great in the College of Imams; though I had devoted myself to the mysteries of nature, never had it occurred to me to think of the Flame with any but the most ardent faith. Now a door that had seemed for ever sealed was thrown suddenly, violently open.

'"Simonides, you know what we must do?"

'I nodded, my heart shaking with fear. The days of footling work were behind us. From now on, our enquiries took on a particular aspect, and with that aspect a fierce, furtive urgency. It was inevitable, of course: your father sought the secret of the Flame. His explorations would know no bounds. Now, from all corners of his kingdoms, he summoned the most distinguished women and men of learning. Each was accorded the privileges of his palace, and each became the subject of his earnest questionings. Some did not understand, finding his manner obscure and puzzling; others understood only too well. The Imams were alarmed, scenting heresy. Your father scorned their fears, but in private he would give way to his own heretical imaginings.

'The truth came to him slowly, but broke over him at last like thunder. How many times had he seen your great-father writhing on the floor before the column of fire? The old man had deceived him! Whether your great-father had been the dupe of his own longings, or whether he had knowingly acted a part, the effect was the same. Never in all his religious devotions had your father known a revelation like this.

'There was no sacred rapture. No god in the Flame. The old tales of the crystal were the merest delusion, fit only for the weak minds of infants.

'For a time, in the joy of intellectual triumph, your father longed to shout his knowledge to all – but only for a time. In science, there is no value higher than truth, but suddenly this was science no longer. It was religion. It was politics. In the Courts of Kal-Theron, a man must learn cunning, and your father had learnt his lesson well. He was no fool – what would it profit him to proclaim the truth? What power had truth against the might of delusion? For delusion, the Prophet had journeyed across the deserts; for delusion, thousands had followed him, and when he died, had accepted without question that his descendants should reign over them for ever. No, your father could never reveal what he knew! In what else was his power based, but in the useless prayers his people mumbled to a column of burning gas?

'Understand, young Prince, that I speak here only of what your father believed. That a man is convinced of something does not make it so, even if that man is the most powerful in all the world.

'In the thrall of this new conviction, your father felt himself free; with superstition behind him, he convinced himself that neither the world, nor the Imams, could place any barriers between himself and his desires. No longer would he submit to the dictates of fate.

'It was perhaps a sunround after your great-father's death that your father tested his powers, with a startling command concerning the brother who had been separated from him in earliest infancy. The Caliph of Qatani, decreed your father, was an important ally, and with Ouabin-evil threatening the empire at every turn, important allies must be cultivated.

'"To this end," said your father slyly, "I have decided upon a mission of friendship, in which I shall personally visit my dear brother."

'Now there was much consternation among the courtiers at this, for never had a Sultan gone forth from Kal-Theron, nay, not since the Time of the Prophet. The scheme seemed outrageous, and foolish too, but your father would brook no contradiction. Indeed, how could he be contradicted, when he was the one who spoke to the Flame?

'Of course I suspected your father's real intentions. That his plan was to steal your uncle's new bride, I had no doubt. How I wish that, there and then, I had taken my courage in my hands at last, counselling him against this folly! He could be a good ruler, and could he not atone for the sins of the past? Were he only to forget Princess Bela, could he not know every happiness?

'As it happened, only one old Imam ventured even the mildest remonstration.

'"Would His Sacred Highness traverse the desert wastes, suffering all manner of appalling discomfort – perhaps even risking the life for which All Unang prays?"

'"I have secured the Line, have I not? Should I fall, there is a son to succeed me." (A hollow statement to some, for was it not the duty of a Sultan to have many sons, for the Line to be truly called secure?) "Besides, if All Unang prays for me, I must certainly be safe," your father added with a smile, and the abashed Imam dared not point out that All Unang had prayed for your great-father too.

'I was among the retainers who accompanied your father upon his progress across the desert. From the first it was an ill-fated mission, with many delays and much illness among nobles and slaves alike. But your father was determined. A bitter fire burned in his eyes and I dreaded what would happen when we reached Qatani. Often my heart was filled with trepidation as I gazed upon the warriors that rode with our vans, and wondered whether their purpose was only to guard us. In the desert, one's mind is prey to many illusions, and sometimes it seemed to me, looking across the sands that stretched behind us, that I saw the distant flash of yet more scimitars, yet more armoured men, following in our wake.

'One night your father called me to his caravan. He had partaken heavily of the Jarvel-pipe, and would have me do the same. I assented, struggling to conceal my reluctance, as he sought my participation in a philosophical dialogue. For a moment I thought he would resume our old relations, and wistfully I thought back to the days of his innocence; then I saw that he shared none of my regret, and thought only of his present obsession.

'Your father began to speak of time, of its mysterious chambers, of its cunning corridors, and though this was wisdom I had once imparted to him, I saw that he would be tutor now, and have me as his pupil. Sadly I studied his new-grown beard as he put to me a series of oblique questions. Could it be that time had a natural course, a pattern into which events must fall? Could it be that events might take a different turn? If this were so, and a man could see it, was it not his duty to repair time, putting things back as they should be?

'I would have retorted that no man, not even a Sultan, could bend the course of time. But such a response would hardly have been welcome. Your father required me only to nod my head in answer to each new question. I did; but of course, I could see where this was tending. Your father had convinced himself that your Aunt Bela's loss was an error in time itself, one that it was his duty to rectify.

'He looked at me levelly through the Jarvel-haze.

'"You are unconvinced, old friend?"

'"Sire, am I to question one who communes with the Flame?"

'"Hah! It is as well I have brought you with me, Simonides, for I see you are a diplomat." Then he grew earnest, and leaned close to me. "Old friend, if you knew what I knew of the fair Bela's fate, you would think me neither fool nor tyrant. Qatani is far away, but still in that city there are eyes and ears through which I may see, through which I may hear. Oh, what a black day when that lovely girl was squandered on my brother!"

'What came next was an outburst of rage, but though it was barely coherent I divined, nonetheless, what your father's spies had seen. His brother, it appeared, was a weak and sensual fool, unworthy of the love of the beauteous Bela. Spurning the natural pleasures of woman, instead it was with catamites that he would vent his lust.

'Naturally I expressed my abhorrence of such vice, but here it was that your father's eyes flashed, and a smile broke through the blackness of his beard. Even now I did not quite understand what was passing through his mind. Then, as the knowledge filled me, I almost laughed at my young master's audacity. Indeed, he believed he could reverse the flow of time, for not only would he seize back the beauteous Bela, but he had convinced himself that she still must be unblooded, pure. Could he be her first and only lover, would he not laugh at time and all its works?

'"Soon, Simonides, all shall be well," he said, "for as I am no longer married, so the marriage of my dear Ysabela was no marriage at all. Let her father deny me now, and he shall lie dead at my feet! For I, who could have all this world might give, want nothing but the love of Ysabela, and nothing in this world shall stand in my way!"

'Bold words; that they were meant sincerely there could be no doubt. Alas for your father, that all his powers were as nothing against the rival no man may defeat. Yes, I speak of Death! For when at last we arrived in Qatani, we found the city in mourning, and when we asked why, the answer fell readily, sadly from every tongue.

'The Princess was dead, and all the prayers in Unang could not revive her corpse.

'For a time, in the madness that seized him, your father would have ordered his armies to destroy the city, razing every building, killing every inhabitant. Only his brother he would have spared, and that so that he might be paraded back to Kal-Theron, there to be tortured on the steps of the Sanctum.

'"Before my people," your father vowed, "I shall hack from his torso the arms that would not hold, that would not cherish my beloved Ysabela! I shall stab out the eyes that would not see her beauty! I shall slice the organs of pleasure from his loins, flinging the flesh to the dogs of the street!"

'Few were the horrors the Sultan would not have visited upon his brother. Only when he learnt how your aunt had died did his frenzy begin to abate. Rumour might say what it would about her husband, but the Princess had died as her sister had done.

'"In birth-pangs?" cried the Sultan.

'"Sire, it is true. In the moment of her death, Princess Ysabela was delivered of a daughter."

'It was the fitting reward of your father's evil that the sister he loved so ardently should have died like the sister he had slighted and abused. Now passion burst from him again, but this time it took a different form. He collapsed, he writhed, he beat the ground.

'"Oh, I am punished! Justly, terribly punished!"

'Later, with a demeanour so blank, so pale that he too might have crossed the threshold of death, your father participated in the obsequies for Bela. Seeing him at that dismal ceremony, standing side by side with his brother, I remember thinking it was impossible for a stranger to tell which man was the bereaved husband. To be sure, seldom have brothers been more dissimilar; but now both looked stricken, and if your uncle had mistreated Bela as your father had mistreated Dona, it seemed that he too had been chastened for his actions.

'So it was that our mission to Qatani ended in a grim but supreme irony. Your father had said he was going forth upon diplomacy, to tighten the bonds that held his brother's realm in imperial thrall. Thus it was, for the visit ended in solemn treaty between the bereaved rulers. It was a treaty not of words alone, for the rulers vowed that when the time came, a new marriage should cement their alliance. The Caliph's daughter, whom he would call Bela Dona, was to marry his brother's son. A ceremony of betrothal was held, in which your father broke down and wept, for even in infancy, the child Bela Dona had in her a shadow of her mother's beauty.

'Your father returned to Kal-Theron a sadder man, and perhaps wiser. To be sure, he was visibly older, and sometimes when he would summon me into his presence he would speak of the days of Mala, of Bela and Dona, as if a gen or more, not a mere few sunrounds, had passed since their lives were still before them. Never again, your father vowed, would he take another bride; but never again, after his outburst in Qatani, did he admit responsibility for the tragedies that had passed. He spoke of these things rather as if some malevolent fate had pursued him and struck him down.

'"Was it," he would wonder, "because I doubted the Flame?"

'To this question I could return no answer.

'So it was that your father became a twisted, embittered man, abandoning the studies that once had brought him such joy. Now, if women and men of learning came before him, it was only to be tried for heresy or treason, before being put to a lingering death. Public executions earned your father much applause. His faith grew fervent. The Imams were delighted. For long orbits they had urged your father, and his father before him, to Holy War; now the apostate kingdom of Vashi and the far Isles of Ananda became, in turn, the objects of vicious offensives. Triumph followed triumph. The Emir of Ormuz and his fifty wives were led back in triumph to Kal-Theron and disembowelled before your father's gates, to the cheers of the multitude. Entrails flowed in rivers down the gutters. Soon a new truth was abroad, kindling joyously through the blazing southlands: that of all Sultans since the time of the Prophet, none had been fiercer of faith than your father. In time he acquired the title that is now his glory, and all were convinced that your father's was to be the greatest of reigns.

'Alas, how strong is the power of lies!'

✳ ✳ ✳ ✳

Again Simonides sat back, his breathing stertorous, his face pale and troubled. What had he done? Oh, what had he done? He had not even told the whole truth, suppressing the story of his brother Evitamus, whose terrible warnings had ruined the ceremony of betrothal. What did it matter, when Dea's repose, in any case, must be destroyed for ever?

But there was one thing, one thing that still must come.

By now the sun had travelled far across the sky. The shadows in the grove were deeper; a chill had crept into the air, but the shivers that possessed the young Prince had little to do with the declining day. The boy looked up, his eyes deep with sorrow, but his brow furrowing as the old man sang softly, painfully:

> —*Sultan of the Stars . . . Sultan of the Moon,*
> *Can we hope to catch you if you're coming by soon?*
> —*Simpletons, down from your spars . . .*
> *You might soar through the heavens in triumphal cars,*
> *But never catch the Sultan of the Moon and . . .*

Familiar as they were, the words seemed strange, infinitely strange, from the lips of Simonides. Dea would have liked him to go on, but the old man broke off and said, a little cryptically, 'That was the seal on your father's greatness. Ten sunrounds ago he stood on the steps of the Sanctum, with his people assembled before him, and declared that the Flame had vouchsafed to him a great and marvellous truth, declaring him to be the last and greatest of the God-Sultans. Sultan of the Moon. Sultan of the Stars.'

Dea looked down reflectively. There were many things he could have asked, but what he asked first was, 'So my father was wrong, about the god in the Flame?'

'Indeed, Dea, I am sure he was wrong.'

'So my father believed in the god again, and the god rewarded him?'

Simonides had to pause before he replied. He had said enough. Too much; so now he said only, 'Dea, indeed we must believe it is so.'

But a last question came, one still more painful. It was a question that had tormented Dea for all his life, beating always just beneath the threshold of his awareness. 'But if my father is Sultan of the Moon and Stars, what am I to be? What *can* I be?'

There was no reply, but suddenly there was fear and not merely sadness in the old man's eyes. Dea turned and saw the Targons, watching them through the trees.

Chapter 49

THE THINNING

'Rainbow? We've lost Rainbow.'

'Don't be silly, Rainbow can't be lost.'

'Then *we* are,' Jem sighed. Slumping down upon a boulder, he tugged his tunic over his head, flinging it aside. 'Whew! Sometimes I think we might as well be in the desert.'

'We are.'

'What?'

Dona Bela did not quite answer. 'It's perspective, that's our trouble. I mean, point of view . . . I mean vantage. If only we could reach a high point. Somewhere to look . . . down.'

'There are no high points. These gardens are flat, flat, flat.'

Miserably Jem looked at the scrubby trees that surrounded them like ragged, prickly fences. He was ill at ease, especially as Dona Bela had brushed against his side. Since the incident of the night before, he had been wary of the girl, for all that she had made no allusion to it. Had he really kissed her? Had she pushed him into the pool? He supposed so; but how many times during the night had he imagined taking her in his arms again? If dreams were real in this strange place, then Jem had made love to Dona Bela many times.

He stood up quickly, retrieving his tunic. The girl might want to escape the place; nonetheless, thought Jem, she was part of its seductions. He told himself she wasn't real, none of it was real; but he knew that wasn't quite true. He plucked irritably at his sodden tunic, realising that he had turned it inside out. The sun beat down above the dusty, dry trees.

Dona Bela said, 'Prince, what's that you wear round your neck?'

'Don't you know? You know so much.'

The girl smiled and left the question hanging. Jem could not forbear from gazing upon her. Her long hair was tied roughly back and she wore only the flimsiest cotton shift, clinging moistly to the curves of her body. How lovely she was! Steadily she gazed back at him and Jem became self-conscious, aware of the sweat that dripped from his hair, that slithered down his face and neck and pale, boyish chest. He turned away, feeling exposed. The girl moved beside him, her fingers brushing against the muscles of his arm. 'There's something you should know,' she whispered. 'I like you . . .'

'Oh?' Jem's voice was hollow.

'. . . but I don't like boys.'

'What?' Jem turned back. For a moment he was confused. 'You just said you like me. I'm a boy. I'm a man,' he added quickly.

'Yes, but I mean I don't . . . *like* boys. I thought you should know, that's all.'

'Oh? I mean, yes . . . no. I mean . . . well, neither do I.'

Dona Bela laughed. 'I thought as much! But Prince, you have a beloved that you seek?'

Jem said bashfully, 'You know that, too?'

'This much I know: that before this adventure is over, you shall find your beloved girl, as I shall find mine.'

Jem's heart bounded. 'Princess, you're certain?'

'To be sure, it must come to pass. It must, or else . . .'

'Or else?'

The answer came like the tolling of a bell. 'We die.'

Jem let his tunic fall back to the ground and looked uneasily into the girl's eyes. She reached for him and they clung together in a tight, sticky embrace. Around them, the shadows of foliage were growing paler, the sunlight more fierce. A stirring sounded through the leaves and sand whirled across the pebbles, stinging their ankles with its spattering, prickling heat.

Dona Bela brushed her eyes. 'We're not lost. We're closer.'

'What do you mean?'

'Look at the gardens here. These red, hard berries where there used to be flowers; these pallid, tough leaves; this desert sand. Prince, this isn't just another part of the gardens. This is . . . this is closer to the edge.'

'It's as if the gardens are . . . thinning.'

'Yes!'

'But wait . . .' Jem recalled the things he had seen in the night, the pool a shallow basin, the gardens withered, the house a ruin. He thought of the guests who were present only sometimes; he thought of all the strange shiftings, changings. He began to understand, and his voice cracked excitedly. 'That's it! The whole place is thinning! Princess, that's why Almoran wants us, don't you see? He retreated from the world into this imaginary estate where he could rule like a King . . . but his dream is fading! That's why he needs us . . . to keep his dream alive! To help him dream his dream!'

'But how?' Dona Bela's eyes were wild, then she heard a sound from nearby, borne towards them on the gathering wind.

'Hush! Do you hear it?'

'A whimpering! Crying!'

'Rainbow?'

334

'He's hurt!'

They pushed through the foliage, shielding their eyes against the scratchy branches, the stinging sand. A dusty clearing opened before them. First they saw Rainbow, lying on his side. Then the stricken, tiny figure that leaned over him, keening.

'Littler!'

✳   ✳   ✳   ✳

How could it be? The little boy looked up at them through tearful eyes, rivulets of snot running into his mouth. At once, almost incoherently, he began to babble, but through the gurglings Jem made out the words, 'I ran away from him . . . ran, I did. He says he's . . . says he'll be King of the world! I told him he was a fool!'

Dona Bela caught the child in her arms. 'How . . . who?'

'Is Eli here?' urged Jem. 'You mean Eli?'

The little boy snuffled furiously. 'Scabs! I mean Scabs . . . and now he's dead!'

'Scabs?' said Jem. 'But how—?'

'Not Scabs!' Littler pointed.

At once, horror filled Dona Bela's eyes. Sand was rapidly covering the recumbent Rainbow, but it was clear enough that the dog was rigid. With a gasp, Jem knelt beside him. He brushed away the sand, then the clustering flies from the eyes and lips. Appalled, they looked on as Rainbow's colours faded. In moments, in another cruel transition of time, it looked as if the dog had been dead for days. Jem stepped back, letting the sand blow across their lost friend. It stung their eyes. But so did their tears.

Littler wailed suddenly, 'He did this! He did this!'

'Who?' cried Jem. 'Scabs?'

'Him!'

Littler was pointing. Jem reeled round. By now, the sand had swirled into a maelstrom, buffeting them back against the remnants of the gardens. At first Jem could see sand, no more; then he saw the vision of a ghostly face, Almoran's face, flinging back its head and cackling cruelly.

Then came the voice, booming around them as if from all directions.

Fools! Did you think you could escape me? For long sunrounds the knowledge has gnawed at me that one day my world must come to an end. How could it be otherwise, without the security of a Threefold Sustaining? Cursed be my brothers, who would not join with me in my design! But now, at last, my dilemma is solved. Only those charged with magic have the strength to be my avatars; oh, how I have despaired that even one should come into my clutches. Now, there are four! Three boy-children, to relieve me of my burden; a beautiful girl-child, to be my bride!

'Never!' cried Dona Bela.

'Never!' cried Jem.

Fools! What need you care for the world outside when I offer you an eternity of sensual bliss? Shimmering Princess, forget your mortal love! Key to the Orokon, forget your foolish quest! Join with me now, in my dreaming dimension, and all you have ever wanted in your lives shall be yours!

'You're mad!' cried Jem. 'You'll never keep us, never!'

I shall bind you by magic! You shall have no choice!

'You're dying, Almoran! Your world is thinning, fading!'

Never, I shall clutch you again! In moments, mere moments, I shall clutch you again!

But in the next moment the face was gone, then the trees, then the bushes too. They were in the desert, with a storm blowing round them. They clutched hands, coughing, choking, stumbling. Wildly Jem wondered what would happen now. Were they free? Had they escaped? How could it be that Littler was here? And how could it be that Littler spoke of Scabs? Questions overwhelmed him, but there was no time to voice them. They must survive this storm, but how? There was nothing they could do but huddle together. Jem grabbed Littler, holding the child against him; but when he would have clutched Dona Bela too, her hand had slipped away.

'Princess?' he shouted. 'Princess, talk to me!'

Then Jem realised: if they had left the dreaming dimension, the Princess could not speak.

'Princess? Princess?'

It was useless. Jem collapsed in the sand, dragging Littler after him. They huddled into themselves, agonised, desperate. Dry sobs racked in Jem's throat and he cursed himself for a fool. Had Almoran taken Dona Bela, snatched her away in the moment before he vanished? That was when Jem heard the high ethereal sound, pealing like a bell above the chaos of the storm.

The song!

> *In my mind there are*
> *Five vanishings,*
> *Vanishing one by one:*
> *One is done in a soaring canopy,*
> *Two is blue down below.*
> *The third vanishing comes in the sun,*
> *The fourth through a darkened glass,*
> *But only after there are*
> *Five vanishings*
> *Shall I be real again!*

Jem cupped his hands round his eyes, struggling to look up. Astonished, he saw the vortex of sand forming itself into a circle, and in the centre of the circle, unharmed, untouched, the radiant, regal figure of the Princess, her dark hair and white shift billowing as her music filled the air. Could this be the key? The key to their escape? Jem felt the heat, searing into his chest, before he realised that the Crystal of Viana was glowing again, as if in the presence of a fellow crystal.

Yes! This was it! This had to be the way!

※　※　※　※

A vast aura, like a magical field, had formed around the Princess. Entrancing, mystical, flashing with the colours of the Orokon, the circle was a cocoon of light. Inside it, Dona Bela revolved slowly. Her eyes and mouth were shut, but still her song echoed in the air, as if a thousand voices had taken it up, repeating its mysterious words in excited, flurrying whispers ... then screeches ... cries ... The next thing Jem knew, Littler was tugging at his arm, dragging him into the pulsing bands of radiance. The crystal at his chest glowing, Jem knelt before the Princess, staring reverently up towards her closed, impassive face.

'Princess! Can you speak? Can you speak in here?'

To Jem's astonishment it was Littler who replied, but it was the voice of the Princess that issued from his lips. While Jem knelt, while the Princess revolved, Littler had drifted upwards, weightless, floating inside the aura, limbs outstretched.

Speak? he intoned. *But briefly, briefly. Almoran is not gone, only gathering strength. He is all around us, and I can barely sustain this projection.*

'Princess, you know, don't you? About the crystals.'

I know only of the strange intimations that stir sometimes, deep within my being. I know that, like you, I am part of a greater destiny, but what that destiny is, I cannot say. This I know: that soon I am to be married, and that with my marriage, the world shall lurch closer to the fate that is ordained.

'Married? But Princess, I thought—'

What did you think? Prince, remember the lesson of the House of Truth. What is false, what is true? I say only that there is to be a wedding in the Sacred City, the wedding of a Princess and a Sultan's son. Then, there, you shall find the answers you seek!

Jem's heart pounded with excitement. 'Princess, this crystal I wear is glowing now, but until its red brother comes into my possession I can do no more than a common man. Mystic force enfolds you. You create this projection. Can you transport us to the Sacred City? Can you free us from Almoran's grasp?'

A low, sorrowful moan broke from Littler's lips. *You know not what you ask! The enchanter is too strong—*

'But he's weakening! We know he is—'

No! No, I cannot sustain even this projection—

By now, Littler was spinning rapidly in the air – spinning, then blundering like a confused insect. The colours of the aura flashed in and out of being. In one moment the desert was upon them again, then the aura; then the desert; then the gardens.

Desert. Gardens.

Desert. Gardens.

Birds and butterflies whizzed though the air, and replacing the echoes of Dona Bela's song came the renewed, wild cackling of the crazed enchanter. Desperately the Princess struggled to sing again, but the words caught in her throat. She slumped forward, coughing. Jem clutched her, holding her as the aura faded to nothing, and the green, searing glow of the crystal died again.

Silence.

No, birdsong.

The rustle of leaves. Water.

Then came the sweet, drifting intoxicants, the rich enveloping fragrances of jasmine, narcissus, lilacs, camomile, lemon trees and cedars and heavy-headed poppies. Jem looked up and saw the House of Truth, brilliant beneath a bright sun, and stretching before it, deep as life, the mysterious waters of the long pool.

Chapter 50

WHEN THE SLEEPER WAKES

We forget most of our dreams, or think we do. Remembered, they stir us to the strangest thoughts; sometimes they leave us heavily burdened, and the day that follows seems thin, brittle, liable to break. Then, with a knowledge deeper than reason, we know that the dream-world is not mere illusion, but a mysterious other world that lies in wait to claim us.

What happens to the forgotten dreams? I suspect they do not really vanish; instead, they cluster in a secret room to which only sometimes we may find the door. I have come to feel that my life in dreams is forming itself into a fugue, a complex pattern of interweavings that one day will make a coherent design. Often now, when I remember a dream, I remember also the many times I have dreamed it before, dreamed it and forgotten. I walk round and round a labyrinth of stairs in search of a room I shall never find again. I kick off from the balcony outside my room and hover high above the world, looking down. Then come the memories of many nights, years of nights doing these things I have never done, being in places I have never been. The dreams seem to say I have been an amnesiac; that the waking world beguiles us with curtains of illusion. They seem so real, these curtains, that we think they must be real. But that is the illusion. I believe we all have amnesia, and spend our lives longing for our memories to return. We are all dead, waiting to come alive again. Dreams prompt us from the darkness. One day, they seem to say, we shall find our way back to the truth we have forgotten. Dreams are our ghosts, and they haunt us.

✳ ✳ ✳ ✳

The night after Almoran's world closed round him again, Jem's mind was filled with dreams more vivid than any he had dreamed before. Waking, deep in darkness, he found that his skin was slick with sweat and the sheets beneath him a twisted mass. He pushed away the gauze that surrounded his bed. On a table close by was a jug of hava-nectar, covered in cloth; gratefully he gulped at the soothing liquid. He staggered up, pacing back and forth, pushing his ragged hair from his eyes. The air, clammy and hot, pressed around him like a viscous medium. Blearily he stepped out through the open windows and saw the gardens glowing lushly beneath a golden, engorged moon. The pool shimmered with the promise of depth.

That was when Jem saw the figure on the lily-pad, standing still and silent in the centre of the pool. A female form. The Princess? But no, it was Cata, naked as he was and ... no, not still, but floating towards him like a memory returning. Now Jem recalled the dreams, erotic reveries that had slipped time and again into frustrating journeys through labyrinths, corridors, dark caves. When would his quest be over? The sense came to him that he had dreamed this quest, long before it had ever begun; perhaps, in truth, he had dreamed his whole life, long ago when he was only a child.

He stared at Cata as if she were a goddess, and thought now that this quest had been for her, always really for her. As she approached, her skin was changing colour, glowing first purple, then green, then ... no, it was the moonlight that was changing colour. Jem looked up and saw five moons in the sky, five moons, five colours: purple, green, red, blue, gold. It seemed to him then that this was reality, this was truth, this moment now. His quest was over.

The lily-pad reached the side of the pool and Cata stepped, smiling, into Jem's arms.

❈   ❈   ❈   ❈

'Polty ... Polty.'

Bean's mind had been drifting again. Many times he had thought of Polty in the old carefree days; now he thought of Polty as he had last seen him, blue-skinned, hair in flames, eyes ablaze with unearthly light. Precipitously, plunging through the caverns of his mind, Bean saw the Polty-monster rearing out at him, bursting with all the hidden evil of the world. Instead of fear, Bean felt compassion. Tears came to his eyes. Poor, poor Polty! What was to become of him? But then, what was to become of Bean? Wildly he imagined himself bursting from his confinement, hunting down Polty, bravely expelling the demon that had taken over his friend.

Bean opened his eyes. Was it day ... night? From the light and the noise that came from above, Bean supposed it was night. In the cell there were no windows, but light of a sort seeped bleakly through a grille in the bottom of the door, at the top of a flight of oozing stone steps. In the day the seeping was greyish and wan; at night, tinges of rancid gold flickered from the lamps in the bar-room beyond. How long had it been now? How many days? From time to time the grille would open, and a hand – perhaps the whoremonger's, perhaps Mother Madana's – would slide in a jug of ferment-slops or a chunk of stale bread, meagre propitiations to the living fetishes who would draw the distemper away from the khan. Curse these people and their superstitions! More than once Bean had tried to plead, crawling up the steps, screaming through the grille; he had soon learnt that it was to no avail. The tars only peered down at him, guffawed that the 'temper must be doing its work, and kicked and banged at the door until they grew tired of it, or the harlots came.

Huddled in the filth, Bean watched the lamplight playing across the floor, shifting with the rhythms of yet another raucous song. In the far wall there was a second door, bolted and barred; evidently the khan had more than one cellar. Often Bean thought he heard voices through this door, youthful voices raised in curses or laughter. But the door was thick and the voices, perhaps, were only echoes from upstairs.

Bean sighed. Cobwebs draped from the ceiling. Rats scurried at his feet. The grille opened and a shower of cabbage-leaves, mouldy potatoes and carrot-tops came scattering down the stairs. Bean fell upon them hungrily and would have scoffed them all, but after a moment he felt a stab of guilt. He reached over, shaking his companion. Was Burgrove awake? Only a groan came in reply, but then, Burgrove had barely stirred from his stupor since their confinement began. It was hardly surprising that Bean, at first, had thought the fellow was dead. He felt Burgrove's wrist, then the face that lolled slackly above the ruined cravat.

Bean started. Burgrove was burning!

Bean scurried back to his side of the cell and huddled deep into himself, shivering, sobbing.

❊ ❊ ❊ ❊

'Cata?'

When he woke again, Jem knew that much time had passed. For how long had he slept? He was alone, fully clothed, and the sheets beneath him were stretched taut, as if he had lain motionless throughout the night.

'Cata?'

No. Of course not.

Jem rose leadenly. Hunger gnawed at him; thirst, too. He gulped again at the hava-nectar and staggered out to the terrace, pushing his hair from his eyes. Outside, the light glowed purple and red. He looked at the gardens, wan and slumped beneath a thin, single moon, as if exhausted after the humid day.

There was a sound of barking.

Jem turned, startled. 'Rainbow? But you died!'

The dog bounded towards him, bold as life. Squatting down, Jem petted the excited, bright creature, but even in his joy at finding Rainbow alive, the young man was aware of an admixture of despair. What could he conclude but that time, here in this strange dimension, was running through a course it had travelled before? Had Almoran trapped him in a treacherous loop, a loop from which there was no escape?

Now came footsteps, sounding across the terrace.

'Excuse me, young master,' said the girlish youth, 'but it is time for the banquet. Your friends have assembled and my noble lord awaits.'

Indeed, it seemed that all was as it had been before. But soon Jem would learn that time flowed forward, if a little oddly, even here.

Chapter 51

TO BE OR NOT TO BE

'Shall I?'

'Why not?'

'Ooh, but shall I?'

'Hardly makes a difference, does it?'

'Think of my figure!'

'Oman, you haven't got a figure!'

'Well, I never!' protested the Caliph, but greed spurred him more than annoyance and, without further ado, he stuffed his little mouth with another jellied eye.

Behind his bronze mask, Vizier Hasem sighed. It was the fourth, perhaps the fifth time during the meal that Oman had played this silly game, slavering as if in anguished indecision over food he had no intention of denying himself. Still, perhaps it was as well that he remained distracted. When he had burst in upon the Vizier that morning, announcing his daughter's miraculous transformation, it seemed that misery would be banished for ever from the little fellow's heart. How rapidly it had reasserted its sway! Soon Oman was cursing himself for feeling even a moment's exultation. To sacrifice a daughter made of mist was bad enough; to give away a Shimmy of flesh and blood, flinging her into the arms of a filthy Ouabin, was a hundred, a thousand times worse.

For much of the day, Oman had railed and sobbed; Hasem, for his part, was troubled, deeply troubled, by the girl's alteration. If he had never liked magic, there was something in this magic that particularly alarmed him. Oman, after all, was such a fool; could his daughter really have been restored? The Vizier didn't like it. He didn't like it one bit; then, too, there was the question of whether this Rebonding would really take place. Spies had sent word that the imperial forces were bearing down rapidly; a battle, as much as a betrothal, might be the climax of the day to come.

Indeed, tonight was a night for distraction ... alas, that their distraction was a fragile thing!

At first, the cracks were fine.

'Isn't it pleasant, Hasem, to dine by ourselves?'

The Vizier agreed that it was. As it happened, six masked ladyboys sprawled about the dining-slab in gorgeous array, while a retinue of black-garbed servants passed back and forth with dishes, hookahs and flagons of hava-nectar. Nonetheless it was an informal meal, considering the lavish and obsequious entertainments they had been obliged, these last nights, to stage for the benefit of Rashid Amr Rukr. In days, stocks of the rarest delicacies had been stripped from the shelves of the palace pantries; carts laden with produce trundled endlessly through the back lanes, while the kitchen courtyards ran with the blood of kill after fresh kill, performed according to Ouabin rites. More than once the Vizier had wondered how they would supply the festivities of the morrow. Whatever happened, the tax collectors would be busier than ever in the moonlives to come.

'What are they doing now, do you think?' said the Caliph.

'The tax collectors?'

'The Ouabin.'

The Vizier shook himself from his musing. 'I understand it is a night of fasting, Your Magnificence – fasting, and certain other preparations. The Sheik, you will recall, must be pure for his part in the ceremony, and all his men must be pure with him.'

'The ointment?' the Caliph said sourly. 'Still, I couldn't have stood another evening like the last one. Those Ouabin recipes are bad enough, but really, the way he was pawing my harem-girls!'

The cracks were growing wider.

'At least he didn't want the ladyboys,' said the Vizier, stroking the thigh of one gorgeous young creature, heavily drugged, whose head lolled behind a purple mask. Why, he considered adding, had the infidel laid a hand on this pretty one, he would have struck the fellow down; instead, conscious of the cracks, the Vizier hurried on, 'But Oman, you haven't even looked at our latest acquisition!'

'The Vaga?' The Caliph's interest quickened and he turned, arching an eyebrow, towards the ladyboy in the purple mask; the cracks, it seemed, were knitting over. 'Bring her to me.'

The Vizier snapped his fingers and the Vaga-boy, like a sack, was hauled by a slave to the Caliph's end of the dining-slab. With pursed lips, the fat little potentate looked the new acquisition up and down. 'To think, and we nearly had her disembowelled! A fine specimen, Hasem! And you say she has the genuine Vaga-mark?'

Curiously, the Caliph parted Rajal's magnificent robes, eager for a sight of the reddened thigh-flesh; instead, he recoiled at the sight of something else. 'Ugh! Hasem, she is not yet clean! Really, what do you think I am?'

The Vizier shrugged. 'Oman, she is new. Must she not pass the nights of preparation?'

'What need has she of preparation, when you keep her in this stupor?

Have the barber fix her tomorrow and perhaps, after my distressful day, I shall turn to this Vaga for an evening's entertainment!'

The Vizier would have protested that this was hardly proper, but at that moment a magnificent, fizzing sorbet appeared in the middle of the dining-slab and other lusts consumed his master's attention.

The Vizier sighed. Freshly-made eunuchs were hardly fit for use; the bleeding was often most distasteful, and the danger of death was high. Still, it was just possible, if the child were well-cauterized, and smeared with the proper potions and creams. He supposed it would be best to keep Oman happy – tomorrow, especially.

A little glumly, he beckoned for a slave, ordering him to send for the barber in the morning.

❋ ❋ ❋ ❋

Marry and burn!
The wheel shall turn!
What bold lover ever needs to yearn?
Seize your treasure from the gleaming py-y-y-re –
Marry and burn,
Marry and burn!

Rashid Amr Rukr smiled to himself, thinking joyously of the ritual of the morrow. In the hall outside his austere apartment, rehearsals continued for the song that was to play so vital a role in the ceremony. He listened for a while, pleased at the cunning words, then permitted his mind to drift, thinking of the triumphs the future would bring.

The Sheik was alone, lying in a slant of moonlight on a simple bed. For a man of the desert, there could be no luxuries; what was it but luxury, after all, that had made his enemies so soft, so weak? Cursed be such decadence! To be sure, he had enjoyed the Caliph's banquets, but as much, he told himself, for the miseries these occasions caused his hosts as for any active pleasure he derived from them. For Ouabin-kind, there could be no pleasure for pleasure's sake. That way lay only weakness, when all that mattered was strength, strength and power.

'But you don't mind borrowing a little of mine, do you, Ouabin?' The golden, glowing creature moved forward from a dark corner of the chamber. 'I had expected to find you deep in meditation – as you promised you are following to the letter the ancient statutes of the Ritual of Rebonding.'

There was no point in dissembling. 'What one does, Golden One, and what one tells the mob, are two different things. Did you not tell me that destiny was with us – and is destiny to be denied? You have seen already

345

my deepest thoughts. What care I for truth when my sole aim is power? But tell me, you are certain that all shall go well?'

'Ouabin, nothing can be certain, for all that we have prepared the way. You will be seen to take the girl yourself, and I trust I shall have no need to intervene. All I say is that your guard must be at the ready, for the Sultan's forces converge upon the city. Even by tomorrow, they may be here, ready to grasp, in turn, the prize that would be yours.'

'You might fend them off, might you not?'

'Ouabin, take care you do not ask too much. With the aura cast by my powers, did I not help you to an easy conquest? I have done what I can, and the task now is yours. You dream of power, yet are you not weak?'

The Sheik's eyes flashed. 'Golden One, it is you who should take care! Would you tell me I am weaker than you? When first you came to me in the desert night, you proposed an alliance, did you not? To be sure, you are devious, and what your purpose may be, your real purpose, still I do not pretend to understand. For me the earth, for you the moon and stars? Do you not beguile me, Golden One? And yet, if I have depended upon your power, so too you have depended upon mine.'

The golden figure turned in the moonlight.

Then came a murmur. 'Ouabin, it is true you do not understand me, and nor is it my desire that you do so. It is true, my powers are far from limitless, and already much depleted. But would I say you were weaker than me? What a question, Ouabin. Really, what a question.'

The creature turned, raising a glimmering arm. A finger pointed and the Sheik's eyes suddenly widened as he guessed what was to come. But there was no time to leap from the fizzing, searing beam.

All night, the Sheik would lie with agony gripping his chest, his eyes hot with tears of pain and rage.

❉　❉　❉　❉

Where had it gone, the buried jewel?

In the incense-heavy gloom of this other Realm of Un, Rajal had experienced pleasures such as he had never imagined before. Again and again, he had longed only to give himself over to the tides of lust; again and again, he had ridden high on waves of sensual joy. By day, it was the ladyboys who tumbled and toyed with him, teaching him their exotic, delightful tricks; at night, the Vizier would return to Rajal's couch, gathering him once again into a deeper, darker rapture. What more could there be? To Rajal, it seemed that all the questions of his life had been answered at last: and the answer to everything was simple after all. His friends, his mission had become the merest blur; of his missing crystal he had no thought. For Rajal, there was only the jewel he possessed already, a jewel he could never lose but only find and find, again, again, again. All

346

through these sensual days and nights, the jewel had gleamed in his mind like the wealth of all the world.

Now its glow had faded and Rajal felt lost. He moaned, clutching his forehead. What was happening? Dimly he recalled the strong slave who bore him like a baby back down the stairs, setting him here to sprawl on this silken bed. Before that? The Caliph's apartments; something about a barber. And before that? Inexplicably, it seemed to Rajal that his dulled brain was sharpening, the mists clearing. He moaned again, longing to sink back into his sweet oblivion.

It was late and the ladyboys were lying down to sleep. Only the dimmest light still shone in the chamber and the voices Rajal heard were the merest murmurs. Softly came the rattling of a beaded chain; the bubbling of an expiring konar-light; the slow, sinister hissing of a cobbera, vigilant in the pit outside.

Where was the Vizier? Rajal felt a slow ache, deep within his being, as of a chasm longing to be filled. His eyes drifted shut. Sinking. Sinking.

A whisper: 'Tomorrow.'

Rajal knew that voice. He opened his eyes and in the darkness he made out, lying beside him, the plump ladyboy he had called Blubina; Rajal was never to learn her real name, or the names, indeed, of any of the others. Tenderly, Blubina stroked Rajal's hair, whispering again, 'Tomorrow.'

'Blubina, what do you mean?'

A tear welled in Blubina's eye, and it was another voice that answered. 'Don't you remember? Tomorrow, the barber comes, and you shall be like us.'

Turning, Rajal found Cheesia – no, it was Fishia – curled on the other side of him, clutching him, fondling him. 'Aren't I like you now?' he murmured. 'How could I not be like you now?'

Fishia grinned. 'Don't you remember what the Caliph said?'

The memory flopped dimly through Rajal's mind.

The barber. Something about a barber.

'Already the Vizier comes to her no more. Poor Sister Raj,' said Blubina, shaking her head, 'her time of pleasure has been short!'

Fishia said, 'Fool, it is but beginning!'

Rajal's brow furrowed, and he looked between them. What could they mean? From Fishia came a giggle; from Blubina, a muffled sob, as she declared, not in anger but in sadness, that her sister was a liar.

'What promises of pleasure seemed to lie before us, when first we arrived in this Place of the Cobras! Ah, but how swiftly those pleasures faded, after the barber came! No more, Sister Raj, will you feel the buried jewel, that once so entranced us all with its glow. How swiftly that glow runs away, like the purple that fills the barber's basin!'

Rajal became aware that his heart was pounding hard. A strange alarm gripped him, and he wondered why it was that he was emerging now from his stupor of befuddlement. He screwed up his eyes tightly, then opened them, closed them. What was happening?

It occurred to Rajal that he did not remember drinking the last of his potions.

Fishia was growing sleepy. Sighing, she said, 'Sister, you speak of jewels, but is not your plump body a-glitter with them, like mine? Jewels and gold and the finest silk and muslin? Sometimes I imagine there is another me, living the life that could have been mine. How I shiver, how I shudder at the thought! Think of the streets, then the life we live here!'

Dolefully, Blubina said, 'But a ladyboy's bloom is soon rubbed away.'

'Sister, what of it?' Fishia yawned. 'To pleasure a potentate, though a fine and noble thing, is but the beginning of our womanly careers. If the diversions of the couch are a glory to me, so too I long for the time when my days as a ladyboy are over. How splendid it will be to be called upstairs, there to wait upon the great beauties of the land! What pleasure will lie in the curling of hair, the cut of a gown, in chains and rings and veils and dainty slippers ... ah, and all the tittle-tattle of a fine lady's life!'

Blubina returned, 'Sister, you may never be called upstairs! What if you are cast into the world again, as many are? Stripped of your finery, you will find yourself a degraded thing, with no place but in the vilest of the houses of ill-fame! No, as you love our new sister, delude her not about what is to be after she is made clean like us!'

There would have been more, but Fishia was sinking into slumber at last, and silence stole over the perfumed scene. It was a fragile silence. Still Rajal could barely move his limbs, but in his mind he felt the dark, implacable mounting of a scream. Then Blubina drew close to his ear, whispering with a new urgency:

'Sister, you had to know. Some say it is kinder to let you know nothing, so that all may pass as if in a blur. Some, like my friend here, will lie to you – secretly even exulting, perhaps, in the knowledge that another is to be rendered as they are. Forgive the envy of one who has been so much abused. I say you should understand, as I wish I had done. In these last days, it has been my task to hold the potions to your lips; whether you think me your betrayer, or your saviour, only the events of the morrow shall tell.'

And slowly Blubina took Rajal's hand, guiding it to the place between her plump thighs. 'Sister, feel. Sister, understand. This is what is to be, when the barber comes. Or not to be. Or not to be.'

The scream came at last.

Chapter 52

TRANSFIGURED DAY

Feluccas.

Not to mention xebecs, caiques and dhows. It was a brilliant morning, with the sun flashing like jewels on the deep, still water. Even now, to the innocent eye, the Qatani docks were a spectacular sight, a riot of sails, flags and brightly painted hulls. From somewhere came the slap of a slow oar; from somewhere the squeak of a winch; there was the gleam of a tar's earring, and the laggardly wail of a squeezebox.

Only to the less innocent observer was there something troubling in this idyllic scene. Something was wrong; there was a strange lifelessness, and its source was not hard to find. All round the harbour, Ouabin stood guard, and the guns that had always bristled from the headlands seemed more than usually alarming now. No ships arrived. No ships left. Trade had halted in the Jewel of the Shore, with the ships and their crews held as if in the grip of the Sheik's strong hand, until his bride was in his possession and he left the city at last.

Captain Porlo stood on a pale length of decking. Buby was on his shoulder; he held a far-glass to his eye. Behind him lay the warren of shabby alleys which included, in its dark recesses, the Khan of the Crescent Moon. Had he been possessed of a prodigality of legs, the old sea-dog would no doubt have explored such regions by now, finding much comfort there; alas, it was as much as he could do to come down to the water, as he did each day, and gaze wistfully at the *Catayane*.

'Me poor wooden lady! Me poor, poor lady!'

Fondly the captain thought of his cabin, that magic den with its lowering ceiling, its tiger's head and rhinoceros horn, its rusty scimitar and brass musketoon. He thought of the charts he had studied so earnestly, and the prize that awaited him at the end of his voyage. To be severed from his *Cata* was more than he could bear. Cursed be Empster, and his wretched quest! Those two lads had been good sorts, the girl too, but Captain Porlo was damned if he would be in thrall to the nobleman any longer, with his endless evasions and strange ways. The fellow was mad, he had to be. Quest, indeed! What had it meant for old Faris Porlo but foreign muck for dinner, and his bowels in constant turmoil? As for his humiliation in the women's wing, it didn't bear thinking about; indeed, the captain himself had refrained from thinking about it ever since.

For some days he had been struggling with a decision. Now he had reached it. Empster? Let him unleash what power he could! What was one man against the *Cata* in full sail and a following wind?

For some moments the captain felt a surge of excitement; then he thought of the Ouabin again and slumped disconsolately against a cracking wooden pillar.

From the other side of the pillar, like an echo of his thoughts, came a deep sigh.

'Cursed be Casca Dalla, curse him, curse him!'

Turning, the captain saw a fellow with a face doleful as his own. Curious, he leaned towards his new companion, and though the fellow was a greasy foreigner, the sea-dog could not forbear from asking him if he was missing a treasure too.

'Ah, my friend, what treasures once were mine, in the days before the wicked Casca took them from me!'

'This fellow must be a villain indeed. Does he keep cobber-as at the bottom of his garden?'

'Cobras? He *is* a cobra! I was an honest man of business, profiting only though my own unyielding efforts. Thanks to Casca, I now face ruin. Thanks to Casca, I have been bastinadoed, and stripped of my royal seal. Captain-sir, what can I do, what can poor Eli do, but start a new life in a far distant land?'

The captain gestured proudly to his Ejlander ship, bobbing on the far side of the gleaming bay. 'Friend, I could bear you to that land, but alas, me *Cata*'s in the Ouabins' grip, and the wretched heathens won't let her go!'

'Pah!' Eli Oli Ali's eyes flashed. 'There're ways around any fellow, even a Ouabin. Why, Captain-sir, if you were to follow me, I'm sure we could escape in your fine ship. Somehow we could find a way . . . why, I'm sure of it.'

The captain held out his hand. 'I declare you be a friend then, foreigner or no.'

Eli Oli Ali flashed a brilliant grin. Moments earlier, he had thought his life was over. Already, a hundred new plans were filling his cunning mind.

'Captain-sir, I have a khan just a little way from here. I know you Ejland-fellows are fond of ferment. Won't you come back for just a little drop and we'll start to think what we can do?'

Briskly, and whistling a merry tune, the whoremonger started back towards the alleys behind the docks. Buby leapt down from the captain's shoulders, scampering ahead.

'Wait up, me dears, wait up!' wheezed the captain, energetically swinging his crutch. 'Remember, there's a limit to the number of me legs!'

❉   ❉   ❉   ❉

'Genie?'

Scabs reclined on a divan beside the pool. His head lolled back and he had loosened his robe, luxuriating in the warm caresses of the sun. A lush redness played behind his eyelids. No breeze stirred the thick, bright air, but the thousand fragrances of flowers, fruits and vines wafted about him all the same.

'Genie?' he murmured again.

Scabs opened his eyes and the little man was there, hovering above the green depths of the pool, cross-legged on the magic carpet. Yes. Still there. If the genie's presence was not quite a comfort, the thought of his absence was disconcerting. Scabs stared warily at the huge turban, the podgy belly, the big sleeves. To think that his destiny lay with this foolish fellow!

The round face broke into a smile. 'Master?'

'I wondered where you were, that was all.'

'Ho? I wondered if you had a WISH.'

Scabs looked suspiciously at the genie. 'Not yet.'

'You WISHED to know where I was, did you not?'

'That was no wish.'

'It was a desire – hm? Is desiring not WISHING? Why, master, I am sure your mind is awash with WISHES. But that is a fine state to be in, is it not? It suggests aspiration – always admirable in a young man.' Jafir lay back on the carpet, his arms behind his head, an ankle propped upon a raised knee. He had produced a Jarvel-pipe, perhaps from the recesses of his big sleeves, and was sucking upon it contentedly. 'Ah yes, how I WISH I were still a young man, awash with WISHES and my future all before me! Well ... it was, before I got on the wrong side of that wicked enchanter. Hm. *I wish I were awash with* WISHES. A fine state – and quite difficult to say, isn't it, master? Can you say that?'

Scabs grinned. 'You think you'll get me, don't you?'

'Master, I don't think. I know.'

The grin turned into a scowl. Springing up on to the ledge beside the pool, Scabs began to pace rapidly, stretching out his arms for balance. *Concentrate, concentrate.* He knew, of course he knew, what his third wish must be. He must wish to be beautiful. But it was not that simple. To say, *Make me beautiful* would hardly be enough. Beautiful? But how? Before Scabs knew it, he could be a beautiful Baba-girl, bound on a slaver for the far reaches of Wenaya. Besides, there were other things he wanted. Oh, he must think, think! It was all a question of wording ...

'Genie, tell me something.'

The carpet wafted forward, keeping pace with the scabious young man. 'You WISH to know something?'

'We're just talking, genie. We can talk, can't we?'

'If you WISH, master.'

'I don't wish!'

The genie arched an eyebrow. 'Ho! You WISH me to go?'

'I wish . . . genie, you know that's not what I mean!'

'Poor master.' Directing the flying carpet in a circle, Jafir orbited slowly round the exasperated Scabs. 'You'll pardon me if I torment you,' he smirked, 'but you see I'm excited. I said you'd left that wretched konar-light behind, didn't I? It's not here, is it? No . . . no? So you see, you can't trap me again. All you can do is ask for your last WISH, and I shall be free!'

Scabs, teetering on the pool's edge, said, 'I might never wish. Where would you be then?'

Jafir laughed, 'Never WISH? Never fear, you will!' The little man hugged himself. 'Oh, what happiness awaits me then! But such a world of choice . . . what shall I do? Shall I return to Qatani, and my dear brother? Well, perhaps, but I'm free now, after all. Shall I magic myself to Kal-Theron, and seize Big Boy's throne? No, I'm sure that would be *far* too easy! Perhaps I shall embark upon a long journey, seeking *new* worlds to conquer . . . one does long to *stretch* after being in that lamp! Hm . . . but then, perhaps I should like to remain with you, my dear, in this dreaming dimension, living the life of a genie of leisure – I mean, a man. But young master, do be careful! Concentrate! Why, I believe you nearly lost your footing!'

'I wish—' Scabs began, his arms wheeling. Concentrate, indeed! How could he concentrate with this fool bumbling round him like a maddening, immense insect? He slumped down, dangling his legs into the cool, green water. Behind him the House of Truth shimmered like a vision of ivory, marble and gold. Birdsong sounded sweetly from the gardens; from the lily-pads came the croakings of a family of frogs.

The genie hovered.

'Genie?'

'Master?'

'Tell me, why are my wishes numbered only at three?'

'Why, master, that is the way. The way, that's all. But are not three enough – more than enough WISHES for a young man like you?'

'You tricked me out of two! I mean . . . I didn't have time to think.'

'Now you do, and you think too much,' murmured the genie. 'Ah, and how you will rant, how you will rail, when thought fulfils you no more than haste!'

'What's that, genie? You're whispering!'

'Whispering? You WISH to know what?'

'I wish noth . . .'

'You WISH nothing?' came the eager reply.

Scabs kicked his legs angrily in the water, splashing the carpet. With a giggle, Jafir whizzed out of the way and for a moment Scabs thought the little fellow had gone. How he hated him! His fists pulped painfully into his ruined cheeks, the cabin boy looked across the green expanse of the pool. In the distance, passing between an avenue of trees, he saw Jem, deep in conversation with the girl called Dona Bela. Scabs gnawed at his reddening knuckles, envy and longing surging through his heart. Oh, the lovely girl! If he were beautiful, would she be his? He had to believe it. But could he?

Jafir swooped back. 'Ho, master, a little more gratitude to your friend might be in order, hm?'

Scabs looked up blankly. 'Friend?'

'Who is your friend, master, but me?'

The cabin boy scowled, but the genie was undeterred and burbled on, 'So, you almost WISHED for nothing. What of it? Why should you WISH for anything more?' He gestured around him, to the house, to the gardens. 'I have brought you to a place of eternal pleasure, have I not? Have you need for anything more? Greedy fellow, that would have another WISH!'

Scabs screeched, 'I wish . . . I wish I had a thousand!'

'What's that?' Jafir's eyes glowed. 'You WISH?'

Scabs rose suddenly, spinning round on the slippery ledge. Defiantly he looked up at the hovering genie. A cunning look came into his eyes and he declared slowly, carefully, 'Genie, I wish for . . . a thousand wishes!'

Scabs closed his eyes, expecting smoke, perhaps lightning. In the next moment he would be transfigured. Now he was just a guest in a rich man's house, a poor, ugly boy, dependent on the charity of his superiors. Was this enough for him? One moment more, and the powers of an Emperor would lie at his command! *Make me beautiful . . . Give me the girl . . . Build me a palace of my very own . . .*

Yes, yes!

But no. Instead, Scabs found himself teetering backwards into the pool as the genie swooped over him with a cackling laugh. 'Fool, you think to trick me? You have WISHED for the one thing I cannot grant!'

'You disobey me?' Scabs thrashed in the water. 'But I'm your master!'

'On the terms of my bondage, and no more! Fool!'

'Genie!'

But Jafir had gone. Scabs lay back, floating in the deep, sustaining water. This water, it seemed, did not sting him as the sea had done; he might have been lying in soft, cool grass. He kicked weakly, propelling himself away from the edge. His friend indeed! The genie was his tormentor, he knew that much. A wicked trickster! If he was to have what he wanted, he must be a trickster too. But how? His heart filled with anguish, Scabs stared up into the cerulean sky. He turned his head and the sun dazzled him; then a face appeared before him, a phantom face with a long, flowing beard.

'Lord Almoran,' whispered Scabs. He was not startled; he had seen the vision before, each day since arriving in this place. Until now it had spoken to him only in oblique, teasing words, of the splendours of this dreaming dimension; until now, Scabs had thought this all very well, but wondered what splendours there could be for him while he remained himself, his natural self.

Child, came the voice, *be not afraid of the one from the lamp. He is in your power, after all.*

'In mine?'

Think of it. Are they not true, the words he says? He brought you here because you sought a place of pleasure. What need have you of his wishes now?

'My lord,' Scabs whispered, 'but my face . . . my flesh . . .'

Child, you have been touched by magic. Do you know what that means? Why, it confers upon you the power to live eternally here in this special dimension of mine. Spend your last wish, and what will you be then? The magic will have left you.

'And then?'

Scabs had been swishing at the water to keep afloat; now he left off, but remained floating. The face loomed closer, but if the words were kindly, there was an urgency behind them too. A power. A command.

I tell you, be not afraid of the one from the lamp. He pretends that the freedom of the world shall be his, once you have wished and broken his bondage. His power, you might imagine, would then be limitless. The case, in truth, is exactly opposite. In his impatience and contempt, did he not permit you to leave behind the konar-light? That was folly, but it is he who shall pay the price for that folly. Without the lamp which is his magical lodging, his power shall be at an end once your wish is made, and he shall become but an ordinary man.

'My lord, why then would he have me wish? This eagerness makes no sense!'

Child, it makes every sense, for the one from the lamp is convinced that sooner or later, whether you will or no, you must spend that last wish of yours. His hope is that you shall squander it here, amongst the splendours and luxuries of this palace, that he might remain here when his magic is gone, and not be abandoned in a place of fear and terror.

Scabs was confused. 'My lord, would you then have me wish, depriving this genie of his magic powers?'

My child, no! Never! Don't you understand? You spent your first wishes carelessly, but while he awaits the third, you hold him in bondage. Hold him you must, if you are to live with me here, for when your own wish is spent, you too shall be lost to the magic that touches you now. Child, think of the power that is yours, and yours alone. Is there not a pleasure in this power? Let the one from the lamp rail, he can harm you not. Wish for nothing. Here in the dreaming dimension, there is no need to wish.

'No need? But my lord—'

It was then, to his astonishment, that Scabs found himself rising into the air. He cried out, but his cry turned to a gasp as he felt himself turning and looking down, back into the waters that still rippled with his own laggardly trail. His reflection shimmered, then cleared, but Scabs saw not the repellent, pustular face that made him avert his gaze in loathing from looking-glasses and windows at night and the polished sides of tankards. The pool disclosed the visage of a handsome young man.

Did I not say there was no need to wish? Child, still your pounding heart. There is no need, I say. You are beautiful; and tonight, in your chamber, the Princess shall come to you.

Chapter 53

THE SUM OF ALL WOMEN

'Pah! Amateur!'

A moan was the reply. 'Oily, the blind!'

'Who does he think he is – Sheik Rashid?'

'Oily, it's too bright!'

Cursing, fumbling for a pillow he had punched to the floor, Polty knocked his hand against something made of glass. With a slow rumble, it began to roll. Polty cursed again and squashed the pillow over his eyes. Really, Oily was the limit! For a moment the fat little whoremonger had been filled with sham respect, wringing his hands over the indisposition of so vital, so valued, so venerated a customer; then he had expressed his horror that the Major-sir should languish like a prisoner in the dark. What, was it midnight? The sky was bright! It was a great day in Qatani's history! Below, the streets were all in a bustle!

A compelling argument; alas, Polty preferred the dark, and Eli Oli Ali, when he battered back the shutters, suddenly forgot the fine customer he was desperate to retain. Instead, he was intent on the crowded street.

'Oily, what is it?' snapped Polty, after a moment.

Bitter envy filled the reply. 'Casca Dalla, driving his Babas to the booths! Pah, they're stale, the lot of them! Virgins? Some bawd's old stock, more like it! Casca struts like a turkey-cock, saying *Eli's finished, Eli's lost his touch.* Now look at him, with Babas like that! Of course I let him think I want, and want . . . do I say, *They're rotten, Casca?* Pah, pah! Let the dirty whoremonger think he's got the better of me! Why, tonight after the Rebonding, when all the fine fellows are out carousing, will they demand Casca's sluts, I ask you, or their old friend Eli's fine fresh produce? Pah, pah, pah!'

Disgusted, Eli slammed the shutters again, then thought better of it and drew one back just enough to fill the apartment with a shadowy light. He turned, troubled, and realised that he must, at the least, secure the loyalty of the Major-sir. Getting back into the palace had not been easy, after all. Really, those guards! It was daylight robbery! Eli must at least make sure his visit was worthwhile.

Once again he was all unctuous concern.

'But Major-sir, where are your friends? By the gods, has even the beanpole fellow left you alone, when you languish so? What manner of men can you Ejlanders be? Why, we Unangs would never be so barbarous!'

Polty struggled upright. He blinked, rubbed his eyes and peered into the shadows. From the square, a street away, came relentless hammerings, heavings, hackings; hasty preparations for the day's great event, they had been going on all night, and all yesterday too. Maddening . . . Polty looked for the glass thing, the orb. Had it stopped rolling? Seemed so. He sniffed loudly, tapped a finger to his nose and announced with as much dignity as he could muster that Lieutenant Throsh, as it happened, was away on a mission, Agent Burgrove too. 'On my particular orders, Oily. My orders, you understand?' Was Polty – an Ejlander, a Major and a Veeldrop, too – to endure the pity of a dirty mixer? With some difficulty, he essayed a smile. 'Your concern is touching, Oily, but I assure you, I am well enough, well indeed . . . well, nothing that a fresh barrel of ferment won't fix. Oh, and I don't suppose you have any tobarilloes?'

At once, the whoremonger was patting his many pockets. Flustered, he thrust forth a brownish, crumpled cylinder – one that Polty had given him in the first place – and fumbled again for a tinder-stick. In the light of the flame, the Major-sir's face showed a curious tinge of purple, or perhaps blue. Why, sweat rolled from his temples, as if he had been toiling, long and hard, in the sun! Eli Oli Ali's brow furrowed, and suddenly he felt more deeply alarmed than before. Nervously he peered round the squalid chamber. Surreptitiously he sniffed the air. The usual foetor, yes, but was there something more? A hint? A whiff? A strange swirling filled the whoremonger's head and he found himself staring fixedly, foolishly, upon the immense stain, like dried blood, that covered one corner of the marble floor. He heard a rumbling and jumped as a glass ball, glimmering in the dim light, began to roll slowly, as if of its own volition, across the floor towards him. With a little cry, Eli Oli Ali rushed to the door, declaring that he would fetch a barrel of the finest Tiralos – at once, and personally – from the Khan of the Crescent Moon.

There was a loud *rat-a-tat!*, and the whoremonger froze.

Polty staggered upright, but slumped back again, scattering ash. 'Oily, you'll see who that is? Really, there's been not a slave to be had in this wing since the Ouabin came. To think, that a Veeldrop must answer his own door!'

Again came the *rat-a-tat!* The whoremonger hesitated; the door opened without him. Disgust filled the greasy face. The new arrival was a fellow he had seen before; an Ejlander, but one hardly so amenable as the Major-sir. *This* fellow had been most impolite when Eli Oli Ali paid him a call, pursing his lips, pointing to the door, muttering that such services

357

would not be required. Pah! A boy-lover, no doubt. Well, let him catch the jubba-fever, and serve him right!

A man had to have standards.

Indignation filled Eli Oli Ali's face as he pushed past Lord Empster, slamming the door. Self-righteously the fat fellow strode down the stairs, almost tripping over the ends of his curly slippers. Then, halfway down, he hesitated. A new thought had struck him. A horror. You could pick a boy-lover, couldn't you? Well, Eli always could, and the Empster-lord looked a fine figure of a man, for an Ejlander. A boy-lover? Never! There could be only one explanation. Casca Dalla had got to him! Cursing under his breath, Eli scuttled back up the stairs, looked round furtively and pressed his ear to the door. Terrible images filled his mind: the Ejlanders, laughing over the fat little mixer; the Major-sir, weakened and open to influence; Empster-lord, extolling the virtues of Casca . . . Now it was Eli's turn to moan. In his distress, he had forgotten the jubba-fever; but then, even if the Major-sir was stricken, he might live for – oh, a moonlife or more! What consolations would he need, as death loomed near!

By now, Eli was feverish himself, if only with a panic of envy and greed. He pressed his ear harder against the door. Damn, but he could barely hear! He thought of the keyhole, and slithered to his knees. In moments, more terrible fears would assail him.

This is the scene he saw enacted.

POLTY (*struggling to rise*): My lord!
EMPSTER (*with a wry nod*): Major Veeldrop. You have forgotten, perhaps, that you were expecting me? Your invitation was specific and cordial.
POLTY: Indeed, my lord. You find me a little . . . indisposed, that is all, but nonetheless you are most welcome. You will take a glass of ferment? (*Looks round, then curses.*) Damn!
EMPSTER *sits opposite, beginning to stuff his pipe.* Pray, do not trouble yourself. May we not keep our heads clear for a little time? Ferment enough shall flow this evening, for all the pretence that it is not allowed.
POLTY (*uncertainly*): Indeed, indeed. It is a great day in Qatani's history.

The orb rolls between them.

EMPSTER: A great day? You think so?
POLTY: I, my lord, think nothing. I mean, we are told it is great.
EMPSTER: Major, you surprise me! Told by whom?
POLTY *coughs, then continues*: My lord, my concern is with trade.

358

We may trade as well, may we not, with a Caliph who
    gives his fealty to Sheik Rashid as to Sultan Kaled?
EMPSTER: Hm. His fealty, and his daughter too.
POLTY: Oh indeed, his daughter.

Coughing again, POLTY *staggers upright at last, beating a fist upon
his chest. He paces to the window. Still come the sounds of
hammerings, hackings, sawings; still the stallholders bring forth their
wares. Flags flutter, strung across the street, and the sky is intensely
pale. After some moments,* POLTY *continues reflectively:*

  Today, all but the most decrepit and diseased shall gather in
  the square. Today, all but the most decadent and disloyal shall
  pledge a new allegiance. So the Caliph shall renounce the pact
  that gives his daughter to Sultan Kaled's son. So the beauteous
  Bela Dona shall plight her troth to a dirty fellow with a flea-
  bitten camel and a tea-towel on his head. So, so. What cheers
  shall split the night! What surging joy! (*Pause.*) Like all joys,
  how empty it will be.

The orb rolls to POLTY's *feet, trembles, then trundles back across the
floor.*

EMPSTER (*arching an eyebrow*): All? Your example is hardly fair.
    You speak of a sham, a forced fealty. Are there not other,
    more substantial joys?
POLTY: I have sounded the joys of this world to their depths.
EMPSTER: You have squandered yourself in debauchery. There
    are higher things, but what do you know of them? You are
    like a deaf man who does not believe in music. Like a man
    born blind, who thinks the world is black because he cannot
    see.

*Until now, there has been a sense of things unsaid, of a confrontation
gathering force. Now it begins, slowly at first, to break forth in words.
When* POLTY *turns back from the window, there is anger in his voice.*

POLTY: There are things I see, my lord. Many things. For
    example, do you think I don't know what you are?
EMPSTER *laughs aloud.* There are many, too many, who would
    tell me what I am.
POLTY *flings his tobarillo to the floor.* Weasel words! But you
    know, don't you, that it was in my power to have you
    punished as the traitor and renegade you are? And to think,
    that once you – *you* – were a trusted member of the
    Ascendancy! The mysterious Lord E—, issuing orders to the

Special Agents! How I trembled at the thought of your displeasure! How I suffered when, it seemed, I had incurred it! Look at you now! A renegade, a traitor, hunted by your own former agents!

EMPSTER (*with a smile*): Hunted? Hardly.

POLTY: We have *hardly* begun. After all, you shall not escape me, Empster. What you have done with the crippler-boy is something I will discover, and discover soon. As for the Vaga, I have every certainty that *his* evil tricks will be punished as they deserve. But my interest now is you. How easily I could have persuaded our hosts to drag you to the dungeons! Have you not wondered why you were spared?

EMPSTER: Major, do you seek to be clever? There are times when I have despaired of Prince Jemany, but really, *you* are stupider by far. You affect to be party to my deeper secrets. Has it not occurred to you that I may know *yours*?

Anger flashes over POLTY'S *face and he steps forward menacingly, but as he does so, the rolling orb halts at his feet. He sways, a hand to his forehead. It is rather as if he has heard a mysterious voice, echoing in his head. He bends, swiping up the orb. For a moment he holds it in his palm, as if weighing it; then, his confidence growing, he tosses it idly up and down during the following exchange. Light flashes from the gleaming glass.*

POLTY *smiles.* But good my lord, we toy with each other. Should I have invited you here like this had my intentions been hostile? You see we are alone, and I can be no threat to you. In truth, nothing could be further from my desire.

EMPSTER: You called me a traitor.

POLTY *laughs.* My lord, an ironic quotation, no more! What care we for the views of the vulgar, when we number ourselves among the world's élite? What care we for the follies of the past, when the future lies before us, and a battle looms? Gentle lord, there is a proposition I would put to you.

EMPSTER: You? To me?

POLTY: Let me be plain. I speak in the name of the First Minister.

EMPSTER: Tranimel?

POLTY: The same.

EMPSTER: Not any more.

POLTY'S *brow furrows.* My lord?

EMPSTER (*mildly*): You speak, I think, for ... TOTH-VEXRAH.

The name has a sudden, alarming effect. Fire burns in POLTY's *eyes and he staggers forward, looming, almost leering, over the noble lord. He holds his finger in the air, and on the end of the finger, the orb spins. Light streaks from the ball of glass, but now, it is clear, the light comes from within. When* POLTY *speaks again, his voice seems strangely altered; increasingly, it becomes the voice of another.*

POLTY: Dear lord, indeed I must believe you know my secrets. But must not you believe, too, that I know yours? Come, let us end all pretences between us. It has been so long; so long, I despaired that we should ever meet again. Sweet lord, will you not take my hand? Will you not embrace me? But why do I call you lord? Is this not a coldness, when in truth, you are my brother?

EMPSTER (*rising suddenly*): No!

The orb spins from POLTY's *finger, but does not fall. Instead, it hovers in the air, then orbits* POLTY's *head like a tiny planet as* TOTH-VEXRAH *speaks through him again. By now,* POLTY's *skin is entirely blue; flickers of flame lap at his temples. By now,* LORD EMPSTER's *customary garb – his long cape, his broad-brimmed hat – is fading, clearing like smoke as the truth of his being shines forth brightly, glimmering, golden.*

TOTH: Brother Agonis, will you be a fool? I said I knew your secrets, and I mean all of them! Do you think I don't know the true object of your quest? You have sought for the Key – so have I. You have sent out your agents – so have I. How you have longed to restore the Orokon, to stand before it, arms outstretched, as the long-lost crystals, once again, glitter in the—

AGONIS (*interrupting*): Hypocrite! Monster! Dare you even speak of the mystic circle, when its sundering was all your doing?

TOTH: Mine? Alas, I see the aeons have dulled my brother's faculties! It was Koros, was it not, who plucked the first crystal from its rightful place? Orok, who dispersed them in the end? Brother, blame me for nothing! Blame our brothers! Blame our sisters! Blame our faithless father!

AGONIS: My father, not yours! If I had spilt my seed into the gutter, and some evil spell had made that seed burgeon and grow into a monster, should I acknowledge that monster as my son?

TOTH: False deceiver, I was fully formed when our father cast me from him!

361

AGONIS: Fully formed, and a monster!

TOTH: Fully formed, and your brother! Oh Agonis, Agonis, what has become of you? Do you not remember those times when Brother Koros was spurned, yet you took his hand before all, testifying to his virtue? How I looked on enviously from my concealment, wishing that it was I who basked in your love! I, the child not suffered even to skulk in our father's vilest corridors. Can you not love me now, as you were destined to do? Are we not struck from the same substance? Are we not alike, alone and questing?

AGONIS: I stop my ears against you! My brother Koros was a good and virtuous being, despised wrongly on account of his visage!

TOTH: Despised, yes! Rejected! And what am I? If Koros deserved your love, does not TOTH deserve it doubly? Agonis, you are a god! I am your brother! Why am I condemned to be a Creature of Evil? Love me, as you loved the dark Koros!

AGONIS: I said Koros was virtuous! Faithless, evil being! What are you, what have you ever been, but vice itself, creeping, polluting, insidious?

By now, POLTY's hair is in flames and his face and limbs writhe in grotesque contortions, but for the moments when TOTH is speaking through him. Still the orb whirls round and round; the room is awash with violent light. Outside, ELI OLI ALI is at once enthralled and terror-struck, alternately slithering to the floor, whimpering and moaning, then scrambling urgently back into place, prodding the keyhole with a bulging eye.

TOTH (*resuming, in a measured tone now*): Brother, I am more than you think, but it seems you will not listen. Very well, as I am a god, or soon to be, it does not become me to beg for love. No more. But think: you call me faithless, but are you not as much a traitor to our father as me? He would have you lie by him in the darkness of his death, yet instead, through all the ages of human life you have wandered through the world, seeking only the one thing you can never find. Ah, if only we had met again sooner! (*He gestures to the window.*) Without, the paltry humans speak of a new pact, a new beginning. But there is a greater pact, is there not, to be enacted here, within these walls?

AGONIS (*bitterly*): Pact? Mine, to you?

TOTH: Brother, I said I knew what you seek. The Orokon, yes:

but why?

AGONIS (*flaming out*): To save the world from you!

TOTH: Smooth-tongued Agonis, I think you care but little for this world. Will you not look into – dare I say – my magic glass?

The possessed POLTY *moves closer, grinning, tempting* AGONIS *to gaze into the spinning orb. For a moment the god is fascinated; it seems he will succumb. Then, with a cry, he lashes out, knocking the orb from* POLTY's *hand. It crashes to the floor, but does not shatter. Instead, it rolls wildly back and forth, as if the apartment has changed into the cabin of a storm-tossed ship. But there is more magic at work, a residue of the spinning. In the middle of the red patch of the floor stands a female form, dressed in a veil and a long, flimsy gown.*

AGONIS (*startled*): The Shimmering Princess – here?

TOTH: Brother, are you sure?

AGONIS: She is garbed like the Princess –

TOTH: But who is the Princess? You know the truth, do you not?

AGONIS: Evil one, I fear where your words are tending!

TOTH (*slyly*): Brother, what is there to fear? Go to the girl. She is merely an illusion, a dream of the orb, but in dreams, may we not sometimes see the truth? (*Wheedling:*) Yes, that's right ... Closer ... Shouldn't you like to lift her veil?

AGONIS (*whispering*): But she is made of mist!

TOTH: I tell you, she is the dream of the orb. Come brother, there is no time to tarry. The vision before us will swiftly fade, and I strain my powers to force my words through the mouth of this flame-haired fool. Quickly now, quickly, draw back the veil.

TOTH *falters. The burning* POLTY *slumps to the floor and for a moment the flames in his hair are guttering. The orb whizzes faster; he swiftly revives, but* AGONIS *falters too. He turns suddenly, rounding on the anti-god.*

AGONIS: Monster, you would torment me with the longings of my heart?

TOTH *affects astonishment.* Torment? No torment! Brother, I said I had a proposition for you ... did I not?

AGONIS *hesitates a moment longer, but* TOTH's *small victory is already won.* POLTY's *face contorts into a leering grin as the greatest of* OROK's *children creeps, like a thief, into the blood-coloured circle.*

With a trembling hand, he reaches up. He snatches back the veil. He staggers back, shocked.

AGONIS: No! It cannot be! She cannot still be yours!
TOTH: She is beautiful, is she not? Brother, why do you quail?

The manifestation flickers, vanishes; AGONIS *lunges at his flame-haired tormentor, clutching at his throat. Round and round them, in tight circles, rolls the orb.*

AGONIS: Evil one, what trickery is this? Pretend no innocence
    with me! Why have you shown me the one I seek? Why
    have you shown me your daughter IMAGENTA?
TOTH (*ecstatic*): Ah! He speaks her name!
AGONIS: The name that beats eternally in my mind, like a
    mantra! In the aeons of my quest, I have learnt but three
    things: that love of this maiden shall for ever fill my heart;
    that you, monstrous creature, are not fit to be her father;
    and that only the power of the Orokon shall ever make her
    mine!
TOTH: Hah! The truth at last!

He breaks away, exulting, but falters again; AGONIS, *wracked with emotion, slumps to the divan where* POLTY *lay before.*

AGONIS (*after a moment*): What do you want from me?
TOTH (*with difficulty*): Oh, very little.
AGONIS: I don't believe it. You deceive and deceive, but no
    more! Do you think I imagine this Unang Princess is, in
    truth, my Lady Imagenta? It cannot be! It violates all
    prophecies!
TOTH (*contemptuously*): What are prophecies, that a god may not
    sweep them aside? But brother, I cannot sustain this
    manifestation for long. Stretched wide across a web of
    awareness, my powers are far from their height. Twice
    already, my grip has faltered, and the flame-haired fool has
    almost slipped free; in moments now, he shall slump down
    again—
AGONIS: Leave him this instant! Go from me!
TOTH (*urgently*): Wait! Brother, listen to me, just listen! This lady
    is *not* the one you seek, yet nonetheless she is an emanation
    of my daughter, and a powerful one—
AGONIS: What lie is this?
TOTH: Your brow furrows? Come, you have wandered for a
    thousand cycles! Have you not seen a thousand ladies –

why, ten thousand – each one of whom resembles your beloved? Some are much like her; others a little like her; some seem barely like her at all, once you draw them close – yet there remains, does there not, a suspicion? A trace? How can it be otherwise, for who, after all, is the Lady Imagenta but THE SUM OF ALL WOMEN?

AGONIS (*breaking down*): Their epitome! And she shall be mine!

TOTH: Brother, I would that it were so! Did not I make her as a gift for you? Why, aeons ago you should have wedded, had it not been for our foolish father! Were my powers truly godly, I would give her to you now; alas, the lady is lost to me too!

AGONIS *looks up, eyes flashing.* You do not know where she is?

TOTH: Have I the power I seek? Only through creatures like this flame-haired fool, and what is he? But brother, when you join with me, think what glory lies before us then!

AGONIS (*startled*): Join? With you?

TOTH: Think of it! For me, the Orokon! For you, the lady! Brother, Listen to me—

AGONIS (*turning away*): No! This is an evil trick! I won't listen, I won't!

TOTH (*grabbing him*): Listen! (*In a voice low and rapid:*) Brother, this very day we may test our loyalties! In the Ritual of Rebonding, shall not three suitors come forth to claim the Shimmering Princess? Each suitor shall bear a gift, shall he not, and he whose gift is most splendid shall win the fair one's hand? Of course, it will be the merest sham, for the human called Rashid has ensured that he, and he alone, can be chosen. But brother, it shall not be! (*Lunging for the orb, he offers it to* AGONIS.) Take this orb, hold it in your palm, let it spin! Brush aside the sham suitors – the one called Rashid, too – and brother, I swear this Princess shall be yours!

AGONIS (*coldly*): Mine? She is the merest emanation, you said so!

TOTH: Not so fast! Brother, have you not guessed? Can you not tell? As the boy-child Jemany is Key to the Orokon, so this girl shows the way to the Crystal of Theron! He who holds her shall possess the crystal! Quick now, quick! Have we a pact?

Again, he holds out the orb, but by now POLTY's *hand is trembling violently, and* AGONIS, *with a cry of 'Never!', rises suddenly, pushing him away.* POLTY *slumps down, writhing, and the orb zigzags wildly across the floor.*

TOTH (*gasping*): Brother, don't be a fool!

AGONIS: A fool? Not to join with you? You say you have sought the Key – but I have found him, and he is mine! You say you send out your agents – but already my children have found two crystals, and soon, I am certain, will seize the third! As for the Ouabin, is he not the merest pawn in my hands? What can you know of my plans, my schemes? Vile thing, you may long for the Orokon, but I shall possess it while you burn in the Realm of Unbeing, where you belong! In what terrible bondage you have placed my beloved I do not know, but soon your evil shall be destroyed for ever, and the Lady Imagenta shall come to me!

TOTH: Fool! Without me, you shall never find her! Hurl me back into Unbeing? Fool, I say! Even now, my powers are growing, feeding from a secret source—

AGONIS: Powers? You are weak! Dying!

TOTH (*desperate, fighting for these last moments*): No! Cruel brother, I have defeated you before, and shall ... defeat you again ... soon, I shall be stronger ... stronger ... (*A last effort:*) Agonis, this I swear: before this quest is over, you shall know my retribution, and fall down and curse that you did not accept my pact! You have had my compassion, and spurned it! Next, you shall feel my ... my wrath ...

A scream fills the air, and the anti-god is gone. Flames extinguished, blue skin fading, POLTY *lies spent, but just before he slumps into unconsciousness, a spasm shakes his chest and he rises up, expelling a stream of reddish, blood-like vomit. Briefly* AGONIS *looks down at him, considering, perhaps, that an enemy, if a lesser one than his putative brother, is at this moment entirely in his power.*

AGONIS (*reflective*): No, flame-haired one, I shall leave you now. The part you play is grotesque, but nonetheless as necessary to this quest as the boy Jemany's or the girl Catayane's. I spare you; as you are a conduit for the evil one, so it is that you deserve compassion, though in truth it is the evil in you that allows you to be such a conduit, as Jemany's goodness permits him to be Key to the Orokon. The one who calls himself my brother says I am a fool. Very well, in time it shall all be clear. I leave you, flame-haired one, to your uneasy sleep.

The golden god spreads his arms wide; a flash fills the air, then he, too, is gone. For moments, the flash lingers in the gloom like a bright, smoky haze, but as it fades, there is the sound of a click. Cautiously, a greasy face peers round the door and ELI OLI ALI *tiptoes into the apartment. A finger toys with his blubbery lips as he looks round uncertainly. Bending down, he reaches out to prod* POLTY, *perhaps to shake him; he thinks better of it. The orb, running down, thuds slowly against the bottom of the wall. The whoremonger's eyes light upon it. Nervously he approaches the strange glass object, looking back and forth between the insensible* POLTY *and the glimmering orb,* POLTY *and the orb,* POLTY, *the orb ...*

ELI OLI ALI: Ah, Major-sir, you are a poor, poor fellow. You want no more of this strange magic. Ferment and Jarvel and tobarillo, that's the medicine for you ... and a Baba-girl or three, but not one of Casca Dalla's, eh? Hm, hm ... Now, when you were speaking in the strange voice, didn't you say the fellow who had this funny ball should win the prize of Princess Bela Dona? Hm, hm ... Now, if I only had a girl so fine ... how could Casca ever compete?

The whoremonger is decided. He snatches the orb and scuttles away.

Chapter 54

AN UNEXPECTED MEETING

'Most sacred one,' said Mother Madana.

'Most sacred one,' mimicked her girls in unison as all of them, mother and daughters alike, abased themselves to the carpet as if in prayer. Cata studied them wryly, catching more than one Sefita or Satima peering up through her hands, entranced. With a shudder she thought of the imbecile caresses that had so tormented her when she was trapped in these apartments. This return visit was a very different affair.

Since her transformation, Cata had gazed upon herself again and again in the looking-glasses, tracing the lineaments of her new face. What stirred her was not vanity, though the face she had assumed was one more beautiful than her own; instead, she wondered if the transformation could hold. For a time the new identity had seemed barely stable, and she would see her face slipping; for a time, she had heard the voice of the Princess, whispering in her mind like a distant echo. By now, the echo had faded and Cata was alone – alone with a task she barely understood. Could she really pass for Princess Bela Dona? There was no going back. She knew only that she must try.

Vizier Hasem cleared his throat. 'Very well, Mother, we may begin,' he said, irritated at the unaccustomed show of piety. In truth, the Vizier had been short-tempered all that morning. Now, not for the first time, he darted a suspicious glance at the girl beside him. Her beauty was dazzling, but was she real? Among the gauze and looking-glasses of her own chambers, she had appeared the creature she had always been, fluttering, almost translucent; the Vizier had to wonder if his poor master had given way at last to the madness that lurks in wait for those who live, too long and intimately, with worry and fear. Protocol made it impossible for him – even him – to touch the royal child, but oh, how he longed to sweep protocol aside!

In Mother Madana's realm, among the brighter light and colours, the girl still had about her something insubstantial. But not entirely. Beneath the fluttering veil the Vizier glimpsed a face that was filled, he was sure, with the flush of life. Could it be true about the Teller's ghost? Dread pulsed in the Vizier's temple, and he wondered what more strange magic might yet work itself out before all this was over.

With barked commands, Mother Madana had arranged her girls into serried ranks, like troops – had troops been given to squirming, blushing and giggling whenever their commander passed by. The Vizier eyed them sourly as his royal companion began her progress along the line.

'They are all ... virgin, Mother?' he murmured.

Mother Madana's eyes flashed and she brushed a hand against the medal on her bosom. 'Really, Your Excellency, it is only the quality-market that Eli and I ... that *Casca* and I cater to here. Innocence is the watchword, is it not, for those who would be purchased for the finest harems? No,' she added with a knowing smirk, 'the wanton arts may be a source of much delight, but those delights I leave to the ladyboys below.'

'Quite,' the Vizier replied curtly, and turned his attention to the business at hand.

According to the ancient statutes that governed the Ritual of Rebonding, a royal Princess, when she appeared upon the altar, must be flanked by two beauteous maidens. Mother Madana took a keen interest in the choice; after all, the girls selected for so special a role would be much increased in value. If she was to be working with Casca Dalla, she must show him from the beginning that she still had her grip on the market. She set her mouth with a determined air. How she would miss her old friend Eli! She had shed a tear for the greasy fellow, but only one: business was business, and even the winner of the Royal Export Medal must strive, always strive, to keep up her place.

Eagerly she pointed out the charms of this or that simpering creature, sometimes reaching out to lower a girl's veil, lift up a chin, adjust a sari or a chain of jewels.

Soon bored by the girls, the Vizier found himself studying Mother Madana. Strange to think this waddling old eunuch had been the most celebrated ladyboy in the days of the old Caliph. Her beauty had been legendary, but not so legendary as her sensual charms. With her silken buttocks and ready tongue, it was said that 'Sweet Madana' could keep a man at the pinnacle of ecstasy, riding unrelentingly on the tides of lust, from the fall of darkness to dawn the next day. Now any man would feel only revulsion for this raddled, fat hag, for all the jewels and silk that draped her, and all the bright ochre that daubed her face. How could it be that she had come to this? With a pang, the Vizier thought of the boy who would perhaps make her a worthy successor. The barber should have finished his work by now.

Cata looked along the line of girls with barely concealed distaste. So far as she was concerned, they all looked the same, but she supposed the Shimmering Princess would take her duties seriously. With a furrowing brow, ignoring the overwhelming feeling that something was wrong somewhere, she pretended to consider the vital question – this one, that one? – when suddenly, from outside, came an anguished cry, and a distant rattling and banging at a door.

The girls squealed.

'Sefita! Satima!' Mother Madana reeled round, startled.

'What? What?' Vizier Hasem, in his preoccupation, was slow to realise the source of the disturbance. Before he could call to her, Cata had darted away, disappearing round a corner of the long chamber.

She knew that voice. She was sure of it.

She skidded down a corridor.

All through the scene with Mother Madana, Cata had felt an impending evil; sensing, just beneath the threshold of awareness, the slitherings and hissings from the cobra pit. Now, all at once, the evil took focus. She cannoned into a door, feeling the throb of the bangings, shoutings.

On the other side it was locked.

On this side, there was a key.

She turned it.

The door was open only for an instant. Cata glimpsed a staircase jutting from the floor below and, swarming up the staircase, burly slaves, girls in gaudy gowns, an enraged barber wielding a razor, and a naked boy, cornered against the door.

He crashed into her arms.

'*Rajal!*'

Quickly Cata bundled him inside.

She slammed the door and would have locked it fast; instead, she swiftly opened it again, standing four-square before the invading hordes.

'Sacred One!' The barber's razor clattered to the floor.

'Sacred One!' cried ladyboys and slaves alike.

They sank to their knees.

Cata slammed the door again.

'Princess, where are you?' came a cry from round the corner. It was the Vizier, seeking her; but a Sefita and Satima, excited by the fracas, had run on ahead. They were almost upon her. Cata looked round wildly.

The storeroom!

'Raj, in here – quick!'

'Princess!' said Sefita, flinging herself through the closing door.

'Princess!' said Satima, doing the same.

Their idol looked at them, and had to sigh. Their eyes were so eager, so wide with wonderment. 'I've seen you girls before, haven't I?' she said, as she banged their heads together.

Cata stood with her back to the door. She thought quickly. If she did not understand all that had happened, she knew that Rajal was in deadly danger. Her eyes darted to the unconscious girls. Sefita was closest to Rajal's size.

'Raj! Into her costume – quick!'

Rajal moaned. 'Oh no, not again!'

'Raj, just do it!'

'But how ... do you know me?' the exhausted boy puffed as together they tore away the girl's clothes. 'Is it ... the crystal? Princess, you must ... give it back to me!'

Cata shook her head. 'Raj, it's Cata! I only look like ... oh, there's no time to explain!'

'Princess! Princess!' came the Vizier's voice again.

✳ ✳ ✳ ✳

'Princess?'

The door clicked open and the Sacred One emerged. Her veil had torn away; she was flushed and breathless, but her beauty, in dishevelment, was still more dazzling. In one circling arm she supported a lolling Sefita; assisting her in the task was a shy Satima, her shoulders hunched and her eyes cast down.

'Princess?' said the Vizier again, his face furrowing. He had meant to investigate the disturbance in the corridor, but suddenly it was forgotten. He reached out, and – protocol be hanged – brushed his fingers against the royal arm. A shock ran through him. It was true, it was true! For a moment he exulted; then he felt a stab of dread. There was something wrong here, something very wrong.

He gazed into the royal eyes with a strange intentness, then jumped as the beautiful girl cried harshly, 'What are you looking at, man? I've been choosing my maidens, haven't I? Now leave me, I'm taking these girls back to my apartments!'

Chapter 55

THE HARSH REFLECTIONS

'Pendants!'
  'Icons!'
  'Bracelets!'
  'Rings!'
So tightly was the crowd packed into the square that the hawkers had barely room to move. It did not matter; each was surrounded by a cluster of eager brown hands, flinging coins recklessly away in exchange for this or that shabby trinket, hastily produced for the grand day.
  'Song sheets!'
  'Sherbet!'
  'Joss-sticks!'
  'Jarvel!'
Already the sun blazed high overhead, gleaming on the gilding of reconstructed galleries, on ceremonial turbans and veils and gowns and line upon line of Ouabin, sabres held erect. In place of the executioner's wheel, the square was dominated by an elaborate arrangement of platforms and ramps, richly carpeted and bestrewn with flowers; high perfumed flames, translucent in the daylight, burned in braziers beside the altar where soon, and for the last time, Princess Bela Dona would appear before the public of Qatani. Some black-garbed women were already sobbing; others maintained a high, strained jollity. The air was febrile with excitement and fear. Even the birds seemed agitated, swooping and cawing strangely through the sky.

'A striking display, hm?' remarked Vizier Hasem, strolling along the curve of the magnificent new gallery. He turned, forcing a smile, to his distinguished guests.

'Vizier, I believe you have used those words before. On rather a different occasion, as I remember.'

'You reprehend me, Empster-lord?' The smile did not falter.

'Never, my friend, but I wonder that you can contemplate this day with equanimity. His Royal Magnificence, I should imagine, is a little more distressed to find his province in the thrall to alien power.'

If this were an effort to ruffle his composure, Vizier Hasem was determined that it should not do so and said only, 'Empster-lord, has not this province always been in the thrall to alien power?'

Lord Empster looked levelly at the Vizier, and might have fashioned an urbane observation about the droll ways of the Ouabin, when another voice burst out, 'Dirty desert swine!'

'Sea-lord, shh!'

Red-faced, monkey on his shoulder, Captain Porlo lurched round a party of white-robed Ouabin. Every bit as much as the square below, the galleries jangled and jostled with life, but round each Ouabin was an empty space, as if from some mysterious field of force.

'You will pardon my friend Porlo,' said Lord Empster. 'He has been, as they say, a little indisposed. Come, old friend – does this historic day not stir your salty blood?'

The captain looked blearily over the scene below. What he said next was not quite a reply. 'Hmph! Ouabin, Qatanis, Sultans, Sheiks? Foreign barbarians, the lot of them!'

In truth, the captain was a little drunk; actually, very drunk indeed. Gladly would he have stayed with his new friend in the khan, where the ferment was the finest he had tasted in these parts since . . . oh, since the night when Lefty met the cobber-as, at least! What a pity his friend had other engagements; but Eli Oli Ali, after all, was a great man. Excitedly the captain looked forward to all that this splendid new alliance would bring. True, he had no idea yet, no idea at all, of how they would escape from the Ouabin. But then there was time, always time. And ferment aplenty while they were waiting.

The old man belched and petted his monkey.

Lord Empster laid a hand on his shoulder. 'You're sure you're up to this, old friend?'

'Up to it?' The reply, if not quite clear in meaning, was alarming in its violence. The captain shook himself free of his benefactor's hand. 'You think old Porlo's not up to it? You think he's a lackey at your beck and call? You think he can't take his courage in his hands?'

It was fortunate, perhaps, that a new voice came at that moment: 'Greetings, nobles!'

It was Polty, shouldering his way through a band of turbaned courtiers. Angry looks followed him, and there might have been protests, but after all, he was an intimate of the Vizier.

Lord Empster's eyes glittered, and he drew forth his pipe. 'And *your* equilibrium, flame-haired one?' he enquired satirically. 'I trust you have regained it?'

'What? The flame-haired one, indisposed too? One would think sickness could never touch one so sturdy!' said the Vizier.

'Foreign food, most likely,' said the captain.

'Vizier, you will permit me a word?' said Polty, with a sidelong glance at Lord Empster.

Reluctantly, the Vizier let himself be drawn aside. Looking expectantly at this strange ambassador, he realised how inappropriate, in truth, his last remark had been. The gallery was in shadow, but even in the dim light he could make out the curious colour that tinged Polty's face and the film of sweat that ran from his forehead, as if heat really radiated from his flame-coloured hair. To be sure, the Ejlander had been upset – so he had claimed – at the disappearance of a certain young lady. But what was a lady? His reaction seemed excessive; then the Vizier, with a stab of alarm, wondered if perhaps it was the jubba-fever, and not mere distress, that consumed the Ejlander.

'Hasem, listen.' Polty's voice was a whisper and he clutched his companion's arm suddenly, painfully. The Vizier would have broken away, but for a moment Polty's eyes transfixed him, blazing as if with fire. The Ejlander's words were barely audible, spat through clenching teeth, but the Vizier made them out clearly enough. 'You know, don't you, that the Ouabin can't have her? Never, never must the Ouabin take the girl! You know that, don't you? Hasem . . . Hasem? This is a charade, isn't it? And the charade must end . . . Hasem!'

There was a fanfare of horns.

'Many things, many things may happen before this day is over,' the Vizier said stiffly. 'Some, indeed, for which I barely dare to hope. But this is not the time to discuss our affairs; I wonder, perhaps, if I should ever have discussed them with an Ejlander. Were this city safe again in the imperial thrall, I think perhaps that I should . . . should *not*. Besides, is there not another young lady, a lady of your own kind, to fill your heart with care? I believe you told me she was your runaway bride, though how any lady . . . but never mind. My master needs me – you will excuse me?'

Jostling like the commoners below, the fine folk in the gallery let the Vizier pass. Polty slumped against the balustrade, rubbing roughly at his discoloured face. All around the square, held aloft, were menacing blades. Why was he suddenly so aware of them?

Blades, glinting in the sun . . .

Reflecting . . .

※　※　※　※

'Mine!'
'No, mine!'
'Give it here!'
'Give it back!
'Pig-face, I'll kill you!'
'I'll kill you back!'

The pushings and shovings might have become something more, with angry strangers beating Blubber and Cheese quite as savagely as they wanted to beat each other. But there was hardly room in the tightly packed crowd; the ceremony was beginning; besides, Faha Ejo swiftly shouldered the boys apart, snatching the stolen pendant from Blubber's fat hand.

'Mine, actually!'

'That's not fair!'

'Shut up and work!'

The words were obscured by the blast of horns, but Cheese and Blubber understood them well enough, squeezing away, grumbling, in search of more treasures. Faha Ejo turned from side to side, staring with cool calculation at the black-garbed women and bearded men who were crushed close against him. Some – his nose wrinkled in contempt – wore little more than rags; others dressed almost as finely as the folk in the gallery; all were intent upon the central platform stretching below the altar, where a line of dancers in white loincloths had assembled, ready for the opening invocations. Faha Ejo felt his fingers itch. With a wry grin he thought of Stork, Fish, Blubber, Cheese ... what a trade they would ply today!

If he remained sad at the loss of Littler and Scabs, the goat-boy did not allow his feelings to divert his mind from business. Cousin Eli had taught him well.

During the stomping and rather repetitive dance, Faha Ejo managed to relieve his plump neighbour of a purse that dangled from a chain upon his hip. Really, such carelessness! In the prayers that followed, with the crowd rippling into a sea of abasement, several bracelets, a fine Jarvel-case and even a woman's ankle-chain which had glinted too brightly beneath her skirts managed to find their way into the goat-boy's pockets. Had there been the space, he would have hopped and skipped. What fine things were prayers! Smirking, Faha Ejo looked back to the platform and saw that the party of holy men had now been replaced by a Ouabin descanter, in full flowing robes, accompanied by an orchestra of tabors and pipes. Hoping they would make a rousing noise, the goat-boy carefully edged his way towards a hawker's basket, foolishly left on the ground by its preoccupied owner.

Beginning as a merry, waltz-like lilt, the descanter's song at first seemed hardly appropriate to an occasion so grave, so spiritual. Then, to the sudden throb of the tabors, came the strident chorus. The contrast was startling, and Faha Ejo – edging closer to the basket of plenty – found himself gazing at the descanter instead, at once strangely fascinated and alarmed.

Time may run swiftly or time may run slow,
Marriage brings pleasures that all men should know:
First fix your sights on the girl you desire,
Win her, enrich her and bathe her in fire!

CHORUS

Marry and burn!
The wheel shall turn!
What bold lover ever needs to yearn?
Seize your treasure from the gleaming py-y-y-re—
Marry and burn,
Marry and burn!

'Your jaw's dropping.'

'What?' A moment passed before Faha Ejo span round, facing the figure that had tapped his shoulder. 'Girl-boy!' With surprise, then suspicion, he looked into Amed's gamine face. 'You said you were sick.'

'I lied. I didn't want to steal on a day like this.'

'What?' Faha Ejo would have been angry, very angry, had any other member of the Unners spoken to him like this. Amed was different. In these last days the goat-boy had been confused about her, not wanting to admit to himself quite how pleased he had been to find her, or be found by her, when he had thought he would never see her again. Besides, Amed had changed since the old days on the Dorva Coast. If she still feared Mother Madana, hiding each time the fat old khan-mistress came down to the cellar, so too she seemed strangely distant, strangely uninvolved. It was as if her life with the Unners were unreal and she was only waiting for another life to begin. It bothered Faha Ejo.

Now Amed only murmured that she couldn't miss the Ritual of Rebonding, and Faha Ejo registered again the new, strange quality in her, something intent and secret. He saw that she was trembling; saw, too, that she was clutching an object in her hand. The konar-light: in the moment she had entered the Realm of Un, Amed's eyes had fixed upon the shabby old lamp, lying in the corner. She had grabbed it and since then refused to let it go. What could she want with it? She would not say; but then, Faha Ejo supposed, the answer was easy: it was the last token she had of her dead father. Amed was strange: at once so strong, but so tender, too. Could that be why she was a girl-boy?

Faha Ejo loved her, but knew that it was hopeless.

Reverently, Amed gazed beyond the Ouabin descanter, towards the empty altar.

The lilting returned.

> *Wives may cost dearly while lovers come cheap,*
> *Still, they bring pleasures that all men should reap:*
> *Ah, for the day when you give her your name,*
> *Clutch her, ignite her and douse her in flame!*
> *Marry and burn,* &c.

✳   ✳   ✳   ✳

'I don't like it.'

'Your cushion?'

'Cushion? What?'

'You keep shifting. Shall I call a slave?'

'Really, Hasem, I mean this song! I suppose the Sheik must intend something by it, must he not? Would he fling my daughter into a fire?'

'I think it refers to his passion, Oman . . . you know, fires of passion?' With forced cheerfulness, the Vizier might have added that the Caliph himself would soon be experiencing those very fires . . . well, similar, if the barber had performed his work by now.

Hasem licked his lips. Such thoughts were enough to divert any man, but somehow, this did not seem quite the time. With brimming eyes, his master was gazing down over the platforms and ramps. His lower lip protruded; he trembled violently; his big turban wobbled from side to side.

'I had the strangest dream last night,' he said softly. 'There was Shimmy, real again, but it was as if she weren't the same . . . as if the lady made of mist had been the real one, after all . . . but how could that be, when the old Shimmy was never real, was she, Hasem?'

The Vizier stood stiffly, registering no feeling other than the merest wrinkling of his nose at the waves of effluvia that rolled up from the crowd. Long sunrounds earlier, the betrothal of the Princess had been an affair for the Court, the Court alone; the mob had never been granted more than glimpses of their idol, and now they were to be privy to something so vital, something so sacred as this Ritual of Rebonding. It was an outrage! Beneath his blank face, the Vizier's teeth were clenched. How he detested these Ouabin ways! In these last days, there had been times when he could cheerfully have lunged, dagger in hand, at Rashid Amr Rukr, and damned be the consequences!

'. . . But do you know, Hasem, that wasn't the worst thing? I woke up and thought, I should be happy, shouldn't I, now that Shimmy's real again? But Hasem, what good is it that she's real, when that filthy Ouabin's going to take her away? Oh, damned be that Teller, and his evil magic! What has he done now, but curse my daughter again?'

377

The Vizier had heard all this before, and was barely listening; but as it happened, his own thoughts had turned in a similar direction. Tightening his grip on the dagger that he carried beneath his robes, he stared towards the curtain that even now concealed the hated form of Rashid Amr Rukr. Cursed be the Ouabin, cursed indeed! What a fine thing to kill him here, before the crowd! Would it not be worth the death that would follow as Rashid's cut-throats rushed to take their vengeance?

'. . . But Hasem, how can I wish poor Shimmy was made of mist? It's a terrible thing to wish, isn't it? She's in danger, but now she's real again, isn't there hope? Hasem, just think if the Ouabin's plan fails! Why, someone could kill him before he lays a finger on our dear, dear daughter! Why Hasem, you could kill him, here and now!'

'Oman, really! And be killed myself?'

The Vizier sheathed his dagger again. There had been times when he longed for death, but what good would his death do, when Oman would be helpless, useless without him? Besides, Sheik Rashid would learn his lesson soon enough; the Vizier was sure of it. At least, so he hoped. New intelligence had reached him, only that morning. No point in getting Oman excited, but . . . but . . . The Vizier permitted himself a fleeting, wry smile.

'If only they would hurry,' he said aloud.

Then he jumped as a slave touched his arm. He turned swiftly. A message! Had an army surrounded the city already? Of course! Oh, that they had ever chafed in the imperial thrall! Could the Sultan let them down?

But the message was of quite a different complexion.

The new ladyboy? Gone?

At first the Vizier thought the Vaga must be dead. Tears pricked his eyes and he cursed that fool of a barber; then he realised the truth, and cursed the Vaga instead. Damn, damn! At this moment, the brat should have been spreadeagled on the Caliph's couch, cauterized, prone and drugged to the eyes.

Affairs of state cause much distress, but nothing annoys a man so much as when social arrangements go awry.

❋ ❋ ❋ ❋

Fame can be fleeting and vanish like clouds,
Death waits to claim us with incense and shrouds,
Life's greatest promises crumble to dust:
Marriage? I still say a man really must!
Marry and burn, &c.

'How much longer?'

378

No answer came; but then, the man who asked this question hardly needed an answer. The ceremony took place at his command. Peering impatiently from behind the curtain, Sheik Rashid had no eyes at all for the clustering mob, for the fine-voiced descanter, or even for the fat little puppet-Caliph who sat on his cushion in the royal box. No, it was only the altar that fixed his attention, and held it fast – the altar, where the Shimmering Princess would step forth, ready to receive her suitors!

Firmly the Sheik clutched the gleaming casket that soon would win him the hand of his bride. In the world's eyes, he told himself, he had fulfilled, to the letter, all the conditions of the Ritual of Rebonding. But ah, what a delicious travesty was about to take place! His mind racing forward, the Sheik looked beyond the dull formalities of marriage to the triumphs that now certainly lay ahead. If he thought of the pain of the night before, he swept such thoughts aside, as if the incident had never happened. A misunderstanding, that was all. The future, that was all that mattered. The future, and glory! With the Golden One as his ally, there would be no stopping him. Within moonlives, he was sure of it, he would take the Sacred City. The Flame would be his! Then what power this frail girl would unleash! With sensual relish, he imagined her body burning to ash in the mysterious fire, revealing the glowing crystal within. He chuckled with glee. With the crystal in his grasp, his power would be endless!

'How much longer? Oh, how much longer?'

❋　　❋　　❋　　❋

Love harbours secrets that some men hold dear,
Others would run from them, crying in fear:
Take, for example, a curious jewel –
Even the brightest of flames must have fuel!
Marry and burn, &c.

'No, not again . . . please, not again!'

The words were Polty's, breathed through parched lips as a lesser flame, familiar to him now, crept its way up the side of his neck. Painfully, surreptitiously, he rubbed his hand against the harsh flicker-ings, as if to extinguish them before they reached his hair. It couldn't happen here, could it? Here, in this crowd? Polty had a terrible suspicion that it could. What could Toth intend for him now?

But Polty knew, of course he did, for one part of his mind was the mind of Toth. Dread flooded him, like vomit ready to erupt. He shut his eyes, shut them tight against the harsh gleamings from the Ouabin sabres, all around the square, reflecting, reflecting, as if the blades were stabbing into his eyes . . .

How long had it been since this possession began? To Polty, the night in the Zenzan woods when he had died and been reborn seemed already an aeon in the past. What exaltation had filled him then, when Toth first gathered him to his heart, like a father, enfolding him in the dark mercy of his blessing. Ah, but what despair had followed soon enough, as Polty realised this blessing was a curse! Was he to be the mere puppet of a vile and crazed creature, bent on the destruction of all the world? He must break free, he must!

The thuddings of the tabors echoed in Polty's brain, painfully, like an ache, as he leaned over the balustrade, his head clutched in his hands. With sharp intensity, he thought of Cata, and moaned aloud. With her love, might he not break this thrall of evil? Polty thought of his last meeting with his beloved and cursed himself for a fool. But next time! Then it would be different! Fervently he imagined himself cast down at her feet, pouring out his sorrow for all that had passed before. Her tender heart must soften, it had to! *Heart-sister, be mine*, he would gasp through his tears. *Your love shall save me. Together we shall fight against the anti-god . . .*

But where could she be? Oh, where could she be?

> *Deserts are places the gods have accursed,*
> *There men live harsh lives of heat, drought and thirst:*
> *Give them a future unburdened from dread,*
> *Rashid and Qatani's Princess must wed!*

> *Marry and burn!*
> *The world must learn*
> *Ouabin power is our sole concern!*
> *Princess Bela Dona holds the ke-e-e-ey—*
> *Marry and burn,*
> *Marry and burn!*

Chapter 56

CASKETS THREE

'Cata, come away.'

'I'll have to go out there in a moment.'

'I'd delay it if I were you.'

'Why?'

'It might be your last moment of freedom.'

'I wouldn't bet on it. Raj, I've got a feeling that things are happening just as they should.'

'Please, no! If they'd happened as they should, I'd be a eunuch now.'

'That wasn't should, that was shouldn't. No, Raj, I think I was meant to take on this new face. I think it's going to lead me somewhere ... somewhere important. Something's stirring, I can feel it.'

'Animal sympathies?'

'The birds are agitated. If the Sheik thinks this is all going to go his way, he's got another think coming, mark my words.'

The pretended Princess had demanded a far-glass; peering round the edge of the screen, she brought it up to her eyes again. Already she had surveyed the masses below; this time she scanned the gallery.

'What can you see?'

Cata shuddered. 'My so-called brother!'

'Polty?'

'He's slumped over the gallery as if he's going to be sick.'

'Good! It might create a diversion.'

'You'd need more than that in a crowd this size, Raj. Why look, there's Lord Empster too!'

'With Polty?'

'Next to him.'

'That makes sense. I don't trust him any more, I just can't!'

They would have said more, but the wedding song was ending. With an appearance of duty, Cata shifted back into place, ready for the screen to pull away, revealing her to the crowd. Behind her, Rajal and a wide-eyed Sefita took the ends of her shimmering train. From time to time, as they prepared for this moment, Rajal had seen the Sefita eyeing him suspiciously, even resentfully, but the girl was frightened and dared not object to things she might have thought to be odd or wrong. To stand close to the Princess was enough for her, more than enough.

A new burst of music rang out, and holy men took the stage again.

'Cata?' Rajal hissed.

'Raj?'

'I think you're very brave.'

'Raj?'

'Cata?'

'You look ridiculous in that dress.'

Rajal flushed behind his veil, but there was no time to prepare a retort. Hidden wires whisked the screen away and all at once the crowd erupted into a momentous cheer. Never in his life had Rajal heard so mighty a sound. The force was like a blow and he almost staggered, clutching tightly to Cata's train as if it could support him. But Cata was swaying too, as if *she* would faint. Had she been too sure of herself? Perhaps now, if not then, Cata saw the dangers that lay before her, trapped in the guise of the Shimmering Princess.

After a moment she breathed deeply and made her stately progress down the stairs. What a regal sight she was, with her loyal women carrying her train! How she gleamed, how she glowed, in her silvery gown! Cheers were replaced by sighs and even sobs as thousands upon thousands of pairs of eyes strained after their idol.

Now, on a stage strewn liberally with flowers, the leader of the holy men took his place beside the bride-to-be. Dressed in robes of black, he wore a fearsome mask with a long corona of spikes and an upraised, flaring trumpet jutting out from the part that covered his mouth. While lesser priests chanted, resolutely but intently, the High Priest raised his arms above his head to hush the crowd into reverence, turned round and round, then intoned through the trumpet that the time had come to test the betrothal of the royal child.

> *Come forth three to contest this hand:*
> *Render void any former vow.*
> *Player, trill on the wedding flute!*
> *If there is a first suitor, come forth now!*

The tune that split the air then was more a pained cry than a trill, and underscored by heavy tabor-thudding. For a time paralysis gripped the scene; then slowly, to the accompaniment of murmurs and gasps, a swarthy fellow in robes the colour of bronze fought his way up from the mob below. Ascending the platform, he held aloft a small, gleaming casket that matched his robes. As if by magic, a spindly plinth rumbled up from beneath the stage; kneeling reverently in the flowers, facing the supposed Princess Bela Dona, the man of bronze set the casket down.

The thudding ceased.

'Ho hum,' said the Caliph, hunched morosely in the royal box. 'Still, Shimmy's done well so far, hasn't she?'

'Indeed, Oman, she performs her part to perfection.'

> One has challenged for Prince Dea's bride:
> Shall another man be so bold?
> Player, trill on the wedding flute!
> Is there a second suitor? Tale be told!

Garbed in silver, the second suitor descended a ramp that curved down from the galleries. For a moment he walked in the air, like an eerie visitor from the worlds beyond; then, as his bronze counterpart had done, he made his offering at the altar, setting down his casket on a second plinth.

Surreptitiously the Caliph sucked on a curly Jarvel-pipe. 'Do you know, Hasem, I really think I'll need that diversion you've planned for me?'

'Diversion, Oman?'

'The Vaga, of course!'

'Oh, indeed,' said the Vizier bleakly; then after a pause: 'Your daughter's women make a fine sight, do they not?'

'Really, Hasem, stop trying to distract me!'

> Two have challenged: with but one more,
> Kaled's son is forsaken, lost!
> Player, trill on the wedding flute!
> Shall the Prophet's Line have to pay this cost?

When the Sheik swept forth in his robes of gold, the mob erupted into fresh and vigorous acclaim, for all the world as if this desert brigand were no vicious conqueror, but a great liberator sent to redeem them. The golden casket flashed in his upraised hands.

'Listen to the baying fools,' said the Caliph, his voice choking with outraged tears. 'Hasem, have they ever cheered *me* like that?'

The Vizier laid a comforting hand on his old friend's shoulder. 'Never mind, Oman, his triumph will be short. To tell the truth, I doubt it shall last much beyond this afternoon.'

The Caliph's masked head turned slowly. 'Hasem, do you know something I don't?'

> Caskets three, for a bride you hold
> Secret gifts and a destiny:
> Player, trill on the wedding flute!
> Bela Dona, look on these caskets three!

For long moments it seemed that all the world was silent but for the birds, wheeling and cawing in the stagnant, blazing air. Cata stepped forward, looking on impassively as her suitors, in turn, opened the boxes that contained their offerings. In the box of bronze was a flashing disc, attached to a swinging chain. It seemed commonplace enough, but the man of bronze effusively proclaimed its properties.

'Behold,' he cried, 'the Amulet of Tukhat! Plundered long ago from the tomb of King Tukhat, greatest of the rulers of Ana-Wenaya, it is a charm against evil, more potent than any the world has ever known. Princess, accept this gift of mine, and no harm shall come to you, even should you live in this world for aeons.'

The second casket contained a bejewelled band, such as a woman might wear upon her forehead. Again it seemed a disappointing offering, but the man of silver was eager to allay this impression.

'Princess,' he boasted, 'I offer you the last of the Lichano bands, retrieved from the furthest reaches of Amalia. For epicycles, tomb-robbers have sought these mystic arcs, that once graced the foreheads of the Lichano Priestesses, massively increasing the powers of their minds. Princess, accept this gift of mine, and the wisdom of the ages shall soon be yours!'

By now, the crowd were in ecstasies, swooning at the magnificence of these splendid gifts, sighing at the dilemma their idol must face. Meanwhile, in the royal box, the Caliph's sorrow had turned into a blazing, impotent rage. 'Fools,' he muttered, 'don't they realise this is all a charade?'

'If they knew it, they have forgotten it. Oman, the mob are fickle, and swayed easily by the calls of emotion. A Princess, a wedding, a splendid display – what price then is tradition, loyalty, reason? Alas, Oman, I fear we see now the folly of a liberal reign! Offer the mob the benisons of trust and choice, and what do they do but abuse the power that has been so foolishly vouchsafed to them? Why, I am certain they love the Sheik because he represents unquestioning, brute strength. They would love you more, Oman, had your reign been more cruel.'

'Oh Hasem, it is you who are cruel!' The little man snatched his mask from his face, mopping his sleeve at his tear-blurred eyes.

'Oman, just wait,' said the Vizier kindly. 'I tell you, the game is not over yet.'

'But its climax has come, has it not?'

So it seemed; at last, Sheik Rashid Amr Rukr stepped forth, gleaming like a vision in his golden robes. Until now, Cata had remained dutifully passive, careful to maintain an emotionless façade; now she felt herself trembling. The first offerings were magnificent, if the claims the suitors had made for them could be believed; Cata wondered how the Sheik could surpass them.

Then she understood.

Slowly, teasingly, the dark Ouabin hand opened the lid of the third box. Could it be? Cata's eyes grew wide with wonder. She gasped, and could not forbear from swivelling round, gaping at Rajal in astonishment.

In triumphant hands, the Sheik held his gift on high. 'Princess, I offer you no mere toy, no trinket of trivial power! What do I offer but power itself, and power beyond this worldly realm? Princess, look! Nobles, slaves, women and men of Qatani, look! For what is this gleaming gift I hold, this great jewel burning with ruby fire, but the stone of power lost long ago by your forefathers, and kept all this time by the wandering Ouabin tribe? Princess, I offer you the powers of the gods! Princess, I offer you the Crystal of Theron!'

'Yes! Yes!' Losing control, Cata burst forward, as if she would clutch the crystal at once; instead, she tripped and staggered back. It was barely noticed, in the excitement that ran round the square like raging fire.

Still the Sheik held aloft the gleaming crystal.

> *Princess, no question can there be!*
> *Silver, bronze? Never! Far more grand:*
> *Player, trill on the wedding flute!*
> *Rashid Amr Rukr has won her hand!*

But Rashid's triumph was not to last.

What happened next was as sudden as it was shocking. First, splitting the air, came a hideous cry; then, like a monstrous bird, swooping above the crowd, a creature with blue skin and blazing hair bore down upon the terrified Sheik.

He staggered back. 'No!'

'Liar! Deceiver!' Searing over the crowd came the voice of Toth-Vexrah, as Polty, aflame with the anti-god's rage, seized the crystal and flung it to the boards beneath his feet. It shattered into a thousand fragments. 'Paste! Worthless paste!'

Waves of astonishment, then anger, shook the crowd. In the next moment, Polty would have launched himself upon Rashid Amr Rukr, wringing the life from the Sheik's neck; instead, Ouabin guards burst on to the platform.

Polty reeled. He flung the guards from him; they crashed into the crowd, but not before Polty had grabbed a gleaming sabre, running it through the body of the screaming Sheik. The Ouabin leader staggered, blood spurting through the gold of his robes; an instant more, and Polty would have finished him off, seized the supposed Princess Bela Dona and ascended again to the skies, completing his victory – or rather, Toth's.

It was not to be: all at once, his powers faltered, his flames guttered, and Polty collapsed among the scattered flowers, the blood, and the glittering fragments of the crystal he had smashed.

✳ ✳ ✳ ✳

There was hysteria below; shock and confusion in the royal box. While the Caliph's gaze darted between Polty and the Sheik, the High Priest seized the moment.

'Nobles, slaves, women and men of Qatani, calm yourselves! Reflect upon the meaning of these happenings. The Ouabin has violated a sacred ceremony, and the god of flame has punished him as he deserves!' He pointed accusingly at Rashid Amr Rukr, who writhed and kicked weakly, struggling ineffectually to stanch with his hands the dark gouting streams of his blood. 'Wounded one, you have no claim on Qatani's royal child. Now, with fewer than three suitors, there can be no Rebonding. I declare this challenge over, and the first betrothal of our Princess the one that must stand. Prince Dea shall be her husband! Mighty Theron, may your blessings descend on Mesha Kaled, Sultan of the—'

'Wait!' came a voice.

The High Priest turned. 'What is the meaning of this?'

In the royal box, the Caliph gasped. 'Eli Oli Ali!'

Breathless, bedraggled, the whoremonger floundered up on to the platform. If he was exhausted from forcing his way through the crowd, it was clear, too, that he was far gone on ferment. He swayed and collapsed at Cata's feet.

Outraged, the Caliph cried, 'What's he doing? Guards! Kill him if he dares touch my Shimmy!'

But before the guards could move, the greasy fellow had heaved himself up on his knees, holding in his hands a gleaming sphere that flickered suddenly into violent life. Above the square, the sky became a churning mass of colour.

'P-Princess!' slurred the whoremonger. 'S-Sacred Lady, hear my p-plea! Be mine, and this Orb of Seeing sh-shall be yours, that shows all that passeth in time and s-space!'

With that, the churning colours resolved themselves into a mountain, a lake, a storm-tossed sea; a populous city, a dark forest, a star-filled sky . . .

'With this orb, ash with the . . . amulet, you shall have no f-fear; then too, ash with the mystic . . . b-band, all knowledge shall be yoursh!' Lurching violently, the whoremonger screamed at the crowd, slurring no more, 'My gift is the greatest, is it not? I have proved its truth, have I not? There are now three suitors, are there not?'

He lunged, as if to catch Cata's arm.

She sprang back.

'She's mine!' he cried. 'The girl is mine!'

Far above, in the galleries, Captain Porlo slumped to his single knee, his wooden leg jutting askew. It was a painful situation, and none thought to help him, but the sea-dog's pain was all in his mind.

His new friend! What had happened to his new friend?

But the contest was not over.

'No! She is mine!'

The voice that came now was callow and shrill, but invested with the authority of desperate conviction. Heads turned, shocked; Eli Oli Ali dropped the orb and it rolled round the platform, flashing and rumbling, through all that followed.

The Caliph's mind was reeling. 'Who can this be? Oh Hasem, what's happening?'

'My murderer!' cried Rajal, and had to hold back from launching himself forward, pummelling the street-boy whose tricks had first left him to be bound upon the wheel, then made him fall into the cobber-a pit, with all the terrible consequences that had followed.

Reverently, the ragged figure knelt before Cata; guffaws erupted as he – or rather, she – produced a battered gift.

'Beloved, I shall be brief. Others have offered you powers beyond those of mortal woman. I offer you *only* the powers of mortal woman. My gift is a konar-light, tarnished and old and shabby, but Princess, this I swear: it is what you seek.'

The crowd lapsed into silence again, laughter dying as confusion spread. Eli Oli Ali would have thrust Amed aside, but something in her bearing made even the whoremonger hang back, wondering; the High Priest looked to the royal box; the Caliph turned, wide-eyed, to Vizier Hasem.

'Beloved, be mine!' Timidly, then boldly, Amed looked up into the face she loved, expecting a look that returned her love. Instead, she saw eyes that seemed troubled, and was alarmed; her alarm only grew as a hand she expected to shimmer like gossamer first reached for hers, then gripped it tight.

But the climax was still to come.

The konar-light clattered from Amed's grasp as a voice came booming from the air. 'Street-child, you mistake yourself. Your heart is good, but I see more than you, and I have the sign that this child really wants. She must come with me, for only with me shall she find her true destiny.'

Suddenly a figure in a dark cloak was standing on the stage, his face enveloped in a misty cloud.

'Empster-lord!' said the Caliph. 'Hasem, how did he—'

'We knew he was a traitor,' the Vizier burst out, 'but—'

'What's that in his hand?'

But only Cata could see as the noble lord cupped his hands and held before her eyes a familiar gleaming disc, stamped with a swirling pattern. Now his voice echoed in her mind. *Catayane, I know you. Catayane, come with me, and you shall meet again the one you love . . .*

Tears filled Cata's eyes; memories flooded her; trembling, she reached for the harlequin's coin, but something stayed her as through her tears, through the mist round his face, she saw Lord Empster's eyes burning into hers, and knew that he was no mortal man . . .

Catayane, I know you . . .

But what did he want? And could she trust him?

Then there was no time to wonder any more.

It was the Caliph who cried out first. From his elevation above the crowd, he saw the powder-bomb flash down through the sky in the instant before the blast.

'Hasem, Hasem!' He scurried back, dragging his Vizier with him as the royal box sagged, almost collapsing into the square below. Another powder-bomb rained down, then another, as the sacred day ended in a chaos of screaming, stampeding, crushed bodies, blood, flying debris.

After the explosions came the Red Riders, bursting into the square on their fearsome black mounts. Shots sprayed the crowd.

'Magic fire-sticks!' the Caliph shrieked. 'Hasem, how—?'

'Ejlander weapons, Oman! Traded for slaves – didn't I tell you?'

'But . . . what does this mean?'

They ducked their heads as shots whizzed past.

'Mean? Oman, we're saved!'

✳   ✳   ✳   ✳

And so was Polty.

Quite what had come over their guest that day, neither the Caliph nor his Vizier understood, but when they next peered over the sagging balustrade they saw him stirring, then rising as Eli Oli Ali shook his shoulder. In the next moment, the whoremonger and the flame-haired one had slipped away into the chaos of the crowd.

Meanwhile, Cata fled back up the stairs. Rajal rushed after her, the Sefita and Amed too; but just as they reached the altar-screen, the Sefita cried out, collapsing.

Rajal rushed to her. 'She's been hit! She's . . . dead!'

'Quick!' said Cata. 'We've got to escape!'

A passage led from the altar back into the palace, but fire blocked the way.

Amed cried, 'We're trapped!'

Wildly she looked down through the shot-holes in the altar-screen. It was the end, it had to be. Amongst the debris below she saw Faha Ejo, Stork, Fish, Blubber and Cheese, snaffling the gifts that the suitors had left; swiftly the street-boys made their escape.

The konar-light!

But Amed had no time even to cry out. Every moment brought events yet more alarming. Now she saw the Ejlander lord, enfolding into his black cape the bleeding, dying Sheik. A Red Rider crashed up on to the stage, ready to destroy the stricken Ouabin leader.

Then came a flash of golden light.

Suddenly the Ejlander and the Ouabin were gone, while the Red Rider collapsed, screaming, to the stage.

✳   ✳   ✳   ✳

The Rider was the only imperial casualty. Victory was swift for the Sultan's forces. When the firing ended, the Riders – Reds in front, Yellows behind – stood across the platform in an impregnable phalanx. In the middle of the long line, one of the Reds twitched away his uniform, revealing a darker garb beneath. A Black Rider!

Terror rose from the remnants of the crowd; up the stairs, Amed blundered forward, clutching Cata. 'It's the end, it has to be! If the fire doesn't kill us, those monsters will! Beauteous one, just tell me before we die . . . are you – can you be – the one I love?'

Cata looked pityingly on the sobbing urchin. 'Girl-boy, I wear the guise of your beloved, no more. I am Catayane, the one you saved; and now, as you saved me, so I shall save you.'

'Cata!' protested Rajal. 'What are you talking about? This wicked boy nearly got me—'

'Boy?' Cata smiled. 'Raj, you're getting confused. I think you mean *girl*, don't you?'

'*What?*'

There was no time to explain; darting to the dead Sefita, Cata tugged at the girl's veil and gown. 'Quick – into these clothes!'

'Why? They're just going to kill us!'

But Amed was wrong. Below, the Black Rider's voice rang out, proclaiming the glorious liberation of Qatani, and the marriage that would bring even greater glory.

'Now, no impediment can there be to the event that was ordained so many sunrounds ago. Nobles, slaves, women and men of Qatani, as you are free from the Ouabin thrall, so your celebrated Princess is free to marry not a filthy desert nomad, but Prince Dea, son of Mesha Kaled, Sultan of the Moon and Stars!'

Terror subsided; there were even cheers.

Behind the screen, Amed adjusted her veil.

'You look ridiculous,' Rajal hissed spitefully.

'Not half as ridiculous as you, eunuch!'

'I'm not a eunuch!'

'Shut up, both of you!' said Cata. 'You'd better get on with each other, you know.'

'What? Why?'

But the Rider was speaking again. 'Further,' he proclaimed, 'I am empowered to state that the wedding of these royal children shall take place in the Sacred City, three Hornlights hence, and that all who would be true worshippers of Theron, God of the Flame, are enjoined to make the pilgrimage for this most sanctified of days in the glorious history of our empire and our faith!'

The fire was lapping nearer. Suddenly Cata stepped forward, pushing aside the remnants of the altar-screen. She raised her arms high, commanding devotion.

'Cata!' Rajal cried. 'What are you doing?'

Cata flung back, 'I've got a plan. If we can't escape, we must let ourselves be captured. I don't understand all the ways of destiny, but I've got a feeling we must go through with this marriage.'

'We?' said Amed.

'I'm a Princess, aren't I? They must let me have my women.' With that, Cata swiftly descended the stairs, before the altar was consumed in flames. 'Come on, girls, we're off to Kal-Theron.'

Chapter 57

GROTESQUE IN TWO KEYS

To the strange chaos of this Ritual of Rebonding, a coda must be added. The scene is far away in Agondon, where a lean, ascetic figure turns away from a looking-glass, cursing. He is a personage, if personage he can be called, who has figured much in the course of this adventure, though never until now has he appeared directly. To the outward world he presents the face of Tranimel, loyal First Minister to His Imperial Agonist Majesty, King Ejard of the Blue Cloth; in truth, he is the form incarnate of the anti-god, Toth-Vexrah.

The evil one is alone in a chamber lit by candles, with curtains drawn and a fire raging. Outside, the day is bright, too bright, and a pall of heat hangs over the city. It will not last for long. Here in these northern lands, Theron's season burns swiftly away; soon the cold will return, gripping Ejland like a mailed fist that has relaxed its grip only temporarily, the better to gain yet stronger purchase. Soon enough, the muddy suppurations of the River Riel will be replaced by a sheen of ice; soon enough, all Agondon's chambers will be shut tightly as Toth's against the world outside, as snow falls and the light comes late, only to fail in the early afternoons. It may be, indeed, that this is the last season of heat Ejland ever knows, as the Time of Atonement draws rapidly to its end, with mere moonlives remaining now until the beginning of the thousandth cycle.

For now, none of this matters to the anti-god. Striding across his chamber, grimacing, clenching and unclenching his borrowed hands, he thinks only of his rage. So, his flame-haired servant has failed him, yet again! To be sure, the projection was unstable from the first. The thousand polished blades, glinting round the square, had seemed a powerful channel, but provided the anti-god with too little focus. Then, too, he was depleted from his interview with Agonis. But there was more, he was sure of it, to this latest failure. He cursed again. Oh, to have clutched the Shimmering Princess! Oh, to have flung her into the Sacred Flame!

But Toth would not give up. He would never give up.

He turned back to the glass, where the image of the sprawled, spent form of Poltiss Veeldrop was slowly fading. By now, Toth knew, Veeldrop had made his escape, scurrying away somewhere, like a coward, to hide; the glass showed the objects of the anti-god's concentration only in the moments when his power flamed out.

Contemptuously he gazed upon his useless servant. In the beginning, the young man had seemed so promising. Could it be that Veeldrop was resisting him? Yes, that was it! Yes, Toth was sure of it! But how could a human so corrupt and depraved have any interest other than evil, pure evil? And what was Toth but evil, if evil was the name for one who opposed the Ur-God, his five vile children, and all their works and ways?

Toth drummed his fingers against the mirrored surface. The stench in his chamber was vile and the heat was stifling, but to him these things meant nothing. He thought only of his humiliation. What a fool he had been, even to attempt to bargain with Agonis! What a fool he had been, to trust Poltiss Veeldrop!

He ran his fingernails, screeching, down the glass. He rushed to the fire, thrusting first an arm, then a leg, into the flames. He leapt up to the ceiling, clinging there like a monstrous, misshapen insect. Once, twice, again and again he beat his head, or Tranimel's, against the ceiling, until the carpet below was covered in white cascades of plaster.

He dropped down suddenly, his eyes blazing, his mouth twisting evilly. No, it was they who were the fools, they – Agonis and the wretched Veeldrop too. If his brother – brother he called him, for brother he was – would throw away all chance of fulfilment, what of it? Let him, he would be sorry!

Veeldrop was another matter. The human was too far away now, that was the trouble. Moonlives earlier, Toth had needed no looking-glass to magic his agent into the fearsome rider of a blue, airborne dragon. But Veeldrop had been in Zenzau then, and besides, was still ardent in his new servitude. Things had changed, and distance of more than one type, thought Toth, was to blame. Now, without the aid of reflection, he was helpless, helpless to control his own slave! Rage filled him again. If only his powers were infinite! But how could they be infinite, without the Orokon?

Again Toth flung himself about the hot chamber, scurrying over floor, walls and ceiling, too, smashing everything that came into his path. Then suddenly he was still. He moved to the window, ripping away the curtain. His eyes flickered over the steaming courtyards below, then down, down through the shimmering haze to the stinking, shrivelled river.

Now, at last, he thought of the heat, then the cold that soon would come. Yes, the final cold, gripping Ejland, never to let go! Soon, soon now, chaos would be here, and with it, Toth-Vexrah would come into his own. What power would then be his, what infinite power, when the

Orokon was his and this vile world, his father's world, was destroyed at last!

Time was on his side; besides, as he had told his brother Agonis, Toth's powers had been feeding from a secret source. True, this source had as yet availed him little; new strength would come to him only, as it were, when his feeding was over, when he was gorged at last and the source was no more . . .

But again, it was only a matter of time . . .

His enemies could not win, they could not!

The anti-god flung back his head and laughed, scurried over the ceiling again, then plummeted back to the looking-glass that now showed him only the image of the debris behind him in this ruined chamber. His eyes flared; the glass clouded, and Toth searched for Veeldrop. Where was he, where was the scurrying rat?

It was as well, after all, that his servant should know there would be no escape.

There *could* be no escape.

✳   ✳   ✳   ✳

'What's happened to him now?' whispered Dona Bela.

Jem muttered, 'He's worse than before.'

'Look at him swagger!' piped Littler.

'Can you swagger at a table?' Jem murmured.

'He can!' sighed the Princess. 'He makes me shudder.'

Littler said, 'Scabs wasn't like this in the Realm of Un.'

Jem said, 'Scabs wasn't like this on the *Catayane*. But then, he didn't have the chance . . . Littler! Don't flick the custard!'

The little boy gave a shy smirk and popped his spoon into his mouth instead.

Jem was troubled. Anxiously he gazed upon the unreal diners, carousing merrily in the hall below them. In the dreaming dimension it was impossible to keep count of days, and how many banquets he had attended since the new arrivals came, he did not know. One thing was clear: each time he was astonished by the behaviour of the cabin boy. In lavish robes, Scabs would sit beside Almoran, chatting with his noble host in a high, affected voice. Smiles played upon the pustular face; pleasantries oozed from the slobbering lips. With a discriminating air, Scabs would hum and haw over this or that elaborate dish, but when it was served to him he would wolf it down like the commonest peasant. Slops covered his costume and the table before him; sauces stained his mouth and his whiskery chin. Through all this, Almoran smiled indulgently, for all the world as if it were Scabs who was the visiting Prince.

Until now, the cabin boy had directed his performance solely at his host, barely glancing towards his fellow guests, seated beside him on the dais. It was as if he had been testing his new-found confidence, rehearsing with his mentor. Now, it seemed, the rehearsal was over. All through this latest banquet, as if granting a favour, Scabs had turned benevolently to his companions, his voice more strangled than before, his manners still more extravagantly absurd. 'Is not the weather most splendidly bracing, Master Jemany?' he would say. 'I declare, I sweated like a pig in the gardens today,' or, 'Littler, my boy, have you tried the lobster? An exquisite foodstuff, I have always maintained. Careful you do not choke upon his sharp shell, though, or the servant shall have to make you vomit.'

Scabs reserved his principal attentions for the Princess. Time after time, Almoran had contrived to sit the girl at the cabin boy's side; now the creature took advantage of his position, plaguing his fair companion almost beyond endurance.

'Come, my dear, let me help you to a jellied eel. Perhaps it may direct your thoughts to something else, something rather *similar* in shape . . .

'My, my, what a lovely hand. How I look forward to the part it shall play, in the intimacies that are soon to come . . .

'Doubtless, my pretty, you're *besieged* by suitors. Tell me, what are your thoughts on . . . marriage?'

Jem fumed. More than once he had longed to lash out, rising suddenly from the table and dragging Scabs to the floor. Only the imploring glances of the Princess restrained him, but it was with an ill grace that he obeyed her.

It seemed the performance would never end. Fawn, fawn went the purple hand; grin, grin, went the green, rotted teeth. In the raw face, between repellent mottlings of red and blue, huge yellow pustules glowed like gems. Could Scabs really believe he was a fine young buck? How could the Princess not cry out?

'This is Almoran's doing, isn't it?' she whispered, as her admirer temporarily left off his ogling, falling instead upon a curried swordfish. How Jem would like to have seized that sword, popping the pustules, one by one! He shuddered, but with the shudder came the thought that he was being unfair.

The Princess was right. This was some trick of Almoran's, it had to be.

'Or the genie's?' he mused aloud. More than once, before Almoran shooed him away, the fat little man had hovered around them, enquiring unctuously if there were anything, anything at all that his master might WISH.

'Not the genie's,' murmured Littler. 'The genie can only grant Scabs his third wish. But Scabs won't wish.'

'He won't?' breathed Jem. 'I wonder why.'

'Perhaps he likes this one too much. This wish,' whispered the Princess, shivering as spluttered scraps of swordfish landed on her sleeve.

'Oh, he likes it,' Jem returned bitterly, 'and the old man's goading him. That much is clear. But Scabs has fallen for it. Fallen all the way.'

'He's a poor boy,' Littler said simply. 'Like me.'

Jem softened, and he fluffed the child's hair. 'You're right, Littler. Scabs is a buffoon, and a grotesque one, but why not? All his life he's been a disfigured outcast – now this. I should sympathise. Once, in a way, I used to be like him.'

'Like him? What can you mean?' hissed Littler.

But this was not the time. Intently Jem's eyes roved over Dona Bela, over Littler, over Scabs; fondly he thought of Rainbow, busy beneath the table with his golden bowl. How could he save them? How could they escape? He was thinking of a plan, revolving it in his mind. But would it work? If Scabs were not with them, perhaps not. Perhaps not at all.

'We've got to get through to him,' Jem said aloud.

'Prince?' said Dona Bela, furrowing her brow.

Littler flicked a gob of custard at Scabs.

Chapter 58

SAIL AWAY

'Another toast to the Major-sir!'

'Oily, you're a good friend!'

'Friend? Pah! Loyal servant!'

'You saved me, Oily!'

'Major-sir, you saved Qatani!'

If this was not quite true, the whoremonger did not care. With an obsequious grin, he filled Polty's goblet again, clashed goblets lustily, drummed his feet on the floor and bellowed to Mother Madana for more ferment, more, for Qatani's hero. Outside, evening was falling rapidly, painting the alley a bruised, ugly purple; gloom was gathering in the squalid chamber. On an ordinary evening, the Khan of the Crescent Moon would have been packed tight by now with lusty, carousing tars; tonight the doors were shut and bolted; Eli Oli Ali and Polty drank alone.

'Eli, think of the trade we've lost!' hissed Mother Madana, thumping down a fresh beaker.

'Trade? You would think of trade, crone, when a great man is among us? Bring us some Jarvel, and light a lamp! See, Major-sir,' added the whoremonger with a grin, 'I took this crone's measure well enough. When first she comes to me, she is all prim protests; now' – he gestured, rubbing with fingers and thumb – 'she thinks only of one thing, one thing! Pah! You're no better than me, crone, and don't forget it!'

The crone may have been tempted to strike Eli's head, but contented herself with slamming down a battered lamp, rather too heavily, between the men. The glass almost shattered and the flame leapt high.

Eli chuckled. 'And the Jarvel, crone? Quick, quick!'

Polty was barely listening. His mind replayed the day's events. Again he felt the pain that had consumed him in the gallery as the terrible possession overtook him. In the moment of his attack on Rashid Amr Rukr, it seemed to him that he had been wholly Toth-Vexrah, with nothing in him at all of Poltiss Veeldrop; he imagined himself slumped, disembodied, across the balustrade, as the anti-god took flight. Then, an instant later, Poltiss Veeldrop lay on the platform, stricken and gasping amongst the strewn flowers. Why the power had failed, he did not know. When Toth had first consumed him, in the Hills of Wrax, the power had been absolute, annihilating. Since then, it had weakened . . . why? Could there be a clue here, that might set him free? Oh, to be free, and in Cata's arms!

Polty moaned. 'Oily, I've been in such pain!'

'Pain?' grinned the whoremonger. 'Major-sir, you are a man of great powers!'

'No powers, Oily . . . no powers!'

'What? You fly, your hair in flames? Major-sir, there were those who collapsed in worship, thinking their fire god Theron had come!' The whoremonger stared eagerly into Polty's eyes. 'Tell me, Major-sir, how do you do it? What is your secret?'

Polty slumped forward, his face in his hands. 'Eli, I burn and burn . . . but something happened today, the possession left me . . . but ah, while I lay barely conscious among the flowers, I thought I saw the orb again, rolling around me!'

The whoremonger's heart lurched, but he said innocently, 'Orb?'

'The orb was there, I'm sure of it . . . but lost to me, lost to me. That's it!' Polty slapped the side of his head. Intently he stared into the flickering lamp. 'The orb . . . it used to be a looking-glass . . . he came to me through the glass . . . glass! Yes, that's it! Or . . . or is it?'

Eli did not pretend to understand; he could only smile and urge his companion to drink, drink and forget his sorrows. Already the Major-sir was far gone; soon he would collapse into a stupor. Good; that would keep him where Eli wanted him while he made preparations for the journey ahead.

There was not much time. Already, perhaps, the Riders might be out looking for the blaspheming mixer who had dared to sue for the royal hand; no doubt they sought the Major-sir too. For a time, Eli had considered flight. But that would be foolish. Camouflage, that was the way. By the morning, they would be part of a caravan of thousands of loyal pilgrims setting out on the way to Kal-Theron. Under the table, the whoremonger rubbed his hands. The bitterness that had filled him after his expulsion from Court had become the merest memory. Eli was not one to dwell on the past, and not one to let a chance slip by. Fresh vistas of glory beckoned.

He reached out, clutching Polty's hand. 'Major-sir, you say I have been a friend to you, hm?'

'A fine friend, Oily.'

'But now you have lost your other friends?'

'Bean? Burgrove? Oily, I don't know where they can be!' Suddenly Polty looked very miserable indeed.

The whoremonger sighed. 'In these Lands of Unang it is common enough for men to go missing, never to be seen again. But repine not,

Major-sir, for now you have a new fellow to assist you in your . . . quest. You shall be . . . master. But let me be your man.'

'Oh, Oily!'

The two men fell into a drunken embrace, which was only interrupted when Mother Madana, at long last, thumped down a bubbling hookah on the table. Polty slumped forward; the whoremonger rose, looking down at his victim in the golden lamplight. Quite how he would exploit the Major-sir's powers he did not know, but there had to be a way. His heart leapt at the thought of Kal-Theron, and the profitable adventures that were sure to lie ahead. Already he had forgotten Captain Porlo and all his extravagant promises to the old sea-dog.

The whoremonger leaned over, prodded the curly hookah-tube into Polty's mouth and turned sharply to Mother Madana. 'He's far gone. Come crone, we leave before dawn – you must help me in the storerooms . . . make sure this chamber is locked, mind.'

The crone lingered.

'What is it, crone? Come!'

'Eli . . . what about the 'temper-cell?'

'Shh!' Rolling his eyes, the whoremonger whispered, 'We leave them to die, don't we? Wasn't that the whole idea?'

'Eli, I don't like it.'

'They're 'tempered already, aren't they? They must be! Now don't be a fool, woman . . . come!'

The whoremonger would have extinguished the lamp, but in his agitation he let it burn on. Polty's hair shone with a coppery glow as he sprawled over the same rickety table where Bean and Burgrove had met their fate. Like a baby, he sucked at the soothing Jarvel, his mind plunging into visions and dreams. Hazily he imagined a cheval-glass, spinning and spinning in its spindly frame; then the glass exploding into fragments, and the fragments cohering into a rolling ball . . .

A voice came. *Poltiss Veeldrop, Poltiss Veeldrop, do you think you shall escape me?*

Polty shifted; the tube fell from his lips.

Footsteps crunched in the alley outside. 'I'll bring the van round . . . now get those ferment-jars ready for loading. Mark my words, there'll be trade aplenty on the way to the Sacred City!'

'Very well, very well . . . oh, you're a monster, Eli!'

A guffaw was the reply, then the footsteps crunched away. There was a pause, but instead of repairing to her task, Mother Madana tiptoed back past the sprawled form of Polty. Looking round guiltily, she made her way to the corner, where she slid back the bolt of a locked door. It was as far as she would go. Quickly she retraced her steps, pausing only to slip the Jarvel-tube gently back into the Ejlander's mouth. She hated

Ejlanders, of course she did; but this one, she could see, was a handsome fellow; her withered hand smoothed his coppery hair. She leaned over, about to extinguish the lamp, but the Ejlander stirred and the old woman fled.

Polty rubbed his eyes. First he saw stars. No, flowers; a stage strewn with flowers, and the orb rolling maddeningly . . . *Poltiss Veeldrop, Poltiss Veeldrop, don't you know you're mine?* Blearily Polty gazed into the glass of the hookah, then into the glass of the sizzling lamp. That was when he saw the leering face, staring at him from the lamp – from the hookah, too . . . *Poltiss Veeldrop, Poltiss Veeldrop, you shall do my bidding till the crystals are mine!*

'No!' Polty leapt up, sweeping the hideous face to the floor. A cackling filled the air, riding high over the shattering of glass. Polty slumped down in darkness, breathing hard. Oh, but his mind was spinning, spinning . . . then he saw something spinning between the flowers, not the orb now, but . . . could it be a coin, dropped from the fingers of the man in black? The coin clattered into stillness and Polty saw the swirling pattern in the gold. He knew that coin – didn't he? But where . . . how . . . what could it mean? Polty searched deep in the caverns of memory[1]. Oh, but there was some mystery here! The Shimmering Princess rose before his eyes and Polty knew only that he must follow her, if he were ever to find his destiny . . .

Polty started.

Fire!

Smoke was thick in the air and flames roared round the shabby chamber. He blundered to his feet. Which way, which way? His senses were a maelstrom, but his limbs were leaden.

He saw a door, standing ajar.

This way?

He crashed through the door, then cried out, collapsing down a flight of steps.

Polty gazed around him in the lurid light. Where could he be? This was not the alley . . . a cellar?

He saw the corpse, filthy, reeking, withered from hunger.

But it was not a corpse. A face turned towards him and a parched mouth struggled to cry out in joy.

Suddenly Polty's mind was clear.

'*Bean!*'

He rushed to his friend, scooping the frail body into his arms. But how

---

[1] See *The Harlequin's Dance*, Ch. 4, for Polty's previous encounter with the harlequin's coin, which later became a talisman for Cata, and a symbol of her love for Jem.

to get out? Could he make it through the flames? A crash came from above as a burning beam fell down, blocking the grilled door.

Polty reeled. By now the cellar too was filling with smoke. That was when the second door burst open and a ragged street-boy cried out, 'Wretches, run for your lives!'

'This way, this way!'

Smoke poured through the door behind them. The fire was spreading from the floor above; curtains of sacking roared into flames. Polty blundered on, blinded, coughing.

'This way, this way!'

A trapdoor slammed open. They were in the alley, fleeing with the boys from the Realm of Un. Bean's throat gargled and his eyes rolled in terror. Wildly he clawed at Polty's neck.

'This way, this way!'

They collapsed at last, coughing and gasping, somewhere amongst the suppurating docks. Bean slid heavily from Polty's arms. Desperately he forced the words from his lips:

'P-Polty, it's Burgrove . . . he's s-still in there . . .'

But Polty had doubled over, shuddering and retching, as a wall of flame concealed the Khan of the Crescent Moon.

❋ ❋ ❋ ❋

'Rum! Scabs, where's me bloody rum?'

Captain Porlo, as it happened, had already drunk his fill, or he would hardly have been calling the name of his missing cabin boy. It was evening, and the bright gold of the moon glittered on the waters outside the open window. On the floor an empty tankard rolled back and forth, shifting in time to the heavings of the waves. The captain's head crashed to the table, narrowly missing the tarnished plate smeared with remnants of salt-pig and mustard, and crumbs of innumerable weevily biscuits. From the sea-dog's mouth ran a line of dribble, and the lids flickered over his milky eyes. Buby shrieked, leaping on to her master's back. Was he sick? Was he dead?

The captain only grinned and hugged the little monkey tight against him, like a lover. No, there was nothing wrong with Faris Porlo. He was happy, and his happiness possessed him like a sudden, ecstatic fit. Earlier that day, back in Qatani, he had known despair. What a fool he had been, to put his trust in that dirty mixer! Quite obviously, Eli Oli Ali was mad, almost as mad as Empster. The captain was glad to be shot of them both – walk the plank, they would, if he ever laid eyes on them again!

The sea-dog felt a little guilty, it was true, about the fate of that lad, Master Raj, and the lovely girl too, abandoned in a heathen land with no way home. And what of the one called Jem? Was he really drowned, or what? Still, they were young folk, all of them, and could look after themselves. Why, think of the number of legs they had between them!

No, the captain would think only of the splendid moment that afternoon when, with the Ouabin in disarray, he had stumped his way desperately back along the quayside, bellowing and waving to the *Catayane*. It had been a young lad in many-patched rags, with a broad stripe of freckles across his nose, who had spotted him first and rushed to assist him. Ah yes, Porlo's tars had not let their good old captain down! In moments, it seemed, it was anchors aweigh, and be damned to them wretched foreigners, Ouabins and Unangs and whatever else they were!

The captain was about to call again for his rum, more rum, when the door opened and he saw, shining in the lamplight, the welcome curve of a fresh, brimming tankard.

'Scabs?' He screwed up his bleary eyes.

Oh, but he was forgetting!

The new boy stepped forward with a gormless grin.

'I be Patches, Cap'n. Beggin' your pardon, Cap'n, you said I was cabin boy now. Now that Scabs is gone, like.'

'Aye, that I did, boy,' said the captain, propping up his head with his fist. 'You won't be an ungrateful scamp like that Scabs now, will ye? Running off like that?'

'Cap'n, no!'

'You be a good lad, Patches. Likes a song, does ye?'

'Aye, I likes a song, Cap'n.'

'Get me squeezebox for me then, there's a good lad. Sit yourself down, eh? Dash of rum? Come on, put hairs on your chest! You're a fine lad, Patches. Just be glad we're not in that Unang-land no more, that's all I can say. No place for a lad, that's not, not with them cobber-as. Got to be good with your cutlass, you do, when there's cobber-as about. One day I'll tell you how I fought 'em off, fought through a field of 'em, to escape that heathen palace. Why, there must have been a hundred if there was one. Whipped off their hoody heads, I did, *whip, whip*, like they was stalks of corn!'

Excitement glimmered in the old man's eyes, but he calmed himself, glugged at his rum, and said, 'But let me sing you a little song.'

So, to the accompaniment of the shrieking squeezebox, the lonely old sea-dog split the night with the shanty he had sung – how long ago it seemed! – for Master Jem and Master Raj. Buby, as if in protest, leapt from her master's arms, scampering about the walls, then hanging from the ceiling as the caterwauling assailed her sensitive ears:

Pieces of eight! Pieces of eight!
Gold and diamonds, rubies and silver plate!
Are they lying in a wreck at the bottom of the sea?
Where, tell me where can me treasure be?
  Yo-ho-hee! A sea-dog's life for me!
  But where, tell me where can me treasure be?

'Join in, lad! Fine song, eh?'

Glugging recklessly at the captain's tankard, Patches could only agree that it was. He nodded, and rum ran down his chin.

'Steady on, lad, that's worth its weight in gold!' the captain guffawed, then roared out another verse, then another.

Patches only grinned, his mind spinning.

'Aye, we be on our voyage for real now, Patches, mark me words!' cried the captain. Then, as if to underscore the point, he sang another verse, a verse he had never sung for Empster's young wards. Tugging his squeezebox back to full length, the sea-dog thought again of the glory that awaited him at the end of this, perhaps his last, but to be sure, his greatest voyage.

And Empster thought he could make a fool of old Faris Porlo!

Crystal of blue – lost long ago!
Powers, they be such only gods can know!
Is it true the glowing crystal holds the secret of the sea?
Where? Don't I know where this treasure can be?
  Yo-ho-hee! A sea-dog's life for me!
  Where? Yes, I know where this treasure can be!

On and on went the joyous cacophony; on and on went the slosh of rum. The *Catayane* sailed on through the heaving, dark sea, bound for the island realms of Wenaya.

※   ※   ※   ※

Dea ascended the pale stairs again. For these last nights, Simonides had slept in his chamber, and much as he loved the old man, the boy had found it a sore trial to wait until he was certain that his companion was sleeping.

What a relief it was when he could finally slip out into the night! Excitement fluttered in the boy's heart as the dark foliage of the roof garden closed round him again. He breathed in, almost swooning on the heady incense of jasmine, javander-root, malak and narcissus. Then he saw the glimmering, frail figure across the broad parterres. Like the devotee of a sacred ritual, he mouthed again the words he had said before. How comforting, how deeply comforting, he found Thal's replies!

'You're real, Thal?'

'Friend, of course I'm real.'

'But I see through you.'

'Friend, I am no less real.' Thal leapt high, high in the air. He passed in and out of the trunk of a tree. 'Should you not like to be as I am? Is my substance not better than the dull, heavy flesh of which you are made? Friend, think how we could laugh, think how we could play, were we both as I am. Think of it, friend!'

'But Thal, I must be married, and be a man.'

Thal laughed. 'Friend, you shall never be married!'

'Never, Thal? You're sure of it?'

'How can you marry, when we must play?'

With that, Thal would grin, darting off like a sprite, and his tall friend would laugh, racing after him. How merrily they would play amongst the dark groves and grottoes, the hedges and parterres, dancing and darting, twisting and turning, tumbling and laughing in the light of the moon! How sad Dea would be when Thal had to leave again!

'Come back, Dea,' the ghostly boy would say. 'Come tomorrow night, and we shall play again.'

'You'll be here, Thal?'

'I'll always be here, Dea, and soon, so shall you. We'll be boys for ever, Dea, and none shall ever find us or harm us again.'

And Dea would hug himself as he shambled back down the stairs, hoping only that this glorious destiny would indeed come soon.

Chapter 59

REEL AROUND THE FOUNTAIN

'Darling? Darling girl, where have you gone?'

His heart surging on tides of joy, Scabs skipped his way through the violets and yarrow, the henna, the bluebells, the luxuriant daisies. Heat, dense and brilliant, lapped round him like water. Incense and birdsong filled the air. Had he ever been so happy? Now all he needed was to find the girl again. Waking, discovering her gone from his side, Scabs had not thought for a moment that she had fled from him. Never! His darling was playing a game, that was all, a delightful game. Well, perhaps she was shy. But then, so was he. Last night had been the first time for them both. But such a time!

'Darling? Darling, I'll find you, never fear!'

Scabs turned a corner and came upon the fountain, the curious undulating flame of rock. Gratefully he leaned over the mossy bowl. He was about to drink, but instead remained arrested at the sight of his reflection, shimmering in the cool, clear water. Since the change had come over him, Scabs had stared again and again at the looking-glass in his chamber, enraptured at his new beauty. The rapture came over him again and he swooned, reeled around the fountain, and sank at last to the petal-strewn ground.

'Oh, darling! Darling, darling girl!'

Scabs wore nothing but a robe of the thinnest silk, secured with a cord; the robe fell open and he ran his hands slowly over his creamy chest. Scabs sighed. He shuddered. Desire had filled him again and he clutched at the column between his thighs, marvelling at the smoothness of the sleeve of flesh. Silk – it was like silk! Ecstatic, moaning, he rolled on to his belly, sinking into the soft, soft petals. There was a moment of struggle; he would have saved his seed for his darling alone; then the memory of her sweet thighs welled in him freshly, and he gave way. Yes . . . ah yes. There would be many times more. Gasping, Scabs lay beneath the dappling leaves. Never, never, had he believed in such happiness. He was a man. And a woman loved him. He whispered her name as the spasms passed.

A barking came in reply.

Scabs looked up. It was the dog called Rainbow, swishing his way through the fragrant foliage. Scabs eyed him with distaste. In his old life, it was true, he had felt an affection for dogs, but mangy mongrels, not strange, brightly coloured creatures like this. Rainbow stood blinking, perhaps a little warily, by the side of the fountain. He barked again and there was a crash of feet.

'Rainbow!' It was Littler's voice. 'I knew you'd find him!'

Scabs scrambled up. Not only Littler faced him, breathless and hot; behind the little boy came Jem and Dona Bela, too. What was happening? Protectively, Scabs moved towards his darling. She stumbled back, a hand shielding her eyes.

'Darling? Darling!' Angrily Scabs turned on Jem. 'What have you done to her?'

'Scabs,' said Jem, 'look at yourself!'

Quickly Scabs drew his robe around him, but not before his companions had seen his naked body. Scabs registered their shock, but not the real reason. Suddenly, boldly, he opened his robe again, flinging it into the foliage. Sobs broke from Dona Bela; Littler turned away; Rainbow scrambled back. Only Jem looked steadily, gulping hard, at the hideous creature that stood before them. Reddened, festering inflammations covered the cabin boy's torso and limbs; his hands and feet were cracked, his joints puffy and oozing, but most repellent of all was the purple, twisted tube, sprouting from a fiery ring of sores, that hung between the cabin boy's thighs. Liquid, like the discharge of some vile infection, dripped steadily from the half-engorged organ.

Scabs grinned, flashing his green teeth. 'I've changed, haven't I? It's this place, you see. Oh, I'll never leave this beautiful place, never!' He moved towards his darling, but Jem blocked his way. Anxiously the cabin boy's voice rose and cracked. 'Darling? Is it Master Jem? What's he done to you? He's done something, hasn't he?' He held out his arms. 'Darling, come to me! Darling, don't you remember last night?'

Jem said softly, 'Scabs, you did nothing last night.'

'What do you know?' Scabs burst out. 'What are you talking about?' He lunged forward, pushing Jem savagely in the chest. In the next moment they were on the ground, struggling, kicking, thrashing.

'Oh stop, stop!' cried Dona Bela.

Uselessly, Littler tried to join the fray; Rainbow barked and capered, scurrying round the fountain.

Jem gasped, floundering. In his rage, Scabs was strong.

Scabs pinned him down. Jem writhed.

Scabs swung his fist.

'No!' Jem broke free.

Scabs smashed against the side of the fountain. Grabbing the naked cabin boy by the neck, Jem dragged him up towards the mossy bowl.

Brutally – but it was the only way – he pushed the ruined face towards the water.

'Scabs, don't you understand? You've been dreaming! It's all just Almoran's trick, that's all!'

'You're lying! I'm beautiful, beautiful!'

'Scabs, wake up! See the truth! Can't you see how Almoran's deceived you?'

Scabs screamed. He broke from Jem, but this time only slumped down, bereft alike of anger and shame, as if all the life had left him. His eyes filled with tears, but he was weeping already; sores had burst on his face and neck, running with golden, thick pus.

A voice came. 'Master, you seem to be in a spot of bother. I do declare, there must be something you WISH right now!'

'Go away,' Scabs moaned. 'Just go away.'

The genie only gave a supercilious smile, hovering close by on the magic carpet; Jem, his face drawn and pale, squatted before the stricken cabin boy. When Jem spoke again, his voice was soft, almost tender. But this was not a tenderness that Scabs wanted.

'Scabs, please. You've got to listen.'

'Listen? To you?'

'We're in terrible danger – the world's in terrible danger. You knew I was on a quest, didn't you? Can't you see we've got to escape this place? We must get to the Sacred City, and can't delay. Scabs, you've got to help us – you've got to use your last wish.'

'Ooh yes, master . . . WISH, WISH!' Jafir rubbed his hands. Leaving his carpet, the genie had moved in closer, perching on the bowl of the fountain, just above the cabin boy's shaking shoulder. He leaned down, whispering into a scabious ear, 'Hm, master – WISH, WISH?'

Jem hissed, 'Leave us!'

'Ho!' simpered Jafir. 'Really, Ejlander, I thought I was just the one you needed! A little respect, hm?' The fat fellow sat cross-legged, expectant. With a smile he studied his fingernails, humming a little tune.

Scabs was sobbing freely now, his face in his hands. Gently Jem pulled the hands away, and stared earnestly into the brimming eyes.

'Scabs, listen! You're the only one who can help us. Don't you understand? Almoran has trapped us – enslaved us. With every day that passes, every banquet, every night of dreams, he's binding us more strongly into this dimension. If we remain here, we'll be locked in an eternal prison, while Almoran lives a life of bliss – with the Princess as his bride!'

Scabs snivelled, 'The – the Princess? You're lying! Almoran said . . .'

Dona Bela took a red, raw hand in hers. She breathed deeply. 'Scabs . . .'

406

'Scabs? Last night it was Jorvel!'

Dona Bela breathed again, her eyes downcast. 'Jorvel . . . Jem's telling the truth. There was no . . . last night. It was all just a dream . . . Almoran's trick. I'm sorry, Jorvel.'

'No!' Scabs snatched his hand away, huddling into himself. He howled like an animal, then whimpered piteously.

'All just a dream? Dear me,' said the genie. 'Perhaps, master, you'd like to dream again? Or should I say, you'd . . . WISH?'

'Cut it out!' muttered Jem.

'Tut-tut! Respect!'

Now it was Littler's turn to kneel before the cabin boy. The little boy's voice was choked with tears. 'Scabs, you were good to me before. I know you're good in your heart. Jem's right. Make the wish, Scabs. Take us to Kal-Theron. Don't you see, this is your chance to be a hero?'

Littler reached out and would have stroked the shivering shoulder; instead, Scabs lashed out, flinging him away. Suddenly furious, the cabin boy leapt to his feet. In the next moment, Jem and the Princess had stumbled back, alarmed; Rainbow, with a protective growl, had rushed to shield Littler, and the cross-legged Jafir, with a splash and a squeal, had toppled into the water behind him.

'Hero? Be a hero?' shrieked the naked boy. 'What do I care about being a hero? What's there for me in Kal-Theron? What's there for me in your stupid quest? You all keep asking me to understand! Don't you understand I was happy here? Happy – for the first time in my life! I was beautiful! I was in love! And you've ruined it! I hate you! I hate you all!' His voice cracked and he swung round, screaming, pummelling his fist against the stones of the fountain. Blood gushed from his knuckles.

'Scabs, stop it! Scabs, don't torture yourself!' Jem grabbed the cabin boy's arm just as it was about to swing back again.

Scabs swivelled round.

'Don't touch me! Empster's lickspittle, that's what you are! What do you know about torture?' Viciously, Scabs flung Jem away from him. 'You smug, self-satisfied bastard! I hate *you* most of all! Kal-Theron? I wish you *were* in Kal-Theron . . . I wish . . . I wish . . .'

Scabs would have gone on to wish Jem anywhere, only not here – in the middle of the desert, at the bottom of the sea, in the Realm of Unbeing, screaming in torment. There was no time – or rather, no need. Like a jack-in-the-box, the genie bobbed up from the water, leaping and cackling.

'Free! Free at last!'

An explosion shook the air, bursting apart the fountain of flame. Water and debris rained in all directions. Smoke billowed. For an instant, Jem was blinded. He stumbled back, but not on to the ground.

407

'Princess! Littler! Where are you?'

The next thing Jem knew, he was rising in the air. He was standing on the carpet, but the Princess, Littler and Rainbow too were struggling to join him, gasping, scrambling, clinging to the edge. First Rainbow slipped back, howling; then Scabs flung Littler savagely aside.

Dona Bela screamed.

Now the cabin boy grabbed her, tearing, clawing.

'Scabs, no!' cried Jem.

'Scabs, please!' cried Littler.

'You won't take her, you won't!'

'Scabs, don't be a fool!'

'She's mine! She's my darling! She belongs to me!'

Desperately, Jem clutched at Dona Bela's hand, but this time, the cabin boy was too strong. With a scream, the girl slipped from the magic carpet, just as it shot dizzyingly into the air.

Jem slumped back, his throat bursting with sobs. 'Fool!' he cried aloud. 'Fool, fool! Scabs, don't you understand you've given up your magic? The Sustaining's gone! Can't you understand, your dreams will crumble?'

But Jem knew that Scabs understood nothing; nothing but the pain of being what he was.

Jem huddled tightly into himself as the carpet whizzed higher, ever higher. The last he saw of the dreaming dimension was the Princess struggling in the cabin boy's arms; the gardens withering, and the genie, realising he had granted the one wish that would destroy his own pleasures, thrashing the ground in despair. The vision of a huge face appeared above the debris, a screaming face with a long, flowing beard; then there was silence but for the whipping of the wind, and all that lay below were the desert dunes.

❄ ❄ ❄ ❄

Even then, Jem was not wholly free of the dreaming dimension. Trapped in that strange place, he had always been aware of paradoxes in time; now the eddying tides of Almoran's magic had one last paradox, reaching out to claim him. Moonlives had yet to pass until the wedding in Kal-Theron; but in the time it took him to fly to the Sacred City – a short time, it seemed to Jem – those moonlives would elapse.

When he came to earth again, he would be plunged at once into the climax of this adventure.

Chapter 60

THE COACHING INN AT GLOTZ

Somewhere along the course of the Wrax Road, where Ara-Zenzau meets the Agonist Deliverance, lies the coaching inn at Glotz. The establishment in question is a tumbledown edifice, set back inconveniently from the road, and infamous among travellers for its poor food, surly service and incommodious rooms. Should one wonder how such an establishment comes to flourish, the answer is soon to hand: for too far, much too far in either direction, it has no rivals, and those without rivals, as much in life makes clear, get away with the most dreadful things. The coaching inn at Glotz would be out of business at once were Nirry to open her establishment next door; as it is, the place receives many visits, from Agondon coaches bound for Wrax and Wrax coaches bound for Agondon.

With one of each sequestered here at present, many a weary traveller faces a night of indigestion, flea-bites and a lumpy bed. For now, though, the dining room is full and the ale flowing freely; this last, perhaps, may serve to mask at least some of the inconveniences of the coaching inn at Glotz.

This inn, let it be known, has no grand place in our narrative, no crucial part to play; indeed, the author would not be thought to have any interest in it at all. True, as shall be seen when his extensive notes are lodged in the library of his old university, he is more than familiar with this inn, having experienced both the fare and the beds on several regrettable occasions during the course of his research; this, however, is precisely why he would not wish to reward with advertisement, let alone to dignify with historic significance, the coaching inn at Glotz.

He should merely like us to listen, that is all, to certain conversations, between certain persons, that are taking place at this moment, on this hot night, within the drab dining-room.

FIRST CONVERSATION

To call him a grizzled veteran seems not quite right; no doubt, at such a description, the fellow would demur, but if he is a coachman, as he seems to be, he is one who has been long in his precarious trade.

Much grey discolours his curly hair and the eyes in his round, swarthy face dart often, anxiously, round the fuggy tavern chamber; is he, perhaps, intent upon his two identical line-boys, who run about noisily, disturbing all the diners? He rolls a tobarillo and hunches close to his earnest, scholarly companion. For a coachman to have established such intimacy with a passenger is strange; one might assume the two men had met before.

COACHMAN: It's been a long time. How can we know?

SCHOLAR: We know one thing.

COACHMAN: What might that be?

SCHOLAR: Why, that things have gone from bad to worse. We don't need reports every day, do we? It was bad enough last time. Arrests ... curfews ... bombs in the Vaga-quarter ... floods in the New Town.

COACHMAN: Why, Hul, I believe you're becoming mystical.

SCHOLAR: How so, old friend?

COACHMAN: You would blame Tranimel for the floods, too?

SCHOLAR: I remember all the things the boy told us, Bando. There are things I believe now, that once – well ...

COACHMAN: Things about Tranimel?

SCHOLAR: Or should we say, Toth?

COACHMAN: Shh ... Raggle! Taggle! Leave the Friar alone! (*He lights the tobarillo that, until now, he has twirled idly.*) Old friend, you have wisdom that will never be mine, but I think there are things that I knew long, long before you. I knew the Time of Atonement was ending. I knew that evil would stalk these lands, and it would be evil from a dimension beyond our own. How do you rate your book-learning now?

SCHOLAR (*producing a tattered little book from his pocket*): Tyranny is tyranny, Hul, whether it comes in the world of men or draws on the darkest of mysterious powers. (*Rifling through the pages, becoming enthused:*) Why, often I'm amazed at just how much Vytoni speaks to us now. I think he might even explain our poor leader, and the way he's changed. Let me read you a short passage, Bando ...

COACHMAN (*with a grin*): Oh please, none of your Vytoni!

SCHOLAR (*with a sniff*): Really, Bando, you don't seem to appreciate that without Vytoni I should never have been part of our great campaign. Why, old friend, we should

410

never have met!

COACHMAN: No? (*He picks up and kisses the tattered book.*) Ah,
then I must bless your great philosopher, bookworms and
all. Bless you, Master Vytoni! Bless you, little worms! But
Hul, did you have to read about our plight in a book?

SCHOLAR: I'm a scholar, Bando. I read everything in a book.

COACHMAN (*puffing contentedly at his tobarillo*): Not everything,
Hul.

SCHOLAR: Oh?

COACHMAN: I've never seen you reading a love story.

SCHOLAR (*innocently*): Bando?

COACHMAN (*gesturing, with his tobarillo, across the benches*): I've
seen you making eyes at a certain young lady. Ho, old
friend, I thought you'd never soften to the charms of the
sex!

SCHOLAR (*flushing*): Bando! I don't know what you're talking
about!

SECOND CONVERSATION

*Two young ladies, extraordinary in the contrast they present; quite as
extraordinary is that an intimacy should appear to exist between them.
One, the one with butter-yellow curls and a plump, excitable face, is
dressed in what one must regretfully describe as a slightly – hm –
common idea of finery; let us assume her to be a person of the menial
orders, who has climbed, or endeavours to climb, to the lower rungs of
the middle rank. Her companion, the lovely girl with long, coppery
braids – it is she to whom the* COACHMAN *has gestured – wears the
simplest of peasant garb, but none could mistake her provenance. Such
a fine, aristocratic nose! Such slender, smooth hands! Strange, the
alliances that are struck up on the road!*

*With the young ladies sits an older lady, stick-thin and grey, whose
peculiar distinction it is to possess only one eye. Evidently an upper
servant of sorts, perhaps she is in the employ of the aristocratic young
lady; though an astute observer might not be sure of quite what role
she plays.*

*There is also – the ladies talk over him – a large-eared fellow, naïve-
looking, but pleasant enough, in a collar that seems a little too tight
for him and a wig that from time to time he will adjust distractedly;
for the most part he sups upon his ale and seems quite content.*

411

NIRRY: Miss Landa, I know you mean well, but you still haven't convinced me. After poor Wiggler's adventures in the war – and mine with Miss Cata – well, we were hoping to settle down to a quiet life, we were. (*Dropping her voice:*) I promised Baines my tavern would be a respectable place, I did, and you know help's hard to find. What sort of place shall I be running, I ask you, if it's filled up with Redjackets?

LANDA: Hardly filled! Nirry, I know you're on our side—

NIRRY: Miss Cata's side? To the death!

LANDA (*with a smile*): Well spoken! You too, Goodman Olch?

WIGGLER (*muttering*): Aye, I've had enough of them Bluejackets, I'll tell you that much. Shift a man the length and breadth of El-Orok, without so much as a by-your-leave? Tramp, tramp, trudge, trudge, all to fight a lot of poor fellows with pitchforks and hoes? It's not natural – and me poor Nirry, having to come and fetch me, like!

LANDA: And Baines? You're with us?

BAINES (*rubbing her hands*): Aye, m'lady. If even my old mistress was sick of those warmongers, I won't tell you what I think of 'em. I'm a Redjacket through and through, and always have been. Don't you go worrying about respectability now, Goody Olch, I'm no shrinking flower. Why, this is the adventure I've been waiting for all my life!

LANDA (*with a smile*): And quite an adventure it's going to be, Baines. Oh, Nirry – dear Nirry – don't you see, we need the tavern? How long we'll be in Agondon before we can make our move, we don't know. Our agents are going to need a place to exchange intelligence—

NIRRY: Eh? What?

LANDA: Well, to meet, and lie low, and . . . oh, you'll see, Nirry! Why, when all this is over, you'll be a heroine, and Goodman Olch . . . you'll be a hero!

NIRRY: Ooh, don't you get him going, Miss Landa. I'm not sure I'd want my Wiggler to be a hero. Besides, he hasn't really got the ears for it, has he? (*Eyes shining:*) Master Jem, now there's a hero.

Pause.

(*Brightening:*) Eh, look what Raggle and Taggle are up to now! Little scamps, aren't they, Wiggler? Make me come over all funny, they do. Seem to like you too, Baines, don't they?

LANDA (*reaching across the bench, clutching* NIRRY'S *hand*): You're a good woman, Nirry. You're with us?

NIRRY *smiles, still a little uncertain.* Only one thing bothers me,
Miss Landa. That fellow in the scarlet – the one that rides
on ahead. We're not going to be seeing too much of him,
are we? I'm none too sure I'd like him in my tavern.
Shouldn't have a customer left by the end of an evening,
the way he carries on!

At this, BAINES *looks wistful, hoping perhaps that her single eye
shall, in fact, be alighting often upon the highwayman;* LANDA *decides
it is best just to laugh, but before she need say more,* NIRRY *detects
her husband's glance straying to another lady, a very strange lady,
who sits across the way.*

Eh, Wiggler, take your eyes off that fancy-piece! (NIRRY *pats
her yellow curls.*) A lady, too, with one of them things in her
mouth! Did you ever see the like? Looks like she's no better
than she should be, if you ask me!

THIRD CONVERSATION

*The lady, and a gentleman. The other ladies in this chamber, we have
seen, present quite a contrast; this lady – the one who looks no better
than she should be – is another. An exotic creature in a heaped-high
hat, with a feathery boa circling her neck, she smokes a tobarillo in a
long holder and declaims loudly to a fashionable young man who
seems just a little embarrassed, from time to time, at his companion's
disdain for what others appear to think. Evidently both are much used
to luxury; they have taken the Wrax stage all to themselves, and
would do well, perhaps, to show a little more concern for the notorious
dangers of the Zenzan roads. One recalls to mind some lines of Mr
Coppergate's:*

> When in the presence of envious eyes,
> I fear ostentation seldom is wise.

LADY: Oh, the colonies! Really, such a hostelry! Freddie, how far
is Wrax now? Do ask the coachman, there's a dear, do.
GENTLEMAN: No closer than last time you asked, I should think.
LADY: Freddie! Freddikins! Are you being cruel?
GENTLEMAN: Hardly, my dear. Only you did ask that question
when we stopped, and I don't think we've started again,
have we? Not unless this hostelry is moving through the
night, even as we speak.

LADY (*with an expressive sweep of her tobarillo-holder*): Oh, you *are* being cruel! You regret coming with me, I know it. You feel you have shackled yourself to an old, old woman!

GENTLEMAN (*flushing, murmuring*): My dear, don't be absurd. (*He grips her hand.*) Could I ever admire a lady more than Miss Tilsy Fash, the Zaxon Nightingale?

So that's who it is[1]. MISS TILSY FASH *strokes the gentleman's whiskers and blesses the day she met, or rather, first established intimacies, with* FREDDIE CHAYN, *scion of a worthless principality, but – oh indeed – a very handsome young man. She says:*

Oh Freddikins, you are a sweet boy, I knew it! I declare, sweetness is your talent.

FREDDIE (*a tad morosely*): It's as well I have *one*. You'll give me a tobarillo, my dear?

TILSY *reaches into her ornate gown, recklessly flicking open a golden box; across the benches, the* FRIAR's *eyes glow.*

You'll pardon my irritable ways, my dear, but these late moonlives in Agondon have grieved me sorely.

FREDDIE: I wonder not; they have grieved me too. Whatever has happened to good society?

TILSY: Exactly! To think, and the Royal Wedding seemed to herald a new golden age. (*The Zaxon Nightingale sighs.*) Poor Constansia! What do we see now but Cham-Charing House shuttered and cold, and all society fawning about that dreadful fat woman from the provinces. What's her name? She's got such a grip on the young Queen ... (*With a catch in her voice:*) Freddikins, I can't even remember her name!

FREDDIE (*with a resigned air*): Jelica. Miss Jelica Vance, that was.

TILSY (*irritably*): Not the girl! I mean the old cow, the fat woman.

FREDDIE (*sighing*): Lady Veeldrop. Umbecca Veeldrop.

TILSY: That's the one. Umbecca, indeed!

These last lines, being delivered at considerable volume, scythe easily through the noisy air. At the next bench, LANDA *has to snap her fingers in* NIRRY's *face, and* WIGGLER *asks if his wife has seen a ghost. For a moment,* NIRRY *sits spellbound, trembling at the return*

---

[1] In the company of the late Pellam Pelligrew, Jem attended a performance by this great diva of the popular ballad in *The King and Queen of Swords*, Ch. 31. That night she sang at the Volleys, but often she gave private performances at the *soirées* of Agondon's finest hostesses, who vied for her services with flattery and expensive gifts.

of old, buried fears. The mistress – a great lady? The mistress – in Agondon? For the first time, NIRRY *begins to wonder, really wonder, just what she will be facing in her new life.*

And what might happen, should the mistress ever see her again.

MISS TILSY FASH *sighs.* Ah, but my love, I must shake myself from this mood. I long only to reach my engagement in Wrax. Performance is my lifeblood, is it not? I must sing, sing! Why, Freddikins, I must sing now!

FREDDIE *fights the temptation to hide his face in his hands as his impetuous beloved rises, looking left and right through the smoky chamber.*

Landlord! Have you no clavichord, no harpsichord, no spinet? The colonies, the colonies . . . Very well, must I perform unaccompanied? I did worse, in my early days in Zaxos!

FREDDIE *does not doubt it, as* TILSY, *making much use of the feather boa, begins to sing. The hubbub of the dining-room falls silent; even* RAGGLE *and* TAGGLE *are still. All are united in astonishment as one of the empire's greatest entertainers enlivens their drab environs with the most celebrated of the many items in her repertoire.*

The King's Old Jester

Fondly I think of the King's old jester
Juggling, joyous, jumping in the air;
All-licensed fool,
His wit was a jewel,
And none, none would it spare.
He had a ready tongue
And he used it among
The great and the powerful at Court:
Burble! Babble!
Went the King's jester
In the days of yore;
Now the poor little chap's
Had a mishap
And he'll burble, babble no more!

415

Sadly, I think of the King's old jester
Turning, tossed out, tumbling down the stair:
   Infinite jest
   Gives a man no rest
But some, some hate its glare!
      To have a ready tongue
      Can be dang'rous among
The great and the powerful at Court:
         Burble! Babble!
      Went the King's jester
In the days of yore;
      Now the poor little chap's
         Had a mishap
And he'll burble, babble no more!

Trembling, I think of the King's old jester
Bloodied, bowed down, binding hands in prayer:
   Wit must be dumb,
   A new King has come,
And none, none shall he spare!
      And so the ready tongue
      Is heard no more among
The great and the powerful at Court:
         Burble! Babble!
      Went the King's jester
In the days of yore;
      Now the poor little chap's
         Had a mishap
And he'll burble, babble no more!

*It is over. There are tears, there is joy, there is a thunder of applause, even
from* RAGGLE *and* TAGGLE; BAINES *hunches over, wiping with her
pinafore at her single eye.*

*Of those gathered in that chamber, only two seem aloof, if
unintentionally, from the general admiration. One is* HUL, *who has found
meanings in the song rather deeper than may have been evident to the
others. It is a song that all know, an old air from the age of legends; but it
occurs to* HUL *that legends may repeat themselves, working themselves
out in new, modern guises. Does* MISS FASH, *he wonders, really know
what she sings?*

Meanwhile NIRRY, *more practical, as ever, finds herself thinking that
the King's old jester reminds her of someone she has met before. Ooh, but
Barnabas was just a Vaga-dwarf, wasn't he? Then* NIRRY *begins to*

wonder if this were really true; then she wonders if she shall ever see the strange dwarf again. Or, for that matter, Master Jem. Or Miss Cata. The tears that break from her eyes now are prompted by more, much more than the song.

NIRRY *clutches* WIGGLER's *hand. Suddenly, she is certain that, whatever the future holds for them, it is not going to give them a quiet life.*

✳   ✳   ✳   ✳

And here we must leave the coaching inn at Glotz. There is more, much more we could say of this place, and of these travellers; the narrative of how Miss Fash and Mr Chayn were subsequently set upon by a notorious highwayman – but fortunately not killed – is one that it pains us considerably to forgo.

But events proceed apace in the Lands of Unang Lia; we can tarry here no longer. Come, away!

END OF PART FOUR

PART FIVE

Into the Flame

Chapter 61

TOUCH OF THE EBAHNS

Konar-lights hissed in the underground passage. Riotous carvings decorated the walls, cut deep into the red marble and growing more extravagant as the golden doors loomed near. Sultan Kaled looked fixedly ahead, conscious, too conscious, of his Ebahn retinue, flanking him like prison guards.

By now, only days remained until the royal wedding. Soon the Princess would be in the city; soon the pilgrims, thousands upon thousands, would gather for the festivities. Tonight's ritual was a different affair, a secret one, but no less sacred. Only the Ebahns witnessed this prelude to the marriage, when the Sultan, shielded from the eyes of commoners, unattended by Imams, heirs or other members of his household, petitioned the Flame for the strength of the new marriage, and the sure continuance of the imperial line. It had always been the way; when he returned, the Imams would be waiting in the palace, bent low, ready to be told that their god, once again, had affirmed that all would be well. How could it not be so?

The golden doors opened and Kaled, just for a moment, looked back. The thought came to him that, since his father's death, his were the only eyes ever to see this long, echoing corridor. He shuddered, glancing to the visors of the Ebahns, wondering why it was that he felt so uncomfortable in the presence of this secret order of guards. It was not that they were blinded; in the Lands of Unang, who would deny that many of those born into the lower orders must undergo alteration? It was the way of the world, and a great privilege for those whose destiny it was to serve the Sultan.

Something else, something more made the Ebahns so fearsome. The Sultan thought of the Novice of the Flame, his son's young friend. Long before the ceremony the boy had known of his fate, but only when the Ebahns gathered about him had his terror burst through. Had the Sultan not felt an echo of that fear? Did he not feel it even now? It was absurd; what was the life of an Ebahn, but a life consecrated to the royal line? What function had such a man but to lay down that life, if needs be, for his monarch?

Then Kaled knew: it was not to their monarch that these guards owed their allegiance, but to the God of the Flame, the Sacred Flame.

The Sultan's eyes set hard. He was, he liked to believe, the most powerful man in the world. Vast tracts fell under his imperial sway; to his people, he was Sultan of the Moon and Stars. Was it right that he should feel a prisoner? Protocol determined every moment of his day. Religion dictated these rituals he followed. True, throughout his reign there were liberties he had taken, but what were these against the customs that held him in their thrall? There had been a time when he had thought freedom would soon be his, a time when a certain truth had exploded, like a powder-bomb, in his questing mind. What a fool he had been! Was freedom ever to be attained in this earthly domain?

It was the Council of Imams, anxious for an heir, who pressed for Dea to be bound to the Line as Heir Unquestioned; with equal ardour, they had insisted that the child must marry, and marry soon. Curse them! To the Sultan it appeared the holy men were impatient for his death, not merely fearful of assassination. All through the follies in the Presence Chamber, as he instructed the boy in the sacred histories, Kaled had raged in the secrecy of his heart. Was he not omnipotent? When his son's little friend had screamed before the Flame, had he not despised the child's unmanly fears? But was he not equally constricted by fear, he who claimed to be the greatest of the Five Sacred Sultans?

Bitterly Kaled made his way through the rocky chambers of the Sanctum, aware of the heavy steps that echoed behind him, and the maddening *jingle-jangle-jingle, jangle-jingle-jangle* of the scimitars that hung ready, always ready, from the golden belts of the guards.

✤　✤　✤　✤　✤

'God of the Flame, look upon your slave. Look mercifully upon him as he cringes before you, as he whimpers and cowers like a beaten cur, affirming before you, now and for ever, the sacred truth: Theron is the true god, and Mesha his prophet!'

The Sultan raised his eyes. Heat coursed through his knees and hands, and through the many windings of his bejewelled turban. How often had he touched his forehead to this floor? Really, it was absurd! But necessary for the Ebahns. They could not see if he abased himself or not, but they could sense, he knew, they could sense acutely. On and on, the words clicked from his lips.

'God of the Flame, listen to your slave. Quell not the pitiful strains of his voice as he writhes before you like the vilest worm that all would crush disgustedly underfoot, affirming before you, now and for ever, the sacred truth: Theron is the true god, and Mesha his prophet!'

What thoughts must have filled the Ebahns as they stood behind the Sultan, their lips opening and closing, chanting in time to the sacred litany? Their minds were trained to think of faith, only faith. None would have imagined the secret contempt that burned inside the Sultan as he hauled himself to his feet, shuffling forward over the jagged, sloping floor. With impassive eyes, he stood before the column of fire, struggling to invest his words with the passion that was required. Indeed, it was absurd! Was he a performing monkey?

'God of the Flame, speak to your slave. Pour upon his paltriness the balm of your voice, as he flutters before you like the frailest moth, affirming even as you sear away his wings that Theron is the true god, and Mesha his prophet! God of the Flame, speak to me of the marriage that is to come, its fecundity and force, as the Line of the Prophet soars ever higher in glory, faith and fame!'

Higher, higher soared the chantings of the Ebahns. The Sultan rocked and swayed. By now, almost despite himself, he had thrown himself into his role. In moments he would stumble back, weeping, moaning, blessing the great god whose words had been vouchsafed to him, and him alone, whispered directly into his brain.

In his cracking voice, in his gestures, the Sultan was the embodiment of his people's faith. If his rapture was a mere performance, nonetheless it was an impressive one. Often Kaled marvelled at the audacity with which he had concealed his loss of faith. For a time, after the death of his fair Ysabela, he had told himself that his god must exist after all, and had punished him as he deserved. Reflection soon banished this base fear. In truth, what could the death of his beloved be, but final proof that no god existed? If there were a god, could Ysabela be dead? No, the Sultan knew he was right; but he knew, too, that knowledge was not, as he had imagined in his youth, the source of all the happiness of the world.

Bitterness had ruined him. He had wanted the glories of science; now they were lost to him. He had longed for love, but love lay dead. His triumphs, instead, had been base ones, meaningless and empty as this column of burning gas before which he now stood, shrieking out nonsense. Sourly he thought of the holy wars, the vigorous persecutions, the public disembowellings; most of all, he thought of the day he had declared himself Sultan of the Moon and Stars. What was this, in truth, but his ultimate gesture of contempt for his cowed, credulous peoples?

Still, it had been a reckless move; only later did Kaled come to see that it had also been foolish. Since then, ten sunrounds had passed and his reign had not continued on the expected course of glory. He had thought that, after his great declaration, his position would be secure. But in the lands that lay beyond the Sacred City, discontent was abroad, fear and danger too, and the Sultan's greatness only made him resented all the more.

As he stood before the Flame now, Kaled knew he had reached a crisis. Already he had used Dea, but was the boy enough? The Flame, he knew, must speak to him again. But what could it say? Simply to condemn the Ouabin would be to no avail. Kaled longed for an inspiration.

But never, never for what happened next.

He flung out his arms. 'Theron, come! Come to me, God of Flame, as you came to my father! Come to me, as you came to his father before him! Come to me, as you came to my father's father's father, and to all the generations of the Line of Mesha! Mighty Theron, possess me as you possessed the Prophet, enfolding me in the rapture of your Sacred Knowing!'

Now it happens. The Sultan shudders, moans. Sweat runs down his face; his robes billow back and the blasting heat sears the bright feathers in his flashing turban. The voice from the Flame is sudden, terrifying, reverberating immensely in the broiling, brilliant cave:

'MESHA KALED!'

The Sultan cries out. He stumbles back. Wildly he turns to the blinded guards. They have heard it too, and fall to the floor!

'MESHA KALED!'

Three times comes the Sultan's name, and with each repetition a dazzling creature grows brighter, brighter, hovering impossibly between the curtains of fire. Can it be real? Flames fizz across the glittering scales and dance from the spikes of the leathern wings. Scaly lips curl into a smile over long, fang-like teeth. Golden eyes bore into the Sultan's brain.

Gasping, he sinks down. 'Mighty Theron!'

'SPAWN OF MY PROPHET,' comes the voice again, 'FOR FIVE EPICYCLES THE HUMANS OF YOUR LINE HAVE OFFERED UP THEIR OBLATIONS TO MY SACRED FLAME. FIVE EPICYCLES HAVE PASSED SINCE I CALLED TO YOUR ANCESTOR, COMMANDING HIM TO RECLAIM MY PEOPLE TO THEIR FAITH. NOW, MESHA KALED, THE FAITH WANES AGAIN—'

The Sultan gasped. 'No! Mighty One, how—?'

'SILENCE!' The Flame shook violently. 'HUMAN, DID YOU NOT SAY YOU HAD COME BEFORE ME AS A CUR, AS AN INSECT, AS THE VILEST WORM? SNIVELLING THING, YOU WOULD QUESTION MY WORDS? MESHA KALED, I TELL YOU THE FAITH HAS WANED, AND NOWHERE MORE THAN IN YOUR OWN EVIL HEART! HAVE YOU NOT FAILED IN YOUR BELIEF IN ME? HAVE YOU NOT FAILED IN YOUR SACRED DUTIES? FOOL, TO BELIEVE I COULD NOT BE REAL, WHEN ALL THE TIME I WAS TESTING YOUR FAITH! YOU ARE DAMNED, MESHA KALED! IN THE DEPTHS OF YOUR DEPRAVITY, YOU HAVE LIED, LIED EVEN BEFORE THIS SACRED EDIFICE, DECLARING YOURSELF SULTAN OF THE MOON AND STARS! VILE CREATURE, THOUGH A THOUSAND EPICYCLES MAY PASS, THAT IS A NAME THAT SHALL NEVER BE YOURS!'

The Sultan could only cringe and cry, clawing with his fingers at the rocky floor. Then he looked up, snivelling, as the harsh voice plunged to a softer pitch.

'FAITHLESS ONE, YOU ARE NO BETTER THAN AN INFIDEL, NO BETTER THAN THE OUABIN, OR THE MIXERS YOU SCORN. YOU DESERVE ONLY DEATH, AND SHOULD I WISH IT, I WOULD COMMAND YOU TO FLING YOURSELF INTO THIS FLAME, AND TO DISOBEY ME WOULD BE BEYOND YOUR POWER. BUT THERE IS WORK YOU YET MUST DO.'

'Mighty One, anything, anything . . .'

What did the Sultan expect now? To be sure, the flame god must order a massacre, a sacrifice, perhaps the building of a massive new temple, or a great crusade to a far-off land. Instead, what was demanded seemed far more modest – more astonishing, too.

'MESHA KALED, THIS IS THE FIRST TIME I SHALL APPEAR BEFORE YOU, AND THE LAST. KNOW ONLY THIS: THAT THE MARRIAGE OF YOUR SON MUST NOW BE UNDERTAKEN WITH THE UTMOST EXPEDIENCY. YOUR TASK IS TO SEE THIS MARRIAGE THROUGH TO THE END. DO THIS, AND I SPARE YOUR WORTHLESS LIFE.'

'Anything, anything, Mighty One . . .'

'NOT ANYTHING, FOOL, BUT THIS!' The Flame flickered, then roared again wildly, 'HOW I LONG FOR THE GIRL TO COME BEFORE ME, DECKED OUT IN THE GARB OF HER WEDDING DAY! THE SHIMMERING PRINCESS IS A CHILD OF SPECIAL MAGIC, AND HER MARRIAGE IS ALL – ALL, IF THE FAITH IS TO BURN BRIGHTLY AGAIN! MESHA KALED, GROVEL TO ME AND BEG MY FORGIVENESS, FOR YOU HAVE CALLED YOURSELF BY A NAME THAT IS MINE, AND MINE ALONE, TO BESTOW! FOOL, IT IS THE ONE WHO WEDS THE SHIMMERING PRINCESS TO WHOM THIS GREATEST OF BLESSINGS SHALL FALL! HE SHALL BE THE LAST OF THE GOD-SULTANS! HE SHALL BE SULTAN OF THE MOON AND STARS!'

✳   ✳   ✳   ✳   ✳

The Sultan blundered from the underground passage. In his desperation, he had forgotten that the Imams would be waiting for him, eager for a message from the god they worshipped. The holy men reeled back, shocked, as he flung himself into their presence. What had become of ceremony? What had become of protocol? Where were the mighty one's flanking guards?

Kaled breathed deeply, looking round the faces that turned to him, astonished, eager to know what could possibly have happened. At this point, another man might have been deeply chastened, sinking to the floor, confessing all his perfidies. Kaled would never be such a man. Already defiance had grown in his heart. Already he despised himself for the snivelling abjection that had overcome him, like a sharp, sudden illness, in the presence of the god – and the Ebahns.

So, he was damned, was he? Very well, then damned let him be!

He drew in a long breath.

He beckoned his Imams to come in close.

'The flame god,' he said, quietly, levelly, 'fears that new treachery is afoot. The Ouabin have infiltrated the ranks of the slaves . . . the ranks of . . . of the Ebahns.'

There were gasps.

'Impossible! Sultan, no!'

'Sultan, how can that be?'

The Sultan did not answer, but only continued, 'He has ordered . . . mighty Theron has ordered . . . that the Ebahns be put to death.'

The gasps became cries.

'The Ebahns, mighty ruler?'

'But tradition . . . protocol!'

'*All* of them, great one?'

Already, Kaled was moving towards his apartments, but he turned back, his voice cracking into a shriek:

'Fools, would you doubt the word of a god? The Ebahns must die! All of them! Tonight!'

※　※　※　※　※

It was done as the Sultan commanded; but that night too there occurred the first of a series of tremors in the earth, radiating out from the Sanctum of the Flame. In the days that followed, the tremors were to increase in severity and frequency. Some blamed the Ebahns, claiming that the fire god could not contain his rage; some said the tremors were shudders of joy, at the thought of the wedding that was soon to come.

If other things were said, they were said only in whispers, and accompanied with looks of bewildered fear.

Chapter 62

GIBBOUS MOON

The heat has dropped, plummeting out of being as if the day before has been the merest illusion, a shimmering in the dunes, a shape traced on the windblown hills. Stars gleam like shards of glass, catching the light of a gibbous moon.

In the desert at night, the darkness becomes an immense overarching dome, implacable, impossibly high, the ceiling of a temple so huge that it spans the world. There is a consuming silence. A stillness. The moon does not flicker, nor do the stars. Immense loneliness lies upon the scene. When human presences stir, they are as inconsequential as the tiny burrowing creatures that live beneath the dunes, even when, as now, they are part of a vast caravan, lying becalmed in the desert night.

Over dune after dune they stretch, the vans, the recumbent camels, the huddled human forms, like an undulating, elongated city of transients. Never in the history of All Unang has so huge a party of pilgrims set forth. There are wizened old men, there are plump matriarchs, there are smooth-limbed young lovers and squalling infants; there are beggars in rags, there are painted harlots, there are holy men and merchants and moneylenders; there are noblemen in vans with gilded sides, flanked by parties of liveried guards.

By day their slow course is measured by prayer, with bells jangling all along the line at Catacombs, Green, Dust, and Wave. After Stars, the great procession does not move again. Later, round the campfires, there is laughter and song; youths wrestle, deals are struck, the old tell tales of the days that have gone. At such times the caravan might be a city indeed, restless with the clamour of ordinary life. The appearance is false: always, beneath other joys and concerns, the pilgrims think of the destiny before them, of the Sacred City, of the wedding, of the blessings that soon shall descend upon them, like rain upon the unforgiving desert wastes.

But not all think of these blessings in spiritual terms.

'It'll be better in Kal-Theron,' Faha Ejo was saying as he strode past a line of tightly shuttered vans. Scurrying beside him was Fish; straggling behind them were Stork, Blubber and Cheese. During Stars the boys had purloined a jug of ferment. By now they were boisterous, and their faces glowed with fire.

'What'll be better, Faha?' said Fish, in an eager, excited voice.

Stork grinned. 'The power of prayer!'

Blubber guffawed. 'The force of faith!'

Cheese snickered. 'The gifts of the gods!'

Faha Ejo turned back, a finger to his lips. They passed a party of pious women, hunched over a cookingpot like enormous black crows. Almost certainly, thought the goat-boy, such women bore with them purses of gold and jewels, hidden beneath their capacious skirts. Alas, that it would be impossible to reach beneath those skirts! All day, such women huddled on a cart, and when they left it they would always keep together. Surprise would be difficult; advances of an intimate nature were hardly likely to succeed.

Faha Ejo smiled and draped an arm round Fish's shoulder, dropping his voice and observing that yes, indeed, in the crowds of the Sacred City, the gifts of the gods would soon fall to their lot. Fondly he imagined the booty that would be theirs on the night of the wedding.

Fish's eyes grew wide. He had always considered himself a pious boy, for all that he found it difficult to observe the times of prayer. Shock filled him at the thought of the sacrileges they would soon be bound to commit, within the very walls of the Sacred City; then shock gave way to a delicious excitement. Oh, but Faha was wonderful, truly wonderful!

'Wait!' Fish reached into his loincloth, producing a greasy orb of glass. 'I've got an idea.'

Blubber grinned. 'Fish's got an idea?'

Cheese guffawed. 'An idea? Fish!'

Stork snickered. 'What idea, Fish?'

'Shh!' Faha Ejo beckoned them forward. Crowded into the space between two vans, the boys looked on as Fish, his eyes straining in the moonlight, stared into the depths of the mysterious orb.

'It's magic, isn't it?' said the boy in the loincloth. 'If I stare long enough, what might I see?'

Cheese grinned. Stork guffawed. Blubber snickered. Only Faha Ejo looked on in earnest, wondering if the Orb of Seeing could really help them go about their thieving ways. He thought of the other treasures they had purloined after the Ritual of Rebonding, clasping the amulet that circled his wrist. The Amulet of Tukhat, the suitor had called it. A protection. A charm. Round Cheese's forehead, hiding in his greasy hair, was something called the Lichano band. From the belt round Blubber's middle, bobbing and knocking, was the konar-light; a swirling-patterned coin nestled in Stork's pocket. They meant to sell these treasures when they got to Kal-Theron, but Faha Ejo had begun to think this plan would come to nothing. Things had changed since they left the Realm of Un. Amed was missing – killed, perhaps, in the raid on the bazaar; Littler was gone too, and so was Scabs. Only the five of them remained. They had bonded closer, and felt embattled. Let them keep their lucky charms, even if the charms were false!

They kept their voices low. 'Do you see anything, Fish?'

Fish's eyes were intent. 'I see a light. A flickering.'

'That's the moon, you idiot!' whispered Stork.

'Shh!' said Blubber. 'Can you hear that sound?'

Cheese peered through a gap between vans. He gasped.

It was an astonishing piece of luck. In the journey from Qatani, the Unners had been on many a mission along the length of the caravan, begging, stealing, hawking trinkets, hiding under vans and in other people's tents, scurrying here, scurrying there, making trouble wherever they could. Their new friends, the Major-sir and his beanpole friend – especially the Major-sir – seemed only too pleased to have fallen in with boys who could provide such bounties of ferment, Jarvel and glinting gold. It was an arrangement that benefited both parties. When needs must, the Unners could pretend to be the pious young wards of the Major-sir; when needs must, solemnly they would swear that their guardian, though an Ejlander, was a loyal convert to the faith of the fire god. How they would laugh over their blasphemous deceptions!

The Unners squeezed through the gap between the vans. In two, nearly three moonlives the shifting city had become to them almost as familiar as the city they had left, but like that city, it had many places they had not yet explored. Indeed, more: for this city was never the same two days running, and as the camels and the vans and the trudging feet made their way over the dunes, so some would move ahead, some would fall behind. There would always be surprises, as the Unners were surprised now. Delighted, too.

By the ashes of a dying fire, lolling in a stupor, was the greasy bulk of Eli Oli Ali. Falling from one of his hands was a ferment-skin; in the other, half-hidden by the mound of his belly, was a purse of glinting coins. On the other side of the fire was Mother Madana, snoring like a pig. The old woman stirred, permitting the escape of a loud fart.

Blubber grinned. 'Is this your magic, Fish?'

'It's too good to be true!' Cheese guffawed,

'Quick!' snickered Stork. 'Before they wake up!'

It was Faha Ejo who took the risk. Darting in, he snatched his cousin's purse and pirouetted away. Sweet vengeance! It should have been easy; in the merest instant, they could have been gone, but for a sudden, sharp tug.

'A chain?' said Cheese.

'Break it!' said Stork.

Blubber wailed, 'You're spilling the gold!'

There was a confused tussle. Stork scrambled in the darkness, searching the sand for the lost coins. Fish floundered; longingly, Blubber eyed the ferment-skin. Did he dare? Cheese tugged him away, but not before the fat boy, with a frustrated grunt, had aimed a swift kick at the whoremonger's stomach.

Sweet vengeance, indeed! Eli Oli Ali doubled over, moaning, but it was Mother Madana who cried out first.

'Thieves! Stop, thieves!'

※　※　※　※　※

'More nectar? Your Royal Majesty, please!'

The Prince only huddled on the many-cushioned divan, his shoulders shaking and his face turned to the wall. Mother Madana looked on desperately. As the wedding day approached, her darling seemed younger, younger and weaker, almost as if some mysterious force were draining away all vigour from his frame. Moonlives earlier, it had seemed that manhood was stirring inside him, ready to burgeon; now, for all his height and the length of his limbs, Dea was a child again, the child she had nursed at her breast.

Looking defiantly at Councillor Simonides, the Targons and the whispering walls, the old woman would have plunged towards the Prince at once, weeping with him and moaning as she swept him into her arms. In the event, she merely lowered the goblet in her hand and stood poised, love surging and crashing uselessly in her heart. Oh, she had to admit it: she had been pleased, very pleased, when Councillor Simonides called her back, admitting that the Prince, as his great day drew near, required rather more than the ministrations of Targons. What were Targons, to a nurse's love?

But still there must be limits to her love, it seemed.

'Go from us, woman,' sighed Simonides at last. 'The claws of childhood cling tenaciously, but the Prince will be a man whether he will or no – go now, go. There is no more you can do tonight.'

Mother Madana shook as the old man spoke and turned, bowing with deep respect. It was not dissembled: no man in the palace filled her with such awe as Councillor Simonides. The Sultan, after all, she had nursed as a child; she could think of him when his voice was high and lisping and sprouting from his face was only the palest down. No such memories mitigated the strange power of Simonides. Eternally, it seemed, he had been the gnarled, mysterious figure she saw before her now, with his sad, hooded eyes and long, flowing beard. Could he understand the distress that consumed her? Was there sympathy in those ancient eyes? The old woman moved her tongue as if to speak, but no sound emerged. Quickly, bearing away the nectar, she made her retreat.

Simonides sat beside the young Prince. His gnarled hand stroked the downy hair. 'Alas, my Prince, I have performed my task poorly, have I not?'

Dea sniffed. 'Simonides?'

The stroking continued. 'Poor child, it is a heavy burden you have been called upon to assume. The common herd, knowing you to be royal, think of you as blessed. They are fools, but how could they ever understand the truth? Royalty is a curse as much as a blessing, a curse you must bear for their sake, like the wound of a god. When you marry, that curse shall descend upon you with all its weight and force. Poor, poor child! I had hoped that, in these last moonlives, I might have inspired in you a new strength and wisdom. Now I tremble at this affliction that shakes you, leaving you enmired in this womanish weakness. My task has been to prepare you for the fate that lies before you; now I wonder if I truly know what that fate might be. Perhaps, in your heart, there are intimations of another. Perhaps there are heavier burdens, heavier burdens still.'

With clumsy hands, Dea wiped away his tears. Blankly he looked up into the old man's sorrowing eyes.

✳ ✳ ✳ ✳ ✳

'Pah! Pah, Pah, Pah!'

Would he ever find those brats? Thieving little swine! Spitting, scowling, scuffing at the sand, Eli Oli Ali roamed restlessly, his greasy face glinting under the gibbous moon. Huddled round a fire were a party of young men, gambling with a spinning coin. He eyed them resentfully. He rounded the corner of a jutting van and saw a band of holy men passing a hookah solemnly between them and debating the meaning of a sacred text. He stumbled past them, shaking his head in scorn. Snoring, slumped in exhaustion, lay ranks of poor folk, footsore and ragged, who had walked all the way from the coast. How many had stumbled in the burning heat, or sunk down to prayers, never to rise again? Did they die easily, secure in the faith that a pilgrim's death was blessed? Fools! They made the whoremonger sick. Let Mother Madana mumble out her devotions; while the crone deluded herself with hypocrisy and lies, her shabby companion would skulk inside the van, eking out his ferment and dreaming of the prospects that lay before them in the Sacred City. Let Casca Dalla do what he would, Eli Oli Ali would be a great man again! Why, he would be whoremonger to the Sultan himself!

It was late, and the camp was sinking slowly into stillness. Eli Oli Ali looked up at the moon. His brain reeled and he slumped against the side of a cart, moaning with weariness. Damn, damn! He had wandered too far from the van, and for what? Curse those brats, curse them! To think, he had been kind to that wretched Faha Ejo! Taken him in! Trained him!

431

There was no goodness in this world, no loyalty, no trust! The whoremonger sank to his haunches, wishing he had brought his ferment-skin. That was when he heard the drunken murmurings, sounding from the other side of the cart.

'But Polty, why haven't you told me this before?'

'Should my side-officer know all my secrets?'

'Polty, yes! Especially one like this! But how can you be sure?'

'I sensed it, Bean. In the moment before Toth's power left me, I knew there was something more to that girl. Something special. She's the key to Cata, I'm sure of it.'

'You mean she knows where Cata is?'

'Perhaps. But somehow I feel it's more than that.'

'More? How can it be more?'

'I can't explain it, Bean, but I had the feeling she was keeping Cata prisoner. Don't you see, if I get to her, I can get to Cata? Bean, think of it! Cata back in my arms! Cata kissing my lips! Cata reciting her wedding vows! Can't you see me on our voyage back to Agondon, bearing her home in triumph?'

There was a distance, a wryness in Bean's reply. 'I don't think she really likes you, Polty.'

Laughter was Polty's only response. 'Poor Bean, when you know the fair sex as I do, you'll understand a woman's coyness. Cata's shy, that's all, but she knows I love her. Why, Cata and I go beyond mere liking!'

'Or disliking?'

Polty grew intent. 'You don't understand, do you, Bean? Cata's mine. She's been mine in her heart ever since we were mere children in Irion. Her Essence is entwined with mine, as mine is with hers. Can't you imagine what that means? When two are one, what meaning can we attach to mere outward words? In her heart, Cata says *I am Poltiss*. As I say, *I am Catayane.*'

'Hm.' Bean's murmur was sad. There was a silence, filled only with the glugging of ferment and the cracklings of the fire.

With a stubby, dirty finger, Eli Oli Ali stroked his moustaches. Hm, indeed. He thought he had seen the last of the Major-sir. Finding him again might be fate.

Might be.

Sip. 'But Polty, how will you get to the girl?'

Glug. 'Bean, what a question!'

'She's a Princess, Polty!'

'We're Ambassadors, aren't we?'

'Not any more. I mean, we're lying low, aren't we?'

Glug, glug. 'Hm. No initiative, Bean, that's your trouble. There's always a way.'

432

Sip. 'Polty?'

'Bean?'

'He's gone, hasn't he?' Bean's voice trembled. 'You know. Him.'

Glug. Glug, glug. 'I told you, Bean, I felt him burn away from me, back on the day of the Ritual of Rebonding.'

Sip. A warmer tone. 'The day you saved me, Polty.'

'That's right, Bean. On that day, something snapped in me, and he was gone. I saw him once after that, then . . . nothing. No, it's not for Toth's sake that I'm after the Princess now. This is for Veeldrop, Poltiss Veeldrop!'

Or, perhaps, for Eli Oli Ali.

The whoremonger judged his moment well. Turning over the possibilities, the greasy fellow had decided that the beanpole fellow might resent him, just a little. Still, what of it? That one silly misunderstanding, back at the khan? Mother Madana's superstitions! He'd tried to argue with the crone, hadn't he, but what good had it done? Women, women . . . no, the beanpole could be dealt with easily enough. The Major-sir was the important one. Down on his luck, yes, but an Ejlander noble, was he not? Quite what Polty meant about Essences and entwinings, Eli did not know, but one thing was certain. For the flame-haired one, nothing could be more important than marrying that girl. What a dowry she must bring! The whoremonger's eyes glinted, and a plan flashed into his mind. Prospects. Possibilities. He blundered round the side of the cart. He flung up his hands.

'Major-sir! It's a miracle!'

Chapter 63

DEAD MAN IN THE SAND

Breath. Rising. Falling.

A heart beating. Pulsing.

Think of these things, only these things.

Simonides was not quite capable of sleep, but when he lay down in the dark he would drift after a time into a species of trance. Sometimes he wondered if even this would be possible without the weariness that now never left him, dragging at his limbs with its intolerable weight. Oh, he was old, old! He longed to sleep, but knew there would be only this wakefulness now, night after night, until he died. Tonight, even the trance was failing him. He stirred, and his eyes flickered open. The old man thought he would welcome death, welcome it into his arms like a lover. Yes, like a lover . . . But there had been no lovers in his long, sterile life.

Simonides stared into the light of the gibbous moon. With no hiss of konar-lights sounding now, the silence was almost entire. From the gardens came only the merest stirrings; even the whisperers in the walls were still. All the world was sleeping; all, but for this fond, foolish old man. Simonides closed his eyes again.

Breath. A heart.

These things, only these.

But his thoughts slipped instead to the young Prince, and the troubled fate that seemed to lie in store for him. What would become of the boy? Could he fulfil his role? What of the empire he was destined to lead? With a thud of dread, Simonides thought of the brothers he had left so long ago, and the powers that he had forgone. In his long years in the royal service, there had been times when he ached to feel again the mystic knowledge, like a potent drug, that once had streamed through his mind and heart. Always he had suppressed himself. Always. Now it seemed to him that the granite walls of a lifetime's abstinence were shaking, cracking. He had said that a Teller's powers could lead only to evil. Now he thought of the boy. His fear for him. His love.

Breath. A heart.

These things, only these.

With a deep sigh Simonides turned his head, looking to the place where the sleeping Prince lay. The moonlight disclosed only a rumpled, empty couch.

❄   ❄   ❄   ❄   ❄

Bean sat cross-legged, smearing his face in his hand. His head hung heavily. His hair was lank and his eyes were hooded. If he was drunk, he was also dispirited. Gazing into the firelight, he peered into the darkness of the desert beyond. It frightened him. What dangers lay out there, in the soft undulations of those sandy hills? If a man were out there, abandoned and alone, he would soon go mad, or so Bean thought. Still, what of it? He could go mad well enough, here by this fire. He smiled weakly at Polty's latest ribaldry and Eli Oli Ali's slimy laughter.

Bean sighed. How happy he had been, on the night that Polty saved him! Burgrove's death had horrified him, it was true, but Bean knew in his heart that he did not really care. Of course he didn't. Burgrove gone, Eli gone, Toth gone too . . . this would be like the old days! That night, as he clung to Polty's neck, as Polty fought his way through the clouds of smoke, Bean would not have cared if they died. To die in Polty's arms! He sighed again, and squinted resentfully at the greasy-faced intruder. How easily the whoremonger had wormed his way back into Polty's favour. Oh, Polty was naïve, far too naïve!

'Tell me the plan again, Oily,' he slurred, an arm draped round the whoremonger's neck.

'Pah! Have the flames burned a hole in your head?'

'Not a bit of it! But I'm not sure how this is going to work. You really think we can abduct this brat . . . this Prince Dea?'

Glug, glug. 'Major-sir, think of it. Mother Madana's sister looks after the brat, hm? Now, when we get to the Sacred City, what's Mother going to do but visit the dear old sister she hasn't seen since . . .'

Glug. 'The Time of Juvescence?'

'Good as. Now, they'll probably look the same, won't they? Being sisters? Well, similar.'

Glug, glug. 'I get it, Oily. All we do is get her to take her sister's place, and the brat's in her grasp – I mean, in ours.'

The whoremonger grinned and clashed his goblet with Polty's.

'You think she will?' Bean said sourly.

Polty slurred, 'Will what?'

'Replace her sister! You mean, switch clothes? Knock her out, perhaps? Drug her, kill her? Her own sister?'

'Details, details!' The whoremonger waved a dismissive hand. 'I'll work on it. Just think: we take the brat, see, and hold him to ransom. If they won't hand over the Princess, the brat dies. Now the Sultan's going

435

to want the brat more than the Princess, isn't he? Son and heir? Stands to reason.'

Bean moaned at the absurdity of the plan. He could see it now: the whoremonger would get Polty into terrible trouble, and soon. They would reach the Sacred City in only a few days, barely time enough to wean Polty away from this latest desperate enthusiasm. Besides, Bean didn't trust the whoremonger, not one bit. Was he to believe the greasy fellow had never known, never even guessed, that Mother Madana had held two Ejlanders captive in the cellar? And were their fortunes now to depend on this same Mother Madana?

Bean turned to the whoremonger, contempt in his eyes.

'I thought you wanted the girl for yourself. Didn't you offer yourself as one of the suitors?'

'Pah! I'd have sold her, that's all. Why, there are those who'd pay highly for a real Princess. Thought it was worth a try, didn't I?' The whoremonger turned, grinning, to Polty. 'Do you know, even now she may not be far away?'

Glug. 'I dare say she's not. We're close to Kal-Theron now, aren't we?' said Polty.

'Pah! Kal-Theron? I mean here, in this pilgrim train.'

'Oily, how can that be?'

Glug, glug. 'I heard some traders talking just today. There are rumours ... well, there are always rumours. But think about it: they have to get the Princess to the Sacred City. Will they bear her across the desert in all the pomp of state, with Ouabin on the loose and who knows who else, ready and waiting to seize so valuable a prize? Think again! They say she's travelling in a common van, with imperial guards disguised as humble pilgrims.' Glug. Glug, glug.

Polty's eyes glowed. 'Oily, that's amazing! Why, if this is true, we might not even have to abduct that brat at all!'

'What, so you're going to take on who knows how many imperial guards?' muttered Bean. 'I don't believe a word of it!'

Polty sighed. 'Bean, who cares what you think? You're brilliant, Oily. I'll get the Unners on to this. We'll find that Princess if it's the last thing we do!'

'Unners?' said the whoremonger, furrowing his brow.

'Say, where are those brats?' said Polty.

The question was answered a moment later when the five boys who had accompanied Polty and Bean on their journey returned at last, laden and jingling, from the night's foray. Slouching round the side of the cart they came, giggling wearily, ready to recount their evening's adventures.

Faha Ejo froze. Blubber gasped.

Eli Oli Ali was on his feet at once. 'You thieving brats!' he burst out, and Polty and Bean could only watch, bewildered, as the whoremonger first lunged at his young cousin, as if to strike him, then tripped and fell face-first into the dying fire. He screeched and leapt up, flapping at his moustaches with his pudgy hands.

Raucous laughter rang round the camp.

✻ ✻ ✻ ✻ ✻

'I'm sorry, my lady, but your friend is dying.'

Astonished, the girl could only look into the physician's kindly face. The scene was playing out around another campfire, far away along the long line of the pilgrim train. On the soft sand, shuddering beneath a simple blanket, lay the ruined body of a young man, barely more than a boy. Clustered round him, bedraggled, dressed in the remnants of elaborate finery, were a second boy, much younger, and a fat fellow, much older; there was also a shabby, scrawny dog. The lady was careful to keep her face veiled, but her despair showed clearly enough in her eyes. She turned back to her friends, then back to the physician. Wringing her hands, she asked if there were really nothing, nothing he could do.

'Lady, you say your party was set upon by Ouabin?'

'It is true, good physician. We were the only survivors.'

'You say you had a long journey, across the desert wastes?'

'It is true, true. For how long we stumbled through the hot sands, I dare not think. How lucky we were to meet you and your good family!'

The physician bowed respectfully. 'Lady, you are kind, but we have done no more than our duty. But pray, you say that, without this unfortunate young man, you should never have survived to meet us?'

'True, so true. There was a time when I had thought him of a different character, but when we found ourselves lost in the desert, he revealed the goodness in him that had lain concealed. Intrepidly he led our party, day after day, until at last we stumbled upon your merciful assistance. How cruel that he should collapse now, sinking so suddenly into this desperate illness!'

'True, indeed, true. But dear lady, for all this, and for all his exertions on your behalf, I tell you this young man was doomed in any case. You look upon him now and I see guilt in your eyes, but his affliction has long been a dire one, and admits no mitigation. That he should die now must not surprise us; in truth, it is astonishing that he has lived so long.'

Tears came now to the lady's lovely eyes and she could only shake her head, wondering at the unfathomable ways of fate. That night, as he slipped into his last dream, she would cradle the dying young man in her arms.

'Dear Jorvel,' she would whisper. 'Dear, dear Jorvel.'

'Dea?'

On the terrace, the moon was brighter. Simonides trembled. Foreboding gripped his heart and he crept forward like a thief or a furtive lover, whispering urgently for the missing boy. Could the Prince have vanished? No, it was impossible. Dea had wandered in the night before, staggering blindly in the grip of his distress. Where could he go but the roof gardens? The old man ascended the pale stairs.

'Dea? Dea?'

Perhaps the Prince was hiding, huddled deep in the foliage. The thought disturbed Simonides. He said the boy's name again and wondered why he was whispering. Then he knew: an intimation, like an echo of his abandoned powers, sounded deep within the old man's mind. Yes, he knew: but long moments passed before he saw what he had feared: the intimation, the echo made real.

Simonides hid behind a screen of tall ferns. All around him, the odours were intoxicating, the jasmine, the malak, the night-narcissus; the fern-fronds were soft as the caresses he had denied himself all through his life. It was too much, too much; but worst of all was the vision, shimmering silver, shimmering gold amongst the ornate parterres. Locked into an unearthly silence, running, leaping, laughing, Prince Dea played with his ghostly companion.

Simonides drew in his breath, but did not speak. Painfully, slowly, he went back below. There he turned away from his own hard couch and lowered himself to the many-cushioned divan. Tears came to his eyes as he inhaled the Prince's smell. Trembling, clutching a cushion, Simonides waited for the boy's return.

✻ ✻ ✻ ✻ ✻

It was never meant to happen. In all the time he had travelled with Polty, Bean had thought it could not happen. Perhaps he thought some special magic protected him; perhaps he had been confused, and told himself that his secret acts had all been in his dreams. But he knew they had not.

Later, he would wonder if he had wanted it to happen. When he had been locked in the 'temper-cell, Bean had longed for freedom, only freedom. But what had his freedom ever been, but a different kind of imprisonment? Perhaps he wanted to break through the invisible wall that surrounded him, whatever the consequences proved to be. Perhaps he was just very drunk.

Bean lay looking up at the hard, unglittering stars. Beside him, Polty's breath rose and fell; Eli was gone and the Unners were sleeping on the other side of the fire. An immense loneliness possessed Bean, and the thought came to him that all his life had been like this, a desperate, lonely vigil of love, watching intently at Polty's side. He thought with disgust of the evening they had spent. Poor Bean! He had thought Polty was his again, and Polty had betrayed him. In Bean's position, others might have resented Polty; Bean resented only the slimy whoremonger. Compassion for Polty welled in his heart, and he rolled closer to his sleeping friend.

Poor, poor Polty! Trembling, Bean's fingers stroked the hair that glowed a dull purple beneath the gibbous moon. Oh, Polty! Bean's touch lingered over the lean, angular face. How different that face had once appeared! Longingly, Bean thought again of that day in the barn behind the Lazy Tiger, and the first time this face – plump, and striped with freckles – had turned towards his own. Perhaps, in that moment, Polty had cast a spell, a spell that was to last for all of Bean's life. His fingers moved to the firm chest that rose steadily, slowly up and down.

Drunken tears flowed from Bean's eyes. Of course, he had known from the first that Polty was evil, a monster in human form. But had he? Could he believe such a thing of his marvellous, magical friend? Besides, what was evil, what was good? There was nothing Polty could ever do that was wicked, not really. Polty just got a bit confused, that was all, and needed a hand to guide him.

Bean's caresses slithered lower as Polty stirred, moaning. For a moment, Bean fancied that his friend had called his name. *Aron, Aron.* Bean's heart surged; but no. Absurd. It was Cata's name his friend had whispered, like a secret, into the darkness. Polty's head lolled; his back arched. The signs were familiar. Bean knew that his friend was dreaming, and knew what sort of dream it was going to be. Yes. Oh yes!

Quite when it was that he had first taken these liberties with his friend's person, Bean could barely remember. For a time, after Polty's return from the Zenzan wars, the side-officer had been careful; only of late, on this desert journey, had he found himself growing reckless again. Sometimes he wondered how Polty could really be oblivious to these intimacies they shared; sometimes, though Polty had said nothing, Bean would sense in certain looks, certain signs, that his friend acknowledged their secret relations. If only it were so!

The dreamer whispered his beloved's name again. *Cata, Cata.* It did not matter. When Polty's hands reached out, caressing his hair, Bean's rapture was complete. He felt as if he were falling endlessly through an enveloping warmth, and never wanted the fall to end. This was completeness. This was fulfilment.

'Oh Cata, Cata ... *Bean!*'

Polty jerked back, suddenly awake.

The rest happened quickly. First there was Polty, screaming in outrage, then Bean floundering up, suddenly sobbing; there were the astonished faces of the Unners; there was Bean blundering away; there was Polty in pursuit, grabbing at the breeches that were slipping round his ankles. Bean turned back, desperate, ready to plead; then came the fist, hard as rock, smashing into his ribs, his jaw, his eye.

'Dirty bastard! You dirty, dirty bastard!'

They had lurched out beyond the shifting city, into the dark undulations of the dunes. Then there was Bean lying on the ground, incapable even of crying out as Polty kicked him in the guts, spat on him, then floundered away, cursing. For a moment Bean thought the Unners were there too, gasping and exclaiming, until Polty angrily barked at them to leave the dirty bastard, leave the dirty bastard like a dead man in the sand.

Chapter 64

THE FIFTH VANISHING

How much time had passed?

Eternities, it seemed, since the agony of the last kick, and the hot, viscous spit, slithering over his skin. It did not matter. To Bean, Polty's hatred, Polty's violence, were eternal too. Now it was tears that flowed down Bean's face and only the burning ache in his ribs prevented him from breaking into guttural sobs. His teeth chattered. The sand beneath his skin was sharp like glass. What a fool he had been! What a terrible fool! Dimly he wondered if the 'temper room had done its work after all, seeding him with sickness; then he thought that he had always been sick, that his whole life was a sickness.

His mind drifted into a blur of pain. He thought of the stars, of the dunes, of the darkness. Slowly the night seemed to turn around him, revolving beneath the gaze of the gibbous moon.

❈ ❈ ❈ ❈ ❈

The ceiling-shutters were open. Flickering into wakefulness, Rajal stared up into the silence of the night.

Watching the moon and stars, for a moment he could imagine he was lying out in the sand, not in the confines of this narrow van. He wished it were true, but the illusion swiftly faded and he became aware again of the cushions beneath him and the gleamings round the walls and the pungency of incense and velvet and silk. The van was luxurious, but how he hated it! He heard the sound of breath, rising and falling. He heard a sound of rustling, and a sigh.

He whispered, 'Cata?'

'I can't sleep.'

'Me neither.'

'Curse this confinement!'

'It's better when we're moving.'

'It must be morning soon. Surely.'

'Hm.'

There was a pause, and they gazed at each other morosely in the gloom.

'It can't be much further now, can it?'

'The Sacred City? How should I know?'

441

'You could ask your father, couldn't you?'

'Raj, please! Don't call that creature my father, not even as a joke. Think it's wonderful for me, do you, getting to visit him?'

'Gets you out of here for the evening, doesn't it?'

'I'd rather be here! Well, rather than listen to endless *Shimmy-this, Shimmy-that* . . . not to mention the caresses! You'd think he'd have got used to the fact that I'm flesh and blood by now, wouldn't you? I tell you, every time I go to that van it's the same. The wedding, the wedding, that's all he talks about. First his excitement, then his fears. Then come his regrets for the past. Oh, and how he goes on about that genie! Then he breaks down in tears, and flings himself in my arms.' Cata sighed. 'At first I was disgusted. Now I'm just bored.'

'Very well, you've convinced me. You'd rather be here.'

'Then there's that Vizier. He's not just boring, he's frightening.'

'The . . . Vizier?' said Rajal.

'Hm. I suppose it's just me, but I keep thinking he's looking at me . . . strangely. It's almost as if he can see through my disguise. I look up from the Caliph's arms, and there he is, that Vizier . . . just watching me.'

There was a silence, then Rajal said distantly, 'I've been trying to avoid him, myself. The Vizier, I mean. He's the one who ordered me . . . well, you know. If you wouldn't like him to see through *your* disguise, I certainly wouldn't like him to see through mine. And mine's hardly as good as yours, is it?

'Well, sometimes I wonder just how good *mine* is.'

'Cata, that's silly. It's slipped a few times, but – well, magic's never perfect, is it?

'Oh? Who told you that?

'The Great Mother, I think. Or perhaps it was Myla.' Rajal sniffed and fell silent again.

It was Cata who spoke next. Her gaze shifted to the sleeping form of Amed, curled up with dog-like contentment on the floor. 'I don't know how she can sleep so soundly.'

'She's happy. Haven't you noticed you make her happy?'

'Don't start! I wish I looked like *me* again!'

'For that matter,' said Rajal, 'so do I.'

'I don't know, I think that costume suits you.'

'Don't start? Don't *you* start!'

They suppressed their laughter. Looking up at the ceiling-shutters, Cata whispered, 'I can't stand being locked up like this! It's nearly dawn. Let's go out.'

Rajal groaned. 'You know what happened last time. Three nights with the shutters bolted! I thought I'd sweat to death!'

'It was good for you. You were getting fat.'

'Fat?' Rajal mimed outrage. 'Shall I wake Amed?'

'Please, no! I can do without her cow-eyes for a while.'

'She can't help it,' said Rajal. 'Imagine if I looked just like Jem. I'd have a few cow-eyes from you, I dare say.'

'I see what you mean. But don't wake her, hm?'

Carefully the pretended Princess climbed on to the ornate table that filled the centre of the van. With the stealth of a lioness she swung herself upwards, clambering on to the narrow roof. From below, beside the van, came the soft grunts of a dozing sentry. Perhaps it had been a mistake to disguise the guards. When they dressed as commoners, their immaculate discipline soon began to decay. With a smile, Cata reached down a hand, helping Rajal to follow.

'If they catch us this time,' he hissed, 'they'll *never* trust us.'

'Who cares? We're nearly there, aren't we?'

'At the Sacred City? You said you didn't know!'

Cata held a finger to her lips. Keeping low, she began to edge her way along the top of the van, then on to the one beside it. Rajal followed, troubled and reluctant. All around them pressed the cold darkness that soon would give way to dawn.

They slipped down from the vans and dashed into the dunes.

❋   ❋   ❋   ❋   ❋

How much time had passed?

Bean jerked awake. It seemed later, much later, though perhaps it was only moments since he had sunk back into oblivion. There was a pressure of vomit in the back of his throat and his heart throbbed hugely. He stared at the moon. He shivered. He huddled into himself.

Then he heard the voices.

'You detect her presence?'

'She is near, near. To be sure, Ouabin, you need not doubt me. Before this night is over, you shall possess your bride. Without the crystal that embodies my powers, it is true that I am diminished in this sub-godly realm. But to find a magical girl – can that be beyond me?'

'Ho! I heard you had long sought such a girl!'

'Fool, would you speak of what you cannot understand?'

'A man's desire for a wench? I think I understand *that* well enough!'

'Hush, I say! Have you not learnt that I am no man, but appear only in man's semblance? Believe then that the one I seek is no mere woman, in your coarse and sensual understanding of the word.'

'Ho! But neither is the woman who is to be *my* bride.'

'Indeed, Ouabin. Perhaps, then, you perceive my pain?'

'Indeed, Golden One. Would I offend a god?'

The words were low, almost whispered, but travelled clearly on the desert night. At first, they meant nothing to Bean, drifting over him unregarded. Then something in their ardour made his awareness sharpen. Bean felt the drumbeat of his slow, heavy pulse. Turning his head, he saw a mysterious glow rising over the humped blackness of the dunes. He rolled painfully on to his belly, crawling forward over the dark sand.

Peering over the dune, Bean saw the two figures, one, glinting in the moonlight, still in the golden, bloodied robes he had worn on the day of the Ritual of Rebonding, the other, golden too, but giving out a radiance of his own.

'Golden One,' said the Ouabin, 'do you see her yet?'

'I tell you, she is near. My powers are depleted, but if I focus on her, only her . . . yes, ah yes. Disguised, perhaps, but visible to the eyes of a god.'

A sabre flashed. 'Come, let us take her!'

There was a hollow laugh. 'Hasten not, Ouabin, she is guarded well. There shall be no crude hacking with primitive weapons. Our attack shall be aimed at the mind, at the heart, a signal to draw forth the one we seek. You would have her unharmed, would you not? We shall wait until dawn, when I sense that her resistance will be at its weakest.'

Reluctantly, the Ouabin sheathed his scimitar. 'To think that I am reduced to this! For a man who has sacked cities, is it not an ignominy to skulk in these dunes?'

'You would shun my assistance? My powers were drained in saving your life, Ouabin. I am not as I was, but remember, you have lost your tribe, your forces, your fame. Without me, you would be a friendless outlaw, with no hope of achieving the desire of your heart. But I have no wish to taunt you, Ouabin.' A smile played across the golden face. 'I say again what I have said before: for you the earth . . . for me, the moon and stars. Have I not told you that your quest is vital to mine? Where should we be without the lady? Now think no more of these matters; think only of the triumph that is soon to be yours. When you clasp your rightful bride, I shall spirit you to the Flame, there to burn away the false treasure, exposing the true beneath.

'But come, I have given you the looking-glass. Stare into my eyes, and you shall have the power you need to secure for it a lovely and valuable tenant.'

The Ouabin stood close against the god, like a lover. When he turned away again, his eyes burned with light.

❊   ❊   ❊   ❊   ❊

'We should go back, shouldn't we?'

'Raj, really! Don't you want to see the dawn?'

'That's why. They'll find out we're gone.'

Cata sighed. 'So? They're hardly going to hurt us, are they?'

'Not the Princess! What about me?'

'You're a girl, remember? It does have some advantages.'

'Many, I'm sure. In fact, I know.'

'You've been converted?'

'I wouldn't go that far.'

Hidden amongst the dunes, Cata and Rajal strolled like sisters, their fingers twined together, their jewels jangling, their gowns trailing in the sand behind them. The gibbous moon was turning pale. A purple glow filled the horizon and Cata felt an answering glow in her heart, a strange happiness that spread through her veins, as if with the intimation that all would be well. She gazed ahead, poised for the raw beauty of blood and gold that soon would spill across the wave-like dunes.

In Rajal's heart there was a different sensation. An ache. An emptiness. His hand went to the place where his crystal should be and he asked obliquely, 'Do you feel her? I mean, do you know she's there?'

'The Princess? I'm aware of a presence. But I know I'm me, not her. It's as if . . . as if I've become a container for something rare and precious, something I have to keep safe, locked away until it's time to bring it forth. A ring, perhaps. Or a jewel. Yes, a jewel.'

Rajal nodded glumly. In these moonlives in the van, he had come to know Cata well. He had heard the stories of her childhood, of her early days with Jem, of the horrors that since had pulled them apart. To all this he listened with a fascinated envy, but when Cata asked for his own stories, Rajal was guarded. Warmly enough he told her of the Vaga-van and his lost sister Myla; he told her of Great Mother Xal and Zady; but there was much, too much, that he could not say. He thought of passions that had churned inside him since childhood and a panic of despair rose to his throat. He thought of what had happened in the Palace of Perfumed Stairs and his shame was all-enveloping. No one – not Cata, certainly not Jem, no one at all – must ever know the truth. He would think of Vizier Hasem and shudder, disgusted, but he would feel a stirring of desire too; then his disgust would grow deeper, for what disgusted him was himself. Sometimes at night, as he lay in the van, his hand would creep to the place where he should have kept the crystal and in a silent, tearful rage Rajal would think, *I have had my punishment. I have had my just punishment.*

But sometimes, he thought his punishment had only begun.

They were sitting, hands still linked, gazing towards the sunrise, when Cata said suddenly, 'It can't be true about the Vizier, can it?'

Rajal's voice cracked. 'What? What about the Vizier?'

Cata said curiously, 'Raj? Are you all right? I mean about the Vizier, whether he's suspicious. I mean, I just thought, no, it can't be true. He'd have said something, wouldn't he, done something . . . Raj? Something's wrong, isn't it?'

Rajal shook his head curtly. 'No, no. I was thinking, that's all. About . . . Amed, actually.' Yes, Amed. She was the one who had started all this trouble.

Wretched little thief!

Cata said, 'You like Amed now, don't you?'

'She's got pluck. I wouldn't say I . . . *like* her.'

'She's annoying, it's true.'

Rajal sniffed. 'She used to be a thief.'

'A thief!' Cata had to laugh. 'I've been things . . . perhaps worse than that. Haven't you done something shameful, Raj?'

He shrugged. 'My life's been hardly so . . . colourful as yours, Cata.'

She squeezed his hand. 'I don't quite believe you. But I love you anyway.'

Rajal took a gulping breath. 'You . . . love me?'

'Jem loves you. I must too, mustn't I?'

Leaning forward, Cata kissed Rajal lightly and smiled. His eyes looked into hers with a dark intentness; a moment later, he had collapsed into her arms, bitterly sobbing, 'Oh Cata, Cata! I'm so unhappy!'

The blood and the gold spilt across the dunes, but now Cata had no eyes for the sun; she did not exclaim over its beauty; she did not feel intimations of a strange transcendence; nor did she see the figure on the dunes above them, looking towards them with glowing eyes. There was only Rajal, poor Rajal. Bewildered, Cata sat stroking her friend, as if he were one of the frightened creatures, the squirrels or robins or quivering lizards, that had come to her in the Wildwood, long ago. But their sorrows had been simple, and she could read them clearly; with Rajal, Cata had no power to understand or to help him. What could be wrong with him? What could be wrong? Gently she rocked him back and forth.

Only when it was too late did she become aware of the presence.

Princess. Princess, come.

Cata stared over Rajal's shaking shoulder. Rashid Amr Rukr held a shard of looking-glass that flashed in the sunrise with a strange brightness; brighter still was the gold of his eyes. In the first moment, Cata felt a surge of fear; in the second, there was anger, and she would have struck out; then the third moment came too soon.

The Ouabin drew back, smiling, beckoning. Cata stumbled upright, letting Rajal slump into the sand.

'Cata?' he murmured. 'Cata?'

There was no reply. Cata felt herself falling forward, as if into a dimension beyond her own. It was something to do with the stranger's eyes, but something to do with the looking-glass too. Her arm swung towards it, not to strike it away but to touch it, to embrace it.

The Ouabin cackled with savage glee.

'Cata!' Rajal cried out now. 'Cata, fight against it!'

Then came another voice. 'Princess, no!'

It was Amed. Coming to find her friends, she was suddenly horror-struck. Starting forward, she would have wrestled Cata to the ground, dragging her forcibly from the Ouabin's enchantment. There was no time. All at once there was another figure, rearing up from the sands.

'Princess! It's his eyes! Don't look in his eyes!'

The new intruder was a lanky, ragged creature, bruised and bleeding and barely able to stand. He lunged forward with the last of his strength, flinging sand into the golden eyes.

Rashid Amr Rukr shrieked. He swung round, striking with the shard of glass.

Then it was Amed's turn to scream.

In the next moment the Ouabin had vanished and Amed too, spirited away into the looking-glass. Her cries died hollowly, unreally on the air as Cata slumped down, gasping, appalled.

The magic was over when the next voice came.

'Princess! Princess, what are you doing?'

Cata looked up. Angrily the chief of guards strode towards her.

Cata looked down. Swiftly she took in the new dilemma. The stranger had collapsed. Rajal huddled over him. A moment more and the chief of guards would see the blood, the bruises, the lanky male form. The stranger had saved her. Somehow, quickly, she must save him, too.

She darted towards the guard, smiling winsomely. 'We're coming back, never fear. It's just' – Cata attempted a high, foolish giggle – 'one of my women has torn her gown. You wouldn't have her guilty of . . . immodesty, would you? Give me your cloak and I'll wrap her up. Then she can come back. I mean, then *we* can come back. Hm?'

The guard bowed reluctantly to the royal will and removed his capacious cloak. On the way back to the van it was still too dark, and he was too busy grumbling, to pay much attention to the huddled form that Cata and Rajal bore between them.

For once, Cata was glad when the door of the van slammed behind her. Only later, after they had bathed his face, would she realise that her saviour from the sand was no stranger at all.

So it was that Amed was replaced by Bean.

Chapter 65

A TALE FOR LITTLE KALED

'Come, old friend. Come, sit by me.'

The old man moved forward stiffly, struggling to conceal the wariness in his eyes. This summons was unexpected, and confused him. It was the middle of the afternoon, and the busiest afternoon Simonides had known for many sunrounds. Pilgrims thronged the city, jostling for places on the great boulevard. Royal guests filled the palace. The wedding, anticipated for so long, was now only a sunset away, and the Sultan had insisted that Simonides, and no other, officiate at the ritual. Much as the old man longed to do so, he feared that his stength might soon fail him – alas, that even the preparations should be too much for him!

His lord and master reclined, with an indolence that seemed, perhaps, a little affected, in the sunlight that slanted through an elaborate screen. He might have commanded a slave to open the slats just a little further, disclosing the historic scene below; instead he preferred not to see the thousands upon thousands of jostling commoners. Perhaps it was as well: if the sight was impressive, it was alarming, too. Over the last day and night, there had been further tremblings of the earth and the air was febrile with excitement and fear. Troupes of doom-dancers were out in force and many feared the hysteria that might break out when darkness fell.

The Sultan patted the space beside him and Simonides sat down. Drapings of luxurious pleated curtains surrounded the immense, ornately patterned couch. Slaves were on hand at once with Jarvel, sherbet and hava-nectar, but Kaled saw no eagerness in his visitor's eyes and waved them away impatiently. He reached out, taking the old man's hand.

'You are well, old friend? You are well now?'

'Sultan, health is not to be hoped for in a man of my years; what is age but a time of afflictions, gathering and growing until at last they prove fatal? I desire only to do your bidding, and see the Prince safely married.' The old man was struggling a little, but smiled and added, 'I am thankful, at least, that the marriage is tonight. After all, I dare say I shall live until the morrow.'

'And for long after, old friend! Speak not of death, when you are so sorely needed – and loved so well. But come, tell me, have you seen my brother? Fat as ever? Still simpering? But of course . . . to think, had I no heir, he would inherit my throne! Imagine it: Sultan Oman! I think the glory days of our realm would be well and truly over then, would they not, old friend?'

Simonides smiled dutifully, then nodded as the Sultan turned his attention to the tremblings of the earth. To be sure, the monarch insisted, these rumblings and rockings expressed no more than the fire god's impatience. Impatience? Why, for the wedding, of course! Fools might speak of doom, but how could doom come, with the Prophet's Line now certain to continue? What need was there for fear? After the wedding, the earth would be still, still and solid as it had always been . . .

'But old friend, enough of this nonsense! Tell me of the Princess! You have seen her too?' The Sultan, it appeared, was determined to establish a mood of pleasantry. 'How I curse – but not really, old friend, not really – how I curse this protocol that keeps her from my view! Dearly indeed should I love to see a girl of such beauty – a girl, I am told, with all her *mother*'s beauty.'

'You shall see her soon enough, when the ceremony begins,' Simonides said warily, and wondered if he would need to say any more.

During all this, he felt the pressure of the Sultan's fingers, stroking, stroking at his withered hand. The old man's eyes were sad as he looked into the dark, bearded face. What a strange man was this monarch! Had tenderness and cruelty, goodness and evil, ever been so hopelessly, desperately intertwined? In the green days of his first ardent faith, Simonides would have been startled by so mixed a nature, and wondered at the ways of the gods; now he knew those ways were more mysterious than he had ever once believed, and not to be fathomed by the minds of men.

As we grow older, the world becomes stranger; so said the Adages of Imral, and Simonides knew it to be true.

Now the Sultan asked after his heir. 'How I envy you, Simonides, how I envy the long days you have spent in the company of my dear boy . . . but do I call him *boy*? After tonight, he is boy no more! But old friend, tell me, do you judge him ready to assume the mantle that shortly shall descend upon him, never to leave him unburdened again?'

'He is a boy of great promise. Alas, I fear he is not strong!'

'Old friend, you alarm me!'

'Had you another son, your alarm would now be less.'

Simonides, perhaps, should have held his tongue, but only for so long could he forbear from stating the truth. The Sultan showed no anger. He merely sighed, and though the afternoon light was declining, Simonides was sure he detected a tear, welling in the corner of the monarch's eye.

'From so old a friend, I hoped not to hear words so cruel. Was I to take another wife, after the loss of my beloved Bela?'

'There are those who would have done, for reasons of state,' Simonides said cautiously.

'There are higher demands.'

'How can that be, when affairs of state are affairs of the gods? What are you, but the world's proxy for that god who speaks to you from the Sacred Flame? Omnipotent you may be in this worldly sphere, but as the most senior of your Imams, I speak with the authority of the sphere that lies beyond.'

'Old friend, I know it, and know you would chastise me. Very well, speak to me as you spoke to me in my youth; tell me of my errors, and the guilt I must feel.'

'Sultan—'

The Sultan laid a finger to the old man's lips. 'I am Sultan, and you disobey my words? Speak to me, I say, as you spoke to me in my youth.'

Simonides breathed in deeply. That the Sultan was playing a game he had no doubt; where that game might be leading, he was not yet sure.

'Kaled,' he began, 'you have made a vow that you think of as sacred, but one that has meaning only in your own heart. The Flame declared you Sultan of the Moon and Stars, but such a title is not only a reward for the glories that have been; with it, too, come responsibilities, to ensure that greater glories may come. Alas, ten sunrounds have passed and your reign has yet to bring those glories. These kingdoms have come to a time of great peril. You speak of the burden that soon your son shall assume, but have you shouldered your own burden as you should have done?'

'Simonides, indeed you are cruel, for but days, mere days have passed since the terrible knowledge came to me that the Ouabin had corrupted the Ebahns. Would you taunt me, that such evil can flourish under my reign? Yet did not the Flame vouchsafe this knowledge to me, as to a trusted deputy? Did not I put the traitors to death, at once and without demur, though it seared my heart to destroy so time-honoured, so sacred a corps? Old friend, you torment me for the blasphemies of my youth, but have I not put that time of doubt behind me? And is this not now a time of especial trial?'

Simonides said sadly, 'Kaled, I would not torment you; only counsel you as you set out on the dark road ahead. With a frail Prince, with a marriage yet uncertain of success, with Ouabin evil abroad in this land, the Line of the Prophet stands in grievous danger. Why, not since the time of the Geden Bride has the future of these lands been so imperilled!'

Simonides, as he delivered this verdict, found himself trembling. What happened next shocked him. As the old man spoke, Kaled's face had crumpled; now, like his son in the depths of grief, the big, dark man abandoned himself, doubling over on his plush couch as the sobs, loud and guttural, broke from his throat.

'Kaled! My child, my child!' Instinctively, Simonides reached out, embracing the man as he had embraced the boy. For long moments he held the Sultan tightly. The declining daylight shimmered around them, enveloping the two men in a golden haze.

'Old friend,' mumbled the Sultan at last, 'will you tell me a story . . . tell me a story, as you did when I was a boy?'

Simonides stroked the dark-bearded face. Pain flashed in his eyes as he recalled the words that must come next. This was a ritual set down in no sacred book, but one more valued once, by a small boy and his tutor, than any of those that were.

He began with difficulty, 'Story? Little Kaled, what mean you by a story?'

'Old man, a tale of what happened long ago.'

'Little Kaled, what mean you by long ago?'

'Old man, I mean the times before I was born.'

'Little Kaled, that was but a short time ago.'

'Old man, I mean the tales of my ancestors.'

'Little Kaled, have I not told you all the tales?'

'Old man, but I would hear them again.'

'Little Kaled, which would you hear?'

The Sultan considered. He sat up, brushing his tears away, and smiled at the startled, troubled Simonides. 'Old man, tell me of the Geden Bride.'

The old man felt a coldness running up his back. Suddenly he no longer liked this game, but knew he was compelled to play it to the end.

He drew in his breath and began.

THE TALE OF THE GEDEN BRIDE

Little Kaled, it was in the time of Bulaq, Sultan of the Red Dust, that there occurred the tragic story I relate to you now. Know ye that of all Sultans of these Lands of Unang, Mesha Bulaq was amongst the greatest, for his destiny it was to unite the peoples of this dry subcontinent in worship of the one true god. All over Unang, from Bulaq's time forth, women and men would bow to the Sanctum of the Flame, and acknowledge Kal-Theron as the Sacred City.

But the ways of the fire god are tangled and strange, for though Bulaq knew such glories, there yet remained a great sorrow, clouding all the brightness of his reign. This was, that though he had fathered many daughters, he had but one son, and none of his wives could provide another. His Imams trembled, for when Bulaq was stricken with the jubba-fever, it seemed to them that the Line of the Prophet hung by a thread; more so, yet more so, since young Prince Ashar was himself a sickly boy and likely soon to die. Bulaq rallied, responding to the ministrations of Unang's finest physicians, but the fever left him with a weakness he was never again to escape. So it was that the Imams urged him that his son, though yet young, must assume at once the mantle of Heir Unquestioned, and take to himself a wife.

Now Bulaq was a proud man, and known to be such. He had never wished to think of the day when he would die, but his faith, he declared, was stronger than his pride. He said it would be as the Imams wished, but that a Prince of the Line could marry no hastily chosen bride. Only the fairest flower of Unang would suffice for the Heir Unquestioned; thus it came to pass that a search began, through all the many kingdoms and provinces that the Sultan, in his glorious reign, had brought under his imperial sway.

Now it happened that, about this time, stories reached the Imams of a disturbing blasphemy that had broken out in the far province of Geden. The Shah of Geden, it seemed, had a daughter of a beauty so bewitching that many would bow in worship to her image, when they should have been bowing to the Sacred City. In righteous anger, the Imams counselled Bulaq that this girl should be destroyed, but Bulaq, in his great wisdom, scorned their advice.

'Fools, what counsel is this? Long sunrounds of my reign have been devoted to subduing the Shah of Geden, binding him to my fealty. Your way would lead only to fresh rebellions, and hatreds that would never be expunged. See you not that this girl is a sign? This girl is sacred, and the bride that we have sought.'

The Imams would have demurred, but Bulaq declared that he had spoken to the Flame, and knew that what he had said was so. Thus it was that, instead of being punished by death, this girl was rewarded with the most splendid betrothal.

Preparations for the wedding proceeded apace and there was great joy through all these lands; for in truth, the cult of this lady had rapidly spread, and when she was married, she could be worshipped without question. When worshippers bowed to the Sacred City, they would be bowing, too, towards the Geden Bride.

Alas, they knew not that tragedy was to ensue, for I have told you, Little Kaled, that your ancestor Prince Ashar was a sickly boy. As is the custom in these Lands of Unang, the wedding was to occur at midnight in the Sanctum of the Flame. All assembled for the ceremony. There was the Chief Imam, who was to perform the rites; there was Mesha Bulaq, Sultan of the Red Dust; most splendid of all, in the eyes of the mob, was the Geden Bride. At last they awaited only Prince Ashar, whose role it

452

was to proceed, last and in greatest glory, down the boulevard towards the womanly vessel who was to ripen the fecund seed of his loins. But young Prince Ashar was never to arrive. Imagine the horror that consumed all when it was revealed that the Prince had died, collapsing in his chamber, mere moments before his marriage!

Terror gripped the mob, for it seemed now that the Line of the Prophet was severed indeed, and doom must befall the Sultan's realms. But the mob were fools, reckoning not with an ancient provision in the marriage customs of Unang. It is true that once a ceremony of marriage has begun, it cannot be discontinued; when a bride is in place at the Sanctum, she must be blooded that night. But should it come to pass that the bridegroom die, or be killed, before he makes his progress to the Sanctum, his brother takes his place; and should there be no brother, then the role must be his father's. Thus it was that Sultan Bulaq that night plighted his troth to the Geden Bride. At this, there was great rejoicing, for if any woman could provide the monarch with the heirs he needed, surely it was the Geden Bride, in whom all saw the perfection, the very apotheosis of womanhood.

Yet there was one who did not rejoice, and that was the Shah of Geden. Standing to the side of the Sanctum steps, the Shah watched impassively as his daughter was married; but in the secrecy of his heart, he burned with hatred for the Sultan and all his ways. Until his lands had been subdued, the Shah and his peoples had been the merest idolatrous heathens. In truth, the Shah was still a heathen in his heart, as events were soon to prove. The ceremony ended and the time came to bear the Geden Bride to the consummation chamber. That was when the Shah's anger broke at last from his control and he stepped forward suddenly, flourishing a large and menacing dagger.

He cried, 'The wicked Sultan has killed his son, that he might violate the virtue of my daughter! This blasphemy shall not be allowed to proceed!'

With that, the Shah stabbed Sultan Bulaq, and would have stabbed his own daughter too, had a guard not intervened at that moment, slicing the infidel's head from his body. The Geden Bride screamed as her new husband, then her father, fell dead at her feet.

Now it was that terror gripped all who were there, mob, Imams, courtiers, guards alike, for at once they saw that these lands in which they lived were lands with neither Sultan nor heir. From this moment on, it seemed, Unang Lia would be plunged into bloody war, and never know again the peace and unity which Bulaq's long campaigns, in the end, had brought. The Line of the Prophet had been broken, and no future remained but chaos and despair. Yet, such is the mercy of the all-powerful one, that this terrible destiny was not to come to pass.

The Geden Bride stepped forward and held up her hands. At once, the sacred lady brought silence to the crowd.

'Women and men of Unang, despair not, for though a terrible tragedy has been enacted here tonight, this is not the end of the Prophet's Line!'

Confusion reigned. All wondered what the lady could mean, but such was the reverence in which she was held that none would do more than listen intently to the astonishing words that now fell from her lips.

She sank to her knees, possessed by sacred truth. 'Women and men of Unang, it was ordained that the events of this night should come to pass, that the Line, which has grown weak, should be purified and strengthened! Know ye, that though I remain a stranger to the consummation chamber, yet I feel nonetheless a burning, like liquid fire, deep within my womb! What can this be but the Essence of the Sultan, passing into my being in the moment of his death? Already, I say, his seed grows within me, and nine moonlives hence, I shall bring forth his heir! Fall to your knees with me, women and men of Unang, and bless the mercy of almighty Theron, God of the Flame, who has set this fiery kernel burning inside me!'

Thus it was that despair turned to joy, for all came to pass as the sacred lady had proclaimed. The Imams saw now that the Geden Bride was no force of ungodliness, to be rooted out and destroyed, but a sacred being sent by the fire god to save Unang in its time of greatest peril. So all, to this day, grant reverence to the Geden Bride, and to the sturdy son she brought forth by a miracle. That son would be Abu Makarish, Sultan of the Wave, and in the fourth epicycle of the Prophet's Line, Abu would extend the reach of Unang even further than his great and illustrious father had done in the third.

In the tale of the Geden Bride we may see the mysteries that destiny holds in store; but see, too, the greatness of our God of Flame, and the sacred rightness of our imperial sway.

Little Kaled, thus ends my story; let me but pray that you profit from its lesson, as many and many have profited from it before you.

❊   ❊   ❊   ❊   ❊

There was a long pause when the story was over. Kaled looked down reflectively, and Simonides wondered what was passing in his master's strange mind. That was when the old man found himself trembling, for the Sultan, after all, was a boy no more, and well aware of the blasphemous interpretations some had placed on the tale of the Geden Bride. Of course Simonides dismissed such interpretations, which only the wicked Ouabin had ever dared to voice. Could it be true that Bulaq, seized with lust for his son's bride, had seduced her before the wedding? Could it be true that Bulaq, indeed, had poisoned his own son, perhaps even at the prompting of his beauteous, but evil beloved? Lies, vicious lies!

Then, with a shudder, Simonides thought of the Shimmering Princess, whose beauty was said to rival that of her dead mother; shuddering again, he thought of Prince Dea, who was, like Prince Ashar, a weak and sickly boy . . . But what was he thinking? The old man cursed himself for a corrupt and profane fool and struggled to smile as the Sultan looked up at last, and took his hand.

'My thanks, old friend, for so fine a story. Man though I am, there is yet a boy inside me, and you have ministered to him well. How can I feel despair at the destiny of this realm, when your tale tells me that all shall be well? Old friend, you believe it, don't you? You must, and so must I. Go now; I am weary and would rest a little, before the travails of this night begin. Embrace me again; then go, go.'

But as Simonides left his master's chamber, he found his heart still heavier than before. The Sultan's words had not reassured him, only convinced him that he had been an unwilling participant in a game he should not have played. A terrible conviction was growing in the old man's heart, and with that conviction came another, more terrible still.

Yes. There was no choice now. It had to be.

Chapter 66

A RICH, BLOOD-LIKE LIQUID

Darkness had fallen. Simonides ascended the pale stairs again. Nights had passed, too many nights, since he had learnt the truth about Dea. For the old man, they had been nights of paralysis. With terror-filled eyes, he had watched as the young Prince played his midnight games. Simonides had said nothing, done nothing; more than this, he had *seen* nothing. Yes, that was it. Now, after the strange game he had played with the Sultan, the old man knew his blindness must end.

He trembled violently, as if with a fever. The powers he must invoke filled him with fear; punishment, he was certain, would descend upon him. But he must see, he must! If Simonides began to think that madness had claimed him, he no longer cared. The old spell filled his mind again, the formula he had never forgotten but borne inside him, like a seed, for sixty sunrounds or more. Now that seed would suddenly, riotously, sprout.

Simonides swooned on the incense of the garden. Silver-grey, gold-grey under the bloated moon, the foliage closed around him. He gazed along the parterres, fighting back the terror, the loathing that filled him. When he last used his powers, his father had died; what dire events would follow now? Oh, but he must hurry; perhaps already he had waited too long. At midnight, Dea would be borne to the Sanctum. Sickness rose in the old man's throat. He swallowed hard. With tremulous steps he made his way to the place where the boy and the ghost had played.

In the chamber below, even at this moment, the Targons would be dressing Dea in his ceremonial robes. Simonides had his own special garb. Hunched and furtive, he looked around him; then, from beneath the folds of his Imam's costume, he drew forth a moth-eaten length of cloth, spangled with stars like the night above. Horror filled his heart as he draped the fatal cape, his father's cape, round his thin, elderly shoulders. He sighed. He shuddered. Dea's robes would be seen by thousands, eagerly lining the taper-lit streets; no eyes, no human eyes, must see Simonides now. Stretching out his wizened arms, the old man shuffled in a circle.

He stopped. He gazed up into the darkness. His face contorted in agony as he forced the rhyme from his lips, imitating the tone of his long-dead father:

> *Theron, god of the sacred flame*
> *Come to the one who bears the name*
> *Of Simonides, servant true*
> *Of all your glories.*
>   *All you do*
> *Shall be reflected in his eyes*
> *That widen to a massive size*
> *To see through mists and shrouding fogs*
> *The workings of your secret cogs*
> *In time that far beyond us lies—*
> *The future of my undefiled*
> *Yet deeply threatened, lonely child*
> *You must reveal to me.*
>   *Theron, come!*
> *Grant me vision or strike me dumb!*

There was a moment of stillness when the rhyme was over. Simonides staggered a little, but did not fall. He stood, breathing deeply, aware of little more than his straining lungs and the heart that hammered like a drumbeat in his chest.

In the next moment, the old man collapsed to his knees, clutching his eyes and screaming.

❋   ❋   ❋   ❋   ❋

The Targons had finished their work. After the bathing, after the perfumes and powders, they had dressed the Prince in his wedding suit. They had bowed obeisance. They had swung incense. They had muttered prayers. Now they had left him.

This, the Prince knew, was his time of meditation. All had been explained to him: he must reflect on the boyhood he was leaving behind, and the life as a man that lay before him. Instead he paced restlessly. How long must he wait? Even through the thickness of the palace walls he could hear the clamour in the streets below, the crowds eager for their frail idol. He turned to the looking-glass, but it had gone. Nowhere in the chamber could he see his reflection. Curtains hung like screens, hiding him even from the gaze of the whisperers in the walls. Flame-red robes trailed heavily behind him. Trembling, he reached a hand to the ruby mask he wore. Oh let this night be over, let it soon be over!

Dea cast himself down on the divan. Struggling to ignore the hungry crowds, he concentrated on the hissing of the konar-lights. Turned low, they filled the chamber with a dark, reddish flickering. He sighed, feeling the tears well behind his mask. But no, he would not cry tonight, he would not! It was almost over. At any moment Simonides would come, leading him down, down through the palace to the litters that would bear them along the sacred route. Dea would not think of what else the night held for him. It did not matter. Nothing mattered now. Had Thal not made him a promise, a promise he had sworn he would never break?

The Prince clutched a cushion, holding it to his heart. A thought came to him: he would never return to this chamber, this place where he had played and laughed and cried, all through the long sunrounds of his boyhood. He did not care. Soon, soon, Thal would be waiting, ready to claim him for that other world. No, his boyhood was not over. After tonight, it would never be over. Dea hugged the cushion tighter.

A voice came. 'Practising for tonight?'

'F-Father! You startled me!'

With a smile, Sultan Kaled sat beside the boy. His eyes were like pools of infinite depth and stars glittered in his sleekly oiled beard. Gently he reached out, prising the cushion from Dea's hands. 'Ah my son, soon something better shall lie against your breast.'

The Prince looked into the deep, dark eyes. Why was his father here? This was not part of the ritual, was it? Rings glittered as the big hands reached towards him again, lifting the ruby mask from the young, frightened face.

'Ah, my son, let me look at you. Let me look at you one last time.'

'L-Last time, Father?'

The smile again. The shifting stars. 'I mean, my son, in a manner of speaking. When I next see you, will you not be translated into a different mode of being? Indeed you shall, for that is the destiny that lies before you tonight.'

Dea gulped.

The Sultan ran a hand over the boy's pounding chest. 'Poor Dea, you stare, and I see the tears that brim in your eyes! You have reached the climax of your life. At the threshold of so great a change, would not even the bravest of men feel fear? Tremble not, my son. Feel no shame. Think of all that fate has prepared for you. The journey down the boulevard. The ceremony on the steps. The dark encounter in the consummation chamber. Indeed, indeed you *must* feel afraid.'

Now the Sultan drew the boy into his arms, embracing him tightly and whispering into his ear, 'Fear not, I say! You marvel, perhaps, that I intrude in this time of meditation. My son, I come in mercy. I come because I love you. It is my mission to ease your terrors, not with mere words, but with something more. Much more.'

He drew back. From the folds of his robes he produced a vial, its glassy sides dark with a rich, blood-like liquid. 'This is my mercy, sweet child.

458

Made according to an ancient receipt, this potion shall remove all the terrors from your heart. The Princess shall be wed; the consummation shall come; all shall happen in the immemorial order, but no fear, no fear at all, shall flutter at *your* heart.'

In those last moments, staring into the infinite eyes, Dea saw himself crying out, pushing away, striking the vial from his father's hand. But he did not. Could not. He knew, of course he knew, what this mercy meant. What could it be but the destiny he had awaited? The Sultan withdrew the stopper from the vial and a sour-sweet vapour curled up into the air.

'Drink, my son. Drink, and your troubles shall soon be over.'

The big hands cradled the boy's head, then stroked his hair as the mysterious potion slipped between his lips. For long moments the Sultan looked at his son, then kissed the boy lightly on the forehead and replaced the ruby mask.

'Goodnight, my son. Goodnight, my Prince.'

✻ ✻ ✻ ✻ ✻

'No!' cried Simonides. 'No, no!'

Sobs wracked his frame as he slumped amongst the flowers, a broken old man, his powers sapped away. He knew what had happened in the chamber below, knew it with a sudden, certain knowledge. Lying there, he wished he might never rise again; lying there, he wished only that his own death would come. Had he not slipped away to look into the future, the potion might never have passed Dea's lips. Cursed be his powers, curse them! To save the Prince's life, he would have given his own; to save the Prince, he would have killed the Sultan. There was no use imagining these heroics now. It was too late, and everything was over.

But it was not.

Mysterious music drifted on the night. Slowly Simonides raised his head. He gasped, brushing his eyes, and hauled himself to his knees. Astonishment filled him, then terror, then hope. What was this new magic? What could it mean? Dark against the moon was a flying carpet; upon it, riding the air, stood a pale youth.

The youth came closer. Closer.

The carpet settled lightly between the parterres.

Simonides gasped. 'Stranger, who are you? Has my magic brought you forth?'

The youth looked at him with equal astonishment.

Fear, too.

'Almoran? But how can it be?'

'Not Almoran, but of equal folly.' Simonides felt his powers come fluttering back. He had thought that all was lost. But no, not all. 'Youth, you are an emissary from my missing brother? Have you met him? Did you see him ... before he died?'

The youth nodded. 'You possess his magic?'

'Speak not of magic! It has brought me only sorrow. And yet ... you bring magic of a different cast. I know it. I sense it.'

The moonlit gardens pressed round them like a cocoon, fragrant and tremulous with mysterious power. Now the youth stepped from the carpet and clutched the old man's hands, drawing him slowly to his feet again. Simonides looked down and saw a green glow shining though the robes the stranger wore.

'Who are you? Who are you, sand-haired one?'

'My story is long, and would require much telling. For days, perhaps for moonlives, I have been lost in a strange dimension; since then, I fear, I have lost yet more time, whirling in the backwash of your brother's magic. Now I sense that time is short, and already the climax of this adventure is upon me. There can be no time for stories now. But old man, you know me, do you not?'

The Teller's eyes glowed. 'It is true, Key to the Orokon. Knowledge floods my heart.' He broke away, beckoning. 'There is much to explain. But quickly, come below. For my young Prince there can be no hope; there may yet be hope for these realms he was to rule. Somehow, his father's evil must be foiled, if your destiny, or ours, is ever to be achieved. Quickly, quickly. I have a plan.'

Chapter 67

THE LESS DECEIVED

'That's it. It's a question of why.'

Rajal smiled. 'No choice now.'

'That's not an answer.'

'Call it a vision. Call it a spell.'

'You've said that before,' said Bean. 'I think I get it. But that's not what I mean. I mean, she can't help the magic that made her this way – at least, I suppose not. But she seems to *want* to go through with it. I mean, as if she really wanted it. Doesn't she love the Prince? Nova, I mean?'

'You mean Jem.' Rajal looked down. 'Oh yes, she loves him. But you see, it's the crystal. I mean, the clue. When the Princess is married, the crystal comes.'

'That's what Polty thinks, too.'

'Hm. He believes it. She believes it. Perhaps it's true.'

'What about the Prince? Nova. I mean, Jem.'

'Jem has to be there when the crystal comes. Perhaps Cata hopes it will work the other way. I mean, if the crystal comes, Jem will come too.'

'Hm. This isn't looking good.'

'Well, no.'

They stood silently for some moments, gazing down at the taper-lit boulevard. All day the crowd had been assembling; there were bursts of song, keenings, prayers. Guards lined the route, ready to hold back the frenzies of emotion. Soon the noble guests would begin their stately procession, then the royal ministers, then the Imams. Soon it would be Cata's turn.

Time was running out.

Bean said, 'I've been thinking about that Ouabin song. Have you? I mean, really thought about it?'

'*Marry and burn*? Oh, I've thought about it.'

Rajal bit his lip. He turned back, peering through the half-opened shutters. In the apartment behind them, teams of slave-girls were completing Cata's elaborate preparations. They had bathed her; they had doused her in pungent balms; they had swept up her hair into complex coils. Now she stood, statue-like, as the red carapace of a Unang bride was assembled laboriously around her. There were paints to apply, pins to fix; there were jewels, flowers, charms. For a time, it had seemed that

461

the process would never end; now it was almost over. Cata had become a ruby vision, a creature who seemed barely to belong to this world. Only the fixing of the veil remained.

Bean said, 'I get the feeling we've been forgotten. What do *we* do at the wedding?'

'Us? Wait out the vigil, I suppose. Like the rest.'

'Down in the boulevard? That's not good enough.'

'I know.' Turning back, Rajal looked across the crowds to the vast edifice where the wedding would take place. How brightly, how evilly it shone in the moonlight! 'I want to get inside that place.'

'Impossible. Think of the guards.'

'Come on, Aron. Nothing's impossible.'

'You think so?'

Their hands lay side by side on the balustrade, almost touching. Rajal felt a curious surge of power.

Bean said, 'I feel so helpless, dressed this way.'

Rajal smiled. 'It saved your life.'

'You saved my life. You and Cata.'

'You saved ours. Remember?'

'I remember.'

They might have said more, but at that moment, echoing through the apartment, came the sound of knocking. The doors opened and suddenly, as if at a command, the slave-girls dispersed.

'Should we go too?'

'I suppose so. But we shan't.'

Drawing back into the shadows, they watched as, with ceremonial decorum, a fat little figure in an ornate chair was borne into the apartment. His taller companion strode behind. Both figures were elaborately robed and wore fearsome masks.

The bearers withdrew and the doors closed.

'Shimmy! Darling Shimmy!' Casting aside his mask, Caliph Oman Elmani held out his arms for the girl who looked like his daughter. Then he laughed, and struck the side of his head. 'Silly me! Did you see how silly I was, Hasem? Here am I, expecting Shimmy to rush into my arms. Poor dear, I'm sure you can barely move, can you? But let's just look at you. Just one more time before . . .' The little man broke off, collapsing in tears. 'My poor baby! My poor, poor baby!'

Cata took several stiff steps forward, her costume rustling and clanking. 'Father, fear not. I am ready for this night.'

The Caliph clasped her hands. 'My dear, I know. Forgive your fond father, but how is he not to sorrow when he loses his daughter? If I bless the magic that restored you to flesh, still I must curse that it took so long a time. What we have suffered! What we have missed! Darling Shimmy, if only we could live through your girlhood again!'

'Dear Father! It is my wish, too!'

On the balcony, Rajal whispered, 'She does it well, doesn't she?'

'You'd never know,' said Bean.

'So we hope.'

While the Caliph sobbed his fatherly tears, Vizier Hasem was pacing impatiently, staring incuriously at the tapestries that hung from the walls, at the richly gilded furnishings, at the looking-glasses that swam with soft, reddish light. By now he too had removed his mask, laying it carefully upon a low inlaid table. Watching him, Rajal felt again the surge of hatred that always overwhelmed him at the sight of this man. His heart pounded hard and he longed to rush forward, striking the cold, arrogant face.

Instead, he drew swiftly away, clutching Bean's arm, as the Vizier flung back the balcony doors. Sounds from the boulevard filled the apartment.

'Princess, do you hear?' The tall man turned back. 'Drumbeats. Cheers. The calling of pipes. Already the Sultan's courtiers make their way to the Sanctum. Soon it will be our turn, and we must accompany you down that long route. Do you tremble, child? Do you rue your fate?'

Puzzlement furrowed Cata's brow. She had never liked the Vizier, but now his tone seemed more than usually cold. There was something dismissive, something sardonic in the way that he addressed her. She stood beside the Caliph's chair, the little man's hand in hers. Slowly, the Vizier moved around them, as if pacing out an enchanted circle.

'No wonder if you quake,' the cold voice continued, 'for much – too much – depends upon this night. Do you know how much? *Quite* how much?'

Cata said, 'My lord Vizier, of course.'

The Caliph said, 'Hasem, what are you talking about?'

'Only about the destiny of these realms, Oman. Tonight you feel the emotions of any father, when the time to lose his daughter comes. Ah, but what greater emotions once racked our hearts! Do you recall the fears this marriage once roused in us? Do you recall the shame, the horror of your daughter's state? Think what rage would have descended upon us, had only the flickering shadow of a woman appeared tonight at this fateful ceremony.'

The Caliph laughed. 'But Hasem, that cannot be! Those fears are behind us, and Shimmy is whole again!'

Now the Vizier stopped his pacing, and leaned almost threateningly towards the little man. 'Really, Oman? Are you so sure?'

Alarm flashed in Cata's eyes. At any moment the bearers would be here, ready to take them down the boulevard. What was the Vizier saying? Could he really know the truth? Why, then, had he kept his silence until now? She struggled for words, but her mind reeled in confusion.

The Caliph tightened his grip on her hand. 'Hasem, I don't know what you're talking about. I really don't.'

'Then look, Oman!' The Vizier darted forward, seizing Cata by the arm. He dragged her to the looking-glass. 'I thought I could keep my counsel, but Oman, as I care for you, I can remain silent no longer! I tell you, the work of this night shall rebound upon us, with consequences worse than any we have feared before! What will the Sultan say, should he learn of this deception? He will blame us, Oman – he will blame *you*, and you will die!'

'Hasem, I swear, I don't know what you're talking about!'

Cata cried out, 'Let me go, let me go!'

'Peace, my haughty beauty! Twist, would you, and spoil your lovely gown? Writhe, writhe, it shall avail you nothing! Oman, look! You see her face? See how it flickers in and out of being? First your daughter's face . . . then another! While you have been blinded by your longing for your daughter, I have watched this girl closely, and been the less deceived! Oman, this is not your daughter! This girl is an impostor!'

The Caliph screamed, 'No! It cannot be!'

'It's true, Oman! Already her magic grows unstable. How long after the wedding shall this false seeming survive? This evil girl would arrogate to herself the powers of an Empress. Think what wrath shall descend upon us, should her impersonation fail! But if it succeeds? It must not, for this girl is evil incarnate!'

'You're wrong! You're mad!' Cata cried.

'Wrong, Princess? Or should I say Cata? Yes, well may you start – you are Catayane Veeldrop, runaway bride of the flame-haired Ejlander! Yes, oh yes, he told me all about you! Before he was consumed by strange magic, how ardently he sought you! How desperately he wondered what had become of you! But how could he have known? How could he have guessed? The fool thought you had become a mere common runaway, like half the harlots that fill the stews! I see now that even he, for all his own depravity, had barely sounded the depths of your evil female magic! Wicked slut, you have met your nemesis now!'

Still Cata tried to break away, but her costume weighed her down. Bands of jewels broke from her arms, skidding across the floor. Desperately she struggled to kick, to scratch.

'Why are you doing this? What do you want with me?'

'Want? Nothing from you, harlot. And soon, you too shall want nothing! Nothing ever again!'

'What are you talking about? What do you mean?'

The Caliph had collapsed, heaving with sobs. 'Hasem, you're wrong! Hasem, I don't believe it! Oh leave poor Shimmy, leave her, do! We were so happy! Cruel Hasem, how could you spoil my daughter's big day?'

The Vizier swung round, kicking his master and shrieking, 'Look, Oman! Look on as the harlot meets her fate! You know it's true, don't you? You know I wouldn't lie? You don't think we can let this girl be married, do you? There's only one thing for it! Remember the tale of the Geden Bride? Yes – that's it, but in reverse! The Princess, in her joy, must suddenly expire, turning this royal wedding ... into a funeral!'

'No! No ... let me go!'

Brutally the Vizier flung Cata to the floor. In the next moment he was astride her, a cushion clutched in his hands. The Caliph screamed. Cata screamed too, but her scream could not escape. Blackness descended. She was aware only of the cushion on her face and the weight of the body that pinned her down.

There was a cry. A blow.

Then another. Another.

Faster. Faster.

The blackness was gone, and the weight too, but on and on went the frenzied hammering.

'Raj ... Rajal! No!'

Cata struggled up, gasping, but it was Bean who pulled his new friend away. Rajal trembled and would have sunk to his knees if Bean had not clutched him and held him tight. The bloody mask fell from his hands as he looked down, horror-struck, at the Vizier's battered head.

'Raj ... you've killed him!'

❋　❋　❋　❋　❋

There was a different thudding.

This time, it was at the door.

'The bearers! It's time!'

The Caliph moaned. He slumped down, unconscious.

Breathless, awkward in her heavy dress, Cata lurched up from the floor. She thought quickly. 'There's only one thing to do.' She pointed at the Vizier. 'Get him out of those clothes. Wipe the blood off that mask ... Bean! You're tallest. Quick, you're going to be Hasem. Raj ... *Rajal! Pull yourself together!* You'll have to hunch up. This cushion ... that can be the belly.'

'What?' Rajal groaned. 'What?'

But Cata was busy with her elaborate costume, struggling to conceal, as best she could, the worst of the ravages.

'Just as well it's red,' she muttered grimly.

The thudding came at the door again.

Chapter 68

RITUAL IN THE DARK

'It's so beautiful!' cried Mother Madana.

'Pah! Why, the wealth wasted on those robes alone would buy a Baba-girl for every man in this crowd! Not to mention ferment for all!'

'You have no heart, Eli!'

'You're the one with no heart, crone! Didn't you promise to help us? Pah, pah! I don't believe you even have another sister! Could a sister of yours work in the Whispering Palace?'

Mother Madana said simply, 'Eli, shut up!'

With glistening eyes she watched the long line of Imams making their way up the ruby-crusted steps, assembling solemnly before the sacred doors. In their golden, bejewelled robes, they were a sight more magnificent than any she had ever seen. But then, she had thought the same of the royal ministers before them, and the noble guests before them, too. How could she see such beauty, and live? How could she bear it when the Sultan came, then the Princess, then the Prince? To the old woman, it seemed that the climax of her life was here at last. All through the journey to the Sacred City, she had felt the faith of her girlhood returning. How bitterly she regretted the impieties of the sunrounds since then, when she had cared nothing for the things of the spirit! Perhaps the destruction of the caravanserai had been no more than the punishment she deserved.

The air was a thunder of thudding drumbeats, riven with sobbings and ecstatic cries. The clamour, like the jewels, like the lights, like the crush, seemed to bear away all thought, all memory, all desire. What did it matter, all the squalors Mother Madana had seen, when she had come in the end to the Sacred City? She had secured her place in the front of the crowd, and would relinquish it for no one. Eli's plans meant nothing to her. Eli meant nothing to her any more.

A voice shouted in the whoremonger's ear: 'You're useless, Oily! Why did I put my trust in you?'

'Pah! Me, useless? What could I do, horsewhip the crone?'

'You've done worse!'

The greasy face twisted in exasperation. Suddenly Eli Oli Ali span round, seizing Polty by the collar, muttering savagely, 'Don't tell me I'm useless, Ejlander! Where would you be if you'd never met me? No harlots, no ferment, no Miss Catayane! Yes, I even had *her* in my grasp, didn't I? Is it my fault you lost her again? Without me, you wouldn't even be here in Kal-Theron now! Look at you! Look at yourself! Here you are, on your night of destiny, and what are you but a quivering ruin? Where's your power? Where's your resolve? Where's the magic that made you fly?'

'Oily,' Polty choked, 'Oily . . . let me go!'

Contemptuous, the whoremonger flung Polty away. The flame-haired one staggered back, cannoning into the crowd. Worshippers turned, enraged, then cheered as the whoremonger spat forcefully into the pallid, stricken face.

Perhaps they thought it was pious outrage.

'And don't call me Oily. I put up with a lot from you, when you had money and power! Look at you now! Just look at you now!'

☀   ☀   ☀   ☀   ☀

'Stop, thief!'

Stop? Never!

If the cry was repeated, it was to no avail. Lithe, laughing, tossing the coin-purse rapturously into the air, the boy in the loincloth weaved away. The noise around him was deafening. Emotion filled the air. The guards thought only of keeping back the crowd.

The Unners had found a paradise, ripe for raiding.

'Hey!' Fish span round as a hand swiped out, grabbing the purse he had just purloined.

Rank breath gusted into his face, laughing.

'Cheese! Give it back!'

'Can't catch me!'

'You bet?'

Heavy bodies lurched against them as they tore away. Elbows jabbed their sides. There were cuffings and cries. Ringing above the clamour came the sound of horns.

The imperial fanfare!

The Sultan was coming!

The crowd surged forward.

Fish cried out, 'Blubber!'

'Fish! Cheese! This way!'

They huddled together.

'It's getting too tight here,' Blubber shouted. 'Soon we won't be able to move.'

'You especially, Blubber!' grinned Fish.

'The rooftops!' said Cheese. 'Faha's up there, hiding the spoils. Stork too!'

'Let's go!'

Only Fish floundered. A hand clapped on his shoulder. Voices shrieked.

'He stole that purse!'

'Dirty little thief!'

'In the Sacred City!'

'On this sacred night!'

Fish kicked. He scratched.

'Stop, thief!'

Stop? Never!

When the rumbling came, moments later, Fish had vanished with the rest of the Unners. The rumbling, of course, had come before, but none had expected it now, just as the Imams in their golden cowls solemnly ascended the ruby steps. A boom like thunder filled the night, but this thunder, terrifyingly, came from below, rippling along the boulevard as if a hideous, enormous creature struggled to break through the crust of the earth. The ground shook. Stones fell. Burning tapers toppled into the crowd.

It was over quickly. In moments, order was restored; in moments, guards had beaten back the hordes that had crashed, screaming, across the processional route. Pilgrims cowered. Some were dead. Some were burned. Some were bleeding. Many abased themselves, muttering portentously of the Sacred Flame, its impatience, its envy, its mystic power.

One curious incident had occurred during the chaos. When the rumbling began, two of the Imams, doddering old men, had been flung from the side of the ruby steps. In the darkness left by a toppled torch, two figures set upon them, brutally and decisively.

'Oily! Quick! This is our chance!'

Moments later, the missing Imams took their place on the steps, their cowls drawn tightly about their heads. From one cowl came a whisper. 'Major-sir? You know I didn't mean a word I said!'

From the other: 'I know, Oily, I know!'

Already their hapless victims lay crushed, unrecognisable, under the feet of the surging mob.

❋   ❋   ❋   ❋   ❋

The tremblings of the earth were soon forgotten, at least by most, as Sultan Kaled assumed his place.

Through the spiky carapace of his royal mask, the monarch's eyes blazed. Gazing along the broad, cracking boulevard, the pretended Sultan of the Moon and Stars thought nothing of the dead bodies, or the debris, or the moans of the injured. Jewels and chunks of stone still fell from the columns above him; dust billowed, but he did not care. All he saw was the distant, brightly lit arc of the palace gates, gleaming like the portal of another world. Through that arc, sailing forward on litters of gold, came the beautiful, veiled Princess, flanked by his fatuous brother and his brother's tall Vizier.

Kaled's heart exulted. Behind him, in silent lines, filling the immense steps, ranged the cowled Imams and noble dignitaries. What were they but the merest grovelling insects, every bit as insignificant as the common pilgrims crushed against the barriers, screaming and moaning? He was superior to them all, but when this night was over he would be superior to all the world! He would be as a god! Even now, it seemed, he could taste, almost touch the power that soon would be his. So, only the man who married the Shimmering Princess would possess, in truth, the title he had claimed, here on these steps, ten sunrounds ago? Very well, let it be so! But he would be that man!

Amongst the Imams, masked by the music and cries, there occurred the following whispered exchange:

'Oily?'

'Major-sir?'

'What do we do now?'

'Hm. Here comes the Princess. The boy's next. They exchange vows on the steps . . . the doors open . . . then they're taken up to the consummation chamber.'

'Consummation?'

'Yes, it's what's you think. They're locked in all night. Meanwhile, we keep a vigil in the Sanctum. The crowd keeps a vigil out here.'

'Oily?'

'Major-sir?'

'But what do we *do*?'

No such questions filled Kaled's mind. As eunuchs helped the Princess down from the litter, it was as much as he could do not to burst forward there and then, sweeping the girl into his arms. Damn this pretence! But the climax of the procession was almost here. In moments to come, the pilgrims would abase themselves before the Princess. Then it would be time for the Prince to join her.

Kaled wanted to laugh aloud. By now Simonides would have gone to the boy's chamber, ready to fetch him from his meditations. By now the old man would have cried out, sinking down in horror and shock. Soon, soon, the message must come! Soon the Sultan must clutch his son's bride, bearing her in triumph to the consummation chamber! His heart pounded as she took her place beside him. The pilgrims bowed, mumbling prayers.

A different mumbling came from behind the Princess.

'Rajal?'

'Aron?'

'What do we do now?'

'Hm. Let's think. We keep the vigil. Meanwhile, Cata's upstairs, fending off the Prince. Or whatever. At dawn, the Chief Imam gets them out . . . takes them to the Flame . . . they bow and scrape to the fire god, I suppose. Then they come out here again. Proclamations. Cheers. Universal joy.'

'Rajal?'

'Aron?'

'I know all that. But what do *we* do?'

Horns sounded. There was a roll of drums. The crowd rose and Kaled stretched forth his arms. Standing in the centre of the ruby steps, he was a figure of awe and fear. Jewels gleamed like stars in his heavy, dark robes and his mask flickered and danced in the light of the burning tapers. His voice, when it came, was like the voice of a god, echoing from a distant dimension. Many gasped. Some collapsed.

'Pilgrims!' cried the Sultan. 'You have come tonight before the Sanctum of the Flame to witness this most sacred moment of my reign. Sunrounds ago, on the brink of manhood, I was brought here by my father to affirm my place as heir; my own son, too, has been likewise affirmed. In this place, I wed my only bride, your Empress, who died so tragically and so soon. In this place, the obsequies for her death were held. Yes, many sacred moments have I marked in this place, but none more sacred than the one I mark now, which ensures the continuance of the Prophet's Line. After tonight, my work will be done. After tonight, my spirit may fly, when it is ready, to the regions of eternity, as did my father's, and his father's before him. Drummers! Send the command along the boulevard! Bring forth my son to the place of his wedlock!'

Rapture filled the Sultan's heart. He could have leapt for joy. Yes, his spirit would be flying to eternity, but not like his father's, or his father's father's! Already he felt himself surging above the world, soaring ecstatically through the vastness of space. Already power seemed to flood his veins. Already it seemed he would never die.

The drums carried their message. Kaled tensed. Now, now, would come the anguished cries, the shocked revelation! Desperately he stared above the heads of the crowd, his eyes fixed on the palace gates.

Then, through the glittering arc, emerged the litter.

Kaled trembled. A cry broke from his lips.

He slumped to his knees.

The crowd thought it was the strength of his piety, overwhelming the man who seemed, that night, to be a great leader after all.

※　　※　　※　　※　　※

Cata breathed deeply. Since arriving in this strange land, she had faced many trials, and faced them with courage. Now, as her suitor bowed before her, fear filled her heart. It was not the boy who frightened her; not his father, nor the crazed crowd, nor the sinister, cowled figures ranged behind her. Rather, she felt the reality of what she was about to do. A terrible foreboding descended upon her as she wondered how this night would end. Trembling, she saw the glimmer of an eye behind the mask.

The boy took his place beside his father.

Simonides stepped forth, standing before a burning brazier. By now the pilgrims had clustered forward, spilling across the processional route. There were no more barricades; the guards had dismounted, sheathing their scimitars. All was a fervour of spiritual expectation. The brazier's flames shimmered and flashed across the bright figures at the front of the steps.

The ceremony began with blessings, prayers and sacred songs. Simonides delivered a long ritual address, speaking of the sanctity of the marriage bond, of the harsh burdens of imperial rule, and calling upon the fire god to bless this union.

'Pilgrims,' he cried at last, 'the moment has come! Tonight, we mark the dawn of a new age! Tonight, we deny the forces of evil, banishing them for ever from these sacred realms! For yes, the dark ones cluster even now, bent on rending what now I join! It is to no avail! They shall have no dominion! Destiny has decreed that this marriage come to pass, and no power in this world is strong enough to prevent it! Children, come forward! I unite you now!'

Cata started as the old man reached for her hand, wrenching her almost brutally towards the brazier. Her eyes blurred, smarting at the flames. Her temples pounded and her face grew hot. She was standing beside the masked boy. At dawn, she knew, they would stand here again, her veil gone, his mask removed. She thought of what lay in the time between and a sick apprehension rose inside her.

From a bowl held by a kneeling slave, Simonides scooped up a glittering powder. He flung it into the brazier. There was a flash. Smoke billowed forth. Cata staggered at the force of the cheers that erupted suddenly from the spellbound pilgrims. In the next moment, the horns rang out again. Immense doors rumbled open behind them and the lesser dignitaries parted, letting first the Imams, then the Sultan, then the boy and his bride pass through the sacred portals, to the ominous thudding of a single drum.

Simonides gripped Cata's hand tightly, leading her forward like a sacrifice.

Chapter 69

IN THE WARM ROOM

The consummation chamber lay at the top of a broad staircase that curved up between walls of glimmering, bejewelled stone. Motioning for Cata and the boy to follow, Simonides slowly climbed the stairs. Below, the inferior Imams arranged themselves in the antechamber; only the Sultan, at this time, ventured to the Flame. From without, there came the thudding of the drum; then the great portals clanged shut, and there was silence. Or almost: even through thickness after thickness of stone, Cata heard a sinister, fiery hiss.

Before them lay a vast, jagged boulder that rolled away, as if by magic, when Simonides raised his arms. They found themselves in a barren hall. Cut deeply in the rock, it was chill and windowless, but harshly bright, lit from mysterious, glowing panels, spaced around the walls. The floor was brightly polished, almost like a looking-glass. At the far end, standing as if at attention, was a party of five elaborately garbed eunuchs.

Cata's brow furrowed in puzzlement.

'Fear not, my children,' said Simonides, 'it is not in this harsh hall that you must consummate your love. In a moment I shall leave you, and the Eunuchs of the Bedchamber shall guide you into the realm that lies beyond. It is a realm of pleasure, but remember,' he added cryptically, 'that upon what passes in that realm of pleasure, the destiny of greater realms may turn. Bless you, my children. I return at dawn.'

The boulder rolled back into place when the old man had gone. Then the eunuchs were gliding towards them, reaching for them with caressing hands, and slowly, strangely, an alteration came over the scene. First the barren rock of the walls was gone, then the glassy harshness of the floor; then, for all the world as if they had passed, unknowing, through a mysterious barrier, they found themselves in a chamber of a wholly different character. Only the glowing panels were the same, but now the light was a soft gold, playing sensually over lush carpets, couches, cushions, laden tables, entangling flowers and vines. Warm breezes wafted on the air. There were gorgeous draping fabrics; there were rich inlaid screens; there were looking-glasses with golden frames; but dominating the chamber, commanding all attention, was the immense bed, strewn with fragrant petals.

A eunuch appeared with two brimming goblets; another with a

bubbling Jarvel-pipe. The ministrations of the slaves would have gone on, proceeding to the last intimacies, but all at once a calm, clear voice came from behind the Prince's mask:

'That will be all. You may leave us now.'

The eunuchs fluttered. They exchanged glances.

Cata was puzzled, too. That voice. That voice.

It came again: 'Go. Leave us.'

The third time, the Prince had to shout.

The eunuchs scurried together, then suddenly they were gone, though where they had gone, Cata could not tell.

She turned, troubled. It was then that she glimpsed herself in a looking-glass.

Her eyes. There was something about her eyes.

She reached up, removing her veil. This time, her visage had not merely flickered. Could it be her false face had slipped for good? Cata looked uncertainly at the boy's reflection, swimming in the background of her own. He was tall for his age, but he was only a boy, wasn't he? To overpower him should be easy enough, once she was out of this constricting gown. She struggled with the fastenings.

The boy laid down his mask and moved towards her. That was when Cata saw the crystal at his chest, searing through his costume with a dazzling green light; that was when she felt a rush within her as an answering power forced its way forth.

When she turned, Cata wore the crystal, Rajal's crystal, that had lain within her all this time, in the part of her that was Princess Bela Dona. The light from the wall-panels faded away; now there were only the crystals and the looking-glasses, too, reflecting back the dazzling, mingling rays of purple and green, green and purple.

'Simonides said this would be a magical night,' came the voice again, the voice that Cata knew so well. 'I didn't know quite how magical it would be.' The loved, familiar hands stretched towards her. Tears sprang to her eyes. 'I've had so many dreams. I've seen so many phantoms. Dear Cata, can it really be you?'

She stumbled forward. She flung herself into his arms.

'Jem! Oh Jem, Jem!'

✻ ✻ ✻ ✻ ✻

Fabric rustled, then ripped. Pins fell. Jewels rolled over the carpet, but not the crystals: they would remain at their chests, clashing and slipping, burning brightly, lighting the chamber through all that followed.

There was laughter; then a sound like purring; then long, low moans. That night, danger had thudded at their awareness like an ominous fist, hammering at a door. All at once, they did not care. There was only this moment, happening now. They fell across the petal-strewn bed, their limbs twining together.

The first time was urgent, a rush of smearing lips and savage, almost brutal thrustings, buckings, writhings. Desperately, Cata clawed at Jem's hair, then his back. Her thighs clutched him tightly, pushing him deeply, deeply into the welling moistness inside her. They rode high on waves of desire. Jem's mind spun and he felt himself speeding like a cannon ball, whizzing uncontrollably to the inevitable, blazing explosion. Sensation darted along his back, along his thighs, sizzling in waves along his clenching nerves.

Cata cried out. She pushed him down.

He reached up, clutching her breasts. He arched back his throat. She arched her back. Their moans rose in unison.

When the spasms came, they first surged and contracted inside her; then, as if they were one being, exploded from him too in a scalding cataclysm.

Deluged in pleasure, they collapsed side by side, their flesh stuck thickly with a thousand petals. Delicious warmth filled the air and still the crystals glowed with sacred light.

Then suddenly there were tears in their eyes as they recalled another petal-strewn place, in the days when Cata was a feral child and Jem a cripple on crutches. How they had longed to find themselves again in the rustling depths of that sun-dappled wood! Jem gazed into Cata's swimming eyes and saw her once more as the dark, ragged girl who had saved him, it seemed to him now, from a barren and bitter life; Cata saw the fair, shy boy who had come to her, like a spirit of love, from the world on the other side of a high but crumbling wall.

For a time they sobbed together, then their sobs turned into smiles, and again they knew nothing but joy.

The second time began with long, tender kisses. Softly, they ran their hands over the sleek lines of their bodies, and desire filled them again.

Later, Jem would recall the dark curtains of Cata's unravelled hair, draping his face as she swayed above him, and the marvellous soft firmness of her breasts. He would think of her teasing hands, then the enveloping warm softness as her lips closed around him. Cata would recall the delicious pain as Jem sucked her engorged nipples, and the mounting pleasure of the volcanic shudderings that racked her frame until the pleasure was too much and they fell back, gasping and shaking, into the petals and the perfume and the running moistness.

Again and again that night they rose to the heights of ecstasy, lost in a dizzying rapture of love.

On and on glowed the mysterious, mystic crystals.

But what would happen when morning came?

Chapter 70

TRIBUTES OF MAGIC

Like rolling, relentless thunder the Flame boomed and roared in Kaled's ears; its brightness seared his eyes. He stumbled. He sprawled to the floor. Outside it had been as much as he could do not to lurch towards the Prince in sudden fury. There and then he would have seized a scimitar, dashing away the boy's head, hacking at his body. There and then he would have grabbed the Princess, dragging her, screaming, to the consummation chamber.

No. Impossible. In those anguished moments on the ruby steps, Kaled had felt the faith of his people pressing upon him, crushing him like an intolerable burden. But it was not only their faith. It was his own. If he wanted to scream that he was their Sultan, that he was supreme, that no power could be greater, it was to no avail. His voice stopped in his throat and he could only sink to his knees, as if in the abasement of a common man.

What a monster he had become! What a blasphemous monster! Once he had believed there was no god in the Flame; now he had tried to cheat that god, denying the fate that had been ordained. What had he thought, that he would rule the moon and stars? In the moment that he had seen his son alive, Kaled knew the vanity of all his schemes. The fire god had punished him again, and this time, he knew, would be the last. The faith of his childhood flooded his heart and he grovelled before the searing column of fire, begging for forgiveness, mumbling and moaning of his worthlessness. He was destiny's pawn, no more; and destiny had decreed that he must die.

At last the Sultan heaved himself to his feet.

He flung himself forward.

That was when a shrieking laugh rang from the Flame and Kaled staggered back, repelled as if by an invisible wall of force. Terrified, he could only abase himself again as the hideous echo boomed all around him. 'Fool, fool!'

Kaled blundered, 'Mighty One! I don't understand!'

But only a laugh came in reply.

❈   ❈   ❈   ❈   ❈

'So, in the end it just vanished?'

'It had to. Dreams seemed real there, but the whole place was like a dream too.' Jem sighed and traced a finger over Cata's upraised thigh. 'Oh Cata, and how often I dreamed of you! Again and again I thought you were there, then I woke and you were gone. I only pray I'm not dreaming tonight. I don't think I could bear it if I woke up now.'

'It's no dream, Jem.'

They kissed, lightly but lingeringly. Sprawled lazily over each other, drinking the nectar from the golden goblets, they had told each other their stories. Frequently Jem had exclaimed in amazement as he learnt of Cata's trials. When she told him that Nirry had fled from Aunt Umbecca, laughter burst from his lips; hearing of Polty's machinations, Jem flamed into anger, declaring that if he ever saw Polty again, he would kill him without question, with his bare hands if there were no other way. Cata only stroked Jem, bade him hush, and said that Polty was headed for his own doom soon enough, with the demonic presence that worked inside him.

She had not even told Jem the worst of it; but then, there were things Jem had not told Cata. For example, he quite forgot to mention his own association with Cata's schoolfriend, Miss Jelica Vance; forgot, too, to refer at all to a certain establishment in Agondon that went by the name of Chokey's. But what did it matter now? When Cata, with a sigh, wished that they had been together all this time, Jem wished the same. They kissed again. They never wanted to be parted; after all, as they said many times that night, laughingly, tearfully, they were married now.

Still, like a benediction, the crystal-light bathed them.

Cata drew back. 'There's just one thing that worries me.'

'What's to worry us?' said Jem. He pointed to the crystal that hung, glowing brightly, between Cata's breasts. 'Quite how you've ended up with that, I'm not going to pretend to understand. But you've got one crystal; I've got another. In the morning, Simonides comes. Then we've got the third.' His brow furrowed. 'Haven't we?'

'I love you, Jem, but you don't think clearly.'

'Cata, what do you mean? Simonides sees the future – well, some of it. He says the Crystal of Theron will come to me in the morning, when I stand with my bride by the Sacred Flame.'

'With the Princess.'

'That's what I said.'

'Jem, are you quite sure we can rely on Simonides?' Cata sat up, suddenly intent. 'I told you I had a vision, didn't I? I knew I had to go through with this wedding, come what may. Only if the Princess married the Prince would the Crystal of Theron ever be found, hm? But that's just it, you see. You thought you were marrying the Princess; I thought I was marrying the Prince. But I'm not the Princess, and you're not the Prince. Not the right one, at any rate. I think our prophecies are at cross-purposes, Jem.'

Jem bit his lip. 'I hadn't quite thought of it like that.'

'All I can say is, we'd better hope for some magic in the morning, or we're in trouble. Big trouble.'

Jem thought for a moment.

He grinned. 'Then there's only one thing to do.'

'Oh?' Cata said archly. 'And what might that be?'

But after that, there was no more need for words.

✳   ✳   ✳   ✳   ✳

Darkness lay over the antechamber of the Flame like a swathing, suffocating blanket. No tapers burned and only the palest shaft of light penetrated from the sky outside, glimmering through a narrow vent in the rock. It was the moon, and its beam fell on the transfixed face of Simonides, who sat cross-legged in the centre of the floor. Deep in meditation, the old man had the appearance of a corpse, propped horribly upright in a dark house.

In a circle surrounding him were the twelve Elders of the College of Imams, prostrated before their leader. Silence reigned; but the silence, like the darkness, was not complete. Always there was the unending, low rumble of the Flame, insisting its way through the rocky walls, and the slow, deep breathing of the vigil-keepers. Then, too, there were those illusory sounds that sometimes come in the darkness. Minds in meditation are distant from the world; it is as well, for some might have been puzzled by the cracking, as of a knee, and the shufflings that sounded in the depths of the night. More puzzling still would have been a furtive sloshing of liquid against rock, and a susurrus that sounded like whispered words.

'Pah! I needed that!'

'Me too. So what now, Oily?'

'Major-sir, I say one thing: don't despair.'

'I'm not despairing, Oily. Not yet.'

'First light. That's our chance. When the first ray of dawn shines through that shaft, the consummation chamber will open again. That's when the old man goes up the stairs, to bring the lovers down to the Flame.'

'He goes up alone?'

'Indeed, Major-sir.'

'But not this time?'

'Not this time.'

479

Once again. Just once again.

Dawn was breaking over the Sacred City as Mother Madana stole towards the Prince's chamber. She glanced behind her; she peered round corners. There was no need. The broad, high terraces of the palace were empty. She heard no voices; no footsteps sounded other than her own. Her heart pounded as the familiar haunts came back into view. Pained, the old woman leaned back against the balustrade, inhaling the heady scents from the roof garden above. Tears filled her eyes . . .

Once again. Again. Just once.

The night's vigil had been too much for her. On the boulevard below, pressed tight with the pilgrims, Mother Madana had told herself she must learn resignation. There would be another child; a child must grow; it was good, it was right. But no. Never, never. Inexorably, a sense of wrongness filled her heart. Could she wait for Dea to appear again on the steps, a man now, and married? She had pushed her way back through the mesmerised crowd, longing only for the chamber where her lost child had lain . . .

Just once again. Once again.

She pushed open the door. Light fell across the rich, soft carpets. The first impression was of a reddish gloom, like the red of the sun that was rising outside. Then came a gleam on a curve of metal, a konar-light perhaps, silent and cold. Mother Madana wiped the tears from her eyes. Terrible raptures filled her mind. She breathed heavily. She staggered forward. She would cast herself down on her child's couch, inhale his scent, clutch his cushions . . .

Again. Once. Just once again.

'Dea, my darling? Dea, it's Lammy!'

An ornate blanket covered the couch. For a moment, as if her fantasy were real, it seemed to the old woman that the Prince really slept – here, now – in this place where, time and again, she had woken him in the mornings of his childhood. She touched the fabric and felt a small shock. Something lay beneath. Something hard. Something cold.

She pushed back the blanket.

She cried out.

In the next moment she was aware of five twittering figures suddenly surrounding her.

✳ ✳ ✳ ✳ ✳

To meditate is to feel yourself to be in two places: at once deep inside the cavern of your mind, and floating free, billowing out into the space beyond. To meditate is to see through the illusion of this world, to glimpse a place where the burdens of time and identity no longer press upon us. Perhaps it is to glimpse the state of death, but to see death not as a thing of terror but as an evanescent, eternal lightness.

Thought vanishes in meditation, but there are random images, and sometimes in the images there are ghosts of meaning. As the moonlight shone against his closed eyes, Simonides was aware of a mandala pattern, churning slowly through the air; then the mandala was a mask; then the mask was a face; then flames came flickering at the edges of the face. For eternities, it seemed, but without fear, Simonides watched these strange displays. Deep within his being, the old man knew his death would soon come. He accepted it. He welcomed it. Perhaps he even knew it would come today, this new day that was beginning now.

Twining round the pallor of the moonlight came a soft creeper of red. Calmly, without flickering, the old man's eyes were open. Yes, the time had come. For a moment he looked on his brother Imams, hunched and silent, who would remain in their abasement until the Sultan emerged, leading them back out to the ruby steps. Simonides rose painfully to his feet and began, in the spreading, dim glow, to make his way towards the consummation chamber. An ominous rumbling sounded from above as the great rocky door slid back at last.

What happened next was over in an instant. When the stranger's hand slipped suddenly over his face, Simonides had no time even to gasp. The second stranger struck him a sharp but silent blow.

Simonides crumpled.

Polty and the whoremonger raced upstairs.

❉ ❉ ❉ ❉ ❉

'I say, I'm puffed! Can't we stop now?'

'She wants to go higher. Come on!'

The fat man rolled his eyes. 'Easy for you to say, my boy. I'm a bit older than you, don't forget.'

'Not to mention fatter.'

'Fat? Have you forgotten I've been starving in the desert?'

'Well, it shows how fat you were before.'

'Well, I never!'

The boy and his protesting, purple-cheeked companion might have appeared to be mere pilgrims. If so, they were pilgrims of an odd sort, climbing away from the hushed crowd, just before the next stage of the ritual was to begin. Ahead of them, rapidly ascending the stairs, were a veiled, distraught girl and an agitated dog. From time to time the dog would turn back, barking.

'Really,' puffed the fat man, 'I wish I had that konar-light.'

'So you'd still be magic?'

'So you could carry me.'

'I'd rub it,' laughed the boy. 'Then you could solve all our problems now.'

They had pushed their way up to the first balcony, then the second. Now the steps were narrow, and the crowds seemed far away.

'Why,' said Jafir, 'does she want to come up here?'

'She's stifled below. She's royal, remember.'

'So am I. In a manner of speaking.'

'It's easy to forget.'

'Ooh!'

They found themselves on a flat, cracking roof.

'Princess, be careful.' Littler reached out a hand, plucking Dona Bela away from the edge. She could not want to fling herself down, could she? But why did she want to come up here? To wait with the pilgrims, perhaps, was too painful for her now, as the terrible climax of the night's events loomed. But could they really do nothing but watch?

The Princess slumped down; Littler squatted beside her. Below, in the gathering light of the dawn, stirrings were visible on the ruby steps, but still silence reigned. Strange, to think that last night the air had been so volatile, with members of the crowd breaking through the barricades, with guards beating them back, with hysteria rising like the smoke from the blurring, red-gold tapers!

Suddenly it all seemed so distant. So unreal.

Littler found himself thinking how far they were from the ground, and hoped there would be no more of those earth-tremblings. With fearful excitement, pilgrims had spoken of the fire god's agitation. His anger. Or restlessness. Or joy. Or sorrow.

Soon, perhaps, the deity would be very agitated indeed.

Littler attempted, 'Princess? It's not over, is it? Not really?'

Pallid in the moonlight, the mute girl turned towards him. Tears glimmered in the limpid eyes. *It's over*, she seemed to say. *Yes, it's over. We struggled all this way, but what could we do? Nothing. My shimmering self is married, be the sequel what it may. Soon, when they open the consummation chamber, they shall discover the truth. What, then, shall be the destiny of these realms?*

Littler sighed. He had tried for so long to keep his spirits high; now despondency fell over him like a pall. Last night, arriving in the Sacred City, they had presented themselves at the palace gates. What was the use? In a city filled with crazed pilgrims, they were just three more. Scornful laughter was their only reward, and the guards had flung them brutally into the street.

Littler sighed again. Softly he stroked the mongrel that lay between them, panting, beating the cracking roof with his tail. Poor Rainbow!

Jagged bones stuck through his sides. His coat was mangy and dun-coloured too, but still they called him by his old name.

If only they were back in the dreaming dimension now!

Jafir stood over them.

'I thought,' said the fat little fellow, 'that the Princess wanted to confront herself, as it were. I mean, the other version.'

'In that crush?' said Littler. 'It's hopeless.'

'Now really, boy,' said the ex-genie, 'you surprise me. Nothing's hopeless. Sometimes all you need is a bit of ... perspective! Yes, that's the word.'

Littler gestured below. 'We've certainly got that.'

'Exactly. We hardly came across that desert, did we, just to give up at the first difficulty?'

'Hardly the first. Besides, I thought you were rather good at giving up.'

'Hmph! To be sure, I was disappointed about the dreaming dimension. Only natural, isn't it? When you think you're in paradise, you're hardly pleased to find yourself in the middle of the desert.'

'Well, no.'

'Ooh, and that journey!'

'We'd never have made it without Scabs.'

They were silent for a moment, thinking of their lost companion.

'We've got to do something, haven't we?' Jafir pursued, adding unexpectedly, 'We owe it to the cabin boy. To his memory.'

'We used to have so much magic,' sighed Littler. 'If only we had just a little bit now!'

The boy would have sighed again, but suddenly the Princess gripped his arm, as if she had suddenly had an idea. She staggered to her feet. She stretched forth her arms and her companions looked on as the mute girl began, astonishingly, to sing. The purity of her voice was like a clarion bell, ringing above the chaos below.

> In my mind there are
> Five vanishings,
> Vanishing one by one:
> One is done in a soaring canopy,
> Two is blue down below.
> The third vanishing comes in the sun,
> The fourth through a darkened glass,
> But only after there are
> Five vanishings
> Shall I be real again!

The song might have been a hopeless, useless gesture, but as the beautiful voice filled the night, something strange began to happen. First came the faintest flicker of light, lapping at the hem of the girl's gown; in moments, a mystic aura surrounded her. Beauty flamed from her tired face; her rags were royal finery.

Rainbow barked, frisking around her. In the rays of the aura, his dun-coloured fur flickered with magical colours again. Jafir was wide-eyed, a hand to his mouth. Littler trembled, wondering what this could mean.

That was when the new figure suddenly emerged, staggering forth from the darkness.

Littler cried, 'Stork!'

Stork did not reply. Instead, he moved forward stiffly, solemnly, kneeling like a worshipper before the shimmering vision. In his hand he clutched a golden coin. Reverently, he laid it down.

'P-Princess, you are p-poor. Accept our w-wealth.'

'Stork?' said Littler. 'Stork, can you hear me?'

But now Stork's companions were emerging too, and Littler could only look on in astonishment as his old friends from the Realm of Un laid down their tributes.

'This ancient amulet shall protect you from evil.'

'This band shall magnify your inner powers.'

'This orb lets you see, see beyond sight.'

'Princess, I give you the konar-light.'

The Unners abased themselves, caught in the magic aura.

Chapter 71

CRAZY FLOOR

Bean's limbs were aching and his head ached too, weighed down by the burden of his mask. In the depths of the night he had been tempted to remove it, but the fear came that he would be unable to attach it again, or would fall asleep with his face exposed. He began to wonder whether it would matter. If the events of the new day were destined to happen, what difference could his own actions make? With itching, dry eyes he gazed down at the pilgrims. How faithfully they kept the sacred vigil! He scorned their folly; but then thought of his own follies and envied, instead, their simple faith.

Rajal was shivering, but whether with the terrors of the night before or the terrors of the day that lay ahead, he did not know. In his mind, again and again, he saw the moment of the Vizier's death. Never had Rajal thought such anger could burst from him, so wild, so unconstrained. It shocked him; he felt sick; he struggled to push the images away. He thought of Cata, and wondered what she had endured. Her sacrifice astonished him; but then, he thought, she was sacrificing herself because she loved Jem. That was something Rajal understood well enough, back from the days when he had been a fool. He became aware of Bean, hunched beside him, and Rajal wondered how much of a fool he was now. Shyly, he sought for his new friend's hand.

Bean was thinking about Polty. He had been separated from Polty before, it was true, but never so finally. Even now, he found himself wondering, would he go to Polty if Polty needed him? If Polty forgave him? Bean screwed up his eyes, blinking away the gathering tears. He could not help himself: the tentacles that bound him to his old life were many, deep-rooted, and strong as iron chains. He felt Rajal's hand and Bean struggled to think of this new friendship, and what it would bring. Yes. This was good. This was right. He could not go back.

Rajal swallowed hard. Not daring to turn his head, he kept his grip on Bean's bony hand as shards of red cracked the desert darkness and the swelling sun gleamed at the far end of the boulevard. All at once a fanfare sounded and the two young men sprang apart, startled. The royal guests shuffled, assuming their proper places. Some, slumped against pillars, were jogged awake. Snores ceased abruptly and the familiar drumbeat began again. Guards moved forward, ready to open the immense iron portals. The pilgrims below were on their knees, bowing and muttering prayers.

When the Elders filed out of the Sanctum, Rajal registered something odd about them, though what it was, he was not quite sure. As it happened, he was never to realise that there were only ten of them, not twelve. There was no time. The Sultan distracted him. Devoid of his mask, haggard, desperate, Kaled blundered to the edge of the steps, swaying like a drunkard. His bleary eyes swivelled over the crowd, then he turned suddenly to the figure he believed to be that of the Caliph of Qatani.

'Brother, it is all over! Brother, kiss me before I die!'

Panic filled Rajal as the Sultan first pulled him savagely towards him, then struggled clumsily to push his mask aside. Rajal cried out. Bean sprang forward. In the next moment, Rajal's mask would fall away, but not before a second distraction came.

It was a mercy. But the mercy was brief.

There was confusion in the crowd. Jostlings. Cries. Astonished, Kaled stared down at the frail old woman who tottered towards the ruby steps. It was Mother Madana – Lammy! Her piteous keenings filled the empurpled, bruised dawn, and Kaled saw that she was not alone, but leading a procession. It was a procession very different from that of the night before. Behind the old slave, ranged in a ragged line, were the Targon Retainers. How they had pushed their way to the ruby steps Kaled was never to know, but perhaps the burden they bore was terrible enough, shocking enough to part even the tightest crowd.

Four Targons raised their hands in gestures of grief; the fifth carried in his arms the limp, cold body of a long-limbed boy.

Kaled sank down. He moaned aloud.

Painfully, Mother Madana ascended the steps. Her eyes blazed with a terrible fire and with shaking hands she gestured first to the corpse, then to the Sultan. 'Murder,' she whispered, then cried aloud, '*Murder!*'

'Lammy ... Lammy,' the Sultan gasped, confused and shocked, lurching forward as if to embrace her, to sink upon her breast as if, once again, they were nurse and child.

She reeled from him. He clutched her, brutally. 'Lammy!'

'*Murder ... murder!*' She struck his face.

It was blasphemy, treason of the highest order.

Guards sprang forward. Desperation seized the Sultan. *Oh Lammy, Lammy—*

'Kill her,' he bellowed suddenly, 'kill her!'

So it was that neither pilgrims, nor Imams, nor noble guests knew that the old woman's last impassioned word, shrieked in the Sultan's face, was not again '*Murder—!*' but this time '*Murderer!*'

A scimitar sliced at her withered head, before the last syllable left her lips. Blood rushed from the stump of the neck, splattering the Sultan's robes.

Kaled clutched his face in his hands, as if his face were a mask that he would claw away. He staggered, then all at once rushed forward, seizing the guard's bloodied scimitar. With sudden resolve he turned on the pilgrims, screaming as if his words were slashes of the blade, 'My son has been murdered! Would an impostor usurp my throne? The traitor must die, and the Princess will be mine!'

Cries rang out as Kaled charged back, crazed, through the iron portals.

Rajal gasped, 'I don't understand! What's happening?'

'The Prince is dead!' said Bean. 'So . . . *who was that last night?*'

There was no more time to wonder. Pilgrims were pouring over the ruby steps. Guards hacked at them viciously. Royal guests and Imams fled for their lives.

Below, the Targons had been overwhelmed. Pilgrims had seized the dead boy and in a frenzy of grief were clutching, clawing at the royal corpse. In moments it would be torn, as if by vultures, into bloody scraps of meat.

Rajal seized Bean's arm. 'Quick! Kaled . . . we've got to stop him!'

They rushed into the Sanctum, just before the great doors slammed, shutting out the crowd, and just before another, lesser confrontation took place below. Two old women – or what appeared to be two old women – fought their way towards Lammy's beheaded corpse. They were never to reach it, but came close enough to gaze into each other's eyes. One reeled back, filled with disgust at the sight of her brother, dressed in all the finery of a court eunuch; the eunuch's eyes blazed as he saw again, and for the last time, the sister who had betrayed his darling Lammy, selling her into slavery so long ago.

A moment more, and the crowd bore them apart; a moment more, and all that remained of their sister, stamped beneath a hundred frenzied feet, was a squelching pulp, running down the steps.

Then the tremblings of the earth began again, more forcefully this time than ever before.

✳   ✳   ✳   ✳   ✳

The crystals were fading.

Soon the only light would be a returning pallor from the panels in the walls. Clutching each other, Jem and Cata lay on the petal-strewn bed as the foliage and the rich furnishings slowly began to dissipate. Leaves withered; branches crumpled; velvet curtains grew thinner and thinner; embroidery faded to a spidery grey. Soon even the bed was gone, even the masks and elaborate garb they had worn the night before. Only the petals did not vanish, but formed themselves instead into a fabric that crept across their limbs.

When dawn came, they were dressed in simple white robes, unadorned but for the crystals that hung from their necks, dormant now. The rumbling of the boulder filled their ears. They lay, embracing, on the looking-glass floor.

'Kiss me, Jem. Think of our love.'

Again Jem sank deeply, deeply into the enveloping warmth of Cata's kiss. He thought of all that had passed that night and knew that nothing, nothing in all his life, could mean as much to him as Cata did now. The quest that lay before him was dark and perilous, but how could he fail, now that they were together? He prayed only that he would never lose Cata again.

It was a prayer that would not be answered. In the depths of their embrace, neither Jem nor Cata had eyes for the figures who stole towards them now, across the bright reaches of the looking-glass floor. The pretended Imams pushed back their cowls, exposing the familiar greasy moustache and the familiar, flaming hair.

One voice came: 'Pah! Still at it?'

Another: 'They're probably just getting going!'

The lovers sprang apart. They gasped.

So did the intruders.

'The Princess? But this is a whore!'

'Jem! Cata! What trick is this?'

There was a scuffle.

Jem lunged at Polty. Polty's fist flew.

The whoremonger went for Cata. She smashed his face. He staggered, but recovered at once, storming down on her. She kicked and clawed.

Reeling from Polty's blow, Jem floundered. He struggled to recover, but Polty, as he had always been, was bigger and stronger.

He punched Jem in the stomach, and Jem fell.

The earth trembled as he slid across the floor.

Meanwhile Eli Oli Ali had pinned Cata down. His fist swung back, ready to strike.

'Dirty whore! What are you playing at?'

Polty plummeted forward. 'She's not a whore, you greasy pig! She's my sister! She's ... she's my wife!' Outraged, he pushed the whoremonger aside, dragging Cata upright. He clutched her, shaking her in desperate ardour. 'Darling! What's happening? Why are you here?'

'Let me go! Just let me go!'

'Darling, it's Poltiss! Your brother ... your lover! Oh, what's that crippler-boy done to you now? My love, you must fight his evil magic, you must!'

Cata screamed and would have torn out Polty's eyes, but he caught her wrists.

The chamber rocked, rumbled.

Cata struggled, but could not break free.

Eli Oli Ali only looked on, astonished. Where were the Prince and Princess? How did that other Ejlander get here, the yellow-haired one? Why, that was the one who'd attacked him in the desert, wasn't it – the one who'd stolen Dona Bela from the van? What was going on here? Anger and confusion filled the whoremonger, but fear was suddenly stronger. He didn't like any of this, didn't like it one bit.

Curse the Major-sir! Let him rot!

Eli would make his escape, and make it quickly.

But then he spied the green crystal, glinting from the bag round the Ejland-boy's neck. The boy lay breathless on the looking-glass floor. The crystal, Eli was sure at once, was a valuable prize. Yes, he would make his escape, but not without payment.

He lunged for Jem, but Jem rallied.

In the next moment, he flailed with the whoremonger.

A moment more, and the fat man was astride him, squashing the breath from his body, but Jem clutched the crystal and would not let it go.

The whoremonger aimed a punch at Jem's head.

Jem's head swivelled.

He saw Cata, wild-eyed in Polty's grip.

He gasped through his struggles, 'Polty . . . stop this! Leave her alone! I don't know why you're here . . . I don't know what you're doing . . . but don't you understand we're in . . . terrible danger?'

Polty was not listening. In the moment he had seen Cata, he had forgotten everything. Waves of love crashed suddenly over him. How boldly, how gallantly he would have borne her from this place, saving her from the thrall of the crippler's dark magic! But Cata kept resisting him, and as she resisted, Polty's love flamed into anger. His image shimmered in the looking-glass floor. His face twisted. His skin turned blue. Flames began to lap at his carrot-coloured hair.

'Bitch!' he screamed. 'Don't you understand you're mine?'

'Never!' cried Cata. She spat in his face. 'I hate you, I hate you!'

'You'll pay for that!' He slapped her, then his hand clawed down, as if to rip open the shift she wore. She writhed; his hand caught the stone that hung from her neck.

The purple crystal skidded across the floor, but Polty, in his madness, never even saw it.

He slapped Cata again.

This time, she crumpled.

'Bitch!' he shrieked. 'Slut! We may be doomed, but first you're going to get what's coming to you! Deny me, would you, for a crippler-boy? I'll show you what a real man can do!'

By now, Polty's head was a blazing beacon. His face rippled and twisted. The anti-god streamed from the shuddering floor, but Polty's anger was too strong, and now his lust was rising too. He had no thought for the crystals or the quest. There was only Cata . . . beautiful Cata . . .

By now the whoremonger had abandoned Jem. Terrified at the demonic vision, terrified at the quaking earth, desperate only to save himself, the greasy fellow had forgotten the crystal. The others had no eyes for him as he made his escape at last, scurrying down the stairs.

But he had left it too late; for it was there on the stairs, a moment later, that he was to cannon into the enraged Sultan Kaled. The whoremonger had no time even to cry out as the scimitar, scything down like the blade of justice, performed its second execution of the night.

The head bounced down the stairs like a ball.

❊　❊　❊　❊　❊

Jem scrambled at the floor, struggling to rise. He gasped for breath. If he must, he would die to save Cata. In an instant, just an instant, he would launch himself forward.

Polty had ripped open his robes and his breeches too. The struggles of the last moments, the slappings and blows, had roused his excitement to an intolerable pitch. Magnificent, glittering, the mighty sceptre that was Penge curved up, ready to take his pleasure. In an instant, just an instant, he would launch himself forward.

Polty looked down at the supine girl. Never, he thought, never, had he loved her so much as he loved her now.

The instant had come.

But it had not.

A furious cry rent the air and Polty turned to see Kaled bearing down upon him, scimitar still dripping from the blood of two killings.

'Impostor! Demon!'

The scimitar slashed.

Polty sprang back, but it was too late. In an instant, just an instant, the blade had sliced through his flesh, severing Penge at the root. Like an eel, the fleshy thing zigzagged across the floor, leaving a bloody trail.

Polty collapsed, screaming.

Blood gushed from between his thighs.

Crying Penge's name, in shuddering jerks he scrambled after the slithering, sundered organ, desperate just to clutch it in his convulsing hands.

490

‘*Polty!*’

It was Bean, and his wail was even louder than Polty's screams. Bean and Rajal had reached the top of the stairs just at the moment when Kaled's blade came down. Now, breaking from Rajal, Bean ran to Polty, collapsing over him, sobbing, moaning.

Rajal reeled. He saw Jem.

Meanwhile Cata cried out, 'Let me go! Let me go!'

This time it was Kaled who had seized her. Curtains of dark hair fell across her face but the Sultan, blind in his madness, had no thought that the Princess of the night before had magically altered into another girl. Out on the stairs Simonides lay unmoving and Eli Oli Ali's head still rocked, gouting blood from the severed veins; here, the flame-haired one screamed on and on; there were the strangers, too, and a mysterious jewel lay gleaming on the floor.

The Sultan didn't care. Nothing mattered but his vow of marriage. Nothing mattered but the Sacred Flame. Ripping a golden braid from his costume, with a swift, sharp action he tethered Cata to his wrist.

He dragged her to the stairs.

'Stop!' Jem scrambled to his feet. He staggered for a moment, dazed; then suddenly Rajal was at his side.

'Jem! Are you all right?'

'Oh Raj . . . Raj, quick! The crystal!'

Rajal needed no urging. A moment more, and the Crystal of Koros was safe inside his tunic.

Jem and Rajal blundered from the chamber.

Jem gasped. 'The Sultan . . . we've got to stop him!'

✳ ✳ ✳ ✳ ✳

Rajal had no time even to glance back at Bean.

Perhaps it was just as well, for what he would have seen would first have caused him anguish, then astonishment, then terror. He would have seen Bean, his new friend forgotten, cradling the shuddering Polty in his arms; he would have seen the sudden gathering brightness from the floor; he would have seen the brightness searing into a flash that shattered the already cracking floor beneath them into a thousand, a million glittering fragments.

Quite what happened then, who could say? Perhaps it was the last of Polty's strange, borrowed powers, burning itself away; perhaps it was the magic of the anti-god, reaching out for his stricken servant.

In any case, in an instant, just an instant, it was over. The brightness was gone, and so were Polty and Bean, leaving only their reflections in the crazy floor.

Chapter 72

THE RUNNING BACK

'The Flame . . . no!'

Below, there was another dazzling light, surging up just as Kaled, with the tethered Cata, reached the foot of the stairs. The earth trembled again and for a moment it seemed that the Flame had burst from its collar of rock, filling the Sanctum with an immense burning ball. Kaled stumbled back, shielding his eyes; Cata twisted away; then suddenly the light subsided, the earth was still, and standing before them, leering, menacing, dressed in blood-spattered robes, was the Ouabin leader, Rashid Amr Rukr!

He whipped his sabre, flashing, through the air. 'Sultan! The girl is mine!'

'Never!' Kaled cried. 'My son is dead! By the dictates of destiny, the Princess is my bride!'

'Fool! You speak of destiny? Your Line has reached its end! You cannot prevail! Bow to me, Sultan! Let me kill you now with dignity, with one sweep of my blade . . . or would you die fighting for your worthless life?'

'Blasphemous dog, it is you who shall die!'

Screaming, and with Cata still bound to his wrist, the Sultan bore down on the Ouabin leader. There was a clash of steel, just one, and the Sultan reeled back. Cata cried out. Fire flashed from the Ouabin's weapon, fizzing like stars round his golden form.

'What trickery is this?' the Sultan gasped, stunned.

'Sultan, I tell you, the gods are on my side!'

'The gods? The dogs, Ouabin, only the dogs!'

Rallying, the Sultan lunged forward again, just as Jem and Rajal came charging down the stairs. Horror-stricken, Jem's eyes were only for Cata, writhing in her bonds, reeling in the strokes that beat the Sultan back.

'He's mad! He'll kill her!'

Jem knew only that he must save Cata or die. Rocky fragments lay all around, shaken by the tremors from the sides of the cave. Jem scooped up a heavy chunk. The combatants were circling each other, parrying. Rashid turned his back. Jem floundered forward. With all his strength, he struck the Ouabin, but the Ouabin did not fall. He turned, with blazing eyes, and swiped at Jem.

Jem leapt back.

It was Cata's chance. She cannoned into the Sultan. He stumbled, the scimitar clattering from his hand.

'Jem!' Cata kicked the weapon and it span across the floor.

Jem grabbed it.

The Ouabin advanced.

Jem leapt back, then back again. All around him, filling the rocky cavern, came the roar of the Flame. He felt the heat licking his back. The Ouabin's magic weapon swooped down, but still Jem did not thrust.

He had a plan.

A desperate one, but it was all he could think to do.

Meanwhile Rajal had found his own weapon. Beside the prostrate form of Simonides, a bloody dagger glinted on the stairs. Clutching it, Rajal turned again to the fray. Terror shook his heart and images of violence flashed back through his mind. Vizier Hasem. The bashing. The blood.

No. No. Push it away.

Darting forward, he hacked at Cata's bonds.

She leapt up.

Rajal clutched his dagger hard, looking down at the Sultan.

'Coward!' came a cry, and for an instant Rajal thought it was meant for him.

It was the Ouabin, shouting at Jem.

Jem leapt back and back.

'Ejlander weakling! Puny whelp! Come on, won't you fight me like a man?'

'A magic weapon! Is that fighting like a man, Ouabin?'

'Taunt me, would you? Die, Ejlander!'

Jem leapt to the side.

The Ouabin reeled round.

Now Jem thrust with all his might. Golden force streamed from the Ouabin. It sizzled along Jem's scimitar, then raced through his nerves. He screamed out in agony, but struck again, then again.

It was enough. A scream rent the air, and Rashid Amr Rukr fell into the Flame.

Rajal spun round, startled.

At the same moment the Sultan reared up, striking the dagger from Rajal's hand.

By the Flame, Jem staggered.

Cata darted to him, seizing him back. 'Jem! Thanks be to the gods!'

Jem sighed, about to fall into Cata's arms.

'Jem!' cried Rajal. 'Look out!'

Kaled jumped forward, clutching the dagger; he would have stabbed Jem in the neck, seizing Cata again, but just in time, Jem swivelled round.

His scimitar slashed, and Kaled fell, head sliced open, blood and brains spilt, like a sacrifice, before the searing Flame.

Jem turned away, nauseated. His hand descended slowly and the scimitar fell.

❋   ❋   ❋   ❋   ❋

For long moments there was only the thunder of the Flame. Breathless, the three companions staggered towards each other, collapsed against each other, held each other tight.

A voice came. 'You have been brave, my young friends, but the battle is not yet over.'

It was Simonides. Clutching his side, his robes sodden with blood, the old man had heaved himself back to his feet and stood, trembling, at the foot of the stairs. He leaned heavily against the wall, his old face seared with pain.

Before they could go to him, there was another voice, its tone very different, sounding from a corner.

'The old man is right. There is, I think, one further piece of business that remains outstanding.'

'Lord Empster!' Jem gasped.

His guardian stepped forward. At first Jem gazed with relief upon the familiar dark cape, the wide-brimmed hat, the smoking pipe; it seemed as if the past had returned and once again he was nothing more than the nobleman's gauche young ward. There had been a time when Lord Empster, for all his oddity, for all his air of mystery, had nonetheless been a prop and stay to Jem, the father he had never known, and the lodestar of his quest. Now Jem remembered the creature he had seen in his guardian's cabin, on the night of the green lightning; then, too, he recalled what Cata had told him just the night before, about what Lord Empster had done during the Ritual of Rebonding.

'You don't seem pleased to see me, young Prince.'

Jem whispered, 'Who are you? What do you want?'

'Such questions!' Lord Empster had to laugh. 'Really, Jemany, you are the strangest young man. You are Key to the Orokon, are you not? Did I not train you for your mystic quest? What should I want, but for your quest to succeed? Really ... what else should I want?'

He turned to Rajal, then to Cata, but both of them, like Jem, had set their faces hard.

'They don't believe you,' breathed Simonides. 'Wicked one, you can deceive for a time, but in the end the truth will be clear. It is clear now.'

'Oh?' Lord Empster drew deeply on his pipe. His tone had lost its merry banter, and an evil power seared from his eyes. 'Know it all, do

495

you, Simonides? I wouldn't rely on your paltry mystic powers if I were you. Senile old fool, what *do* you know?'

There was no reply. Simonides was sinking to the floor, blood flowing freshly from the wound in his side. A terrible moan escaped his lips, while all the time Lord Empster kept up his intent, staring gaze.

'Stop it!' Cata sprang forward. She struck the nobleman's face, and as she did so, the wide-brimmed hat fell from his head. Beneath it he was hairless, and his skull gleamed strangely. But there was something else, too. Something more. Lord Empster was changing, once again becoming an inhuman thing. The clouds dispelled from around his face; his cape fell away; suddenly, the golden creature flared out.

Cata gasped, staggering back, then gasped again as the creature plunged towards her, dragging her to the Flame.

'Leave her!' cried Jem, but before he could intervene, a sharp pain racked his chest and he doubled over. It was the crystal, glowing green, burning into his flesh with a heat more violent than it had ever possessed before. He glanced at Rajal and saw that the purple crystal was glowing too. His friend collapsed, convulsing.

A rumbling shook the ground.

'You've done well, Key to the Orokon!' laughed the creature that had once been Lord Empster. 'Two crystals already, and a third . . . I think we're on the brink of the third, don't you? I had hoped the Ouabin would do my work for me, for my powers are dissipated by my long tenure in this secondary world. Ah, but my folly shows only how weak I have grown! I should have known the Ouabin was a useless fool and that I must do what he has left undone, releasing the red crystal from this dross of human semblance! Come, Princess, let me purify you in the Flame!'

Cata struggled, but the creature was too strong. He lurched back, ready to fling her forward.

Jem and Rajal were helpless, paralysed by pain.

A second rumbling shook the ground. The Flame was flickering immensely, its roar ever more furious.

'Fool!' cried Simonides. 'Fool, look at her face!'

'You call me fool, old man?' spat the creature. 'Do you think I can't see through this veil of false seeming? This girl's appearance has changed, and changed again, but inside her is the Essence of Princess Bela Dona!'

'Again I call you fool! Golden One, your powers indeed have waned if you believe the legends of the Ouabin tribe! I have seen the destiny of this day, and I tell you, if you fling this girl into the Flame, the lady you seek shall never be yours!'

Fury blazed anew in the creature's eyes, and perhaps he would have destroyed the old man. Instead he cried out, 'Lady? What do you know of my lady?'

'You call my powers puny, but I know who you are, and I know what you seek. Agonis, through all the long history of this Time of Atonement, have you not wandered this world in secret, seeking always for the lady you have lost? Once you were most blessed of the gods, but look at you now! Before, in the Vale of Orok, the anti-god deceived you; in your future, I foresee, he shall deceive you again, for in your hunger and madness you shall sell yourself to him!'

'Liar! Old fool, what can you know?'

'It's no lie, Agonis! All along you have seduced this boy, this young Prince who now lies stricken, pretending you would help him save this world! In truth, you would deliver this world into the power of Toth-Vexrah, for you would give him the Crystals Five, would he but give you his daughter Imagenta!'

'Old man, you know not what you say! When my sisters and brothers went to war, was I not the only one who did not fight? Unang fool, can you not understand that I am the god of mercy and compassion?'

By now, the ground was trembling relentlessly. Debris fell from the cracking cave; again, Simonides sank down, gasping. The old man was near death, but he flung back brutally, 'Mercy? Compassion? Yet you would fling that child to the Flame?'

'The girl must die, that millions may live! What is she, but a container for the crystal that is within her?'

It's not true, Golden One! None of it's true!

This time, it was not Simonides who spoke. The voice was a new one, a female voice, but not Cata's. With the voice came a cloud of orange smoke, filling the centre of the shaking chamber. Rooted in place, clutching his crystal, Jem had listened in amazement; now, his amazement could only grow as he stared up through the clearing smoke at a group of familiar figures.

One was Littler. One was Jafir. One was Princess Dona Bela, with a konar-light in her hand. Rainbow was there, too; dun-coloured again, he darted forward at once, barking angrily at the golden god.

The voice of the Princess resumed, ringing out regally. How it was that she could now speak, Jem did not know, but he soon guessed the answer. Circling her forehead was a silver band, gleaming and pulsing with each word she uttered. Her lips neither opened nor closed. If Dona Bela was not yet whole again, nonetheless she was close to the magic that would restore her. Her destiny was at hand.

She went on, *Golden One, I tell you that girl must not die, for though there is a secret buried within her being, it is not the one you seek. Kill her, and the crystal shall never be found!*

Agonis looked between the struggling girl in his arms and the girl who looked exactly like Princess Bela Dona. He lashed out at Rainbow, kicking the dog away. 'This is a trick,' he spluttered, 'an evil trick! Simonides, this is some magic of yours!'

'Believe the girl, Agonis,' gasped the old man. 'Believe her, for she speaks the truth!'

'Lies! Treachery! Die, Shimmering Princess!'

With that, the sky god would delay no longer; but it was then, just as Cata was about to burn, that a sudden knowledge exploded in Jem's brain. He clawed at his chest, tearing away the crystal that seared his flesh.

'Cata . . . the crystal! It's our only chance!'

He flung the glowing stone through the air.

Agonis flung Cata into the Flame.

Her arm flailed out. She caught the crystal. Dazzling beams shot from her hand and suddenly she was back on the cave-floor again, her eyes searing, her hair streaming back, advancing on Agonis with the crystal glowing in her upraised palm.

The god stumbled back. 'It is the avatar of my sister . . . *Viana! What are you doing? Viana! Don't you know me?*'

'You've gone mad, Agonis! You're evil! You can't win!'

Now Rajal rose up too. The power of Viana gave him strength; clutching his own crystal, he advanced on Agonis.

'Koros! You, too? Brother, how can you . . . how can . . .?'

Green rays, then purple, seared the golden god. He crumpled to the floor, his substance turning to smoke. It seemed that the rays were destroying him; in truth, he was summoning the last of his strength to vanish, as he had vanished so many times before.

In the last moment, he screamed out, '*Fools! You won't defeat me! I'll be back, do you hear me? I tell you, I'll be back! The Orokon shall be mine!*'

He was gone. Only the echo of his voice remained, but still the two crystals glowed and glowed.

※　※　※　※　※

What happened next took only a moment. Suddenly Rainbow was barking urgently. They reeled round. They gasped. The Flame! As if it were a living thing, the Flame darted out a fiery tendril. Like a monstrous serpent, it slithered across the floor. Its aim was unerring, and Jem was caught in its coils. He screamed; he bucked and writhed, but there was no way to resist as he was drawn up, like a cinder, into the roaring column of fire.

The earth trembled again, still more fearsomely.

Cata collapsed, beating the ground.

Dona Bela's voice rang out: *Genie! Quick! Save him!*

498

Littler cried, 'Princess! Say *I wish*—'

'It's useless!' said Jafir. 'Many WISHES are within my power, but against such mighty force, I am helpless!'

'He's dead!' shrieked Cata. Dust and debris rained around them, but to Cata, there was only the agony that consumed her, more terrible than the Flame or the quaking earth. 'He's dead! What does it matter now? What does anything matter?'

In that moment, Cata would gladly have died too. To have come all this way, to have been through all this, only to lose Jem when it seemed they could at last be together, was too much, too much. What did she care for the world now? It was doomed anyway, without Jem!

Yes, she would gladly die, too!

Cata struggled upright. Tears blinded her eyes as she staggered towards the Flame.

Suddenly Rainbow was barking again. He launched himself at Cata. She lurched, falling to the floor.

Then it happened.

'Look!' It was Littler who saw Jem first, whizzing and whirling inside the Flame.

Jem flailed, as if beating at walls.

He screamed out his defiance.

'I don't understand!' shouted Rajal. 'What's happening?'

Jafir cowered, covering his face. 'Magic . . . terrible magic! We must run, before the Flame takes us all! Princess, WISH we were gone from here – WISH, girl, WISH!'

'No!' It was Simonides. 'The Prince fights for his life . . . but there is one way . . . one way . . .'

Rajal rushed to him. As he cradled the dying old man in his arms, the purple light of the crystal poured like an aura around the grizzled head.

'Old man . . . what is it?'

Simonides reared up for one last time, his words coming in a wheezing rasp. 'The Flame would destroy him . . . destroy him, rather than yield up its secret! Prophecy tells that the crystal shall be found when a shimmering girl is brought before the Flame . . . Fools have believed the crystal is . . . the girl! But my Imams . . . my Imams were right all along! The crystal . . . the crystal is . . . the Sacred Flame!'

Rajal's mind reeled, still uncomprehending. But what should they *do*? In desperation he would have shaken Simonides, but as the old man pronounced the words *Sacred Flame*, a chunk of rock detached itself from the ceiling and crashed down, striking his head.

Rajal leapt back, splattered in blood.

All this time Jem whirled and whirled. All this time, the tremors grew more violent. Suddenly there was a mighty explosion, ripping out the roof of the cave. Suddenly Jem was lost to view, shooting skywards on the column of fire.

'Jem!' Cata cried.

'Princess!' cried the genie. 'Please, WISH now!'

That's it! said the Princess. *I know the way! Genie – I wish . . . I wish to be united with my Essence again!*

'What?' burst out Jafir. 'At a time like this?'

Rainbow leapt forward, snarling.

'Do it!' shrieked Littler.

'Ooh, very well!'

The genie twirled about and clapped his hands. Orange clouds billowed up and just for a moment the chaos around them was still. In that moment, a silvery, glowing light surrounded the Princess, then possessed her being entirely. It was as if her whole body were a looking-glass. She turned, unseeing, first to the genie, then to Rajal, then to Littler . . . each saw his reflection in the shimmering glass, distorted against the dazzling backdrop of the Flame.

The Princess turned to Cata. The reflection became clear.

Cata moved forward, astonished, transfixed.

'Wh-What's happening to her?' gasped Rajal, then cried out Cata's name, reaching out helplessly, as suddenly she fell forward, disappearing into the glass.

'Wait!' said Littler. 'It's not over yet!'

The glass clouded; a thousand colours swirled in its depths. A song, pure and ethereal, sounded on the air, Dona Bela's song, that spoke of the vanishings that must come before the Princess could be made whole again.

Then the orange smoke billowed up again, and Cata was falling back to the cave floor, and the Princess returning to human form. As they separated, Rajal saw a phantom shape, the shape of a third girl, flickering and stretching on the air between them.

Sinking to her knees, the Princess cried out in her own voice now, 'My Essence! It's over . . . it's all over . . .'

'But Jem,' Cata choked, 'what about Jem?'

As if in answer, the cave was shaken by an explosion yet more mighty than the last. There was no time to cry out. There was no time to flee. The Flame seared into a white-hot beam; a crevice opened in the floor; lava poured from the ground.

Rubble rained down. The cave collapsed. In an instant, just an instant, everyone in it was killed.

Everyone.

Cata. Rajal. Bela Dona. Littler. Rainbow.

Even Jafir, who could not retreat into the konar-light in time.

An instant earlier, Jem had whirled in the air, billowing at the tip of the Sacred Flame. Free of the cave that had confined it until now, the Flame seemed to stretch above the very sky, into the blackness that lay beyond. All around him, Jem saw the stars, then the gleaming disc of the moon, so close he could almost touch it; but to touch it, he knew, would be to sear away his being, to destroy himself as Kaled had destroyed himself in his longing for a power beyond his reach.

Jem turned and turned. Far below, he was aware of the Sanctum, ruinous with its roof blown out; he was aware of the boulevard and the Whispering Palace and the dark, mysterious city that surrounded them. Renewed rumblings threatened at any moment to level the city with the dust of the ground; at any moment, Jem knew, the Flame would sustain him no longer, and he would drop down, down.

It seemed that the moment of his death was near, but it was then that Jem heard a ghostly music, borne up from the world below on the juddering column of fire. It was the voice of the Princess, and the song she sang was one Jem had heard before.

> In my mind there are
> Five vanishings,
> Vanishing one by one . . .

Joy flooded Jem's heart, for suddenly he understood the mystery that had lain, all this time, behind this strange adventure. The Princess was *not* the crystal, but when she was whole again, the crystal would be found.

Triumph burst from Jem's lips, just as the second, shattering explosion tore apart the night. Then he was crying out, falling down through a white-hot, searing shaft. As he plummeted, his dazzled gaze saw the Sanctum collapse, crashing into nothingness; he saw the bursting lava surge from the ground and vast chasms cracking open, all along the boulevard. The palace shook. Buildings crumbled and fell. Jem saw the ruined ground, surging ever closer.

Deep, deep he plunged beneath the earth. It seemed he would fall for eternity, and as he fell, he was aware of Toth-Vexrah all around him, reeling and writhing, swooping and darting in the semblance of a mighty wingèd serpent.

Fool! came the voice of the anti-god, a hideous, crazed screech. *Take the crystal, would you, take it now? What can it avail you, when your friends are all dead – yes, even the female you love more than life, crushed beneath the ruins of the Sanctum! It's over, Key to the Orokon! Take the crystal, take it if you will, but you can never prevail against me! Take it, take it – but when you take it, you* extinguish the Flame! What then? Don't you know this Sanctum is a storehouse of power, and when the Flame is extinguished, all that power is mine?

Jem bucked; he twisted; he blocked his ears; he cried out. It was useless. On and on came the taunting, monstrous voice, shrieking of the evil that soon would triumph, of the horror that would rain down on all the world.

How I have laughed at those Unang fools, bowing and scraping to the Sacred Flame! Imagine if they knew, imagine if they guessed, that all this time their prayers had been not to Theron, god of fire, but to TOTH-VEXRAH! *Yes, Key to the Orokon, it's true! My brother Theron vanished into The Vast long ago. What did he care for this paltry world? Nothing! So it was that I, in the semblance of my brother, projected myself from the Realm of Unbeing, appearing in the desert to the Prophet Mesha. Yes, it was I to whom the Unangs prayed, I who spoke to the Sultan from the Flame! By now, as in a bank vault, massive concentrations of spiritual power are stored inside the Sanctum. The faith of millions, for generation upon generation . . . and when that power is liberated, it will all be mine! What fear have I of you, Key to the Orokon? Take the crystal, take it, take it! Your triumph shall be brief! Soon, I tell you, soon, I shall see you crushed at my feet, and the Orokon shall be mine!*

'Go from me, go from me! I defy you!' Jem cried. 'My ancestor Nova-Riel destroyed you before – I tell you, Toth, I shall destroy you again!'

Fool, fool! My powers then were as nothing to what they will be now! You shall never save this world! I shall tear you apart like the insect you are!

Now Jem felt agony tearing at him as all the heat of the Flame seared his senses, as all Toth's torments ripped and gouged at him. Still he plummeted down and down. It seemed he could only be falling to his death; then suddenly there was a sphere of light, dazzling his eyes, and the column of fire around him was contracting, shrivelling into the glowing sphere; then the sphere itself was contracting, compacting . . .

Jem's hands flailed out, and just in the moment when he would have crashed against rock, shattering into a bloody pulp, his hands clutched the crystal that had been the Sacred Flame. His powers had prevailed!

He whizzed up, rocketing into the sky again. Beams of light shot from the crystal, bathing the world below in a searing red. That was when Jem knew, really knew what had happened in the last explosion; he saw the ruins of the city beneath him, and saw that Toth had told the truth when he said that Cata and all Jem's friends were buried in the rubble and flowing lava. Had they all died, that he might find the crystal? It could not be. It could not be!

Jem railed. He cursed his destiny. He cried aloud. But that was when the magic burst from the crystal, the magic the crystals would always bring, in the moments after they were found.

Time was running back. Buildings rose from rubble again; lava slithered back into the earth; chasms knitted over.

Slowly Jem whirled down from the sky. In the next moment he was standing in the Sanctum again, shuddering, convulsing, clutching the Crystal of Theron in his hands.

Chapter 73

ANGELS OF ASHES

'Miss Landa, are you sure this is a good idea?'

'Last chance, Nirry. Agondon tomorrow!'

'I know!' Nirry wailed, as if this were a reason *not* to embark upon the present escapade. Doubtfully she looked behind her. Their latest coaching inn was lost from sight now and the woods had closed around them, eerie and rustling in the light of the moon. Nirry shuddered as ferns and trailing branches brushed against her nightgown like sinister, caressing fingers. 'I say, we couldn't get *abducticated* in these woods, could we? Now that really would make me fed up, it would – to come all this way, only to go and get *abducticated*, just before I got to see my tavern!'

'Don't worry, Nirry, I think you'll see your tavern. I just hope you'll see Miss Cata, too!'

'Very well, Miss Landa. If you know what you're doing ...'

There was still a tinge of doubt in Nirry's voice. Moments earlier, when she had started awake to the hand on her mouth and Miss Landa's face hovering over her, her brain had reeled in astonishment. Struggling out of deep, pleasant dreams of her tavern, Nirry had not at first remembered this meeting. What astonished her now was that the plan could be real; she had thought it the merest fancy of the strange girl's, that was all. Could it be true that Miss Cata had vanished in a flash of light? Could it be true that she could come back, in a second flash, if Miss Landa could only work her magic? Heathen mumbo-jumbo, Nirry called it. But she knew there were many strange things in this world and after all, Miss Landa had been a good friend to Miss Cata.

Miss Cata was missing, that much Nirry knew. If they could save her, they had to try.

Landa pushed rapidly through the undergrowth.

Nirry puffed behind her. 'You're sure she wasn't just ... *abducticated*, Miss Landa?'

'What's that, Nirry?'

'Miss Cata. Them Bluejackets could have grabbed her, they could, while you weren't looking. While you were all wrapped up in your ... your worshipping, I mean.'

'I've told you, Nirry, I saw her drawn into a column of light.'

'If you say so, Miss Landa.'

Landa stopped suddenly. 'This is the place.'

'How do you know? I mean, it's just another tree, isn't it?'

'No tree is just another tree, Nirry.' Landa turned, clutching Nirry's hands. 'I slept too long; already there are glimmerings of light in the sky. Nirry, we haven't got much time. I know it's hard for you, but promise me – just promise me – you'll give me your belief.'

'Belief? Well, I'll try, Miss Landa. I just hope my Wiggler doesn't wake up, is all I can say, and find me gone. Why, he might think I've been *abducticated*, and make such a fuss as to wake the whole house!'

Landa smiled, but her eyes, shining in the moonlight, were earnest. She squeezed Nirry's hands, almost too tightly. 'Belief, Nirry, belief. Think of Miss Cata. Think how much you want to see her again.'

'That won't be hard, Miss Landa!'

'Good girl. You're a link, Nirry, do you understand?'

'I'm a what?'

'Never mind. I just wish I'd thought of it before, that's all. There's so little time. Now just follow me, Nirry, do what I do. And think of Miss Cata. No matter what happens, *think of Miss Cata.*'

Nirry nodded, then gave a little squeal as Landa dived into the undergrowth. Lying flat on her belly, the strange girl was still.

'Miss Landa,' hissed Nirry, 'are you all right?'

'Nirry, remember! Do as I do.'

'Ooh very well, Miss Landa. In my nice clean nightgown, too!'

In the moments that followed, Nirry's surprise could only increase as Landa moaned and caressed the earth, her long braids mingling with the roots and fronds and grasses. A fine way to carry on for a young woman of breeding!

Worse was to come.

'*Ul-ul-ul-ul-ul!*'

It was heathen stuff, that much was clear. But then, thought Nirry, poor Miss Cata had been a bit of a heathen too. Ooh well, no point in ruining a nice new nightgown for nothing now, was there?

Nirry's blonde head popped above the ferns. Imagine, if the mistress could see her now!

'*Ul-ul-ul-ul-ul!*'

❄ ❄ ❄ ❄ ❄

Where were his friends?

Jem turned, looking about him, as the crystal in his hands faded slowly to a duller, darker red. Like the city outside, the Sanctum had been restored, but only to the way it had been before the last explosion. Debris covered the cracked floor and amongst the debris Simonides, the Sultan and the beheaded whoremonger still lay, dead as before. The roof was open to the sky, and the bright light of a new morning shone through the settling dust. Only one thing had altered: where the Flame had burned there was a raw, smoking pit.

It was Rainbow who emerged first. There was an excited barking and the dog scampered forward over a ridge of fallen rock. His coat was dusty, but beneath the dust, Jem saw that Rainbow had assumed, once again, his bright pattern of stripes.

Littler came next, then the Princess, then Rajal, all of them covered in dust and ash. Solemnly Jem embraced them all, but when Cata came, he rushed into her arms, laughing, clutching her tightly. They kissed, long and hard.

The Princess looked on enviously.

Littler cleared his throat. 'Where's the genie?'

There was a sound of scuffling amongst the rubble and Jafir floundered forth, spluttering, coughing and very annoyed. 'It's the konar-light,' he complained. 'Where's it gone? Really, I think I'd be much safer in there! Now where, where can it be?'

Littler spotted the dull glitter, lying in the dust. He seized it.

'That's my home you've got there!' protested the genie. 'Dearie me, look at those dents! Well, it's still my home . . . Give it to me, hm? Hm, little boy?'

'Aren't you forgetting something, genie?'

'Forgetting something? What?'

The little boy gestured to the Princess. 'The third wish.' He counted on his fingers. 'One, to bring us here. Two, we've just seen.' He stuck a third finger, his middle finger, under the genie's nose. 'That still leaves one, doesn't it?' Littler strode towards the Princess, thrusting the konar-light back into her hands. 'I think Her Highness can speak for herself.'

Jafir rolled his eyes, but what could he do? He could only obey the command. So it was that there was a fresh burst of smoke and an instant later, Princess Bela Dona held Amed in her arms.

'Oh Amed! Where have you been?'

'The Ouabin had me trapped in a glass. But my love, my love . . . I could see you all the time! Oh, how I've feared for you! But now . . . to find you real . . . to be in your arms . . . now I must fear these womanish tears, that burst like twin fountains from my eyes! Oh my love, my love . . .'

'Fear no more, my darling,' sobbed the Princess. 'Dear Amed, we'll never be parted again!'

Littler smiled. 'I think we're about to have a happy ending.'

'Yes, if you give me back my konar-light,' said Jafir. 'And throw it away, will you, once I'm inside? Somewhere where no one will find it for

506

'. . . oh, epicycles. I need a rest, I really do!' He grabbed for the lamp, but Littler gave a squeal and, for the sheer fun of it, darted away through the piles of rubble.

'Come here, you little thief!'

Absurdly, the fat fellow started in pursuit. Rainbow frisked and barked, delighted at the chase. Round and round they went, circling the embracing lovers; then Littler skidded in the dust and the lamp clattered from his hands. He would have grabbed it again at once, but something else, something horrible, arrested his attention. The little boy gasped.

Lying in the rubble was a severed head.

A familiar, greasy head.

The genie had no eyes for this unfortunate discovery. Exulting, he swiped back the konar-light. In the next moment, he would have disappeared into its depths again, when a voice he knew called nervously from a half-collapsed doorway:

'Hello? Hello, is anyone there?'

Jafir started, turning slowly to see a podgy, bedraggled little man, dressed only in an undershirt, peering into the ruined Sanctum. Even Littler turned, looking on in astonishment, for the podgy fellow was the very image of the genie. Sweaty, breathless, the stranger waddled forward. At first he was a little dazzled by the sharp sun, glittering on the slowly floating dust. Seeing the genie, he saw only the remnants of his fine garb, and thought him, perhaps, to be a courtier, a dignitary, a royal guest.

'Dear, dear me! Thank goodness I've found someone. Really, I don't know what's happened! If I'd known how far that tunnel runs . . . well, it must go all the way under the boulevard, and . . . ooh, I won't tell you how many times I thought it was going to collapse! Why, I don't think I've ever had such a dreadful night! And poor Hasem . . . first he goes mad, then . . . poor, poor Hasem! Those wicked Ouabin must have got to him at last, is all I can think! Disguised as slave-girls, would you believe? What a wicked world this is! The only thing I don't understand is why they didn't kill me too . . .'

The torrent of words ceased at last and the little man slumped down on a boulder, wiping his forehead.

'Oman?' came the genie's voice. 'Oman, is that you?'

The question, of course, was purely rhetorical. It could hardly have been anyone else.

❈   ❈   ❈   ❈   ❈

'Viana-Vianu, Viana-Vianu—'

'Goddess of the living, consume me like a fire—'

'Goddess of the dying, grant me my desire—'

'Viana-Vianu, Viana-Vianu—'

'Ooh, Goddess, please bring back Miss Cata!'

The declamations rang loudly into the woods, twisting and twining into a strange, unearthly music. It was working! A mysterious green glow burned like phosphorus, rippling through the roots and fronds and grasses. Nirry's heart was pounding hard. Landa reached out, grabbing her hand. They joined in a dance, capering and cavorting. The phosphorus burned on, growing brighter; now the green light was rising higher, raging through the branches of the oak like fire; now a column of dazzling brightness came spinning between them as they danced round and round. Violent, impossible teemings of life fizzed into being beneath their feet; then, spinning in the column of light, was the image of a crystal – a green crystal.

'Miss Cata! Ooh, Miss Cata, where are you?'

'Goddess!' cried Landa, 'we see your sacred symbol, the embodiment of your power! Sacred Viana, bring our sister back to the path she must follow! All-merciful one, guide her—'

Explosively, power surged up from the earth. The women cried out. Torn apart, they were flung to the ground. Wildly the beam of light began to flicker. Cutting across the greenness came a flash of red, then another, then another. Suddenly the elements were a churning maelstrom. Ferns were flattened, flowers torn free, in the violence of the shrieking, downrushing beam. Branches and vines twisted and contorted, dancing in a terrible, crazed ecstasy. Through all this, the crystal span and span.

Nirry screamed. 'What's happening? Miss Landa, what's happening?'

Desperately she clawed at the roots and grasses. Like a sail in a storm, her nightgown billowed about her.

'Nirry, hang on—'

'Miss Landa, I can't—'

'Hang on, just hang on—'

With one hand, Nirry clung to a sturdy root; with the other, she grabbed at Landa's robes.

❈　❈　❈　❈　❈

Rajal looked down, scuffing the floor. By the flame-pit, radiant in the light from the sky, stood Jem and Cata, totally absorbed in each other. In the centre of the chamber were Bela Dona and Amed; by the great doors, the Caliph and the genie had been joyously reunited. Even Littler, it seemed, had forgotten his distress of moments earlier; after all, he must surely have been glad that his wicked father could never shout at him or beat him again. Running about in the rubble, the little boy played with Rainbow, delighted at the dog's splendid new coat.

Rajal felt a sinking in his heart, then a sudden, indefinable surge of feeling, at once hope and fear. Trembling, he slipped towards the stairs; but when he reached the top he found no one in the consummation chamber. His shoes crunched forlornly over the ruined, bloodstained floor.

'Aron? Aron?' Rajal whispered, but it was only for the sake of saying the name. He looked down at the cracks beneath his feet and for a moment, until the illusion faded, he thought he saw the image of his new, vanished friend, clutching tightly to his evil master.

Rajal sighed. There had been a time when he thought he loved Jem. Now there was another he loved, and this love, he knew, was something true, something real. But it seemed equally hopeless. With sad steps he made his way back down the stairs.

It was as he reached the bottom of the stairs that Rajal looked up and saw something frightening. From behind Jem, curling up from the ashy pit, came a last, fluttering tendril of the Flame.

'Jem! Look out!'

Jem spun round, but in the same moment the Flame darted forth, twining its coils not round Jem, but Cata. Jem lunged forward, but the heat was too much. He staggered back. Cata was dragged towards the dark pit.

'Cata! The crystal! Remember the crystal!'

Struggling in the scorching bonds, Cata forced her hands to the crystal at her breast.

'*Sacred Viana! Defy this evil!*'

It was then, as Cata cried out, that the massive bolt of lightning, green and dazzling, stabbed down though the ruins of the roof.

When the flash subsided, the Flame had vanished; but so, too, had Cata.

※　　※　　※　　※　　※

It was over – all at once, it was over. Suddenly the terrible magic was gone; gone were the lights and the swirlings of the air; gone were the wind and the billowings of the branches, the ferns and the ruined flowers. All these things had disappeared, but in their place was a dishevelled, familiar figure, clutching a glowing green crystal in her hands.

'Miss Cata?' Nirry breathed. 'Miss Cata, is it really you?'

Cata's eyes were wide with wonder. 'Nirry?' she murmured. 'Nirry . . . Landa?'

She swayed and collapsed.

'Miss Cata!' Nirry started forward.

'The green lightning. Landa ... Landa must have taken her back. She meant well, but ... oh no, no!'

Jem slumped down, his face in his hands.

Rajal went to him.

'Jem?' he said gently. 'Jem, what do you mean?'

But it was Amed who spoke next. While Rajal was upstairs, Amed had gone to the dead Simonides, sadly embracing this uncle she had never known, who looked so like her dead father. Tenderly she had closed the corpse's eyes and run her fingers over the long, flowing beard.

Now she rose up and said softly, in a voice not quite like her own, 'Prince Jemany, your beloved is gone, and cannot be summoned back. One day, yes, you shall meet her again; indeed you must, if the crystals are to unite, for she took with her the crystal of the green goddess, and shall bear it with her now until the end of this quest. Hold this knowledge in your heart, Prince Jemany, and take strength from it. For now, you must put sorrow behind you. You have found the third crystal, but two more remain. The times grow desperate, and already a new adventure waits to claim you.'

With that, Amed's eyes closed. She staggered a little and would have fallen, if Bela Dona had not been there to take her in her arms.

'My love? My love ... what is this power in you?'

Rajal sighed. 'I'm sorry, Jem.'

'I know, Raj, I know. But Amed – or was it Simonides? – is right. I'll feel sorrow later. Now, the quest must go on.' Jem looked down to the crystal in his hands, then to the crystal at his friend's chest. 'Oh Raj, up till now we've been fools, blind fools! Just look at us. Porlo's gone. Empster's betrayed us—'

'You mean Agonis—'

'We're on our own now, Raj. And the stakes are higher.' Quickly, Jem told Rajal of his vision of Toth, and all the new horrors the anti-god had threatened. 'I hoped I'd defeated him, at least for now. But the way that tendril of fire came back ... already, perhaps, his new powers surge through him. He says we may as well give up now. But we can't ... Raj, if he wins, it's the end of everything.'

Jem looked up, hoarsely crying his defiance to the air.

'Can you hear me, Toth? I'll never give up! Never! Empster ... Agonis, can you hear me, too? It's my quest now ... mine, not yours! I've found three crystals and I'll find the rest! The Orokon shall be mine ... mine ...'

There was no reply but the echo of Jem's voice, ringing round the vast, ruinous chamber.

Rajal bit his lip. He clutched his friend's arm and said softly, 'Jem, I'll be with you. I won't fail you again.'

'Again, Raj?' Something flickered in Jem's eyes, and once again he found himself wondering how it was that Cata, last night, had possessed the purple crystal.

This, he decided, was not the time to ask.

'I mean, I won't fail you,' Rajal said quickly. Brushing at his eye, he added, 'Where's the next crystal, Jem? Wenaya?'

'That's right, Raj – the islands of the west. Have you seen the maps? Hundreds of islands – hundreds. And somewhere amongst them, the blue Crystal of Javander.'

'You'll find it, Jem. You're the Key, remember?'

'It gets harder, Raj. It gets harder all the time.'

'I know.' Rajal scrambled back to his feet, reaching out a hand for his friend. 'Jem?'

Jem dusted off his robes. 'Raj?'

'You know Wenaya? I think our first problem's just going to be *getting* there.'

Jem looked thoughtful. 'Actually, Raj, I'm not so sure.'

Chapter 74

SAY HELLO, WAVE GOODBYE

'Really, young Prince, is it *quite* necessary to climb all these stairs?' puffed the Caliph Oman Elmani, looking up towards the palace roof. 'I mean to say, I enjoy a garden too, but I'm sure the ones below are just as nice.'

'They don't have magic carpets in them, Oman,' said the genie.

'Magic carpets? I could do with one now!'

'Come, Oman, you know I can't fulfil your *every* wish. I've told you, I can't bring people back from the dead, I can't stop them being born, I can't change your life from the beginning . . . and I can't be making magic carpets whenever you take it into your head to want one. Oh, and don't expect me to go conquering other countries, either. If that Vizier of yours was right about one thing, it's this: limits, Oman. There've got to be limits.'

'Couldn't I even have a litter, borne by slaves?'

'I've supplied you with some new regal raiments, haven't I? Quite a boon, when you were virtually naked. That will have to do for now, hm? We'll sort the slaves out later.'

'Hmph. You're cruel, Jafir, positively cruel.' The Caliph's little mouth set hard, then softened. 'Still, I'm glad you're back. After all, I'll be Sultan now, won't I? What I'll do without Hasem I don't know, but at least . . . well, life goes on, doesn't it?'

'We hope so,' muttered Rajal, following behind the striding Jem. 'We can't be sure, can we?'

But the Caliph did not hear the ominous aside.

The roof garden closed around them, with its thousand fragrances and rustling leaves, its hanging vines and many-hued flowers. Luxuriating in the lush incense, they pushed their way through the thick screens of foliage, entering the domain of arbours and grottoes and mazes and parterres. It was a place where, in a time that was already history, a boy had sat at an old man's feet and listened to the secrets of his father's youth; a place where, that night, though no eyes would see them, the boy and his playmate, gossamer-thin, would leap and run and laugh beneath the pale light of the moon.

It was as they rounded a corner of a tall hedge that the party were startled to see a dirty young boy, very much alive, dressed only in a loincloth and darting across their path.

'It's Fish!' cried Littler.

'Who?' said Jem.

Littler raced ahead. 'Fish, come back!'

In the event, it was Rainbow who caught him. Exuberantly the dog leapt up, ripping off the ragged loincloth. Coins and little ornaments and gemstones sprayed the ground.

Fish stood shame-faced, covering his nakedness.

Princess Bela Dona looked upon him, surprised.

Slowly his four companions emerged from the foliage. Blubber struck Fish in the back, forcing him to kneel; then all the boys were kneeling, contrite, before the Princess. Between them, they had been carrying several clanking sacks; now, as they lowered the sacks to the grass, one fell open, revealing a glittering cargo of gold, silver and pewter.

'Faha Ejo!' gasped Amed, seeing her old friend.

'Whatever's going on here?' said the Caliph, approaching.

Princess Bela Dona raised an eyebrow. 'Hm. Faha Ejo, perhaps you can explain?'

'The guards weren't about. We thought we'd explore the palace,' mumbled the goat-boy.

The Princess laughed. 'I see you have! But what are you doing in the roof garden?'

'We thought this might be a good base for operations,' said Blubber, squirming. 'Didn't we, Faha? Nicer than the Realm of Un, I mean!'

'I'll say!' said Littler.

'Besides,' attempted Faha Ejo, with a sly smile at the Princess, 'your father doesn't actually *like* the Sultan, does he?'

The lovely face twisted into a mischievous smirk. 'Boys, I'm afraid the Sultan's dead – well, the old one. His poor son, too. Do you know what that means? It means this place belongs to my father now. And me.'

'Oh,' said Faha Ejo. 'Oh.'

The Caliph's brow furrowed. 'Thieves, indeed! And we haven't even moved in yet! Jafir, I don't suppose you could clap these boys in irons, or something similarly appropriate? I dare say Hasem would have insisted upon disembowelling them at the earliest opportunity. Why, in deference to his memory, I think perhaps it behoves us to do just that!'

The Unners quailed, but before the genie could even roll his eyes, Princess Bela Dona had laid a hand on her father's arm. Leaning close to him, she whispered in his ear. When she stepped away, the little man's clouded expression had brightened and he held out his arms rapturously to the five boys.

'Heroes! My dear boys, you're heroes!' Beaming, he turned to the others. 'Did you know, these brave boys saved my daughter? I declare, they shall keep the treasures they have purloined; but more than that, I shall make them my daughter's personal guard!'

Amed had been smiling at Faha Ejo; now she burst into delighted laughter.

'Jafir,' added the new Sultan, 'I don't suppose you could manage some livery?'

'Ho hum, I suppose so,' grumbled the genie.

※　※　※　※　※

The great central parterres that had been so sinister the night before were dazzling in the bright day. Looking around him, Jem almost imagined himself back in the dreaming dimensions, longing only to lie down and sleep amongst the fragrance and the colour and the rising heat.

But the quest called, and there was no time for dreams.

Dubiously, Rajal inspected the carpet. 'Jem, are you sure this is a good idea?'

'It flies, Raj, believe me.'

'That's what worries me.'

They turned to the friends who were ranged all around them. It was Princess Bela Dona who led the goodbyes, embracing Jem fondly.

'Prince, you are a good man, and the world needs you. Every day I shall pray for your quest; pray, too, that one day you shall find again the girl to whom I must also owe my enduring gratitude. I only wish I could help you in other ways.'

'Princess, your prayers are enough.'

'Perhaps, but let me give you something.' The Princess reached into her robes. 'What this talisman is, I do not know, but I sense it is the most valuable of the gifts I have been given. Take it from me, please, and bear it with you.'

She pressed the object into Jem's hand.

Jem looked down. It was the harlequin's coin.

'Princess, by what route this precious thing came to you, I cannot know, but my thanks are greater than I can express. This gift you give me is a token of my beloved.'

The Princess turned to Rajal, removing a golden band from her wrist. 'Koros-child, this is the Amulet of Tukhat. In the course of your adventures, I sense you have encountered terrible things, and suffered much; this amulet, if legends are true, will protect you from harm.'

Two more gifts remained. The first was for Littler; the second, for Rainbow. The Princess kneeled, smiling, before the boy and the dog. 'Little boy, with this mysterious orb you shall possess the power of seeing from afar; to our particoloured friend, I give this object called a

Lichano band, which he may wear as a collar. Already it has given voice to a girl who was dumb; what powers it will grant Rainbow I do not know, but soon enough, I dare say, you shall see.'

Jem's brow furrowed and he said, concerned, 'Princess, these are fine gifts you give, but you know this boy cannot come with us. He is a mere child, and our quest is perilous.'

The Princess said only, 'Have I not armed him for what lies ahead?'

'Princess, no. His place is here.'

Jem had been whispering, but Littler had heard.

'Jem! You can't mean that! After all we've been through! And Rainbow ... think what Rainbow's been through, too!'

Jem knelt down. He took Littler in his arms and felt the child's sobs; then he pushed him firmly away.

Jem and Rajal took their places on the carpet. Now it was really time to say goodbye.

'Poor Rajal!' Amed said wryly. 'I'm afraid I was a bit of a trial to you! You forgive me, don't you?'

'Oh, I forgive you,' smiled Rajal. 'I've had worse things to put up with than you, Amed.'

'Really?'

Rajal did not elaborate. If he thought again of Vizier Hasem, he struggled to put the memories behind him. To have murdered the Vizier gave him no pleasure, and he wished he could call back the anger that had driven him on, pounding at the Vizier's head, long after the man must have been unconscious. But after all, the Vizier had been about to kill Cata. This would have to be Rajal's justification, and he only hoped that it would be good enough for his conscience in all the life that lay before him. But then, thought Rajal, that might not be long; then, too, he might do far worse things before his own death came. He thought of the dangers that they had yet to face and found himself shuddering, there in the heat and brightness of the day.

'Say, Vaga-boy?' came a voice.

It was Fish, pushing his way forward. In their splendid new livery, all the Unners seemed barely recognisable, but none more so than Fish. Impulsively he thrust a bag of gold into Rajal's hand, grinned, and said, 'You can never have enough, hm?'

'Indeed,' muttered Faha Ejo. 'Fish, what *are* you playing at?'

Fish only shrugged and fell back shyly.

The Sultan clapped his hands. 'Jafir? You *do* know which way's Wenaya, I suppose?'

'Really, Oman! Of course I do!'

For the last time, Jem saw the familiar orange puff of smoke. In the

515

next moment, the carpet was rising, at first hovering slowly, as it had done before.

'Goodbye!'

'Goodbye!'

'Good luck!'

But the scene was not quite over.

It was in the instant before the carpet soared upwards that Rainbow, with a joyous bark, darted away from Littler, leaping up beside their departing friends.

'Rainbow!' Littler wailed.

Then suddenly the little boy had launched himself forward too, clawing desperately at the edge of the carpet. They were rising higher and higher, whizzing up through the air.

'Genie! Do something!' Jem cried.

The genie only flung up helpless hands.

There was nothing for it but to drag the child aboard.

Littler had nearly fallen to his death, but he was laughing as he scrambled into a cross-legged position. Below, the Sacred City became smaller and smaller, disappearing into the merest golden gleam amongst the red immensity of the mountains. Before them stretched the vast reaches of the desert, and somewhere, far away, mysterious islands in a glittering sea.

'I knew you couldn't go without us,' grinned Littler.

Rainbow barked delightedly.

✳   ✳   ✳   ✳   ✳

'You could have *done* something, couldn't you, Jafir?' said the Sultan, as they watched the carpet soar away.

'I told you I was tired, didn't I, Oman?'

The Sultan raised a suspicious eyebrow.

'Oman, the boy wanted to go! To tell the truth, I gave him a little push.'

'Poor Littler,' Faha Ejo was saying. 'He doesn't know what he's got himself into.'

Cheese said, 'Who would have thought he was such a fool?'

Stork said, 'I h-hope he's not going to be s-s-sorry.'

'Rather him than me,' said Blubber. Smoothing his new livery, the fat boy began to wonder aloud what sort of food would be served in a palace, and whether there would be eels, so far from the shore. In any case, he was sure the portions would be huge. 'I think we've got the best deal, hm, boys?'

Fish looked down sadly. 'Oh, I don't know.'

Blubber only laughed and rubbed a hand over his stomach, which began to rumble alarmingly. Hearing the rumble, the Sultan laughed too, and declared that indeed a banquet was in order. After all, there was much to celebrate.

As they wove their way out of the gardens, the little man looked up again at the sky, where the carpet had now vanished against the dazzling pallor.

'Oh Jafir, I see a splendid future before us! Only,' he muttered, 'there's still the problem of Shimmy.'

'Problem, Father?' said the Princess, overhearing.

Her father smiled tightly. 'Marriage, my dear!'

The Princess winked at Amed. 'Father, I don't think that's a problem any more. Well, not for us, at least.'

Her father wailed, 'Shimmy, we're royal! Think of the Line!'

The girls only laughed and ran on ahead, racing each other down the stairs. Later that afternoon, when the banquet was over, they would retire together to a luxurious apartment, turn the looking-glasses to the walls, and begin the marvellous process of exploring their two bodies which at last were equally real.

The Sultan shook his head. 'Dear me, what a blessing is a daughter – but what a burden, too! Ooh, and that friend of hers can't really have the Telling power, can she? That's what started all this trouble . . . dear, dear me!' More mutterings followed, but then the little man looked up brightly. 'Jafir,' he blinked, 'I know I'm asking a lot, but I don't suppose you could help me out again in a certain matter of . . . the succession?'

The genie's look was grave.

'Jafir!' wailed the Sultan. 'What about last time?'

'Oman, I told you there were things I couldn't do. Suffice to say that . . . well, let's just say that Vizier of yours was a versatile fellow.'

'Jafir? Jafir, what do you mean?'

The genie only laughed and would say no more.

The Sultan glowered, but was not really angry. There would be time enough later to worry about the trials that lay ahead. Side by side with his double, with little waddling steps, the great monarch made his way back down the stairs. He was happy; but every so often he sighed, shaking his head again, thinking how bewildering life could be. He thought again of the events of the last day, and sighed more deeply than before.

What a shambles of a wedding, after all that planning!

Here ends the Third Book of THE OROKON.
In the Fourth Book, Sisterhood of the Blue Storm,
*Jem faces his most daunting challenges yet, while back
in Ejland, as Cata fights new battles of her own,
we meet old friends – and old enemies.*